Kir~~

Ash an(

Auth
Email: em̲...~~...com
Website:<u>http://www.richardnell.com</u>

All material contained within copyright Richard Nell, 2019. All rights reserved. No part of this book may be reproduced or transmitted in any form or by any means without prior written permission from the author.

The following is a book of fiction. Names, characters, places, and events are either the product of the author's imagination, or used in a fictitious manner. Any resemblance to actual persons, living or dead, or actual events, is purely coincidental.

Cover art by Derek Murphy

Orhus

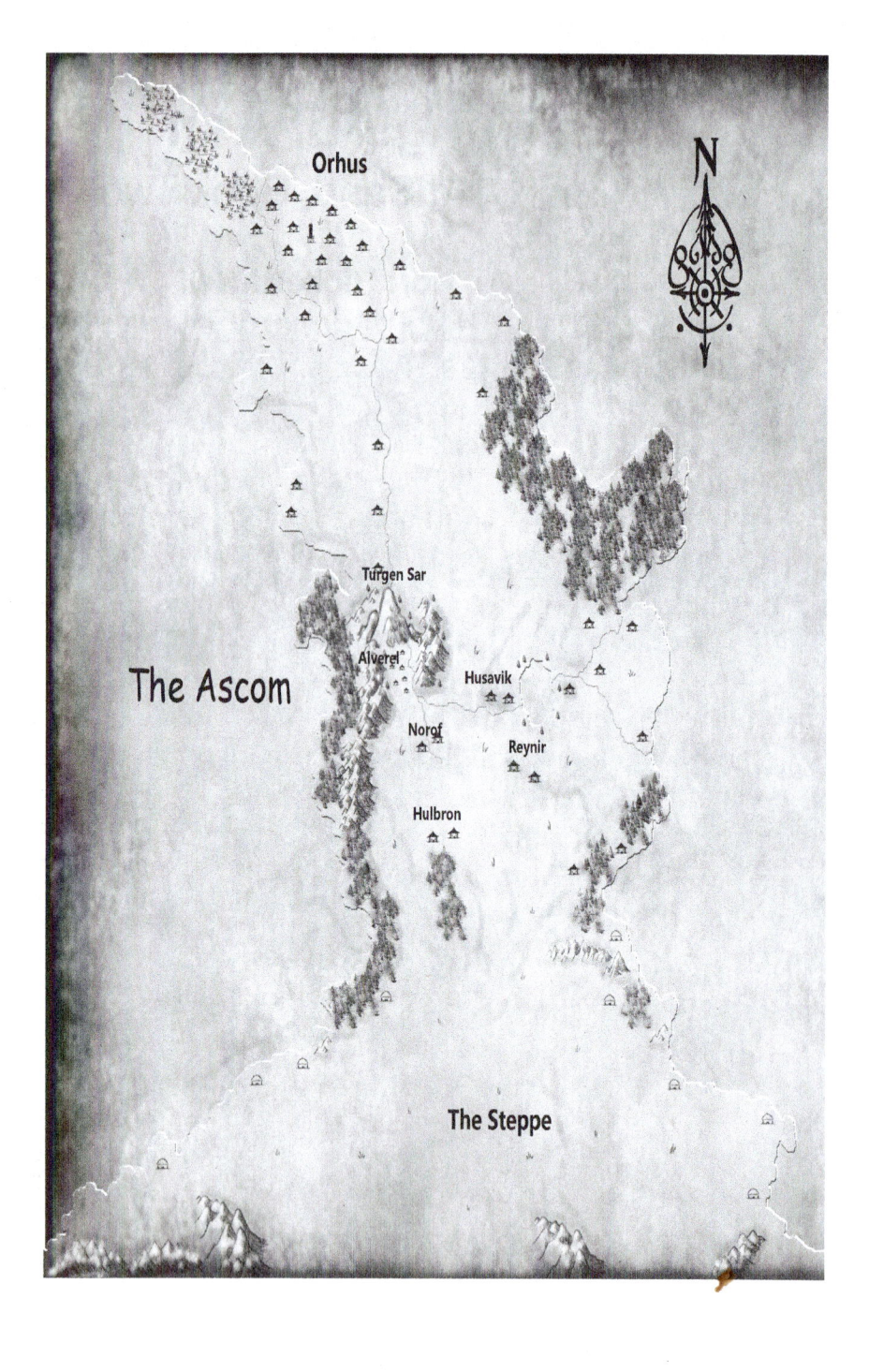

Turgen Sar

Alverel

The Ascom

Husavik

Norof

Reynir

Hulbron

The Steppe

Naranlon Border

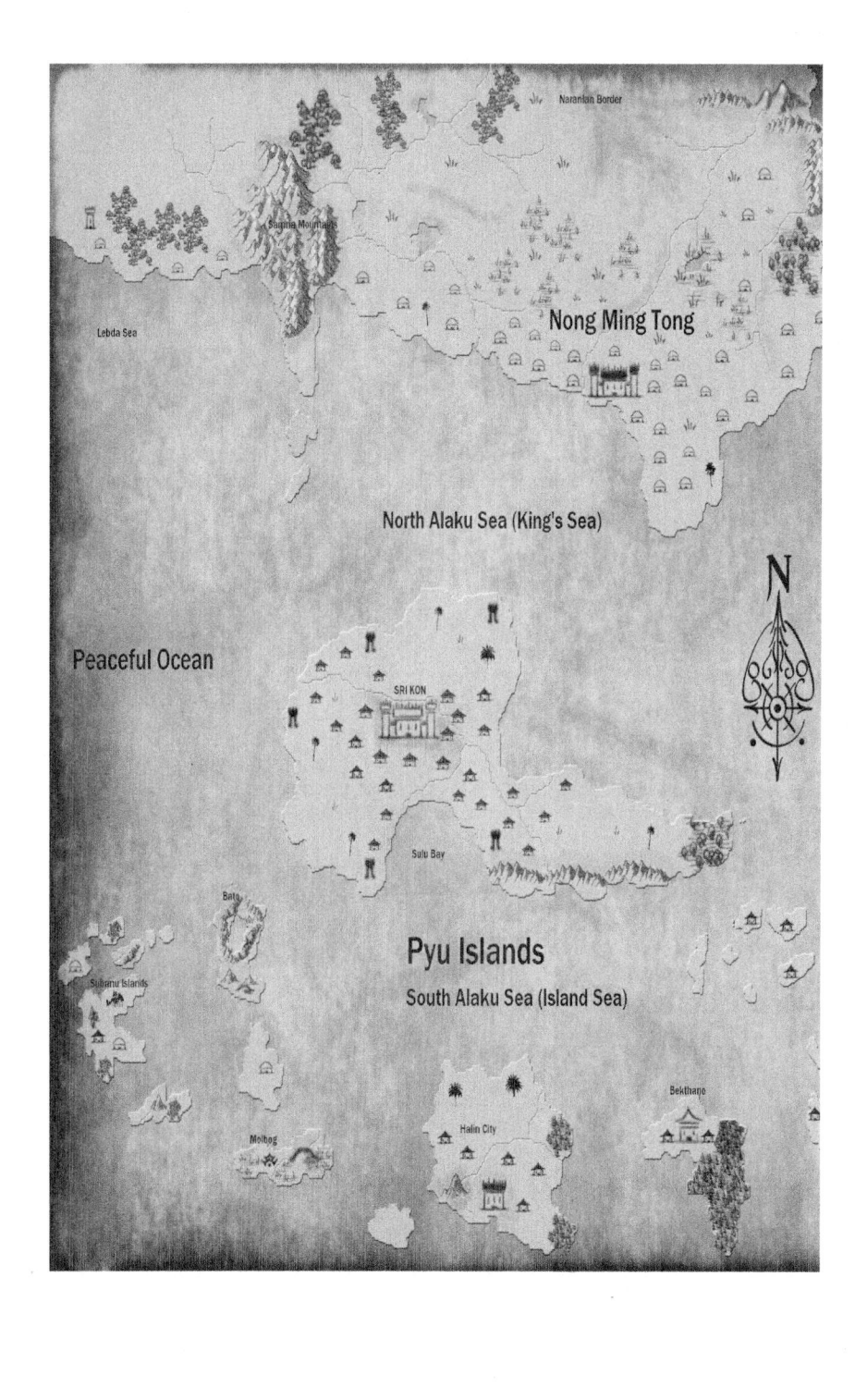

Saynia Mountains

Lebda Sea

Nong Ming Tong

North Alaku Sea (King's Sea)

Peaceful Ocean

SRI KON

Sulu Bay

Batu

Subanu Islands

Pyu Islands

South Alaku Sea (Island Sea)

Molbog

Halin City

Bekthano

Praise for Kings of Ash

"Kings of Ash triumphed over its predecessor in almost every possible way."
Novel Notions

"I give this series my highest recommendation."
Fantasy Book Review UK

"Ruka just might be one of my favorite characters in any book I've read in years."
The Nerd Book Review

"Emotional, heartbreaking, and bloody. The story is unpredictable and addictive, proving Ash and Sand will be a series of surpassing excellence."
The Grimmedian

"If you're looking for epic high fantasy that's vivid and grand, you will cherish this series."
Kreativejoose

"This was one of my most anticipated books for 2019 and it definitely lived up to and surpassed my expectations."
Amazon Review

"Nell delivers a heart-wrenching and devastating story with real, believable characters you care for despite their monstrosity."
Goodreads Review

pted family killed in revenge by Ruka after they attack and rob in the night. She decides to devote her life to the Galdric Order, ing off her small facial deformity.

o succeed in her apprenticeship, Dala allies herself with the ntmen of Orhus, particularly their leader Birmun (the fallen son of nief), whom she seduces. She builds their resolve with hatred and rder, and uses them to intimidate the other girls into making her a estess. She chooses High Priestess Kunla as a mentor.

Dala accompanies Kunla to defend from allegations by kayag' (Ruka's runeshaman alter-ego) at the valley of law. The ley erupts in violence, Ruka catches and kills Kunla, and Dala lieving Ruka is a servant of god like her), saves him in his ment of weakness, promising one day he will see why.

ka

Ruka (the single-born, Noss-touched son of a rich, Vishan woman) ws up in the frozen steppes of the Ascom, isolated on the skirts of a Southern town called Hulbron with his mother Beyla. ey are eventually persecuted by a priestess named Kunla, and ced to journey to the valley of law for justice. Beyla dies before y reach it.

Ruka is made an outlaw at the valley. He is forced into the wild, coming a murderer, thief and cannibal to survive, until he meets d saves a traveling skald named Egil.

Egil offers an ill-fated, get-rich-quick scheme to become a 'rune-aman', which Ruka transforms into a plan of rebellion and revenge. tortures Egil into submission, and begins gathering like-minded iefless warriors with rune-weapons and words of prophecy.

At the valley of law, Ruka at last takes his bloody, savage revenge High Priestess Kunla, then flees to the coast and sails into the idless' sea to face the gods, or just to die.

Years later, Ruka returns. He finds Egil and tells him he has found

Note from the Author

For those who've been waiting a year or more for this sequ[el,] is a (very) brief summary of the important plot points and [characters] of book 1, *Kings of Paradise*. With such a large book, man[y things] will of course be left out, but hopefully this remains useful.

(Arranged by the three main characters: Kale, Dala, and R[uka.])

Kale

1. In the islands of Sri Kon, Kale (the fourth and youngest [son of the] king of Sri Kon) is forced by his father into marine training t[o toughen] him up. He does very well, winning 'Head of the Bay' and d[efeating] the belligerent Sergeant Kwal (eventually executed by the [king), as] well as winning the affection of his childhood friend Lani (a [princess of] the neighboring kingdom of Nong Ming Tong).

2. Kale is then sent against his will to a 'coming of age' ritua[l at a] near-by Batonian temple. He meets a strange, young monk [Eka] who teaches him to meditate and discover his 'Way' - the pa[th of] 'they who stay', which begins his journey into an almost limi[tless] spirit-based magic.

3. After completing the monk's tests, returning and consumm[ating his] love with Lani (who is secretly the crown prince's betrothed)[, Kale is] banished to the Naranian academy to spare him from castra[tion or] execution.

4. At the academy, Kale survives imperial and temple intrigu[e with] the help of his friends (Asna - a Condotian mercenary, and C[anit - a] Mesanite warrior), though his mentor Amit (actually the Empe[ror's] uncle) does not. He vastly increases his spiritual powers, lea[rns that] a foreign army (Ruka) has invaded his homeland, and decide[s to] return home to do what he can.

Dala

1. Dala (a Noss-touched, low-born Southern farm girl) has he[r]

a new world, and that together they must again rally an army of bandits to seize it. After an undetermined amount of time, they do just that, with Ruka swearing to keep his word to an 'island king'.

Part I - The Past

1
An 'endless' sea. 425 GE (Galdric Era). The Past.

Ruka knew his death rose with the sun. His skin had peeled and burned, dried and cracked now with lines of blood. His small, square-sailed ship floated listlessly for the seventh day, and he saw nothing but sea on the horizon. The wind, and even the birds, had abandoned him.

Water seeped through the deck. Ruka bailed it numbly as he'd done since it began. Or, at least, his body did.

In Ruka's mind he was far away, and surrounded by dead men—men he'd killed, and who now lived in a special place with him he called his Grove. Ruka's Grove was a dark, deep forest much like those he had lived in as a boy—somewhere between imagination and reality, a secret world where Ruka could be safe from the cruelty and terror of his homeland, the Ascom, the land of ash.

At least that is how it started. Now his Grove was filled with walking corpses—the men, women and children Ruka had killed, still bearing the wounds he'd given them in life. None ever spoke, though they toiled in silent tasks, and they watched him. They watched him now. Their eyes said 'you will join us, murderer. You will join us soon'.

Maybe if you came out and rowed, or helped bail water, he thought bitterly, *I wouldn't be in this predicament.*

The dead never looked ashamed. They looked like vultures preening next to a graveyard.

And maybe if you left me alone, he added, *I could think of a way out of this.*

But in truth he knew this wasn't true.

Long ago he'd thrown the other man sailing with him—the previous 'captain', whom he'd abducted—into the sea to conserve water. He had not intended for the man to die, but sharing their meager drink would have meant death, as would drinking the growing briny pool beneath his feet, or any attempt to swim, or to break away on a smaller raft to paddle. The sea had many storms, and just as many nights full of huge waves. Ruka would survive neither.

"At least we killed Priestess Kunla," his body mumbled with cracked lips. His body could speak on its own without his mind, and they sometimes disagreed, but not this time.

Priestess Kunla had been the High Priestess of the South, a powerful woman of the Galdric Order who had killed his father, persecuted his mother, and made him an outlaw those many years ago. Yes, Ruka had killed her. But her death didn't bring him comfort, nor bring his mother back. It didn't put an end to the misery and cruelty of the world which created her.

"I'm too tired to bail, we have to abandon ship."

His body dropped their bucket, shuffling to the starboard side to untie their 'life raft'—a small, pitiful collection of planks, with a box of dried pork, some rope, a tarp to block the sun, and a paddle. *It won't save us*, he thought, but he didn't bother stopping it.

"We will last slightly longer," it muttered, mostly to itself.

Stubborn to the end, he thought with a sigh, but in truth felt admiration. Ruka respected the will to live.

With shaking limbs, they pushed the raft into the water and eased themselves over to land on top. His body secured the few possessions and itself beneath the tarp, and tied it all down with rope. "I must rest," it said out loud, "and then I'll row us where you say."

Some of the dead men smiled now in his Grove—or at least those without ruined jaws.

Think this is funny? Ruka rose up with a metal sword and hacked at a few, then broke their gravestones out of spite.

He had always thought a free death would be easier—dying on his own terms, by his own will. But it was too soon. The world was vast and mysterious, and he knew so little. *What makes the waves? What is the sun? How big is the sea and what is beyond it?*

He found now he did not wish to die without these answers. He found it as compelling as the promise of a little boy to his mother that he'd change the world and be free.

Will I ever see you again, Beyla? And will you approve of what I've done? Are there truly gods and is there an afterlife? Or when I die will my bloated corpse feed the fish, and then nothing more?

As he floated out and rose and fell over the currently peaceful waves, Ruka thought on his mother. He could remember everything he had ever seen or heard, touched or smelled or tasted. So he closed his eyes and breathed Beyla's scent, and heard her voice, and touched her hair. He thought on her lessons, the tests of memory that he'd always passed, learning to snare rabbits and find water and firewood and how to cross the snows. He remembered the genius of things that grow.

How do they sleep for the winter, Mother? Ruka the child had asked this of the grass and the trees, wishing he too could sleep until the sun warmed the frozen plain. *And how do they drink when they sleep?*

He walked to the huge, dark cave in his Grove that he'd hoped one day would attract a bear, but never did. *Why can men not sleep for the winter, like plants and beasts?*

Was it from lack of trying, he wondered, like crossing the sea?

He picked his way around the rocks, into the gloom beyond the widened mouth. Darkness had never bothered Ruka, and he could still make out the shapes of the walls, the teeth-like pillars attached to the floor and ceiling. He found a snug, protected nook in a corner, hidden by a large lip of hanging stone, and settled in.

They are nearly dead, the sleepers. Ruka calmed his breathing. *They awake grey and thin, starving, to hunt for food.*

He didn't sleep much anymore. He had to concentrate on a single thing—or play with numbers and symbols to distract his mind. *You will sleep now for days, or weeks—until I tell you to wake.*

He felt his body resisting, fighting for control, its fear of sleep like the fear of death—as if all acts of letting go led to some unpleasant end.

Death is not truly death, he coaxed.

"Not for you, maybe," it mumbled.

I will wake you before the end, no matter what. I promise.

He felt his muscles slacken. Soon the breathing from his body matched the breathing in his Grove. And though the lunacy of this did register in his mind, he ignored it. Things were always madness until they were true. *If men can sleep like bears, I, Ruka, will be the one to do it.*

Even if he did he knew the waves could kill him. The sea could be vast beyond all mortal understanding. Or there could be no other land. Or the world could be a ring after all.

He smiled because it made no difference. He could do no more. He willed his body to slow its breath further, to grow cool and quiet, still and calm. *I do not fear the cold, my body is nothing but flesh and bone.*

Alone beneath a bright blue sky, Ruka floated helpless amongst gentle waves. In his Grove, the darkness of his cave spread further—stilling the dead, and even quieting the birds. The warmth in the air fled from an icy breeze as winter came to paradise. His fake sun drooped and fell, the skies above his forest of trees clouded with a long night, and in that moment, Ruka knew purpose transcended death. It was bigger than him. And it certainly didn't need his body.

But best kill me now, and be sure, he thought to the gods, if they existed. *Because I haven't forgotten you, or my promise. And I'm still coming for my mother, and your children, in this world, or the next.*

* * *

When he opened his eyes his tarp was being ripped away, his raft dragged onto white sand by strange, near naked, brown-skinned men. The sky shone clear and shimmered like the air above a fire, the sun prickled hot on his skin. Clucks and jabbered nonsense filled his ears, and men bound his hands and feet with rope.

I'm alive. He meant to shout it, but his body was still cool and helpless. It opened its eyes so he could see, but didn't truly wake.

In this helpless state he was carried across a long, empty, sweltering, beach. He was stuffed into a kind of wagon, and rolled by the strange little men along a bumpy road.

Is it the land of the gods?

He paced in his Grove and did his best to see through cloudy eyes—to turn his head to see white crabs and colored flies and a hundred unknown things. *But I will know them soon*, he beamed and laughed at the sullen dead who stopped staring and walked off to other things.

The warmth of the air renewed him, though his lungs struggled, and his body quickened and deepened its breaths. By the time the wagon stopped, and the group of brown-skins were heaving him off onto a thin sheet of soft fabric, he could move.

They startled as he sat up. They babbled and pointed and fret like children as if they didn't know what to do. Their fear curled his lip.

If these are gods, or the sons of gods, I'll eat my raft.

Then one had a spear and thrust it down at Ruka's face, pointing at the sheet and motioning to lie down.

"Water," his body said through cracked, bleeding lips.

Hands pushed him back, and after feeling the weakness in his limbs, he decided not to resist. *Not yet*, he warned his body. *Let me watch, and learn, and get you food and water.*

He noticed the men darted their eyes round as if concerned who might be watching, so he tucked that knowledge away.

They lifted him up in the sheet with groans, and carried him inside a greenish wooden house on a hill surrounded by huge trees with wide, drooping foliage. He'd never imagined such healthy plants, as if when squeezed they'd drip out water and sap like rain. *Oh mother if you could only see such things!*

He set some dead boys to work in his Grove expanding the garden, hoping to examine it all more closely later. He would perhaps need to clear more trees for space, and in the real world such different plants would fight for sunlight and moisture and exchange disease, so perhaps in his Grove he should separate them.

While he worked they dragged and tied his body up more thoroughly in a room without windows. Only metal grates on the door and walls let in some light from elsewhere in the house. There was no bed, just a mat on the floor, and it reeked like sweat. Before they closed and locked him in they left a large pail full of water, and a bowl of white grain-like food. He had to kneel on red, swollen skin and eat and drink without his hands like an animal.

The grain was near tasteless and the water clean, incredibly clean, which suited Ruka fine. He finished it all at once, stopping rarely to breathe and swallow, not caring at the loss of dignity but careful not to spill.

When he sat up, he saw broken fingernails on the door and froze. He noticed old blood stains on the wood beneath him, then what looked like ants but bigger swarming over flecks of maybe skin in a corner.

He heard sobbing and peered through the obscured gloom of the grate. Beyond were three girls—he wasn't sure how old, but it seemed young—and despite their misery and filth, their perfect brown skin made them beautiful. Their round, smooth features and dark hair to him were all marks of fine breeding. He felt his eyes roam their mostly exposed bodies in ways they shouldn't, felt his body stirring. He let it bear the full weight of his disgust and judgment.

"I must rest," it said, and tried to lie down on the mat. But Ruka kept it up and its eyes roaming, senses sharp, letting his mind race out and around the mystery of this new world. *How is it ruled, then, to allow such places? And how large is it? How much food do they grow? How do I learn their language quickly? And do they know my people are across the sea?*

He heard cruel laughter in the house, then moaning and the fleshy thuds of violence. He smelled human filth and urine and wet floors wafting in from every hole in his shoddily crafted cell. His body twitched, preparing to chew at the ropes, or to work at loosening them. *Not yet*, he soothed. *They've given us food and water, and for now that's enough.*

Still, the instinct to flee was strong, and probably right. Was this a stockade? The last time Ruka was held in one he lost a toe. Was it some kind of holding place for criminals and outlaws? But then why were there women? Surely they would hold their women somewhere better.

It must be disfavored women, like my mother, he decided—those who'd broken mating laws and stayed to face punishment, suffering the wrath of lawmakers or 'gods' instead of running away like Beyla.

He sat in the gloom and listened to the slaps of skin on skin, and the dull moans of suffering. And though this world might be new and alien, these things were not. Ruka searched his mind and found the fleshy sounds a perfect memory of his youth—memories of a weak and useless father's night-visits to his mother's bed, memories of lying still by a dying hearth as a man who was nothing took his mother's love. *It is rutting,* he understood, *the sound I hear is rutting.*

Rage took him then, quiet and deadly, as the world re-shaped. The concept itself was blasphemy, no matter a woman's crimes. Even the 'chattel' of the Galdric Order forced to 'Choose' loyal soldiers or chiefs as mates lived as Matrons in their own houses. They were not trapped in cells like animals.

His joy at being alive vanished, his hopes for a better place than the Ascom destroyed. *Men are men,* he thought, *and meat is meat.* He recalled the images of the foreigners he'd seen, looking intensely at their eyes and mouths and smiles.

In truth his captors were small and soft, with fat bodies and ignorant stares—the kind that thought the weakness of others made them strong. Yet here, somehow, they were like Imler the Betrayer—like the man who nearly brought a land of warriors, a land of ash, to its knees. *They have the power to hold women against their will.*

Ruka brought the wood, the grates, and the plants to his Grove to study later. He repeated the alien-sounding words of his captors, and went to the rune-hold he'd made, which contained most everything he'd ever heard or thought. Dead men were dutifully taking notes for him—scratching new words down on thin rock using runes that represented sounds. He re-read all the Northerner's conversation, and their attempts to give orders.

'Theesaka'. Did this mean 'lie down'? Was it one word? Or two or three? He noted it as 'possible', and made another spot for 'certain', which for now was empty. He had so much to learn and understand.

For a short, measured moment, Ruka nearly forgot his purpose. But he reminded himself that he was young, and the world more vast than he realized. He had plenty of time to master this new land, then return to his own, if he chose. *All things have their time, and their place, just like your garden, Mother.*

First he needed knowledge, and to re-gain his strength. Then he would escape this prison.

His body suggested they make a river of their captor's blood, as well, then maybe see if they tasted like pig. There seemed to be no need, of course, and Ruka hadn't had to eat a man in years. But he had to admit, he *was* curious.

2

They ignored him for a day, except to stare through the door-grate and goggle. It was also difficult to tell them apart, but Ruka focused on their features like he might with animals. He watched for skin-marks and nose-shapes and hair-lines and named them accordingly. His guards became 'Wide-nose', 'Bald brow' and 'Teeth', because these things were obvious. He smiled when he wondered what they called him.

There were other men, too, but these came and went—maybe just to stare at Ruka, or maybe to rut with the captive girls. They'd stick their eager faces up to the bars and gasp with wonder, sometimes speak, and the guards would laugh.

Ruka tolerated this. His body offered to snatch one man's hair and twist his neck till it snapped, but he declined. There would be a time for violence, oh yes, but he must choose it carefully.

"Maybe for now if I plucked out an eye, they would understand."

Ruka smiled, but this was all bravado. With his hands tied as they were, he couldn't do much but ram his head into the grate. And even if he managed to get free and kill them all, then what? Where would he escape?

He tried to remember his 'sleep' on the raft, and found he had no knowledge. Had he drifted for days? Weeks? Did he wash up on the coast, or had these men found him in the water?

Without this, he may not easily return home. He might need his captors alive and capable of speech he could understand. And besides, for now they were feeding him. Every time he emptied his bowl they filled it—usually they watched him eat, and seemed pleased.

He had many more words now for the 'possible' stack of meanings, but he was patient. 'Wide-nose' liked to talk, and his endless stream of alien sounds were getting clearer. Sounds for 'I' and 'him' and 'we' and 'yes' grew closer to being certain in Ruka's mind, and studying them occupied his thoughts.

So occupied, in fact, he hadn't noticed the silence, and the swish of light, soft fabric. His door unlocked.

Behind it stood another small, pudgy brown man like all the others, but this one wore blue clothing so thin Ruka could see his nipples, which puffed out like a woman's from floppy slabs of fat on his chest. He had a knife in his soft, little hand, and his face was a mask of friendly deception.

Ruka lowered his eyes, hoping to look as un-threatening as possible. He extended his hands as if to beg for release.

The man turned to the three guards, then almost screamed at them, gesturing wildly and frothing at the mouth. He again plastered that false, friendly grin on his face, and bent to a knee. He gently took Ruka's hands, gestured with the knife as if asking for permission. And then, unbelievably, he cut the ropes.

Every muscle in Ruka's body screamed for blood, and he saw fear in the man's eyes. *Are you brave, or stupid, 'Nipples'?* He supposed it didn't really matter. He smiled and nodded as gently as he could, then rose to his feet.

The little chief cut his feet-ropes and withdrew, seeming to understand for the first time the enormity of his prisoner. He showed the briefest signs of regret, but covered quickly and gestured for Ruka to come out.

They led him to another room with a large table, this one covered in food. Nipples beamed and gestured, slid back a chair, and poured cups full of something dark. All the guards glistened with sweat. They were armed, but Ruka ignored them and sat.

He began to stuff himself, though he recognized nothing except some fish. It smelled good enough he didn't care, and the dark liquid smelled alcoholic, but seemed weak, so he gulped it down at once.

For a moment he considered that it could be poisoned. But then, why bother? They could have stabbed him to death in his cell.

Nipples watched him with wide eyes. The men all talked and laughed, but it didn't slow Ruka down. The pudgy chief tried speaking in a tone that implied questions, trying again and again as if Ruka could understand. Minutes passed this way, Nipples getting redder and redder as Ruka made no attempt to respond.

He used the time to eat a whole fish, then two plates of mystery greens, and a few hunks of grey meat. Then he started on the mushy white grain and some kind of fishy soup. Finally finished, he leaned back and looked at his captors.

The guards were dripping now. Their brown skin glowed red, and Ruka felt treachery in his bones, but couldn't understand it.

He realized as he looked at them, they held a faint blur. He blinked but it wouldn't fade. He realized even the skies in his Grove had fogged, the sounds of the birds growing distant and distorted. His stomach roiled, and in panic or perhaps rage reached out to seize Nipples by the throat. Except Nipples had crossed the room at inhuman speed.

Ruka tried to stand and lift a chair as a weapon. In the Ascom it took days to kill a man with poison, yet he felt oblivion rising up to strangle his world, inevitable as winter.

Why didn't you just poison my white mush while I was bound and helpless? Their incompetence galled and enraged him. He would be killed by fools.

He heard their same infuriating babble, and felt their hands grabbing at his limbs, and still he tried to note their words for his rune-hold, just in case. *If your poison doesn't kill me*, he thought, *you'd best run far away...*

* * *

Ruka dreamed of the sea, and then brown men in boats and choking on water funneled down his throat. Then he woke in chains, surrounded by four walls of pitted stone.

For a few moments he forgot where he was entirely. He called out for Egil—a handsome teller-of-tales from the land of ash, a former servant, and a cripple at Ruka's hand.

But Egil, like all of Ruka's retainers, was probably dead. They had fought and likely died in Alverel—the circle of law—when Ruka rose up in rebellion and killed the lawspeaker and a high priestess, and slew many men before fleeing North to the sea.

This felt like another life, now, though it was no more than a month away. Or so he hoped. The sea-crossing took only a few weeks, even with the wind's nearly fatal delay—but how long had he slept on the waves? He couldn't remember.

He stared at the square walls around him, smooth and thick and the height of five men at least. There was nothing else in the room except Ruka, his shackles, and a bowl of water. But as his eyes followed the sheer rock, he saw, with some surprise, there were people above. He was in a pit.

They stared down at him, and gestured. They spoke and laughed and ate. They looked clean, and even above the stink of his dirty floor he detected scents of spice that reminded Ruka of his mother's cooking.

As he moved and looked at them they pointed, exciting amongst themselves as he rose up to his water-dish. A chain attached to metal rings clattered across the floor and apparently bound him by the ankle, but he could still use his hands enough to lift and drink.

He wondered at the poison the little cowards had given him. *A most useful trick, he thought.*

Ruka's body laughed, perhaps because it was still alive. His crowd of watchers at first seemed pleased with the show. But he filled the 'pit' with his strong voice, and they pulled away at the sound as if he'd cursed, or thrown a rock.

"You're clever little buggers, aren't you?" He shouted. "Very good."

His body raised the water-dish in salute, and drained the rest, still smiling and laughing.

"I'm still alive, brother," it said out loud, sounding pleased.

Ruka blinked. *What did you call me?*

"I am Bukayag. Surely you know that. And are we not both the sons of Beyla?"

Bukayag. The man Ruka had become. The fake name Egil had given him those years ago to evade the law, and assume the role of a rune-shaman. Bukayag 'the arrogant seer, re-born'. It had all been nonsense, just a ruse, and yet…

I suppose we are like brothers, he thought. Ruka had always wanted a brother as a child, even the murderous, rage-filled kind, and even if he'd made him up.

"Before, I had no name," said Bukayag, "now I do. I exist." His body, or maybe his brother, stretched then sat down.

In any case Ruka knew he was right. His body was always doing things he hadn't strictly told it to. The men of ash said it was because he was single-born—that he had eaten his twin in the womb. Perhaps it was true, perhaps it joined them somehow, like the dead in Ruka's Grove.

I'm sorry if I ate you brother, he thought, *I might be a monster.*

Bukayag shrugged. "Maybe it was me who ate you."

Ruka thought on this and supposed it should be terrible, but made him feel better. He felt a sense of justice—right from the start they'd been in it together, killer and killed, just the same. He dug a grave with all the others and put 'Bukayag' on the post, just in case.

Don't worry, brother, I'll think of a way out of this pit.

"Good. Best do it quickly."

Bukayag lay down in the filth without concern, resting like on the sea to conserve his strength.

Keep your eyes and ears wary, if you can, Ruka 'told' him.

"I shall try," he mumbled.

Ruka left him to it, trusting him, and feeling a warmth in that trust. While his brother rested, he practiced climbing the rock walls of the cave in his mind.

3

After two days of water and gruel, guards came with spears and shackles.

There were four of them, all wearing thin leather padding, carrying poorly forged blades of maybe bronze. They yanked at Ruka's chain till he rose and followed.

They dragged him past a trough—a big wooden bucket used for feeding animals in the Ascom—where a dozen other filthy, half-naked, half-starving men jostled for food. Then through another metal door, into another dirt-floored pit.

He struggled and lingered long enough to examine the hinges and lock, and the thickness of the metal. On the other side of this new pit-room stood a big brute of a Northman, with two guards of his own holding chains.

Crude wooden clubs lay in the center of the dirt-caked stone. All around the top of the pit stood fine-smelling, fine-looking watchers, many of whom Ruka recognized from before. He noted their clothing, their faces, the other people they watched, and who laughed when who spoke.

All at once, the guards released the chains. They sprung away and slammed their clever metal doors behind them, and the big brute ran forward with fear and violence in his eyes. He scooped up a club along the way, raising it up with a wordless, language-crossing shout of bloody intent.

Ruka did not move. He could feel his brother's urge to kill—to seize the smaller, terrified man and rip him to shreds. But he knew that was what his captors wanted. No doubt it's what they expected from a big, monstrous looking creature. And in that moment Ruka was sure these people had never seen his kind before.

At the last moment before the other man struck, Ruka lunged, catching the forearm as it swung. His attacker moved much too slowly, and much too boldly. Ruka took the meat of the man's arm, held him back with it, and squeezed. He held his eyes as he squeezed harder, and harder, until the bones of the arm flexed and threatened to snap.

In the briefness, and in the obvious mismatch of the contest, the cheers of the small crowd faded. The filthy prisoner lost all his courage in Ruka's grip, as had so many others before him. He dropped his weapon.

Ruka crushed until his foe whimpered and sagged, until the contest of strength was so obvious and unequal it became obscene. Then he motioned back to the other side of the pit, and released him to flee back to his corner.

Ruka lifted the discarded weapon as he scanned the crowd. He watched them closely, looking to see who was pleased, who wasn't, and where the eyes turned.

The tribe's hierarchy was soon obvious. One man alone became actively ignored—peered at only with the corners of eyes. *There you are,*

Ruka thought, *chief of the pits.*

This chief was older than most. He was well groomed, with the stature of a man who once liked to fight, but now liked to eat. The crowd tried to watch him without watching. They seemed worried, but some at least looked amused. Almost pleased. Perhaps these were his enemies or rivals.

From the moment he'd entered the room, Ruka had begun to practice throwing a club in his Grove. He moved a target and tried again and again in the training field he had labored in since he was a boy.

The pit above him had no railing, and the distance was short. Men began shouting at the other prisoner, who had scurried back to his side and huddled on the ground. Ruka waited for the chaos to grow. *Be ready, brother, your moment is soon.*

The crowd kept up its calling in harsh tones, others turning to one another and laughing perhaps to soothe the mounting tension. At last the chief spoke, and all eyes turned to him.

Now!

Bukayag launched the weapon hard at a smiling-man closest to the edge. It was not a tool designed to be thrown, and its flight was awkward, but it struck. It hit the man in the gut and no doubt did little damage. But damage was not the intent.

The terrified watcher startled in surprise. He jostled his neighbors, who themselves panicked as he stumbled against them. They knocked him forward—the only place they could push—and he lost his footing. With a wild, useless flail, he fell into the pit.

The crowd cried out in horror, and Ruka paced forward in measured steps. He knew the door behind him was complex. It had several latches and required a key, and would take the guards far too long to open.

None of the fine-smelling, fine-dressed watchers carried weapons—at least nothing except perhaps knives small enough to be hidden. He did not think they had the skill or the instinct to throw what they could down to intervene.

'Smiler' moaned and turned over to his back. He held his wrist as if he'd broken it in the fall, and his face was bloody from where it bounced off the stone. But he was very much alive.

With one hand, Ruka reached down and lifted him by his neck, amused at the slight weight. He was heavier than Lawspeaker Bodil, perhaps, but not by much. Ruka wondered if he would crush as easily.

The guards had entered now with swords drawn, but waited across the pit. Perhaps they waited for orders, or perhaps from fear of the big white demon. It made no difference.

Ruka looked up and waited for the chief's eyes. *This is for you,* he meant to say. *I am a killer, but I am not mindless. I can be useful.*

He squeezed till the flesh of Smiler's neck shrunk—until the harder structure inside crushed and popped to half the size it should be. He dropped the poor man to suffocate on the ground, and started on his grave in his Grove.

The crowd gasped and shrieked. Many covered their mouths in horror, though some few of the men still looked pleased.

The dying man writhed and squirmed on the ground, his mouth leaking blood as he made his last, desperate strangled sounds. Ruka felt a sudden anger at the reaction above.

Why do you recoil? He wanted to scream. *Isn't this what you came for? A dead man in a pit?*

They cared only that the man who died was one of them. *We are none of us safe*, Ruka wanted to tell them—a hard lesson learned well in the wilds as an outcast. Such was the nature of all living things.

But he didn't know their words, and in any case his point to the king had been made. He put his hands out and knelt, hoping the guards didn't beat him to death.

They ran forward and seized his chain. Something hard struck his shoulder, then his sides. Ruka hardly felt the blows, and Bukayag laughed.

"I will take it, brother, never mind."

Thank you, brother. Be patient, and trust me now. We will survive.

Bukayag nodded, covering his head and hunching down to deflect the hits as best he could.

At last the chief called out, and the attack stopped. He pointed down at Ruka and spoke, then pointed at the dying man and spoke some more. All were silent, as if ashamed or at least uncomfortable. Then the chief laughed. He laughed alone, and the onlookers forced smiles with white lips and white faces, clapping with hands that hardly found each other.

The guards made Ruka stand, yanking his chain until he followed. They walked him back to his pit, treating him more gently now that they were not being watched. Soon enough they were gone, and he was alone again, battered and spotted with blood on the filthy stone.

Bukayag didn't mind. Ruka watched all the faces again from the perfect images of his memory. He watched the chief again and again as he laughed, and tried to place his words. He saw the fear in the eyes of even the women standing on the ledge, the shiftless hands and postures ready to run, ready to hide. Slowly, he understood.

This man was not a chief at all. He ruled alone, and with fear. He fought men like dogs for amusement, and to terrify his followers. This man was like Imler the Betrayer. This man was a king.

Ruka leaned his body back against the cold stone as his mind raced.

"Do you have a plan?" It wasn't fear in Bukayag's voice, only impatience.

Ruka didn't. At least not a good one. *We are nothing to this man.* The realization frightened him. *He does not see our value, nor does he care to try.*

"Then we must escape." Bukayag looked at the smooth, stone walls.

Ruka's attempt to climb his cave had been largely unsuccessful. He would need metal tools to dig hand holds or pierce the rock. And they were watched every moment.

"Then we kill a guard." Bukayag sniffed and lay down. "We take his sword and keys, and fight our way out."

Yes. It may come to that. But I believe there are hundreds, maybe thousands of warriors. A king must have a proper army.

Bukayag looked around the cold, deep prison, then closed his eyes and let out a breath. "Doesn't matter. This is not how I die."

This seemed a ridiculous thing to say, yet it gave Ruka some comfort. It reminded him of his purpose, and that such things could mean more than the limits of flesh. He glanced around his Grove at the expanding limits, thinking of the mysteries yet to be solved in the land of the living and the dead. He took strength from his brother and repeated again and again. *This is not how I die.*

4

Arun the ex-monk, killer, and thief, wore his favorite pirate mask. Its name was Noose.

"Drink, Noose?" said the newest member of the Bahala Crew, a smile on his ugly baby-face.

Arun leaned on a rail over-looking the famous Trung fighting pit. He closed his eyes, putting his head in his hands.

"Just get me some tea."

'New Guy' snorted and took other men's orders, and Arun kept on pretending he was more hung-over than he was.

"Who do we like?" said another of the boys, waving a fistful of tickets. Arun tossed a hand as if to say he didn't care. But of course, he'd already placed his bet.

The Bahala's complement of kidnapping, extorting, murderous criminals were not a trustworthy lot. Arun's gambling custom was a monthly display of wanton debasement, then he'd come to Trung's slave-show reeking of rum and sex with red eyes and single syllabic words. Once properly shielded by the farce, he would slink off as if to retch, and quietly wager around half his savings. This time, though, he had bet it all.

"You're one stupid, dependable lush, my friend."

The Bahala's captain slapped a meaty palm on Arun's back, and he grunted in response, gulping saliva with a fake spasm.

"Which whorehouse you hitting anyway, eh? Damned if I don't fancy myself a spin."

The captain was a city-native, and equal parts paranoid and curious, so it was hard to say which this was. Anyway, Arun never told anyone anything he didn't have to.

"Not sure, Cap. I think a few."

The fat man roared and slapped Arun's back again, turning to the men to repeat 'I think a few!'

Arun wasn't exactly faking the debauch. Most of his life he'd been trapped at the monastery with old men and boys, forbidden from touching himself, knowing nothing about lust or love or vice of any kind. These days he made up for lost time.

He had a few regular girls who cleared their nights for his visits, stocking up on drink and sweets and toys, taking turns with glee till even his well honed stamina wore down and he slept like the dead.

Arun loved them as he loved all beautiful women. He brought them gifts, he overpaid, tipping at least double the cost. And if they ever had trouble with a customer or a pimp while he was gone, he 'intervened' on return, and added a few more notches to 'Noose's' reputation.

Of course he'd *killed* his share of women—such was the life of a pirate. He killed children and holy men and cripples, too, if the price was right, or because the boat was sinking and who had room for broke bloody prisoners. But he didn't enjoy it.

"Entertainment, gentlemen?"

The girl's voice was sweet and playful, like a child's. Arun stared from the corner of his eye. A teenage fight-piece passed out a different kind of ticket. She was barely clothed in what might be fishing net, her skin and hair shone glossy with paints and oils, her smile flashed to show crooked teeth that somehow made her even more appealing.

"No, thank you." Arun stood straight and smiled, weaving to maintain the illusion of drunkenness.

A few of the crew pawed at her hands for tickets, but nothing else. Everyone in a place like this knew the girls belonged to local gangs, and that to smudge her meant buy, or bleed.

Fight-girl smiled back as she passed, and Arun breathed in, hoping for her perfume. He smelled only the dirt and dried blood and booze of the pit.

"They're stepping out," said New Guy, handing Arun his tea. The crowd of nobles, pirates and other degenerates waved their tickets, pointing below.

The captain whistled. "Just look at that monster!" he yelled, barely heard now over the frantic last moment betting of the crowd.

Arun grunted and hardly looked, as if he didn't really notice or care. But 'The Monster', of course, was why he was here.

A week earlier, a flesh-peddler bragged they'd found an albino giant, and that they'd sold him to the slaver king.

"Took damn near five doses to knock it out," said his man, shaking his head as he remembered. "Poison makes 'em choke, sometimes, so you've gotta be ready. We let 'em out, and he comes peaceful-like and sits, 'cept the monster just kept fuckin' eating! Headman tried every tongue from here to Naran. Didn't hardly blink. Nothing. He just sat there an' spooned it in with these…" he shook his hands for effect, "these big, pink palms like you never seen, Noose. You wouldn't believe it."

Arun had seen many strange things, however, and *did* believe. He'd seen old monks who could wrestle strong warriors to the dirt like children; he'd seen men bend iron with their flesh, and once, a little boy who maybe lived forever.

So he walked down to the pits and bribed a prison guard to take a look. Together they snuck down into Trung's slave pens while the stock fed, watching the huge man bend to take his supper like a beast.

He was still shackled and held by four guards, and even so the other slaves gave him wide berth as if afraid. Arun watched him, and watched him. He inspected his wide, hardened feet, his pink, callused palms, his black hair sprouting like fur. Whatever the man or creature was, he was not an albino.

His short hair looked a common black, most of his skin a color between cream and wood. Every movement he made flexed a bunched or corded muscle, his body so fatless he seemed half-starved. His whole head lacked symmetry, with queer lumps and crookedness from forehead to jaw. Yet it was his eyes that held Arun's attention. His eyes had bright, near slit pupils, and the almost yellow color could still be seen in the gloom.

Arun watched in fascination. The giant had at last finished his supper and rose up as if the pits were his, and strode to his cell as if his captors were his servants.

In that moment, Arun knew he saw something special. In truth he wasn't much of a gambler, but he could always read the grit and mettle of a man. With only a glance at a man's eyes he could often see how far they'd go in the name of violence, how committed to their own cause. When he looked in the savage's eyes—his far distant stare, boring into the world as if seeing through to some other realm—Arun saw a lord of death.

"All on the Savage," he'd whispered later to his usual bookie, betting damn near every coin he had.

It was riskier than ever before, but he'd grown tired of waiting—tired of murdering for scraps and sharing the company of common pirates. And he felt a sureness and madness he couldn't seem to stop. His hands moved as if in a dream as they spilled a small fortune in island gold—every ounce of wealth he'd stolen and saved since fleeing Bato and the monks, and a life of joyless discipline.

The bookie's brow raised as he licked his lips. He vanished the coins beneath his trays to weigh them and glanced around. "To win or place?"

"To win," said Arun. He'd stared again at the wooden board etched with steep odds and still felt compelled, as if he weren't truly in control. It was four-to-one against the savage. And whether this was ignorance or because of the favorites involved, he had no idea. He knew only they were wrong.

He allowed that 'The Hand' was down there, and 'Three-toed Braun'—both who'd survived a dozen scraps only losing bits and gaining shallow scars. No doubt the odds would change slightly when the crowd had their first good look at the thing, but they wouldn't have much time.

Arun already pictured his own ship and crew—a future filled with choice and power and everything he ever dreamed. It was just one last gamble, one last risk, and then it was done. One more win and he'd be free.

The bookie's greasy forehead was sweating as he smiled and held up the ticket. He looked nervous. *But it's hot*, Arun remembered thinking, *nothing to be worried about. Nothing out of the ordinary.*

He'd gone to this particular man because he had a noble patron and rich customers. He had few masters and could be discreet, and because he had every reason to be forthright or else lose his reputation. But by the time the man said, "Good luck," his smile and tone no different than always, Arun's gut flipped with unease.

"Here they go," said the captain now, bringing Arun back with another rude slap. The men all pushed up against the rail to see, their drinks slopping on the already wet floor.

Arun watched knives drop from the slave-handlers' hands to bounce at the fighter's feet; he watched the giant stoop down and lift his like a child's toy, glancing at his enemies as if only curious.

Arun saw the half-looks and glances of the fighters. He saw their nods and silent agreement as it passed to each an instant. The flip in his gut turned and flopped like a dying fish.

The five veterans aimed their paths toward 'The Savage'. Their feet and knives pointed at a single target.

They all knew, Arun realized in horror, *all the regulars*.

He closed his eyes. The pit-fighters below were survivors because they avoided killing the other champions. They played by a certain code and so protected themselves from death. And all the real gamblers here understood: they'd kill the outsider first.

Arun staggered against the rail, held up mostly by the other pirates. The world spun but not from the drink. *I'll be right back where I started. Another broke pirate who gambled away his blood-money and went back to the sea like any other stupid slave or peasant.*

Arun's hot tea spilled on the skin of his sandaled feet. His ambitions shook, their foundations caught in a great wave or an earthquake far beyond his control.

And for the first time since he'd left the monastery, the ex-master of the Ching did something he'd sworn an oath in blood to abandon—an oath he had kept though near drowned in the Coastal Sea, and as he'd lain stabbed, and alone, in the gutters of Sri Kon. For the first time since Arun had abandoned his faith and his only family in the world, he closed his eyes, and prayed.

5

Ruka heard the shouts before anything. Light and men waited beyond the narrow, metal-gated mouth that stunk of rot and blood. He stopped and felt the urge to fight his way free, to turn and run as he once had when surrounded in a field by other starving outcasts, not knowing what he'd face.

Perhaps it's better to fight here, he thought, *then to try and take a weapon and navigate the pits.*

But he couldn't be sure. His escorts prodded him with sticks and grunts when he delayed, though they were being careful—as if they sensed he might choose this moment to strike. They had left him bound by ankles and wrists in a shoddy iron, but it was enough to hold him. If he fought them and failed he would be punished.

After his stunt in the pit they left him to wallow in his cage. He had no watchers now except the guards, who moved him away from his own waste only to feed on mush in a bucket. Without the sun he couldn't know the true passage of time, but he had a dead boy track the time in his Grove by pouring water through a narrow wooden tube, and count the drops. The dead were patient.

By this count he had estimated it was three days before men came with nets, clubs, and hoop-ended poles, which they managed to slip over Bukayag even as he raged.

They shuffled him through the feeding room, a tunnel lined with torches, and finally here to an open gate. Now he stepped through into another pit, and his ears filled with chants, and the roar of bloodthirsty men.

This new stone cage was huge, with the same smooth, high walls. The watchers above numbered in their hundreds, displaying a mix of clean and dirty clothes and faces. They pointed down and called as they saw him, eyes widening, mouths jabbering in excited talk too conjoined and cluttered to be understood. Some threw bits of greens and maybe bread onto the blood-stained dirt and straw. For a moment Ruka considered falling to his knees and eating it, but soon realized it looked and smelled as rotten as the ground.

Ruka's Chief Guard, a man the others called 'Kaptin' and who had never beaten Ruka or treated him cruelly, came forward.

Sweat shone on his brow and stained the cloth at his neck. The others stood behind him with their sticks and hoops, sweat pouring from their soft bodies. Kaptin held up a key. He motioned at the shackles and at himself, and his meaning was clear. *Be calm, and still, and I will unchain you.*

"Teemada, ka?"

Ruka felt Bukayag's urge to pull the manacles apart, to rage and leap at this lesser thing before him and tear out his throat. But violence now would not serve him.

Kaptin seemed an honorable sort. Even in the depths of hell, it seemed, decent men could be found improving it. Ruka relaxed. 'Ka' seemed a way to form a question, but also meant yes.

"Ka, Kaptin."

The man raised a brow in surprise, but nodded and came forward. He gestured for his men to follow close. His hands shook and he dropped the key once and turned a bright red.

At last he came close enough to push the key into Ruka's manacles, turning until an internal latch clicked. The metal came apart, and Kaptin glanced back to his men, no doubt realizing, just as Ruka, they were vastly too far to intervene. He stared into Ruka's eyes, and froze.

Ruka grinned at him. He did not know the word for honor, but gestured towards the gate with a nod.

Kaptin left the manacles and sprung away. He seemed to recover his wits and screamed at his men, no doubt rebuking their useless efforts. Then the gate closed.

Ruka unchained his ankles and rose up free for the first time since he'd killed the watcher in the pit.

Five more gates creaked and shuddered as men cranked impressive rope winches, and five more prisoners came in through other gates. The crowd cheered for all of them in ways they hadn't for Ruka. The men looked well-fed and scarred, with large muscles wrapped in fat. Ruka couldn't help but think: *their prisoners eat better than my people.*

He understood he would have to fight them to leave this place. The sons of Imler sometimes fought dogs or cocks in the same manner, but never men. Again he marveled at the cruelty of paradise. He wondered too if it was every warrior for himself, or if Ruka had to fight them all.

In his Grove he lined up five dead men in the training field. He gave them blunted knives and clubs and tried to take them all at once. Weapons bounced off his head and neck and chest before they fell, and he knew if he fought them this way then his wounds might kill him even if he won.

Bukayag sneered, which perhaps meant he was excited. He twitched their muscles and cracked their joints, the shudder of blood lust rising up Ruka's spine.

A large knife dropped from the ledge above. Ruka tested the edge and found it wanting, but thought he could drive it through flesh with enough force. He tested the weight and grip, and decided if Vol— god of craftsmen —truly existed, then he had left these lands long ago.

The other prisoners claimed their own blades and moved out from their gates. Their steps were slow and short, their bare feet crunching or dragging over rotten straw stuck in the sand. They watched each other; they watched the ground and the walls, and they picked paths through the clutter with care. But Ruka saw their glances, their feet, and the direction they held their knives, and he understood. He would have to kill them all.

We must be careful, brother. Keep moving, fight one or two at a time, don't let them cluster. And stop only stabs—the edges of these knives are too dull for cuts to matter. Oh, and take the one with three toes first.

Bukayag breathed and nodded. He had killed before, of course—he had ripped Priestess Kunla apart with his bare hands, his strength monstrous and frightening even to Ruka. But he had never truly fought, not like this, never in battle. It didn't seem to bother him.

He beat his chest with an open hand, letting the slap of his own flesh echo like a drum. He roared like Noss burning in the mountain, and charged.

* * *

Arun jumped like everyone else when the savage screamed. His voice was deep, but the shout rose in pitch as it lingered. The sound of it stood little hairs on Arun's neck and arms and he saw the same was true of others. He knew he'd heard it before, or something like it, in nightmares never quite drunk away.

The savage's shout wasn't the lust of battle. It was the cry of a husband whose wife was kidnapped; the cry of a father who'd found his family slaughtered by pirates. The giant's scream was pure horror.

At the sound, the gathered men's cheers for death fell flat and silent. The other fighters paused or winced back half a step. In the strange, momentary silence and stillness, the giant sprinted out from his gate.

He crossed the distance to Three-Toed Braun in moments, lifting him with one hand on his neck, using the other to stab again and again as he carried then hurled the big pit fighter to smash against a stone wall.

He looked back at the others, face almost bored, then bent down and took a second knife as his prize. He turned on the others, and spit on the ground.

A few fools in the crowd cheered. The other fighters clumped together and wiped sweating brows with forearms, no pretense now that this was anything but a contest of four against one. Still the gamblers remained in near-silence, until a single voice broke the strangeness.

"Kill him! Kill the fucking ape!"

"Get 'em!" called another pirate, too close to Arun's ear.

The words sounded harsh with hate, and soon picked up behind a hundred disjointed voices. The insults morphed into 'demon' and 'cum skin' and a hundred other vile things till they rose to a roar that drowned thought and sound.

Arun remembered to breathe. He remembered his future rested on these knife-tips and the fate of the man or thing below him.

The Savage circled now and kept his distance, seemingly oblivious to the crowd. He lunged and withdrew, as if probing for weakness, but the pit veterans held. At every advance they gathered and held up their knives, at every withdrawal they followed as one. On and on it went as the crowed jeered.

"There's four of you, take him!" called New Guy. His hands squeezed and thrust in jabs, as if he'd ever killed a man honorably and from the front.

The dance kept on. The pit fighters slowly pushed the gap, trying to direct their enemy towards a wall so they could pin him down. The giant abandoned his attempts and withdrew. He fell back, foolishly, and no doubt just as his enemies hoped. They followed, feet shuffling together in the sand, and Arun felt his hand crushing skin on his forearm as he gripped it.

Near the wall, the giant stooped and seized Three-Toed Braun, or at least his corpse. He lifted it up above his head as if it weighed nothing, blood dripping down to his shoulders and face. Then he lunged forward, arcing the body back then forward like a rock, and he *threw* it.

Arun at once thought the distance impossible. But the body sailed through the air, the strength to do such a thing incredible, inhuman. Two pit-fighters failed to move, bowling over as they caught it.

The giant raced behind his throw. He hacked with his knives like clubs at the scattered men till the first took a blow and stumbled. The savage kicked him back and stabbed at the rising men, gouging forearms and faces as more blood sprayed to the sands.

Get back! Arun almost screamed at him as the stunned fighters rallied.

They closed and made frenzied swings and jabs of their own, too close and panicked now for skill or coordination. These men had earned their places in the pit, had survived when other men fell. Some few blows connected, hard and fast and spraying blood from the giant's flesh. But for every hit, he retaliated.

He seized and spun his foes away as he battered and maimed them, planting his feet as he caught arms and gouged throats or chests. The men he struck solidly didn't rise.

Soon only 'The Hand' was left. He plunged his knife in a downwards strike, and the giant dropped his weapons and caught his arm, then the other. He stared down at the smaller man's eyes as he squeezed both wrists, and the veteran sagged and screamed .

Arun walked towards his bookie. The little man's booth was down some stairs on another level, the pit only visible there through a grate. He found him pale, and sweating. He licked his lips as Arun approached.

"You don't look well," said Arun, extending his ticket. "You might see a physician."

"Sir, it...the, fight. It isn't yet..."

A sickening crunch sounded from the pit, and the crowd groaned. Arun kept his ticket out.

"Congratulations, sir," the bookie whispered, looking increasingly green. He turned away and handed up an exchanger's chit with the number of a veritable fortune, and his mark.

"Thank you."

Arun took it with steady hands. He'd redeem it later—*much* later—when his crew and the other pirates were long gone. There would still be risk of getting robbed, perhaps, but then Arun had little fear of common thugs.

How many men in all the world could kill five veterans of the pit like that?

He had won a small fortune in the space of an afternoon, and yet it was this thought capturing his thoughts as he wandered out to an angry crowd.

He followed the swell of bodies from 'Trung's hole' to a warm sun, wondering who or what this giant was, and where he came from.

His thoughts soon clashed with memories of his teacher, old Master Lo, who'd twist his ear and ask what benefit knowledge served such a stupid boy. But he thought now as then *there is always benefit, you ignorant old prune.*

Despite the crowd, he pushed his way out from the cave and across the 'plaza', which was really just a patch of crushed rock outside Halin city, filled now by scum and the vendors who catered to them. It all connected—the cave, and the pits, and an underground river that came up in Trung's fortress.

This was just one of many things Arun knew and shouldn't—one of many secrets he might sell to the right buyer at the right time. *Like the secret of The Savage? Or can I somehow sell the man himself?*

"Ride to the city, sir?"

A leathery urchin displayed his mouth of broken teeth, carrying a wheeled-cart behind him. Fifty more stood scattered around the plaza shouting for business.

Arun ignored them and walked on through other wretches selling water and rum and sweet meats or pastries covered in flies. *Just take the money and run*, said a small, hopeless voice in his mind, which he'd never quite sorted as wisdom or fear. But soon enough it went quiet as it always did, ignored behind plans and ambitions that lead to fortune, or ruin.

In truth the dream of his own ship and crew was only a small dream—a consolation, a 'good enough' accepted by lesser men with lesser skill and courage. Arun had chosen that dream first because to admit to wanting more seemed laughable, ludicrous, unfounded in reality. And yet...

And yet he had risen from nothing. He had youth, wealth, and ability, and with luck and wit and his own two hands he had already defied his birth, his fate, and the 'wisdom' of old men. So why not more? Why not further?

He followed the well-worn path along a high ridge above the sea, then stopped and looked back at the jutting rock that formed Trung's caves. *What is your value, demon of the pit?* he wondered. And who would pay it, if they knew?

The answer was clear enough. The giant was worth more than just his own value. Already Arun ticked through the names of corrupt guards in his mind, and formed a mental map of Halin's fortress. The sheer boldness of the shaping plan inspired him more than it should, he knew. But a man could only be what he was.

Will you let me save you, Savage? Or will you snarl and bite at my hand?

He would have to act quickly, either way. For who could say how long the barbarian would last in prison? Or if escape was even possible? Or if the pay-off was worth the risk? Should he just tell a man who might be interested, or did he gamble, one more time?

He breathed out and watched sea waves break on rock below. It was an act, he knew, this moment of stillness—a self-delusion perhaps meant to convince himself he had choice. But he had made his choices long ago, and not unhappily.

Arun, ex-master of the Ching, would risk all. He would gamble his essence and fate and match it against any other man or woman in the world, and show his worth, even against a king. That was his Path. His *ojas*. His Way. And only death would stop him.

6

After the pit-fight, Ruka sat in his prison and ate what he thought was chicken.

Starving prisoners brought it and took away the bones with hungry eyes. He wondered how much they'd stolen, but didn't blame them. They cleaned his shallow cuts and wiped his body down with wet cloth, and they were so miserable-looking he left them to it without a fuss.

This 'king' has decided we have more value, brother, but only in the pit. And we won't last forever.

Bukayag nodded but said nothing. The blood of the fight had seemed to sate him, and in any case there was nothing for him to do. They were still trapped and guarded with no escape; they were still at the mercy of a ruthless butcher who ruled alone and fought men like beasts.

I'll give him to you, brother, Ruka promised, *though I don't yet know how. He can smolder in the same fires as Kunla.*

For now all he could do was wait. In two days by Grove reckoning, the guards returned, this time with hairless dogs.

Kaptin brought them himself, one under each arm. He nodded in a gesture Ruka had decided was respect, and so he returned it. Then the little creatures were released on the floor.

They seemed harmless things—longer in the snout than the fang, with plump, elongated bodies and stretched, weak necks. They bound into the pit without leashes, sniffing at the filth and stains before coming to Ruka's hands without a shred of fear.

They climbed into his lap, licking his arms and face and chest. Their tongues were rough and wet and he almost laughed at their boldness. He'd always wanted a pet as a child.

"Next year," his mother always said, and he'd knew she lied but understood. It was hard enough to keep themselves alive.

He let the bizarre, friendly creatures lick him, amazed at their reaction to a stranger. They explored the prison, nibbled each other's ears and tussled before finally settling down on his lap to rest.

All the while, he felt eyes above.

The pleasure of the animals fell away as the men watched, and he knew it wasn't allowed in the world of the living—not in a world that ate weakness and spit out.

It's a test, brother. A trap of the mind. They mean to shackle us with affection.

Bukayag said nothing, perhaps because he felt none.

The men watched Ruka as Ruka watched the dogs. The 'king' sat in his padded chair, sipping from a crystal cup and looking down with a cold stare and a cruel smile. For a time, Ruka focused on his Grove.

He sat in his mother's garden, fighting the hopeless rage and isolation threatening to swallow him. He knew as he had always known that gentle things weren't allowed. He knew the creatures would be used to control him, to break him—to be taken away or killed once they'd earned his love. He knew he should have ignored them entirely, and had already done too much.

He picked spinach and squash thinking perhaps later he'd teach Stable-boy-From-Alverel how to make his mother's soup as a break from the forge.

Please, brother, he nearly wept. *Do this thing for me. They must see no weakness. But be gentle, please, and be quick.*

Bukayag blinked awake and smiled at their captors. He lifted two dogs by their necks as Ruka's tears fell and trapped in the crooked indents of his face. For a moment the animals yelped and squirmed, then Bukayag crushed their throats. He tossed them away, and yawned.

The king jerked forward, and laughed.

Ruka covered his ears and forced his brother to stare up at the man's thick, curved lips, his fat belly shaking as he spoke to the others. The watchers settled deeper in their seats, re-filling their drinks and eating round, plump fruits from platters held by half-naked women.

Ruka dug his dirty nails into his palms. *When I am free*, he thought, *I will wipe that smile from your face, and show you the true meaning of suffering.*

He sat in the darkness and seethed, but soon couldn't stop from thinking of Egil and a night of screams. Through the heat of his anger he felt hypocrisy and shame, and thought perhaps such things could never be justified. If so then one day Ruka would pay, and without complaint. But this cruel king would be the last. First he would let Bukayag take this man in his hands like the dogs, and he would not ask for mercy.

For now he sat in misery with the twisted corpses of the animals, wishing he could pet their fur. He had never killed a creature save for a man he did not intend to eat.

Later, the pit's iron door clicked again.

Bare, brown legs moved into Ruka's view on the tapping of wooden shoes. He looked up and saw a girl wrapped in soft, dyed fabric that looked cut from a single strip of cloth. It clung to her flawless, smooth skin. Her terrified eyes flit about the pit.

Kaptin entered behind her. His face held a labored calm, and his eyes went at once to the corpses of the dogs. He put a hand to the girl's shoulder and held her firm, almost in a protective gesture. Then the king barked from above.

Kaptin's eyes found Ruka's and held them. It brought memories of a gathering hall in Hulbron, with a knife to a priestess, and a chief testing his resolve.

Oh yes, Ruka wanted to say, *I will kill her, chief of the pits. I will kill you, and your king, and the whole world before I fail Beyla, before I become another suffering, helpless slave like you.*

But he did not speak their words, so he only growled. The girl shook at the sound, her careful smile breaking beneath her fear.

Ruka was familiar with his effect on women. He had imagined perhaps in this new world he might be seen differently. But he knew this as foolish. He glanced at his blood-stained clothes and manacled legs, the piles of his own waste left in the corner of the room. Here he was a monster rotting in the depths of hell, and he did not blame her.

Kaptin's arm firmed even as his eyes glazed, and he pushed the girl forward.

Ruka did not know precisely what they intended. Perhaps they meant her to sit with him and remind him of life and the possibility of more than fighting other men in a pit. When she came closer and he did nothing, some of the watchers laughed and made thrusting gestures with their hips.

The girl put a trembling hand to her shoulder and slipped the fabric to the grimy floor. Ruka blinked, staring at her utter nakedness save for gold rings on her wrists and ankles.

His eyes roamed without thought. They paused and probed in ways that brought heat to his face. It was the first time he'd ever seen a woman without her clothes except for his mother. And all at once, he understood.

The thought struck him numb. They meant to rut them like dogs, or horses.

He had heard of outcast boys being abused in the Ascom in such ways, though he had never seen it. And those were just boys.

In the Ascom, to take a woman in this way was a crime so great, a stain so deep, that a man would suffer forever in the afterlife.

Do you not have mothers? Daughters? Ruka thought with horror. *Are there no laws against such things? Are you even men at all?*

"I'll kill her after," Bukayag whispered, "so our jailer will see no weakness." He licked his lips. "By now it's obvious there are no gods to fear."

Ruka twitched at his brother's words. They weren't his, exactly, but they had still come from his mouth.

Doing anything they wish is weakness. And this thing is evil. I won't let you.

Bukayag curled their hands into fists and squirmed against the wall.

"*Why not?*" he hissed, and the venom behind it surprised and frightened Ruka. Kaptin startled at the sound, and the girl paled.

Because she could be our mother. There is no difference. What sort of men don't protect their mothers and daughters from such a thing?

"*Outcast men!*" Bukayag rattled at his chain. "I've never even touched a woman except to kill, brother. Give this to me. All women are daughters, all are mothers. What of it? Ours is dead."

Ruka found no words in the silence, but his answer was clear. Bukayag stood and kicked a dead dog across the pit.

"I take your pain, I kill your enemies. How am I repaid? We're in this *pit* because of you. We should have killed those fat little pigs and escaped before. Now we're stuck in this fucking stone-trap and we'll die here. I want a woman before I'm nothing. I want it. I want this. *Give it to me!*"

Ruka breathed and took control of his body. His brother wasn't entirely wrong, but that didn't matter. Ruka would not let his final act be submission and torture. He saw the fear from the girl and the guard, the wonder from the men above. The silence held and Ruka sensed Bukayag struggling uselessly against him.

I can hurt you brother, in ways even you can understand. But you can't hurt me, not in my Grove. Don't forget that.

"I haven't," Bukayag choked. Ruka seized control now and quieted his brother. He leaned back against the wall as he had after the dogs, as if he didn't care—as if the girl didn't interest him.

The king didn't wait long before he gestured forward, eyes twinkling with pleasure. His fellow watchers stood now with food and drink all but forgotten.

Kaptin's face had turned red, his face flickering with images of Chief Caro, both their honor trampled out of fear and weakness. And like Caro, he obeyed. He pushed the girl forward perhaps harder than he'd intended, his anger truly at himself.

She trembled as she lurched forward. She recovered and reached out to try and touch Ruka's chest, tears welling in her eyes.

I'm sorry, Ruka thought, wishing he could say it. *I don't wish you harm, but you must refuse. Please refuse and face whatever punishment comes, even if it means your death. Die by their hands, beautiful cousin, and not mine. Be brave, here and now when it matters, for the brave live forever, and in death you will be truly free.*

He growled low again, but she ignored it. Then she reached down towards the swell between Bukayag's legs.

"No," Ruka said in his own tongue as he shook his head. *Don't do it,* he almost prayed, *don't make me the one to choose.*

She smiled grotesquely through the tears, paints congealing and running down her face. She tossed back her long, thick hair as she rubbed against him in a revolting attempt to seduce.

For a moment he did nothing, understanding very well why his brother wanted her. Ruka was a young man, too. He felt the pull of lust, the longing and misery of rejection and solitude. But they would not defeat his purpose.

He clenched his hands, knowing Bukayag wouldn't help him now. He would have to see and feel, to remember the life leave the girl's body until the day he died. And perhaps he owed her that. Perhaps the details of the dead were the duty of the living.

He lifted his arms and seized the girl's neck, feeling the soft, moist flesh with his own hands. He watched the dread and listened to the air squeeze as he closed the pathways in her throat. The pressure swelled in the pools of her perfect brown eyes, and she stared at him as if surprised.

"I'm sorry," he whispered, holding back his tears, knowing his curse was to see and feel this moment until Noss left his mountain—not one image or smell or inch of skin forgotten.

He held on and squeezed, very gently, until the struggle stopped. He held her and looked Kaptin in the eyes until the man's jaw clenched and he looked away. Then Ruka dropped the girl's corpse to the dirty floor with the dogs, and the waste.

Only then did he go to his Grove. He built the girl a grave, adding some tree bark and flowers, labeling it 'Girl in pit'. He drew Zisa's rune because she'd been beautiful. His tears made a patch of mud by her sign.

"I will not be a slave," he whispered later, long after Kaptin and the watchers left him alone, perhaps bored with the show.

"I will not be a slave," he said more loudly, hearing the metal door close and lock again—hearing the voices, laughter and babbling fade down the pathways above.

In his mind he rose and climbed from the darkness, learning every secret of this place. He gathered his strength as he had once intended in the land of ash, and one by one he butchered these corrupt, cruel men like a vengeful god. This thought, at least, brought some comfort.

Ruka knew he was not a good man. He had killed and tortured and lied, and if he had not been born a monster then perhaps he had become one. But if he could kill this Trung and all those like him—if he could cut away evil men like blackened flesh, or rotting toes deadened by the frost, then perhaps, perhaps the scales might balance. At least then he would have a purpose worthy of his mother's sacrifice. It was worth a try.

7

After the girl in the pit, the king starved him for three days. Then came more men with nets.

Bukayag resisted, roaring and bloodying the small-army of guards as they claimed him. They beat him with their hoop-poles in anger once they'd shackled him, then they bound him with loop after loop of rope, hands trembling even as they handled his chained-up limbs.

Good with knots, Ruka decided as he watched, then went to his Grove at once to try and copy them while his body was half-carried to a new door, and a new pit.

There in the dark he saw strange, rusted instruments of fear and pain lining the walls. The specific purpose of each was not always obvious, but Ruka soon got the idea. In one corner a man hung upside down from a rope by his feet with a metal saw half-way through his abdomen, a trench of gaping red flesh opened from his crotch. Ruka could still hear him breathing.

Another lay tied to wooden boards with a vertical v-shape top. His limbs were splayed, chained with metal weights, and the sharp angle of the wood dug an inch into his chest. A third man sat strapped to a chair, a metal rod protruding from swollen lips, blood dripping from the corners.

Bukayag jerked and thrashed at the sight, but Ruka knew it was useless. His new guards smiled, talking and laughing now that he'd been secured. They settled him on a sturdy chair with armrests, and strapped his limbs to it with leather at the wrists and ankles.

Other men here spoke to the guards and dismissed them. They wore aprons like butchers, their faces masked by scarves. Ruka decided these were to mask the smell of their work, noting the distinct, gag-inducing sweet-rot of decayed men. No laughter or words passed between these 'torturers' as they lined up tools in wooden trays.

Despite their masks, to Ruka they seemed no different than smiths or farmers with houses and families. They seemed ordinary men performing a task. And though he thought them cowards, he didn't hate them.

As they prepared, he thought of Egil and his own amateur attempt at breaking another's will. Again he felt the shame, then the questions of why and if and what else might he have done. Egil had become a useful servant, yes, that was true. But had there been no other way? And if not, could Ruka now protest his fate?

"I will bear it, brother."

Bukayag breathed for them and showed no fear. But Ruka looked at the tools and expected not to live.

He felt some guilt for not giving his brother the girl in the pit. It may have been their only chance—a brief moment of pleasure before misery and death. Had it been pride that made him resist? Was the girl being taken against her will not better than being killed? Ruka found he did not know.

"It is meaningless," growled Bukayag. "There is only fear and failure. The world is cruel to the weak. How they suffer does not matter."

Ruka sighed, disagreeing, though he could think of no good reason why.

He looked to the top of this new pit and saw the same collection of padded chairs. This room had two doors, and by referencing these against the lay-out of the area in his mind, Ruka knew they led to rooms or pits he had not seen. But this did not help him. He could see no way to escape.

"They won't hurt us badly—you'll see. I'll bear it."

Bukayag sounded almost excited.

Soon enough the torturers began to bow and scrape and babble, and Ruka saw the king had arrived. They met each other's eyes, and the king looked amused. He wore a thin shirt that exposed layered fat, which matched the grotesque, drooping mounds on his neck.

Ruka sneered, thinking: *if I'd found you in empty Ascomi hills, 'king', you'd have fed me for a week.*

Two torturers seized his fists. He pulled at the ropes and straps and chains but the chair hardly shook, so he clenched his fingers together with all his might.

The men strained to pry them apart with both hands but failed. Two others with plant-like sticks beat him about the legs, the flexible shafts seeming designed more for pain than real damage. When this too failed they moved up to his knees and his chest, his head and face, until he tasted blood in his mouth.

Bukayag spit it out and laughed.

"Is this all you have, little cowards? Sticks and knives? Skin and fingers?"

Ruka sighed and left his brother to his task. He buried some of the new Northern plants in his mother's Grove-garden, not sure how much to water or if there'd be enough sun. After, he walked to his house, which was much grander than its humble beginnings.

He'd finished two levels now, and dug a basement around the cellar. He'd re-done most of the walls with stone and made new rooms for guests, or for reading, and one for children and their toys just in case. The beds were now all sturdy things with proper frames and mattresses. Pillows lined the wood-based furniture that he'd carved himself and strewn throughout the larger spaces.

All around him dead men cleaned and dusted, equally proud of their work. Ruka liked to take some meals here in the kitchen. It was just pretend, and his corpse-guests never ate or drank, but he felt it still good practice. Here in his house he liked to do things properly.

"Pass the salt," he said to Girl-from-the-pit, who had appeared whole with only a few bruises on her neck from where he'd choked her.

They smiled at each other, and unlike some of the others, she didn't seem to blame him.

Ruka complimented the chefs. He wasn't sure exactly what the meat was, but he didn't care. It tasted like blood, in any case, with the torturers beating him still with their sticks.

From the corner of his eye, Ruka saw the torturers give up on his hands and move to his nine toes. They pulled off a nail with metal pliers, and Bukayag laughed and wiggled his fingers before he clenched them again and winked.

Ruka sighed, and didn't intervene. It would be wiser to show pain and terror, he knew. But since they were likely dead regardless, he let his brother have his fun.

* * *

A crippled killer has no value.

Arun watched as the fools pried and thrashed his prize. He strained against the door, still and quiet, forcing sense to overcome desire.

Damned idiot, he thought. *Why damage him? Stupid man. So wasteful!*

King Trung sat comfortably as the pale savage turned red from welts, bamboo sticks thwack thwack thwacking a rhythmless beat.

Will they butcher him now, then? Am I too late? Or can I pluck him out before the king's eyes?

Arun did not know, but feared to risk it. He clenched a fist and waited in the darkness, breathing against his mask. If he did nothing and the man died, then all his work and preparation and risk already meant nothing. But he knew he had no choice except to wait.

First, Trung needed to leave. If he saw Arun spring on his torturers, he'd run to his bodyguards, and in moments a hundred swords and eyes would come running, all of them warned and watching for a big white creature Arun maybe couldn't quiet or conceal.

He could call it all off, of course. He had spent a small fortune already; and yes, he could have bought two boats instead of one before all the bribes. But to attempt, and fail? Unthinkable. Better to live and gamble again, and for now, *right now*, he could wait. The damage to the barbarian was still slight. And the king might yet leave. *Or a rock might fall from the sky,* Arun thought dryly, *or the earth may erupt in some fiery explosion.*

He forced a calm he did not feel, and took slow, steadying breaths. He waited as the torturers plucked two nails from the barbarian's toes; he watched as they lifted blades and pokers and held them inches from the barbarian's strange eyes. But the man did not wail or flinch, and the torturers set down their blades. They lifted their bamboo rods and knocked them against his flanks as if they tendered meat. But all the while the crazy savage only laughed, or spit blood, and grinned.

I need him to run, and fight, and swim, Arun thought. *Not possible if he's ruined; not possible if he's driven mad.*

Throughout it all, the king stared at his prisoner. When the barbarian had borne more pain than any man had any right to bear with good grace, he laughed, too. He shook his head in disbelief, and perhaps pleasure.

"Enough! Enough!" He waved his hands. "What a wonder! Let's not ruin him. But keep him from food or sleep till I return. Perhaps he'll be more docile."

The chief torturer stood from his work, red and sweating. "Yes, lord, very wise to stop now; he would have broken soon."

Arun almost choked on his spit.

But the king nodded as if it were true. He eased his fat belly up in the way of old men, aided by grunts and a rolling stand, and Arun heard the happy whistling of his exit down a near-by hall.

For the first time all evening, Arun smiled.

"Get the guards, they can move him back," said the head torturer as he pulled down his scarf and wiped sweat from his cheeks.

Arun fingered his short throwing spears, his hands dry and steady now that violence loomed.

No, he thought, choosing his targets. *No, I think not.*

8

Ruka watched as a shadow cut a torturer's throat, then tossed a plant-spear through another.

He left his Grove and his supper to come back and watch, blinking as he tried to understand what he saw.

Soon he realized the shadow was just a man in dark clothes, very tall and thin compared to the others. He had been hidden from Ruka's eyes because he stood almost behind him, and very still. But who he was and why he attacked made no difference. He was killing torturers. That made him Ruka's ally.

Bukayag filled the pit with their own pretend shouts of agony, drowning out the sounds of the dying men to cover the shadow's attack. The shadow leapt from man to man throwing knives and slashing faces and throats, leaving only the faint moans of suffering, and the dripping of fresh blood.

Ruka shivered at the rare feeling of surprise.

The shadow stood before him with one bloody knife raised, then he stooped low and cut at Ruka's many loops of rope. Once finished, he rummaged through corpses for a key to the metal shackles, and took no pause to rest or enjoy his victory. In moments, he set Ruka free.

Bukayag stood. He stretched his arms and cracked his neck as Ruka inspected them. His skin looked a bloody mess, and his toes throbbed, but in truth he hadn't been badly damaged.

The shadow bent forward rather purposefully at the waist, and held up a a knife. Bukayag seemed keen to plunge it into the shadow's chest just to be safe, but Ruka mimicked the bowing gesture, and took the blade.

He scanned the tight-fitting, black fabric sheathing every piece of the man's skin, and in the gloom, even for Ruka, the shadow's dark eyes were hard to see. Darkness seemed to gather in his clothes, and Ruka marveled at the fabric and whatever trick made it possible.

The shadow put a finger to his mask where his mouth should be, and hissed softly. Apparently 'quiet' was a universal gesture.

Ruka nodded, then followed his savior through one of the unlocked doors. His feet were bare, and he tried to move stealthily, but his skin slapped or crunched against the dirty stone no matter how he stepped.

The shadow, on the other hand, seemed made of air. His knees bent, arms held out; he stepped strangely, as if he rolled forward on the edges of his boots—if the tiny slips of black fabric on his feet could be called boots.

Ruka decided he looked like a fox stalking its prey, and grinned. He summoned the many images in his mind of the lithe hunters of his homeland as he'd seen them in the steppes, and the comparison felt right.

The shadow led them through many more doors and sloped passages, all poorly lit by the curious glass-candles, and always higher. The shadow led him on, slowly but with confidence, twice passing through rooms with dead servants tucked neatly into corners or under tables.

You've been a busy little fox, Ruka thought, looking at the expertly slashed throats, and seeing little sign of struggle.

They kept moving, up and up now until the scents on the air turned from blood and squalor to spice and cooking. Ruka heard voices and laughter, clatter and kitchen-work, and the shadow would sometimes hold his hand up and stop. He entered one room alone, and when he came out to lead on, the noise had ceased.

Ruka smelled fresh blood as they passed. It covered the faint odor of sweat and soap with copper, and as he passed through he saw two young women lying together in death. It seemed the fox had slaughtered them as a man might slaughter sheep.

"And so?" Bukayag whispered, as if annoyed. Ruka had no answer.

Room after room, hall after hall they moved forward, everything made of perfect-cut square stone. Ruka added it all to the map in his mind, and their escape began to seem so easy he cursed himself for a fool. They had not seen a single guard, nor even an armed servant.

Soon the rooms had huge colored bed-sheets hanging near or over windows that revealed a fog-filled, moonless night. The window-slits were too small to crawl through, and they moved on, skirting intricate, glossy-surfaced tables and chairs. The richest hall in the Ascom was a sty in comparison.

Statues made of metal or stone sat on raised, wooden platforms next to life-like creations of half-naked women, or strange, animal-like monsters. Dyed images of men lay on flat, paper surfaces hung from nearly every wall, haunting in the dim light.

For many long moments, Ruka could only stop, and stare. The skill of it all made a mockery of the crude statues and carvings of his people, and it made no sense to exist in the same place as Ruka's captor.

Does ugliness seek out beauty, he wondered? *Or is it just more noticeable when it does?*

The shadow held up his hand, and turned his head as if to listen. Before Ruka had time to consider, the fox sprung to motion, sprinting to the wall to disappear behind one of the bedsheets.

Ruka hesitated because he did not think he could move so quickly, or quietly. He heard voices the same moment a group of young, armed men rounded the corner from a more brightly lit hall ahead.

They stopped, and stared. Ruka stared back.

One man he recognized—a watcher from the pit. His dark, thick hair was oiled, his clothes brightly dyed and clean, covering a body unfit to wield a sword. The rest were warriors, garbed in leather armor with small blades on their hips, and maybe knives on their belts.

The stunned moment passed. The men drew their weapons.

* * *

Arun clenched his jaw and held back the curse. He had accounted for the princes. There was no reason for any of them to be here, and yet here one was. This meant not just him, of course, since princes hardly wiped their asses alone, but four of the Trung family's bodyguards—some of the finest warriors in Pyu.

Arun stood behind the tapestry, frozen for a moment between order and chaos, life and death. Once again he had to choose his gamble, and quickly. The barbarian chose first.

Without a word, the savage charged. All four bodyguards leapt before their prince, holding their ground and drawing curved swords.

Arun blinked, still frozen. The attack was madness. These weren't pit-slaves with dull little knives—these were trained soldiers, hand-picked from thousands of other men. The barbarian would be hacked to death.

Still he closed the gap until he stood a man's length apart, then swung back his arm with the pitifully short knife held high. He threw it, and the weapon sailed across the room, far off-target over the heads of the men. For a moment Arun nearly closed his eyes in pain at the foolish, incompetent attempt.

Then the lantern behind the prince shattered as the iron connected. It fell off the stone catch and broke, spilling flaming whale-oil down the wall and over the prince. The stink of fish filled the air, then the burning hair of the crown-prince, who screamed in panic.

Two guards turned at once to help him, cutting off flaming silk and smothering the flames with their bare hands. The other guards came forward with murderous stares, and the giant turned and ran.

Arun watched from the shadows still undecided, but he believed he understood—the giant wasn't running away. Just like the pit, he had a purpose.

A single other lantern hung near the window. It flicked lonely shadows in the breeze of the moonless, pitch-black night, and all eyes turned towards it.

The giant crossed the room in four huge strides, sparing a brief look back towards the men. His golden eyes slit, almost glowing in the firelight as he smiled. With a flick of his huge hand, he tossed the lantern out the window. In its absence, all went dark.

The same, horrifying laughter from the pit filled the night. Again it stood hairs on the back of Arun's neck, and he crouched low and opened his mouth, using every trick to amplify sound as his eyes became all but useless.

He heard the guards shuffling blindly. He heard the giant walking as if without care across the room. Then he heard stone grate against stone, and a grunt. He twisted his head back and forth trying to understand, readying two knives as he stepped silently away from the tapestry.

Heavy footfalls crossed the room. Blades hissed through the air in futile terror as the guards seemed to huddle together, perhaps to ensure they didn't accidentally kill one another. The prince still whimpered in agony.

Arun flinched as the squish of something huge and heavy cracked against flesh, and bone, and men screamed in blind panic.

The barbarian laughed again, the sound now more like a child at play, but in the deep tones of a man.

Arun blinked and believed he understood, thinking of the corpse of Three-toed Braun hurled across a pit. Somehow the giant had lifted a statue. He had *thrown* it as he had thrown a full-grown man. He had crushed a person to death with a massive chunk of Trung marble.

The guards reacted as any sane men trapped in the dark with a giant, monstrous killer. They turned and fled. Panicked footfalls followed the wall, soon disrupted by grunts and dull thudding and violence.

Arun moved to cut them off—he knew which hall they would flee towards. He raced low across the room and waited, then seized the first man and pulled him to the floor. A sword clattered to the tiles, and the ex-monk grappled both his opponent's arms as he took him flat to the ground. He jerked and bent the joints until bone snapped, dragged a knife across the man's throat, then held him until the resistance stopped.

Air rushed past him as something huge sped past. For a moment he wondered only how the giant could run so quickly without light. But the how made no difference, all that mattered was that he could.

Arun rose and followed to the dim light promising safety in the next hall. The savage had already caught and killed the last guard. He held the crown-prince against the wall with one massive hand, the lantern with the other.

Blood pooled from a headless corpse at his feet, the curved-blade abandoned beside. The giant's face was almost touching his victim's—his bright eyes staring as he squeezed the prince's neck. He was whispering words Arun couldn't hear, and no doubt couldn't understand anyway.

The prince was wide-eyed and dying, his feet lifted from the stone floor. He thrashed and flailed against his killer, but the attempts were feeble. His eyes rolled back and his tongue lolled while his urine mixed with the smell of blood and fish in the air. The hall and the corridor silenced.

The dangerous barbarian was not laughing anymore. His jaw had clenched, his eyes searching before him, his body held stiff with effort. He dropped the dead prince as if he'd forgotten why he'd held him, and his face lost all expression. Then he looked straight at Arun—though it was all but pitch-black where the ex-monk stood—and pointed down the hall, as if to ask 'is it this way?'

Arun nodded reflexively, and somehow, the man saw that too.

Perhaps he is a demon, he thought with a shiver, *or an evil spirit in a man's flesh, or the bastard son of a foreign god.* But it made no difference, it was too late for an exit now.

Arun led on as before, first down the corridor then to a room over a sheer high wall. This was one of the king's many decoys—a fake bedroom designed to lure assassins, or to house guests where he could kill them quietly. But tonight there were no guards outside—only fifty feet of silk rope bundled beside one of the few windows big enough for a man.

Arun climbed down first. The barbarian struggled and seemed not to trust the rope, but he mastered his fear and lowered himself strangely, holding his weight almost entirely with his arms.

They crossed the moat on wooden planks to avoid the piranhas, chests down as Arun paddled with a single oar and showed the savage to avoid the water. Then they took the rampart stairs to the outer wall, slinking past the empty post of another bribed guard, and dropped to a pile of clothes.

An animal-cart pulled by two men waited as instructed, and the pair slipped inside without a word. Arun had ensured enough room to sit, as well as provided rice and water in clay bowls, and loose cloth shawls big enough even for the giant.

We are almost free, my friend, he thought, noting the barbarian looked longingly at the food, but did not touch it.

Will you let me take you across the sea, or are you a demon sent to tempt and destroy me? And if not, will the richest man in Pyu reward my gamble?

Arun knew he should be thrilled. He had perhaps been the first man of the isles to break a prisoner from Trung's prison—the first man in a thousand years to take what he wanted from a royal palace and survive.

Whatever the pay-off, whatever happened next, people would whisper of the thief who stole the giant in the night for a hundred years.

Yet all he could hear now in his moment of glory was the killer's laugh; all he could think was the giant's horror turned to glee, flipped at a moment's notice amidst the chaos and blood. And Arun felt the same fear and thrill he knew so well when the stakes were high, when life and death seemed the same. He looked out at the night and the buildings flying by, the sleeping citizens and their simple lives, and he smiled without regret.

9

After their escape, Ruka and his new benefactor went to the coast. Bukayag wanted his head.

"Let's kill him and take his ship," he muttered as the little man loaded them onto a strange, sleek vessel with disjointed pieces somehow lashed and bound together with a single sail.

Ruka sighed.

And then what?

"Then we are free. We've been outlaws before."

Not here, Ruka countered. *Not in a place where we understand nothing. Where would we hide? I have seen no forests, no mountains, no plains. We must be patient.*

The shadow—rather, 'Ah-rune', as he had seemed to indicate was his name—had tried speaking to Ruka as they'd traveled. He was more clever about this then the former captors, gesturing with his hands at himself, or at other things, repeating one word till Ruka said it back. He even managed to ask for Ruka's name.

These conversations added more words to Ruka's collection, and certainty to a few. He understood more than he let on, of course, but Bukayag was right not to trust too much. Whoever this man was, and whatever his motives, no doubt he hadn't risked his life out of altruism, and he had already demonstrated his talent for killing.

Where are you taking me, Shadow-fox? And will I be a prisoner there again?

It was hard to imagine any place worse than the pits, but in this strange new world of cruelty and paradise, nothing would surprise him.

For now, he could do nothing. Instead he inspected the night sky and the sea, his memories of the palace and the boat beneath him. He could tell the 'main' hull was shallow, long and thin, with even shallower 'little hulls' flanking on both sides. The sails looked entirely unconstrained by framework—completely free in the wind, held only by a complex system of ropes.

And the speed!

Once out into the open waves, Ruka and his new companion nearly *flew* through the water, tacking faster through the sea in high wind than Ruka could have imagined. The 'little hulls' gave a width and balance that mocked the waves, yet almost rose up above the water as the wind moved them, so that the drag was slight.

Do you see how much we have to learn? Ruka pointed, feeling his brother didn't truly appreciate the ship's brilliance. *We will not survive without knowledge like this. We must be careful until we master this place.*

Bukayag said nothing, and Ruka closed his eyes and rose up to feel the coolness of the night air. Even when the sun was down this land was hot, and despite his life-long desire for a world warmer than his homeland, he was finding it hard to bear. His skin constantly glistened with sweat, and each breath felt labored as if drawn through a damp cloth. He hoped only this was summer, and the hottest the weather turned.

As the sight of land moved further and further away, Ruka felt uncomfortably trapped, and helpless. He could barely swim, and there were no other boats that he could see. When morning came the land was entirely gone. Blue, calm water covered every horizon, and the sun beat down with a still fury Ruka had never known.

He and the shadow took turns hiding under a tarp, and their boat kept moving well with the wind, which held steady, if mild. But once the sun drooped again, and the land returned to view, Ruka's new friend looked back and forth and rubbed his fingers together as if anxious.

Many other boats dotted the new coast. The long, flat shore and the signs of men reminded Ruka of the Ascom, but here he saw huge wooden buildings, man-made stone walls built into the sea, and docks that stretched out floating for impossible lengths. He covered himself in the strange, thin fabric, and hunched, hiding his skin and size as best he could.

They docked as far off from the busy port as possible, but still there were men waiting. Ahrune unlatched a board from the boat. From beneath he removed a box that clinked with metallic sounds, and he plucked several round pieces of maybe silver before tucking it away beneath his clothes. He spoke with the men and seemed to pay them, then gestured for Ruka to follow along a worn stone path leading away from the coast.

The wet, salty scents of the sea soon replaced with cloistered humanity. Ruka's stomach growled at the smell of cooking meat, and he could see smoke rising in the distance. But nothing could have prepared him.

They crested a steep hill rising from the coast, and beyond it lay a city more vast, more colorful and beautiful than anything he had ever seen. Buildings sprawled in organized chaos into the horizon in every direction, a great stone fortress lodged in their collective heart.

By their design, Ruka could not even understand exactly what the buildings were. Some had multiple roofs of colored tile, stacked as if a forest canopy had grown straight up in layers. Streets of flat rock wound between them without a trace of the dirt beneath. And all about them, inside them, coming and going and standing on balconies and reaching out windows—clogging every ounce of rock and wood as far as Ruka could see —were little brown islanders.

The children he could see were plump, and healthy. They laughed and ran through tall grass along the pathways leading to the city, or beneath rough-barked trees that drooped with branches heavy with lush, green leaves like ladles. In his Grove, Ruka fell to his knees in open awe.

Even in the real world he had stopped to stare. The men jabbered and waved him onward but he ignored them. He reached down and scooped a hand into soft, black earth, knowing in the Ascom, such soil would be fought over by every chief, and every matron, until the blood of a thousand sons stained it red. But here it looked largely ignored. It held weeds, and a stone path.

Oh, mother, he thought. *Here is the paradise that was promised. It is a world beyond our frozen wasteland. It is the end to an endless nightmare. You were right. And your ancestors were right.*

He held back the tears as he thought on his purpose—first only to survive, and to avenge, and to make good the sacrifice of a holy woman who had spent her life to save her son. All his life he had clung to this with a desperate need, the barest hold on a dangerous cliff as he dangled from its edge. But perhaps no longer. Perhaps here, across an endless sea, lay the answer to a shattered life.

Oh Beyla, beautiful Beyla, you were right to save me. There is meaning to what I've done. Paradise exists. And your son has found it.

He rose only when he felt he could control his trembling, and followed the men again, knowing very well where they would take him.

They passed the playing children, then the young women carrying baskets to the shore or the river that ran through the center of the city. They passed thousands of people ranging from light brown to a deep black, and Ruka hunched as best he could and tried to hide, but still attracted stares on every street.

The crowds seemed to squeeze his body like a bedroll made too small. To distract himself he tried his best to note everything—the sheer, colorful clothing, the strange shapes of the buildings, the plants hung in decoration. He noted none of these people carried weapons, not even the men. He noted no one seemed afraid despite being surrounded by strangers, and wondered if they had no outlaws or criminals, and if men even fought duels for offense.

By the time they'd crossed the section of city in their path, he believed himself prepared to enter another war-fort and face what followed. But as the huge, grey walls loomed, his feet slowed and his brother hissed.

Beyond would be another great war-house of rock, another king and another pit, and all his traps, locks and torture chambers. Bukayag flexed his hands.

"I won't be imprisoned again, brother, not while I still draw breath."

Ruka felt much the same, but what choice did they have?

Ahrune slowed now, too. He followed Ruka's gaze and seemed to understand. From his belt he drew a small sword, and stooped down as he had in the pit, holding the blade much like Ruka had as he gifted a rune-sword to an Ascomi chief.

Bukayag breathed, and clenched their jaw. But after a long, tense wait, took it, and troubled Ruka no more.

This place might be different, Ruka soothed. *We won't eat or drink until we're sure—and if we must, we will fight to escape, or die. I promise you that.*

Despite the words he found himself sweating from more than just the heat. He didn't want to die—not now, not anymore. He wanted to learn every truth this new land had to offer, to plumb these foreign minds for every scrap of knowledge, and decide if the world were worth saving after all.

He couldn't do that fighting slaves in a pit, or if some new king stripped his flesh in a torture chamber. And more and more, he was sure, he couldn't do it without Bukayag.

10

Arun couldn't seem to stop his hands from shaking. It was the waiting, of course, and the lack of control. He had sent a message to his buyer before he left Trung's city, but with nobility, there were no guarantees.

The men waiting at the docks at least confirmed interest. Arun was at the city's mercy now, and his prize could be taken at a pittance, or indeed for nothing at all. Still he dared to hope. The young king had a reputation for being fair and reasonable, and he'd been the best choice.

When 'Rooka' waited at the entrance to the fortress, though, Arun cursed himself for a fool. *Of course the castle scares him,* he realized. *He's just been tortured and fought like a dog in one!*

Yet they *had* to go in. They'd been followed all the way from the docks and there was little doubt what would happen if they ran. Arun thought he could escape, perhaps, by charging into a crowd and changing his clothes or cutting through houses and alleys. But not the giant. No, the huge, strange man was surely and truly trapped. So Arun handed him his sword, and it at least got him walking.

They entered the outer fortress, with checkpoints manning each gate of each layer of wall. All stared but let visitors pass into the informal market inside. Arun soon saw 'common' men hiding swords, and keen-eyed 'merchants' selling too little for too much. Boys came begging, their hands darting about as if for loose coins or trinkets, but their true purpose was clearly to search for blades.

Arun understood every step took him further into a well-made trap—a maze of death designed by a shrewd, paranoid mind.

Once at the inner fortress, they took a side entrance into the palace. There were more guards but no questions as they passed into a garden-filled courtyard. Servants here pruned perfect bushes or swept fan-brooms over dustless paths. No one looked at or bothered them except an older man with oil-slicked hair and a trimmed goatee.

"Come this way, please."

Arun felt the tense, menacing movements of his companion and wondered if he'd sensed the danger too. He wondered if at any moment the giant might panic, draw his new sword and hack a bloody path towards the sea. But Arun hid his concern. He smiled and gestured forward with his hand, using all his will and training to be calm as still water. The giant nodded.

They followed the old butler to a marble hall, then beyond to a double mango-wood door, and into the room behind.

There, perched on the throne, was the most beautiful woman Arun had ever seen.

"Thank you, Hina, you may leave us," she said, voice smooth and sure.

Arun sensed the man's hesitation and didn't blame him. Whatever else the two men now in his mistress' presence were, they were certainly dangerous. Still he left without a word, and the three of them seemed alone. Arun wondered if there were guards behind curtains or fake walls, and if he was a step away from death.

"You have fortunate timing, *Noose*," said their hostess. "The king has just welcomed another official son. He's feeling rather generous."

Arun bowed low, flashing his most charming smile.

"Then I am pleased, my lady."

She exposed her long, pale neck as she cocked her head.

"Don't be. It's why I came instead, and I'm never feeling generous."

"If all I receive is the gift of your beauty, my lady, I will feel more than compensated."

The woman laughed, though it didn't touch her eyes.

"Piss on my beauty, pirate. Show me your monster."

Arun bowed and gestured for Ruka to remove his hood. The look in the man's golden eyes was unreadable, but he obeyed.

To the woman's credit, she kept her composure as she inspected.

"Not quite an albino, is he? Can we speak with him?"

"No, my lady. I don't believe so. I've tried several Pyu dialects and a few of the continental tongues."

She frowned. "Then what good is he?"

"He's very clever, my lady. Perhaps there are linguists that can help."

"Linguists cost money. You bring me useless expense." Her gaze went up and down the huge length of thick barbarian. "He probably eats like a bull."

"I expect he does, my lady. But this bull has horns. I've seen him kill five veterans of the Halin pit, alone, using only a dull knife and his bare hands."

The lady shrugged her exposed, perfect shoulders, and crossed her long smooth legs.

"So he's dangerous and hard to control. More expense. I don't think I want him."

Arun bowed, happy to play through the ritual of haggling.

"I understand, please forgive me for wasting your time. We'll go and see another family."

The woman's dark brown, almost black eyes stared, then she laughed. The sound was harsh, and condescending.

"Oh, I'm *keeping* him, pirate, I'm just not sure I *want* him, or that I'll *pay* for him. Perhaps I'll cleave his ugly head to ease my mind."

Arun's jaw clenched and he made some effort to relax. Apparently this was a different kind of game. But pirates played such games and he was used to these, too. He stepped forward but kept his smile, waiting till she met his eyes.

"I'll happily kill you, and die today, before I let you rob me."

His words hung in the air, and Arun readied his senses to hear the first arrow whistle, ready to pounce and do exactly as he promised. The lady looked from one of his eyes to the other, and smiled.

"I like your courage, pirate. You and your monster may stay here in the palace tonight. I'll discuss your fee with the king. Is that acceptable?"

Arun stepped back and bowed, knowing it would be the most dangerous night of his life.

"More than acceptable. Bringing a smile to such lips as yours is reward enough, my lady."

The pleasure stayed on her face, and she nestled back in her chair, lithe as a hunting cat, though she said nothing.

"May I have the pleasure of your name, my lady? And I should like to congratulate the king on his new son in person, if I may."

At this the noblewoman's pleasure seemed to vanish, and Arun feared he'd blundered.

"How well spoken you are for a pirate," she said, standing to cross the room. "But I tire of the charade, *ex-brother of the Ching*. Oh yes, I know exactly who you are. Understand this—I am Princess Kikay, the king's sister, and I am your master now. I am all that stands between you and death. You will meet my brother soon enough, and perhaps your politeness will save you. When you praise the infant prince's name, you may refer to him as Ratama Kale Alaku."

11
Mesanite Hills. Malvey - the Blue City. 1580 AE. The present.

Osco, third son of Harcas, and Devoted warrior of the Mesanite hills, kept to the ten thrust technique. It was important he do his duty as a husband, but sex was for health and making children, so he did his best not to enjoy it.

Still—he couldn't keep from looking at the strong, prominent lines of his wife's face and shoulders, or from feeling her lithe body beneath him. Having been away so long, he knew if he looked into her dark eyes, or kissed her, he would be lost.

Liga moaned correctly. She did her duty to preserve his honor, just as he did. She'd suggested they couple quickly because Osco's father would send for him soon, and he might die before they met again. She had always been wise and practical. The perfect wife, save for her beauty.

"Are you alright?"

Osco startled at the question, then noticed he was bleeding from a minor wound on his leg, the blood staining the sheets.

"It's nothing."

He looked back to the wall. In truth he was exhausted and wounded from many days of hard marching, and Liga quietly did her best to scoot up and help with the thrusts. She always knew exactly what was needed.

Most noble girls in Mesan married at fourteen, but Liga had been eighteen and nearly a priestess when Osco proposed. Her family—the Hirtri—had been thrilled, expecting no one would have the courage or perhaps the arrogance to take her. And it was true her beauty tempted Osco to lust—at least for the brief time he'd spent with her in Malvey. But in truth it was her discipline and loyalty that truly stirred him. The less she'd tried to tempt him, the more he respected her; and the more he respected her, the more difficult it was to leave.

But to Osco of the Magda, son of Harcas, difficult was nothing. He finished in silence, rose from their small, firm bed that he'd shared so rarely, and dressed in civilian clothes.

"Make a sacrifice this afternoon, and pray for a daughter. Our people will need more children."

"Yes, husband. Everything is prepared."

He paused, and turned back to her, thinking *of course it is.*

The house was also flawless—the servants waiting to greet Kale and Osco's father, the kitchen ready to host a feast; Liga had contingency plans if they moved to another wing, as well as warriors ready to kill Osco's guests, if required, and resources for a dozen other possibilities.

"You've done well, wife, as always."

"I do my duty, husband."

She said the words without pride, without false humility. Osco allowed himself to smile. He resisted the urge to reach out and touch her beautiful face, or her short black hair, and he could see the same longing in her eyes. But she did not reach out for him.

The perfect wife.

"If I die," he said, hoping his words conveyed the depth of his respect, "my family will find you a new husband, and you will receive as much of my estate as I can give you."

She bowed exactly right, draping an arm across her breasts with natural modesty. There was nothing left to say.

* * *

"Welcome, Prince Ratama."

Kale smiled and bowed to his friend's father in Pyu fashion. Asna gave his ridiculous curtsy.

As soon as Lord Harcas Magda—Head of the City for this year—had greeted them, Osco went off to 'visit his wife'.

Kale wasn't surprised his friend failed to mention her in their time at Nanzu, the Imperial Academy of Naran, but he was still skeptical of his often duplicitous ally, so he followed the son with his spirit while his body smiled at the father.

Asna had moved into a ludicrous bow, hand sweeping down and back to rest on his hip. The general's eyebrows twitched.

"We don't see many Condotians in the hills. At least not since the war."

By this Lord Harcas meant the war with the Naranian empire—the war where mercenaries like Asna's people helped plunder and ravage Mesan's crops and merchants until they all nearly starved to death, and eventually surrendered.

"From what my grandpapa say, mighty lord, you often not see them *during* war. It was problem, yes?"

Kale held his breath, and Harcas stared. He was the spitting image of Osco, and his face moved about as much.

"We have a feast prepared, Prince Ratama. Please." He stretched a hand out towards the plain stone hall behind.

Kale much rather preferred to turn and leave immediately. His people and family had no time to waste, but he knew this rudeness would cause offense, and he needed this man and his warriors.

"Thank you, my lord," he bowed again, "of course I'll stay."

Kale was rather pleased to be bowing because it let him hide his surprise. His spirit had followed Osco up a flight of stairs into a bedroom, and with about five polite words between them, Osco and his wife—who apparently was real—removed their clothes and climbed onto their bed.

As the touching started, Kale's spirit fled away, but he felt a blush on his cheek, and fought a grin. *Must have missed her, my friend, to be so eager—not so reserved as you think.*

Harcas and his retinue of silent guards clacked hard boots down the grey corridors, taking Kale and Asna to a large, square room filled with plain wooden tables and benches. Perhaps fifty men and boys of several generations filled the seats, backs straight as castle walls, speaking quietly. They silenced at once and rose up to stand with hands at their sides, eyes locked at nothing on bare stone.

"Be seated."

Harcas obeyed his own command first, taking an empty space on a backless bench, his table no different than the rest. He gestured for Kale to do the same.

"We are all equals here," he explained, "but I am first."

Kale had grown quite accustomed to 'more equal' since entering the continent. He didn't much like the falsity of it since everyone knew the hierarchy anyway. On the isles people were rather more direct with their rankings

Polite conversation began around the table, and Kale listened with his spirit. In their native tongue the men discussed their houses, children, and training; not a word was said about their guests or the 'miracle' that Kale produced outside.

"Do you like goat?"

Kale blinked and smiled politely at his host. Servants brought out round metal trays with plain brown rice, a lentil soup, and a sauceless meat.

"I've never tried it, General—I'm sure I will."

The men dished themselves, so Kale did the same. He took a few bites with his host watching. The meat was dry as sand and tasted mostly like charcoal.

"Very good, thank you."

The man smiled perfunctorily.

"Our cooks avoid excess spice—this way you taste the flavor of the meat, and the cooking."

"Mm yes." Kale added some water to his spitless mouth.

"So tell me," Harcas' fidgeted and he had yet to touch his meal. "Could my people destroy Naran with your miracles, Prince Ratama?"

Kale swallowed and managed not to choke. After so many months of Naranian tedium and endless chatter, he was not prepared for such directness. But it was kind of refreshing.

"Possibly."

The king or general or 'Head of the City' reacted without even an eyebrow twitch.

"And you can teach us? How long will this take?"

Kale swallowed again and felt the impolite urge to vomit. "I can. But I don't know how long it will take."

"Your best guess then, please. A few months? A year?"

As he kept chewing Kale realized how hungry he was. He made good use of navy habits—stuffing food in his mouth and chewing without taste. By the time he was ready to actually speak, Osco entered and took the empty seat on his other side.

"Every path is different, my lord," he finally explained. "I can't say for sure, but there should be progress in months, not years."

Harcas nodded, but gave no indication. Kale thought perhaps he found this satisfactory, but then who the hell knew with these men of stone.

"That was quick." Kale whispered and welcomed his friend with a smile. It was hard to tell, but the general's son seemed rather pleased with himself. "That wasn't a compliment."

Kale grinned at his friend's eyebrow twitch, but his smugness soon waned as he felt his body sweating around his stomach. He tried to soldier on, ignoring the heat on his brow as he took several more bites. He tried the soup but tasted only salt, and somehow it was so thick it hardly helped with the dryness of his mouth.

"I think I'm going to be sick," he said quietly.

Osco's eyebrows raised in alarm.

"Unadvised, and exceedingly shameful. Overcome."

Kale breathed and tried not to roll his eyes, or swear. He glanced at Asna, who looked at his own food with undisguised contempt and hadn't touched it. He shook his head when he noticed Kale's glare.

Bloody hillmen, he thought, *and bloody Condotians. And bloody goats. This is awful.*

He regretted thinking about the goat at once. He ran a hand over his face and found more sweat than he realized. He shook his head and noticed his vision swam then started to blur until it got hard to sit straight in his chair.

"Are you alright?"

Harcas' voice. It held something now, some deception. Or was it fear?

"Water. More water."

Kale's mouth felt strange, as if it were almost numb. He blinked fuzzy eyes towards his host, and his gut went cold. He thought of his father.

"*Royalty must never trust too quickly,*" he had told his sons a hundred times. "*And if possible, not at all. Especially friends, and allies, especially when they feel safe.*"

Kale would have laughed if he didn't feel like vomiting. It was poison. They were trying to kill him. The thought hadn't even occurred to him.

He wondered what Farahi would say if he saw him now. He imagined the square, stern face, jaw clenched in contempt. '*You thought me harsh, paranoid, and now look at you. Trusting fool. Walking corpse.*'

Kale rose to his feet scattering food and dishes, the clay bowl of his soup shattering on the floor. His limbs felt weak, his breathing labored. The other men were crying out but the sounds seemed suddenly far away and mushed together. They didn't matter. Only the poison mattered.

How does it kill? You've heard it over and over! Damn boring tutors, damn stupid wasted youth!

Obviously he'd swallowed whatever it was, and his tongue had numbed but didn't swell; his throat hadn't burned, though the flesh there seemed numb, too. He knew you could sometimes weaken and outlast poison; you could draw it from a wound; you could bleed it, or take an antidote.

He burned his thoughts and watched himself through his spirit's eyes, gasping and swaying on his feet. He realized it was too fast, whatever it was. It was already killing him. Soon he expected it would numb his heart and lungs as it numbed his mouth, and his breath would stop, his blood clog and stick like sludge in a gutter. Then he would die.

Except he couldn't die. Not now. People needed him. Lani needed him.

He opened the windows in his spirit-house—the imaginary place that represented control of his mind. He made a blank canvas of night on a calm, white beach, until the world became only the moment before him, and the still air around him, the feel of his feet on stone.

Why I do it matters.

It was a lesson he learned well in a Batonian monastery with a mean, old monk. He closed his eyes, knowing no one would save Pyu if not him. No one would use God's miracles to make the world a better place if not him.

And yes, he might be too late, he might fail. But not today. Not before he did at least *something*, before he helped at least *someone*.

He reached out all around him for the threads of power that made up the world. Some shimmered in the air, some circled around the men at the table, more pooled beneath the earth or far above it, harder to reach but almost endless in strength. Kale had no time, he had to be quick.

He seized the threads in the air and pulled at every cup, every bowl, every glass, draining the liquid into the air and pulling it to his body. Water hovered and flowed like little rivers till they reached him, pouring into his mouth, eyes, and nose to drown the corruption taking root.

Dishes and men scattered as the air shimmered with moving heat, and soon Kale could see their breath misting in the cold air.

He watched his eyes and ears start to bleed, the blood flowing out even as the water flowed in. His body wracked in agony, convulsing as it tried to expel again and again. The men around him backed away—all save Asna, who came closer and drew his sword.

Kale didn't know if he meant to protect, or kill, but there was nothing he could do.

The numbness taking over his body began to ease, replacing with fire.

When he could stand it no more he released the liquid, and his body vomited again and again, ejecting water stained with goat, lentils, and blood.

He sagged forward, arms on the table, forehead resting on his hands as he took deep breaths, ready with his spirit now to rip apart anyone and anything that got too close. Finally, he looked up with his own eyes.

The men were leaned back against the walls, some mouths agape in horror. Asna stood poised and ready to kill, but his eyes and sword were turned towards the hillmen.

Kale sagged roughly to his seat. He looked at his own blood dripping down around his chair, and felt it smeared across his face. He swallowed the pain shooting through his guts, and his sore throat.

"Let's speak plainly." His voice sounded weak and hoarse, so he amplified it and threw it out to every man's ear as he had in the courtyard of Nanzu, making it a little more menacing, perhaps, than he'd intended. "The goat was terrible."

12

The scene was bizarre, maybe grotesque, but Osco's rage overcame.

"What were you *thinking*, father?"

His mind flooded with memories of being chastised as a boy—being the one in the chair staring at his feet as his father paced.

They were alone now in a side-room off the hall, a place where servants usually ate and waited while the family dined. Harcas seemed far too relaxed, considering, and his lack of fear or at least embarrassment only infuriated Osco further.

"I was thinking I don't want my people destroyed. I was thinking I don't trust your miracle-worker. And even if I did—he may die before he's useful. Or he may not be able to teach us as he claims."

"Then why not simply reject him? Why try to kill him?"

Harcas showed not even the subtlest signs of shame, or regret.

"The emperor sent birds to every city for a hundred miles—there's a vast reward for him alive, or for his corpse. I'd planned on the former, at least until his little display. I did not think it possible to capture such a man."

Osco pointed a finger as calmly as possible towards the hall where Kale waited with the family.

"Capture him? Kill him? You're lucky he didn't just butcher every last one of us. He still may. I certainly would have in his place."

His father's face at least acknowledged that. But he shrugged.

"How could I know he resists poison? I used ten-breath dew, and plenty of it. It should have killed an ox."

"He's a damned miracle-worker! You shouldn't have risked it." Osco felt sick, disgusted. He wanted to say 'and if you chose to do it, how could you *fail*?' But his father's earlier words overshadowed everything else, and he clenched his jaw before he spoke.

"Now tell me, since when do we call that tyrant 'emperor', father?"

The man rolled his eyes as if it didn't matter. It was like a dagger to Osco's heart.

"What's the difference. Tell your 'friend' to do whatever he intends to do, and leave. He is not welcome here. I'm still your father and lord of this house."

Osco stared and tried to find some trace of the man he once knew. Had he truly been away from home so long? Had the world spun and changed with him oblivious at its center?

His father looked greyer now, and fatter, but otherwise much the same. Could all that Osco knew and hoped and dreamed be destroyed in just a few short years? Could a man's faith be broken so quickly, so quietly?

Earlier that morning, he would have said no. But truth was truth, and here he was.

"No, you're not. Not anymore."

The old man that was once Osco's father scoffed.

"You're not my heir. And even if you were, you can't just seize power from me."

Osco sneered. He dropped every shred of respect from his tone, for he had none left.

"I can do whatever power allows, as I've been taught. I will go and tell my miracle-wielding ally that you and all my brothers still intend to cause him harm. He will rip you apart, and I will be lord."

The older man watched him intently now, still and silent.

"A bluff."

Osco blinked. He couldn't understand the man who raised him ever believing those words.

"You will sign over all family authority to me. You will retire to the country, and you will never return to Malvey. Do this, or you will die."

He banished the image and memory of his father in his mind and walked from the room, then ordered his uncle to retrieve the proper documents.

The man hesitated.

Osco hurled a bowl across the room, shattering the silence with a hundred shards of flying clay. He stepped forward and unsheathed his knife.

"I see Naranian gold has softened all your spines. But please believe me, it has not softened mine. Go now uncle, or watch your sons and brothers die."

The old, maybe even wise and kind scribbler fled, and the rest did not move.

Kale still looked awful. Between his pale face and the streaks of blood he resembled a walking corpse. His eyes had gone bloodshot, but when they turned on Osco they weren't angry. He spoke with the same soft, gentle voice, pleasant even with a rasp.

"I'd like to leave now. I understand if your soldiers can't come with me."

Osco couldn't seem to process how he felt about this strange island prince. He respected his power, sometimes his wisdom, and yet he lacked the ruthlessness required to play games of state, and perhaps to survive them.

"They are promised. By oath of a Magda, of a Devoted." He said this for his family's benefit. "They *will* go with you."

Kale nodded and said nothing. Together they all waited for what felt like hours—men who had taught Osco to be a man sitting in shame, or anger. His uncle returned with the family seal, with documents transferring Magda authority to a new heir, and a glass horn of red ink. Harcas looked one last time in Osco's eyes, and at Kale's quiet calm. He signed.

"I will be leaving with Prince Ratama, as planned," Osco explained. "My wife will choose a regent to serve as Patriarch until my return." He kept his voice matter-of-fact, but in truth his mind spun in fear.

He asked Asna to take Kale back out of the fortress and down to the soldiers—who'd already agreed to make war in Pyu, knowing nothing of treachery—then he returned to his wife hoping she'd not yet left for the temple.

"I have usurped power from my father," he said to her with no other explanation. "I am now head of the Magda. You will manage all family business on my behalf until I return, and after 'consideration' you will choose my cousin, Duvi, as regent."

Liga's face showed surprise, but otherwise remained carefully blank.

"As you say, husband. But Duvi is six years old."

"For all practical purposes, you will rule in my stead." Here he paused, unsure how to say everything that must be said—to warn her properly against treachery and violence and death, and explain how far she might have to go. "My family...they will not accept this. They may try to kill you, or destroy the documents, or any number of other things. I give you full authority to do what is necessary to maintain control. Speak to your family, tell them they will soon rise to preeminence and that the Magda are fallen. Use all the wealth of our house, kill anyone you must. It will not be easy."

He knew his words were insane, overwhelming, impossible. Liga stood from the desk and the documents she'd been scribbling.

"I understand, husband. I will speak to my father and brothers. We will protect Mesan. Is there anything else?"

Osco blinked. *Is there anything else!*

"No. No. There's nothing. May the gods protect you."

"And you, husband."

Osco found he was speechless. He was unequipped to honor such a woman. He stepped forward and took her in his arms, which seemed acceptable, given the circumstances. He used every ounce of will to hold back the tears of pride.

"There is no greater wife in all Mesan," he whispered. "You shame me. You shame my family."

Her arms gripped him correctly, holding him, but not clinging or trembling.

"Your family perhaps, husband, but not you. Never you."

He allowed that praise without rebuke, just this once. Then he banished all selfish things and held her at arm's length.

"We will free our city, Liga, or die trying."

She smiled, support and comfort written over her face and eyes. He wiped a thumb across her smooth, dry cheek.

The perfect wife.

He strode from her chambers for what he expected to be the last time.

He turned his mind to a foreign prince, a long, difficult road across an enemy empire, a foreign sea, and a foreign land. He doubted very much he would see Liga again, at least not in this world. But very quietly, and yes, very selfishly, he hoped he would.

* * *

"I couldn't have killed them," Kale admitted as his friends all but carried him through the city gates.

"Couldn't have, or wouldn't have?"

Kale glanced at his 'friend', and wasn't sure.

"Let's say both."

He coughed, then considered the fact that the men being discussed for miracle-assisted death were the entirety of Osco's family.

"Would you have asked me to?"

He thought he knew the answer, but still, he wanted to hear it. Osco's brow tightened, and he looked away.

Kale knew it meant yes, but didn't know what to do with that knowledge, and felt too ill to consider it.

In fact he'd never felt so weak in his life. Water was the only thing he could keep down, and drinking it made his head spin, keeping time with the waves of shivering and stomach pains. He suspected the poison hadn't entirely gone, and he'd have to suffer through the remnants.

He forgave Harcas Magda at once for trying to kill him. It was a mistake to come here—a mistake to allow others to take on such risk. Kale hadn't even considered that the emperor might punish Mesan, maybe destroy them, just for helping him. It made him feel like a fool. Warriors too felt fear, he knew, especially old warriors with ruthless minds—for they knew what they themselves would do.

He looked around and saw hundreds of trained killers surrounding him. He saw a mercenary who murdered for sport and profit, and who earlier in the day could have betrayed him and this would not have been surprising. And he saw a young man willing to slaughter his whole family for an idea.

All his friends were soldiers, or the allies of soldiers. And yet how could he fight violence without violence? He had no answer, and expected none. He would kill to create peace, and hope his reason mattered.

But was this not the same reasoning Naran had used to subdue Osco's people? Was there truly any difference? And what was the limit to such an ideal?

Kale sighed. He did not know.

He had followed Osco back to his wife with his spirit before they left Malvey, and he had heard their words of deadly commitment, then watched her hide away the official documents of betrayal. He had even lingered and watched her weep and wrap her arms around her chest in solitude, then mask herself in Mesanite stone before summoning guards and servants.

He'd watched, too, the reaction of Osco's family when they'd been left alone. They had not wished Kale dead. But they believed that the emperor would kill them all—that he'd kill their wives and children and neighbors, and grind their city into the dust.

The emperor of Naran was perhaps a tyrant. He had likely killed his own uncle, Kale's friend, for being a nuisance, and his people had expanded their power over neighbors and allies since men wrote records of such things.

But Naran itself was most impressive. The Naranian *people* received the best education in the world; their women could rise to prominence in government; their servants could be born peasants and die aristocrats, rising on merit alone. The emperor himself could be replaced by 'lawful revolution', which meant simply 'successful revolution', and had happened two generations ago, though it had no doubt taken thousands of deaths.

Osco's people, on the other hand, were born to their caste. A man born a commoner died a commoner. And whether farmers or merchants, craftsmen or servants, no matter what they were seen as nothing by the warriors and all those with power. Five families ruled the Blue City with complete control, and any man who raised a spear against them lost his head. Mesanite women were wives and mothers; they served their husband's house, or they joined a temple to serve a god. They had no other choice.

Kale walked amongst them in body and spirit as they left the city. He saw illiterate peasants surrounded by mountains and desert and harsh laws. He saw slaves, he saw misery—he saw people who starved during drought, who made little profit when there was rains, and lost their hands or lives when they stole something that belonged to the upper class.

It was not a place he would live, or choose for his children. Whatever it was that made a man like Osco willing to kill or die for his people and city, it was not their greatness, nor fairness, for it seemed to lack both, save for the quality of their warriors. But then who was Kale to judge? Were his people so much better? And what was better?

Peace was better, he had to believe that. His people, at least, were not warlike. Their greatest heroes were explorers and spiritual men, not warriors. *And yet here I am, coming to sweep away men's lives with allied soldiers and miracles. The sorcerer-prince.*

His small army of Mesanites were gathering now into lines outside their city. Each man carried a leather pack strapped to his shoulders that sagged beneath the weight. Donkeys were being latched to the front of fifty wagons, braying and honking and kicking at shins.

The soldiers would need to march across half a continent, through hills and who knew what else avoiding roads and other travelers.

Before the end they would no doubt need to send men in groups to towns for supplies, or raid farms or countryside. They would have to send out scouts to kill anyone who saw them just to be safe from imperial spies.

And even then, it was probably hopeless.

To take five-hundred men through Naran without notice or resistance seemed unlikely, and if successful, still they would have to cross Nong Ming Tong; they would have to bargain for ships with a king who could betray, or avoid him and attempt to hire pirates. All this just to arrive at what could be their doom.

For whatever foreign force had taken Sri Kon had somehow overcome or bypassed the greatest navy in the world. Kale's father controlled a thousand warships, with twenty thousand marines patrolling the seas beneath a complex system of leadership which should function without the king.

The city itself held three-hundred thousand people, likely more, and though the army was small and inexperienced, it could muster a few thousand soldiers in less than a day.

Kale believed that whatever attacked his home was a small, elite force, because anything else was inconceivable. Somehow this small group of elite warriors must have taken the palace and the royal family, and now disrupted everything by holding the fortress. He believed this in part because it meant his family might still be alive, and because the alternative was impossible.

To have conquered Sri Kon so quickly, and with overwhelming force, would have take tens of thousands of men. It would have taken at least several hundred ships, organized and well supplied and skilled and knowledgeable of Pyu waters. But there was no such sea-power in all the world. There was no such people or men or force. *They must be few in number.* Kale closed his eyes. *They must be.*

Another wave of nausea tried to spill his already empty stomach, and he prayed his actions hadn't just caused the destruction of Osco's people. He thought about Li-yen, the girl from Nanzu who should have been more, and about Lani, his childhood lover—now his brother's wife. *If my brother still lives,* he thought. *If Lani does.* He tried not to think about his infant son with Lani, who he had begun to think of in his mind as Tane's son to protect his own sanity.

He let a soldier help him into the back of a wagon, and smiled gratefully. Then he focused his mind and his breathing, picturing a fire enveloped by a canopy of night. He rested this way until the windows of his spirit-house had fully opened—the air and sun coming through to fill his inner-eye with warmth and power. He crawled outside and beyond himself, watching his small army roll through the hills in perfect order.

The future and the past were beyond his control, yes he knew that. What he could do, now, he must do, and not be distracted. He knew it was up to him to do what was necessary. It was up to him to master God's miracles, to understand the threads of power and the rules and the raveling of the world.

First, he thought, *let us see how far the mind can wander.*

Kale hurled his spirit forward, leaving the trappings of the earth, gliding out and South towards Lani's homeland and the palace of the farmer king.

Perhaps he could guide the army's route—perhaps he could blow winds and rain over their tracks and bring fog to hide their passage. And maybe, if he was careful, he could prevent more innocent deaths with his power. He could save unwitting herders and farmers from Osco's scouts and the emperor's wrath, and at least reduce the harm he would cause. It was something. It was not nearly enough.

13
The Royal Palace of Sri Kon. 1561 AE. 19 years previous.

Kikay blew on her soup, which signaled a servant to replace it with a cooler bowl. The king and the pirate slurped at theirs, silver spoons clicking on the porcelain. The barbarian stared at them.

"It would seem your friend isn't hungry, Arun. Perhaps I was wrong about his feeding costs."

Their guest scrunched his rather handsome face and smiled, glancing at his merchandise. "He may have customs we don't understand, my lady. Perhaps he won't eat with a woman."

True to form, the 'king' laughed at that, and Kikay shot him a glare.

"Then he will go hungry. Are you enjoying your coconut soup, pirate?"

"Like a mother's milk, my lady."

Kikay felt her scowl deepen because she didn't like this man. She didn't like the way he looked at her, or how he spoke, his easy charm and arrogance or his bewildering competence. She had never heard of another brother of the Ching abandoning the Way once so far down its path. And yet…

He had also managed to spring a big clumsy giant from the very depths of Trung's prison—a place she had lost more than one skilled spy and assassin. And if he could get in once…

"Tell us," she leaned forward, noting the subtle flick of his eyes towards the split in her dress. "How did you manage to free your prize and escape Halin?"

"We pirates have our ways, my lady." The ex-monk shrugged. "Perhaps we could first discuss the matter of my fee?"

"All in time. I only ask because, as far as I know, you are the first thief to ever succeed in coming out of that place alive. Isn't that interesting?"

At this code, several guards stepped out from the hidden walls with bows and spears at the ready. The King, or rather one of his doubles, simply pushed back his chair and walked away.

"Put all your weapons on the table, pirate, and if I were you, I'd do it slowly."

Arun raised a hand towards the giant as if for calm. He smiled and unfolded several blades from his clothes, placing them down in a neat line.

"Please be very cautious, princess. Our friend was tortured by the last royal family. It has left him…most anxious."

Kikay rolled her eyes.

"I don't care if your friend is anxious. Have him put his sword down, or I'll fill him full of arrows."

"Happily, my lady." Arun's face grew a bead of sweat. "But I believe he would rather kill me. We're already in danger of violence, I think. Please be *quite* cautious."

Kikay looked at the barbarian's bizarre, ugly face. She couldn't read it, but a quiet voice told her to be wary. She took a breath, knowing Farahi would remind her to be patient.

"Very well."

She gestured, and the guards put away their weapons, but moved forward to collect Arun's knives. They gave the barbarian a wide, anxious berth. When the room had stilled and Kikay nodded, at last the real Farahi emerged from his viewing room, calm as a Bato breeze.

"You'll have to forgive my precautions," he said. "You are either a man of great talent, or a ruse sent by Trung to kill me." He signaled for the guards to back away, and took the seat furthest from the barbarian. "Either way, you're a man to be taken seriously, yes?"

Kikay felt the same anxiety she always did when her brother was in danger. He wore several metal plates beneath his silks, but the monk was possibly skilled enough with his hands to reach him and twist his neck before he died. *I should have had them both tied up or chained. I will suggest it for next time.*

Their dangerous guest stood and bowed, smiling with his soft, quick eyes.

"I expected nothing less, great king. But please be careful with the barbarian, he is a wounded tiger in a foreign land."

Farahi nodded, disinterested as ever in small talk or anything other than his purposes.

"I'll buy the barbarian and pay you fairly, but that's not why you're here."

The pirate's lips curled.

"You want Trung dead."

Kikay winced in her seat. Of course he knew. Farahi had long ago quietly told any thief or pirate in the isles he would buy stolen merchandise from Trung's castle. But what he truly wanted was proof of a man who could get inside.

No doubt the pirate had arranged all of this purely to establish his credentials. To take a big savage from the prisons was about as impressive a gift as a man could make. Now he would ask for a price beyond imagination.

"I want his heirs dead, too," Farahi said, "as many as possible."

Arun raised his eyebrows, nodding very slowly. "That could be difficult. His sons are guarded, and not often together. But his first heir is possible, yes."

Farahi shrugged. "That is acceptable. Name your price."

Kikay watched the greed sparkle in the pirate's eyes. She decided again he was too clever and skilled to be useful—too ambitious to be trusted. Farahi wouldn't listen, of course. He had gained that look of impossible certainty, that intense and far-away stare that told her he had moved beyond and decided already, so bent now on his goal.

"I'll need some time to consider," said the pirate, and Kikay nearly spit.

As if the treacherous little villain hadn't considered it a thousand times. No doubt he'd been dreaming of this day for months, or even years. Men were so predictable. They waved their hands and denied their ambitions or their motives, but in truth they never truly changed their minds.

She looked at her brother and took a deep breath, imagining the hours of near-useless debate. She could always go to Hali, she supposed—the king's concubine. Whenever a man's passions interfered with good sense, a spent penis was a good tonic.

But she looked the king's eyes and saw the iron that sometimes made him great, if also vulnerable—the mark of a man not afraid to make decisions, and bear the cost.

She looked, too, at Arun's easy smile, and the effort to conceal a fragile pride. With the right prize and mask she could perhaps understand his dreams, change his ambitions, and bend his future to her will. But in the end, a scorpion was a scorpion, and she wasn't yet sure what sort of beast he was.

At the thought it became impossible not to glance again at the blotchy giant sulking and staring at the end of the table. He stared back at her with his strange, bright eyes. She looked away.

"Take all the time you need," Farahi said. "In the meantime, you and the barbarian will stay here at the palace as my guests."

The pirate smiled, and why shouldn't he? He was safe now, secure in his knowledge that the richest man in Pyu wanted his help. No doubt he'd sleep deep with dreams of wealth.

"Of course. Most generous, my lord."

Kikay thought perhaps she'd have him killed once he'd accomplished his task, if he survived. She'd save a great deal of coin, or whatever other ridiculous reward the man wanted, and wipe out a threat in the same stroke.

She held back her smile, wondering exactly how she'd trap an ex-master of the Ching, but sure she'd find a way. There were other killers, other low-born men of talent willing to do what was necessary to rise. The thought gave her some comfort, and she settled back looking forward to the duck she'd heard the chef boasting about for days. Then she jumped as the giant leaned forward, and blew on his soup.

Farahi and Arun stopped talking, equally fascinated as a pale-faced servant replaced the savage's plate with a new bowl from the fire-heated pot.

The giant watched it all carefully, then at last lifted the new bowl with a lopsided grin. He drank, steam rising as he took great gulps and emptied it, removing his hand for the first time from his sword.

"Soup. Good," he said, his sounds almost correct, his voice strong and deep. At the sound of it a near-by servant dropped a tray of appetizers, and the giant smiled. "Like mother's milk."

Kikay blinked in the silence, trying to recover by re-arranging her lap-cloth. After another moment, she remembered to close her mouth.

14

Ruka wasn't precisely sure what he'd said. He knew the words referenced soup, but considering the reaction of the matron, he might have said it tastes like horse piss. It didn't really matter. The point was the same: I can learn your words and how to use them. It worked well enough.

After, they'd all jabbered at him as if with these few words he had mastered their tongue. He'd responded once or twice but mostly shrugged and ignored them. Then they left him alone for a time, and he ate a series of new and incredible dishes of food brought by their servants.

Now he sat on the edge of an opulent bed—similar to the one he'd found in a rich farmer's home near the coast of the Ascom. His stomach felt stuffed in an unfamiliar, and rather uncomfortable way, and it drooped his lids and sapped his strength.

He ran a finger over the wood base of the bed's crossing boards, then the carved, flat, square edges and posts at the corners. He lay on it for quite some time, feet dangling off the end until curiosity won out, and he cut into the huge cushion that covered the entire base. He wanted to know what made it so soft. The answer was feathers, down feathers, as if from hatchlings. He marveled at such a thing.

They'd given him his own room, which contained the bed, a 'cupboard' on the floor with a deep bucket for waste, a smooth table holding water and fruit in clay bowls, and a large, unbarred window. They'd even left him Ahrune's sword, and a servant with a noise-maker, who seemed to gesture if rung he'd come running. Ruka almost dared Bukayag to tell him to flee.

After the 'revelation' at supper that Ruka could speak, 'Keekay' and 'Farahee'—formerly Long-neck and Square-head—had assaulted him with words. The dead men in his Grove frantically searched for meanings and sounds in his word-lists, and though time was slower in the world of the living, it had been difficult. He'd made them understand his name. They'd introduced themselves. For now, he could manage little more with any certainty.

It also became clear that Ahrune was trying to sell him, or had already. Why exactly these people should pay, Ruka wasn't sure, but they seemed a better breed of owners, and if they kept him fed and gave him time to learn it was more than enough.

He'd spoken up in the first place because he hadn't liked the way they ignored him—the way they referenced him with tones that implied something lesser, with subtle glances as towards a rude guest, wary but not afraid. Perhaps he was still just an animal in their eyes, but now at least he was a *talking* animal, and that surely made a difference.

He went over everything again and again in his mind, everything he'd seen and heard for the past few days. It would take time to understand. But it seemed, at least for now, time was something he had.

Sleep, brother, we're safe in this war-fort. It is different than the other.

"I do not feel safe. This place is a prison."

There are no bars, brother, no chains.

"There is more than one kind of prison. You should know."

Ruka snorted because he supposed that was true. He used the thin folded coverings of the bed to mop at his sweat, then drank all the water from his bowl. There was never any sediment in the water, he'd noticed, not even the faintest hint of dirt. He had no idea how they managed it. But he intended to learn.

When he'd lain long enough to grow restless, he rose and reached for the small and only door, forcing Bukayag to leave their sword behind.

"It will be locked regardless," his brother growled.

Ruka reached for the smooth, rounded handle. When it turned, he grinned, and stepped out to find two guards holding spears. They stiffened when they saw him, and for a moment he only looked out at the world lit by a sliver of moon.

The halls had the same clear-glass candles that smelled of fish as the previous war-fort. Ruka raised his hands and moved slowly, gesturing down the hall as he made a walking motion, assuming the guards would jab their spears at him till he turned around.

Instead they bowed and followed, staring at his ripped, stained pants, and his welt-marked, naked chest.

"The illusion of freedom," Bukayag whispered, "don't be a fool."

Ruka imagined the guards exchanging glances at his alien words, but he didn't look back.

Instead he focused on the breeze blowing across his skin, slick still with sweat, and the pain flaring from every plant-stick gash and bruise. He stepped with bare feet along the cold stone, feeling his pulse in the place his few missing toe-nails should be.

In his mind he looked again at the torturer's faces as they'd seen his feet. By their expression, he believed they'd never seen the wreckage of frostbite, nor perhaps the hardened callus and wear of a man who lived half his life as an outcast in an open plain.

He mapped the palace halls as he walked, as well as the features of the land outside. High buildings dotted the landscape, their slanted roofs pointed with strange carvings. The huge river snaked towards the sea, the strong current audible even from the fortress.

Ruka took deep breaths because it seemed easier at night, and the walking refreshed him. His mind wandered even as he memorized, considering all the things he could learn from these little brown Northmen— these lucky inhabitants of paradise. *We must see their larger ships*, he decided, *and their maps, if they have them.*

But this was only one of a thousand things he wished to know. He would somehow need to find the words and men to discuss winds and seasons. *And farming, and irrigation; and stone-masons, artists, blacksmiths, priests, builders and fishermen!*

Ruka realized he was almost running by the concerned pants of his guards.

His pulse raced, but not from the effort. They stood near a balcony now that overlooked the city, and the incredible light of it drew Ruka to the railing. His sentries sagged against it, bracing spears as they put their hands to their knees. Ruka grinned at them.

He looked out in open awe, a feeling so new and indescribable, closest perhaps to the warmth of a fire on a cold back. *Hope*, he thought it, surprised, trying to feel some version of it from his childhood, *perhaps the feeling is hope.*

The wind beside his head hummed, and for a moment he thought it nothing—only an insect, perhaps. Then one of his guards fell back with a thin black shaft of wood stuck in his throat.

The night filled with buzzing and the clatter of wood on stone as Ruka threw himself backwards, dragging the other guard with one hand. Little arrows dropped beside them, then metallic ringing roared as hooked, anchor-like weapons latched to the balcony railing.

Ruka and his guard found their feet. They were far enough back now to avoid the arrows, or whatever they were, but with so many hooks they were clearly vastly outnumbered. Bukayag woke as if from a sleep, his fists clenched and a growl in his throat. He wanted to fight.

We are unarmed, brother, and these aren't criminals with knives. We must run.

"I grow very tired of running."

The young guard's eyes had widened in panic, locked now on the bloody, gurgling death throes of his ally. He stood poised and rigid, twitching as if each second he considered fleeing, then rejected it.

Ruka searched his word pile and gambled without being certain.

"Where king?" he tried to say. The boy's eyes widened further, if that were possible. He mumbled something Ruka couldn't understand, then shrugged.

But the words didn't much matter. There was no time. Somehow the intruders had already climbed up.

Black-hoods and long sticks emerged from the balcony, and more buzzing and hissing sounds filled the air as Ruka fled down the hall, one hand on the back of his guard.

More sounds came from ahead—more hooks landing on balconies along the outer wall.

These corridors were too long and narrow, the fall too steep to jump off the side. Ruka knew he'd be shot to death before he ran out of range, too. But he couldn't run past them fast enough. He was utterly trapped.

In his Grove, he stood in the training ground before a dozen dead men holding bows, practicing trying to dodge the missiles.

No, he thought, catching arrows to his body no matter how he tried to dodge. *We will need a shield.*

"You don't fucking say."

Turn back. This hall goes on forever and there's nowhere to hide.

Bukayag seized the guard by the neck and spun him, sprinting and hoping he could rush past the few up top behind him and round the corner. But Ruka knew it was too late. At least five little Ahrune-like shadows had climbed the rail and gathered by the wall, mouth-tubes at the ready.

It's too high to jump off anywhere, and there's no moat here.

"We can use the guard as a shield."

Ruka had already considered it. But the boy was thin and unarmored, fidgety and afraid. He wouldn't cover them well. He would fight, too, and if he lived he would despise them and say who knew what to the king.

The shadows were coming forward, and there was nowhere to run.

"We can't die yet," Bukayag growled, or maybe whined. "There's too much to do."

The shadows moved forward firing their tubes. The dead men in the practice field fired their bows.

In his Grove, Ruka lifted a huge, square shield from his armory. It was thicker than he needed, made to stop swords and axes and perhaps to stand in a wall with other men. But, of course, it didn't exist.

He had toiled over the edges, the boss, the grip, drawing runes carefully when he was finished—but here in the world, here where it mattered, it was all in his mind.

Bukayag didn't seem to care. He raised his empty arm—as if imaginary Grove-steel from the land of the dead could protect him just as well, as if imagination worked the same as reality.

And why not, Ruka thought, enthralled. Had Ruka not already done the impossible? Had he not overcome sleep, crossed an uncrossable sea, and rested like plants and beasts? If Ruka could do that, couldn't a world exist where a man's will became truth? And once imagined, didn't thought itself make it true?

Take it, brother. Its yours. Show me how.

Ruka closed his eyes and willed it so, then stood in open awe as his shield shimmered and faded from his arm. Imagination in reverse.

He grunted as the walking corpses' arrows struck home, blunted tips pummeling his chest. But in the real world—the land of the living—he heard a sound like a sword ringing free of its scabbard.

Sparks flew and lit the narrow corridor. Molten iron formed as if pulled from the forge and struck by a blacksmith's hammer. The flames arced and sizzled in the air as the image of Ruka's attackers vanished behind a wall of darkness.

Ruka hardly noticed as the darts bounced and rattled and fell away. He stared at the curved, rectangular shield from the land of the dead—a shield cut, forged and inscribed with runes by his hand in an imaginary smithy.

And this, brother, he whispered, still in awe.

Ruka lifted a short, stabbing sword from his armory, and Bukayag reached out his other hand. His eyes glazed as fear replaced with bloodlust. He grasped it as if he had always done so, dragging back his arm until nothing became something, two feet of tempered iron hissing and sparking into being from a scabbard of air.

The light and sound came heavy now, lighting the hall like flashing lightning, every inch of the blade scraping the air as if cutting a path towards existence.

Bukayag lowered his guard enough to see his enemy. The little shadow-men stood in the hall staring, their tubes momentarily forgotten.

"You'd best build a few graves, brother," Bukayag snarled.

Ruka agreed, but it could wait. The moment his brother seized the sword, he had gestured at the dead to light his forge, arranging his tools across the closest bench. *I'll make some armor,* he thought. *But what are the limits? What else can I bring?*

Bukayag's hands twitched as he focused on his first target—a man trapped before his fellows in the narrow passage.

Ruka glanced and suggested he stab and bash his way through to the railing, and cut those clever little hooks from their ropes. This seemed good enough for Bukayag. They charged together.

15

"Tell me exactly what you saw."

Farahi's tone was calm, and familiar, as if he spoke to a friend. In fact he didn't even *look* upset, which reminded Kikay why they worked so well as a team. She'd been ready for executions. Maybe a lot of them.

"Men…in black silks, my lord, they used hooks to grapple the Western balconies in the visitor wing."

Kikay fanned herself. She didn't care what the man saw or how he felt or what any of the men involved had to say, but Farahi was insistent. The attack seemed over, at least. Guards and soldiers swarmed the palace like flies, and bodies were being piled up all over the fortress.

Now they sat in one of Farahi's 'safe rooms'. Like all of them it was small and uncomfortable, with only a few simple tables and chairs surrounded by thick stone walls. Kikay felt trapped, and oppressed.

"Good," said the king, still calm and patient. "Now tell me about the barbarian, Togi."

He'd have never remembered the man's name on his own, but Kikay had whispered it as they brought him in. The fool's skin was red and dripping with sweat.

"He…he left his room to take a walk, lord."

"Armed?"

"No, lord. He wore nothing but his filthy savage clothing. We followed as ordered." The king nodded and said nothing, so he went on. "His legs…he is very fast, lord. Taffa…that is, the other guard on duty, said we should stop him because we could not easily keep his pace. But then he waited for us at the balcony, and we stood beside him."

"Good. Tell me about the corridor."

The man's red skin was slowly paling, and he swallowed at nothing.

"He…we tried to run, but were trapped by the…assassins, lord."

"And then?"

"It…he…" the man glanced back at his superior officer, who stood equally pale-faced at the door. "He used sorcery, my lord. I'm very sorry, I can't explain it properly."

Kikay rolled her eyes, but her brother didn't. He just waited, as usual, patient and curious, the same expression whether he discussed rice yield, war, the weather, or 'sorcery'.

"Tell me what you saw, Togi. You will not be punished."

"He…made weapons with fire, lord. From nothing. I saw it with my own eyes."

"And then what?"

The man blinked, as if he had expected a different sort of follow-up question.

"He…well, he killed them, lord. He killed all of them."

This wasn't true, though perhaps it seemed so to the guard. Dozens of the assassins had entered other areas and not just the visitor wing. Many had moved elsewhere as soon as they arrived, so the savage only fought a handful on the balcony.

"Tell me how," said the king.

"I…could barely see, lord. It was dark. Everything happened so quickly."

"Just tell me what you saw, and what you heard, Togi."

The officer waiting at the door looked ready to scream out in fury, or maybe faint.

"He…he was laughing. He killed many with his shield, I think. He'd… *knock* them off the balcony, or…crush them, against the wall, or just swing the edges, like an axe."

"Good, and then what?"

"We, well, we kept running, lord, all the way to the bedrooms."

"Did he receive his wounds there on the balcony or later?"

"Both, I think. My lord."

Kikay didn't much give a damn where the savage received his injuries. If it were up to her she'd just kill the wounded barbarian *and* the guards *and* the pirate and be done with it.

In fact she had acted the moment the attack begun. Arun was already imprisoned, and she'd told her torturer to prepare. The palace elite roamed the grounds, and half the army now patrolled Sri Kon. On her instruction they would bribe, intimidate, or kill their way to the conspirators, and before the sun rose tomorrow, she'd know how so many men infiltrated the city without alarm. And if she didn't, more men would die.

"My lord, I'm sorry I nearly forgot…before the barbarian…before he attacked, he asked me, very badly but in our tongue - 'Where king?'"

Togi looked on the verge of tears at his monarch's long, silent expression. Kikay stared at her brother with wide eyes, but he did not look back. At last he spoke.

"What did you tell him, Togi?"

"I…I said I didn't know, lord, because of course I didn't. But if I had I wouldn't have told him, lord."

Farahi nodded, his temporary surprise banished again behind the stone.

"Thank you, soldier, you're dismissed."

The young man bowed and retreated, his commanding officer seizing him at the door to flee together.

Farahi flicked a hand at his bodyguards which meant 'clear the room'. He waited until he and Kikay sat alone in their chairs.

"I suppose you think I should have them tortured."

"At best they are incompetent," Kikay snapped. And, anticipating his next questions: "Their families are powerless. I never choose palace guards from families with any wealth or influence, particularly because most want you dead."

"The problem is," Farahi sighed, "I believe him."

"You believe everyone."

The king rolled his eyes, standing to pace with his hands behind his back. Kikay for now held her place, and softened her tone.

"They were too close this time, Fara-che, we should make an example of the entire shift."

She knew he wouldn't, of course, but it was worth saying.

"I don't think they knew they were close. They attacked half the palace. It was wild, desperate. The treachery was in the city where it always is."

"Not always," she said, even more gently. Island lords had tried to kill Farahi more times now than she could count. But her brother's stomach pains and vomiting, his scars and many nightmares—they were reminders enough. Her warm tone affected him, and he walked to her, putting a hand to her cheek.

"I'm fine, sister. My wives still sleep. My children are undisturbed. It was a desperate attack by Trung and his allies, and it failed." His face hardened. "Do you think it was a coincidence?"

Kikay did not believe in coincidences. Nor did she believe in luck, or sorcery, or mercy.

"I think the barbarian is beyond dangerous. Whether he intended to kill or protect you, whether he just killed them for fun, or perhaps because he wants your trust, I think we should put him down."

Farahi stepped away and sighed, returning to his pacing. Kikay supposed not wishing to kill one's savior was only natural.

In truth, the assassins almost succeeded. Servants still removed a small heap of bodies from the hall attached to the room her brother shared with his concubine. The assassins had checked every room, and it seemed clear they didn't know where Farahi was. But if more had survived to reach that hallway…

The couple moved nightly, but this night they had chosen the visitor wing. If the barbarian hadn't made a great bloody racket smearing assassin corpses all over the halls, they might never have heard and fled further in. Farahi's guards might have died too quickly, too quietly, and the king of the isles might very well be a corpse, just like everyone wanted.

"Somehow he managed to sneak in a shield and sword," Kikay reminded him. Farahi shrugged at this, but the concern was clear in his eyes.

"Arun might have arranged it to make him feel safe. Or they might be friends and have a way to speak. Perhaps they set up the 'capture' in the first place."

Kikay raised her eyebrows and stood, walking across the room to where the barbarian's weapons rested on a table. It took both hands to lift the sword.

"And where exactly do you think Arun got *this*?"

Farahi glanced at the thick, yet razor-edged blade, the metal glinting slightly blue in the torchlight. He had brought a blacksmith in to look at it instantly, annoying Kikay because it seemed this was more important to him than the damned attack.

"That's why I won't kill him, sister. He may have things to teach us."

Kikay let out a breath, angry at the logic, and at the useless smith for lifting the blade like a monk at prayer and failing to explain it.

"We don't need shiny new blue swords or complications. You have the most powerful military in Pyu already. We don't need or want change."

Farahi smiled.

"But change comes, sister. What we want is irrelevant." The king approached and lifted the shield—so massive it rose above him though he held to to the floor. His jaw clenched from the effort.

"If there's more men like this one, are we not wise to befriend them?"

Kikay set the strange-colored metal back on the table and shook her head.

"You heard the guard. This 'man' laughed as he killed—*nine* assassins, Farahi! Even half dead from wounds he kept fighting. Does that sound like the sort of men who seek allies? Who seek peace?"

"We'll see," her brother let the shield drop, careful not to crush his toes. Kikay noticed blood crusted on the sharpened edges, and a couple of teeth.

"At the very least put this savage in a cell. Put him near Arun so he can hear the screams as we torture him, and so learns to fear us."

Farahi put his hands behind his back as he walked away.

"If he lives," he said at last with a nod.

"If he lives," Kikay agreed.

The king spoke over his shoulder as he left through his secret passage. "I wouldn't want to be your enemy, sister. Tell me what you learn from the monk."

* * *

Arun was a god-damned fool, apparently, and he'd die screaming.

He sat chained to iron bars, his arms held above by rope, knowing he had no leverage, and no escape. He should have known Trung was prepared to kill Farahi, that he'd have allies amongst all the petty, Alaku-hating lords, and spies on every island.

Likely they'd hoped the guards would be distracted by their visitors—that they'd be looking inward, rather than outward, and so they'd struck in force. And even if the plot failed the king of Halin would have known what would happen to Arun. The plan was cruel, wasteful, but effective. In other words, classic Trung.

And I'm a god-damned fool.

Farahi's guards had seized him in the middle of the night. He'd been half-drunk on palace wine, comfortable and deep in sleep, thinking the danger over and the deal secured.

Now his arms were stretched up above him by ropes, his clothes stripped, his feet chained to the floor. A big, thick butcher of men sharpened his tools in silence.

Arun almost laughed. The pirate-king! He couldn't have been happy with just a few boats, oh no, couldn't have been satisfied with freedom and wealth and living on his wits in the open sea with scoundrels and whores. He'd wanted more, just like always, and so he'd had to gamble. Now they'd torture him to death to be sure. It made no difference he wasn't involved, or that he'd tell them the truth. He was too dangerous and maybe involved, and that was that.

King Farahi's resolve and lack of mercy were legendary. The man had probably murdered his whole family just for power. What was one more nameless pirate to the list?

His prison and torture chamber looked completely different than Trung's. Here there were no 'observers', no rusty tools or sycophantic slaves serving a tyrant's amateurish whims. Here there was good light and clean tools and a washed, stone floor.

A thick bull of a man stood patiently at the only table. He held a blade up to the near-by lantern, then blew off a fleck of metal dust before placing it back to his whetstone. When he was satisfied, he pushed his table to Arun, wheels beneath not even creaking as they moved.

"I assume bribery is out of the question?"

Arun tried to keep his tone light to control his fear. He met the man's eyes, and in an instant saw a reptile without pity, or reserve. He saw only a true master of cruelty, employed and paid well for his talents, then left alone, and undisturbed.

"I am King Farahi's Master of Torture." His voice held no sign of emotion, nor pride. A shiver raced up Arun's spine.

"And here I'd thought you were the gardener."

The butcher didn't blink, or smile. He spoke as if reading from a script.

"When I am satisfied you have provided honest answers to my lord's questions, the process will cease."

The process.

Arun supposed that sounded nicer than 'bloody, agonizing maiming.'

"Has anyone ever satisfied you and lived, Master Torturer?"

"Do you understand?"

Arun sighed. "I understand."

The butcher's pupils shot back and forth, never staying still, never moving even near Arun's face. Instead he looked him up and down as if considering a flank of pork.

"Were you or are you in any way involved in any plot against the king or his family?"

"No," Arun breathed out, knowing his answers made no difference.

The torturer lifted a curved-handled razor.

"Were you or are you involved in any act of deception concerning your dealings with the king?"

Arun took another deep breath and tried to find calm. He'd been a monk in Bato for many years—a disciple of the Enlightened, taught to master his body and mind to ignore the corporeal world. Of course, he'd never been a particularly *good* monk.

"No," he said, trying to drift far away. But he still jumped when the razor touched him.

It didn't pierce his skin. The torturer began to shave him, almost gently, from neck to knees, patient and precise. Afterward he washed Arun's skin with cool, clean water, and rubbed him down with alcohol, which burned fiercely. He did everything slowly, carefully, and in silence.

"Is there anything at all you wish to admit to me before I begin?"

"I have nothing to admit. And I will still kill Trung for your master, if he wishes. Tell him that."

The torturer at last met Arun's eyes.

"You have no use to my master now." He stepped away, putting his hands on a wooden wheel almost like a mill, and turned.

Metal screeched apart from above, and four iron shafts descended from the low ceiling. They were attached to prison-like grate roof and sides, which soon enveloped Arun in iron. Only his arms stuck out the top. The torturer seized them and released the rope, sliding his arms down into two slots before shutting them in more iron.

Arun could move his arms a little, but the manacles stopped him from bringing them through the grate, and his body was completely trapped. The wheel had also slid open a panel in the roof, and sunlight poured through, covering Arun with morning warmth.

The torturer left the room and returned with what looked like a single shoot of bamboo.

He placed it beneath in a large pot, the tip of the plant several inches from Arun's groin. He fussed and angled it just so, adding water and stroking its bark and whispering like a proud father.

"This breed can grow a foot or more in a single day. It will enter your body and move through your flesh as if it were soil. You will die slowly. If you attempt to move, or disrupt the growth, I will remove your hands, your feet, and your eyes, in that order. After that I will hold you in place with clamps. Tomorrow, I will ask you my lord's questions again. Do you understand?"

My body is nothing, Arun looked up the sunlight, feeling the warmth and closing his eyes as he imagined a quiet, temple life. *There is only the spirit.*

He held his former master's lessons in his mind, wishing only he still believed them.

"I understand."

The big man nodded. He sat in his chair across the room. They watched the plant grow together.

* * *

The bamboo touched skin just behind Arun's testicles, and he nearly moved. "Ask me your question again, Master Torturer." He felt the sweat dripping down his neck, and armpits. "I'll tell you the truth."

The butcher sat perfectly still save for his pupils, which shifted around as if they had a mind of their own. He hadn't spoken since the start, and didn't seem as if he would.

Arun took another deep, settling breath. He wasn't afraid of death, exactly. But life was such a glorious game of chance, and he would have liked to see what came next.

Slow, agonizing death by bamboo, that's what's next.

He thought of the unpredictable insanity of this, and couldn't help it, he laughed.

"I've really always been lucky, you know." He knew the torturer would ignore him, but nevermind. If he was going to die he'd say his peace. "I'll miss women," he sighed. "Especially whores. Have you ever had a beautiful woman lie to you, friend? Her deep, brown eyes wide and staring into yours, not a hint of shame? No. I suppose not. I'll miss rice wine, too, and sugar-cane. I always liked food, any kind of food you please."

He closed his eyes and thought back to old Teacher Lo—he and his brother's first trainer at the monastery. Would all that old bastard's fine words hold up, he wondered, if bamboo sprouted through his gut?

"I bet my brother's in morning song, welcoming the sun," he whispered. "Or stretching his limbs out to dance for his students." He smiled and wished he could see him now—wished they'd parted on better terms, and that he'd said goodbye. But at best Arun would be a failure in his brother's eyes now. At worst a heretic.

The thought depressed him in a way he couldn't express, nearly sapping the last remnants of his good humor. He'd been so lost in his mind, embracing every last painless free moment, remembering his past, that he hadn't noted the slippered feet on cold, marble stairs.

"Still alive, pirate?"

Arun blinked as beauty filled the gloomy, evil little pit. He saw sleep bruises under Kikay's eyes, her hair tousled, her cotton nightgown resting over a silk shift beneath. She had her arms crossed as if cold, and her voice was gentle. Arun smiled without a hint of mask.

"For a little while, princess."

She returned the smile, but looked away. "I don't believe you're guilty, Arun. I know you're clever—I think you'd have fled had you known about the attack, or taken part in it."

"Then let me go."

Her long, loose hair tumbled as she shook her head. "My brother doesn't care. He wants an example."

"I can be much more useful than an example. String up one of the assassins."

The torturer perked up, as if he'd smelled something rotten. "Please speak with the king or don't interfere...my lady." He bowed as genuinely as he'd read Arun his script.

She ignored him.

"He won't believe anything you say. And he won't trust you to do what you promise."

The bamboo was doing more than prickling flesh now. Every moment it seemed an increasingly firm 'support'. Arun closed his eyes, not seeing an escape.

"I'll do whatever the king requires to prove my loyalty. I have no reason to lie. I am a mercenary, my life is..."

"*There's nothing!*" she interrupted, angrily, as if she'd been considering this all night.

Sweet girl, Arun thought, seeing at last through her mask—seeing just a terrified young woman doing what she must. *I can't imagine what it's like to live here trapped with the Kinslayer King.*

No doubt the toughness she'd shown before was a brave-face for guests while her brother dangled her out like bait. Arun looked on her fragile beauty and reminded himself she was no more than twenty-three, her husband dead, her whole family gone except the brother that killed them a few short years go.

Of course she had to pretend to be loyal, but she probably hated him.

"You're a failed monk—you betrayed the Enlightened." Kikay sighed. "He'll never trust you."

Arun's mind raced, and he surged against his chains as it clicked.

"Yes, I'm a failed monk. Tell him to send me back to Bato a prisoner. I'll re-take the tests, I'll do whatever they ask to prove my honesty. Let the monks decide if I live."

The Alaku princess searched his eyes, then looked away again, turning back with at least some hope.

"Maybe. Yes, maybe. He respects the monks."

"Enough." The Master Torturer rose and looked straight at Kikay. "Until the king tells me otherwise, you're forbidden from speaking to this prisoner. I am master here, my lady, in the king's name. Leave us."

Arun blinked in shock at the tone. Kikay withered.

"My apologies, I'll speak with the king." She bowed slightly and turned.

"Do hurry," Arun called, as casually as possible, noting the bamboo's persistence growing stiffer by the moment. *Save me,* he thought, *and perhaps later I'll kill your brother for you.*

She spared a look at the bamboo, then his eyes, and ran for the steps.

Arun almost sagged in relief. He realized he might be useless to a woman by the time she returned, but he couldn't help himself, he watched her curves as she ran, and held her smile in his mind like a prayer as he breathed out.

When he was ready he re-focused on his flesh, preparing to harden himself as he'd done a thousand times to snap boards and bend iron in training. The masters of the Ching could shatter stone with their palms and feet, and bend iron with their necks.

But never with their balls.

He held back the laugh at the insanity of life, and the pure, beautiful chaos of it all. Well, he supposed, controlling his breathing, there was a first time for everything.

His torturer stood with arms crossed, pupils floating, and glared.

* * *

Arun felt the growth rising against his flesh, pushing, exploring, stiffening against him. Then he was back beside Lake Lancona while Old Lo poured salt-water in his eyes.

"Keep your eyes open, boy."

"It hurts," he'd whimpered.

"And what is pain? Does a stone fear water? Fear salt?"

"N-, no, teacher."

"Tell me why."

"Because a stone feels no pain, Teacher."

"Maybe it does, and you just can't hear its cries. Be a stone, boy. Do not move."

Arun had done his best. The rusty sprinkler in Lo's hand had been used both for watering plants and little boys, its wooden handle smooth and faded from use. He remembered wondering if the man or the tool was older, but he never talked back. He was always polite and respectful, and he'd never breathed a word about running away before he did it, not even to his brother.

Bastard boys were always running away. No one would have thought much of it if Arun hadn't been selected for the Ching, and so close to becoming a monk in truth. Anyway, the running came later, far later, after a hundred cruel tests and meaningless exercises. He'd suffered for years under that man.

"Don't move!"

The voice was the butcher now. Lo had his arrogance and his tests and natural meanness, but measured against whatever lived in this torturer's heart, the old monk seemed harmless enough.

"Clear your thoughts," whispered Lo again in the recesses of Arun's mind. "Be still. Let the water flow over you, shape you, but do not resist. You are a flat stone in a river."

Fuck you, old fake.

Arun's mind had never once 'cleared'. Most days he'd thought of taking the sprinkler and beating his teacher to death; sometimes he'd thought of stealing a boat and sailing away, far away, to a place with all the food he could eat and soft beds and maybe a mother and father who tucked him into it at night. He'd held his eyes open through sheer will.

"Very good. Now don't blink."

He *hadn't* fucking blinked. But not because he 'stilled his mind' or 'became like the rock' but because he'd been so angry, so wretchedly tired of being weak, he had said to himself 'I am the master of my eye, not this old man, not this pain. My eyes will not close'.

"Yes, boy, empty your thoughts, still your mind."

Not once in all those years had Arun understood what that meant. And later he'd swum that damned lake with open eyes and a busy mind, just like he'd walked over hot coals and snapped wooden beams and danced the Ching with a busy mind. Just like he'd sat through morning prayer and afternoon prayer and evening prayer while he thought about naked girls and drowning Old Lo with water from his sprinkler.

Now here he was. And what the hell was bamboo, anyway? Nothing. A piece of wood, a stupid plant, a lesser little form of life with no spirits or Gods, helpless to stop one single swing of one single machete. That's what intended to kill him? Intended to invade the only thing Arun could call home? Well, he thought, let's just see who cares more.

He flexed every muscle from his chest down to his toes, twitching each separately as he'd learned painfully over a decade to do. The bamboo was sharp, he knew, that was the danger. His skin must be hard, so hard that the tip would hold and force the stalk to bend. He breathed out and lifted his torso a fraction of an inch. He cried out from the sheer bloody trapped rage and effort of it.

"Move again, prisoner, and I take your hands."

Arun opened his eyes long enough to stare. Oh how he would enjoy killing this man when the time came. And by all the spirits and gods, he promised, it would come, because fate never spared anyone, especially not someone like this—not someone who deserved it, not in the end.

The ex-monk found the muscles in his gut and around his manhood and flexed them, then settled very slowly, and very carefully, against the plant. He watched the other man's eyes, which focused on the sharp, firm, round top of the plant pressing against his prisoner's skin.

'Bend but do not break,' Arun imagined the old man saying, 'be as the bamboo'!

Fuck you, and the bamboo, and this fat, shifty-eyed monster.

Arun breathed. Life became the passing of single moments, or perhaps it always had been and Arun just never noticed. Even now his mind wandered, thinking of all those he'd killed because fortune was fickle or because they were weak creatures in a world that tested strength.

He felt each moment as if failure loomed—as if justice and fate pushed at him through the stiff stalk of a plant, and that his skin was torn and his body impaled already, blood running down his leg and pooling on the sunlit floor. But thought was useless. He had but a single task, a single purpose, and it was obvious. Life could never be more clear and beautiful.

"Stop it."

The torturer's hands flexed and his brow looked sweaty.

"Stop what, my friend?"

Arun exhaled as he spoke. He smiled at the glorious look in the monster's eyes—a hungry carnivore trapped in a cage, terrible ambitions thwarted.

The bamboo was slowly starting to bend. The torturer stared and stared, his face seeming to bend with it, pupils floating around his eyes as if he'd been smoking opium. His hands clenched white as he stood watching, his breathing getting heavier.

Without another word he turned and walked to his tray. He lifted a claw-like contraption of knives, dipped it in sour-smelling liquid, and returned to the cage. He paused long enough to stare again at his bamboo, then raked it across Arun's chest deftly between the bars.

Arun screamed and shook more in rage than in pain. He breathed and kept his body tense, yelling again and again at the waves of pain rolling down his flesh. The cuts seemed shallow enough, but he yelled because he was trapped, because he was in the grip of a madman, and a living thing was trying to grow through his groin.

He felt his muscles shaking imperceptibly, then the urge to swat at the pain like a mosquito, a shiver on his skin as the wind rose hairs on a man's neck. He screamed again at the fury of it, the betrayal of his body. Finally he flinched. Not enough to lose control of his muscles, but enough.

"You moved." The big man was covered in as much sweat as Arun, like an addict too long from his pipe, expression locked now in the foggy haze of his passion. He put the claw down and returned to his tray, and very slowly, very deliberately, he lifted a butcher's knife.

"I will take your hands now," he almost groaned. "But you must leave the stumps out of the shackles for me to bind them, or else you will bleed to death. Do you understand?"

Arun's heart pounded. His stomach rose in terror because he knew it was too soon. Kikay couldn't have found the king and convinced him yet, let alone returned, and she was the only thing in the way.

He's going to do it. He's going to cut off my bloody hands. Enlightened help me.

With eager yet halting steps, the torturer jerked towards the cage. Arun knew the monster was savoring his fear, that he lived for it, that he needed it somehow. But it didn't matter. Arun couldn't stop the watery trembling of his bowels, the tightness arcing through his muscles. He was giving this awful man what he wanted and by all good spirits he didn't want to lose his hands, please no. He screamed again in rage, trying to let out the trapped, helpless terror with the only thing he possessed that could escape the iron bars.

The butcher smiled at last. He brushed sweaty fingers over Arun's manacle locked hands and raised the cleaver. Arun cried out again, but this time, not in terror—but out of sheer, insane hope. Over the butcher's shoulder he saw a shadow.

A huge silhouette stepped into the gloom from the stairs, a shuffling scrape of callused foot against the stone of the basement. The butcher blinked, then turned.

"Loa, pirate," said a voice, deep and sonorous. Arun nearly wept, and laughed like a madman.

"Loa, Ruka."

The savage was half-wrapped in white and red bandage, his bright eyes half-closed as if he'd been drugged.

Oh God, Arun's mind filled with terrible, hopeless thought, *perhaps he's only come to watch. Perhaps he hates me, perhaps he thinks I've betrayed the king and his rescue was just a ruse.* And then: *Or maybe he likes torture, who knows what he thinks, he's a god damned savage!*

Ruka leaned against the wall as if exhausted, or in pain. He was unarmed. A gash across his side appeared re-opened just from coming down the stairs.

The torturer gripped his knife and his massive chest heaved. He gestured up the stairs.

"Go. Go back to your room! Go *now*! Understand? Go!"

He gestured again and waved the blade, speaking as one would to a feral dog.

The giant's bright eyes opened slightly and shone in the light. He inspected Arun, the cage, the bamboo and the little tray covered in clean, metal knives. All at once he sneered and rose to his full height, as if whatever pain he had felt simply disappeared.

"No."

With that he stepped forward, eyes locked on the butcher's. The two big men leaned like hunting cats. Their faces were hardened in concentration, violence lurking in their limbs.

Arun tried to push past the trembling in every muscle—past the waves of pain from what smelled like lemon juice dripping down his chest-cuts, and the urge to scream from still being so thoroughly and utterly trapped. He felt the strange joy of hope and salvation, and the fear of its failing.

Ruka approached on shaky legs, his hands up and open, his eyes wary. He stood at least a foot or more taller than his enemy. His muscles were taut, corded and terrifying, and Arun knew the awful strength in the man's body. But he was badly wounded, and unarmed.

The butcher was thicker, and though fat, moved like a wrestler. He stepped and circled like a man no stranger to violence. He raised the cleaver to swing once, twice, but held it back. He faked a lunge, faked a dash to the side, and moved away. Finally he surged ahead.

He almost leapt and shouted, one hand sweeping out as if just to distract. He swung his cleaver, and Ruka stumbled to the side but seemed too weak to move away. The blade sprayed blood.

A piece of flesh squished to the ground. Ruka roared and charged, his bloody hands closing around the thick neck and forearm of the butcher. The two big men spun and flailed and fell to the floor. They grunted and growled like animals, striking out at each other with elbows and knees, one arm each devoted to the cleaver, holding it up as if some delicate jewel.

Arun's heart felt like it would burst. He strained at his bindings knowing nothing he did mattered, that his fate lay in other men's hands. He cursed himself for a fool, playing the game of kings, hating his greed and the knowledge that if he survived this moment that the flood of victory would please him just as his terror fed the butcher.

And there he waited, a plant sticking under his groin, some barbarian he'd meant to sell fighting tooth and nail for his life. *What a strange, insane world*, he thought, *what a beautiful, terrible world.*

The butcher screamed.

Ruka's jaw opened and closed on the butcher's face as he chewed, tearing flesh like an animal. The cleaver came free and Ruka flung it across the room. He brought his huge, bloody fists down again and again until his enemy went limp beneath his blows. Then he seized the thick neck, and squeezed.

It was the slowest death of Arun's life. He trembled, waiting for the gurgling last sputters of the dying man. Finally Ruka rose without a word. He shook like a new-born calf before plodding to the cage, his body coated in blood, his left hand missing its smallest finger. He knelt and took the bamboo pushing against Arun's body, bending it down and away. Then he lifted it entirely from its pot, stumbled back across the room, and rammed it through the torturer's gut.

Without looking back, he stumbled up the stairs with the audible sounds of swallowing whatever bits of his enemy's face he had still in his mouth. He left Arun alone, but safe, weeping and utterly speechless in the dark.

16

Ruka woke on a wide bed with his feet propped on a table. Someone had wrapped his wounds—or rather, wrapped them *again*—including the even more freshly wounded hand.

Nine fingers to match the nine toes, he thought. *At least now in one way I'm symmetrical.*

A young, half-naked boy waited at the door. He looked at Ruka's open eyes and bolted out, and soon returned with an older man who spouted gibberish. They replaced Ruka's bandages and doused his wounds with water, offering Ruka a sweet-smelling alcohol, which he ignored. The terrified boy made a show of holding Ruka down while the old man sewed.

"Still alive, brother," Bukayag said at last as he woke to feel the pain.

Ruka smiled. *Still alive. At least for now.*

The old man noticed his good humor and began to sweat. His eyes twitched as Ruka's brother grinned at every stitch of their flesh as if willing the needle forward.

"If they come for us," he hissed when it was done, "give me a sword. I will fight to the death."

Ruka only nodded, knowing the attempt would be pointless. His brother feared the new king would punish him for the attack, or for the torturer, or just because he thought him a threat. It had been a very long night.

First they had hacked and bashed their way through the shadow men, taking a dozen wounds from darts and little knives on ropes and throwing blades. Then, later, after they dragged him to his room, after the healers and questions he couldn't understand, he'd heard Ahrune's groans and screams.

He'd left his bed, slinking past the half-sleeping, incompetent guards who thought him near death. He followed the direction of the sounds to find another room for torture. He grit his teeth, disappointed.

Beneath all the civilization and stone, beneath the dark caverns of paradise, still things were the same. The fat, unarmed islanders sat on their white sandy beaches ringed by killers with sharpened knives.

As he looked at the devices conceived for pain, he'd thought again of Egil and a night of screams. Even without this shame, the little shadow-fox had saved him, and nevermind his reasons. Ruka owed him a debt.

But I should have summoned a weapon, he thought, angry at himself and whatever drugs he'd been given that dulled his mind and senses.

He had underestimated the squat little killer. In future he knew he must take care not to judge all foreigners from their lesser brethren, and be more cautious. He only had so many toes and fingers.

But he had survived. He had crawled back towards his bed, the guards finally finding him in a panic and calling for help to lift him up.

And all the while, through everything, he'd been busy in his Grove.

Many failed pieces of armor lay scattered and discarded around his forge. He started with metal plates surrounded by corrugated ring, all in theory resting over leather padding. He shaped it knowing fear and intimidation mattered, angling and sculpting the pieces to be animalistic, the helm open and spiked at his face to look like the head of a bear. He inscribed it with runes like the legends of old.

The dead collected everything he needed, bringing ore and water and tools; they hunted and skinned animals in the forest, salting, watering, and oiling the hide. They chopped wood, mined coal and iron from the caves for smelting, expanding the clearing to begin new buildings.

Now that Ruka had brought the worlds of the living and the dead together, the possibilities were endless. Could he bring something larger? A wagon? A ship? What were the rules? What were the limits?

In the real world, the young boy fed Ruka fruit and white-grain and then chicken with trembling hands and wide eyes as Ruka gestured for more and more. When he left, Ruka slept.

It went on for three days. Three days of rice and wound checking, bandage changes and water. Then at last came the men with spears.

The little islanders shoes slapped on stone in a pack from the hall, and the door opened with a jerk.

Bukayag fully intended to seize a sword and hack his way to freedom, but Ruka held him. *They would not have treated us or fed us if all they wanted was death, brother. Be calm.*

Spear-servants stepped inside, and behind them another old man in fine silk robes. Behind him, the king himself.

"Loa, King Farahee."

Ruka bowed as best he could from his bed, and the square-headed monarch smiled thinly.

"Loa, Ruka."

In one hand the king held a wide, flat disc that looked like clay, in the other a small, smooth white rock. Neither looked like weapons.

Farahee smiled politely and sat in a chair placed by his guards, holding the clay tablet on his lap. He rubbed the white rock across the front, which left a mark or some kind of symbol that was not a rune. He leaned forward and made a sound, like 'Ah,' and waited.

Ruka looked at the warriors, then the old man, all who stared with blank faces. He shrugged, and made the sound back.

The king nodded as if pleased, then drew another.

'Eh', he said this time, and Ruka repeated it. The king nodded and drew another.

And so they went. When the tablet was filled the king wiped it with a cloth dabbed in water, and started again.

In total he drew seventy-two symbols, seventy-two different sounds, all ending in one of five 'base' sounds. Farahee then re-drew the first symbol, and waited.

Ruka thought it best to display some value, and also—he was rather bored. He reached for the tablet, and though the men with spears grunted and thrust their weapons, the king seemed to understand and slid it onto the bed.

Ruka took the white rock and drew his name with the right sounds, then spoke them. He drew the correct spelling of Fa-ra-hi and Ki-kay and Ah-rune, which he corrected to spell more like 'Ah-Ru-Neh' with three symbols because 'n' was apparently its own sound.

Then he spelled Lo-ah, and thi-sah-kah, and a dozen other words and sounds he'd stored as certain in his Grove, and now had symbols for.

And as he did he began to forget, at least for a moment, that he sat wounded before a king in this strange land drawing alien symbols. In his mind he returned to the land of ash where he learned runes by firelight.

He was wrapped in old thin furs, hungry and shivering. His mother sat before him, blue-lipped and reading from the Book of Galdra. She clapped her white hands in wonder.

"I'm so proud of you, Ruka." Her words and look filled him with warmth even now. "You're a very special boy. Do you know that? You must know and remember how special you are."

Oh yes, he thought, *very special*. Deformed, and cursed. Marked and single-born. All the others in the world to remind him.

Farahi was smiling and nodding at Ruka's efforts, his wide eyes and warmth a pale reflection of Beyla's.

This king wanted something, just like the first. No doubt he'd play his own games and twist Ruka's invisible chain as Bukayag feared he would. But he seemed patient, and clever, and willing to teach.

And if he would teach his words then perhaps he would bring books, too. Ruka had seen many placed in large, wooden boxes, standing in rows like livestock. Perhaps here, despite being a man, and single-born, and cursed and an outcast, he could learn their contents. It was only a goddess of laws which prevented it in the Ascom, and here she did not exist.

He knew he should focus on the task at hand, but he couldn't seem to hold his thoughts steady even as he drew Northern runes. The floodgates of his memory had opened—the endless images of youth flowing through unwanted.

First came the memory of a father, mysterious to the eyes of a child, now plain, pathetic, and disgusting. He remembered the half-looks, the silence and shame—the clear image of a man who knew what was right in his heart and yet lacked the courage to make it so.

Ruka blinked back the tears. As a boy he had thought himself to blame. He had believed his mother's pain and loneliness were the result of his curse. But as a man, Ruka knew no priestess, no law, no power on earth save death could stop him from doing what he thought was right. He had no sympathy for his father.

And how could a man forgive, he wondered, if the memory of his wounds were as fresh as the day they spawned?

He thought perhaps this was his true curse—to remember. Other people never truly forgave, he thought—they only ever forgot the details, the feelings, the failures. But this was not a path open to him.

In the real world, Farahi had introduced the old man, who bowed and began speaking what must have been questions in a series of words and sounds. Ruka did his best to listen.

He realized, amazed, that many of the words were different entirely from the others—that the sounds were not any of those Farahi had taught him, and that they must be from some other tongue. He realized, with some excitement, they were trying to find sounds he would understand.

If a collector of such words existed, then there must be many different peoples, many different ways to speak. The world must be even more vast than he believed.

Ruka understood none of it, of course. Some sounds he recognized as from the pirates, which meant even on an island near-by they had different words. He shook his head at the fruitless attempts, and when the old man had exhausted his words, he unfurled a flat parchment covered in shapes and symbols. Ruka understood what it was at once.

He had begun something very similar in his Grove—a map of the Ascom with the coasts, mountains and forests drawn. Compared to this wonder of colored dyes and intricate detail, though, his own work was crude, and childish.

The king pointed to a small series of what must have been islands and said 'Pie-yew', or 'Pyu'. Then he pointed at the largest and said 'Sree-con', which was perhaps spelled 'Sri Ko-N'. Then he waved a hand over the parchment, and waited.

Ruka understood this, too.

'Point at the map,' the king meant, 'tell us where you are from.'

For one of the few moments in his life, Ruka hesitated. It was not that his mind had not told him of the possibilities, of the dangers, and opportunities, for already it began a list. It was that he could not decide on a very simple question: *Do I owe my people any loyalty?*

The king looked at Ruka's eyes and seemed impatient. To buy time, Ruka looked at the old man, then the door, before meeting the king's stare.

Farahi's calm face cracked slightly as if amused, but he nodded and spoke, and the old man bowed and left, and even the spearmen stood further away.

Ruka decided, whatever his feelings, whatever his reservations or loyalties, he must trust this king. He could see no reason for these people to venture South, no true threat to a land of frozen tundra and hard men from the soft sons of paradise.

So he pointed to the edge of their world. He dragged his finger off the Southern sea, beyond all the islands until his hand moved off the leathery map to the bed. He couldn't judge the distance, but he made his best guess.

"Ascomi," he said, wishing he had the words to say more.

The king blinked and sat back in his chair. His face grew very still as he looked away, staring at the wall as if trying to rip some answer from the stone. To Ruka's eyes he seemed worn, or perhaps, resigned. At last, he nodded.

"Ascomi," the king repeated as he let out a breath.

Ruka watched him closely, fascinated at the strange reaction. It was as if he knew, or at least suspected. They looked at each other, and the king seemed fascinated, too.

Finally he rose and gestured at the bed, saying words that might have meant 'eat, and rest'.

Ruka did not know how to thank him and so said nothing. The king left him with the marking stones and servants, and before night fell they brought him paper and ink, books and blank scrolls and clothes.

He marveled at it all, bewildered as his world spun and grew and re-formed with islands and new seas and a great continent so vast it dwarfed the Ascom several times over.

In the morning, the old man returned, and Ruka sharpened his mind, turning it to words and trinkets and books, all thought of the past or revenge or hatred gone, replaced for the moment by a thing he had lacked since Kunla died: a new purpose.

Ruka had finally found a cause worthy of his talents. He would learn this world and everything ever understood by men, because only then could he decide what to do with it. He would show these terrified and unworthy lesser things what a man could do, then take their world by the throat. What he would do then, he did not yet know, wishing only he had Beyla to advise him.

But on his fourteenth day in paradise, after a long and restless night of heat, Ruka's education truly began.

17

Ruka learned the island tongue in a week, but he pretended two. He did not know how long it took other men, but by the reactions of his tutors, he assumed considerably longer.

He pronounced the sounds terribly, of course. And he did not yet know a great many words, nor understand the strange formulation of many rules and exceptions. But it was enough, and the rest would come.

The eyes of his chief tutor, 'Master' Aleki, grew more narrow as the days passed. Many times as Ruka understood or formed words he would almost spit and raise his voice as he demanded 'where did you learn this?'. By his expression he did not believe the answers.

Such was the way with mediocre minds, Ruka decided. His questions, too, began to wear at the man's patience.

"How big is world?" he asked, and Aleki stared.

"Our sailors say the known world stretches from Samna to Naran, mountains to mountains in the West and North."

"And beyond?"

"Nothing. Only the sea."

'And across sea? Is world ring? Sphere?"

"Perhaps it is flat," snapped the older man, though without conviction

Ruka dismissed this. He had seen the curve plainly, mountains slowly falling beneath the horizon as the distance grew. The world was rounded, that was obvious, either a ring or a sphere. Sphere seemed more likely, or else men would have found a way off the edge.

"What created world? Gods? What is sun, moon, and stars? Why does sea move and how? What is disease and what makes seasons?"

At first Aleki tried to answer such questions, but he soon discovered Ruka expected exact detail. He wouldn't settle for metaphor or approximation or assumption, he wanted answers, explanations.

For all their wealth and knowledge, Ruka soon understood these 'Pyu' lacked them just as the men of ash did. The old man spouted gibberish about gods and spirits and legends which in some ways interested Ruka, but this too would be mostly nonsense—more ancient wisdom for curious or perhaps fearful minds, but mostly without merit.

At night they left him books on Pyu history and myth, though what he truly wanted was to understand their buildings, their ships, and their cities. He knew he must be patient. He read what words he could and stored the rest to ask his tutor, providing a list each morning to the wide-eyed old man.

"Night is for sleeping," he scolded as if with a child. "You are the king's guest. You are expected to rest and maintain your health, or he will be displeased."

Ruka only shrugged, and carried on. He did even more than it seemed, for he worked in his Grove even as he studied, expanding the clearing for the many new buildings he expected to begin.

Sometimes he walked at night, too, because the days were suffocatingly hot, and the sun scorched his skin. His guards followed but never stopped him, and he toured the palace grounds, especially the gardens.

Servants here kept bushes and flowers, vines and trees—so vast and intricate they were the size of fields in the Ascom. It seemed in Sri Kon there were men whose sole task in life was to maintain beauty. Ruka thought it a most honorable profession.

Indulgent, perhaps, in a world where others starved, but still—had he found an animal that sacrificed for beauty, he would have been overjoyed. It seemed a reason for mankind to survive.

There were others like this, too—men and women who devoted their lives to music or art, much like the skalds of the Ascom. Here they seemed far less rare, which he supposed was a sign of wealth. Most of the islanders did not think of life as a struggle. They did not act as if starvation and suffering were a single season away.

In the veneer of immortality that seemed to encompass everything here, Ruka saw how a man could lose himself in the show—how he could forget the drought and snakes and disease that lurked, always waiting, and turn his eyes from the death all around him.

Every day he wished to see how those outside the palace lived, but he couldn't leave, and always returned to his room.

After the first huge moon passed, Ruka was invited to sit with the king.

His wounds had begun to heal, and he wore mostly the soft, smooth 'silk' of the islanders now in a loose wrap as shown by the servants. It helped with the heat, but not much.

Ruka had largely memorized the palace grounds, but the king's retainers did not take him to the main hall. Instead he was led up several flight of stairs, up to an outer wall and a tower rising above it.

"Loa, Ruka. Come and sit with me."

The king sat in one of two chairs set out facing East above the city. He was dressed in rich, blue silks that almost matched the color of the sea on the horizon. Rays from the un-risen sun lit a thin, cool fog.

Ruka bowed as the islanders did and sat. The king inspected him.

"I'm told you are learning our language very quickly, and that you're a very good student."

"Thank you. Yes. Good teacher. Many books."

Farahi smiled.

"You can already read books?"

"Yes, king, a little."

"Do you have many books in Ascomi?"

"No. Some. Few." Ruka shrugged, unsure how to explain the book of Galdra, and that if other books existed he did not know of them.

Farahi smiled politely, and gestured at the table. "I thought we would play a game, and watch the sun rise. This is a test of mathematics, mostly. Do you know that word?"

Ruka shrugged because he had read it but did not completely understand. He could count and manipulate numbers in his mind very well, but this seemed simple enough and not requiring many books.

The king explained though that mathematics could be very complex, and Ruka's curiosity piqued at once. The king's smile broadened as he leaned closer to the table.

He explained the rules of the game with gestures, motioning how the pieces would be set around the board, explaining patiently how the rules changed as more pieces entered, and different shapes on the board added complication.

"They multiply, you see? And they are worth more along the edges. They get more important very quickly. Pieces here are worth two of these, and these two of those. The pieces placed at the very end are what truly matter."

Ruka believed he understood. He counted the squares, and the pieces, and the 'barrier' squares which would surely require strategy. To him it felt like a battlefield.

The king placed a piece first, and when Ruka followed Farahi watched his four-fingered hand.

"Sorry, for your finger." He moved another piece. "It wasn't my intention. And I'm not angry about the…dead servant. Understand?"

'The dead servant'.

These kings had little regard for their followers, Ruka knew. For a moment he again wrestled with the butcher in the pit, wounded and slick with blood, pain lancing up his arm. He nodded, and took his turn.

"You have many calluses," said the king. "What was your profession in your homeland? Were you a sailor? Farmer? You have rough hands. Understand?"

Ruka flexed his fingers, then relaxed them. In truth he did not know what to say. His hands and even his body did not reflect reality as they should.

Over the years, he had slowly begun to accept his body shaped little by little from the toil in his Grove. It made him stronger, body hardened and roughened by toil. He didn't think he had the words to describe 'shaman', or 'outcast'.

"Hunter," he said, and shrugged. "Warrior."

The king nodded, then looked at his own hands.

"Mine are soft," he sighed. "Rich hands. Perhaps I should be proud of this. But a man should be rough, eh?"

Ruka did not catch every word, but understood the meaning.

"Man learns with books, or hands. With books, he keeps fingers."

Farahi met Ruka's eyes, a broad grin stretching across his face. He placed another piece. "And what would you like to learn, Ruka? What interests you?"

"Everything, king. All things men can know."

Farahi smiled and leaned back. "And why should I teach you? My people are traders. What do you have to trade?"

Ruka had not considered this and had no real answer. These people were so rich and powerful. He had little to offer them save as a warrior. But surely one man was not so useful.

"Teach me the secrets of your blue metal," said the king after a pause. "Your sword, and shield. For that knowledge I will teach you all that you wish, anything in my power."

Ruka felt his brow raise. He had seen many shoddy weapons thus far, but assumed this more choice than anything—cheap armaments for a people unaccustomed to fighting. But if they had poor iron, then perhaps they had room for other improvements. And if Ruka learned what they knew, perhaps it would all seem less impossible.

He glanced at this new island king, and decided him a different breed than the other. He was clever and difficult to read, and most certainly dangerous. But Ruka did not fear a dangerous man, nor judge him. Indeed, it was the opposite.

"Agreed. We trade."

Farahi smiled, and casually moved a piece to block Ruka's strategy. It seemed a strange move because it interfered with a plan far away. Ruka frowned.

"Good," said the king, a sparkle in his eyes. "Know you are my guest, Ruka. You are to be respected, and treated well by my servants. Understand guest? You are not my prisoner. If anyone mistreats you, you need only tell me."

Ruka nodded because he understood. In the Ascom, expensive horses were treated well.

"Today I will send you to my craftsmen," said the king as he leaned in his chair, distracted by the tip of a yellow sun rising from the sea.

Ruka nodded absently. His mind raced up and down the game board for a new strategy. He saw several choices, and decided at once.

The king glanced at his choice and smiled. He said quietly, as if for his own private amusement.

"We shall see who teaches who."

* * *

True to his word, that afternoon the king sent Ruka with a pack of men outside the palace. Some of his escort were nervous warriors sheened with sweat, the others carried books and thinly veiled expressions of disdain.

He did his best to withhold excitement as they left the palace walls, walking amongst the bustling, sometimes staring townsfolk.

He took in every detail he could, noting faces and clothes and the design of streets and carts and buildings. He saw smoke rising from the direction they were headed, and with every step the noise and activity grew until it seemed every structure was a beehive filled with jabbering foreigners and their toil.

Ruka's procession took him into a half-exposed row of huge stalls, with many tables full of discarded bits of clay and wood shavings. He also saw stacks of almost perfectly flat or round, transparent stone, and he lifted one, marveling, then saw the look of concern pass around the worker's faces.

"That is very brittle, Ruka. Easily broken. Be careful," said Aleki.

"What is it?" Ruka turned it in his hand, feeling the incredible smoothness.

Some of the old men smirked or rolled their eyes, and the tutor cleared his throat.

"Glass. It is made from molten sand. We use it for decoration, jewelry, cups, plates, beads, and so forth."

Molten sand? Incredible!

"And this?" Ruka lifted a strange wooden stand full of round stones. Again the old man winced.

"That…is a calculating plate. The stones represent numbe…"

"I understand."

Ruka set it down and walked past the tables to what looked like furnaces and ovens, as well as anvils and a few troughs of water. In many ways it resembled his own smithy, though of course this was considerably larger.

"These are craftsmen employed by the king," called Aleki. "Come this way first and we'll see the…Ruka…where…"

Ruka strode straight to the huge, round furnaces spouting heat in waves from open faces. Strong men layered in soot and sweat stared as he approached, their gloved hands suddenly idle.

"Why open," he pointed. "How control heat? What is fuel?"

The men glanced at one another. One wiped soot and sweat from his brow and cleared his throat with a glance at the cluster of palace men.

"Wood," he grunted. A few of the others chuckled.

"And air, how control air?"

When the men stared at him he motioned as if stoking a gallows. When still they blanked he puffed up his cheeks and blew towards the furnace.

"The heat is all that matters, Ruka," said Aleki, now a little red-faced as he glanced at the others.

Ruka looked around at the islanders, and their stares—the great furnaces stocked constantly with the hardwood he now saw piled behind.

He looked at the baked clay, the unwieldy shape, the open areas. And he laughed. For the first time since he'd landed in Pyu, he felt at least, for a moment, to have found solid ground.

He grunted, and waved in dismissal at the old, soft-handed men in robes who had likely never touched a hammer or a forge.

"I make proper iron. Do you have…" He had no idea what the word for 'coal' was. "Black rock, for burning?"

The smith nodded. "Some." His face was at least a little interested. "Iron is expensive and difficult to use. We have little enough." He glanced at the tutors. "Mostly we make bronze here."

"Yes." Aleki cleared his throat. "Bronze would be better, Ruka, and far more useful to improve, since it…"

Bronze!

Ruka almost rolled his eyes. If iron were rare here, then perhaps the Ascom had more to trade than he thought. They had several deposits, and far more than they could use.

"King said iron. Ruka makes iron. Get large piece. And fanners. And potter. We close furnace. And need clean water." He waved in disgust at the dirty troughs.

Ruka assumed the men would comply and now ignored them. He considered bringing tongs and hammers and bellows from his Grove, but thought better of it. Better to leave room for improvement in the future. Drawing the tools from nothing would overshadow his current efforts.

He considered what to make and decided a sword would be too difficult and take too long. Besides, it seemed hardly any of the islanders used them. A good, thick steel rod, perhaps, might serve his purpose. He smiled at the shape forming in his mind, then noticed the men had yet to move.

"Guest of king," he said, as if annoyed. Then louder, making each word clear. "*Guest of king.*"

Aleki smiled politely but without his eyes, and Ruka stared down any of the old men who would meet his gaze.

"Black burning rock," he said again. "Ore. Fans. Potters. Water. Now."

Aleki clenched his jaw, but gestured towards the smiths. They bowed, and moved to their tasks.

The team of island smiths and potters accomplished what Ruka needed with astounding speed. Carts full of coal, wood, tools, and smelted metal wheeled to his disposal in moments. Many of the near-by men came to watch, and once or twice Ruka noticed chiefs or foremen red-faced and shouting before later coming to see for themselves.

First, Ruka and the potters completely closed the furnace. They disconnected the grate, and stuck a metal catch to hold it open when required. To temper iron properly required a heat so hot it might even burn or melt through the bottom of the islander's clay furnace, but they would find out soon enough.

Next, they set up two fanners, but Ruka also sent men to fetch wineskins and leather. He thought perhaps with a little effort he might make a bellows, because the air from the fans would not easily reach the fire.

In truth, he did not know why exactly air was required. All he knew—from many, many experiments— was that metal become brittle without it. The more air as the metal smoldered in the heat, the more malleable, and the less brittle hardness.

For this effort he wanted some balance between the two, but since he intended only a rod good for bashing, he wished it to be just soft enough to crush anything he struck without snapping. It made little difference if it dented, so he could make it almost impossible to break.

The islanders loaded their furnace with coal and some of the hardwood, and then waited. Ruka arranged his tools around the table as he did in his Grove. He scrubbed the wood, he scraped the hammers and tongs and files for every speck of dirt or sediment, then replaced the water in every trough. Whatever the exact rituals of steel, he knew, uncontrolled elements were a mistake.

As the heat from the furnace grew, he stripped off every layer of wrapped silk until he wore only his loincloth.

The men stared at his body with wide eyes but he no longer cared. The smiths at last brought him a huge clump of ore, which he submerged into the hottest embers of the sweltering flame, and waited, counting water-drops in his Grove. Much could be learned by sight, but he had a rough estimate of time for every single step—from heating to blowing, cooling to hammering: each step had purpose.

He snapped his fingers, and the smiths jumped and met his eyes.

"You help hammer." He rolled his shoulders and stooped, lifting the anvil with a grunt to place it in the center of the cleared space. He released a breath and stood, and saw the men staring with open-mouths. He supposed the anvil *was* rather heavy.

After enough water drops he inspected the color of the iron, removed it with the tongs and placed it on the anvil.

"Long, and thin, like spear," he said, and began hammering. The smiths approached and took their positions, awkward at first, but soon found their rhythm. One man held the metal with the tongs and turned it occasionally without instruction, and it was clear they were all very skilled.

They soon began a sort of humming chant as they worked, and grinned when Ruka joined. They heated the iron, and began again. They heated the iron, and hammered again.

In truth the heat was barely enough and the process went on and on. The smiths dripped with sweat from the toil and the sweltering furnace while the robed men sat on crates or wood-piles and chattered amongst themselves.

When the ore was at last vaguely shaped, Ruka told them they must be careful now. He blew more air with his make-shift bellows, submerging the iron in water before heating it again. The smiths watched him in silence, eyes quick and curious, the soot and sweat of their faces forgotten.

Ruka checked the hardness as best he could. It seemed the ore they used was slightly different than what he was used to, and he noticed small differences in the color of the flame, in the reaction to the heat, and even the hammering of the metal. The result was more imperfect then he'd hoped, and would require considerable testing to understand. It was darker than he wished, too, which meant more brittle, with hardly a trace of the malleable blue of his Ascomi steel. But it would serve.

Finally he stepped to the oak table and set down a smooth, three foot length of tempered, island iron. The smiths stared, captivated.

"Good," Ruka grunted, flipping it over as they examined together. "Very good." He nodded to the men, who grinned and returned it. He watched their pleasure, and for a brief moment he simply stood and basked in the shared moment of competence, sensing the strangeness of standing so far from home, and in the company of strangers, yet feeling the strength of the pack.

"The sun is nearly gone." Aleki glanced at the rod and rose from his seat. "It seems a rather lengthy and expensive process to make a single iron…club, Ruka, which is useless, and we would never do in any case. What we truly need are better nails and clamps for ships and buildings. Perhaps tomorrow…"

"Useless?" Ruka lifted the steel, annoyed as the brittle feeling of unity he had shared swept away. He walked to the rack of weapons and lifted a bronze blade.

With a grunt he chopped down and bent the flimsy thing against the floor. He struck again, and the thin, vastly inferior metal snapped.

"Useless?" he growled, then stepped to the pile of rock and smashed a chunk from it, hitting again as he broke apart stone and ore. He smashed the spears and tables next to it. He held up the rod, which wasn't even scratched, and grunted between his heavy breaths.

"Warrior is useless. Unless there is war." He held it forward. "Take. Gift. For king."

He took the time to bow to the smiths, then gestured at the half-sleeping guards in the direction of the palace, and walked out into the night.

18

After the craftsmen, Ruka learned with Aleki and his men of books for another full moon.

He grew his words and understanding of the rules and subtleties of the islander's speech. He read of ancient gods and spirits, of a sea-faring race of men who had traveled the world until they arrived at the islands of Pyu, led by a sort of prophet they called the 'Enlightened'.

These people had their heroes, too, like the Ascomi had Haki the Brave. Pyu heroes however were not warriors. They were often men much like priestesses, or explorers, their greatest a trickster named Rupi.

Ruka was interested, but to him it seemed largely the same nonsense his people invented to explain the world. Buried in such myths and stories there existed truth, perhaps, wrapped in some useful mixture of practicality and illusion—the perfect meal for the human mind. What truly intrigued him was the timing.

By islander reckoning, they had been in Pyu now for two thousand years. Where exactly they came from was not clear.

The scholars knew the continent to the North was far older, and had been inhabited since time immemorial. Their books described a dozen races and kingdoms, city-states and chiefdoms—even an 'empire', or a king of kings.

Ruka asked Aleki many more questions he could or would not answer.

"How many people live in Pyu? How many in Naran? How many in the world?"

Each made the man squirm.

"We do not know. The last census was in the king's grandfather's time, and there has not been another. As to Naran, or the world, no one knows."

"You must have a guess."

"I try not to *guess*."

Ruka stared in silence, thinking *you guess all the time, about everything, you stupid fool.*

Aleki cleared his throat.

"Naran is very large. Perhaps three million people, though I expect this number means little to you. And the world..." He shrugged, and scoffed. "Perhaps...triple that. Why does it matter? It's very large."

Ruka goggled because he suspected it would be even more than Aleki believed. The same pride his own people shared would no doubt inflate the man's sense of his own importance. He held back the reflexive sneer at the question of why it mattered.

Aleki had his uses, but like many of the other islanders he believed his knowledge of the world all but complete, and the last few details of little importance. Ruka knew they were so very wrong.

He knew fear and pride prevented men from seeing how ignorant they were, how ignorant every creature truly was of the mighty world around it—of the things he could not see, touch, or hear. Ruka expected there were many new seas to cross, many mysteries so complex he could not even begin to ask the right questions—perhaps far more complex than he could comprehend. But he intended to try.

At night while the islanders slept, Ruka sat on the same balcony he had once fought assassins for his life. His guards leaned sleepily on their spears, and he read by moonlight.

Farahi had a vast library filled with thousands of books, and had made them available without boundary. Ruka intended to read all of them.

He started with mathematics, eyes wide like a child learning stories of a far-away land. He read of shapes and symbols representing numbers so vast he could not imagine them, Aleki was right about that.

The Pyu had 'formulas' to calculate shapes in the real world, to understand the weight and strength of wood or stone, or the correct angle of their construction, and could use it all to plan building or ships. These apparently worked perfectly every time you used them, and could be calculated without much effort. The knowledge opened a window in Ruka's mind, and he did not know if he should laugh, or weep at his own ignorance.

In his Grove, he began testing everything. He would need to know if things could be improved by using stronger materials, and expected they could.

His old tutor was right about the nails and the clasps. With Ruka's iron perhaps they could build in ways they had never imagined before, and perhaps the future might change for them as well as the Ascom.

With Farahi, trade seemed possible. Perhaps the men of ash could bring their iron and their salt, or their lumber from huge and untamed forests. Maybe they could serve as warriors to their island neighbors, too, or conquer the weakest with permission. The possibilities were endless now.

Ruka was left alone and free to roam the palace as he liked. Servants brought him all the food and water he wished. All the while, Bukayag stayed silent, dazzled by complexity beyond his interest or understanding—civilization and a future forged perhaps with more peace than bloodshed.

Ruka was learning much, but he still wished to see more of the world, and even more of the islands.

He knew at some point he must gather all he'd learned and make order from this new chaos, but he could handle more. He read on architecture and sailing, astronomy and geography, warfare and earthworks.

In the back of his mind, already he wondered if he should ever return to his people. If he owed them anything, if he would not prefer instead to stay in this new world and bind himself to this king. He did not know, and for now, did not care.

When Matohi came again—what the islander's called the full moon—

the guards came to summon him, and Ruka rose expecting another meeting with the king, excited to discuss all that he'd learned.

* * *

"Loa Kana, and Hoilo."

The young guard grinned and bowed politely as they gestured down the corridor.

Speaking the islanders words at all still seemed to entertain the servants. That Ruka remembered their names and could pronounce them seemed endlessly fascinating. He supposed anyone would be delighted if their pet learned words.

This time they took him North around the palace—to a different wing than his previous visits, up near the fortress itself. He found Farahi sitting at another small table covered in their game pieces, scribbling at paper over a wooden board. He wasn't surprised to see another clear view of the horizon.

"Loa, Ruka. Sit with me."

Ruka obeyed, settling in the larger chair. Farahi's face held no indication of his mood, as usual. He gestured at the board as if Ruka should begin the game.

"I've seen your iron," he said, after several moves. "It's very impressive. But Aleki tells me you can be very disrespectful."

Ruka shrugged because he was, and didn't try to be otherwise.

"I dislike arrogant men."

"Surely you mean *other* arrogant men," said the king, and Ruka squinted.

No doubt even a more honorable king like this one expected his servants cowed, and docile. Ruka supposed he should round his shoulders. He should bow his head in fear and submission and be a proper little retainer. He did not.

"Competence is not the same as arrogance, King Farahi."

He moved another piece, and the king watched him. The skin around his eyes crinkled, and the stone face cracked.

"Here on these islands, men like to exchange light pleasantries before they move on to meaningful things. I might, for example, ask after your health, or how you slept. Do yours do this?"

"Yes." Ruka placed another piece. "I dislike it."

The king smiled. "Me too." He leaned back in his chair. "Very well. I'll speak plain. I wish to know more about you now that you know my words. Tell me about your homeland. Tell me about this 'Ascom' beyond the sea."

Ruka looked out at the blue haze of the water, already tinged with a red rising sun. He pictured an endless field of white, and marveled that such places should exist in the same world.

"Have you ever seen snow, King?"

"Once," the islander nodded. "In the mountains of Nong Ming Tong."

Ruka breathed out as he recalled winter in perfect detail, seeing again his time as an outlaw. His first season he'd been trapped between the forests near Hulbron, and the mountains near Alverel. He'd lived in fear of travelers, and wolves, afraid every meal would be his last unless he could steal or hunt and somehow escape the consequences.

"Imagine this sea as white as a mountain peak, smothered beyond sight in all directions. Imagine a wind raging across it so cold, and part of storms so dangerous, a man might be lost and blinded, frozen not a hundred paces from his home." Here he paused, feeling a shiver despite the warmth. "There is never enough food, nor fuel. Death is quiet, and everywhere. Children are not given names until they are two years, and poor mothers often focus their attention on the strongest. Men fight and die for glory, for dishonor, for insult or excitement or revenge or hate or curiosity because they do not much value their own lives. And why should they. They cannot feed their own children, they cannot change the cruel reality of their existence." He felt a bitterness in his voice, and he looked at the king and saw something he did not expect. Pity, perhaps, or at least empathy. He did not know what to do with it, and stopped speaking.

"And you, Ruka, how did you live in this place?"

The king's voice had become more gentle, as if he knew the answer. Ruka at once tasted the dead flesh of a boy he'd murdered. He again stabbed the farm-house boys to death, tore Kunla apart with his bare hands, strangled the lawspeaker, killed warriors near Alverel, and tortured Egil in a night of screams.

"I was an outcast," he said, struggling for words. "Then a shaman...a kind of priest, and warrior. My mother...I had only a mother, and she is dead. I am alone."

He wasn't sure he should be so honest but felt no reason to lie. He glanced at the king, who sighed and moved another piece.

"I too lost my parents. A king knows what it is to be alone." He smiled politely. "Often I feel like an outcast."

They played for a time in silence, and Ruka felt the slow, impending feeling of being maneuvered to inevitable loss. Often he felt as if the strange island king were only waiting for his turns—as if he knew already what would happen, though he showed no impatience. In all his life he had never felt another creature his equal in simple feats of mental strength. But in this complex game with this man, no matter what he did, he could not win.

What does he want from me, Ruka wondered. *What is he planning?*

The iron seemed to interest him, though perhaps not as much as it should have. Was their time together just curiosity? Was the king of paradise bored and looking for entertainment?

"So," Farahi said at last, "you fled your home to an unknown sea. You expected death. Instead you have found a new world. Now what do you want, Ruka? Do you wish to return?"

The king's keen eyes locked onto Ruka's, as if he were truly interested—as if the answer mattered.

Ruka blinked because his mind raced in a thousand directions. It was still spinning with the chaos of a world grown a hundred times in size, still reeling from so much newness and possibility.

What did he want? He wanted everything. And sometimes nothing. He wanted to climb from the mounds of snow that had buried him. And yet it seemed with every piece of ground he covered, with every new hand-hold that wrenched him up from a frozen tundra, the horizon only grew. New problems and chaos arose in every direction.

Be free, Beyla had told him, *tell your own story. And not these unworthy men, nor these terrified women can stop you and your mind and your old gods.*

Back then, it had served him well. But it seemed insufficient. An animal was free, but no animal had ever built a city, or forged an iron claw. No animal could live in both ash and sand.

Ruka did not know if he could forgive his people or be forgiven—if he could transcend his past when he could not forget a single moment.

He stood in his Grove and watched the dead, and soon they abandoned their tasks and crowded together, watching him in return. He felt shame as he looked on their wounds. How could he ever be free of them? And should he be?

Redeem our suffering, he wished they'd ask. *Redeem us, and redeem yourself.*

But the dead could not speak. Ruka wanted only to somehow justify all he'd done—to balance the scales of his darkness with greatness, and with deed. Perhaps the prophetess had the right of that. Perhaps only a man's deeds truly mattered.

"My people," he said carefully, "their lives…are difficult. They are very poor. Each day and each season is a fight to survive. It is another world from this." He waved a hand at the city and the great fortress of stone, not knowing how to truly explain. Farahi nodded.

"We will speak more of your people, Ruka. I wish to learn, to understand, and perhaps even to help." He waited a moment to emphasize this, then looked away as if deciding how to proceed. "Until this moment you have technically been my slave, my property. Do you understand this?"

Ruka nodded, he had assumed as much without knowing the word. He read of Pyu slaves and bristled though he wasn't surprised. As monstrous as the notion seemed, apparently all the world save for the Ascom had them.

Farahi met Ruka's eyes.

"Now I release you." He slid the paper he'd been scribbling across the table. "You are a freed man of the isles, and you may go anywhere you wish. But, I offer you a path, if you wish—to serve in my court, with my family. You will be paid and housed in the palace as my guest unless you wish to live elsewhere. You may read anything you wish, and all my son's tutors will be available to you." He smiled. "And you and I shall keep playing Chahen. Would that please you?"

Ruka watched him, feeling speechless. He felt Bukayag's distrust, and knew even wrapped within generosity and perhaps kindness lay manipulation and the desire to make Ruka his retainer.

But he saw something else in the king's eyes, too—a hope that this strange foreign man before him would say yes, and not because he had something to gain, or because of some master plan, but because he was lonely. Perhaps he did not play Chahen with others, or share the sunrise, because in a way he truly was an outcast. Ruka was moved by the thought.

"That would please me. I accept."

The king nodded as if unsurprised, and only mildly pleased. But Ruka caught the jerk in his shoulders, the almost tremble of his hand.

Ruka knew fear when he saw it, even on this man of stone. He couldn't understand it, for they were surrounded by guards, and in truth Ruka meant the man no harm.

"Good. Now there is only the matter of what exactly you will do. Aleki tells me you had many practical questions about Pyu architecture and construction. If you do not object, perhaps for now I will send you to my Royal Chief Builder. He will teach you anything you wish to know, and give you some practical experience. Is that acceptable?"

Ruka shook his head at the word. He did not have the tools to relay his gratitude.

No doubt he was being manipulated, yes, of course that would be true. This king would have his demands like any other chief, and would do nothing out of generosity alone. But even in Trung's pit of hell there was a man of honor. Perhaps so it was with kings. Maybe Farahi Alaku was a man improving his world—a worthy chief who saw truth and merit, and rewarded it. Perhaps even an outcast might serve him with pride.

"It's acceptable." Ruka placed another piece on the board and looked away to hide his emotion. He would not forget Beyla, or Bukayag, or that the world ate weakness and spit it out. But the world had changed, and perhaps for the better. He thought with time, it may even give him cause to hope. He said nothing and blinked away the water threatening his eyes, because men of ash did not weep, and old customs died slow.

19

1580 AE. Somewhere in Naran.

Kale watched from above as a thousand jackals circled his lions. Despite everything—all of Osco's tricks and the deaths of farmers and scouts and innocent travelers that crossed their path, the emperor had found them.

They'd abandoned their wagons a week ago. They even butchered and ate their dying donkeys on the move, cooking with torches held under copper pots. Kale tried to keep up, tried to share the burden with the men who served his cause, but even if he wasn't still weak from poison, and unable to eat much of anything but soup and rice, he'd have failed.

Besides their packs and gear, Kale was the only thing the Mesanites still carried. It gave him time and energy to help in other ways, floating out over untamed, green trees that spread like fur over the backs of uncrossable mountain beasts. He flew over ground that always rose or fell, never laying flat and always leading to more.

He saw huge, ancient trees next to sloped fields or lakes with murky, freezing water that the men said didn't warm. He'd never seen snow until he left Pyu, but here it crowned the mountaintops even in summer, and he reached out to feel its coolness with his spirit as he soared above with the birds.

He froze at the sight from one such peak, feeling both small and god-like, nothing and everything all at once. Naran held cities so vast they sheltered more people than all of Pyu, but it also had mountain country ruled by wolves and bears, plains ruled by lions, and jungles ruled by nothing. Even with his spirit stretched to its limit, and his view from the tallest peak, he saw only a tiny portion.

"There's so much," he whispered, holding back tears. Too much. Perhaps a world so vast could never be ruled by one man, or one people, or even one God.

Osco marched at his body's side, and his eyebrows looked impatient. "Are there men blocking the bridge to the East?"

Kale blinked, and flew closer. Yes, there certainly were. Every bridge in sight had become gathering points, with exhausted, rag-tag bands of scouts drawing like insects from every direction.

Some had already attacked. Arrows flew at their camp from the darkness, others tried to grab supplies before running off, and maybe cut a throat on the way. The main body of Osco's men never stopped or gave chase, but his lightly armored 'skirmishers' had murdered their way across the empire. And there were losses.

It was hard to tell exactly since they were always gone or moving, and Osco didn't bother giving reports. Kale thought at least thirty of his men were dead. Most were just 'missing', but these weren't the sort of soldiers who ran off.

Others had died in raids or random attacks, many others were wounded. These marched now with arrow-shaped wounds wrapped in cloth and not a sound of complaint. Others had become sick, perhaps from water sources poisoned by the Naranians, or perhaps just from bad luck. The hillmen called it 'Flux', but Kale's people called it 'brown fever' because it meant shitting yourself until you recovered, or died.

Osco asked Kale constantly about troop numbers, about river width and currents, or surrounding cover of trees or hills. Once he'd learned Kale could scout with his 'mind', his appetite for details turned voracious. He'd asked how long Kale could 'roam', how much time to rest, how far could he travel, how much could he see, and could he teach other men to do it now? He'd accepted 'no' as the answer to the last, but his asking and his eyebrows showed concern.

"We are trapped," the general's son and maybe now general announced. He raised a hand and stopped the men. "We'll rest here a moment to recover strength and plan, then we attack that bridge." He stared back behind the army with a squint, then shrugged to himself. "If you need rest, islander, take it. What can you do to help us?"

With his spirit Kale watched the few hundred Naranian soldiers preparing make-shift walls. It took little strength now to explore in this way, and despite the weakness in his body, his windows would be wide.

"I can do a lot of things. What would you prefer?"

Osco's eyebrows raised. "I would prefer you wiped out all our enemies with flying icicles, or burned them to death with lightning."

Kale glanced at him and sighed, mostly to himself. He didn't want to kill anyone.

But then whether from swords or arrows or threads of force a man couldn't see and probably didn't believe in, dead was dead. There was no escape.

"March across the bridge. Do what you have to, and then keep moving South. I'll do what I can."

Osco didn't look pleased by this, but nodded. Kale glanced at the sky.

It held few clouds, and the air was dry and cool. The bodies of the men held power, as well as the trees, the earth itself, and the river. But compared to Nanzu, this place held only a fraction of the power Kale had once used.

Rope-thick strands led to the mountains far away, humming with a force so vast and wild it terrified Kale just to feel it. But did he dare pull?

Higher, on miles of wind-roads traveled by birds, he sensed something just as endless, just as world-shaping. But were men meant to even know such things? To change them?

Am I meant to, God? Is that my path? Is that my Way?

* * *

The rest was over rather quickly.

Kale picked apart his thoughts until all he could feel was beaded mat, the air in his lungs, and the slight breeze. Then Osco was saying "It's time" and the men were forming shield-lines, unstrapping weapons, and telling jokes.

Most of the Mesanites looked only a few years older than Kale's navy recruits, which seemed impossible, and comparing them felt ridiculous. His people trained the teenage sons of merchants and fishermen to keep their heads and man ships in war—they trained civilians to follow orders, chase down pirates, and stay alive.

Mesanites turned little boys into fearless killers. They dragged children from their mother's skirts, threw them in a ring, and said 'fight, or die'. And that was apparently just the start.

None of these men were anything but soldiers. They were the sons and great-great grandsons of soldiers. Their 'over-families' provided them with wives and income, and their gods would honor them in death. Their only concerns were loyalty and glory, and Kale had heard them with his spirit as they marched—they expected heroic deaths at the side of the 'sorcerer-prince'; they expected their names to go down in legend, sung by their children with tears of pride. They felt rare privilege killing strangers on foreign land, all for a cause not their own. It all turned Kale's weak stomach.

The march to the bridge was short, and the Naranian scouts were still poorly prepared. They'd cut down trees and laid them in bundles across the wide, stone crossing; they'd gathered and scattered rocks, though these were still thinly piled. Such men were used to setting traps and ambush, perhaps, but left the heavy fighting to others.

Kale floated his mind out and across the bridge. The leaders of the few hundred men were arguing, no one quite sure who was in command.

'We can't hold them, there's too few of us,' whispered some; 'the emperor commands us to protect the bridges!' came the retort; finally: 'those are Mesanites!'; 'we should fall back and gather more warriors'.

Every man had a bow, and seemed to at least agree they should use up their arrows. They'd built up deadwood at the foot of the bridge, but it wasn't much of a wall.

"Shields!" Osco shouted as his men entered bow range, and the same square blocks they'd demonstrated outside Malvey now formed on the bank. It took only moments, then the block was moving, shuffling forward with measured steps, breathing out with a sound like 'hoo' as their right feet landed.

Kale had been squeezed inside, blinded by flesh and iron. He used his spirit to see. He watched the first wave of arrows, then cringed at the sound of hard rain on a tin roof. He knew he could reach out and snap the arrows, but didn't think he needed to. Mesanites took the missiles without alarm, not a single man dropping or even losing pace as the arrows landed and bounced away from their shields.

They took several volleys but soon made it to the bridge, pushing fallen trees into the water, stepping around or over rock piles, adjusting their formations easily. The scouts kept shooting, but now Osco's men stepped out from their protection and returned it with their smaller bows.

Kale protected these as he could from return shots, snapping the arrows or guiding them into the dirt.

Some of the scouts soon fled towards the trees. Most ran alone or in small units of three or four to the call of 'cowards!' from their fellows. Others fell back, moving down the road on the other side of the river and re-grouping.

A small force stayed at the end of the bridge, guarding the last 'wall' that would at least slow the Mesanites down.

Osco's front rank broke apart and threw their javelins. Many skewered the defender's upper bodies before they rammed the deadwood, toppling most of it at once.

The scouts began to scream and panic, and as these men broke or died the 'battle' seemed already over.

Kale, though, sensed danger as he'd done in Nanzu before a dozen assassins tried to kill him. He reached out with his spirit and felt nothing, saw nothing to alarm him. But the ground, he realized, it smelled strange. And it was sticky, and dark.

The air crackled, and the remnants of the deadwood scattered all around the Mesanites feet. Everything around them burst into flames.

Kale panicked. Threads of heat sprouted all around, and he swept his spirit's arm through all of it, seizing at everything he could touch as he hurled it away.

A roar followed like wind through a tunnel, and Kale felt the men around him lean and stumble against the force of it, half-panicked themselves from the fire rising around them, but too disciplined to break formation. With a huge whoosh of air, everything burning took flight.

Some of the scouts beyond the bridge managed to scream. Red and orange flame spotted with flying tar blew in a wide cone through the air. The men in its path seemed to vanish. The flames roared past them, over them and to the trees beyond. The dry, summer-heated woods, now spattered with tar, and densely packed with fuel-filled needles, lit at once.

Kale watched, surprised as everyone else, as the forest began to burn. He had not even pulled at the mountains, nor the strong winds above, nor the river. His windows had barely moved. His energy remained wide and ready to seek out more light, more energy, more death. Smoke rose before him, and his Mesanites butchered in the flickering shadow, as the world around him burned.

"Woe to the enemies of Mesan!"

Osco took up the shout as the enemy fled, and the men answered.

Soldiers with tar-stained boots—singed but unharmed—stepped over and around the dying, thrusting spears down or chopping with the sharpened bottoms of their shields to deal with the wounded.

Kale walked on, stunned, and horrified, not just at what he'd done, but that his allies made sharpened shields just to kill wounded.

Asna was patting his arm, the Condotian's weapons still in their sheaths. Osco slapped his back, wiggling his eyebrows in encouragement.

"Half-way there, islander," he said, then jerked his head towards the flames. "Do what I can, he says."

Asna laughed and joined in the back-slapping, and the Mesanites raised their voices in a marching song, the battle all but forgotten.

Kale looked and didn't think they'd lost a single man. He watched the fire spreading and wondered how far it would go, how many people would die or lose their homes, how many animals, how many hundreds and thousands of years of trees.

He wondered briefly if trees suffered too, and if that mattered. Yet didn't God burn them on his own with the sun? Didn't he make the threads and the fuel and Mesanites and everything?

Kale missed Amit desperately in that moment, and Li-yen, Tane and Lani, Thetma and Fautave. He wanted only someone to speak with who didn't think killing was easy, and glorious—someone who could hold him and say it was alright and not his fault. Except it was.

He thought perhaps he could stop the fire, but destroying was far easier than protecting. Stopping it would sap the strength he'd desperately need to survive.

Before him lay a long road filled with enemies, and more were gathering already, perhaps even an army near the borders of Nong Ming Tong. God knew what lay beyond.

"I'm sorry," he whispered, repeating 'why I do it matters' in his mind like a sacred prayer. But in his heart, he knew, he could still be wrong.

20

By the Kubi river. 1562 AE. Six months after freedom.

Ruka pointed and slashed his finger at the river's East bank.

"No, we make it angled, like this."

Blood rose to his face as it always did far too easily in this heat. He knew his voice was too loud, his tone too harsh.

Chief Builder Hemi squinted, and the king's builders snuck their hundredth 'look' since the morning started, unmoved from their parallel positions across the Kubi.

"It must be diagonal to the flow to maximize the length of the crest," Ruka explained, "do you see?"

Chief Builder Hemi stared, unblinking. Ruka held back his sigh.

For a moment he pictured his last meeting with the king and cursed him. They watched the sunrise and played Chahen once a moon, just as Farahi promised. They discussed their lives or the many things Ruka learned with his tutors, or the efforts with Chief Builder Hemi. And every time, no matter what he did, Ruka lost. Every strategy he chose, no matter how boldly or cautiously he advanced, Farahi always seemed to predict, and counter him, all the while giving 'advice'. The man was infuriating.

"You must occasionally take an *indirect* route to your aims, Ruka. Learn to influence Hemi—negotiate with him, compromise. You must preserve an islander's...face, his honor, eh? While he does as you ask."

Ruka had clenched his hands and nearly thrown his piece over the balcony.

"Why do you let the river flood?"

The king blinked, and smiled, though Ruka hadn't intended to be amusing.

"We don't *let* it. It happens. There isn't much we can do."

"You don't try, so how could you know."

They'd argued, and Ruka had explained his thoughts to control the flow, and shore up the river banks, all inspired by watching Pyu fountains, which made him even angrier. Farahi had eventually shrugged.

"Even if you're right, that's a tremendous project."

Ruka said nothing because yes it was, and so what.

"Convince Hemi first, and we can discuss it."

"Hemi is a coward and higher in station than intellect. Convince him how."

Farahi laughed at this, the act from him always brief and sharp, like unexpected pain. When Ruka said nothing the king shook his head.

"You haven't been listening. Use your patient voice. Give men what they want when it benefits you or costs you little. Start with that."

Ruka was not aware he had a patient voice.

It had taken four days just to convince Hemi to look at the river together, and every night he grit his teeth and accomplished a hundred tasks in his Grove thinking the living lazy wretches unworthy of their ancestors.

He could hardly believe the king's words and suggestions. In the Ascom a chief did not need to 'convince' his retainers of anything. He demanded, and was obeyed. Words and schemes were for women because for them violence was forbidden. For men, the stakes were far greater, and in any case men had farms and villages and mines to manage, and no time for such nonsense. To Ruka it was all cowardly, Northern horse-shit, devised by weak, corrupt little...

"And how do we build such a structure *in* a flowing river, *exactly*?"

Ruka blinked and stared at the pot-bellied little Chief of the builders. He tried to take just one full, satisfying breath, and to tolerate the hot afternoon sun of Sri Kon without the desire to strangle the closest stinking, sweating islander he could grasp. Eventually he sighed, trying to do as Farahi suggested. He stooped to show Hemi what he meant with sticks in the sand using his best 'patient voice'.

The man wasn't as incompetent as Ruka initially believed, of course, and had not earned his position entirely without merit. He was a middle-aged bureaucrat with three wives living in three houses filled with his children. He was an 'Orang-Kaya', a land-owner with voting rights, and had business partners and friends all over Pyu. He was a plump, arrogant creature, grander in position and demeanor than knowledge and intellect. But he was not incompetent.

Hemi spit black tobacco-y goo on the ground as he peered over Ruka's sticks, face blank and eyes half-closed. "It won't hold," he said flatly, "and even if it does, it'll disrupt fishing and I still don't see the point."

Bukayag finally woke at Ruka's rage and whispered in their native tongue.

"Enough. I'll drown him in the river."

Ruka prevented his brother's attempt to rise and do just that. He breathed and watched the birds till he felt calm, then turned back to his 'master'.

"You don't need to see it, Hemi."

In his Grove, a team of the dead already cut the stone 'steps' that would form the base of the structure. They prepared the ground and fired the huge clay siding that would rise up above the river bank like a half-closed pipe.

"Buy property along the river," he said, as he met the man's eyes. "Tell your men I'm a fool, if you wish. The king will pay you, and you them. Do as I say, and by next year the flooding will end. In a few years, when the property remains undamaged, prices along the river will soar. Claim the credit with anyone who matters. Say somehow you managed it despite my interference, and you will be the hero who tamed the Kubi." Here he shrugged. "If we fail, sell back the property for what you paid, and blame everything on me."

He knew his tone and expression had been wrong—that he challenged the man's pride and dared him to refuse unnecessarily. But they were alone, and he expected men like Hemi were a practical sort.

"My only concerns are for the workers and the people who rely on this river." The Chief Builder spit and shook his head, arms crossed. "But if the king wishes it, however ill advised, let no man say I refused." He rose and waved a flabby arm.

Ruka promised him that in his homeland such things already existed, and that the king desired one here. Both were of course lies.

There was nothing like this back home. Rivers did not often flood in the Ascom. Ruka had watched water flowing through the islanders round pipes, or over v-shaped notches, steady and controlled into fountains and pools, even as pressure built from behind. For a time he had wondered why they didn't do the same with rivers but assumed there was an answer, and it had just been one more question amongst many until the wet season brought a flood.

Then, along with everyone else, Ruka had watched homes and docks and lives swept away, and Farahi only shrugged and said it happened often. For this disruption the Pyu blamed their gods, or in any case did nothing, and so their reasons made no difference.

When it was over, Ruka took long, wooden sticks and walked the Kubi. He measured the depth, the width, then floated leaves and timed them. He traveled from one side of Sri Kon to the other to see how high it could rise safely upstream, the height, the depth at the sea, what would happen if the water moved, if the banks could be raised, how many people and buildings and animals would need to be moved. Then he made his plans.

Now he stood from his sticks, towering over the islander beside him.

"Bring your workers back, Hemi. The markers are adequate."

Hemi rolled his eyes. "Why did I bring workers if we aren't using them? We could have driven in your bloody stakes ourselves."

Ruka felt the frustration easing now as he looked out at the opposite bank. He had the agreement he needed, he knew, and already saw it all constructed in his mind.

"We will need them, and more." He handed Hemi a note he'd prepared with all the stone, wood, and tools they'd require. "We're going to need more men because the season fast approaches." He turned to look at the man, knowing the effect his words would have. "The first thing we're going to do, Master Builder, is divert this river."

Hemi's jaw dropped, and Ruka knew he should have handled it all differently, more carefully, and in any case shouldn't enjoy the shock. But he couldn't help himself. Subtlety was for the weak.

* * *

"So, tell us about your day."

Ruka glanced at Kikay—especially the distaste oozing from her eyes.

They'd invited him to dine with the royal family, and now he sat at a huge, rectangular table in another of the king's many dining halls. The king sat next to his concubine, Hali, which was different than a wife in a way Ruka didn't quite understand. His young sons sat with their nursemaids, save for the youngest, who giggled and smiled in his father's arms.

Kikay would have already spoken to Hemi, of course, or whoever her spies were. No doubt she'd warned Farahi of Ruka's 'madness' before their meal.

"It was productive, Princess." Ruka skewered a piece of herb and salt covered chicken correctly, then spooned it to his mouth correctly. When no one spoke he chewed and swallowed. "The plan will work. But we will need to move the river. Temporarily."

Even Hali's eyes widened. Kikay looked at her brother, but he was ignoring them both and making faces at his infant son.

"And how…," Kikay's face had turned a pleasant shade of pink, "*where* exactly will you divert it?"

Ruka shrugged. "Not far, and not all of it—only enough to build the weir."

The princess and perhaps great matron of Sri Kon shifted in her seat.

"And you have done this before? Successfully?"

"Of course. In my homeland. Many times."

She stared and stared, and he knew she did not believe him.

Farahi lifted his youngest son and set its feet on the table, taking the spoon out of its mouth as it slurped. "I hadn't realized your interest in irrigation, sister."

The pink gave way to a shade of red, and Kikay's hands squeezed closed on knife and napkin. "You're just going to allow this? *Move* the Kubi?"

"Why shouldn't I?" He held the boy up and nudged it forward.

"Because it's disruptive and risky and dear spirits there's *more important things to do*."

"More important than the health and safety of my people?"

Kikay shook her head and looked away. "King Trung breaks your laws and you do nothing. Your *many* enemies gather around you and you do nothing."

"What would you have me do, sister? They want me dead, only dying will satisfy them." Farahi's voice never raised or changed despite his sister's fury. He smiled at the boy and its mother. Kikay stood.

"Send the navy, the army, and *kill him*! *Tomorrow!* What on earth are you waiting for?"

The various servants spread about the hall clinked and scuffed to a stop, suddenly very interested in the tapestries, floor-tiles and windows.

"Do you think Trung hasn't considered that, sister?"

"He's overconfident. He believes in his own family's myths and thinks his allies bolder than they are. But his navy is half the size of ours."

"Yes, he seems weak, and yet provokes us. Do you think King Trung a fool, sister?" Farahi tickled his son's ear and it giggled.

"No, not a fool. But he's arrogant because of his friends and his name."

"Or perhaps you are."

Kikay's eyelids splayed. She threw her knife across the room, pointing a painted finger straight at Ruka.

"I'm tired of your god-cursed pet. I'm tired of his projects, his ugliness, his disruption. He's unnatural. He knows too much, and too fast, and he has put some *spell* on you, Farahi. Why won't you *listen* to me?"

Special, Ruka thought, yes, always special. *Cursed by Noss. Marked. A demon.*

"That's enough, sister."

Finally the king's voice held a mote of emotion. Kikay sneered.

"Why all the new guards, brother? Don't you think I've noticed? You're afraid of him, that's why, and rightly so."

Ruka considered this, trying to decide if he had seen more guards since he arrived. Perhaps, yes, but not while he and the king sat and played their games. Surely that meant he felt safe? Still, the thought annoyed him.

'Why do you care', he almost heard Bukayag growl. But the truth was he did not want Farahi to be afraid of him.

"I have more guards because my own lords are apparently trying to kill me again, sister." The king rose with the boy in his arms. "As with all new and difficult things you fail even to try to understand." Farahi looked at Ruka. "Tell my sister—how many languages have you learned?"

Ruka felt entirely uncomfortable to be caught between them, but it seemed here as in the Ascom, a king ruled alone. If he had to choose his allegiance, the choice seemed clear enough.

After he had learned Pyu common, Farahi had suggested he try other tongues. These had come just as easily, the words now gathered and organized in different rooms in the Grove's rune-hall, labeled and corresponding into what he thought were related groups.

Ruka put his knife and spoon to the table and sat at attention, trying to look at least like a tamed beast.

"Seven, Farahi."

The king snorted. "Seven tongues in six months. And whose idea was it to heat our iron purely with charcoal, to change the forges, to add air to make what my smiths call the greatest metal in the world?"

"It was mine, Farahi."

"And tell my sister, have your people really moved great rivers and built 'weirs' as you suggest, or is that your idea too?"

Here he hesitated, but not for long. "They have not, king, but I assure you it will work."

Farahi strode across the room with his son in his hands, stopping beside Ruka's chair. "Take him." He looked at the guards. "Leave us."

Hali jerked towards the child, but stopped.

Ruka thought back to the last time he had touched another human being without killing them, and knew it had been many years. He had never held a child, but stood and extended his hands as he'd seen others do.

The boy, Kale, seemed pleasant enough. He didn't cry or fuss as a stranger held him, even one as strange as Ruka. He was soft, small enough to crush with one hand, and to Ruka he looked like a girl.

Pyu children, and it seemed children everywhere but the Ascom, were usually single-born. But this did not make them aberrations. The child smiled and reached as if to suck at the one pinky Ruka had left. In the Ascom, he would not yet have a name.

"I trust him, sister." The king looked at Ruka as he spoke. "He is not some rabid beast, nor some unnatural monster. He is just a man. A brilliant, worthy man. And he is my friend."

Ruka returned the look, feeling stunned. It hurt his chest somehow, to be called this Pyu word 'friend'. It meant informal allegiance and perhaps made sense in a land where you were born beneath a chief without your choosing, in a world where kin was not all.

He thought of Trung and the dogs and the girl in the pit, then he thought of his mother.

The world is dark and cold and cruel, my son. Take it by the throat and throttle it.

It had been good advice, once, and needed. But in this moment, he did not wish to.

Kikay stared at him with hatred in her eyes, and the boy's mother sweat with fear. But the boy's father, a great king and a wise man, looked at Ruka with a smile and kind eyes.

In that moment he thought perhaps the world could truly change with words, and perhaps by constructing weirs and better ships and forges and with great minds in friendship, building instead of tearing down.

The world eats weakness and spits it out, said Beyla. Then she had died in a field.

Ruka knew this too, was true, as he knew Bukayag smiled with the same lips as Ruka. He remembered the taste of a man's flesh even as he bounced the boy on his knee. And in his grove, uncertain, hopeful, and terrified, Ruka wiped away his tears.

* * *

"I'm sorry."

Farahi sighed over his book. He and Hali were finally alone, and he could hear her brushing her hair too hard, and sitting too still.

"I knew he wouldn't hurt him. I wouldn't have done it if I thought there was any chance." Farahi scanned the same page in his book without reading. Kale was with his nurse-maid now, his brothers in another room, all likely asleep, all guarded by expert men.

"I trust you."

"Then what's wrong?"

Normally when she was angry she would say 'nothing' and he'd have to push, and only much later would he have the truth of it.

"You and Kikay." She spoke over her shoulder. "You should fix it."

Farahi set down his book, and sighed. As usual, Hali surprised him, and though at the moment it annoyed him it was one of the reasons he loved her. And, of course, she was right.

"I will try."

She looked at him through the mirror, finally, and smiled. She shrugged the straps off her shoulders so her thin shift slipped down as she brushed. His eyes followed.

"Tomorrow I'll take her sailing," he added, "just the two of us."

The shift kept slipping and she arched her back, shaking out her long hair as she put the brush down.

"And?"

"And I'll apologize for what I said tonight."

She stood, slip falling to the floor. Then she was naked and crawling towards him along the sheets like a cat.

"And?"

"And I hate this game." He threw away his book and waited, knowing he wasn't at all convincing.

"You like winning it. And?" She'd stopped, and he watched her curves from the front, the mirror behind.

"And I'll tell her all about my plans for Trung."

Such as they are, he thought, *and I didn't say when.*

She smiled and kept coming, sliding up his legs till she lay on his chest, kissing up at his neck. "You win," she sighed, as if resigned, and her eyelids drooped as she stared into his eyes.

Farahi never needed to tell her what he wanted or how. She read him like he read his books, her reaction to his every touch instant, as if they had been husband and wife all their lives.

They made love until the candles dimmed, the game long forgotten, and slept like the dead.

Farahi dreamed his mad dreams of death and destruction. He woke as he always did before the city rose, creeping from the bed so as not to disturb his lover. Later he sat alone at one of many desks in a room that faced the sunrise as he wrote down what he'd seen.

He had died again, of course. This time he had been older but not that old, and still ruling the isles. A great storm blew across the Northern sea from Nong Ming Tong, impossible and unnatural. He saw ships that looked like his, friends as enemies and enemies as allies. But it was vague and unclear and maybe impossible. Perhaps it was just a dream.

When he woke from such things, his first thoughts were always of Hali and her son. He knew he cared for them too much. He gave her too much influence, favored her father far more than he deserved, ignored his wives and hardly even slept with them since Hali arrived. No doubt they whispered to their families or servants and all his enemies knew of his affections. *And so what?*

In truth his position as king was all but secured. He had two important wives, both now with young, healthy sons. His navy was trained and finally paid properly and less corrupt than it ever had been under his father. On Sri Kon, there were few men left who dared oppose him openly, and none of the islands dared challenge Sri Kon. Yet he could do little but stay in power, and the many problems of the isles continued to swell.

Trung's boldness said much. The old man was losing his mind, arrogant as Kikay thought, or he had friends and a plan. It was no secret that Sri Kon's many nobles hated Alaku sons and their century-long rule. Perhaps the local lords would revolt if Farahi went to war, though he'd planned for this and might have enough men to deal with both. He could hardly believe how much they hated him, though he knew it wasn't actually *him* they hated. He was the last Alaku, and they'd been so close. He was a constant reminder of their failure, and the status quo. But they were fools to think killing him would improve their lives. Only one could be king.

"My lord?"

Farahi recognized the voice of one his bodyguards, so he kept watching as red and gold pierced through cloud and darkness, hung for a moment in morning perfection—when light and life won their victory over the endless night.

He imagined a knife entering his back while he looked away, and thought at least it would be a good way to die.

"What is it?"

"The barbarian, my lord...he is outside. He asks to see you."

Farahi never chastised his servants for calling Ruka 'the barbarian'. Despite all his gifts it remained an accurate description, and in any case didn't bother the man.

Farahi chose not to show his surprise at the uninvited arrival. He had not yet brought Ruka here to play Chahen, but at this point, he put nothing past his newest servant.

"Let him in."

The soldier's sandals shuffled as he obeyed, and Ruka's footsteps echoed through the rampart gate. He would have to stoop as usual to enter, his massive height impractical in most Pyu buildings.

He bowed his tiny bow that was more like a nod, and sat beside Farahi awkwardly in a chair made too small for him. He was barefoot and glistening with sweat, the coarse, dark hair more like fur exposed on his chest and limbs.

"Still not used to the heat, my friend?"

"I am not." Ruka grimaced as he finished squeezing his bulk into the wooden frame, looking prepared for it to snap.

"How did you find me?"

The giant squinted his eyes as if uncomfortable with the light. "With my white-demon magic."

Farahi smiled and almost laughed, perhaps because he was tired.

"You expect some mental miracle." Ruka shrugged his sun-burned shoulders. "It is the best, safest view of the East in this wing. You are not so unpredictable, Farahi. Except in Chahen."

Farahi nodded, and they watched the sunrise together in silence. In truth the foreigner's words disturbed him because he spent a great deal of time and effort being unpredictable. Ruka was a creature of intense logic and observation, though, and if he predicted this than Farahi had erred.

Must I give up beauty, too, to protect the future?

He looked at the strange man who might be his friend and thought on the even stranger months they'd shared—the disbelieving blacksmiths, language tutors, historians and academics of all stripes.

"He is lying, my king," said Master Aleki in the second week. "He knew these things before and pretends now to learn. No man can learn so much and so quickly."

Farahi had said little and been prepared to accept this, but he had urged patience. He no longer believed he was lying.

Ruka could now draw a vast map of the known-world—in perfect detail, with rivers and cities, forests and mountains, exactly and without pause. He knew the huge maze of the palace better than the servants. He questioned everything—how the islanders made their ships, how they cleaned their water, how they handled waste and floods and great waves and droughts and where they grew their food. Sometimes, his questions haunted Farahi's dreams.

He took a deep breath and broke the silence. "Why are you here, Ruka?"

This seemed a good question for the giant, both now and perhaps more broadly, but that bigger question could wait.

Trust was important to establish first. Unlike Chahen it was not composed of mathematics. Trust did not have tiles or pieces; it was a deep, dark well, and a man need draw a hundred times before he drew the hundred and first with certainty.

Ruka shifted and his chair creaked. If anything he'd gained weight since he arrived, yet still his muscles were sharp and angled, though he seemed to do no exercise.

"I told Chief Builder Hemi to buy property along the Kubi," he said, as if it pained him. "He may do so, and he may tell his friends. I thought you should know."

Farahi snorted. He understood without asking why, and didn't much care. In all his dreams he had seen the project succeed.

"Tell me what it's like in your homeland today. In this moment."

His 'guest' made no sign of thinking first as anyone else would have done. The words seemed just to come as if plucked instantly from his mind.

"It is winter, and very cold, king. The lakes and rivers have frozen so solid now that a thousand warriors could cross them together, save for the mountain river men call Bray's Tears. It lies furthest North, and I believe is heated beneath the earth."

Farahi shook his head. He struggled to imagine the Ascom, though everything about it fascinated him. Ruka had spoken often of the weather, the gods, the people, and Farahi balked at the very existence of a place so untouched by the world.

"How do your people survive it? Truly? Are they like us or are they a different race of men entirely?"

Ruka paused, as if seriously considering this. "They are different, and yet the same. To survive they store up salted meat and bread, letting it freeze in the cold then warming it by the fire when needed. In the far South, it is even more difficult. Hunters travel and build houses out of ice, walking on the snow with wide wooden shoes, or in carts pulled by dogs, tracking beasts or cutting holes in the ice to fish all winter."

Farahi closed his eyes in memory, thinking of his one and only journey to the continent as a boy. Even then he had thought the world so vast, so complex, that he would never understand it. But now already it had grown, and if new land could exist to the South, why not elsewhere? Perhaps there were whole new continents yet to be found, new peoples with new ideas.

How mysterious and wonderful it all was, he thought. But also how dangerous.

"I would like to see the pirate, now that I can speak to him," said the giant after a pause.

Farahi kept his face passive to hide his surprise. Ruka had not asked once since the night with Kikay's torturer, and he had to admit a certain curiosity.

"Arun is still with the monks. Bato is a holy place. Foreigners are unwelcome there."

"But perhaps not a king's servant. I will do whatever is required."

Ruka's boldness never ceased to amaze. But a man who understood his own worth did not bother Farahi.

"I will try to arrange it." He paused as if to think, though he had planned a version of this long before. "In return you'll take Kikay with you. For both our sakes, I expect you to do everything in your power to befriend her."

The giant twitched an amber eye, and Farahi fought a smile through long seconds of silence.

"Your sister dislikes me. The feeling is mutual."

Farahi cleared his throat to prevent the laugh.

"She dislikes everyone. But she is clever, loyal, and dangerous. She could have you killed already, my friend, or worse. You must learn to work with even those you dislike, or you will spend your life fighting enemies."

They looked out at the fading half-moon for a time, the sun rays spread below like a lady's fan.

"I will try."

Farahi nodded, thinking of his same word to Hali in the night. He pat the man's shoulder as he rose.

"Better to succeed."

His guards bowed and followed as he left the rampart to face his day, mind turned now to court and how best to isolate Trung from his allies without force, and how to begin the fledgling steps towards alliance with King Kapule, and a thousand other things.

Tomorrow, he hoped, he would still have a sister, as well as a strange but brilliant foreign friend who had come from an endless sea. And perhaps, if he was lucky, even a half-monk killer with Trung's name on his lips.

But a king must be ready to lose anyone, he knew, especially those he loved. It was worth the gamble for the future he desired, the future his people deserved. And two out of three wasn't bad.

21

They woke Kikay before breakfast and put her on a boat with a killer.

Her dead son's birthday was a day away; her blood had come earlier than expected, and her face was bloated from crying. She had a hundred merchants to soothe, intimidate, and bribe because island lords kept attacking ships and saying it was 'pirates'.

I don't have the time or patience for this nonsense.

But Farahi was insistent, and also the king. Neither meant she had to like it.

She glanced at Ruka as he leaned out over the front of the prow like a child, almost giggling in the sun-touched spray and bouncing boat. The morning at least was beautiful, but the savage ruined it just with his presence.

It particularly annoyed her that Farahi hadn't even asked himself. He'd sent a *messenger* with one of his bloody notes:

"Please, sister, try to see his value. The pilot is deaf so you are free to speak as you wish. I don't ask you to trust Ruka. Learn his uses, his weaknesses, *understand* him. Do this for me, and I will listen to your advice."

Kikay had crumpled it and tossed it in the sea for Roa. Bloody arrogant shit of a man. Farahi had an infuriating habit of being right, which Kikay respected and loved but also sometimes hated because it led to his always thinking he knew best, even in matters beyond his insight.

Kikay breathed in the salty air of the sea and adjusted her cushion. The day was warm, windy, and increasingly cloudless. She wore a wide-hat and held an umbrella to block the hot sun—a sun she hoped fried the barbarian like an egg.

If they had ignored Farahi's wishes and sailed in silence for the brief journey while she worked, she'd have been perfectly pleased. But no, the barbarian ruined that too.

"Princess Alaku." He sat across from her with all the grace of a falling rock. "I will not insult you by acting friendly. You mean little to me."

She met his discomforting stare and shook her head. "I'm *devastated*, savage. I just think the world of you."

He ignored her tone. "We need not be enemies. Perhaps we can learn from each other."

She took a deep breath and exhaled. "Very well. Here is your first lesson: I can utterly destroy you, no matter what my brother says or wishes. So let's begin with some advice. Don't speak to me, or get in my way, and while you're at it tell my brother not to waste my time with your nonsense."

The barbarian squinted, and Kikay almost grinned from the pleasure of annoying him.

"You need only move past your prejudice, Princess. I can be useful, to you and your brother. I intend to be."

Kikay scoffed. And here she'd thought *Farahi* was arrogant. "If you could hold my umbrella, savage, that would be *most* useful."

With that she put Ruka from her mind and looked back to her ledger and a list of merchant names, marking how she'd handle each, and calculating expected costs.

The wind blew at her papers and pulled at her hand as she held up the shade, but she managed, lost in thought. Could she start setting traps for the various 'pirates'? Could she turn the court against Trung with 'evidence' of wrongdoing? She'd prefer to send the entire fleet and destroy him utterly, but Farahi was adamant. There would be losses and risk, yes, and what of it? They had too many ships and marines and losing some would reduce the expense.

The sun blotted out and Kikay jerked in surprise. Ruka's fist closed around the stick of her umbrella before she'd noticed him move, and she pulled away. Her ledger bounced off her lap and half carried off over the edge of the hull, several papers scattering in the sea.

"Shit!"

She clamped down on what was left with both hands and lost her hat as the chin strap slipped. She stared up at the barbarian, who glanced at the papers with perhaps some form of chagrin.

"I'm sorry, I meant..."

"To *frighten* me? What did I tell you? What did I just say?"

He was so close she could smell his thick foreign sweat.

"I did not intend, I meant to hold this, to show...to do as you asked..."

"Look at you!" Kikay stood and almost screamed. "You're disgusting! You're so ugly your own mother must have started at the sight of you! *Of course I jumped*! Have you learned no manners with that big, *impressive* brain of yours?" She grabbed at the umbrella in his hand. But he had stilled utterly, as if paralyzed, and didn't let go.

Kikay glanced at the barbarian's strange eyes and saw the hurt. He looked suddenly like a child ready to sit in the corner and sob. Her anger slipped away as it always did, replaced with regret for the outburst, and perhaps some contempt for his softness.

"Alright, I'm...", she meant to say 'sorry', but lost her words.

Ruka released the umbrella with a violent jerk. He reached for her and froze as if in agony, then staggered across the small boat, causing it to sway enough Kikay had to grab out for balance.

With a wild cry, he ripped a long knife from his waist, seized the pilot by the hair, and with one savage stroke, half severed the man's neck. His blood spattered the wood, the sail, and the rudder.

Ruka screamed and stabbed the dying pilot again and again before ripping the head off completely with a horrifying tearing sound. The suddenly insane savage roared, throwing bits and pieces of the man off the side like chum. All the while, Kikay did not move.

Her stomach fluttered with illness at the shock and the display. Her legs felt weak, because she understood all at once that she was trapped on the sea with a madman.

Ruka was muttering to himself in nonsense sounds, or perhaps in his own tongue. His teeth were bared, his head shaking back and forth, voice stopping and starting with growls and hisses.

Kikay's mind wouldn't seem to work. She felt helpless, trapped in a cage with a wild, diseased animal. She could only stare at the pool of blood that used to be a man.

Ruka put red hands to his spotted face. His eyes rose slow and steady till they locked on hers.

"That should have been you, you god damn fool." His chest heaved, his sharp teeth exposed. "Our mother loved us," he hissed. His tone was deeply bitter, emphasized, as if daring her to disagree. He was shaking, his sounds suddenly accented.

"I...I'm sure she did. I spoke in anger."

Did he say us?

The giant came forward, struggling with every step. Kikay had backed as far away as she could, and considered leaping into the water, but she was too slow.

Huge hands batted away her protests and wrapped around her neck before she could scream. His lips curled back like a dog's, and he bent her backwards, half over the water.

"Beyla was kind and brave, good and loving. She was *nothing* like you, princess, or like me. I know that torturer was yours, oh yes. I know you play the fool, but the servants live in fear of you, and no doubt the whole of Sri Kon. I know your games and deceptions and what lies beneath that mask. Monsters can not hide from monsters."

He breathed as if fighting the urge to crush her neck, his muscles straining though the pressure of his grip did not change.

"You will never. Ever. Speak of my mother. Never, ever, *ever, ever!*" His chest rose and fell. "Or I will teach you the truth of suffering. Do you understand, pampered princess?"

Kikay nodded because she could not speak. She felt only the slippery filth on Ruka's fingers and now on her face and hair, and the closeness of his face and his rotten breath mingling with hers.

All at once he let go and backed away. His face scrunched as if confused, hands still out and half curled around an invisible neck. He looked at the blood-stained boat, and his eyes looked full of regret.

"I...I'll clean...this, and take us to Bato," he said, his voice was far away now as if describing a dream, flawless Pyu sounds again. "The pilot," his mouth opened and closed and he looked, perhaps, ashamed, "he died of a sudden illness." The savage scooped pales of water and scrubbed at himself, then the blood-puddle.

Kikay reached down and cupped sea water with her hands to wash her skin. She closed her eyes and tried to control the trembling. She knew she must not show fear before a wild animal.

"I noticed he'd looked pale," she said, when she felt her voice would be controlled. "Then he shook and coughed up blood, and within minutes collapsed and died. I…I didn't wish to travel with a corpse, so you threw him overboard, for my comfort. Thank you."

The giant said nothing, throwing the last of the pilot's body into the water.

"I'll say a prayer now," Kikay said, still trying to return to herself. Her mind at least began working again and she knew the pilot's family would have to be compensated. "Did you know his name?"

Ruka shook his head. He finished cleaning himself, then moved to steer the ship, his back turned away from her.

Kikay asked the good spirits to hide the pilot's corpse from sea gods, lest they raise him as some deep terror. And she asked them, too, to protect her from this madman, and let her live to see dry land again.

As she prayed she made herself and the spirits a sacred vow, that she would put deep if she had to: if she lived to see the shores of her city, she promised, Ruka would one day die screaming.

She understood Farahi had been tricked, maybe even influenced with some foreign magic, and every moment in this thing's presence put him in danger. Her brother was a great man, and a great king—the king Pyu needed and deserved. But he needed protection, from himself, from his enemies, and from his 'friend'. As ever, Kikay intended to see it done.

* * *

Arun sat cross-legged on the beach. He fought down his impatience with thoughts of now—birds laughing as the tide left their supper, the strong warm breeze and dancing shade from palm leaves above.

No matter his attempts at calm, however, he felt the tingle of nervous pleasure when he saw Ruka's boat.

A messenger from the king had arrived earlier and asked the monks to allow the visit. Old Master Lo had spit and frothed and spread his ire to a few of the elder monks, but ultimately, they had to agree.

Arun wondered if the giant could speak many words now. He wondered, too, if he would be angry about the night of torture and losing a finger to save Arun's life.

In the past months of reflection, he'd had considerable time to think on his past. He examined his choices and deeds, successes and failures.

The monks seemed entirely less hateful than they had in his youth. Instead of ignorant tyrants and cruel old men, he saw a simple people surrounded by beauty, choosing lives of discipline and worship for different reasons.

It had shamed him, at first. Arun had taken their teachings and turned them to his own profit with no other purpose, no higher meaning except escape. And escape from what? He still did not know. He had caused pain, and death, and when all of it slipped through his fingers he'd had nothing at the end.

But he did have one thing, he'd eventually realized: he had saved Ruka from torture and death, whatever his reason; then he had been saved by him in return. It felt like one lonely balance of fate and justice in a lopsided life, something even the monks respected. Every day that single deed sat warm and still in Arun's gut like a morning meal.

So he'd sat on the rocky Batonian beach trying to still his mind, and not just his body. He had focused on the horizon most of the morning, losing his patience many times in anticipation. It was at least a start.

Now he examined the ship—a civilian outrigger, sleek and narrow, pontooned with a single sail. It cut across the waves with ease in the strong wind, and Arun realized with amazement that Ruka was piloting. At the rear of the boat sat a woman in colored silks.

Arun's mind and heart raced as he fought for quiet. It had to be Kikay.

After the torture, she had returned as promised and found him by the butcher's corpse. He'd been trapped and bleeding, his tormentor dead and sprawled beside. She hadn't spoken or panicked. She put soft, gentle hands to his cheeks and held his eyes. Then she'd struggled with the winch but managed. And once he was free, his muscles throbbing from the awkward angles and effort, she had whispered in his ear.

"It's alright," she'd brushed his skin, "you're safe now. You're safe."

They'd spoken only once more before Farahi sent him to Bato. She snuck into his room, her fear plain as day. She begged him to succeed.

"Please don't fail because of pride. You must impress the monks to gain Farahi's trust. I need your help. Please. I'm so alone here."

She'd broken down and told him about her brother's 'sorcery' and madness, his lust for power and ruthlessness. Arun held her and said he'd do what he had to. He said he'd come back and help her, and at the time he thought his words simple lies—another con for another rich matron, this time to save his skin. Now he wasn't so sure.

He watched Ruka steer to the small docks, lashing rope near as fast and snug as any seaman. He stepped off to the pebbles and dirt with sandaled feet, skin ruddy but somewhat browned, in thin cloth shorts and shirt like some giant, monstrous islander.

"Loa, pirate."

Arun bowed to hide his smile.

"Loa, Fellow Traveler. Do you speak some of our words now?"

"Yes. Most. Have you become a priest?"

Arun rose with no expression. He was astounded at Ruka's words, which seemed almost perfect even in sound.

"We monks don't preach, if that's what you mean, especially not to barbarians."

The giant nodded and came forward, raising his left hand to spread his four fingers.

"You owe me a finger of debt. I'd like to see the island."

Kikay stepped off the boat behind him. She raised her skirts with one hand, held an umbrella with the other, and set down lightly on the swaying dock. Her long hair blew in the breeze, eyes shining in the sun.

Arun walked past Ruka as if pulled to help her across.

"Loa, Princess." He bowed, deeper than before. And she smiled and nodded, but seemed unwell, perhaps pale. "Are you alright?"

"I'm fine, thank you. Just the waves. It's nice to see you again."

Arun saw the fear spreading out from her eyes in bags and wrinkles too soon for her age, misplaced on such perfection. He felt an anger that surprised him as he wondered what Farahi had done to her.

"Our friend here fancies a tour." He smiled, and tried to put her at ease. "Would that please you?"

The mask of her false bravery fell away at once, and the young woman emerged, eyes sparkling.

"Very much."

Arun took her hand, perhaps too eagerly. "You're safe now," he whispered, realizing he meant it. She clung to his arm like a life-raft.

Ruka walked ahead without waiting, up the narrow path that lead through rock to water and beauty.

He wouldn't know, of course, that no distant foreigner had ever done so. Though perhaps with a man like Ruka, he wouldn't much care.

For a moment he recalled the statue-wielding giant crushing men in the dark. He saw the dead prince strangled in a corridor, and the butcher as his face became meat in Ruka's jaw.

And yet the same man had risked his life and saved Arun's, and now brought beside him the most beautiful flower in the isles.

Life was so very strange, and beautiful, and for a moment Arun was just glad he lived to experience it.

* * *

"Welcome to our humble monastery."

No doubt Old Lo meant this welcome for Kikay, not Ruka—a woman in this case being the lesser of two evils.

The other elder monks stared at the foreigner with ill-concealed wonder and contempt.

"Thank you, Teacher, it's nice to see you again," said the princess of Sri Kon.

Arun blinked in confusion at her use of the word 'again', and the warmth in her words sent a wave of jealousy racing up his spine. *She's just being friendly; Lo's the king's old mentor*, he reminded himself.

"And this...this must be Ruka."

The old man glanced upwards briefly, displeasure dripping from his tone and face. In private he had referred to Ruka only as 'The Filthy Mongrel', and at first argued apprentices should follow him with salt and water to purify every speck of earth he touched.

'The Filthy Mongrel' hunched inside the temple, but still stood far above the Batonians. His cat-eyes almost glowed in the dimly lit entrance, slit and glazed, moving over everything.

"I would like to see all the floors and rooms," he said, voice bouncing off the cloistered walls in perfect Pyuish, disturbing several monks at morning prayer.

Arun held his laugh as Lo's face twisted.

"Here we introduce ourselves to our elders, lest we risk being rude."

Ruka's head turned down, gaze roaming from Lo's callused feet to his wrinkly bald head. Then he spoke again, this time in Batonian.

"In my homeland, the old die before they are a burden."

Arun comprehended this as slowly as everyone else. He focused on still water and rising steam to prevent himself from howling with pleasure.

Lo fumed in the stunned silence, and though Kikay surely did not understand what was said, she put a hand to his arm.

"Ruka is still unused to our ways and words, Teacher. Please excuse any unintended offence."

Unintended! Arun almost laughed out loud.

Lo looked at her and blinked his way back to reality. "How may we help you, Princess Alaku?" he said, voice tight.

Kikay nodded deferentially and smiled, and Arun couldn't help but stare at her lips. She opened her mouth to speak, but Ruka—seemingly bored of the exchange—grunted and walked towards the stairs.

Lo looked at Kikay, and then anyone and everyone, as if someone might explain.

"Stop! Some rooms are forbidden!" He shouted at last, lurching forward on his walking stick. "Stop! Stop right there! Stop at once!"

Ruka did not stop. Instead he crossed the room in only a few strides, then moved up the circular stairs two or three at a time as wide-eyed monks scattered.

"You will stop *this instant!*"

Lo gave chase, hands raised as if to pull the giant back with his spindly arms. Arun and Kikay followed with one or two of the elder monks, enthralled by the show and because what else could they do.

Ruka's sandals thumped and slid their way up the stairs without slowing, and Arun and the others reached the top and found him standing in the testing hall—a place where young men and masters came to seek their ancestors wisdom. He had stopped, and now stared ahead with fists clenched.

A tall monk in adept robes blocked his path. Arun saw who it was, and couldn't begin to decipher the mixed emotion rippling through him.

"Very sorry, but you must go back."

Tamo's voice was calm, his face older but even more serene than Arun remembered. He looked healthier, and thicker in the limbs.

Where have you been these months, he wondered. *Why haven't I seen you, brother?*

In the same language he shouldn't speak, Ruka answered, almost as if pleased to be challenged.

"If you can stop me, priest, you deserve to." Without another word he advanced, massive hands raised with fingers spread.

"Tamo, don't!"

Arun hadn't meant to speak. Then he was moving forward and pushing past Kikay and throwing back his robe.

His brother moved faster. Tamo leapt at the wall, then changed direction. He grabbed Ruka's arm and swung past him, curving the limb and wrapping his arms around its joint in an instant. He flipped over till his feet were behind Ruka's head, his whole body stiff and locked like a splint, toes on the big man's shoulder.

For a moment Ruka looked utterly confused, grunting as he sunk to a knee, his arm back and dragging Tamo like an anchor.

"Do not move."

Tamo's thighs and shoulders bulged as the robe tightened and the giant's limb bent closer to snapping.

The larger man snarled like a beast in a trap. It wasn't pain, or fear, but rage. He stood, and despite the angle and monk's full weight, lifted Tamo entirely off the ground. Then he swung him like a club.

Arun dashed forward. He chopped down at the back of Ruka's knee as if smashing coconut, and Tamo released his hold, pulling his head in before its date with stone wall. He flipped over in a blink and lunged.

Ruka caught him. He'd buckled to one leg again after Arun's strike, but he still had leverage to thrust the monk at the wall.

Flesh pounded against stone, and Arun struck again and again at anything he could, striking until blood smeared across Ruka's scalp and the top of his ear tore. The giant reached back, and when Arun met his eyes he saw no recognition, not even the hint of a thinking man.

Tamo was still twisting in Ruka's grasp, feet wrapping around his neck while Arun dealt with the other arm.

The giant rose and spun, taking both brothers with him and ramming against the closest door, shattering the hinges and sprawling all three of them inside. One massive hand squeezed noose-like round Tamo's neck, the other held Arun at bay.

But the monks worked together now. They had wrestled all their lives as children, and then as apprentices. Tamo hardened his neck and stilled—the same neck that bent iron rods for practice, and Arun twisted the giant's other arm, flipping over, laying flat on the ground with the joint raised and weak. With violent speed, Tamo chopped down on Ruka's shoulders, seeking the pain points. He struck again, and again.

Ruka took blow after blow and for a moment Arun watched feeling helpless, as if they fought with a bear or at least some inhuman and unstoppable thing. At last the giant gasped and released, his face a mix of pain and confusion as he sagged down to lay on his back.

He looked into the room now as if the fight were forgotten. His eyes roamed the thousands of symbols on the walls used for testing memory and patience.

"Beautiful," he said, his voice hoarse.

Arun breathed with relief as he saw the man again emerged from the beast, all trace of anger seemingly vanished.

"I think you can let go now," his brother said, laying back against the wall, a hint of boyish smirk unmasked behind that awful calmness. Arun did the same.

Kikay and Lo appeared in the shattered doorway, the old monk mouthing toothless obscenities, the young woman covering hers with a polite hand.

"I think that's the end of the tour, Ruka."

Arun slumped, thanking all good spirits they'd fought in a well-lit space lacking weapons—or statues—no idea what had just happened, or why. But he hoped dearly he'd never have to try it again.

22

Ruka banished his brother and stared at the walls. In his mind he watched Bukayag struggle against the monks again and again. Both the fight and the room were fascinating, world-changing.

It seemed he had things to learn here even of violence, though such close hand-to-hand meant little in war, or against men with swords and armor.

Still—two little Northerners had trapped and knocked the mighty Bukayag senseless, and if it weren't for the pain shooting through his torso, shoulder, and several places on his head, Ruka may have laughed.

But this scuffle was a minor distraction. What mattered, what truly seized the slowly firming earth beneath Ruka's feet and spun it like an angry god, was the room itself.

The walls before him were like a huge carving, as if a single piece of enormous stone had been hollowed out from within and placed here. The shapes and symbols were physical things, not carved in like a rune, but emerging as if cut away from stone like statues. They weren't just sculptures, however, nor meaningless artwork made for beauty alone—they were symbols, and perhaps words.

The Batonians had runes.

Thousands covered the room from floor to ceiling, perfectly spaced and consistent. It covered the whole Ascomi tongue, and more. Ruka almost pointed as he recognized symbols, an excitement rising in his breast.

Edda's mark! And Seef, and Bray, and Noss!

He could make no sense of it. It was impossible, and yet here they were, just as a single book in Farahi's library had described.

"You must leave at once, for this…blasphemy."

The old, miserable looking priest seemed ready to burst, but Ruka stood and ignored him. The young priests or warriors stirred but stayed down, eyes widened with surprise perhaps because he'd stood so quickly.

Ruka almost scoffed at them—as if this small tussle could bring him true pain and suffering—as if a few strikes of a palm would be enough to keep a man like Ruka from his purpose.

Though, he had to admit, it did hurt.

He rolled his shoulders and winced because Bukayag was pouting like a child, and he'd left Ruka to feel the wounds and bruises he'd earned in the hall. But pain didn't matter, minor wounds didn't matter. He had come here for this.

The Batonian 'test' room lay before him. It was mentioned in a single book on 'Ancient Religions' from Farahi's collection. At first it seemed just one of many books Ruka pored through as he memorized and created in his Grove's growing library. Then he'd recognized the runes, and nearly revealed his amazement to Aleki.

They'd been learning of religion, old and new, from the continent and the isles—mostly the words of the 'Enlightened', or an ancient Pyu prophet of sorts. Among other strange things, the islanders believed a man could defeat death with enough thought, or at least the right *kind* of thought.

From the continent they had embraced a view that the world and heavens were in perfect harmony—that action brought reaction, good brought evil. But like the Ascomi, they had ancient, terrible gods. They had ocean-boilers and child-eaters, imperfect beings that hated and loved and feared like men, different only in scale and power, cruelty and greatness.

All the old stories were written in some version of the island tongue, and without any to truly stand out—that is, all except one.

The hero Rupi, who tricked the gods for fire, fought off sun-beasts, and did a hundred impossible things—his story had been first written in what the islanders called 'Old Batonian'.

What mattered were the symbols. The islanders now all shared the same symbols, but 'Old Batonian' had a language with a thousand symbols for different words. And when he'd first seen them, Ruka choked on his spit.

Most of the symbols had extra loops and slashes, curves or angles, but still—they were unmistakable. They were runes. He'd asked his tutor all kinds of questions: How old is the language? Where does it come from? Who are the people there? Where did *they* come from?

But the man was little help. He seemed not only disinterested but perhaps annoyed at questions about an old, meaningless dead language. Ruka had at once formed his plan to see it for himself.

"Please, Ruka, do as he says."

Arun rose now to his feet, legs bent and ready in a fighting crouch.

Strangely, Ruka couldn't seem to read anything meaningful on the walls. He knew the symbols, but they weren't arranged in any sort of pattern that formed words he understood. Perhaps the patterns had changed, he realized, or perhaps it was a code, or perhaps whoever drew them had not meant to say anything at all. He couldn't help but feel disappointment.

There are answers here, Ruka thought, *or perhaps pathways to better questions.*

But he needed time.

"If I was your student," Ruka said without looking away from the walls, "you could punish me. You could educate me properly." He met Lo's eyes and waited, then at last knelt down and bowed, head on the floor, as time slipped quietly through the room.

He hoped his earlier arrogance and rudeness had been enough to entice the man to accept this to punish him.

Give men what they want when it benefits you.

Ruka grinned into the floor, thinking *very well, Farahi, I will try to learn.*

"You wish to seek *Enlightenment*?" the old man said, his tone pinched and raised at the end.

"I do."

Ruka kept his head lowered and tried to control his anxiety. He did not know what he would do if the old man refused. He counted drips of his water-counter and tried to be patient, tried to ignore the almost palpable incredulity of the islanders.

"You will swear to obey me in all things?" said Lo after a long pause.

Kikay stepped forward and almost stomped. "Teacher, please, this..."

"Is not a woman's business." Lo snapped. "You will swear?"

"I swear it."

"Then I accept you. Take off your clothes and lie down on your back."

Ruka almost snorted. He had expected pain, or possibly a task so self-destructive he would be forced to refuse. But humiliation made sense. It was a weapon of the weak.

He obeyed, careful with his damaged ear as he stripped off the cloth shirt, bunching it with his shorts in the corner. He was glad his brother still slept.

The islanders all stared at him, and he remembered the feeling when he'd first become 'Bukayag'—the unwanted eyes of townsfolk after hiding in the hills for years alone.

"You will lie there until I tell you otherwise, and from now on you will call me Master."

"Yes, Master," Ruka said at once, etching every new rune in stone in his Grove as his gaze swept the ceiling.

Then Lo was telling Kikay the 'savage' would stay till the monks said otherwise, and that the king could have him when he'd failed or quit and not before. She'd fumed, and jabbed a finger though Ruka assumed she must be thrilled.

Then he was left alone. He lay mostly naked on the cool, dusty floor, staring at foreign symbols, ancient and across the sea, yet used for words by his own people.

Why, he thought, *why why why and how, and when and do we come from paradise, or do they come from ash? Were we enemies? Friends? Once the same? Did your world chase us away, or did we chase you here?*

He saw his mother dead and frozen, thawed and rotten come spring, picked down to bones by maggots and wolves. He saw a broken, starving people turned hard and cruel by the cold.

And then at last, the question that truly mattered, the question he had asked a hundred ways a hundred times and never answered, the question on his tongue before he knew how to speak, and perhaps on the tongue of every man of ash.

Who is to blame?

* * *

The priests sewed up his ear and scalp then starved him in a little room with one barred window. For two days he lay on the floor beside the tiny bed too small to hold him. When Lo tried to sneak in, Bukayag rose up and stared.

The old man met his eyes. He tried to hide it, and perhaps it was the realization they now stood alone together in a very small room, but Ruka saw his fear.

"Why are you here?" he said without coming all the way inside.

Ruka held back his brother's venom, thinking *I could ask you people the same.*

"I am here to learn."

Lo seemed to consider this for a time, then frowned. "What can you do?"

"Anything that a man can do, Master."

The old man showed his toothless maw, which was perhaps a smile. "You are arrogant and rude, and certainly wrong."

Ruka shrugged because he supposed that could be true. The old man turned and hobbled off without another word, and Ruka sighed and lay his body back to rest while he worked in his Grove.

Since he'd first seen the war-fort Pyu men called a 'palace' he'd begun a great project of his own. The dead already began to stack the walls from blocks cut in their quarry. They pulled these with ropes and rolled them along tree trunks—just as the Pyu.

Other teams of the dead cleared forest, or dug into the earth to make room for underground floors. Ruka at first thought the moat a decorative waste of effort, but he had read most sieges ended with the invaders digging tunnels beneath, and thought a deep moat would make this difficult. Starvation and disease were the next weapon of choice, so he'd use the river, and make wells, and fill a hundred cellars with supplies. The dead didn't eat or sicken, of course—but it was good practice for the real thing.

He'd also begun sculptures in the Pyu style—starting with images of his mother, of Egil, and Aiden. One day he intended to make a sculpture of all his men, particularly those who died because of him but he hadn't killed directly. It seemed at least a small way to honor them.

He would also build the weir, expand his armory, construct the new forges and stables and glassworks and brickworks. The immensity of the task made him smile, undaunted, though he never had enough time nor enough workers, and his plans always outstripped his means.

Bukayag resisted their urge to sleep. They didn't talk about the monks in the hall, though Ruka felt his brother's urge to kill them, even if it meant sneaking into their rooms with cold steel.

He'd never allow this, and felt only contempt for the thought. He respected the monk's bravery, their victory and prowess. Arun had saved them from Trung and his pits, and though his reasons were perhaps selfish, the deed mattered more.

"We should be bringing more from our Grove to the world," Bukayag grumbled. "We should be testing the limits and growing our power, not wasting time in this shithole."

Ruka smiled, thinking now that his brother was active again, he was awfully chatty.

All things in their time and place, brother. We have much to learn.

"I'm *tired* of learning. We have everything we need. Let us return, and conquer the Ascom."

Ruka blinked at this, perhaps surprised to hear it spoken out loud. In truth he had already considered it.

Yes, he had knowledge and power now to perhaps arm a great horde of outcasts and lesser men with the forges of the dead. He could bring word of this new world, converting greater men to his cause in a new campaign. He had more than Imler ever dreamed possible, and the Order had grown weak.

I have everything, he thought, closing his eyes, *everything except a reason.*

"Don't just lie there, come." Lo arrived again as the sun rose, and gestured to follow.

Ruka blinked away a neglected exhaustion, rising with a groan to duck through doorways and down the stair-wells till they walked on fresh-cut grass in a ring facing the lake.

The view here rivaled the path down from the rocks, which was already a sight to behold. The Batonian lake seemed almost a perfect circle, surrounded by small, fire-spewing mountains like Turgen Sar—the mountain of all things.

Was it another tie between these people and the children of ash, Ruka wondered? Or just coincidence?

A boy sat before them in the grass holding a pear-shaped instrument, much like Egil's lyre. He bowed to Lo and plucked at the four strings with his right hand, placing down fingers higher up with his left. The sound was strange but pleasant, and they sat and listened looking out as steam rose from the water, and the sun dipped down behind its mountain ramparts.

When the playing stopped, Lo smiled and met Ruka's eyes.

"Since you can do *anything*, foreigner, here—play the peepa."

The boy bowed and extended the instrument.

Ruka looked at it and at his 'master', then glanced at the boy. He'd watched his hands as he played and knew many of the movements, able to summon them exactly if required. But it would be like speaking in a foreign tongue. His movement would be clunky and unpracticed and useless.

Perhaps it was the view, or the warmth, or the pleasant music, but Ruka gestured at the instrument and laughed. It wasn't truly a matter of practice.

His digits were too thick, and too rigid, and he was missing a finger. Even with effort he could never play like the boy.

"I can't," he said, shaking his head. "Your lesson is learned."

The priest glared at him as if he felt otherwise. "And what lesson is that?" he snapped.

"Humility," Ruka said, feeling more amusement than shame.

The old man smiled at him, his toothless mouth a gaping hole of darkness. "Oh no, my poor, ignorant *apprentice*. That lesson has just begun."

Lo took Ruka on a tour of the island, where he was out-done at every turn by little brown priests with pleasant smiles.

Some could balance perfectly on wooden beams. Others leapt through the air holding their weight with toes or fingers; others swam like fish or held their breath long after Ruka surfaced sputtering.

There were priests who could sing like birds, or catch sturgeon with their bare grip, and yet others who could bend bronze with their flesh or climb trees like squirrels.

The old man sneered after Ruka's every failure, but in truth he began to enjoy his own defeats, and the skill of the other men's displays. His pleasure seemed to annoy his master.

"You grin like a fool, which you are. So strong and mighty but out-done by a boy who still wets himself at night."

Ruka laughed because it was true, and quite amusing, and Lo's face twisted as he huffed. He took Ruka to a cluster of rough-barked trees, pointing up into the canopy.

"Catch that monkey with your hands," he said, then settled on a rock and picked at his gums, as if angry to provide the test.

Ruka had already seen the creatures on Sri Kon and thought them fascinating. They seemed very playful and clever, and harassed the merchants of Farahi's island as they stole and made mischief from merchant squares to soldier's barracks. He admired their intelligence, and their agility, their curiosity and their courage. In many ways, they reminded him of men.

He watched them as he practiced throwing again and again in his Grove. When he was ready, he withdrew the hidden blade from his ill-fitted 'apprentice robe', and took aim.

The blade spun fast and true, and pinned one animal to its thick branch, straight through the chest. It sagged without even a howl of surprise.

Lo goggled, mouth working soundlessly as he pointed at the blade.

"Use your hands, I said! *Catch him*, I said!"

Ruka walked to the creature and snapped its neck to be sure it wasn't suffering, holding it up in display.

"I threw the knife with my hands, Master. And it seems well caught."

Lo blinked with his mouth still agape. He leaned forward as if he might spit or retch, putting his old wrinkled hands on his knees. He leaned against the closest rock, and howled.

"That's true," he managed, wiping away a tear. "That's true, yes you did."

Ruka smiled at him, liking the old priest far more than he expected. "Meat is meat," he said. "Sacrifice should not be wasted. Tonight I will cook you monkey, Master."

The old man looked up and shook his head, his fit coming to an end as he stared and stared. With a grin, at last, he nodded.

* * *

For two more days Ruka was assigned tasks next to apprentices half his age. Together they cleaned chamber pots, cut and peeled vegetables, and scrubbed the temple until their knees were raw. Ruka enjoyed it all immensely, and hadn't realized it was meant as will-testing tedium until the boys started to complain.

He only shrugged, and continued, even cleaning at night while he worked in his Grove. When an elder monk finally approached at dawn and told him to 'leave all that noisy brushing and go to sleep, you idiot', it seemed the test was over.

On the third day, Lo came again.

"Today you dance the Ching, Ruka."

Men of ash had no word for 'dance', but it just meant rhythmic movement.

"Yes, master."

"Brother Tamo will be teaching you. Do what he says."

Bukayag tightened their jaw but Ruka ignored it, and bowed. This time they brought him peacefully to the room of runes.

Tamo knelt by the windows watching the sunrise. He turned and bowed as they entered, his face serene and friendly, no trace of anger at Ruka, no avoidance of his eyes.

"Once you have performed to Tamo's satisfaction, you will see me again. You will not eat until you do."

"Yes, master."

Ruka studied the room again and found it the same. He wondered with excitement if the test might help him understand, or when they would end so he could explore the island and learn more himself. Then Tamo rose and started moving.

He was slow, and purposeful, his stance strong and balanced like a warrior. After several thrusts, twists and steps he stopped and waited, and Ruka did his best to imitate it. Then Tamo began again, adding another movement.

This repeated over and over. Tamo made a total of forty-nine movements or sets of movements that took thousands of water-drops of time, the finer steps somewhat difficult with Ruka's nine toes. He did what he could.

As the sun reached its peak outside the window, flickering the men's shadows as they moved over the creaking floorboards, the routine finished. Tamo bowed again, gesturing for Ruka to step back. Then he snapped forward violently, hacking his way through the movements at full speed.

Ruka had been practicing in his Grove even as his body learned. Time was slower in the realm of the dead, and he had moved through the routine several times. His body was sweaty and tired, though more from heat than exhaustion. His size and height meant he could never truly mimic the young, lithe priest; his muscles were built from hammering and lifts, sword-swinging and shield-bearing—not holding his weight at awkward angles.

Still, he watched, fascinated, and in his Grove he tried.

When the monk finished his spinning and settled on his heels, Ruka stepped forward at once. He noticed the man's surprise, the serene and gentle features breaking just for a moment as he considered what to do. But he bowed, and stepped away.

Ruka realized he had not been expected to attempt it, and supposed other men might not remember so many movements all at once.

In his Grove, Ruka had ten toes and fingers and practiced in his training grounds. He led his body, watching Tamo again in his mind. The dead watched him and said nothing.

He let Bukayag help him move in the room of sun and ancient runes. It felt different, somehow, from throwing knives or climbing walls or forging steel or murdering. It was easier, more natural, if slightly surreal.

Ruka felt very close to his brother in that moment, as if perhaps in most ways they were not separate men. It felt much like Farahi's palace when he'd first taken a shield and sword, nothing to something, thought to reality. He wondered if perhaps his Grove was not so different and separate as he once believed, just another truth existing in parallel—like life and death, opposite and conjoined, neither with meaning except for the other.

Ruka moved to the Ching for a few moments simply because he could, and because it was pleasurable. Though it was difficult, it did not require a purpose.

He saw beauty in the light and the strain, thinking how incredible to be here in this warm, strange place of mysteries. He wondered on his fate, and the gods, and the creation of the world. But for a moment, perhaps, it did not matter. Ruka felt a sort of peace in the Ching, knowing the feeling would fade and perhaps did not truly exist, just as joy and perhaps love did not truly exist, and yet did, though they could not be seen. Then he sighed, and stood still, because all at once the dance was over.

Tamo stared at him like the dead men in his Grove. His face grew very calm again, and he bowed and motioned to stay. He left the room, and returned after a time with master Lo.

The old man's face was blank like Egil's when he'd meant to deceive. His milky eyes searched Ruka's face just as Tamo's had.

"There is but one test left, apprentice. Are you ready?"

Ruka had been ready for anything since he was a boy. He thought of his mother dead in a field, or of standing on the lawstone, and cowering beneath a tarp on the open sea. He was ready to die. He was certainly ready for some priest's test.

"Yes," he sighed, watching the harsh light of the drooping sun.

"Remember the symbols," said the old monk. Then he explained how they must be drawn exactly in reverse in the matching room beside.

Ruka nodded, then walked to the new space. It was covered in empty, square blocks on floors and walls, a mirrored reflection of the testing room. Ruka wondered how any ordinary man should hope to accomplish such a task, but he supposed it didn't matter.

He picked up the chalk and began, trying only to control his shaking limbs as he filled the emptiness with something, blank space with meaning, one by one across the floors and walls while Lo and Tamo watched him in silence.

"Don't finish them!" He heard Egil in his mind the first time he'd written a rune—the poor, ignorant fool, afraid of a false prophet's god. He felt wetness creep to his eyes.

"It…it matters why." Lo spoke as if by rote, his voice shaking.

Yes, Ruka thought, *why and how and when and where, it all matters.*

His heart hammered in his ears, and his pace increased now. He scratched the lines so quickly the quality decreased, the edges squiggled and weak as he raced to the next. His hands shook and he began drawing the same symbols in his Grove, tracing them on tablets as the dead ran to fetch more.

He was in a hurry because—at last—he understood. In the right pattern, and from the right direction, the symbols formed words.

The earth seemed to shift beneath his feet, as if waves crashed against him—as if Tegrin the star god stirred the seas with his iron rod. Ruka cursed himself for a fool, racing to read words and sentences of an ancient people made thousands of years before. He had not seen it.

When he was finished, he stood back and looked about the beauty of the room, the simplicity of the test. Nothing had changed, and yet everything—Ruka knew the story of his people.

He read the last words of island men, the final epic of people who called themselves the Vi-sha-n. The symbols he'd written were now a mirrored reflection of the first, the changing order emerging meaning from the runes.

It seemed the Ascom's words were in truth an ancient tongue, perhaps lost to these 'foreigners'. They had been held in trust by arctic colonists—

preserved as if in the ice for an age of men.

They read like Farahi's books, up and down rather than left to right, and backwards. But read properly, it weaved a history like the book of Galdra.

"We are the Vishan," it started. "We are the divine blood, children of the gods. We are all that remains of a butchered people. We few are they who go across the sea. This is our story."

Ruka could not read every word and meaning. Some runes he had never even seen before, or perhaps they had changed beyond his recognition. But he understood enough.

The story described a people murdered and chased, routed and butchered by some foreign invader. They told of a great war of heaven and earth, a bitter defeat, and a final attempt to cross the uncrossable sea to escape.

The Vishan had run from misery and death. They had been men and women of paradise fleeing usurpers, fleeing a butcher. A traveler. *An Enlightened.*

But they had survived.

Ruka's heart felt heavy but glowing with pride. His ancestors had fallen, but they had the courage to face the sea, to risk all for their children and descendants. Now, maybe thousands of years later, here one stood.

"Remember us," said the Vishan, in their final words. Only that: "Remember us."

Ruka swore it as he had once sworn to a dying woman in a frozen steppe. He would remember every symbol, every line. It was as if he'd been made to do so.

He dropped to his knees in both the lands of the living and the dead, feeling for the first time what a man of faith might feel—a reverence, perhaps, for a thing he loved but could not touch.

It was as if they'd written the message just for him, as if they had somehow known, and waited, an ancient people crafting him from ash and clay over two thousand years. It was a love note, a silent plea, the last words before a suicide.

I will remember, he promised again, feeling trapped in forces far beyond him, like a fish caught in an ocean current. He clenched one fist and Bukayag the other, seeing justice form on some distant shore, land at last from a stark and endless sea.

His mother had been right to save him. He was not a mistake.

He stood in his Grove and faced the dead, no longer feeling shame. He was not a demon cursed to wander the earth. His darkness had a purpose, his gifts tools for a task left undone, two thousand years in the making. His deeds could be redeemed.

Beyla had carried an ancient vengeance in her womb. She was the holy matriarch of a wounded tribe, the last she-wolf chased into the steppe, the great fire of ash in her breast never dimmed. She had loved a dangerous child, and paid the cost. She had given her life for her people.

But we survived, Ruka thought, feeling his pride spread to the men and women of ash, despite their harsh laws and mistakes and hardness. They too had survived. They had faced the misery of the Ascom, raising children in a long and unbroken line to make Beyla just as she made him. They had honored the dead, and were worthy. In the end, they had won.

Ruka felt himself wrap in purpose like armor, untouchable and strong. First he had lived only for survival, then revenge, and finally knowledge. All were inadequate. They had all been the closest branch next to a blinded thing, grasping for anything at hand. This was the first that had meaning.

Whatever it took, however long and how much he need sacrifice or suffer—Ruka knew the final purpose of his life would redeem him, as it would redeem the dead and the past and the frozen tears of ten thousand mothers weeping at their infant's graves. Ruka would bring his mother's people home.

23
1580 AE. On the border of Nong Ming Tong.

Kale watched King Kapule's commander with his spirit. The Tong army was ten thousand strong, fanned out across the plains in good order, well-fed and bristling with bronze and iron.

"What's the message, sir?"

The Tong general sat under a shaded veranda, sipping water as he fanned himself. He shrugged.

"The king has a non-aggression treaty with Naran. We enforce it. Nothing else."

"Understood sir. And if the Mesanites try to cross the border?"

The general smiled. "My orders say nothing else, Captain. Quite specifically, I'd say."

The younger man returned it. "Yes, General."

Kale breathed a sigh of relief, and pulled back to his senses. Osco and his men had nearly reached the borders of Nong Ming Tong. They had some small hills to protect them from sight, but with few exceptions they stood in an open plain of grass and farmland.

At least two thousand Naranians stood in their path.

"The Tong won't stop us." Kale blinked his tired eyes and ran a hand over his greasy face. "We need only push through the emperor's men."

Osco's eyebrows quirked. "*Push through*? It's not a jungle, islander. That's a great deal of soldiers."

"Yes I know. I told you their numbers." Kale tried to push down his frustration. Win or lose, there'd be more needless death, just like Amit, just like the burning forest, the fallen hillmen, the farmers and merchants and scouts. *Just let me go*, he wanted to scream in the emperor's face. But nothing was that simple, not with kings. Maybe not ever.

"Can't you just…form your square and keep moving? Cross the border and they can't follow us."

Osco shrugged. "Possibly. They are lightly armed and tired…"

"And lady-men," Asna added, all smiles now that it looked like they'd make it.

"Yes. Well. We either form a 'square', as you say, and they may shoot at us but otherwise flee. Or they will stand, and we will have to kill most of them. Or, we charge and hope to break them. But if they hold and surround us, it could be…unpleasant." He looked at Kale as if to say 'can you do something about that?'

"I'll do what I can."

Osco's eyebrows frowned, and Kale let out a breath. He looked away, readying himself for another spirit-flight.

They had time, he thought. The enemy waited and more reinforcements were coming, but they weren't yet close. He flew out towards the Naranian line, searching for their leaders.

He crossed over a mix of dried up marsh and plains that he knew stretched to the sea. He reached out with his mind and felt nothing but wind and the tingling that clung to wool blankets. The sky looked clear, though something lurked there far away that promised a flood. As he flew he tried looking lower, sifting the earth with his hands out to touch threads lurking in the soil. He found nothing—only huge, hardened cords of earth that fit like fingers in a fist. They felt solid, locked, as hard to move as a mountain with a shovel.

He flew over the haphazard line of the enemy scouts to find a cluster of men arguing behind them.

"And I tell you they're not half the fighters you think they are!" A young man with a red face pointed a finger at the others. "I've seen Mesanite princes in Nanzu with my own eyes. They missed their targets. They failed out in tournaments, ended drills and competitions with the lowest scores. I'm telling you they've grown soft!"

Kale blinked in confusion, then thought back to his friend at the warrior college—Osco had never scored high in anything. In fact, he had missed simple shots before a group of students. At the time, Kale thought it just nerves, or maybe anger...

But perhaps all Mesanite nobility did this, and had since becoming 'vassals'. Was such depth and constancy of deception possible? Kale could see no other explanation. For a moment his mind blanked in open awe.

"They're in armor with broad shields," said an older man. "And we have what? Knives and spears?"

The younger man and his supporters looked unmoved.

"With respect, Captain Toda, these are not the Mesanites of your youth. And yes they have armor and shields, but they've had to drag them halfway across Naran. Look at them! They can hardly hold them up!"

Kale nearly snorted.

"And what will the Emperor say if we let them cross, eh? Will you face him for us, Captain? In Death Hall? Will you say 'yes we outnumbered the enemy four to one, Emperor, but we were poorly armed and *tired*!'

Kale saw enough shame in the other men's expressions to know their answer. He closed his eyes and returned to his senses, knowing the enemy would fight, and that every man on this field would pay a cost for it—Kale included.

Whatever power he used in this place would be difficult. There were rules. Any strength he drew would come mostly from the air, or from the men's bodies. It would burn bright and fast and end in death and misery— blood boiling and bursting beneath its own weight, squeezed by force both small and endless, and who knew exactly whose. Kale thought he could snap arrows, twist spears, and break bones, but little else safely.

"You'll need to form your square," he said to his ally. "We'll have to engage them, and hope they break."

Osco's eyebrows weren't encouraging.

If you're watching, Kale looked the unknown heavens that perhaps held Ru, or powerful spirits, or evil, spiteful Gods watching the conflict with glee, *please protect these men, friend or foe. Protect them, and just let us pass.*

* * *

Asna wore his armor for the first time since they'd started marching. It was only leather padding, and relatively light compared to the Mesanite's mix of iron and bronze plates and chain links. He strapped a buckler to his left arm, a heater to his back, and layered his legs and arms with knives.

Two good swords in scabbards dangled at his hips, and he spit when the Mesanites offered him a bow. *God damn fools*, he thought, *attacking archers on a god damn plain. No wonder they never caught grandpapa.*

Their enemies were skirmishers, really, not infantry. Osco and his men would traipse about while being shot to hell, charge as the enemy fled, and then get shot to hell some more. In any case no sane man stood against the advance of Mesanite heavy infantry and forget their numbers. So yes of course the scouts would run.

Yet here they all were, everyone formed up like it was otherwise. *Yes very good, very impressive, you're all very brave.*

The imperials stood in a ragged line. The hillmen stood in a perfect rectangle. A silence settled between the men, intense and anxious as the infantry entered the edges of the archer's range.

"Tooooee!"

Osco shouted in his ugly goat tongue, and hundreds of stomps and shouts answered as the men advanced.

Shitting hell. Shitting goat mucking hell. Why am I here? How did this happen to me?

Asna marched because he had no choice. He huddled under his 'allies' shields and spared a look at Kale beside him, hoping the islander read his displeasure. *You'd best drown me in gold and fish-women, princeling, or I'll...I'll...you'll bloody what, stupid idiot? You're bound to him now. You're a criminal everywhere else that matters.*

Asna, son of Fetnal, son of some other bastard and no doubt a bunch more, banished all his natural instinct to flee. It tugged at his ears like his aunts guarding their raspberries or his cousins' virginity, and he took deep breaths.

He was here because of fate and fortune, and because he had done a thing his people lived all their lives trying to avoid—he had committed.

Thunks and pings made him flinch as the first arrows fell against thin metal shield. The hillmen didn't hurry, didn't slow, didn't even cry out or grumble as other men would to bolster their courage.

Asna's world became only the crunch crunch crunching of boots on dying grass, the metal screeching of shield slapped and rubbing against shield, the thwacks and zinging of arrow-tip ramming against the infantry's barriers.

Soon it would be screaming and sharpened edges cleaving bone and Asna would be in true, open battle for the first time since he was a boy. *Unless they run*, he thought, *which they will.*

"Or my mother loves goat-cock," he yelled. But no one heard in the advance, or would have understood him anyway. He flexed his fingers and wiped at his brow.

The arrows slowed as the Mesanites advanced. He assumed the enemy was falling back and re-positioning, no doubt surrounding the square to fire their arrows until their fingers bled and their quivers emptied. With a sigh he risked a hop to look over the heads and shields of the men around him. Though his glance was brief, he could hardly believe it.

The skirmishers held. They had their spears braced in three ranks, the men directly before the Mesanites holding and ready with their bows discarded.

Do you think this will save you, lady-men? Asna almost laughed aloud. Perhaps it was a trick, like the fuel-sodden wood on the bridge. Perhaps the dry field would light before them. *But the islander will protect us, yes? Yes. Nothing to worry us.*

Still his hands shook, heart racing but not from the run—for even his allies' 'charge' dripped as sap down a tree. In this last moment he basked in the shade of shields and strong arms, in clean air and clean clothes, knowing all would soon taint and sharpen with messy deaths.

Again without a word, the Mesanites slowed to a crawl. Their shields lowered nearly in unison, and without instruction, every Mesanite in range hurled his javelin towards the waiting enemy.

The Naranians were shieldless. They wore no armor save for cotton and leather with perhaps a few, useless bucklers. Their spear-wall tore faster than frayed cloth.

Men cried out in surprise and terror as the deadly throwing spears pierced their bodies. Then the hillmen charged.

Their shields led the way, smashing and shivering spears, brushing them away like cobwebs. In every gap, in every faltering stab from the enemy, hillmen stepped through to lance Naranian guts with their stabbing swords, then fell back in line.

The heavy infantry made no shouts or calls. They fought in silence, eerie and terrifying save for their grunts and growls. They bashed and stabbed, withdrew and advanced, folding their enemy like smiths hammering bronze, moving step by step through a field of blood with practiced ease.

Asna was impressed, and yes, a little frightened, and suddenly, very bored.

He rolled his shoulders and dropped his shield. He unsheathed both blades at his hips, pushing out from the cover of his fellows with a few Condotian swears to slip out the flank.

He knew the sides of Osco's square were the only places the lady-men had a chance. If they had any sense they would push here and try at least to slow the butchery enough to stop the advance. Perhaps there the fighting would be fierce, and chaotic. Perhaps there would be glory.

If you are watching from hell, Papa, time to see how a real man fights.

"I am Asna Fetnal," he called out over the din, seeing with great pleasure the skirmishers had begun to wrap around the square as he'd predicted.

He slashed aside a boy's spear-shaft and severed his wrist.

"All will fall before me, starting with you!" Asna pointed a curved sword into the chaos of skirmishers, vaguely at some man he couldn't reach, and in any case didn't intend to. He turned the other way and charged.

* * *

Kale felt the deaths around him. The heat seeped out of men to cool and mix with dirt, clumped and trodden, mud tinged with red. He'd never seen war, and this was small but already terrible. It would be worse where they were going.

"Please just stop," he whispered.

His empty stomach heaved at the smell and noise and movement and he put a hand to his face. He imagined his fig tree in Nanzu, sitting with students as he focused on his breathing.

If there was only wind or clouds, or something, anything he could use for spectacle—some way to shatter these men and make them run.

He reached out to feel again and failed. He hovered up with his senses to look down at the square of discipline all around him fenced in by spears. It was like a wolf-pack pecked by chickens. So far, he couldn't see a single dead Mesanite.

Then he saw Asna.

The Condotian had run out alone, out of formation. He was already half-surrounded, chopping spears and hands with his curved swords, narrowly avoiding death from an arrow shot.

"Fall back you damn fool," Kale whispered with his spirit.

The Condotian jerked, confused, and in his distraction death lunged at his side. Kale snapped the spear in half before it landed.

"Islander! About time!" The mercenary backed away, half a dozen spears fanning out to skewer him. He pointed a sword and looked to the sky, then laughed. "God is with me!"

Before Kale had time to react, the Condotian charged.

Iron-tipped shafts thrust up but he ignored them, reaching around them for the kill with no thought of safety.

Kale swept the tips aside to save his life, barely, and Asna slashed a man's throat. Blood sprayed over men too shocked to withdraw.

"I am death!"

Asna abandoned defense entirely, not even flinching at his enemy's thrusts.

Kale didn't know what to do. He pulled the weapons away in panic, or raised them straight in the air, or plunged spear-tips into the dirt, catching two arrows before they landed. With every stroke, Asna murdered.

He threw himself forward, racing across the ground and cleaving at faces and chests, his movements erratic but efficient, his swords perfect for the task.

"Stop," Kale whispered, too distracted to project it.

With his spirit he watched one man against fifty, twisting from side to side, laughing and slaughtering anyone he reached. Kale broke his enemy's weapons in mid-air, knocked them from their grasp, or turned them aside only to protect his friend, but also leaving the unarmored scouts exposed.

Asna began singing in his own tongue, which Kale understood with his spirit. The sounds were lyrical, flowing, even beautiful. The words were monstrous.

"Send the city up in flames, spit in their face, spit in their face. Raise your torches, hope remains, spit in their face, spit in their face..."

He'd snarl a verb as he hacked off a limb. "Spit in their *face*". Then twirl and catch the next line and take half a head.

"It's the Anointed!" shouted one of the scouts. "He uses his magic!"

In the small clearing of bloody men on the Mesanite's flank, men were running now. They pointed and shouted. The archers tried to bring Asna down as space around him cleared, but Kale caught the arrows.

Asna sheathed a sword and threw knife after knife, then turned back and raced down the line of enemies pinning in the Mesanites.

These men stood in formation. They faced the infantry, attention consumed with jabbing at shields and anything exposed, trying desperately to slow the advance and protect themselves from retaliation.

Asna was free, ignored, and unopposed. He cut backs and sides, hamstrings and necks. The spearmen were shieldless, armorless, trapped against the square. Every stroke of Asna's sword killed or maimed. When at last he seemed to tire of hacking men to death he simply switched arms, walking now instead of running to save strength, moving down the line butchering, singing, 'spit in their *face*,' 'city in *flames*' as he chopped.

Some turned to face him, and were cut down by Osco's men. Those that held faced Asna's scimitar.

Heads swiveled and heard the singing, heard their fellows dying. They saw no support or reinforcements; they saw the column of heavy infantry still advancing no matter what they did. Many turned and fled, and soon the whole flank broke apart.

The Mesanites finally came apart to chase, strength re-surging as victory loomed. They rolled out and down the 'outside' square of scouts still holding, poking holes and bashing over the enemy with their shields as often as their swords. It all ended quickly.

Kale soon heard only the moans, the weeping, the begging. There was an awful smell, like a butcher or a harbor. He looked upon a whole field of men in pieces, their blood feeding the soil. Osco's soldiers moved across it finishing the wounded, ignoring their pleas.

Kale felt utterly numb. He tried to think back to the moment he had turned his miracles on the enemy and found he couldn't. He had meant only to help, to protect; he reacted because his friend and ally was in danger and what else could he do?

The action had come without thought, like dancing the Ching with Master Tamo in a room of symbols and sunlight, like an infant holdings its breath under water. *But I must accept blame*, he thought. Surely he had destroyed those men as sure as Asna.

The 'windows' in his spirit-house were near sealed and so he fled back to his own senses. He looked on his blood-soaked friend—the friend who had saved him from assassins twice, and who just killed or wounded maybe a hundred men with his own hands while singing and laughing.

Asna's curved blade was raised in the air splattering gore. His clothes looked dyed red, his silks and frills dripping all around him. Mesanites shook his shoulders and laughed, patting his back, raising their swords with his and chanting in their tongue.

Kale was glad not to be watching with his spirit, because he didn't want to know what they said. He thought back to the beach—to navy life and fighting with Thetma while boys hooted their names.

Does nothing ever change, he wondered? But he knew the answer. Nothing ever changed, save for the stakes.

The memory of Thetma was unwelcome, for he was likely dead, too, sunk beneath the waves of the Alaku sea. Sergeant Kwal, Kale's enemy in the navy, was dead. The Exarch and his servant were dead. The martial students, the assassins, Amit and no doubt Lani and Kikay, his brothers and father.

Kale wept for the dead while his men roared in triumph. He saw perhaps fifteen hundred cold Naranians in a field of dry grass, with only five hundred to run and live and tell the tale.

Many Mesanites had been wounded by arrows or spears, or bones broken in the clash of shield and body, wood and iron. But there was not a single dead.

Kale knew little of battle, and of war, but he knew this in itself had been a miracle. *The Condotian and the Sorcerer-Prince*, he thought, a legend written in blood. They would re-tell it, perhaps, without the prince's tears.

24

With the enemy routed and the wounded seen to, Kale and his allies crossed the border into Nong Ming Tong. Half of Trung's army followed watching, but at a distance, sending only one messenger to announce their 'escort'.

Kale went to his wagon to meditate and let the men pull him. He didn't want to talk or even look at anyone, so he focused on the terrain, which bristled with summer heat.

Every step seemed dryer, and more barren; stream-beds lay jagged with stones, empty and dead; grass stuck out like straw, clinging to the soil by yellowed roots. The air shimmered. The men's lips cracked and even Osco carried his helm.

Their march passed farmland parched to ruin, dull-eyed merchants rattling dust with stick-thin donkeys. Kale's people called this place the 'Rice-basket of the world', but he saw no sign of that here—he thought the good land must be further to the coast.

"I want to thank, friend." Asna approached him very late in the day, his posture cautious. "What we do together," he looked off into the horizon. "Glorious, yes? Glorious."

They both knew Kale wasn't pleased, and that he'd been an unwitting participant.

"You seemed very sure I could save you, and that I would."

The Condotian smiled.

"No. But faith, yes?" He put a hand out to rest on Kale's shoulder. Sweat trickled down his brow, and not just from the heat.

Good, Kale thought, you know you've pushed me, and you know I could rend you skin from bone, and you think perhaps I might. He met the mercenary's eyes.

"I wouldn't try it again."

"No, no, of course. Rest my friend." Asna bowed his ludicrous bow and twirled away in courtier fashion, shrugging at Osco, who ignored them both.

Kale settled back to his silence, sweeping his gaze out over the tumblebush and skinny trees that looked like starving peasants. A soldier handed him water and twice-baked bread, holding it out as if in sacred offering.

'I am just a man', Kale wanted to say, but he couldn't speak their difficult tongue. He took it and smiled, thinking of a thousand corpses picked by vultures and maggots and feeling more like vomiting than eating. But he was alive. He had to eat to keep his strength because he had things yet to do.

He'd lost weight—more weight, as his appetite dwindled, his stomach still weakened by the poison. The hard muscles of navy life had begun to round and soften, his chest growing leaner and fatless, ribs now poking out slightly beside.

"How far to the king's city?"

Osco's voice broke Kale's thoughts.

The general's son was far from his home now. He knew of the comings and goings of other places, but likely he had never walked their lands.

"Several days," Kale said, but wasn't sure, or at least not exactly.

He came this path in the opposite direction with Amit, first from Sri Kon to Tong with his father's ships, then with King Kapule's escort from the coast on foot. He'd been hurt still from a fight with his father's guards, and from being forced away from Lani. It had felt a very long trip indeed.

But he smiled as he thought of Amit—the old crickety-legged scholar who made every step that Kale did. He'd kept them moving, tired in body but never in spirit.

"If I can do it, certainly you can," he'd say, contempt and humor mixed inexorably in his voice.

"You're not hurt," Kale had whined.

Amit had stopped, eyes wide, finger prepped for wagging.

"Boy, I once walked for a week, puffy and half-blind from a snakebite, mad with hunger and wounded, straight through a swamp. Now get up."

Kale laughed now at the memory, though he hadn't at the time. In fact he'd pouted and kicked rocks feeling sorry for himself like a child.

And what are you doing at this moment?

He took a deep breath, and burned his thoughts.

Opening the windows of his spirit-house was getting easier—the 'muscle' of his power was sharpening, firming, even as his body withered. He breathed and floated up and out with the ashes, then sped out and over the road watching everything. He sensed a great flood still waiting in the distance, lurking in dark clouds held back by wind, penned as if by God himself. But this was not his current concern.

How far can I go, he wondered? *And how many threads can I gather?*

He thought often now on Ando's words—the Batonian 'boy' who taught him to meditate. Nishad, he'd called him—'they who stay'. *Stay where? And where is there to go?*

In truth he was afraid to learn. The thought of being trapped when his windows closed still shook his chest and tightened his throat. But he knew he must at least push the boundaries to grow.

He raised his arms and soared above himself, higher and higher until the men below became a swarm of ants on a dusty plain. He looked into the perfect blue sky and wished he could feel the wind with his body, but regardless, the sight was incredible—the feeling freeing, and terrifying, like leaping from a cliff to the sea.

He had risen faster than he expected. His spirit was growing, lengthening, quickening. He blew past birds in flight, hollering in joy at the speed, but glad that he was nothing and weighed nothing, and did not intrude on the little creatures.

For miles in every direction he saw a countryside begging for rain. He came upon towns that stretched on like cities, sparse and sleeping, streets spotted with guards and meager shops.

Beyond he found more fields—endless fields of different crops, some seeming as large as the whole of Sri Kon. But he flew on. He flew until field became gravel and paving stone, brick and wood and the taming pathways of man. Every road seemed to lead the same way, a thousand rivers pouring humanity into a great sea. For the second time in his life, and from the first time from above, Kale saw Ketsra, the farmer-king's hall.

It was said to hold a million lives, and seeing it now from above Kale believed. A motley canopy of clay or mud, sandstone or brick houses checkered every patch of earth. Narrow streets wound between them filled by people and animals, tarps and bazaars. Clothes dangled on lines between floors and windows making the city look like a web weaved of dyed cloth and livable earthworks. At its Southern edge was the sea, which called to Kale and whispered freedom and home and a thousand thoughts he forced from his mind. Instead he flew down to inspect the palace.

It looked much like Farahi's, though this was connected to the city and far less protected. The gates lay wide open, walls built half-heartedly and small, courtyards filled with people and merchants, animals and sound. It had no moat, no secondary or tertiary walls, no curved angles or maze of inner fortress, not even a throng of spears or men-at-arms.

A line of women with baskets and children were the largest crowd, standing at a huge clay silo that rose up as tall as the palace. They held pouches, waiting for baskets or scoops of grain doled out by sweaty, smiling guards. It looked organized, but tense.

Kale swept in and through the open entrance at the front. The yard might be welcoming, but the palace itself was thickly piled stone strengthened by wide outside tiles, topped by hard plaster roofs to prevent fires in a siege. It was square and unimaginative, but sturdy-looking.

He flew further inside to a gathering of cleaner-looking men in fine linen and silk. These stood at ease, huddled near a door flanked by swordsmen.

Kale saw the trinkets and baubles outside, the artwork and sculptures and weapons hung from marble carvings—all the heirlooms his own family used to display their wealth, ancestry and power.

With no further evidence required, he knew he'd found the Tong king. He passed straight through the door.

* * *

"Tell me," said the King of Nong Ming Tong, seated on a throne so thick with silver and cushions it looked like a cloudy moon.

"It is unclear, my lord."

Kale floated in the center of the room and watched a man in black, jewel-studded robes lean over a bloody table.

With careful attention the man picked through a chicken's guts as if panning for gold, weighing and feeling fleshy chunks before placing them back.

The king smiled, seemingly relaxed. He wore a layer of healthy fat like a uniform, squeezed in more layers of what looked to Kale like women's silks from ankles to neck, with even more swaddling his head, so only his face remained in sight.

"Do you know why I sent for you, seer?" The king breathed out as he spoke, as if he'd lost interest.

"My lord is concerned for his people." The older man spoke calmly, but his neck glowed as red as his nose.

"Of course. I mean you *specifically*. Frankly, I've never liked your chicken guts. They're messy, and they stink. But you see I've killed all the others. They're down with the dogs."

A bead of sweat, perhaps, grew on the seer's brow, but he stood with surprising poise. "My lord may kill me if he wishes, of course, but it will not bring the rains."

The king's eyed widened momentarily, but shrunk again.

"Ha. Now that I believe. But then it won't stop them, either, and I'll feel much better."

He waved a hand, and guards took the seer's arms and escorted him away, his rich leather shoes squishing on the tile.

Kale watched, and weighed.

He flew down through the floor looking for dogs chewing on human bones, or prison cells filled with filthy seers. But the palace was large and he found neither, so he returned and watched some more.

King Kapule dealt with a dozen visitors discussing trade. He handled them deftly, apologetically, giving each little more than promises and charm. After, he would look out his windows and sigh, and when he'd summoned the strength he'd wave at his guards and bring in another.

Kale knew Kapule was at least fifty. He wore the years badly. His eyes bulged with red veins, his skin puffed and bruised beneath them, his babyish face lined with worry.

On a whim, Kale whispered with his body, trying to project it over the vast distance and make the king hear. The older man didn't even flinch.

He'd never tried to truly speak with his spirit, but he did so now. It felt strange, and heavy, like wearing shoes after a season of sandals. But it worked.

"I'll bring your rain, Farmer-King," he croaked, "because your people suffer. I will be there soon."

The man jerked in surprise, a knife appearing in his pudgy hand from a fold in his robe.

"Are you alright, sir?"

A bodyguard formed as if from nothing from beside the door. He moved like a viper guarding its young.

"Yes. Yes…I'm fine." The king shook his head and pat the servant's shoulder as if he did it often. "But I'd be better if it rained."

"Yes sir." The guard didn't smile, then he strode around the room barking orders at hidden guardsmen to sweep the palace for danger. "Disarm everyone," he hissed.

Kapule raised a hand as if to protest, then seemed to change his mind and settled back down in his mountain of pillows. "Don't kill anyone," he sighed, resigned, as if it didn't really matter.

Kale pulled back to his senses, uncertain how he felt.

* * *

The army marched. The men's water ran low then out before the week was done, though they stopped at every well along the way. Lips went from dry to cracked and bleeding, tongues bulged, and what little the soldiers pissed came out the color of sunlight. None complained, except Asna.

"What good is gold if I die in hell-hole?"

Kale rather agreed with the sentiment, but there was nothing to do but go onward.

At first locals feared their small army as it passed, but when the men kept good order and their hands to themselves, half-naked children soon came tugging at legs. Some begged, some stared, others just followed in silence, dirty faces cast down in misery, twig-like legs good only for a mile.

They traveled a road Kale had seen from the sky. From his height he hadn't seen it clearly, but now discovered it flanked on both sides by men in wood collars staked to red dirt. Hundreds, maybe thousands of such men hung over empty barrels or slumped against the ground.

Most looked dead, probably just from dehydration and the sun, others moaned, cried, or wailed. Guards sat near-by under tents drinking water. Some held back families that came too close to their dying sons, husbands and fathers.

"Who are these men?"

Kale stepped to the guards with his soldiers behind him feeling a sudden rage. He could speak Tong, but not particularly well.

"Thieves," said a glassy-eyed spearmen in an officer's cap. He looked on the clustering group of Mesanites with entirely less fear than seemed prudent, and shrugged. "They all stole food."

Kale felt the pull of violence at the man's casual tone. The urge to burn his thoughts and float free, pull at the sky and rend these men limb from limb felt as strong as his thirst.

But he tried to remember patience. He stood staring, feeling Osco's hand on his arm as if trying to calm him, and he felt the truth and horror of it all. He had seen the countryside, the drought. There were simply too many mouths to feed, and people would starve and fight and nothing anyone could do would stop any of it. He could give no justice or answers in that stark reality.

He felt as he had when his navy brothers couldn't read, or as a great wave drowned Sri Kon's coast—noblemen drinking as the fishermen died.

But at least his father hadn't. Farahi the evil sorcerer had never sat idle while his people suffered. He had tried to save those he could, even on the fateful night when Kale slept with Lani, and ensured his own banishment.

Kale turned from the scene of horror and walked on, passing the dead and dying with his eyes turned to the road. He was being watched, and followed by an army—his first act in Tong couldn't be killing his ally's soldiers.

Before the sun fell they entered Ketsra on the main road that ran to the palace. Humanity clogged it from tip to hilt, spilling off to side streets and jamming these too.

Osco looked down into the city and sighed, sharp eyes no doubt seeing details and options and plans Kale couldn't begin to form.

"If we take the men down that madness, there will be many injured locals," the Mesanite said without tone.

Kale sighed, knowing the warrior was not suggesting they avoid it. He was simply stating a fact.

"We leave them here," Kale said, and started down the gentle slope to the main entrance.

In his mind Kale saw the staked and dying men, the doomed 'seers', the viper-guard at the king's side.

He swallowed and felt poison coursing through his veins, burning his gut again in Osco's hall. He began to understand his father's fears, his paranoia, his terror of the game of kings.

"We leave them here," he said again, more forcefully, as he stepped towards his father's 'ally'. It occurred to him then that he had taken Kapule's daughter without his consent, and perhaps the man had already heard this rumor. He took a deep breath.

"Asna, stay close to me inside."

The mercenary grinned and stepped forward, checking straps holding knives around his body, and the looseness of the swords at his waist. Kale pictured his singing and his sword chopping men in a deadly rhythm of violence, and he tried not to feel ashamed.

25

"Ruka, I'd like you to meet someone."

The old monk had knocked for the first time, and no longer tried to surprise him in the mornings. Ruka blinked in the dim light and returned from his mind, putting away his Grove-work to focus.

After the test, he had been given all the food he wished but otherwise ignored by the monks. He wasn't sure why or what they intended, but he sensed little enough danger.

"Yes, Master."

Lo nodded and led him down the stone steps and corridors, across the green temple grass and dustless pathways, until they stood beneath palm trees by lake Lancona.

"Wait here," he said, and slunk away, leaving Ruka to watch steam rise and smell the salt.

The heat still bothered him, and the moisture in the air felt oppressive, but the beauty was almost overwhelming.

"Stolen beauty," Bukayag growled

Ruka knew in a way this was true, but also false. Did such a thing belong to men at all?

Questions like this were beyond Ruka's brother, though. They stood together on the sand and felt the breeze, waiting a long time in silence. The sun crested the volcanoes, and soon cleared the small mountains to bathe the view in the fading colors of what ashmen called fall, but these islanders called 'dry season'.

Ruka worked in his Grove while he waited. He wondered sometimes what other men did to occupy themselves during the banalities of life, but he supposed they had their fantasies, or their escapes, or perhaps for them memory was a tool requiring constant maintenance.

He'd almost finished a dry-dock now on what would one day be a river. The dead were fastening oak boards, curved and overlapping, joggled, caulked and bolted down with steel rivets. He would build new and better ships mixed and matched from Pyu and Ascomi styles. Their sleek but sizable hulls would cut through the sea, reverse if needed, and run shallow enough to beach, all while holding a hundred men.

"You're very patient," spoke a boy's voice. It disturbed the sounds of the animals and the water against the beach. It seemed unsure, and on the edge of manhood.

Ruka turned to find a tall, skinny teen in robes with acne on his pale brown face.

"No," he said, "not truly. I was busy."

His lips felt strange as he spoke, and he winced and licked them. He had not intended to say this out loud.

The boy smiled, then gestured down a path around the lake. "Will you walk with me? My name is Ando. What is yours?"

Again Ruka found his tongue moving before his mind could decide. "My name is Ruka, son of Beyla."

The boy's eyes narrowed. "That is a strange name, at least to these islands. Tell me, how did you pass the wall-test, Ruka?"

The boy's eyes seemed somehow brighter now, and menacing. Ruka felt little hairs on his neck raise, as if he were watched by some hungry pack of predators. He felt his mouth moving and tried to stop it.

"I..." he coughed, and growled, but failed. "I memorized the symbols."

The air seemed to shimmer in Ruka's vision, and with every step he felt heavier. The boy seemed to swell in size beside him, all his shyness vanishing as if only an illusion.

"That's quite a gift," his voice was louder now, and deeper. "Where are you from, Ruka, son of Beyla?"

The question felt snapped like the end of a whip. The air was thick and viscous and Ruka felt his body sweating.

He ran towards his mother's house in his Grove, wanting only someplace safe to hide. He slammed the door and put his forehead to the wood, summoning a Pyu map of the world to his mind. He relaxed his control.

Speak for us, brother, there's something very wrong. There is power here or from this boy, something that controls me. I can't fight it.

Bukayag woke, and blinked.

"An island," he almost spit, as if unbothered by the boy's power. "Far to the North. Beyond Naran."

Ando's eyes narrowed, then flared. His body shimmered as heat rising from a fire, his voice growing deeper and echoing even in Ruka's grove, scattering the birds as the dead men looked up from their toil.

"*Where are you from?*" the 'boy' repeated.

Ruka fell to his knees on the wooden floor. *The Ascom!* He wailed. *The land of ash, from across the sea!* The words felt pulled from his churning gut as if expelled.

"The North," said Bukayag, "a small place called Tinay. I left because I didn't want to fish."

The boy who wasn't a boy stared and stared as if ready to draw a blade and drive it deep into Ruka's gut. At last he smiled, calm again. Bukayag did the same.

"I'm curious because you remind me of someone," he said, as if this explained everything. "But the world is very large."

Bukayag nodded, and they walked together along the lake until Ando spoke again.

"Tell me, Ruka, why have you come seeking Enlightenment?"

Ruka sat trembling in his Grove, but the boy's voice at least no longer felt like a crushing weight.

"I didn't," answered Bukayag. "I came to see a friend, but once I saw Bato I wished to stay longer."

Ando's smile didn't touch his eyes. "It is a very beautiful island, I don't blame you. Well. It was very nice to meet you, Ruka, son of Beyla, of Tinay. Perhaps you'll visit me again."

"Yes, perhaps."

Bukayag returned the boy's bow with the faintest movement and turned away. Sweat trickled down their armpits and beaded on their neck, and they nearly fled, not stopping or looking back until they reached the far side of the lake.

When Ruka felt sure they were alone, close to the rocky outer beach and the cliff-like drops to the water, he finally relaxed.

"By the mountain what *was* that, brother?"

Even Bukayag's voice was tight with earnest fear. Ruka had no answer. Was Ando a man with powers like Ruka? Was he a God?

His people claimed that 'beyond the world-ring is a realm beyond mortal ken.' They believed in gods and half-gods and star-kings, but Ruka had never seen any proof. *Except the land of the dead, and my own strange powers.*

Perhaps Ando was proof otherwise. The thought filled him with doubt, and fear, reminding him of his own ignorance. The feeling eased slightly as he walked.

He couldn't make you speak, at least. Together, perhaps, we were stronger.

Bukayag gripped a stone and threw it into the water. "Barely."

They sat on the lake's edge together seeking calm. Ruka knew his brother was right about his Grove. More than ever he knew he needed to test the rules and push himself further. Perhaps there were other Ando's. Perhaps there were other men or Gods with great powers, and one day they might come with more than curiosity.

He left his mother's house and returned to the drydock, putting a hand on the prow of his first war-ship's hull. It was held upright with clamps and wedges but soon would float in water drawn from wells.

He allowed himself a moment of exhaustion and weariness. He had so very much to do.

In his mind's eye, a hundred war-ships already circled the Ascom. These would be both fighters and transports, ships with hulls shallow enough to sail down Bray's river, but large enough to hold his retainers and supplies and horses. With enough warriors, he would be able to control the fertile ring, all the way to the valley of law.

Farahi ruled his world with sea power, and Ruka could do the same. All it required was the materials, and the manpower—both of which he had in his Grove. Why couldn't he bring something larger than a sword, or armor?

Why couldn't he wield an endless war chest, and buy the loyalty of every coastal chief? Why couldn't he build an armada of ash?

"Ruka!"

Arun's voice echoed over the water. Ruka spotted the pirate or maybe monk holding his robes as he ran, skirting over rocks and footpaths in a straight line towards the coast. Sweat glistened on his brow. His eyes were wide, veins thick and clear as he came closer.

"The palace..." he straightened his robe as he arrived, and swallowed. "A messenger came. There's rebellion. Farahi...the king's palace is under siege. We must go to him."

Ruka stared and said nothing because in truth he didn't understand. He knew much now of architecture and ships, and many other things, but he did not know the games of kings. Were such things common?

"Did you not hear me? We must go, right now, nevermind the monks. The king is our future."

Ruka stilled and considered this. His mind went out beyond the death of Farahi, circling, looking for paths back home without his help. It would be harder, much harder. And perhaps with Farahi's help, with the wealth and knowledge of Sri Kon, the men of ash could reclaim their birthright without war.

And, he is my friend.

This last thought came slower, colder, and quieter. It felt different than before—at a distance behind runes on an ancient wall, a bitter history of conquest, and by a sea between paradise and misery.

'What can we do?' he said with a shrug, knowing in truth they could likely do a great deal, but curious what the man would say.

Arun seemed to sense the deception.

"Think of the reward," he said, his eyes shining like Egil's at the chance of wealth those years ago.

Ruka smiled, knowing what the man really wanted. Or rather, *whom*.

"I care nothing for wealth, pirate. But I will come, if you ask. You will owe me. Far more than a finger. Swear it on your god."

The monk's eyes narrowed and Ruka thought of Chief Caro in Husavik's hall. *Swear to help my mother*, Ruka'd told him, his knife to their precious priestess. Though Arun was a murderer and a thief, if he promised, Ruka would believe.

"I swear," said the monk. "Another life, that's what I'll owe you."

Ruka extended his arm in the Ascomi fashion. The smaller man raised a brow, but seized it vaguely correctly.

"A man's word is his honor, pirate. It is all he has in this life."

Ruka began walking to the armory in his Grove. When he arrived he slipped quilted leather over his arms and torso, standing with hands extended while the dead sealed him in chain and rune-etched plates. He eased his helm down, looking out through a visored steel mask made to resemble a cave-bear, its 'teeth' crossed with thin, jagged bars.

"Hold it up," he said to the Boy-from-the-stables-in-Alverel, who raised a replica of shoddy Pyu-forged iron.

Ruka hacked down with his own latest sword, made lighter because islanders wore no metal armor. Even with less weight, the enemy's crude metal bent and soon snapped, and the Boy grinned with his eyes. Next he lashed a steel rune-shield, made broad and thin, to Ruka's wrist and elbow.

"Do you need a weapon?" The pirate asked. He was already pushing their boat out onto the beach, unfurling shoddy knives and spears from a roll of dirty tarp. Ruka answered with a stare and prolonged silence, and Arun cleared his throat."Well, let me know if you do."

Ruka stepped over the lip and sat as the boat swayed from his weight. There was little wind, so he lifted two oars, pushing them through the tide as Arun fiddled with the sail. The handles felt good in his hands—solid, like sword-hilts freshly molded, and with every stroke he hacked through Northern iron in his Grove, leaving scrap and ruin in his wake just as Bukayag left the waves.

"Are you supposed to be leaving again, monk? Is it not against the rules?"

The man who could be a shadow smiled, though he looked sad. "Rules can be broken."

Ruka nodded, thinking how very true. It prompted memories of a dead priestess, birds soaring into an endless sea, men sleeping like plants and moving rivers and a hundred other 'impossible' things.

I'll help you, Farahi, he thought, *then you'll send me home. And perhaps together, we'll see how many rules can shatter.*

26

"I told you. I *told* you, Kikay."

Farahi gripped the rail of his fortress rampart and tried to control his breathing. Despite every dream and intuition it was a mistake, his sister had finally broken him down, and he had sent a fleet to sweep the routes to Halin.

He thought at least if he sunk a few of Trung's 'pirates', and a few of the other lords at that, it might give the old tyrant pause. He knew his ships would be scouted, maybe lured and trapped, and so he sent nearly his whole navy—an almost unstoppable force—in two prongs.

As expected, it *had* been a trap. Just not for his fleet.

The 'rebellion' started within a day of his navy's absence. Some were clearly locals, others mercenary. Only the Enlightened could say where they'd been hiding so many weapons.

They stormed the courtyards wreaking havoc with torches in a large, coordinated assault. They had simply walked through open gates of the outer walls, killing guards and servants indiscriminately as they dashed wildly ahead.

Farahi was not entirely unprepared. He had summoned his personal troops to the palace the moment he'd sent his ships. The inner fortress was sealed, his few hundred men held the moat and inner walls, and the 'rebels' found themselves on the wrong-end of the final gate.

Now it would take them days, maybe weeks to tunnel under, if they even knew how. Farahi's fortress had its own well, plenty of supplies, and his personal guard included sappers who would counter-tunnel and sabotage the enemy's efforts. These 'siegers' had no rams or towers. Even if they managed to build some they still likely lacked the numbers to storm the walls.

Farahi therefore had only to wait for his fleet to return. When they did, twenty thousand enraged marines would surround the doomed brigands, and promptly butcher them.

"We were reckless, and now I look like I can't protect my own city," he sighed. "Another drink?"

Kikay winced and came to the balcony, looking down over the siegers as Farahi poured squeezed oranges and Bekthano rum into her glass.

"We'll make examples," she said. "And we can have some admit to Trung's conspiracy in court. Let these raiders rape and butcher the ungrateful dogs down there. Maybe they'll be reminded why they need you."

She took the drink and swallowed most in a single gulp. By her expression, Farahi knew she was more angry at herself than anything, but she likely meant this disregard for the people.

Kikay could rage or wail like an actress, then shrug it off and eat her breakfast cool as a Bato breeze. In truth she despised the commoners of

Sri Kon. This wasn't news to Farahi, however, and he'd made his point.

"Tell me what happened with Ruka."

Kikay's eye twitched. They hadn't had time to speak of it except for Kikay to say he was staying with the monks and that any chance of a cordial relationship had failed. Farahi sent a spy at once, fearing she'd had the barbarian killed.

"Nothing. He made an ass of himself, then asked to stay in Bato."

"Did you talk?"

"No we didn't *talk*." She turned to face him. "Brother, despite your naive belief otherwise, some people will never get along. I've told you your pet scorpion will sting you, and he will. Perhaps not today, or tomorrow, or even a year from now, but he *will* sting you because that's what a scorpion does. Pretend otherwise if you like, but I won't." She dumped the rest of her drink over the rail. "Now I need to prepare a hundred messages for when this siege lifts. So if you're done rubbing my nose in this?"

He waved her off, thinking *the siege won't just 'lift', sister. We're going to butcher them, many our own people turned against me because they've been wronged by us, or because their selfish, stupid lords paid them, and they're too poor to fear death properly.*

Chaos below was only a matter of time now. The 'rebels' would come to understand, just as he had, that they had no hope of taking the castle. They would see torture and execution were coming for them and that escape from Sri Kon was impossible. In rage, they would turn their attention on the citizens. They would rape and murder and drink themselves into oblivion to push down their fear.

And what could Farahi truly do?

The 'greatest king of Pyu' stood stranded behind his walls, helpless and useless as a child while parts of his city burned.

He supposed he could sally his soldiers out to fight in the streets. But perhaps Trung hoped for exactly that. Perhaps a fleet of assassins waited, all the rest of this violence mere subterfuge to create an opening, a single moment of fatal surprise.

Must I suffer this, too, to protect the future? Farahi curled his fingers into a fist. *Must I become so cowardly I lock myself away from all dangers to protect my people's children?*

He stood frozen on the rail, watching, debating. When he could wait no longer, he summoned his sergeant and asked for advice. They walked through city maps and choke points, considering what the citizens would do now with the palace trapped—whether they'd stay locked in their homes, or flee to the outskirts.

Farahi thought of fishermen drowning in great waves, laughing as the sky darkened and all the merchants ran. He knew they would not flee. Islanders did not fear death and tragedy on their doorsteps, for it was always there.

They would go to work, open up their shops in the city-square and hawk their wares, even to the enemy soldiers. They would live their lives as usual, hopeful and calm in spite of danger, right to the end.

Farahi closed his eyes and thanked the soldier, telling him to be ready if the order came.

He looked up at the falling sun, standing still as the light faded to a dull red and Sri Kon settled into evening. He stood still and silent as a statue, waiting, until the ring of men thinned around his castle, and the screams began.

* * *

Arun led them as he had in Trung's dungeons, though Ruka knew every street of Sri Kon.

There was no need for silence now that the fighting started, but still the monk stalked and slid through alleys, motioning without words, slitting two throats before Ruka raised his hands to fight.

"Take a weapon," he'd said as they'd pushed up onto the coast, but Ruka walked on unarmed.

"Focus on saving your princess, pirate, you needn't look after me."

He'd watched the surprise in Arun's face, and nearly shook his head. Men thought themselves so clever, so unpredictable, but their desires in life were few.

Together they trekked through the city and saw many houses in flames. A few corpses lay in the streets, and soon they passed groups of men and boys lying dead in piles. Some had women and girls dragged off beside them.

'Raped', Ruka knew, thinking such an act should not have a word. But word or no, the thing was the same. He decided the men who did this had destroyed the very purpose of their civilization. They had defiled the very thing that gave them all life, and given up the right to be men. They deserved the death that would follow.

Arun led them past the piles of corpses in silence, but the mood had changed. They crossed the river and crept near the temple, always careful because they couldn't know how many men were nearby. The raider's purpose seemed only cruelty and destruction, for they had no carts or wagons, nothing to steal with, nothing to hold their plunder.

It also seemed as if they attacked the rich houses first, as if they knew the city well. Ruka thought it must be common men rebelling against their wealthy neighbors. But he felt no pity or sympathy for the Pyu 'poor'.

Farahi and the temple gave food away for nothing, and even the poorest in the isles had something in their bellies. They had warmth enough just from the sun; they had good clean water to be drunk from the great river or the many wells. And if these people had any right to violence, then Ascomi poor could butcher all the world.

The two men stalked to a dark corner of Sri Kon's square—an open street ringed with shops and carts at the foot of the outer palace gates. At least fifty warriors stood guard, and did not wear Alaku blue and silver.

"Shit." Arun leaned against the sandstone wall and closed his eyes. "If they have guards, it means they've held this safely for some time. We might be too late."

Ruka doubted that very much. He knew little of the game of kings, but he expected Farahi and his sister were very good at it.

"There's more gates, pirate. Straighten your spine."

Arun perked up and stared with a squint. "I'm going to climb my way into the palace. I expect you can't follow." Ruka looked at the walls and said nothing. "Our deal is off, then, you've been quite useless."

Ruka stared until he felt the man's discomfort. "Our deal remains. I'll see you inside shortly."

Arun snorted, muttering 'lunatic savage" in Batonian as he snuck round the corner. "I won't be there to save you this time," he called.

"You think very highly of yourself, pirate," Ruka called back. He watched the men outside the gate, and waited.

In his Grove the dead lined a hundred weapons on racks in easy reach. They fired the forges just in case, then gathered at different distances on his field for target practice.

He breathed and summoned his memories—the feel of hard, leather wrapped pommel, the heavy sag of metal and padding against his skin.

Ruka smiled as he thought of the impossible things he intended, and his faith that it could be so.

In a way he forged his own religion in the land of the dead—a belief in concreteness, a belief in the possible. The purest faith there was. *Believe it to be real*, he thought, *and it will be so.*

Wet heat flared from his skin as Bukayag's body wrapped in leather hide. Sparks and light followed, then the flare and spray of steam as it all weighed down with chain-linked and plated steel. He brought a shield but not his sword, then pulled down the single whale-oil street-lamp and doused the fuel in dirt.

He stepped, ready now, from the alley to open square. In his Grove he lifted a throwing-spear from its wooden grooves—one of many now in reach, sharpened and weighted to pierce wood and flesh with ease.

Bukayag held back his arm and walked forward just as Ruka did, the spear flaming into existence mid-throw as they released together with the might of both.

The steel sailed forward as if launched from a bow. Ruka seized another and threw again, both spears flickering with fire through the air, lighting the dark night before the first one struck. The target turned to look, then flew from his feet as the missile pierced his chest.

The others started shouting in alarm. They hunched and scattered, searching and readying bows. Some loosed arrows at nothing, or at every dark mound in the gloom.

Ruka didn't fear their arrows in any case, and threw more spears. Sparks lit his body, and soon the men pointed and turned their attacks in the right direction. Flimsy arrows bounced off Ruka's shield, one off his arm-plate, though most clattered and missed.

He started killing any man he caught standing still. Others drew blades or lifted spears and charged across the square, frantic steps uncoordinated and rushed without clearly seeing their foe.

Ruka skewered the first and second with a single throw. The third reached him, and he swiped his shield's edge into the man's face, splattering blood and teeth and battering him half dead into the paving stone.

Ruka drew a chopping sword in the mid-swipe of his arm, cutting through a man's spear-shaft and deep into his shoulder. With a savage kick he knocked the foe back from the alley, twisted and hacked a neck with the backstroke.

With every kill he fell back into the alley swinging, feeling a few useless spear-tips rattle against his shield till he plugged the space. Only one or two men could approach. Two tried, and Ruka cut them down.

Others fell back hurling rocks or spears or knives, all of which clattered like hail against Ruka's steel.

As they fell away, he dropped his sword and threw more javelins. The first pierced a man's gut, straight through to skewer him to the earth. Bukayag saw it and laughed his laugh.

He drew a new sword as fire rained down from its scabbard of air, and readied for more. Island voices were crying 'Demon! Demon!', so Ruka screamed like Noss to make it true. He charged from the alley swiping at any not wise or fast enough to flee.

At least thirty men turned and ran, wild-eyed into the night.

27

Arun untucked the climbing kit tied to his back. He wore sandaled foot-spikes now, but kept his hands free, dousing them in alcohol to dry and remove grime. He chalked his fingers, wiped some off, and chalked again.

Farahi's walls were huge and sheer. Most of it was square stone blocks cut and stacked then held in place with mortar, coated in whitewash and plaster. They were too high to throw a hook.

Arun stood for a moment on the ground to seek holds and grooves, then, deciding on a path, began to climb.

His hard fingers clawed and locked at corners and indents, scraped out dirt, and held his weight as he spread his limbs out flat and flexed. Even amongst the monks of the monastery, he had been an excellent climber.

Soon all thought was gone—there was only the wall, the next hold, the nearly invisible path above. Hand then foot then knee, dig then thrust, lift and splay.

Time lost all meaning until Arun's hand touched flat rock at a new angle. Then he had both hands on top and pulled himself to the safety of a horizontal world, where every movement didn't contain the chance of death. He raised his body straight up and over the rampart without looking back. He kept his spikes and moved on his toes down the unmanned ledge and steps, through the courtyard to the next wall.

More rebel guards sat about the outer courtyard, tense and wary with weapons held or close at hand. He held back the swear.

It would be simple enough to sneak along the rampart and hide in the shadows, but who knew how far in the rebels were? And if they controlled other gates, then perhaps he'd have to climb those too.

But he had no choice. The only way was forward and the Alakus—and all the wealth they could lavish on their loyal protectors. For a moment Arun watched and waited to see patrols. He saw nothing, but soon heard shouts and fighting back from the square. He ignored this for a moment, assuming some sort of clash with civilians. Then he heard a scream birthed deep in darkness—a familiar voice locked forever in the pits of Arun's mind. A madman judging all the world.

He crept back to the wall-walk behind and peered over the ledge, for a moment seeing only the dim silhouette of the guards and buildings.

Then fire like a torch lighting sparked in the night, and a man sheathed in polished silver walked to the square alone. He was lit by flames as he threw maybe spears at the rebels.

Arun realized dead and dying littered the street. They looked like meat on sticks in a large, square serving tray. Maybe ten, maybe more. Men fled from the lone figure screaming 'Demon', 'Demon', towards the inner gate and more allies. Others ran to the city sprawl.

Ruka—for surely it was him—walked without hurry towards the open entrance, now cleared of rebels. He stepped over wounded and dead men, past the blue-green Feet of the Traveler, the perfect grass and bushes and trees to the first courtyard.

"I serve the King of Pyu," he growled to the new and larger group of men before him, his voice deep and dramatic. He reached out an empty, metal fist, flames filled the air, and suddenly he held a sword. "Run," he said, "and live."

The night stilled and Arun blinked, unsure of what he saw—unsure even of his own eyes and perhaps his mind. Seventy, perhaps eighty men stood against one, and the one threatened them with death.

For just a moment it seemed almost possible they would turn and run away, as if they shared the same sense of dread as Arun, and the pit-fighters, and the gamblers. But they stood.

They looked to each other and shook off the strangeness, forming into sloppy angled lines, with the runners from outside hiding well behind their fellows.

Ruka snarled and stomped and clanged his sword against his shield, as if pleased.

"Come and die, then. Who is first?"

Certainly not the runners. These shook their heads and backed away even as the others advanced, hands trembling on their weapons, further and further away.

Arun felt enthralled, knowing he must be watching Ruka's mad death—that the only possible outcome was fifty Trung rebels dragging the giant down to the ground. Yet somehow, he didn't believe it. Even as he watched them close the distance and the giant stand, he couldn't.

Several of the runners in the back cried out and seemed to fall.

Arun's eyes whipped back and forth across the group trying to see as men cried out in alarm.

Blue and silver silk and iron raced across the courtyard, even as the black shafts of arrows rained from the sky. Men came running from the closest gates and ramparts, or from hidden doors and corridors as a horn blew. These were Kings-guard—draped in Alaku colors, trampling leaves and garden, charging with swords and pole-blades high in feral screams.

Still Arun did not move, even as the rebels turned and panicked and Ruka charged as if he had known, or perhaps did not care.

Only the knowledge that Trung's assassins would be surely lurking and that Kikay might be in danger forced Arun's muscles to react. He turned towards the inner courtyard, trying to banish the madness he'd witnessed, and ran a hand over his many knives.

* * *

The 'invaders' split in half, and Ruka charged. Many simply tried to flee past him, away from Farahi's guards. Ruka cut through flimsy blades and spears, often with the same stroke that maimed the wielders.

Others tried to fight him, bouncing blows off his armor. One spear-thrust hit square against the chain-links guarding under his arm, and pain shuddered through his chest.

He jabbed the edge of his shield into the man's nose with a crunch, then moved out from the open ground to put his back to the wall. He knew with such numbers all they need do is seize him together and drag him down.

But they were confused and panicked. His strangeness, the dark, and the ambush had them trapped and dying. They were ignorant of armor and metal so hard and sharp. They thrust spears at him because it felt safer, and easier, and even as the weight and heat dripped sweat down his body he slaughtered any man who tried.

The two layers of armor was sweltering even in the relative coolness of the night. He felt like a pig covered and roasting in the ground, and hoped the fighting ended soon so he could send it all back to his Grove. If he even could.

But for now there was only battle—for Bukayag, glorious and sweet as he dominated other men and splashed their blood on the uncaring stone. He screamed and laughed and showed men the vicious price of ignorance, the cruelty of strength wielded against the weak.

At last he emerged from the wall over a ring of corpses, panting with nostrils flared to approach the king's soldiers. They stared at each other as their blades dripped with a shared enemy's blood, and some few finished the dying.

"Your city burns. Will you stand by, or put these murderers and traitors to the sword?"

The men's eyes took him in and perhaps on any other night would have been afraid, but their bloodlust was up. Their captains gestured and the men spread out into red streets, many at Ruka's side.

He knew they hated, and why. These were men of Sri Kon, and must have sat upon their king's high wall cursing, helpless with rage in the palace while they feared for friends and neighbors. Ruka looked at the bright killing moon, and knew there would be no mercy this night.

He led those who followed, his eyes finding rebels even in the deepest dark. They quickly found the loudest, wildest men, drunk on wine, detached from sense by fear and anger, lust and greed.

The kingsmen impressed even Bukayag. They cut off noses and lips, hands and genitals—they staked men to the ground and left them for their victims.

"They're yours," they would say to young sons who'd lost their fathers, or watched sisters raped. Each scene of horror left them colder.

"I will bear it," Bukayag whispered. "I will wake you when it ends."

Ruka closed his eyes and knew he shouldn't.

But he was tired of the heat, the pain, the armor—of marching through a foreign place just to kill. He went away to his Grove and slept in his mother's house, leaving his brother to butcher and stand tall as if half a man's weight in steel were nothing. Tomorrow, he knew, he'd feel every bruise and muscle stretched to tear.

Feeling guilty, for a time he helped the dead build graves. There were so many now they had to expand the fence. Ruka at first thought it should always be him—that he should give each man or woman he killed his full attention. But this feeling passed. It seemed right the dead should care for their own homes like living men, and he left them to it.

He wandered away to see others finishing the ship, reinforcing the stern, good pine tar made for proofing slathered by hand along the ribs. The sail and ropes would be next, and very complex, and they would need his help to start.

The ground of his palace was taking shape now, too, the earth dug and leveled and delved more deeply than he'd believed possible before he'd come to Pyu.

Soon they'd dig moats and criss-cross the walls and levels to disrupt tunnels and sieges like the 'Mesanites' of the continent. Ruka had read of these and other things in his books—even a giant, flat 'bow' built to launch arm-sized arrows vast distances, used in battles and in sieges to deadly effect. The world of men was just full of innovation.

Finally he walked back to his mother's house. He lit the hearth and spread out furs, and lay down with the Book of Galdra as he had so many times as a child, humming one of his mother's lullabies. He summoned perfectly the smell of her hair, the feel of her arms as she rocked him to sleep. He tried not to watch as Bukayag slid a begging rebel down the shaft of a pike.

* * *

Ruka blinked and almost yawned, as if waking from a dream. His legs were sore and trembling, his arms and back aching with strain. He looked at a stone-tile floor in confusion, then realized he was kneeling at Farahi's feet. Arun knelt beside him.

"Twice now you've spilled blood for me, Ruka, though just a humble servant in my palace. How should I reward you?"

Kikay sat at the king's side, aloof, in a chair of green, sanded rock like the 'Enlightened' feet, and a dress of scant purple silk. The hall was empty otherwise—just another plain chamber of tables, chairs and banners the king cycled through at random.

Ruka scrambled for something to say. He felt disoriented and lost, wondering how much time had passed and what exactly his brother had done. But he knew he must adapt. He accepted what was happening because he had no choice, and settled on what he truly wanted.

"I ask only for your help to return home, King Farahi."

He almost laughed as Kikay sat up, clearly thrilled. The king's face, though, dropped, subtle as it was.

"A humble request. Is my hospitality so poor?"

"No, king, but my place is with my people."

It hurt Ruka's jaw to talk. He realized his hands were blistered and bruises covered his arms and no doubt elsewhere.

Farahi breathed and looked away. "First, finish your weir. Then, if you still wish it, of course I'll send you home."

Ruka bowed his head, wondering if when he finished this task there would be another waiting, and then another, and always just 'a little more time' and 'this one last project'.

The king looked to Arun next.

"My sister says you scaled my walls and killed two assassins tonight, Master of the Ching."

The monk bowed low and said nothing.

"These were careful, dangerous men who waited for my soldiers to leave, yet you found and bested them. Most impressive." Farahi paused, his voice turning less pleasant. "Except, I understand, the monks had not yet released you."

Arun still said nothing and kept his eyes on the floor.

"What to do." The king rose, wandering back behind his chair to a table hidden from view. He lifted one of Ruka's javelins, which had apparently been gathered and piled behind him. He balanced it in his hands and pricked his finger atop the point. "Tell me, pirate. Are you afraid of dying?"

"No more than other men," Arun responded at once.

Farahi nodded and approached. He moved past and around them, bouncing the javelin's length on Arun's shoulder. He leaned and whispered, and Ruka heard it, too. "And what of my sister's death?" He held there as seconds passed. Then he jerked to a stand, arm back—and flung the spear hard at Kikay.

The monk uncoiled, hand thrust up. He snatched the steel like a fish from his people's lake, and spun on the king, ready to kill.

Ruka stood at once, his hands outstretched and ready to seize the smaller man and at least hold him. He felt a moment of fear at the thought of being struck by his own weapon. He did not know if he could take it back, or if the agile little monk would pierce his guts with his own creation.

Guards poured in from doors both real and fake, and Ruka almost sighed with relief.

"Kill me, Arun, and she'll die skinned and screaming," said the king.

Kikay sat rigid as glass on her throne, as if subdued with fear and ready to break.

Ruka watched them all, every face and detail stored away to examine later. Farahi's stone was all but impossible to pierce, as usual. But in Kikay Ruka saw deception. He had seen her once trapped in true fear, and this was not how she looked.

A ruse, he realized. *A patient, clever ruse.* His respect for the Alaku siblings grew.

Arun's grip, though, wavered. He did not see it, and did not know.

"Or serve me," said the island king, "and she'll go on safe and whole. And so will you."

The monk's eyes flared then blanked. The javelin rattled to the floor. Guards scooped it up and went to haul him away, but the king waved them off, and returned to his seat.

"You didn't tell me you made an arsenal, Ruka."

Farahi's voice was so steady, so normal, despite his momentary flirt with death. Ruka admired the man even more, though he wasn't sure what to say.

Any rebel survivors would swear 'the demon' made weapons from fire, but Farahi wouldn't listen. He would assume Ruka had stashed arms and armor in the city—forged them in a smithy somehow with his own hidden coins, or brought them from his homeland and hid them long ago. He would find some logical explanation, confined to the reality he understood.

"I like to be prepared, king."

Farahi stretched his lips in a pleasureless smile, nodding his square, symmetrical head. "I think that's more than enough excitement for today. Thank you both, now go back to your rooms." He stood and waved at his bodyguards, then left out a door that looked like a curtain.

His sister paused then followed him. Before she disappeared, she turned with a brave smile, and one last lingering look at Arun.

Ruka watched this, too—very carefully—and saw the shy flick of her eyes, the downward slant of her face.

His mother had given such looks to useful men—a gaze that promised interest, mixed with a false sort of weakness. It was vulnerability mixed with hope, innocence with guile. And though a wide sea stood between both women, the look seemed the same. *A clever queen's beautiful, terrible lie.*

The monk smiled back and bowed his head low. He did not see what Ruka saw, or perhaps, did not wish to see it. He was a fly trapped in a spider's web, and had not yet tried to move.

A push in the right moment could knock the man free, no doubt, and drive him to rage and treachery. But a more useful time would come. Ruka could wait.

28

Three months passed as Ruka built his weir.

The season changed from dry to wet; a huge moon signaled the islander's version of a spring festival, and all over Sri Kon feasting and merriment disrupted the norm. Traders from Nong Ming Tong came in clusters of huge grain ships, their wealth and sailors and merchants filling the foreigner's square of the city and bringing more abundance and cheer than Ruka could have imagined as a boy. Chief Builder Hemi whined through all of it.

'Not enough time', 'not enough men', 'too much mud, or rain, or heat', he said at the dawn of each new sun. Ruka was surprised Bukayag didn't strangle the man. In fact his brother had been oddly quiet since the rebellion. Perhaps 'sated' was the right word.

Despite the whining, their great project continued, and Hemi proved to be most useful. He'd even become rather friendly.

Every day his men dug trenches and reservoirs upstream with competence and speed. At night, before going home, they'd drink rum or beer in common halls, and just as often as not, Hemi would go with them, and never failed to invite Ruka along.

'Good for morale' said the chief of the builders. Then he'd rant for hours after a glass of something stronger than he was, and complain about his wives and his children, trade and the nobles, typically in that order.

He told Ruka that Farahi was stringing up rebels in court—that he made them point broken fingers at Trung and others for treason. He said trade and all travel to Halin was banned. The nobles banged their fists and swore loyalty publicly, then gathered and moaned because it was wine and gaming season, which was renowned on Halin, and who wanted politics and war?

All of them ignored the rules and squabbled. Young lords and princes disguised as pirates attacked coastal vessels, robbing merchants traveling East and West and even those heading to the islands. Smugglers went to Halin anyway, and all assumed things would go back to normal soon enough.

But Hemi, apparently, knew differently. Pyu's kings trained their navies like farmdogs, he said, though who knew for what side when the time came.

"War in the isles is coming," he'd promise to empty cups. "No one alive's ever seen a real war, my friend. May the Enlightened help us all."

After such proclamations of doom he'd always finish with a religious gesture—like Ruka's people and the mark of Bray—then shake his head as if at man and all his folly.

Ruka did not begrudge him his fear. He had not seen true war, either, though at least his people knew violence and hardship, so it would not be so shocking. Even in the Ascom, soft-bellied builders were never fond of war.

Day by day the weir took shape in good earth next to the Kubi. The men grew accustomed to Ruka, or at least stopped staring, and when he'd shout orders out across the mud they'd answer 'ka' as they would for Hemi.

All the builders were common men, yet had 'wives' they'd been allowed to choose. They had children to feed, masters to pay, kin to support. They were decent men with modest homes and modest vices. And to his surprise, Ruka found he liked them.

Many were good story tellers. They practiced nightly, matching and raising one another with tales of 'loose' women and gambling, silly children and stupid bureaucrats. They were not braggarts like Ruka's people, and their stories were never to build their own reputations. All listeners expected a certain humility, a certain mockery of one's own deeds and life, or else soundly thrashed them even before it ended. Ruka was astounded at the way the men spoke to each other. They laughed and insulted as a matter of course, howling with pleasure as each found new and harsher ways to point at another's flaws. Such words would bring men of ash to violence.

Despite the typical good humor, though, the mood could turn sour. The builders spoke of the 'Night of Demons'—their name for the rebellion—of dead nephews or neighbors or friends with pregnant daughters who had been 'shamed' by the rebels. Ruka knew by 'shamed' they meant 'raped', and thought compounding suffering with scorn seemed a foolish tragedy.

He listened closely to the men when they spoke of Farahi. They believed their king had summoned an army from the underworld clad in human masks to put down the doomed uprising. "He's an unholy sorcerer," said a man once, which seemed generally agreed. "At least he's ours," toasted another, and many laughed. No one blamed the guardsmen for their cruelty, and no one thought the 'Bear-Headed-Demon-Lord' that led them was Ruka.

Time went on, fast and steady.

Each night Ruka stumbled back to the palace and his room, his new 'bodyguards' in tow. Since the Night of Demons he was followed everywhere by silent men who informed him they worked for the king. Whether these were to watch him, or protect him, he wasn't sure. In either case they didn't bother him so he paid them no heed, working and drinking with Hemi and the builders, each night dropping his exhausted body onto his gaudy bed in the palace.

He met with the king only once, and then only briefly. Farahi informed him he would be very busy for the next few months and that they would renew their game when things were less hectic. His expression had been friendly, almost apologetic, but his eyes looked tired and drawn.

Ruka started noticing subtle changes around the palace. Young, female servants became the norm all around his room. All were pretty girls who glanced up shyly then looked away as he passed, their clothes thin and bodies fit. Ruka felt his brother's desire and understood—it was like Trung's dogs. Farahi dangled 'privilege' to be earned by submission. As was his way, he did it very subtly, very cleverly.

"A pleasant prison is still a prison," Bukayag growled, "a slave to pleasure still a slave."

Ruka wanted to but could not disagree. Several times he also sought Arun but couldn't find him, and hadn't since the night of their 'rewards'. The servants would look surprised then baffled when he asked.

"There's no one by that name in the palace, Master Ruka," they'd say, then dash off as if fearing some disease.

Meals were now always given in his room. He could eat in the kitchens too, but the servants would chew in silence and look at walls, shuffling off with half-full plates. The girls drew Ruka's baths with warm water on request; they swept his floors every day, washed his sheets and dumped his pots. Otherwise, they ignored him.

On the days Hemi and his workers rested Ruka wandered the city.

After the initial shock of the size and complexity lessened, he was surprised to see Sri Kon was so free of dirt, and assumed it must be the rain. Even in the 'dry' season it poured more than the Ascom, and far more heavily with each fall. Plants abandoned as weeds, full of juices and springing up like his homeland's thistles, grew even in shade near buildings, despite being trampled.

People gawked at Ruka from docks to the square, rich or poor, holy or base. His only respite came in the Alhunan temple—a gaudy thing raised from marble and clay, supported by pillars made from wood and stone and cut to resemble angry gods. All around its edges was a soft, yellow metal they called gold, which seemed to sheath even its roof-tiles and walls. Priests roamed the grounds and corridors wearing silks and jewels better suiting a princess, and made the white cloth shawl of the Galdric Order seem plain and austere.

Despite their pomp, these men smiled and welcomed Ruka without a fuss. They let him walk their temple and left him alone to peer at huge statues of fat, smiling monks in the inner circle. Some of the statues were gold, too, or at least plated. Ruka wondered what the holy halls of the Galdric Order looked like, for he'd never seen their bastions of power save for the ancient rocks at Alverel. In any case they would not be so grand, nor surrounded in such splendor, of that he was sure.

Sometimes he even knelt with the monks as they hummed. Their throats buzzed with a deep growling drone as they swayed up and down, hands together in a frozen clap. Their teachings were all peace and wisdom, balance and order, a sort of endless fate that spun like a wheel, good luck and bad turning high or low. Only the gods gave the wheel pause.

Island gods however were not great creators or wise guides, but disruptive and petty things, both jealous and cruel. The Pyu-priests blamed all terrible things on higher powers, all good on the works of men. Ruka sympathized, but disagreed.

We do both, and they do nothing, he'd thought. *You're all wasting your time.*

He found it utter arrogance to thank themselves for all their success. On the streets and beaches of paradise Ruka found complacency everywhere. Roads were plugged with too many carts going too many ways; dead dogs festered near street-side produce; the incredible coins were made with weights and textures mismatched and sloppy, faked and refused. Street-gangs owned by merchants threatened neighbors, or bribed officials, and yet were not obliterated. Orang-kaya played favorites or conspired to manage prices, ballooning city costs and ruining things for all. There were laws, but poor enforcement, and it all ran in daylight without fear.

Ruka knew if his people wasted like the citizens of Sri Kon, half would starve in one season.

Despite their great learning and access to the world they still had superstition and nonsense like his homeland. They believed in spirits and baubles and religious habits meant to ward off trouble or focus luck. Cripples and madmen were abandoned as 'cursed', left to linger in alleys and beg or steal for food like strays.

The islanders themselves were small, weak, and more sickly than Ascomi. Illness seemed to plague them constantly, but still they lingered. The least amongst them were not culled by the elements, but protected by their kin and their laws. And their women—their women birthed single-sons, not twins or triplets, with very rare exception.

With enough food and shelter, in a few generations, the men of ash would out breed them.

What the Pyu *truly* had was rain, and heat. They had beaches low and sloped as if made for shipping, and dominance of an important sea. All of this was natural, 'from the gods'—who they said hated them. Near everything they had stemmed from fair weather and fertile land, and they were ungrateful.

It was these thoughts in his mind on the night of his last rest day—perhaps a week before he and Hemi meant to release the Kubi over 'stone steps', and change river-life forever.

He'd been storming back to his room with balled fists from the city to sleep, mind lost in thought, when a red-faced messenger shouted from the street.

"Master Ruka! Here!"

The young man was armed with a long knife and wore the king's colors. He was sweat-soaked, his voice hoarse from use. "The king," he gasped, pupils flared, "the king asks for you, right now."

Ruka glanced at his ever-present bodyguards, then the anxiety in the young man's eyes, and felt a moment of fear. He wondered for a moment if he should flee, expecting the king had lost his patience, and would now demand Ruka's permanent loyalty, or offer him death.

It may also be Kikay making her move. She had never liked him, and he'd known she would not forget their boat-ride and the dead captain who could have been her. Ruka had lost control of his brother in his rage, and felt shame. But there was nothing he could do.

He took a deep breath and made his decision. If it was Kikay, then that was Ruka's 'fate', and he deserved to face it. But he would not go quietly. He would fight for his life, such as it was. If he failed then he failed, for one day he knew he would pay for all his deeds. Perhaps it was now.

He followed the guard at a jog, unsure in any case how he'd make it home without the king's blessing. In his Grove, he stood in his armory, and the dead layered him in steel.

29

The servants led Ruka through palace gates with tense guards in tow. Butlers and cleaners hid in shadows, and the air buzzed with silence. It was 'Hotu', the Pyu calendar name for a half moon, but few lanterns were lit. Ruka felt a concreteness, a stillness in things as just before blood was spilled and futures ruined—a heightened sense of now.

"This way." The same runner that found him took the first floor stairs in twos and threes.

Ruka followed recalling exits, as well as which guards were likely on duty and which hand they held their weapons with. He pictured a map of Farahi's fake rooms and tunnels to use if needed, though he hadn't seen them all. He knew the three possible shifts guarding tonight, and the faces of every man.

They jogged down empty halls in the Royal Wing, not far from where Ruka once killed assassins. The knowledge that he had nearly died in these islands several times did not escape him, and he wondered only if this would be the last.

He was finally stopped outside an unmarked door flanked by bodyguards. Ruka waited because this did not mean Farahi was inside— often the king left his elite to watch over empty rooms, and to meet him involved subterfuge and false locations. But Ruka heard voices inside.

The messenger knocked then backed away as if afraid, and Ruka gripped a sword and shield in his Grove.

Be ready brother. The walls are close so I will give you short, stabbing blades. Kill quickly and do not linger, we will need to move as we fight.

The door opened, and Ruka nearly drew something from nothing, prepared for assassins and treachery and mortal combat.

"Let him in."

Farahi's voice. It sounded tired, the words said as if in after-thought.

Ruka saw old robed physicians huddled inside over a table, picking over glass jars and bickering in quiet voices. Kikay sat rigid in a corner with neatly stacked papers on her lap untouched, eyes drifting, accusing.

Farahi knelt at the side of a bed surrounded by pails and vials. He held his concubine's hand as she lay still, her eyes closed and breathing fast, her skin pale and moist.

"She's been poisoned," he said, keeping his face turned to hers as he brushed his fingers through damp hair. "My physicians say there is nothing more to be done." His voice was calm and far away, the only sound now in a hushed room.

Ruka was no longer afraid, and ducked inside to kneel beside them. In Hali's pale skin he saw images of his mother lying in a mound of furs. He spoke softly. "Do you know how?"

The king shook his head, smiling as if it were funny.

"She was unconscious when I found her." He waved at an empty corner. "There were broken plates. She must have dropped them as she fell." He brought his eyes—with some effort—to Ruka's face. "I should prefer it if she lived."

Ruka expected something approaching threat, but was instead struck by the raw, tender, even humble look. He saw a kind of madness too in the king's eyes, a terror and rage buried beneath the surface, magma waiting for this man of stone to crack and loose his fire. Ruka knew why the palace felt like a graveyard, and why sweat shone on every face.

"My mother was an herbalist," Ruka said, knowing the danger just as well as the king's trembling physicians. "But I must try to learn the poison's ways, Farahi, and I can promise nothing."

Kikay almost snarled.

"Now your creature's a physician? If so, for all we know he poisoned her, brother. Send him away."

The king pinched his wide nose. "Out. Everyone out, except Ruka."

The physicians almost ran.

Kikay scattered papers as she stood, pretty face twisted, green-dyed nails digging into her palms.

"*Everyone* must suffer for this. *All* must fear us more than they hate, more than anything. Hali's dying because we've been too soft. How many times must I say it, brother? How many times? Let me punish them. The Orang-Kaya. Our lords. The islands. *All* of them."

Farahi's moist eyes blinked. "Not now, Kikay."

"Not now? Not *now*? If not now then when, brother? *When*?"

"Not now!" The king surged to his feet and Ruka heard servants scatter beyond the door. "Do you hate our people so much, sister? How many corpses is enough? I thought this would end. Must you take each chance to spread cruelty?"

Her eyes blazed. She came forward and faced the king square, eyes up and locked on his. Her voice hushed like Ruka's had with a knife at Priestess Kunla's groin.

"Perhaps you'll hate them, too, when your precious Hali dies."

The king's pupils flared. He balled a fist, but relaxed. Then, as if in cold decision, he struck the matron of Pyu, open-handed and hard. She hardly flinched.

"I'd die for you, brother. I'll take a few slaps."

She turned and walked tall, sandals tapping stone across the room, and closed the door behind her.

Ruka leaned over Hali's bed in silence. He felt the blood pulsing through her throat, then lifted her lids, smelled her breath, and looked in her mouth. He couldn't truly be sure what she'd been given, nor of anything.

She seemed much like old warriors on jimson weed—as if she hallucinated beyond control, trapped in a dream while her body withered.

He looked at the jars labeled with Pyu names—foreign plants and mixtures he didn't know or understand.

"She's pregnant," said the king, who sat still and distant again, "if that matters."

Ruka took a deep breath. He was digging through his mother's garden in his Grove while the dead brought grinders, water and glassware made since his time in the isles. For all he knew, it would burn up when he tried to draw it. So far he'd only tried steel and leather—sturdy tools made of sterner stuff than plants and potions.

"I'm going to attempt to wake her, Farahi."

He said it because he knew he had no choice but to try. Waking her was all he believed could be done with any likelihood. The king's face rippled with hope as he sat forward.

"Will she live?"

"I do not know. But I will open her eyes."

The dead went to work. All around him they crushed seeds and roots meant to slow and ease death, calm fevers and madmen, then mixed them with charcoal.

If Ruka was right, Hali could perhaps be soothed from her dreams. Her heart would beat slower, her breathing relax, and perhaps once woken she could drink and vomit and flush out the toxin from her gut or blood. Or perhaps her heart would simply stop.

"If you save her, Ruka, I'll give you anything you want. Anything. I swear it."

Ruka heard the tremble in the man's voice, and held back his brother's sneer. He wished he could put it away, to forget the word weakness and all urge to exploit it. Not with this good man, not his friend.

"I would try regardless," he said quietly, then stood and went to the physician's table. He made a show of mixing potions and smelling plants, but in his Grove he held the mixture in his hand and closed his eyes. He imagined how it would look in the land of the living, how it would feel grasped in warm flesh.

Heat and moisture tingled in his hand at once. Unlike weapons and armor, the vial *dripped* into being as if in the rain. It started as dew, then droplets, beading to pool in his palm without spilling as the glass appeared and filled with a murky blackness, corked with cloth, just as he'd imagined.

He did not pause to dwell on another impossible thing, instead moving to Hali's bed and lifting her chin. He oozed the dark liquid into her mouth and rubbed her throat as it clenched and swallowed.

Ruka and the king knelt there together, as if in prayer, as the young woman fought for her life.

"Tell me about your children," Ruka said, hoping the man would remember what he had.

Farahi's smile reached his glazed eyes.

"Good boys." He looked at Hali's stomach. "Tane is six now. He chases his tutors with a stick. He charms the maids for more toys, and teaches his brothers bad habits."

Ruka tried his best to smile. He imagined fatherhood and brotherhood — a life where 'extra' anything was possible, and where resisting it was a virtue.

"Rani and Manu are serious, and too much like their father. They sit and watch Tane for hours." Farahi leaned forward and held Hali's hand. "Kale..." He laughed, and his eyes welled. "Like his damn mother. Won't eat, won't sleep. He fusses and fusses till he has his way, which is always."

"Uhhhm."

Hali's head twitched, eyes fluttering then darting about the room.

Ruka blinked and saw his mother lying in her furs, calling for him with a half-frozen mouth.

"Fara-che?"

The king squeezed her hand and his face transformed, as if he had never been afraid.

"I'm here. You've been poisoned, my love. We need to know how."

She turned her head and moaned. "I don't...I had some tea, maybe, I don't know, Fara-che. My stomach."

Her anguish hardened the king's face. "Who brought it, Hali? Where were you?"

"Bring me my son." Her eyes went wide and she clutched at his arm.

For a moment Farahi froze, then the hardness dissolved, and he was up and screaming at the door for Kale and physicians.

They brought the boy wrapped and sleeping, hair longer than when Ruka saw him last. His fat had slimmed enough to show his mother's features.

The physicians flooded and purged the king's concubine as she tried to hold her son, who woke up and cried as he looked at his parents. She called his name and took him as she rest, sometimes humming a low, sweet song.

The king paced and raged and bargained with spirits and gods. He threatened his men with death if they failed. He swapped from lord to man, back and forth, holding his lover's hand or hair or the buckets as she expelled. When the chief physician said it wasn't working—that 'maybe what the barbarian did made it worse', Farahi screamed.

He threw the man to the tiles and beat him with his fists despite Hali's weak protests. It went on and on, and when he turned back, red mixed and smeared across his cut fists. He left the man unconscious on the floor. His eyes promised worse, far worse, as if this violence were but a drop in an endless sea.

"Who was it?" he demanded. Again Hali said she didn't know.

Who is to blame? Ruka sat silent and alone in his miserable empathy.

Who is to blame?

Hali's vomit soon turned to blood, and the king begged her not to die. He took the child away, banished the physicians again, and brushed her hair.

Since the beginning, Ruka had counted water-drops in his mind because knowledge was useful, and perhaps next time he could do better.

In less than a hundred more—despite the king's pleas and threats and Hali's promises she felt better—she fell asleep again, and ceased to breathe.

The king's lover died white and fetid, slick with blood, sweat, and tears. She had been alive, young and beautiful but a few hours before her death. It was a fact without comfort, or pity, or perhaps meaning. But it was the truest thing Ruka knew.

Farahi stumbled from the bed then the room as if drunk and without a word.

Ruka sat alone and looked at the corpse. He thought: *I could have killed her, and built her a grave. She could have lived with me in the land of the dead, and perhaps that is better than nothing.*

But it had not been his decision to make, and impossible to explain. He locked the image of Hali's face in his mind, thinking perhaps later he would carve a statue of her beauty to stand forever in the land of the dead. He expected this would bring the king no peace.

30

Servants shuffled against doors and walls, staring at the ground as Kikay stomped past.

She had no plan except death for the first man, woman or child to look at the red welt spreading across her cheek. Her legs took her down empty halls and stairwells, away from light, people, and especially Farahi.

She walked down into darkness and terror where three innocent girls hung naked and sweating.

"Stretch them up."

Her new master of torture tugged at ropes as Hali's maids wept.

Kikay lifted a spiked iron rod. She beat the youngest across the legs, and meant to strike once, maybe twice, but kept hitting. Then there were screams and begging and all the girls crying out so weak and pitifully.

"Stop," she grabbed the girl's thick, beautiful hair and yanked down hard. "Stop!" she screamed and pulled back to keep hitting, moving up from long legs to slim sides and arms, then the flat stomach that had never birthed a child, till the girl's toes painted with blood and the spikes shone in torchlight.

"Who did it?" Kikay shouted, panting. Only two girls were left to answer.

"Please, please my lady we don't know. We don't know! We loved Mistress Hali! *Please*!"

"And what were you doing while someone killed your *beloved* mistress?" Kikay hissed.

They cried and she almost knocked out their teeth. The oldest kept talking.

"She...was to see the king. We were warming a bath."

"And who told you that?"

"She did! She told us herself!"

Kikay snarled and threw the rod clattering across stone tile. She wiped her hands on the torturer's apron, and picked up a jagged knife meant for sawing.

"You'd best think of something useful, and quickly." She put the flat of the cool metal against her cheek and closed her eyes. When she opened them the oldest had her face scrunched in some mixture of fear and concentration.

"There was a teapot," she breathed out hard, as if she'd just realized. "We didn't make it, she never asked."

"Then how did she get it?" Kikay came forward with the blade, setting it down gently on the girl's wrist.

"I don't know. Please, please I don't know."

"You don't know much of anything, do you?"

"No, lady, please. I don't."

Kikay took the knife away and shoved it back on the spotless table. She sighed.

"Keep them here. I may free them, or I may butcher them and put their heads on stakes. We'll see." She ascended from the gloom, followed by pleas for mercy and more pathetic weeping.

Obviously, the teapot was the answer. She could go back and tell the physicians, but no doubt it didn't matter now. As usual Kikay tried to see the positive from tragedy, and at once knew Hali's death was a mixed blessing.

Yes, the woman had her uses—she could whisper words in moments a sister could not. But she clouded Farahi's judgment, and made him weak in ways he should be strong.

Kikay glanced at herself and saw blood drying in patches on her dress and her shoes. For once she didn't care. Shadowy walls and portraits of Alaku kings flew by her in dim light as her legs took over, the feel of night air against her skin all the purpose to move she needed.

Should she start the killing tonight? She couldn't decide. Should she gather up servants and guards, sending long knives in the city for Alaku enemies in their beds?

She could convince Farahi tomorrow once she had results. When she had Orang Kaya blubbering and pointing fingers at neighbors and allies he would agree with her methods as usual.

Then she was standing at a thick, hidden door made to look like shelving. She unlatched the painted metal lock and pushed through, closing it behind to shuffle in near darkness for an opening beyond. It smelled like old sweat.

"Loa, Kikay."

She no longer liked how her lover said her name—so familiar and unafraid.

She stripped off her underclothes and found him with her hands, pushing him down to the floor with her mouth on his to straddle him. He was strong, and dangerous, and she knew she could only do this because he allowed her to.

A shiver raced up her spine at the thought. She wanted her knees scraped to blood on the wood floor; she wanted nails digging paths through her skin and iron hands groping her flesh. She bit his lip hard and put his hands up her dress, reaching back to grab his crotch. She massaged till he was ready, then stripped down his pants just far enough.

She rode him and clawed at his face, choking his neck and shoving her fingers in his mouth as she thrashed and bucked against him. When the release came at last she stood without a word to lay on the small, spartan bed against the wall.

He slipped beside her in silence. Then he was spreading her legs with one iron grip on each thigh.

She'd never been so aggressive with him before—so, *honest*—never once taking off the mask of a princess who needed protection in their encounters, which were frequent and not unpleasant.

Instead she'd been sweet and gentle, acting more for him than her as she finished the seduction. In the past she had moved as he wanted, looked in his eyes and whispered and asked to be held in the night as he wanted. Perhaps she had 'made love' like Hali and Farahi.

Now though she clenched her jaw and took a fistful of his hair as her mind drifted through the names of Pyu lords whose children she would take.

She writhed against him, then reached for a half-empty wine bottle she knew would be on the nightstand, wrapping her lips around the mouth to gulp down swallows.

Her spies would know schedules and favorites, tutors and nursemaids. The children would all need to be taken at once before word spread and families hid them. But it was possible.

That Hali was unimportant made no difference. What mattered was that she was family, and by all the gods and spirits, Kikay vowed that every man and woman in Pyu, innocent or guilty, would learn the price of dead Alakus or their families.

Time had passed and she was slick with sweat and shaking. She pulled her lover off, utterly spent, and drained the wine. Mentally she went over all her agents and how many would be needed and across how many islands, knowing with such a grand scheme and risk some would fail, or disappear, and others defect. The cost to her network would be immense.

A lantern lit and Arun looked down at her face.

"What do you need?" he said. She saw there some mix between pirate and Ching master, lover and protector, victim and addict.

"I want you to kill Ruka," she said, curling herself around him again. She was surprised to see resistance in his eyes.

"Why should you want that?"

"Because he's a monster, and because he frightens me."

The pirate said nothing, gaze moving back and forth across her face. Then he reached out and seized her hair, pulling her down as he moved back on top of her.

"He *should* frighten you. So should I, Princess."

Kikay almost gasped as he took her again, harshly, violently, every thrust a slap of flesh that bounced off stone walls.

"I know what you are," he said, much later, staring into her eyes. "I want you anyway."

She said nothing but turned gentle again, drifting fingertips down the lean, fatless length of his muscled back while he rested.

"I need you," she said later, when the time was right. "I have no one else I can trust."

He smiled and stroked his fingers down her cheek, soft as a Bato breeze.

"Remember that," he whispered, picking dried blood from her hair, and moving a knife she hadn't seen from under a pillow to drop on the floor.

Her heart beat faster, and she kissed him, no longer sure if it was for him, or her. In truth, she didn't care.

If this dangerous man killed Ruka—if he stalked the shadows of the palace and obeyed her, becoming her eyes and knife and iron fist that made men vanish and fear, or butchered children on her word— well, she'd be whatever he pleased. Nevermind that she liked it.

31

Farahi stumbled from the bedroom he knew he'd later have closed off forever.

So much future, he thought, *so much future gone in an instant.*

He felt it snuffed out like a candle in the last breath of a cold concubine who should have been a wife, a first wife, at his side with honor and respect. *Even in my thoughts I can't say love. Thank you for that, Father.*

The memories of the night were already haunting him, as if somehow they could override the now and his perception of the world. He had never seen so much blood except his own.

He turned and loosed the contents of his stomach at the thought, but kept walking. He wanted to see his sons and then realized he couldn't remember where they slept. He laughed, and wiped his eyes.

"What sort of father can't find his children in his own home?" he spoke to the gloom.

Farahi's children lived in the same peril he did. All their short lives they'd been trapped in the shadow of treachery, always on the move, always careful, pretending it was a game. They were innocent except for Tane. Already Tane saw through the lies and made up his own. *He'll be a better king than me*, Farahi thought, *if I live long enough to see him crowned.*

Even in his misery Farahi glanced down the corridors for danger. He saw the servants had not followed him, and he wept now that he was alone. He took deep breaths and imagined a white-sand beach and a fire.

Farahi emptied his mind, just as Ando had taught him.

He succeeded for a time but soon couldn't focus—unable to stop the knowledge that this would be the perfect time for assassins to strike. He growled and took a clay pot from its stand beside him, throwing it to shatter against the wall.

"Can I just grieve as a man for one night?" he shouted. He breathed again and closed his eyes, and remembered his lessons—lessons he knew had saved his life a hundred times, and saved him still.

"Only when you can act in the now while always thinking on the future will you be safe, Farahi. That is the way of kings," Ando had told him.

It all felt so long ago now. They'd sat dangling their feet in salt water, practicing focus and the three spheres of The Way—learning to imagine the future and all its possibility—to see the threads so clearly they felt real.

Meanwhile the old Alaku patriarch and all his sons except Farahi had been fresh corpses, lying on some island or floating in the sea, killed by enemies or pirates, or just strong waves.

Half a million Pyu had waited in stunned silence. Half a million mouths had asked 'will there be war?' as the new boy-king wept for his family—as he tried and failed not to be terrified, sitting in a place meant to make children men as his whole world watched, and plotted.

"Who can I trust?" he'd asked Ando—the boy-who-was-not-a-boy—the ancient thing Master Lo said was a spirit, or a God, and had taught wise men and Alaku kings since any could recall.

"Trust yourself, trust your own strengths," he'd said, his hand resting on Farahi's shoulder by lake Lancona as monks pretended not to watch.

But Farahi wasn't sure he *had* strengths, save perhaps for patience. His father had always preferred to call this 'cowardice'.

"A prince must act, Farahi. There are never perfect plans or perfect knowledge, but a prince must act as if it's otherwise."

Farahi hadn't agreed—not then, and not now. All his brothers liked to 'act'—to chase girls, or pick studies and tutors and officer postings like dogs with bones while Farahi waited, and watched.

'Would a man sail without direction?' he'd wanted to argue. 'What is the *purpose*?' he'd wondered, but always been too shy to ask.

"A king's task is to stay alive and have sons. And then it's to keep those sons in line. And then if there's any time left he can do something useful."

The king had been speaking to his heir, of course, who'd been shoving spoons in his rice bowl like flags as his brothers giggled and Farahi watched it all in silence.

Doing 'something useful' seemed to father the *least* important; keeping his sons in line the most.

Farahi had—rather, *used* to have—seven brothers, all of them older. All had wives and children and positions in the navy and court. Some dabbled in trade, others traveled the world as diplomats, or fought personally at sea as pirate-hunting swashbucklers like father as a youth.

And then, in a single afternoon, they were dead. All of them. Gone, like a stone in the sea.

Seven princes and their mothers and sisters fed the fish with their bodies, all perished on a single ship because they thought they ruled the world, and acted without caution.

Farahi was single back then. He was childless and deedless. He'd preferred books and lessons from old men with grand stories, or afternoons on the beach with his sisters watching children play in the waves. His father had no time for him, and even less interest.

A 'fat boy who acts like a girl' he'd once heard him say to his mother. Farahi had felt her shame through the study door. He'd pretended it didn't matter, but later slept with prostitutes to prove to himself he could, and never ate to excess again.

Then one day his father was dead. Everything that turned the world and mattered and that people said he must be or do was gone. None of it mattered, as it turned out, just as Farahi predicted. His brothers, too, were dead. His mother was dead. His sisters were dead save for the one who hated all the world.

Now Farahi staggered against the corridor wall, swearing as he stumbled over dirty clothing left in a pile. Just the thought of his sister could sometimes disturb him.

Kikay the 'Unhinged' the court had called her in whispers after their family's death. In truth, Farahi knew it wasn't so. Kikay had always hated.

She hadn't been much damaged by her family's death. She wasn't love-sick from her old, politically useful husband's passing. Even as a child her words had been venom for anyone not family. When Kikay rose to power at Farahi's side, she was finally let loose.

In the days and nights Farahi wept and wished for anything but what was thrust upon him, Kikay gave him strength. She too had been chosen by fate, at once wielding her charm and beauty and cunning to prop up her brother and help cement his rule.

Farahi had been too weak back then, and he knew he'd be dead now without her. In those first years he'd never asked how or why when her reign of terror began. Instead he'd given the nod to admirals, lenders and loyal Orang Kaya to follow her orders as if they were his own.

Where was 'control your bloodthirsty sister' in your list of kingly duties, father? Did you forget to mention that?

Farahi sighed, and kept walking. These were old problems, old concerns. Though she had made many enemies and sewn the isles with mistrust, Kikay was not to blame for this night of fear and blood. Farahi was.

Hali was dead. His love was dead. And she was dead because of him.

At last Farahi found his way to the cellars—sandaled feet stepping sure though his vision blurred with tears. He banished the guard there without meeting his eyes, descending into the cool, moist vault of wood and wine. High, curved rafters stretched out nearly beyond sight, and in the great clutter of barrels he at last felt truly alone. He slumped against one of five hundred or more of the casks, a jug in each hand, and drank.

His father had been a dangerous drunk. Farahi had seen his sour moods and foggy memory and judged him, so as a man he'd always abstained. But not tonight. And maybe never again.

He drank and drank without waiting, until he was hot and spitting, pushing his face against anything cold, tearing at his hair as he thumped his head on beveled edges.

"I'm sorry, Hali," he whispered to the dark.

He thought of their first night together—still unofficial, her with a face already lined from laughter, body taut with silks to show a figure carved from a young man's dreams. She'd agreed to dinner and nothing more. She'd come with no chaperone, smiling and serene like the day he first saw her in the palace grounds. No doubt she'd expected a night of kingly charm and further wooing while her father waited to sign the official papers—a royal concubine, with royal children!

She'd been thrilled, as most any common woman in the isles would have been thrilled. But not so her old father.

Hali's ancient patriarch was a humble merchant with a single ship. He knew he had no power, nor any influence to meddle with a king once his only daughter left his house. Hali had been the jewel of his eye, the last remnant of a wife died in birthing, and all he could do to protect her from intrigue and court was to say no.

And he would have, too.

Farahi had seen it in all his visions—the different ways he'd try to convince and fail, no matter the bribe or threat. She was just one woman, of course, and so he could have done nothing and found another concubine, or been more disciplined. Instead he acted, and lost his patience, and took her honor.

Half-drunk, eager to impress, naive and still on the edge of womanhood, Hali had given in. For Farahi it was like a madness—a fall through sense with lust that had him stripping her dress off despite the weak, frightened protest. He'd undressed her right there at the dinner table.

The servants had fled in surprised panic. Until that moment, their new king was young, but stoic. He had acted prim and correctly, with three wives he slept with rarely and properly in beds in one position said the best for making children. The servants had known only a king who did not drink or gamble or fondle serving girls or nobleman's daughters—not a man who took commoners without consent.

But that night he had. He'd moved in and kissed her when she'd said he was handsome, sweeping aside a dozen dishes to crash on the floor, throwing her on the table as he pawed at her clothes.

"Not yet," she'd begged, eyes wide, no doubt too afraid to resist a king. "Please be patient, Farahi!"

Patient. The word itself had sent him diving off the cliff. 'A prince must act' he heard his father say, that disapproving face. He'd looked to the future as Ando taught him, which seemed even easier when he'd been a younger man. He saw this beautiful woman taken away because he did nothing, because he was *patient*, and did what was right. Or maybe that was all excuse.

Maybe he had just smelled her skin and hair and saw her bare legs spread just so. Maybe he'd imagined a future where she sat naked and writhing against him, wet and eager, and couldn't look away. One day he knew she would want him, and not like his wives or the women he'd paid. Perhaps he'd mixed that future into the present, ripping aside her small-clothes and thrusting as she said 'no' but all he heard from the future was 'yes'.

He'd kept her in the palace, afterward, and her father had no choice but to agree and make it official lest she be shamed.

In his heart Farahi knew he'd raped her that night, or at least close enough. They had never spoken of it in this way, and Hali had smiled at him in the morning and stayed in his bed each night without tears. But he had done it. Yes he knew. And in so doing, he had killed her.

The simple, wise merchant who'd had the courage to deny a king would get another royal letter. It would be solemn and sealed with royal wax, with all the same decorum and honor, and it would say he'd lost his daughter for the second time.

That Farahi loved her and her son made no difference. Just as it made no difference that later, perhaps, she had loved him too.

Hali was dead because Farahi was a man, and a king; she was dead because he had acted when he should have thought, and because he had gambled. She had lived in one version of the future—a perfect future where all Farahi's plans succeeded, and saved his world from death and madness.

But now she was dead. And he wept for her, but not only her. For that greatest future died with her. Farahi wept for that, too.

* * *

Later, when the moon's light mingled with the sun, and the wine jugs lay shattered on sanded wooden boards, Farahi rose.

His mouth felt coated in dry slime, the air oppressive and thick. He felt clearer at least, himself again despite the pain. Hali's death came back like a fresh cut re-opened, but he climbed the stairs from the cellar and pushed past the bodyguards who'd found him and stood watch.

'I had some tea, Fara-che.'

Hali's maids were like her sisters. They went twice a year as guests to her family home when she'd visited her father. She spoiled them with gifts and time away and a hundred other things she shouldn't have done with servants. Farahi knew they never would have betrayed her.

He knew this almost for certain, even without his visions. But he had seen Hali die many times. Oh yes, he had seen it, and tried to prevent it—and he knew there were very few reasons for her deaths.

The many possible futures stitched together in Farahi's mind like the threads of a great quilt, smothering the man he wished he could be. It made him suspicious, perhaps even paranoid, for near every man and woman carried in their heart the capacity to betray.

He knew his wives often sat for tea and fruit in the afternoon, and frequently invited Hali. No doubt this was a gesture of peace from practical women who'd seen their husband's new-found joy. But he had never trusted them.

Farahi's wives were all political marriages. They were daughters of enemies or shaky allies he'd needed turned to solid friends, at least for awhile. And it was never his love they wanted, though they'd have taken it—it was his favor, and his influence.

He denied them both, instead keeping them hidden away and plodded out in court when needed, because all were ambitious and cunning and had to be managed. He had given each a prince, then left their beds cold and empty. He knew they all hated Hali.

His steps quickened in the hall and he willed himself to be steady.

"Follow," he hissed at guards as he passed. The men startled when they found their king near jogging, his eyes red and a growing troop of armed men gathering in his wake.

Kura—the queen and Tane's mother, would not be guilty. Her son was the heir and no king of the isles ever changed succession laws. Favor or no, love or no, she need only wait and her son would ascend. One day, with the right control of his marriages, she would be queen mother and feared by all, her respected family's rise assured.

But Cyntha and Turua were jealous, scorned, and lesser wives. They would never be true queens, nor given official positions. Their sons would not be kings unless Tane died, but Tane had come from the womb plump and squealing, eager for the breast and never sick for more than a week in his life.

Farahi stomped through the palace scattering breakfast cooks and serving girls, twenty men at least behind him with hands gripped tightly on scabbards, ready to kill but not knowing why or who.

He imagined Hali sitting with the women whose children all played and slept together. He imagined her unafraid and sipping her death while her killer watched and secretly laughed. In his mind, he watched her murderer show concern for her fluttering stomach, asking about the baby growing in her belly.

His hands clenched and his pace increased. In a single thread of the future he saw his guilty wife groggy-eyed and confused as the guards walked and buried her in a hole to wait and fear. He saw the trial, the family in shame, the side deals to save their honor as best he could and maintain peace.

Then he was at Cyntha's door. He was bursting through, dragging her from her bed screaming with his own hands tangled in her hair. Next he had Turua, and he strapped them both to chairs in a bedroom that held an empty crib.

"Please, please what's wrong!" they cried. He said nothing and let them fear. Soldiers blocked the hall outside with weapons drawn, and he closed the door.

"One or both of you killed Hali," he said, watching their faces. "Admit it now, or I swear on my sons you'll die suffering, and in terror."

They stared at him in horror. They wept at the 'news', denied, begged, assured their love and devotion and how could they kill her when they didn't even know she'd died?

Then he asked how they liked their tea.

He had his guards heat the pot in Hali's room, pouring it into deep porcelain mugs meant for water, and when he met Turua's eyes, he knew the truth.

She opened her mouth to speak but he'd crossed the room, slapping her across the face with a half-closed hand hard enough to tip her chair. Then he was straddling and crushing her, blocking out the changing futures in his mind as the daughter of a king coughed and choked and shook. She died in his grip, and her sister-wife wept like a child.

He stumbled from the room knowing it meant war with King Saefen and maybe all the Molbog, and the timing couldn't be worse. He knew he'd be sending men to die because again he acted like his father, and like Kikay—like a bloodthirsty tyrant that ebbed and flowed instead of living the laws as he made them.

He knew too he had taken a concubine he didn't need—that he'd loved her when he shouldn't, and killed for her memory though she'd have asked him not to.

His guards took the corpse and untied his innocent wife, walking her back in a daze to be locked up and held till Farahi said otherwise. They did not question him. Not anymore—not after so many years of his victories, of his survival, of his beating the odds when every man in Pyu said the Alakus were finished.

He hated himself because he would need his sister now, one more time. He would need to kill and lie so others could live, and then to become the king he should have been all along.

It was a king he would despise—hard, and ruthless, who sometimes overlooked but never forgave—who judged all, who oversaw all, who brooked no lies or violence except his own, final, but fair. When not fair, then at least victorious. It was the only version of him that could save the future.

No more love, he thought, holding back the grief. No more favor or watching the sunrise or hoping for the best. The worst was coming, Hali's death had confirmed it, and he must choose the lesser evil.

Long ago Farahi had seen two futures for his people, each with a thousand threads leading to inevitable doom.

In the first came Naran. This death for Pyu was slow, but sure, and could be made tolerable with surrender. The other was far worse. All his life it had been almost a mystery—a nightmarish fever-dream with foreign strangers and a dark sky full of ash.

But it was this dream that was coming, Farahi knew that now. Though perhaps still it could be managed.

Farahi knew in either case he must unite the isles, no matter the protest. He must make allies beyond the seas that bore his name, on the coast and further. And maybe, just maybe, he must embrace a strange genius whose life was so frightening and full of threads—whose tapestry seemed so great and wide it might wrap around the world and crush it. *Or he could be the answer. He could save the isles, and more, much more.*

No matter what Farahi did, many would now die. He had only to choose to let it be in some other man's time—to turn away from the peril and pretend he did not see, or else to face it.

Farahi saw the man he could become after Hali's death. He could grow gaunt and reclusive, letting his sister rule Sri Kon with an iron fist until the doom. But Ando had come to him, not Kikay. Fate had thrust this responsibility upon him, and his people needed him. They deserved a chance. Farahi would bear it, and so must they.

In that moment, walking through the hushed halls of his ancestor's palace, he gave up all the things that made men human. He became a king, and only that, with a purpose far beyond one man and his dreams. He watched the threads of the future changing, twisting in his mind's eye as he committed.

Tomorrow, he thought, *I will bury my joy in the earth with her beautiful corpse.*

Then he would find a way to take control of the isles—but not as all the Alakus had done before him. Not 'unofficially' and with restraint, for this was not enough.

Farahi would bind the lesser kings and city-states beneath his banner formally, imposing laws he would enforce with an iron fist until the islanders learned to curb their corruption—until they became master stewards of their beautiful isles, and worthy of their fortune. *Worthy to be judged.*

It would be cold and endless toil and death and danger. It would require a great king to face a barbarian from a frozen land, and ask to be weighed, and measured. But he would do it. And only then might the Pyu survive.

32

"Release!"

Ruka called from his position on the highest bank, and the many foremen took up the call. All along the make-shift diversions holding small lakes of the Kubi's water, the builders leapt to action.

The first teams pulled iron catches and slid wooden doors, opening spillways that would race back to the river proper. As they did, water roared and ripped chunks of earth along its path to the sea, mud-spattered men following it cheering and running to see their triumph, or perhaps disaster.

The half-pipe overflowed at first, sloshing water out and around the weir's 'steps'. But it ebbed quickly, sediment circling before the drop in spirals then flowing down as it should. Soon the Kubi moved along its original path, flowing through the construction and new walls at the lowest edges most prone to flooding.

"Bugger all the gods in their arses." Hemi put his callused hands to his red scalp, face a mix of fear and disbelief. "It's bloody working!" The men cheered, and he reached up blindly to grasp Ruka's shoulders but managed only upper back.

"Of course it is." Ruka glanced down, his face calm. Very slowly, he allowed a smile.

Hemi saw it and laughed in crescendo, finishing with a cough born no doubt from his filthy habits.

It was funny because—several times—they had almost failed.

As dry threatened to turn to wet, the waters of Pyu had risen again. The men carved out new channels, widened others, fighting a war with the tide that split every man's hands and lips with toil, all eyes on the surface as it bulged.

"Of course it is, he says!" Hemi aped and clapped his hands. "I'll be bloody rich!" he announced more loudly than he should have.

"You're already rich, Master Builder."

"Well I'll be *richer*!" Hemi's worry drained and disappeared with the unblocked river, and Ruka smiled without purpose. He was glad he hadn't let Bukayag kill the man.

Over the months of effort he'd seen Hemi was a good leader who treated his workers with care. Builders did and always would die in their jobs, but Hemi was a man who paid fairly and tried to prevent it. When he failed he often looked after widows and children, sometimes paying dowries for new husbands, or letting whole broods live in his homes. He'd even married an ex-foreman's widow because she was old and plain and had five children. He treated all as his own.

"To the South now, at least, the river shouldn't flood." Ruka looked out on the water flaring white with air as it moved through his dam. "But we should build another, smaller weir further upstream, and perhaps spillways to the North. After that..." he shrugged, then noticed the other man staring.

"You're a damned bloody madman savage, you know that?" Hemi coughed again, leaning down with his hands on his knees as if tired. He shook his head and stood. "Why don't you let me buy you a drink, first, then we can go on world-shaping. Maybe a few drinks, eh?" He raised his hand high so the men could see, shouting over the roar of the water. "Two weeks pay, boys! And tonight a drunken debauch!" His workers whooped and spread the news to the stragglers. "On the damned king!" Hemi added, laughing with genuine pleasure. Ruka nodded, but did not share it.

Now that he'd finished he would face Farahi, and the unspoken would become spoken. He would not be permitted to leave.

After Hali's death they'd not met again. Every day Ruka labored with Hemi and his men, then returned to the palace. His access to tutors at least had been restored, and he had never been denied the library, so each night he spent learning as much as he could.

But Farahi was a practical man, and a powerful king, and when he saw the value of the weir he would not simply give up his new servant. Ruka would ask to leave, and Farahi would find some excuse.

'Wait till after the war' seemed most likely, since from dawn till evening every person on the island seemed to rise and whisper of its coming.

'Farahi killed his wife, another king's daughter, with his bare hands!' they now said, 'and he killed his concubine too!' they agreed, for some 'unholy ritual'. Ruka never bothered to correct them.

It seemed now the 'Molbog' were angry and breaking treaties and ignoring court summons like the Trung. 'Pirates' were attacking Sri Kon's merchants, or kidnapping or murdering, or poisoning their wells. All the islands suffered.

Trung, it seemed, had many allies who hated Alaku dominance. Hemi even whispered of a 'Triumvirate'—a sharing of power between three minor kings, though none seemed to agree on who the third was.

In any case it seemed Farahi was losing control. Even the builders sometimes muttered in their cups that maybe a Trung should be king after all—that maybe a 'kinslaying demon-summoner' angered the gods and would bring Pyu to ruin in the end.

Ruka refrained from pointing out, if bitter war truly came, it would be they and their sons first drafted.

* * *

That night in a worker's pub Ruka drank three rums for each of Hemi's. As usual he half-sat, half-leaned so the cheap chair wouldn't snap beneath his weight. He threw back cups with two fingers, ignoring stares from locals who weren't builders, and the smells of so many half-naked, sweaty bodies.

"My wives will kill me before Trung's army, wait and see."

Hemi smoked like a winter chimney when he drank, thick scoops of tobacco wrapped in paper staining his fingers yellow. He did most of the talking, too.

"Let's move to the continent! Ha!" He made a face and raised the pitch of his voice to a mocking, whiny squeal, then slid his elbows across the wet table. "Women, Ruka," he raised a finger to help drive home his wisdom, "women are like children, my friend. Everything is urgent. Everything is now."

Ruka nodded and threw back another cup from his collection. He thought of his mother suffering for years, of her trek across a frozen wasteland alone except for an infant, all to protect the future at the price of her own life and happiness.

He pointed at the door which meant he had to piss, then stood and made his way in a zigzag, trying not to crush anyone.

He weaved through the alley, night air cool and pleasant against his skin after the stuffy pub. He was dressed like the islanders now, wearing only shorts and sandals and sometimes a silk shirt to block the sun, but not tonight. He tromped through dirty sand and braced his shoulder against a tree that grew huge fruits all year.

Would it live in the Ascom, he wondered? Or would the winter choke its life like so many other things?

They weren't far from the beach here. He looked out at the waters of paradise, wondering if perhaps he should just stay at Farahi's side for a time. Ruka was a young man, and he had time. He could regain the king's trust and attention with the weir, perhaps return to their games and conversation.

The thought threatened to wake Bukayag. It seemed a great deal like acceptance, and could lead to the worst kind of betrayal. His mother had not taken the easy road. She had given all, just like her ancestors and theirs. And for all his flaws, or whatever he might wish, Ruka was the only man in all the world who knew the truth of the Vishan. It made him responsible.

Remember us, they whispered from the grave—brave men and women he would not exist without—survivors fleeing conquerors to a foreign sea and a frozen hell.

Ruka looked at his missing toe and finger and wondered what else must he lose for his mother's purpose. What else must he suffer, and sacrifice, and why must he alone bear the burden of history?

He blinked and felt a tingle on his neck. His body's vision swam from the rum, but in his Grove he was sober and scrambled for a weapon. He flexed his legs and torso and coiled to strike, feeling the air disturbed as a knife flew past his shoulder, sinking into the tree.

"You're dead," said a quiet voice from the shadows.

Ruka looked at the length and edge of the blade and *greatly* doubted that. But he smiled.

"Loa, pirate." He turned slowly, thinking perhaps in truth it would be wise to kill the dangerous man. "How is your princess?"

Arun snorted. He wore his black silks, though his face was uncovered. Knife-handles poked from his hip.

"I owed you a life, my friend, consider it paid. Kikay wanted your head."

Ruka sighed, not surprised, exactly. "You know what she is, pirate?"

"No different than you or I, savage."

Bukayag bristled at being compared to *anything*, but Ruka dismissed this as arrogance. Anyway, he knew it was wrong. He stepped them forward and crooked their neck. "No, not like us, pirate. We can be monsters. But your princess has no choice."

The ex-monk's eyes narrowed. He stepped away and almost growled. "What do you know? Don't speak of her."

Ruka smiled at the tone—for it rung hollow, and desperate.

"I know many things I shouldn't. I know Farahi would never harm her, and that they deceive you. I know she loves only him in all the world, and that you're just her *pet*." He spit the last word, and the monk's face twisted but his eyes revealed the truth.

"I take what I want from her."

"Is that why you freed me, pirate?" Ruka stepped forward again, or maybe Bukayag did. "All your efforts to seduce a princess? To be her toy? Is that the end of your ambitions?"

His words pierced his own chest, ringing in his ears. *Is this place the end of mine?*

"No."

Arun's voice sounded hollow now, his protest so familiar.

Ruka breathed and stretched his mind out to the future, seeing his meeting with Farahi, then his wild and bloody escape from Pyu. He would steal a ship and cut a path through the sea to freedom, that was clear enough. But there was far more. He had a new legend to spin, a land of ash to conquer or maybe unite, and then the isles…

"Join me," he said, watching close as he spoke, noting every line and sparkle and twist of the shadow's face. "Join me, pirate, and one day you will have Kikay in your power. And then anything else you wish, because one day, you'll be a great lord. Perhaps even a king."

The monk stared into Ruka's eyes, a small twitch like a fish trying to slip its hook. Ruka saw the limitless greed, untempered by reality, and he knew he could own this man without the torture once required of Egil. Arun was a man of vision.

No doubt he would make his own plans and try to twist things to his benefit. This was to be expected. He could have no conception, no inkling of the future and the tides of change to come.

"How." The ex-master of the Ching asked as if only curious—as if he pretended not to believe, and not to care.

Ruka smiled.

He told him of his people, at least in part—of great warriors across the sea, ready to flood across weaker peoples and make their claim. He told him of fat-bellied kidnappers in a house on Trung's island who would be needed first.

"Help me escape, pirate, as you once did in Trung's dungeon. I will raise an army of monsters in my homeland, and together, we will change this place forever."

33

Ruka knelt before Farahi for what he hoped was the last time. They were in his huge official audience hall, the same room used to hold court. Blue carpet stretched in a line from doorway to throne; pillars made from an almost clear but opaque stone dotted the path on both sides, and Ruka waited to the king's left to be called.

Hemi knelt beside him. Kikay sat at Farahi's right, as usual, both siblings in full royal panoply of Enlightened blues and greens and Alaku silver. The surviving wives were nowhere to be seen.

Many guests sat in the wings beyond on high-backed benches with plush cushions. These would be lesser lords, Farahi's officials, Orang Kaya and their broods.

Servants had given Ruka clothes to wear—expensive silks in Alaku colors, stitched with circular patterns marking him as a vassal of the throne. They were huge and fit him correctly.

His guards had escorted him here from the palace, and before he'd entered he'd been taught how to behave: *Bow once to the king, and once to the sister. Wait until called. Keep your eyes on the floor.*

First he'd waited outside the hall by the door for his summons, unsure of what would happen, but expecting a small reward and a new position along with polite imprisonment. As he stood watching from the side entrance, one of Farahi's messengers had approached and whispered in his ear.

"The king offers you a place in court," he said. "You may take land and an estate, Pyu brides and concubines. You would be given a generous income, as well as time and resources to pursue your own projects, and weekly meetings with the king. Do you accept?"

This had been far more generous than Ruka expected. He'd nearly asked what the terms of refusal were, but of course, he knew very well. *A man should always have a choice,* he'd thought wryly. Instead he nodded.

"Thank the king for his offer. Of course I accept."

The servant nodded and bowed low, looking very pleased to give his lord good news.

Then Ruka and other servants or guests were summoned inside, and now he knelt in the courtroom. Other men were being honored, too.

Red-faced youths accepted praise and kiss-cheeks from Kikay, then promotions and metallic amulets from the king. Grey-haired men with straight backs and perfect bows added more prizes to their thickly covered coats. All were called 'Pirate-hunters', but Ruka expected they were really 'winners of skirmishes against enemy fleets'.

It all took forever. Ruka worked in his Grove as the islanders displayed their pomp and ceremony, rich food and drink served through the aisles as fire-dancers and musicians entertained.

"And now, for the great minds of wood and stone." Farahi raised his voice and smiled. He beckoned Ruka and Hemi closer to the carpet. "Chief Builder Hemi of the Karim, and his foreign protege—welcome, our masters of the Kubi!"

The crowd clapped politely, staring and whispering as Ruka rose. They would all know of him now, of course, working openly as he had. But he supposed it was something else entirely to see him.

The few steps from his waiting position to the front felt long, and uncomfortable, and the silk swished around him like a woman's dress. He bowed as instructed, then dipped to his knees before the king officially. He glanced up enough to see Hemi giving a friendly grin.

"How to reward such audacious men?" The king looked about the room as if an answer were forthcoming.

"We are humble servants," said Hemi, eyes turned down to the tiles, "no reward is necessary."

Farahi ignored this and waved a hand at servants waiting by his dais. "For the Master—new trade to hold in trust and tax for the crown."

An older butler scooted forth to offer what Ruka assumed were deeds to some kind of shipping route. The audience clapped without enthusiasm, and Hemi bowed and accepted.

"To the apprentice and foreigner," here the king paused. Silence dragged until Ruka looked up to meet his eyes, and there was a sly curve on Farahi's lips. Ruka recognized it, for he had seen it often—the last gesture before a clever Chahen strategy crushed him, and ended their game. "To our friend, and ally—our guest from the sea who loves and misses his people." The king's eyes shone and Ruka was surprised to see maybe real emotion. "To you," said the king, "I give a ship, a crew, and this silver. Go back to your home with my blessing, and my eternal friendship. May you return to us one day soon."

Two guards staggered across the dais with a large, wooden chest. One opened the lid, and the crowd gasped. Ruka couldn't tell if Hemi or Kikay's eyes were wider. He looked at the unquestionably large sum, and his mind raced.

Here in the isles, it was most common for a man to be paid in gold, not silver. But Ruka's people did not. They had no gold in the Ascom, Ruka had told him this. He believed the king was sending a message. He was paying in coin that could be spent in the land of ash. He wanted mercenaries.

For a moment Ruka still did not understand the deception. Farahi could have voiced this openly and in private. Why show it in court and make a different offer first before he entered? In fact why not send a delegation to the Ascom himself, an 'escort' with Ruka to translate?

He looked at the king's sad smile and saw no answers, his mind racing and trying to understand the clever island's king angled mind. He glanced at the far more open Kikay and saw a swelling rage, and began to understand.

The unofficial spymaster of Sri Kon had eyes and ears everywhere. In the sibling's quarrels, no doubt Ruka played a prominent role.

All at once, the many moons of feeling abandoned began to make sense. Farahi had been ignoring him deliberately to appease her.

But now—now he honored Ruka publicly to show his true intentions. With the ship and the silver, he was asking for help with his enemies, paying entirely in advance, and letting Ruka sail away. He relied only on their friendship.

It seemed mad. Foolish, even. But Farahi was not a fool.

The future twisted and pulled at its chains in Ruka's mind. The death and blood he thought was required turned to air, and vanished. Farahi would let him return in peace, and with a fortune. He had never lied. His words were not empty.

Perhaps his offers of help were not empty, either. Perhaps with the great king's power, new crops from around the world could be shipped and tested in Ascomi soil, growing further South. Perhaps they could even import soil and change or improve the land itself. Ruka saw wells and aqueducts sloshing clean water beneath the earth so they would not freeze; he saw flat-stone roads and thick-walled houses filled with healthy families. He saw children, even boys, learning to read Pyu books without fear. Tears fell from his eyes in his Grove.

With Farahi's help, it was possible. Island wealth and builders could ship across the sea to help his people. The island king was a trader in his heart, and the men and women of ash could trade. Ascomi warriors could help secure the Alaku throne. They would sell him iron, salt and lumber in return for food and supplies. It would not be enough—not the ending the Vishan deserved, but it would be a start.

He's a good man, brother. A powerful man. If he helps us, if he truly helps, we need not soak his world in blood.

"Thank you, great king. I..." Ruka fought emotion even in the land of the living. "I promise...my people will not forget your kindness. I will not forget." At this he held Farahi's eyes, and found the smile was not forced.

In his Grove he walked to the now-constructed copy of Master Lo's training room. He had traced the runes exactly, to interpret and finish the history of his people. He re-read it now—the doomed Vishan, chased and butchered by usurpers.

Remember us, they said, but only that. They did not say avenge. They did not say destroy the children of our conquerors. *Remember us.*

The dead mouthed these words in silence, and Ruka heard the same plea from the frozen face of Beyla's statue, and perhaps, in the memory of all living things.

He rose and seized the chest to lift it with one arm as the two guards goggled. He winked at Hemi, and looked to Kikay to see the hate filling her eyes. He thought of Kunla, or the mothers of Hulbron, Lawspeaker Bodil or the family that rejected him. None of that mattered now.

In the end, words and feelings misted like boiling water, and there was still only deed. Only action.

He bowed low to Farahi, and turned from the hall without applause. At the exit he found a new servant waiting at the door in plain clothes.

"A ship is already prepared, Master Ruka. The crew and captain are assembled. You are to go at once."

Ruka shook his head as he thought of Farahi and their games. The king acted in haste because he was afraid Kikay would try to kill Ruka before he left. He acted now so it would be too late, a step ahead of Kikay, and a step ahead of Ruka. The clever bastard.

Together they walked through the palace halls, through the courtyard without stopping even at Ruka's room, then to a wagon pulled by guards in the king's colors.

He glanced at the sky and the swaying palm trees, seeing the winds were up and even mostly in the proper direction. He almost laughed. *Does the man outwit the heavens, too?*

The beach crashed with choppy waves, grey sky above it clouding the sun. Many boats were moored along the coast waiting for fairer weather, but the fishermen paid no heed, bouncing along in their tiny vessels.

Farahi's servant took them to a mid-sized trading ship with two sails. Ruka knew the islanders called it a 'junk', which did not indicate its quality, but rather once meant 'cat'. He supposed it implied 'sleek', and 'quick', but in any case the hull was almost u-shaped, the sails rigged for battens that extended the bat-wing-like sails forward beyond the mast. The design was meant for open sea, and heavy winds. It was sturdy and strong. It was perfect.

A young, muscled sailor stood at attention near the dock.

"We're provisioned for a month, sir. We leave on your command." He unfurled a parchment bound in leather casing, using his body to shield the wind. It listed the ten crew's ranks and names, ship contents and specifications.

"Captain Kwal, is it?"

Ruka inspected the scroll, then the man, and liked what he saw.

"Yes, sir."

"Good. Take us South, Captain. One stop will be required. It will not be simple."

The man bowed with a practiced ease, but grimaced as he rose. "There is one additional man on board, sir. A Master Eka—sent by the king 'off the books'."

Ruka nodded, sighed. He readied a knife in his Grove. Perhaps Kikay still somehow managed to get one of her own men on board—no doubt to kill Ruka at the earliest opportunity. He would have to be dealt with.

Ruka dropped the chest, and two sailors sagged as they took it. Then he stepped across the gangplank and onto the deck.

"He's in the cabin," called Kwal, a jerk of his head at the only shelter not inside the hull. Then he barked out orders at the men with a loud, sergeant's voice to untie and raise the sails.

Ruka stopped and readied himself for violence with his hand on the door's latch. In a way, he supposed, it would be almost comical to die now. He would have been so close to freedom, and a new life, and so much knowledge and purpose vanished in an instant.

Bukayag nearly growled at the thought, and they walked in together.

"Loa, savage."

Ruka stared for a moment and scoffed. 'Eka' sat at a small table holding a bottle of rum. He faced the door sitting in one of two chairs, the only things in the room except a cot.

"Loa, pirate."

Ruka took a seat in a chair made with extra legs and a long back, clearly made just for him. His 'friend' and maybe enemy now looked exactly like a sailor. His pants and shirt were tied off at the knees and elbows, his feet bare, his lean, hairless, muscle-plated chest uncovered.

"And whom do you serve today, Master 'Eka'?"

Arun swigged the bottle, then offered it. "Myself, as always. And the highest bidder, which currently is you. Or maybe Farahi. Honestly it's hard to keep track."

Ruka met the man's eyes and probed for weakness or deception and found both, and neither. He grinned, deciding in the end this was the best and most honest answer he could hope for.

"Good enough." He threw back the bottle but plugged it with his tongue. Arun laughed.

"You saw me drink, my friend, it can't be poisoned."

"You might be tolerant," Ruka watched him, still ready to kill. "Or you might have the antidote, or some other Ching deception. I shouldn't even have touched the bottle." He handed it back.

"More rum for me," Arun seized and drank deep as he wiggled his brow. "This will be a long trip if you don't trust me, savage."

Ruka nodded. On that they agreed. It might be a long trip regardless.

"Trust is earned, pirate. It requires deed. We sail to Halin. There you will swim in darkness, find and take a man who once imprisoned me, and return in darkness. He must be alive. I expect he will have guards. Do that, and I will trust you."

Arun cleared his throat and took another swallow, then reached into his pants pocket. The motion nearly sent Bukayag crashing over the table to crush his skull, but the pirate removed only paper and tobacco.

"As you say." The pirate rolled his cigar and spoke without looking up.

"Trust. And one Ascomi bride, when the times comes." He grinned with one corner of his mouth. "Unless they all look like you, of course." He finished rolling and grimaced as he seemed to realize he couldn't light it.

Ruka blinked at the request, and nearly laughed out loud. He considered explaining that men did not *barter* for women in his homeland—that only women chose their mates, and even then, it was complex. But he imagined a strong, Southron Matron crushing Arun between her thighs, and smiled.

"Very well. My trust, and one Ascomi bride. Agreed."

He reached out and slowly took Arun's cigar, then from his Grove drew the blue-steel knife he'd readied.

Sparks hissed from the air and lit the paper as he put one end to his lips and drew smoke. He put both down on the table and watched the pirate's widened eyes.

"In future, 'Eka', I would remember who you bargain with. And I would be very careful."

With this he rose, noting his 'friend' completely stilled, his eyes and face smooth as the Lancona. For just a moment Ruka smiled with his teeth and let the monk see his brother's eyes—the wild, mad thing who remembered every hit from every palm in a Batonian temple—and wanted only to draw a Grove-sword and scream blood and murder and rip the monk to shreds.

Then he blinked and re-took control, and became a man again. He opened the door, intending to inspect the ship, and spoke over his shoulder.

"Keep the blade. It will remind you."

34

Two days on the sea

Ruka stood in the moonlight and a light rain as the deck of his Pyu ship swayed. His former captor shivered on hands and knees before him, panting and soaked.

"Loa, Nipples."

Captain Kwal and his men held fishing spears in a half-ring around them. Arun stripped off his own wet clothes and sagged in exhaustion. All smiled at Ruka's name choice.

"What...who..." The fat, squat pirate finally looked up and froze. "I...I..." His skin went as white as Ruka's as the blood drained.

"You won't be harmed," Ruka told him, and meant it. "But I have questions."

"I...I...yes," Nipples shivered and rose up to hug himself, prompting a few spear-thrusts near his face.

Ruka was impressed Arun found him at all. He was equally impressed he'd managed to get him out and put him on a stolen fishing boat—as impressed as he'd been when the islanders got them to Halin at all, and in darkness. Both things were tempting to attribute to luck. And perhaps partially that was true. But it was also exceptional men.

The impressive Captain Kwal had laid out a detailed map of Pyu waters and guessed at Trung patrols. He had kept near rocks and reefs, skirting them even in darkness with men lined up on the edges calling out depths. Kwal himself would tangle up in ropes for safety and hang off the prow, one hand raised to warn the man steering. Ruka had expected to provide assistance with his night-piercing eyes, but they hadn't needed him.

"Get us moving," said the young captain to his men. "Trung's scouts are still on patrol."

The sailors raised anchor with blinding speed, sliding to posts across the slick wood, clambering up ropes and masts. The islanders seemed born for a life at sea.

They moved across the swaying deck and clung to their ropes like monkeys swinging from vines, displaying an almost reckless skill Ruka would not have believed if he had not seen. With a growing pride, he knew they would make the Ascomi worthy allies. Both peoples had their flaws, their room for improvement. But together, perhaps, the sons and great-grandsons of the isles would be braver, stronger— both masters of land and sea.

Ruka dragged 'Nipples' out of the rain and into his cabin. He asked nicely where the pirate's men found him drifting those many months ago. The answers weren't helpful.

"Please, please, why would I lie? They found your raft on the shore. The tide blew you in, please!"

"He doesn't know anything." Bukayag hissed in their own tongue, hands clenching in anticipation.

Ruka reluctantly agreed, but he'd said he wouldn't harm the man, so kept his brother restrained. He busied himself over maps in his Grove on a simple rectangular table.

Kwal had what he called a 'sea-book' from Farahi—a careful series of notes on the furthest known voyages to the South of Pyu, filled with landmarks, winds, currents and tides in various seasons and seas. Added to Ruka's own experience on the journey here, it was perhaps enough. He had come in summer, though, and now returned in spring. That mattered, but the Ascom was large—if he kept straight South, he expected they would strike land. It mattered little where.

They had oars if the wind failed them, though these weren't ideal—their 'junk' sat high in the water and was made for the wind. The hull's oar-holes were small and conceived for minor efforts as needed in port.

There could also be spring storms that would rip them apart—the same storms that drowned the coast of Sri Kon in an often yearly tribute to the smallness of man. Ruka supposed they could land on some other island and pick another season, but the sailors may have families and orders, and no interest at all in delay.

And what will I do with these men once we arrive, if we arrive?

The people of ash believed that they alone were the children of gods. How would they react to the dark-eyed and dark-skinned foreigners, and a world rich beyond comprehension, where men ruled as kings by birthright?

Ruka dragged Nipples by the armpit to the edge of his ship. The man wriggled and screamed in protest, but whether and how far the man could swim was not Ruka's concern. Without pausing, he threw him over the railing. He would make it to the dinghy, or drown.

The cold of the wind and rain on his face felt pleasant and like home, and he ignored the crew's stares.

The men of ash would see this enormous ship and panic just at the sight of it. They would not believe that the world was so vast, that they had once come from paradise, that the Vishan were islanders, that a foreign temple held runes with all their gods and symbols. Not any of it.

"We'll make them understand, brother, with the sword if we must."

Ruka sighed, and glanced at the islanders—his crew and perhaps soon his retainers, and frowned.

Only the gods knew what they would think of his dirty, ignorant people. They would see men who killed each other over scraps and words and almost anything at all—folk who lived in squalor with little wealth even amongst the great families. *Will they think us animals?*

Bukayag bared his teeth. "They will fear us, as they should."

Ruka rested his hands on the railing, looking up at the moon and knowing the day and week by Pyu gods and reckoning now before his own.

He wished he could see birds flying South, and for a moment longed for the simple days of revenge and escape as he'd fled away North.

No doubt Beyla would have known what to do, even if she was wrong.

"We have our plans," said Bukayag.

Ruka wondered if his plans were like a handful of sand, grains slipping through his fingers as soon as he squeezed. He intended a hard path of maybe blood and greatness, driven and designed by him for a people who may not want it. And what would he do if they said no?

"It makes no difference," said Bukayag. "We will do what must be done, and give those who deserve it justice." He used this last word like a slur, and Ruka knew any excuse for bloodshed would do.

I'm the only one who knows, he thought, *no one is asking for justice.*

Bukayag growled. "I know, brother. *I* know."

Ruka sighed. *We'll deal with Trung, as I promised you. I'll put him in your hands and let you rip his bones through his skin. But after that, I do not know.*

He let the cold sea spray catch his face as he leaned off the ship. He reached his hand to wipe his eyes and felt the flesh curved and wrinkled on his brow. He felt down past the lumpy cheeks to a bulging jaw, crooked teeth exposed and locked. He supposed Bukayag was smiling.

* * *

They were at the Southern edge of Halin when sails crept into sight.

"A patrol. They're coming West and fast with the wind—they've seen us, sir." Kwal stopped squinting and yelled at the men to turn South-West. "I don't know if we can outrun them, sir, we'll see." He unhooked a rack covered in tarp, exposing swords, bows and bundles of arrows.

Ruka took a deep breath and glanced at the drooping sail. The wind was low, and none of them could do much but wait.

In his Grove he gathered javelins and armor, then walked to his ship-builders and told them to pool up buckets of pine pitch. He chastised himself for not reading and learning more about Pyu naval warfare—he'd been too busy with basic principles and building his weir, and he'd only read a fifth of the books in Farahi's library. But he had his tricks. And he supposed flaming arrows were flaming arrows.

"Do what you need to, Captain. We'll fight if we must."

The intense young man nodded, but it was clear he'd rather escape.

Ruka watched and waited while Kwal and his men pulled at ropes and angled the rudder, pivoting and 'tacking' against the weak wind. The wood creaked and the square canvas stretched, soon like a huge bird battling the breeze. The silent race continued most of the morning.

"They're a coastal vessel and pumping their oars like madmen," said the captain bitterly. "They're too quick and we're too heavy with supplies, but we'll see how brave they are."

He went back to the rudder and made a head-long dash South towards what the Pyu thought was endlessness and death. He raised Sri Kon's silver flag high and watched his enemy's outline loom.

"Make ready," he said to his crew, who were sweating from the chase and fear but armed themselves in silence.

The islander's bravery and competence again stirred Ruka, as well as their devotion to their tasks. He had no wish to see such men die here before seeing new lands and mysteries. He glanced at the sun.

It was high and clear, the enemy close now to bow range. In his Grove Ruka set up targets and walked the distance measuring. He fired test arrows, but had little practice with the weapon, and decided the draw could only be so strong before the wood snapped.

"Lower the sails, and tell your men to take cover," he said. Kwal, paused, but obeyed. Arun watched it all, waiting beneath the cabin's roof smoking one of his cigars.

Ruka first stepped to the stern and brought a shield from nothing. He held it out over the water so the sparks missed the ship. He knew the crew could see but no longer cared. They would serve him in truth before the end, by choice and not by order, and in any case Farahi would know Ruka's powers soon enough.

For a time he waited at the stern, shield held high as Trung's ship approached.

By the make and outline of the enemy he knew the distance, so he turned and counted paces in his Grove. The small sail grew, then the sight of the narrow paddles wrenching their way through the sea.

Four hundred. Three fifty. Three hundred.

The dead moved a wagon along the ground while he threw javelins drenched in pitch. At two-fifty, the enemy's flaming arrows splashed and sizzled into the water. A few bounced off the hull.

"Throw the arrows off if they land, and put out fires," Ruka called, though he probably didn't need to.

Halin's ship moved closer, slowly but surely, every pull of their oars another gain on the sailing vessel.

Two hundred paces. One fifty.

The enemy's missiles were more on target now. Some bounced to burn on the deck or cargo-coverings, but Kwal and his men scrambled under shields to toss them off, dousing charred marks in buckets of sea water.

Ruka at last tensed and moved back, giving himself space to run. When he had enough room, he surged forward at a sprint, torso angled to be jerked up in the throw. He released as he struck the rail, growling with the effort, pulling a throwing-spear from nothing mid-throw.

Sparks flew but paled next to the true fire burning in flight—the weapon already soaked in fuel by the dead. Blue flames roared, dimmed by the rush of air.

Ruka jogged back to his spot without watching, and checked the distance. He angled his throw and ran again, shield still in his off hand, raising to block a batch of well-placed shots before the release.

This time he watched and saw the first steel spear plunged deep into hull, completely in flames and out of the sailor's reach. The second he put into the mast, the flames leaping up quickly into sails.

He smiled as he watched them, knowing his foes were already dead. He looked back at his men and almost called for them to huddle under their shields and simply wait.

But he looked back at the coastal scout and saw it hadn't stopped or turned. It kept coming, oars yanked through the sea to a steady drum.

Ruka looked at the ship and examined every memory of every design of island ship, seeing again that his enemy was a kind of warship, but designed for speed and ranged warfare—not for closing with an enemy.

He stared at the bow, and soon Kwal stood beside him. They breathed together. The enemy ship had an outline of wood like a cap on the front. Lines were traced around a hidden bulge, like a shell, with something else beneath. With horror Ruka realized it was a cover, a ruse—to hide the true purpose of the fast, sleek vessel. It was a giant ram.

He leapt back and yelled at the men to brace themselves, to turn, to make sail or by god do something, anything. But it was too late.

The drum stopped and the enemy crew cried out in triumph and maybe terror as they struck.

Ruka's junk shook and shattered from the rear, wood spraying and giving way to the reinforced bronze ram now revealed as the cap splintered,

He flew from his feet, senses reeling as men screamed over the crunch and groan of the wood. He lost track of up and down as the world spun, not knowing if it was him or the ships that moved. He bounced twice along the hull and crashed against the mast.

"For the king!"

He heard men yelling and hoped they meant Farahi. Iron and bronze and wood clashed as the men raced together with daggers and clubs, the sounds of their vicious fighting mixed with the roar of flame.

Stand us up, brother. We have little time. Stand up!

Pain shot through Ruka's leg and back and every movement was agony. Bukayag shook his head, and snarled. He punched the deck to rise. Ruka knew his leg was broken, and perhaps his ribs. Bukayag didn't care.

Take these.

Ruka lifted two killing swords in his Grove, and his brother took them mid-cut as he swiped at the first Trung pirate in reach. The blade took the man's arm off without slowing, and Bukayag howled with an open mouth full of blood.

Our ship is doomed, brother. We take theirs, or we'll die at sea after all.

Kwal and his men were already fighting bravely, and had handled the clash far better. They were outnumbered and shaken, but from all the rowing the enemy were no doubt exhausted.

Ruka couldn't see Arun, but if he was alive he'd be murdering his way to safety.

Clear us a path, brother. We need to put out the flames.

Bukayag roared and charged into the fray, stabbing and hurling men back as they tried to close. Trung's sailors fell back in panic just at the sight of him. He was blood-soaked and wielding swords as long as an islander's torso, roaring as he limped straight towards the enemy without fear.

To Ruka the violence seemed a blur of gore and hacked limbs. He paid attention only to his goal, and together with his brother leapt across a broken gangplank on a dangling rope.

The enemy's sails were in tatters, burnt halfway already by Ruka's fire. He saw Arun hanging off the hull, hands wrapped in cloth, straining at the burning javelin. It came out and he plunged into the sea.

Bukayag seized another man and hurled him overboard as he staggered for the mast, then rammed his fist into another's face, blood spraying on the sparse white canvas that still remained. He dropped his last sword and clutched the flaming spear lodged through solid cedar. His arms and back bulged as he strained and growled.

"Take it back, brother! It' too deep, I can't move it!" His voice was choked and desperate, a lion roaring in its cage.

Ruka felt his skin singing. He closed his eyes and thought of the first tools he'd taken to his Grove—axes and saws, wood-files and scrapers. They hadn't been real, only images in his mind from seeing them as a boy. But they had appeared. Nothing had become something, imagination made manifest.

Ruka tried to picture this one specific spear in his mind, but he couldn't focus. He smelled burning flesh and maybe it was his. He cried out in his Grove for his brother to stop, to let go, to find another way.

Please, he cried. *I can't. I've lost something Ruka the child once had. I can't bring it. I can't! Let go!*

"There is no other way," Bukayag held them fast to the burning iron. "Succeed, or watch us die."

Ruka fled further from the reality of the world, running into the woods of his Grove, away from the clearing made by the dead into an untamed wild. He fled into dense spruce that scratched his skin, wondering how far it went, too afraid in truth to try. The trees ended almost quickly, and he saw a lake he hadn't known existed. he knelt on the muddy bank and plunged his hands into the water.

Like the river Flot as a child, it burned as ice on his skin. He took sharp breaths and looked down through the water hoping to see the bottom. But it wasn't like the clear, blue beaches of Pyu that could be pierced by eyes to see a world that spun and rested below. It was Ascomi water—dark and green, hidden and cold beyond comfort or desire, required but never enjoyed.

He spasmed with a laugh as he looked at it, thinking even in his mind he was trapped. Even in his Grove the paradise of his forebears was lost forever. He shivered and wondered why he couldn't imagine warmth instead. Why hadn't he as a child pictured a perfect land of sun and plenty? Why must he look out at a lake that stretched forever into mists, near frozen and lifeless, good only for bland, bottom-dwelling fish, toothy monsters lurking in the muck and algae of a still, fetid pool?

Fish in Pyu were colorful things—a mix of blues and reds or metallics, shining in the hot sun as they twirled as if for an audience. They reflected the beauty of a beautiful land, proving just another mockery in an unfair world.

Ruka wanted the new world in the depths of his mind—not just the plants and war-forts called castles, or the tools or the clothes. He wanted a warm, Bato breeze; he wanted a hotspring steaming beside resting mountains. He wanted Girl-from-the-pit to dangle her feet with him while she tossed her hair, so he could see she was happy and in a perfect place he'd built for her.

He saw no reason it could not be so. He would bring it all back, one grain of sand at a time, and if he did then perhaps he would have made a paradise in truth. Perhaps the land of the dead required sacrifice from the living—the unmaking of the world. Imagination in reverse.

There are rules, he thought, *even in the land of the dead, there are rules.*

Ruka looked beneath the cold water and saw his javelin in his hands. He pulled it from the lake, watching it vanish in his brother's world as swift as it was called.

Bukayag wasted no time. He ran to the bronze ram still lodged in the sinking junk. "A long-spear, brother, give me something to pry."

Ruka walked in a daze to his armory and obliged, and his brother pushed it down between the hulls, levering the steel shaft between the mashed wood of the two ships.

Arun was back on board now and did the same. He met Ruka's eyes, and there was only purpose—the will to live. Ruka didn't bother considering how the man climbed up.

Kwal dove over his doomed ship's rail, hands clasping for safety. His half-dead crew fought on behind him, oblivious, keeping the ten or so remaining attackers busy.

With a scream of effort, Bukayag took another spear and used both to push off from the sinking boat. The wood creaked and fell, separation speeding the intake of water as the hull made sucking sounds.

Some of the Trung crew now noticed the shifting ground and panicked, running back to reach for ropes or leap at gangplanks. Arun turned and cut down those who made it, until the distance and height lurched from one pace to five, swaying in the waves and making all movement difficult.

Two others leapt but fell to float in the sea and wait to die. Unlike the Ching-master, they would have no chance to climb a moving hull. All at once it was over.

Bukayag released and Ruka slumped on the enemy's flat deck, feeling as if the fire still burned on his skin, as if his leg and chest were being crushed. The last of the crew were fighting on to their doom, soon to be pulled down by the sea, or their foes, to drown in bitter duels to the death.

Kwal bled from several stabs and cuts. He lay still but his chest rose and fell with life as Arun sat and threw away wet tobacco, looking unharmed but miserable.

Ruka realized his fortune of silver was gone—sinking now to bury itself in sand, ignored by the fish and crabs who had no use for it. *Just like men*, he thought, *ignorant of power beyond their understanding*.

A month's worth of supplies sunk alongside his fortune. The coastal fighter would have much less stored, no doubt—enough for patrolling near shore and perhaps only a few days at sea. They may not have new cloth for sails, nor lumber for repairs.

He lay back and groaned, staring up at the cloudless sky. He felt tempted to wallow in the teeth-grinding horror of pulsing heat in his body, or in the losses and ill-fortune and ignorance that put him here.

Instead, he laughed . Despite everything, he was still better off now then when he came North. He was much more than an Outcast with a dead mother and the loneliness of the frozen steppe. He knew more than any man or woman of ash in two thousand years, and he was still alive.

"Pirate," he managed, already focused on his Grove and sending the dead to weave new sails, "check for food and water below. We will need it."

He heard nothing but the distant sound of men in mortal struggle, and the splashing of Trung's ship in the sea. But if the dangerous shadow rose and obeyed, Ruka wouldn't have heard him anyway.

35

Kale hadn't taken more than two steps into the city before grabbing Asna's arm. Ketsra was a madhouse.

The farmer-king's city had looked like an anthill's surface from above, and now Kale saw the plugged, filthy tunnels below. He felt trapped instantly in the throngs of sweaty, bustling bodies, donkeys and oxen, dogs, carts and make-shift bazaars that stretched out and blared with competing sounds.

Osco and Asna had it worse. Compared to Kale they were almost country boys, and their eyes shot back and forth for danger, lost in the hot, stinking tide of foreign words, colors and smells. Asna held one hand on a knife, the other on Kale's shoulder, and muscled through beggars and merchants with his shoulder or hip, heedless of the damage in his wake.

They stopped only to drink. Kale spotted a man hawking water and nearly bowled through a dirty-looking boy in rags as he crossed the narrow street. Osco plucked coins from somewhere under his belt as Kale and Asna gulped down ladles of warm water.

"Yes, good, drink thirsty travelers!"

The stubbled, mostly balding vendor had dark-skinned guards beside his cart and barrel, but he smiled widely. They all wore armor too thick for the heat, holding clubs stained with old blood. Their eyes looked as wary as Asna's.

Osco paid what his eyebrows clearly thought a usurious price. He softened when he took his turn, tilting his head back to let the water coat his throat with a groan.

"When we meet with the king, ask him to send my men water."

Kale nodded, thinking 'they're my men, too,' but he said nothing. Again they picked their way through the chaos.

Despite the weather, the people here dressed with grotesque modesty compared to islanders. Men and women seemed soaked in sweat and reeked of it—their clothes were stained yellow from necklines to armpits, backs to bottoms. They wore colors and fabrics meant clearly for fashion, not comfort. The men wore thick hats with dark dyes, their shirts wrapped too heavy to breathe, shoes enclosing their feet entirely. Women at least wore brighter colors, more like the peacock-river Subanu, but equally sheathed themselves in layers, till only faces and hands showed.

It made Kale think of Li-yen and her dresses, then Lani and her immodest silks. Thinking of Lani was harder. She was a Kapule daughter, though she dressed and acted like his people now—a foreigner perhaps in her own land. Kale knew she may never see her home again, and may not even be alive.

He wondered how his father would handle King Kapule if he were in Kale's place. What would a man like Farahi do with Kale's power? Would he demand Kapule's help? Would he threaten to wipe out half the palace in a show of 'divine' strength?

Kale supposed it was an option. With his spirit's senses he found power everywhere here. It squeezed together beneath the earth, shimmered on the surface with the sunlight and the life, rhythmic and strong flowing in from the sea.

The promise beyond the clouds made him shiver—power so vast just to sense it made him sweat with a thing he hadn't felt since the day Amit died —an unreachable thing between intuition and understanding. It surged through him as he thought on all the people yet to die, the decisions and bargains yet to be made.

Who was he to make such choices? Who was he to negotiate with kings and conquer islands and claim titles? His hands trembled and he wondered if Asna could feel his fear on his shoulder.

They reached the palace near dusk. The gates were open wide but still daunting, and the silo Kale had seen from the clouds still had a small line of basket-wielding women. Guards stood or sat by tables in shade playing dice or gawking at girls, weapons leaning on fences. Kale nearly scoffed. *What's to gawk at? Their ankles?*

The trio walked through it all undisturbed. Here they became just more faces in a crowd full of travelers and tourists, merchants and bodyguards— a blend of foreigners so diverse and thick that even a Condotian mercenary strapped with iron was ignored.

Kapule's influence stretched to every port on the continent, and it seemed his court was filled by foreign officials. With Farahi's ships and laws keeping seas safe for decades, coastal-trade had become the most prosperous business in the South, with Nong Ming Tong next to Pyu at its center.

Not for the first time, Kale wished he'd listened more to his damn boring tutors. Even though they were Lani's people, he knew little enough of the Tong. Between his father and Kapule, though, he knew they managed to export more rice than anywhere in the world. Only the Enlightened knew what the drought and loss of peace had done.

They walked through the gates, then the courtyard that could have passed for a merchant-quarter, then through the inner doors flanked by men with spears. Finally they were challenged before the king's hall.

Men here were garbed in silk and linen, heavy with jewelry and surrounded by servants. Most drank tea and socialized on plush furniture, or sat at paper-filled tables arguing. The guard who challenged them looked more bored and short-tempered than concerned.

"This area is off limits. Who are you, sir?"

Kale had once felt a perhaps childish anger at not being recognized or given his due respect. But he didn't feel it now. He summoned his father's voice and tone, stood tall and proud despite the stiffness in his back.

"I am Ratama Kale Alaku, Prince, Sorcerer, and Regent of Pyu. Tell the king I bring his rains, and seek his help."

It took all his will to say this without turning red. He felt more than saw Osco's subtle eyebrow raise.

The guard before him kept well composed. He had the good sense or perhaps experience to wipe off any surprise or contempt.

"Please wait here, Prince Ratama." He motioned at a servant for refreshments, then pushed past waiting visitors with an impatient grunt, sneaking through the crack he made in the double doors.

Kale followed him with his spirit. He wanted to watch Kapule receive the message.

The viper-like bodyguard, long blade in hand, almost cut the messenger's throat as he came in unexpectedly.

"I'm sorry my lord, but an Alaku prince is outside. It is the youngest, I believe."

He then passed on Kale's message precisely without inflection, and after a pause, Kapule dismissed a heavy-set, continental Northman with a wrist-flick. He smoothed his face in concentration, arranged himself on his pillows, and waved to proceed.

"The king will see you now," said the servant on return. "But leave your bodyguards here."

Asna's hands moved noticeably on his blades, but Kale pat his shoulder.

"I'll be careful." He reached for the courage he was faking, then held out his spirit's hands and grasped the strongest threads he saw. With a gentle pull he whispered in both his friend's ears with his spirit. "I have great power here. But if I need you, I'll open the door."

The warriors blinked in surprise, but nodded.

Kale readied himself to throw Kapule's men away, but he truly hoped he wouldn't have to. He followed his escort through the still-barely-cracked double doors.

* * *

The room smelled like freshly cut wheat, or maybe flour, and Kale thought that not an accident. He looked straight at the viper's eyes as he entered, turning his head back to the shadows and staring just to throw the man off.

The guard slithered forward once spotted, hands raised as if to search Kale for weapons, or maybe just strangle him. Kale wondered if all kings had men like this ,or Farahi's 'servant' Eka at their call. *Maybe just the successful kings.*

"That won't be necessary," Kapule called from his pillow-throne. "Welcome, welcome Ratama. Always good to see a friendly face in such troubled times." He rose and spread his arms, ambling forward to seize Kale as if he were a long-lost nephew.

He even looks like a baker, now that I think of it. But he doesn't announce me, or use titles. A bad start.

"Loa, King Kapule, and thank you."

Kapule pulled back to arm's length and inspected his guest as one might a gift, or a slave.

"Not a whiff of Farahi! Ha!" He turned towards his pillow-mountain, making it half-way before looking back. "How is your father, young Alaku?"

Kale blinked.

"I...don't know, your grace. I was hoping you could tell me if my father and brothers live." *And Lani,* screamed his heart.

The king nodded, then shrugged and climbed padded satin to his seat. "I'm afraid not. The invaders chase away my scouts, and my people aren't much for Alaku waters."

The invaders. The way he'd said it—so casual, so obvious. *Then it is real, truly real, Sri Kon has been taken by foreigners.*

Kale expected this, of course. Somehow hearing Kapule say it made things more visceral, and more imminent. But he'd come here for a reason.

"I intend to drive off those invaders, my lord." He hoped it sounded more confident than it felt.

The farmer-king said nothing at first, just watching, his hand stroking a porcelain figurine of maybe a turtle by his chair. "I heard about your troubles on the road," he paused, and watched Kale's eyes. "My men say you trounced some bandit scum. My congratulations."

Kale blinked in confusion. He returned the stare and eventually understood, or at least thought he did—no doubt it was best not to *officially* have slaughtered a host of Naranians, and therefore not *officially* be the emperor's enemy. Or in Kapule's case, harboring said enemy. 'Bandit attack' seemed a wise fiction, though Kale had little patience for it.

"Ah, yes. The two thousand 'bandits' who attacked a group of heavy infantry. They were no trouble."

Kapule smiled at this, and Kale hated the trace of pride he felt. He burned the memories of the dead and dying, the flaming trees and the march of terror.

"I'm afraid these are not bandits in Pyu," said the king. He rose and walked to one of his many windows, sweat visible on his cheek in the light. "There's a whole foreign navy. My scouts say they have five hundred ships —proper ships, mind you, as built by men of the sea."

Again the king looked at Kale, whose mind blanked at the number. *Five hundred ships! From where? And who? And how did they approach or even build such a fleet and land without being noticed, or seen, or attacked?*

"It is quite possible that each ship holds a hundred men," said Kapule. "If so, they might have...say...fifty thousand?" Here he shrugged, as if to say 'a few more or less doesn't matter'. "How many soldiers do you have?"

Kale didn't answer because he couldn't understand. He was being told a fleet the size of Pyu's entire navy—the most powerful fleet in the world—had simply appeared from nowhere. That an impossible force had been gathered in secret, fed, armed, and sailed in secret, into dangerous waters known only by the islanders. It was impossible. It was a thing that would take years, decades, and untold resources. *And yet they are here.*

The king sighed and returned his gaze out the window.

"I don't doubt your courage. But, even if you had the ships, *even if* you managed to land, how would you fight such a force?"

Kale took a deep breath because he truly had no idea. He felt his fear and anger surge then fall away through despair.

But in that expectation of failure, that knowledge of having nothing to lose, he found something solid, something obvious. It was the same feeling beside Old Lo's impossible wall. It was the knowledge, perhaps, that what was needed was insane, that what it demanded was unfair. In a way, this was comforting. It meant he must cheat.

"I'll fight them with magic," Kale said at last, losing interest in the rules of etiquette or what his father might do. He waited until Kapule met his eyes. "As your ally, I want you to give my men food, water, shelter, and physicians for a week, and then enough ships and sailors to take them across to Sri Kon." He didn't wait for a response. "In return, I or whichever eldest Alaku is still alive will marry whichever daughter you please, fulfill your arrangement with my father, and your grandsons will straddle both thrones as intended."

Kapule glanced at his viper, and Kale wrapped his spirit's arms around threads of power in the air. The king's uniform of mirth strained at the jowels, drooping than snapping back in place as he forced a smile.

"Straddle both thrones? What an interesting notion. Tell me, sorcerer and regent, what if you should just die? What if you lose my ships? How then do I benefit?"

Kale knew this was reasonable, but he found he had no patience left. He whispered with his spirit in the king's ear. "*If honor and friendship are inadequate, then in payment I'll summon your rains.*" He stepped forward with his body as the king startled and spoke out loud. "If I live, I'll return each year you need me, and your crops will be assured."

"My lord?"

The viper bolted across the room to strike, perhaps unsure but seeing panic in his king and reacting.

Kale wasn't interested in a comparison of force. There was no comparison. With the smallest thread, he flung the guard back to tumble across the tiles, knife rattling away as the king's gaze followed.

"It would be much better," Kale broke the silence, "to be my friend."

He waited, knowing in his heart he would take the ships, if necessary, and sacrifice five hundred Mesanites if it meant saving hundreds of thousands of his people from misery. These foreigners would have leadership—Kale could find these and rip them apart. If he must he would float above the others with a great storm of death until they fled back to wherever they came from. He need not kill them all.

The king sweat visibly, but mastered himself. He raised a hand to calm his snake.

"I am, as I have been for years, a friend to the Alakus. Of course I will help you. I have *already* helped you."

Kale was surprised to sense no deception in the man's words.

"Helped me how?"

The Farmer-King managed a toothy grin. He came forward, slow and steady, draping an arm around Kale's shoulders with all appropriate caution.

"You have more men than you think, my young friend."

The king used his arm to urge Kale to the Southern window. It seemed it overlooked the harbor, which Kale had vaguely observed with his spirit, but didn't truly inspect.

The beach was busy, cluttered—the sand more tan than white. Warehousing and docks spread out as they did in Sri Kon, though here Kale knew the sea sloped faster. Shipping was constrained further out and bottlenecked by access to the shipyard, vessels lined up to load or offload goods, pay their fees, and tie in to spend the night. The shipping ranged from small fishing boats to huge freighters—classic hulled, oar-powered galleys, to double-sailed outriggers in the Pyu style. He saw nothing particularly out of the ordinary.

In fact he was about to ask Kapule to explain himself, then he saw them —far off down the coast, flagless, lashed together in clustered rows on smaller, older looking docks. There were Pyu warships.

He saw scouts, rammers and fire ships, even the biggest flagships meant for boarding and command. There were a hundred, maybe more, though it was hard to tell.

"They're your father's," said the king. "At least half his bloody fleet was away when the attack came, out on some damned bloody ill-timed 'training exercises', so they say. Most ended up here."

Kale felt his heart beat down to his toes. "How many men? How many marines?"

The king glared. "More like how many greedy, pot-bellied stomachs!" He shifted and scratched his own ample gut. "Ten thousand," he shrugged, "maybe more. Pigs and whoresons, the lot of them. I've been feeding them for months, *ally*, not to mention putting up with impregnated peasant girls, angry fathers, and drunken brawls. And you can be very sure my bean-counters have kept track of every grain. Every little expense!" He jabbed the air with a finger.

Kale felt suddenly sheepish about hurling the guard across the room. He resisted the urge to hug the man, and the king seemed to notice the change, and grinned.

"And, just so it's all abundantly clear, I'll give you five-thousand *more* of my best marines on my own ships, with enough food and water to keep you supplied."

The king watched as Kale tried and failed to respond, as if amused. He softened his face and squeezed with his plump arms in an almost embrace.

"Your father is a wily, black magic wielding sea-lizard, Kale. Once perhaps he was my enemy. Today he is my friend, my ally, and yes secretly perhaps my family. And if that clever cockroach is dead I'll eat my hat." He smiled encouragingly. "Now let's get you on that island with your army, and your...magic. You'll rally the city, yes? There should be local lords and many thousands ready to rise up when they see you. You'll overwhelm the bastards and show them a good island navy, neh?" He gave a fatherly back-pat. "Now, would you like to meet your men? I'm sure they'd like to see their prince."

Kale nodded, still stunned from the rising and falling through despair and hope. Half the fleet was gone, perhaps, so the chances his friends from marine training were dead were also half.

"After we see to the Mesanites," he answered, resisting the urge to send his spirit to look for his friends now. He knew the men would be scattered and hard to find and maybe somewhere in the city. And he'd need his full attention for Kapule. *Men are most vulnerable*, he heard his father say, *when they feel safe.* Even now he held onto cords of power—it was not a lesson he'd forget again.

Kapule's friendship could turn to betrayal in an instant, no matter what was said, or sworn, or done. Kale needed to watch for Naranian assassins, too, lurking in shadows, or enemies of his father who might still kill an Alaku even as their homeland burned.

And if I die, it all falls apart. Because perhaps I am the last of my kin.

With a small, thin thread, he flung open the doors to remind Kapule what he was dealing with.

"Gather my men by their ships, I'd like to address them." He stopped and waited for the king's attention. "When I'm finished, I'll summon your rains." He paused for the challenge that didn't come, and was thankful for that. "Warn your people, my lord, and tell them to watch the skies. The monsoon may not come gently."

The Tong king nodded slowly because—Kale supposed—what else could he do? Sane men didn't claim such powers before a monarch.

"If I promise them rain," said the king, "five hundred thousand men, women and children will stand waiting in the streets until it comes." His eyes hardened, boring into Kale as if digging for the moisture there. "Gods and spirits help us both if I'm lying."

Kale nodded slowly, trying not to feel as if he was mad to promise such a thing. He knew the city was already on the brink of riot and chaos, and that Kapule did all he could to prevent it. Kale wondered again at the 'Seers' imprisoned or perhaps killed somewhere beneath his feet, but burned the thought, and walked towards his men.

36

Osco watched his friend pace. It wasn't like Kale to be so...active. Usually the prince sat and crossed his long legs in that ludicrous pose, soaking in the 'energies', or whatever exactly he called 'resting', with a sort of serene intensity.

Now he covered the fat king's opulent guest-room in hurried strides, arms crossing and uncrossing, womanly eyebrows furrowed.

"You asked to see me." Osco stood at a soldier's ease, feet apart and arms behind, the waiting in silence getting too much.

"Yes, I..." Kale didn't look up, but his eyes looked glassy and far away. "Osco, I may not succeed tonight." He moved along in a straight line from the gold wash basin beside him, to the massive, curtained bed. Osco frowned.

"That would be inadvisable."

His friend scoffed but kept moving.

"Nevermind that. How would you attack a force five times your size? How would you re-take Sri Kon, if it was you?"

It is me, Osco thought. And 'I wouldn't try,' was not likely the answer the prince wanted.

"I would learn my enemy first, islander. What does he want? What are his weaknesses?"

"And how might you do that quickly?"

"I would watch him with my flying, invisible, mind-eyes, if I had them."

Kale flicked a hand.

"I will. Tomorrow. For now I need my strength and focus. What else?"

Osco sighed. "I don't know. I understand little of ships, and nothing of these invaders. You should speak to your men."

As Osco spoke he was reminded to be concerned. His infantry had never set foot on a boat. From what he understood, they were likely to be ill in the crossing, and if they had to fight some kind of naval battle they might be worse than useless.

His ignorance of his enemy frightened him. Were they real soldiers, like Mesanites? Or were they farmers and peasants given swords and told to fight?

"Perhaps you should 'meditate'. You seem agitated."

Kale glared then looked away, worry and thought lining his usually smooth face.

He'd been changing since they left Nanzu, and perhaps since he'd killed teenage assassins sent by a foreign priest. It was intense, and volatile, but a thing Osco had seen many times.

A young man's first taste of his own power was a heady potion. Mixed with crisis, freedom, love, burden and change—even for those new killers of lesser means it was a strange time, both terrible and wonderful, full of meaning yet cold and lonely. It would certainly be worse for a man with miracles. But the solution was no different, and they had no time to wait.

"Pick it up." Osco unsheathed and threw his long-sword down to clatter and scratch across the priceless floor. His friend stopped, met Osco's eyes, then stooped to obey.

Osco drew a second, shorter blade from his waist.

"You waste too much time thinking. Attack me."

Kale hesitated, and frowned. "We both know how that ends, I have no…"

"Then *die!*"

Osco rushed and slashed down at the prince's pretty face, knocking the pitiful attempt at deflection aside. He stopped the killing blow an inch from skin, and they both stood frozen, violence and quiet mixing with the fading light through the king's silk curtains.

"You could be dead now, *mighty sorcerer.*"

Osco panted from the will to stop—the urge to kill so strong since his training as a child. Kale's fading body shook with adrenaline as Osco pulled back the sword.

"You worry on tomorrow and why and what if and maybes. No man is all powerful, not even you, and one day you will feed the maggots while the rest move on." He sheathed his weapon, ramming it home to banish the violence in his arms. "If you fail, we adapt. Your worrying is pointless. You have power, great power, now. Use it while you can."

He turned and walked for the single door, banishing thoughts of his wife and wondering if his family buried her yet in a shallow grave.

If Kale dies, he thought, *it's all been for nothing.*

He nodded at Asna on his way out. The Condotian was hidden in a corner strapped with knives, one out and seemingly ready to plunge into Osco's heart. *Good,* Osco thought, *at least one other man is ready to do what's necessary. Perhaps we'll keep this damn fool boy alive.*

"And King Alaku," he stopped at the exit and looked back to see his friend still stunned, "*act*, always, even by yourself, as if you will succeed. If you die, your wrongness makes no difference."

* * *

Kale sat in one of the many colorful, embroidered chairs placed for guests. A few drops of blood leaked from the line in his neck left by Osco's sword, and Asna handed him a clean rag. He took it and stared at candle-flames, warmth trickling through him to flood his cold limbs.

"Should I fetch him back?" Asna's tone implied he meant 'for punishment', but Kale shook his head.

"No. He's mostly right." He looked up to make sure his friend was listening. "I'll be lost in my mind tonight, Asna. You'll have to protect me, and maybe carry me back to my room when its over."

The Condotian bowed his bow.

"You can trust in Asna."

Kale smiled. It seemed surprisingly true. At least so far.

He lay his head back and wished he wasn't required to consider the loyalty of his friends at every moment. Then he looked down at his plain, dirty initiate robes, and wasn't sure what to feel about himself, either.

Was he a prince? A priest? A sorcerer? He had no idea.

Whatever he was he had no interest in the gaudy decoration of kings, even if he understood their purpose. Clothes were a silent, subtle expression of power, and identity, no matter how you chose to think of them.

God only knew what Farahi would say if he saw him.

Do you believe in a foreign god now? Have you abandoned your family, your people? Have you given up your wealth and responsibility?

Farahi was not prone to excess, but then his 'show' was his bearing and his dress in court. He sat silent and far-away, robed and draped in an ancient heirloom, feeding the legend of a sorcerer-king—aloof and untouchable, all-seeing, all-knowing.

But Farahi was *not* a sorcerer. He had to convince others with tricks and mystery because they were all he had. Kale was not pretending. This thought still made his heart race—the ridiculous, impossible reality of it.

Only a year before he could never have imagined soaring through the sky, through walls, speaking to men far away, or pulling power from the heavens or the earth to crush and smite the world like a god.

In his heart he knew, or at least felt, it was too much for one person. It was too much power to have no explanation or rules except those Kale discovered himself. And what would happen if he moved those threads dripping power in a far-away sky? Would he doom one people to save another? Would someone else pay a price?

He laughed because Osco would kick his ass back to Nanzu if he heard these thoughts, but the laughter brought him no comfort. His loneliness dwarfed all comforts of friendship. It was not Osco with such power, not him who would carry the burden of things done and undone. It was Kale. Only him.

He hoped Osco was right about one thing—that guilt and humility and shame had no use. Surely lions didn't feel them, he thought. But perhaps men should have better role-models.

He rose and stripped off his robes, picking up soap shaped like fish to scrub at the dirt and blood with the water from his gold basin.

"I fetch servant," Asna said, sounding almost embarrassed.

"No," Kale looked back and smiled to assure him, then hummed a tune from his youth while he lathered, naked as the day he was born. He supposed Osco was sometimes right about power.

It meant at least he didn't have to apologize for the things he knew were right, the simple things. If somehow he lived and became king he decided he would wash his own clothes and empty his own pot, and to hell with what people thought because, after all, he could rip them apart with air.

When he was finished he wore the robe damp, knowing soon they'd all be soaked and it wouldn't matter anyway. He asked the attendant for a plain meal—rice porridge and soup, and maybe some fish, if they had some. He ate for the first time in days with an appetite and good humor, looking out his window at the lights of Ketsra, and the growing crowds of people moving to the streets.

"It's time," he said to Asna, rising and putting his hands in his cuffs like Amit had when they'd met. *I miss you, 'Master Asan',* he thought, *and I wish you could stand by me tonight.*

But his path was no longer beside old, wise scholars in a quest for truth and harmony. Instead he was flanked, then surrounded, by young warriors.

He smiled at Osco to say he wasn't angry. He wished his friend understood that he didn't judge him because he couldn't judge anyone. *I am nothing,* he thought, *and neither are you. We are all dust in the wind, and one day we will blow away and sleep in the mountains and seas.*

They walked down to the docks together, through a busy yet quiet courtyard, with hundreds of merchants staring and whispering. Mesanites in full kit cleared them a path, their hands and shields out to gently but firmly push gawking bystanders aside.

"That's him, that's the prince!"

Many pointed and strained their necks to see past the guards.

Kale smiled and bowed at the shoulders to a few, but he mostly kept moving, eager now to end the spectacle and give these people what they desperately needed. *I will be the king of small things,* he thought happily, *and it is the god of great things who will water these lands, not me.*

The moon lit their path, nearly full and a week perhaps from Matohi and a time of celebration in Sri Kon. Kale thought of his navy brothers and their debauch, drinking and eating in the Lights and Sky, then sitting with Lani and saying a goodbye that was really a beginning.

Osco would tell him to ignore such thoughts, and be fearless, Ando would tell him to burn them and live in the now. Instead he let the feeling rise up and choke his throat. If love and joy were not worthy of remembrance, then surely nothing was.

He thought too of all the other young lovers with broken hearts, the children dying from disease and starvation, his old life of comfort and wealth he hadn't earned, and the many days of happy life and beauty. He wished he could share those days with the starving, with the hopeless faces staring at him with faith in their eyes as if he could change it all.

I would, he tried to say, *I'd give it all away if it helped, but it wouldn't, and I can't.*

He felt tears down his cheeks and knew his father would be horrified. He felt Osco's confusion, and embarrassment, but more he felt the heat and threads and misery of the crowd, parting and reaching for him with half-dead children in their arms, hoping he had the power to heal, to change things, to give them salvation.

He reached past his guards to touch swelling or welted sickness, wishing he could draw it out like poison and scatter the suffering to the wind. He said nothing because his throat had tightened. He cupped cheeks and smiled, and ran his hands over old backs bent from toil. *I am just a man*, he wanted to say, but couldn't, and maybe if it would help someone to believe than what was the harm?

The walk was slow-going but sure, each pace sloped down towards the beach and a platform raised up for Kale to climb. The ten thousand survivors of Sri Kon's navy had massed up, now waiting for their prince, looking at the snaking, begging crowd of Tong in Kale's wake with wonder.

He climbed wooden steps to the raised podium, looking up to the dark gray clouds and closing his eyes as the crowd hushed in a wave.

They wanted words of comfort, or majesty, no doubt. They wanted a speech from a prophet to raise their spirits and banish their fears.

But tomorrow, the hungry would still be hungry. The weak would still fade as their families watched, and there were no words to comfort death. Kale had no answers, or reasons. He had only threads of power to pull, and gods to beg for a miracle.

He said nothing. His spirit floated up and raised its arms, squinting in the almost blinding light of the terrible, beautiful thing stretching up through the grayness, rainbow-like but tangible chords spanning the length of a thousand stars. He floated and reached, wrapping them like ropes in loops around his arms.

He breathed and imagined a calm fire on a beach with his brothers, smiling at Tane while he burned his doubts.

Please be gentle, god, whoever or whatever you are. Please help me and these people and give them life.

He leaned back in the air, and then he pulled.

The threads stretched taut like ropes connecting full sails, but nothing happened. He leaned back and reached again, this time in every direction—for the motion of the waves, the heat of the crowd, the shifting of the earth. This was a place of power, and he tied it around his body like armor.

"Move, damn you," he whispered, trying not to think of the misery and death his failure would bring—and knowing, too, that he would die before he let that happen. He felt his body stagger and hold the rail, warmth sapped all around it, the breath of the crowd growing visible in the air.

The beach began to shake. Kale's spirit roared in effort, and he could hear the spray of water, the clap of thunder. Ropes of power tied around his arms pulled back as if resisting him, as if someone or something stood far away and pulled back.

Kale knew he couldn't release—that he wouldn't, even if he could. All those gathered around him covered their ears though Kale could no longer hear. He heard only the groaning of the threads of power like rope, shifting about him, straining against his spirit.

The crowd hunched in pain and he knew they'd heard him somehow, as if perhaps his spirit had screamed in every ear.

There's more heat in the water, and in the sky, he thought, *and there's life and wind and the crowd can bear more!*

"Islander!"

Kale thought he heard Osco shouting but wasn't sure, so loud now was the rising of steam, or perhaps the spray of sea or the pounding of blood in Kale's ears. His vision pulsed with darkness but still he pulled.

Even if I kill myself and everyone around me now, many more will live. I can not stop. I will not stop.

He blinked at the thought, wondering if Farahi thought the same—perhaps this was the same reasoning if his father had used to justify murder and torture for some higher purpose he alone claimed to know.

It was a splinter in Kale's mind—a rock under a heavy shoe as he strained with all his might to keep his feet flat.

He lost his balance. His body collapsed on the rail as his spirit left the ground—as the threads whipped him forward, dragging him up, and up, faster and faster, like an octopus' tentacles pulling its victim in to swallow whole.

The clouds raced towards him, then passed him, his false eyes somehow wet with tears from the wind.

Whatever threads held his spirit to his body snapped, ripped asunder as quick and quiet as hair snipped with shears. The windows of his spirit-house slammed shut with him far, far away, terror convulsing through him as he felt caught in a riptide. He didn't even have time to scream.

37

"This is Lani, nephew. She's going to live with us in the palace. How do we welcome guests?"

Kale bowed and was supposed to touch the little girl's hand, but didn't. She looked as shy as he felt and he hid behind Kikay's skirts as he often did with strangers.

His aunt laughed and shooed him away, holding both their hands as she walked to the royal beach. She gave them buckets and straw hats and a finger waggle. "You're going to be friends, yes? Now play in the sand and be nice. I'll be over there." Then she walked to a servant and whispered and Kale blushed in the silence.

Somehow, he knew, it was only a dream, or perhaps a memory within a dream. He'd met Lani when he was six years old but couldn't remember it exactly.

She got busy right away, digging out hardened clumps and shiny stones and easing them down to the bottom of the pail. Her soft hands with their filed and lacquered nails seemed so wrong in the dirt, and he couldn't stop watching her, even then.

"What are you doing?" he tried to ask like he didn't care.

"I'm taking some home for my mommy. I bet she's never seen white sand."

He'd been silent, thinking 'what other color would sand be?', and that it would be nice to have a mom.

"That's nice," he said. She smiled.

Then he turned, startled, because Kikay was practically spitting in a servant's red face, much too close to him to be polite.

"I'm sorry, my lady," he said, "the king has ordered all your messages to be approved."

"Don't you think I know that?" She was using her angry voice—a thing he'd learned to flee from as a boy. "I want you to take it anyway, do you understand?" Her rage melted away to something like tears, her head tilting, chest rising. She stroked the young man's cheek where the spittle flew. She licked her fingers and whispered words Kale couldn't hear.

Then the sky darkened with clouds too black to be real. The tide swept up the beach like it was flowing down-hill, splashing over Lani's back in a spray of white and sound.

"Kale-che!" she screamed.

As the water dragged her she was no longer a little girl. She fell back as the water sucked away, tossing her pail in panic and scattering the stones.

"Lani!"

Kale reached but couldn't move.

In an instant, the waves tumbled her back and under the tide, wiping all trace of her except the lingering scent of vanilla, and dented sand.

Kale looked back and still saw Kikay stroking the servant's arm, laughing now and ignoring the waves.

"Help her! Please! Help us!"

But his aunt couldn't hear him over the roar of crashing water. And when he tried to move again it was only his spirit, not his body. He floated out though he hadn't intended to, rising higher and higher till the beach all but disappeared in a white swirl of cloud—up past birds and into air that misted with his breaths. The sun shimmered and vanished. The sounds of life disappeared into a cold and endless void. Kale blinked in the darkness.

This isn't real, he thought. *What was I doing? Where am I?*

He remembered bright lights, danger, and the sadness of strangers. The details hid behind an ache in his eyes that spread to his temples and scalp, pulsing like a heart trapped inside a drum.

Nishad, he heard a boy's voice whisper, *they who stay.*

Kale recognized and trusted the voice, but couldn't remember why. He squinted, trying to see something, anything in the black canvass all around him. He felt fear, because he knew now that he had 'gone', or was 'going'. He knew he didn't want to.

Eyes twitched in the corners of his vision, and he spun to see them clearly but lost them. Shadows emerged in man-sized shapes, somehow darker than the absence of light. He could move here with his spirit and fled them. But he did not know where to go.

Where is my body and my spirit-house and my windows?

He flew blindly, terrified, hoping only to out-run whatever it was he could see or feel lurking in the void. The creatures whispered and hissed and screamed, their inhuman voices without meaning as they reached for his feet, brushing his skin with what must have been claws.

Their touch was fire. Kale flew faster, he reached out for threads of power but found nothing. He scanned in every direction, feeling no up or down in this nightmarish world. But far below him, he saw a light. It looked faint and blurry, but he knew the darkness was death and he flew on without hesitation.

As he neared it, he remembered: *I was pulling at threads, that's what I was doing; I was using my magic, and I was surrounded by people.*

The 'air' he crossed numbed his face and hands, and a pair of shadow's claws raked his back and neck. It was hot, sharp, the contrast to the wind making him feel like he burned and froze at once. But he couldn't scream.

He thought back to his navy brothers—swimming past pain and reason and fear to win a distance-race. He remembered ducking waves and pulling his heavy body one arm at a time while all the others fell away. He thought of riding the wind and flying to Ketsra, alone and free except for winged-things who couldn't see or harm him.

It wasn't only his life he fought to save, somehow he knew that—it was a hundred-thousand lives waiting, counting on him.

The light grew wide and clear, now encircled by rings of greens and blues and greys. Kale hurled himself without slowing. More shadows tried to catch him, surround him, and he didn't care what this place was or where, knowing only that life was better than death.

He stopped 'flying', and fell, dropping through cool mist with half-closed eyes, wanting only to curl up and weep at the pain coursing through him. But the mist ended. He saw good, green earth but felt helpless to slow his fall. He crashed head-long into mossy dirt, sinking into it as if he were a stone thrown by some angry god.

His head throbbed, his face thawed but tingling, his skin on fire just at the touch of his clothes. But he was alive. The fall seemed not even to truly harm him. He crawled out from the crater he'd made, moving pull by pull to a cold, dark place surrounded by huge, blurry trees.

"Hello," spoke a deep, pleasant voice.

Kale twisted for the source but found he could hardly move. He groaned, which he'd intended to be a greeting. He tried again.

"Help."

His sight swam, dull as it had been when he first 'reached' out with his senses in Nanzu. Then he was lifted off the ground in strong arms. He felt the coolness of rain on his skin and wondered when it started, feeling somehow the rain was important.

"You're safe now," said the voice, "I'll take you to my mother's house."

Kale bobbed his head enough to see his savior. It was a giant with pale skin, whose yellow eyes shone in the dark. These stared down at him, not with cruelty, nor with kindness, as if he simply observed.

"I've never had a guest," said the giant, sounding pleased. "But you are most welcome here."

The sounds echoed, and Kale lost even the strength to hold up his eyelids. As sleep or unconsciousness took him, he looked up at a jagged-tooth smile and a distorted face. The bright eyes faded like lighthouses on some distant shore, and Kale thought he still saw shadows lurking at the edges of his vision. But he could do no more. He shivered in the cold, and closed his eyes.

Part II - Ask the Trung

38

Ruka brought venison from his Grove, but it arrived black and stuffed with dead maggots. He threw it overboard with the equally undrinkable Grove-water before the other men saw, wondering why it was so.

In the past two days they'd nearly finished all meager drops and scrapings left by the former crew, their barrels moldy and poorly kept, rat corpses kicked away into corners. They must have just been returning home.

Unless it rained soon, and Arun managed to fish, other worries need not be considered. All three of them would die of thirst, or hunger.

But they had other problems. Their new ship's hull was damaged. It was built for coastal skirmishes, not weeks or months in open sea. Arun was the only one healthy enough to search, to set sails, to turn the rudder and make repairs. Kwal at least gave instruction sitting or lying down, still pale from pain and blood loss. Ruka tended their wounds. He also built and salvaged missing supplies from his Grove.

The other men watched this but neither said a word. Ruka laid out sail-cloth and frame on the deck from nothing, sparks and steam rising from his outstretched hands. He passed Arun steel hammers and nails and silk rope from his curled fists as heat rolled from his hands in waves.

The act of passing was painful to his wounded body. Indeed holding or touching anything was torture. But Bukayag took it.

Ruka brought herb poultice, too, and rubbed the clumped, stinking mixtures on Kwal's wounds before his own with the backs of his hands. "It will prevent corruption," he said. The man nodded without complaint or question.

The first evening he set his own leg and braced it with wood as the others pretended not to stare.

"Do you need help?" Arun asked only once, very quietly.

Ruka shook his head as he popped the bone into place and tied it tight without a sound. Bukayag took that, too.

"What will we do for supplies?" his fledgling servants grumbled as morning came on the second day.

Ruka still did not know, though he searched his mind for answers. In the Ascom fresh water was scarce. His mother taught him to boil unknown sources in pots before using it to drink, or even wash, if you could manage it. But it still required fresh water. It was the salt that made sea-water useless, and all he had was sea-water.

"Just keep us moving South," he said, and scooped up pailfuls of sediment-filled water from the salt-lake in his Grove.

Somehow, he would need to remove it.

He tried different methods, first transferring from pot to pot as he tried to strain it. Removing dirt with tight-weaved grates or fabric was not so difficult, but no matter what he did, the taste was salty.

But he knew there was an answer. All things had answers with enough knowledge. This was the closest thing to faith Ruka had.

He boiled more pots and tried to think of something so small it might strain salt, but somehow once submerged in water the crystals dissolved and became part of the water itself. He stood watching, lids covering his pots as he considered. Droplets fell from the edges and sizzled as they struck the fire. Ruka froze. Water could become steam, but could salt?

He collected the droplets, tasted them, and smiled.

He brought the pots and lids from his Grove to sit on the deck, as well as a metal stand to hold the wood-fire above the vulnerable hull. He had Arun fill pails with sea-water, dump them in, then set them beneath the off-center lids.

As the fire boiled, the water rose as steam and droplets fell having abandoned the heavier crystals, and collected.

"Taste it," he said later when they had half a pail.

Arun tried it, then grinned for the first time since they'd changed ships.

Ruka shook his head and nearly cursed himself for a fool, thinking it such a simple thing. No doubt the methods could be improved. It might be useful even on land, but for ships they could use such methods to reduce the need for barrels and barrels of storage.

"We might survive the crossing without food," Ruka said, "but I'd rather not try. I'll make us something to catch fish."

The dead—at least those with unbroken fingers—were already threading huge ropes into square netting. In the world of the living, Arun nodded, a thing growing in his eyes now like Ruka's first retainers—a wonder, perhaps, or deference born from a secret wish for a master.

In truth, Ruka wished men never felt this way. He wished they were stronger, and better than they were—that he could find ways to make them do what was required without fear and awe and greed. But he had yet to find them.

The softer power his mother had wielded seemed only useful against the weak, and dependent. There was also the island way—choosing roads that benefited most, relying on collective interest and a peaceful nature. But interests could change, and such a comfortable people would quail at the first sign of doom or tragedy.

No. Men needed struggle, and a firm hand. They needed the worst amongst them culled, laws enough to keep the rest only from degradation, enforced by strength but tempered by mercy.

Perhaps in the future there might be better ways. But for now, Ruka would gather the best and strongest and help them rule. Men like Aiden and Farahi, and great matrons like Beyla. Then he would turn his eyes to Grove-magic and mystical island monks, and all mysteries unknown in the world.

It will be your legacy, mother. I will help build a world shaped by your sacrifice, and it will rise above the darkness of ignorance. But first, I must tame the pretenders.

Ruka sat and winced at the pain in his leg. He waited for the foreigners to meet his eyes, knowing he would need these men, and to gain loyalty there must always be a form of truth. The warmth and light of the mid-day sun was not the burden it once was, and he let the heat warm his face.

"Since it seems as if we might live," he said. "There are things you must know. With a bit of wind, there is perhaps one full moon before we reach my homeland. On arrival I intend to gather a small army on the coast, load them into several ships we will build upon landing, and sail to destroy the Trung. We will sail in four months." He let that timeline register with the men. "Now is the time for questions."

Arun snorted but didn't seem alarmed. Kwal's tone was plain, and respectful.

"Why do we need more ships, sir? I thought the plan was subterfuge and murder, not conquest."

A plan can be both.

"I need them for plunder, Captain. I intend to capture as many young women as will fit on board."

The young sailor's brow raised at that, his face stretched like a man who heard news he didn't enjoy. The pirate just rolled tobacco.

"Why women?" Kwal said with a careful tone. "There will be a treasury. If we can manage it, surely that is more valuable."

"You Pyu value the wrong things," Ruka answered. "In the Ascom, women are worth far more."

Arun lit his smoke with the fire on Ruka's stand, puffing and laying back on his elbows. "Do you have allies? Resources? What do we use to build the ships and hire men? If you hadn't noticed, we've lost our silver."

Ruka smiled with no attempt to mask Bukayag's arrogance. In truth he felt annoyance already at the doubt and questions though he'd prompted them. He flicked his gaze towards the sails and pots and tools he'd pulled from nothing.

He'd seen the man's greed the moment he'd done it. Arun's mind would have leapt instantly to gold and silver, and the same lust had entered his eyes as Egil's when he'd found a Vishan boy who could draw runes.

Small men, he thought with scorn, *and their small ambitions.*

"I have enough," he said without a hint of doubt. "More than enough."

He watched dead men with picks and hammers in his Grove. They were digging down beneath his cave, hunting for precious metals he somehow knew would be there. Already they made piles of ore flecked with metals. Others constructed a special furnace with molds to keep his Grove-coins consistent. He would do far better than the Pyu.

Farahi's minters had not controlled the mixtures or heat as they should have. Their coins crumbled and blackened, chipped and varied. Merchants were forced to weigh, inspect, and bargain. It was better than the Ascom, but it could be vastly improved.

Ruka lay his body flat to rest while he toiled. No matter what he did, his fate was still in the hands of the sea.

If a storm came they would all certainly die; if they failed to fish and the winds didn't oblige, he might be forced to eat his companions, and to kill them would require all his strength. For now he stilled like the plants and beasts escaping winter, hoping only to buy time.

If necessary, he could start with Kwal, who was injured and weak. But if he ate Kwal then Arun would no doubt fight him, and damaged as he was, a fight with the Ching master may not end well.

He sighed at the thought, closed his eyes, and hoped for fish.

39

Altan stood on the peak of his farm's highest hill. He watched the boat on the horizon and wished he was on it, knowing but not caring that the men aboard were likely cold and hungry, tired of their fellow's stink and habits. He sighed, turned to look at the squealing pigs outside his barn, and squinted against the falling sun.

"I suppose someone has to feed you."

He trudged downhill with his slop in freshly washed buckets. It was mostly leftovers from his family's daily meals, which they produced in embarrassing amounts. The youngest twins still preferred to throw their pork and fish rather than eat it, pelting siblings and walls and laughing as the dogs scampered madly for pickings. His Matron, Noyon, gathered up the dirtier pieces and stored it for the animals. Altan wished she'd make them eat it anyway.

"Boys your age in the South would kill for that," he'd say, and his children would all roll their eyes.

"In the South they kill for anything," once said the oldest, now seventeen, voice dripping with confident disdain, and Altan reminded himself how little they'd all seen of the world.

He hurried to open the feed slots and toss his heavy load. The sows whined and lined up in their order of size and aggression, the single boar waiting in his place up front. Altan had no time tonight to sort them out, but tomorrow he'd have to separate his stock into pens and make sure they all ate their share. Left to their own devices, pigs would let the weakest starve, no matter how much food you gave them.

He left the buckets for his sons to deal with later, hurried to the site of his new house and covered up the foundation with wooden planks. It would rain tonight, or perhaps tomorrow, and he'd rather not deal with a mud pit. He covered the boards with old, cheap furs, stitched together by his parents from half a dozen breeds of beast. It should be his sons doing the work, he knew, but there was still time for that. When the rain dried they'd come down together as a family and he'd show the boys how to build a frame, how to square off the ground and carve proper walls for storage.

It would be a fine home—large, and warm enough to hold four women and their families, if the Mother graced them. When his daughters took mates they'd be offered first choice, but who knew what they'd decide. They might Choose the Order or move to a town; they were more educated than most, and there was always need for teachers and birthers, or they might try their luck as merchants and take a portion of Noyon's wealth to start. None of this bothered Altan, he and the land earned her plenty, and his sons would stay at least until he had son-in-laws.

He smiled at the brightness of his children's future, feeling a pride and grace that made him kiss his knuckles in thanks to the Goddess, but there was no time for idleness.

The ship he'd seen rounding Cayer's Rock would be close to his shore. He scrambled around freshly planted fields—mostly durum and coriander, though the wheat was sicker every year from disease and he should plant something else. *Damn the chiefs and their quotas and all ignorant townsfolk*, he thought.

Meeting sailors was more important than ever. The income offset his weakened crops, and he and a neighbor had been running a supply trade of sorts for years.

The coast of Altan's land was a good slope and protected by trees—so he'd built several docks and kept it readied with fresh water and grain in barrels; his neighbor cut and stocked lumber, rope and cloth, coming by every few weeks to re-supply and settle the costs. They found merchants ideal customers—always loaded with useful goods or silver, always knowledgeable of a thing's worth so the haggling was short. They split the profits, with Altan receiving a fee for handling the exchange.

In truth he was pleased to do it. He loved hearing the men's stories, often inviting them to his home for a meal or a night if they seemed honorable. It made him long for a life with more danger and freedom—a life where a man could pit his wits against the sea and weather and forget the politics of land and chiefdoms and priestesses. But he would miss his family.

For now he unfurled the furs covering his goods, pushed up a white rag on a stick to signal his interest, then waited on a bench trying to make out his visitor. He hoped there was news of last year's harvest in the East, or perhaps the men would have a skald of sorts to tell his children stories.

He stood on the bank and looked and looked at the outline of his guest. But no matter how long he stared, he couldn't quite understand the shape of it.

The sails were wrong, first of all. Perhaps they were damaged. They looked rounded rather than square, as if the wooden frame had fallen apart. And they were *huge*, he realized, as the distance lessened.

He stood watching, and soon the sun shrunk to a sliver, and though the boat was shrouded in gloom, it became clear: this was the largest ship Altan had ever seen.

He felt a sudden panic, but wasn't sure exactly why, or what to do. It would be some new creation, he supposed, something he'd never seen from the East. He knew much now about the usual visitors and local sailors, but by no means was he a sea-man.

How many men could be aboard such a thing, he wondered? And why make it so large instead of simply using another ship?

The answers left his mouth dry, and his bowel's gurgling. He ran back to his house shouting through the yard.

"Get weapons! Boys, get out here, *right now!*"

Altan scrounged in his shed for axes and anything resembling a spear, his youngest sons came first and asked foolish questions as they played.

"Where are the damn bows," Altan muttered, hating himself. "Why are there no god-cursed bows in the North?"

The eldest twins finally came up panting.

"There's a ship," he said as he met their eyes, "I don't recognize it."

"We're ready, father," said the older second-born, and Altan smiled. Carst was always best in a crisis.

"Good lad," he pat the boy's shoulder and handed him a scythe. "Tell your sisters to sharpen some knives, bar the door and guard it. Then tell your mother to take the horse and run to the neighbor's for help, then get my wolves."

The boy nodded and ran off pale but steady, and Altan took the others down to the beach. He stopped at the hill and felt his breath catch. His sons froze in their tracks at his panic.

Somehow—impossibly, considering the distance he'd seen it—the boat had already arrived.

Its hull looked half destroyed, and even bigger than he'd imagined. It had rammed wildly into the sand with no attempt to slow or dock. The sails had no frame, drooped now and held by more ropes than Altan had ever seen, somehow stretched across the mast but otherwise free.

"I see no men or tracks, father," said Galin, the first-born youngest, now thirteen and a serious boy who only spoke when he was sure.

"Nor I." Altan gripped his old axe—the only one not made for cutting wood. He tried to keep his thoughts in the now, and not on old crimes and miseries, and the vengeful dead.

"There!"

The oldest pointed and they all looked together. Altan saw a body laying on the beach. It looked thrown several man-lengths away from the ship with no footprints, sprawled flat down on its front.

Altan felt the urge to turn around, and run.

Without explanation he considered for a moment packing up his family and leaving his wealth and farm without looking back. But his son returned with their four wolf-dogs snarling, leashed but snapping for an unknown foe, feeling their master's fear. Their courage renewed his own.

"Come." He started down the bank, eyes searching trees and bushes and tool sheds, counting the men who might be hidden and knowing it was few.

His own trials in combat were not forgotten. *I can handle what comes.*

He looked at his young but strong sons and well-trained dogs and knew they'd do him proud.

So why do I feel so afraid?

* * *

Rise, brother.

Bukayag lay cold and helpless from the weeks of Grove-sleep. Ruka tried to look through the blotchy greyness with his own eyes but failed, blinking away tears and trying to take in where he was. The ground did not sway, it seemed. Did this mean he was on land?

He moved an arm beneath him and lifted it to his face. He found dried blood and maybe sand—but not island sand—it was coarse and yellow and mixed with dirt.

He heard voices as if through water, genderless and unknowable except for tones raised at the end as if in question. He ignored them, going back to recall failed attempts to fish and what might have happened to Arun and Kwal.

He remembered failing winds, then rain and waves battering his coastal hull near to breaking. He knew they'd survived this and limped along the sea with water but no food while Ruka rested. But after that, nothing.

Bukayag managed to raise their head, spitting and coughing as his hands went to the earth to lift. They heard dogs barking and Ruka felt Bukayag snarl in answer.

"Are you alright?"

The voice sounded closer now. It spoke in Ruka's native tongue with the staccato'd sounds of a Northerner, and Ruka didn't know if he should celebrate, or curse.

"Water," he answered, reminded for a moment of his trip the other way and being captured and bound in silk ropes by pirates.

"Be calm," said the voice. "Are there more of you? Are you alone?"

Ruka tried to shake his head but lacked control. A shape loomed close and blurry with something in its hands and Bukayag almost struck.

"Easy, brother. It's your drink," said the voice. Ruka grabbed and gulped from what felt like a wooden cup, knowing his need was too high to worry on poison.

"I need to know if you're armed, and if there's more of you. But if you're honest, and peaceful, we'll help you. You have my word."

Ruka thought that rather reasonable, considering. Bukayag just balled a fist.

"There's...two men on board," he managed , not bothering to add 'I hope'. Then he used the last few drops of water to wash sand from his face. The blurry men gasped.

Ruka's pulse picked up and he blinked till his vision cleared, thinking *I'm a damn fool.*

He took in the wide eyes of four teens holding farm tools, and a muscled farmer with a war-axe.

They stared and he knew it was at his birth-mark, his now open yellow eyes, and his deformities—their fear and superstition showed plain on healthy faces. *I have been in Pyu too long*, he thought.

"Be calm," said the farmer as the dogs hunched.

Ruka's reminder of his difference, even in his homeland, sent a flush of heat through his body, and he felt his brother's anger.

"I am Bukayag, son of Beyla." Ruka stood tall and threw down the cup. "I am Vishan and Rune-shaman. I mean you no harm."

The man and boys froze and stared at his strangeness, and perhaps his size. Ruka knew it always best to act when others failed, so he turned with clumsy limbs to inspect his ship, hoping with a few moments rest to climb and search for his foreign servants.

The sound of hooves interrupted him, splashing along the coast.

Bukayag crouched to the sand, one hand closing around a sharp, black rock.

"Get me a sword," he hissed. But Ruka felt a weakness in his mind, too.

The air in his Grove was hazy and swamped in fog, and the mere thought of pulling something from nothing bounced his empty guts.

"Be calm, be calm," soothed the farmer, more urgently.

Ruka blinked still trying to clear his eyes, then he saw the riders more clearly—settling on the long hair.

"Priestess," Bukayag growled, his toes curling sand as he braced, ready to charge, ready to kill everything he saw with his bare hands.

Ruka looked for a white shawl and saw nothing. He knew it could be covered by her clothes, though, and time dragged as he weighed the risk of climbing back aboard, swimming out, or trying to arm his brother.

One of the boys yelled as if in surprise. The four wolf-hounds howled and surged forward, crossing the sand in leaps as their lips drew back to reveal huge fangs.

"No! Down!" cried the farmer. But the dogs charged on, thralled now by the hunt and the pack and the fear.

Bukayag rose up and snarled.

He bashed the first with a violent, desperate swing with his rock, and caved its skull. The second clamped on his still-wounded thigh while he dropped his weapon and caught the others.

Bukayag roared and crushed both animals in his hands, fingers curling around the necks like Lawspeaker Bodil's.

The fourth released its bite, leaping up Ruka's body using his leg as a stand, its wide jaw stretched and reaching for his face or neck.

It jerked before it could strike, whining as it fell, crawling away with short kicks of its hind legs. A blue-steel knife jutted from its side.

Ruka looked and saw Arun slumped over a rail. He was thin, face drawn, yet still managed to seem smug.

Bukayag looked at the others and saw no sign of further violence. He collapsed and stared at the chewed flesh of his still-broken leg, and sighed.

"Let's try your way," he muttered. The pain rushed up so fast Ruka almost moaned. He put his hands up with open palms and looked to the farmer.

"Peace. I swear to Nanot, we've not come for violence."

The farmer dropped his axe and came forward with face flushed. "I'm sorry..." his eyes searched the wound, "my son...he...it was an accident."

The horses had arrived now and their riders dismounted. The woman was healthy and sun-dark, perhaps thirty-five, wearing common clothes; the man was lean and holding a butcher's knife with shaking hands.

Just more rich farmers, Ruka snorted. *You're as jumpy as those dead dogs, brother.*

"We're starving and wounded," he said, wondering if Kwal was still alive, and noticing the farmer's gaze had strayed to the brown-skinned foreigner half-dead up above. "I can pay well for your help," Ruka added, not sure if it mattered to this man.

"Who is your chief?" demanded the black-haired Matron in a strong, sure voice. What she meant was: 'are you an outlaw?'

Ruka considered picking one at random or hoping Aiden of Husavik still lived. Though he paused, feeling the urge to spit and say he needed no chief.

"His name is Bukayag, Noyon," said the farmer, and the woman's eyes widened along with the horseman's.

Ruka watched their faces in silence, surprised for a moment they knew who he was. He wondered if they had heard the 'Tale of the Last Rune-Shaman' as spread by Egil or some other skald. Or perhaps it was his murderous exploits in Alverel they'd heard of. *What have the priestesses said in my absence?*

"You can stay here until you're ready to move on," said the farmer, "whatever you can pay will be fine." Then he motioned at his sons to come help him lift.

"They're going to tend to us, pirate," Ruka called to Arun in Pyu Common, watching the family exchange looks.

The Ching master groaned, then lifted himself enough to look down. He spoke in a voice hoarse from disuse. "Your women. They aren't so ugly. I'd been picturing you with breasts."

The farmer and his sons groaned as they lifted Ruka to his feet.

He looked at the half-destroyed ship, the dead dogs, and the Pyu islander, half-corpse but still making jokes. And perhaps it was his crossing an uncrossable sea for the second time—or surviving kings and gods to return from paradise to a land of ash—but Ruka pictured himself as a woman, and smiled. He spasmed and laughed, carrying on even when the farmer's boys startled, and nearly dropped him.

40

Two weeks later.

Bukayag the Bastard. That was what the Order called him. He supposed Imler already took the 'Betrayer'.

They said he'd been killed in Alverel two years before, then spread the news of his crimes and death with skalds along the Spiral—the major roadway of the Ascom.

His limbs, they said, were hung in the corners of the continent, his head staked next to the holy rock of law as a warning to all other outlaws and religious rabble-rousers. Ruka wondered what poor, deformed cripple they'd used in his stead, and if he'd been killed quickly or suffered in display for a crowd. His hosts didn't seem to know.

"Keep it straight!"

Altan barked at his sons, neck and shoulders bulged with the weight of the long, oak post in his grasp.

Ruka watched and stopped himself from guiding it down the support hole, knowing the man wanted his sons to learn. Earlier he had provided an iron rod hammered into the center of the post to strengthen the hold, which he'd convinced Altan would let him add more weight to the roof.

A thousand more improvements could be made from his own experience and watching the Pyu, of course, but now was not the time. In the future he would make a guild of house builders—set standards to guide all men in the ways of safe, warm walls and hearths, whether made of wood or stone.

The boys circled with their father, pushing and angling till the post slotted with the iron and slid down on its own, grinning as they wiped the honest sweat of toil, though the morning was cool.

It was nearly summer now. The coast of the Ascom was temperate, barely freezing in winter but never truly hot—at least not as the islanders of the far North would reckon. If the sun hid behind clouds, no matter the season, it could be cool. But after his many months in Pyu, the cold mountain breezes felt like home to Ruka.

A strange thing, he thought it, to miss a land that called him outlaw and nearly destroyed him. And yet, it was the truth.

He'd missed the forests and snows and open plains without a man, woman or child for days; he'd missed the crisp, dry air so refreshing it could wake him from the deepest sleep as a boy. *Back when I slept*, he thought.

He closed his eyes and filled his lungs with it. Near two years without a proper breath. Already his skin dried and began to pale, covered now always in long cloth shirts and pants, but he felt comfortable and at ease.

"A few more before lunch," Altan said, walking to the heavy pile of posts near-by, his sons trudging behind.

One would be placed—rather sloppily—every man-length or so

surrounding the whole house. It would have oval sides and a sloped, thatched roof, built much in the same way as Ascomi ships.

But not her *new* ships, Ruka thought with a smile, waving at Altan as he walked down to the coast to his foreign servants.

"Loa," Ruka called, leaning on his stick as he eased his leg down the slope to the sands, clenching his teeth as pain raced up his ribs.

"Sir." Kwal gave his half-bow, crisp and formal as always, bandages now hidden beneath Ascomi clothes.

"How are we doing, Captain?"

"Better if it wasn't so god-cursed cold," said Arun, now wrapped in winter furs and huddled against a bank to avoid the wind.

Ruka's gaze swept the mostly-patched coastal vessel, then the skeleton of the first new ship.

"It's summer, pirate, stop embarrassing yourself. How many men do you think you'll need, Captain?"

Kwal shrugged. "More is better. I'm not a ship-builder, sir, but with trial and error and enough men and supplies, we can manage in your timeline."

Ruka nodded, as ever admiring the man's competence and plain-speaking. If the young marine said he could manage, Ruka had no doubt that he could. He'd been clear since the start about what he knew and what he didn't of construction, always undaunted by the task.

But only if I can get him enough men and supplies, Ruka thought. He wondered again if he could drag a ship whole from his Grove, built in his mind entirely by the dead. Perhaps the question was *how*, and not if.

"In this land *you* are the Master Builder, Captain. I'll get you as much as I can."

Ruka walked back to the farmer's main house, gritting his teeth as he near tripped over weeds and grass-clumps, stomach rumbling from a morning without breakfast.

Altan's daughters sat outside weaving and patching clothes on stools. They were all pretty like their mother, but the first-born twin, Ana, had a courage that let her smile at Ruka politely while her siblings gaped or stared at the dirt. It gave her a true beauty in his eyes.

"Bukayag," she said, and he tried to control the flush because perhaps he'd been staring. She approached him clutching her work, composed and without shyness. "Mother said these were for your men." She held out thin summer-wool blankets, her eyes firmly aimed at his, and not down or roaming his face.

"Thank you, Ana." He smiled and took them, and her hand absently touched his. The skin was cold but soft, and the feel of it stood hairs all over Ruka's body.

Girl-From-Trung's-Pit stared at him in his Grove.

Ruka imagined the green and purple bruises on her neck instead wrapped around Ana's like a collar, and he cleared his throat, and turned away.

"Sit and eat," said Noyon as he stooped and entered through the thick, open door, leaving his boots and walking stick outside so as not to track dirt. "You can leave those on," she said, as usual, and he went in without them as usual, moving to his place on one of the long benches around the low-burning hearth.

He resisted the urge to brush dirt from his seat. This was a rich house and certainly cleaner than most farms, but he had begun to notice the filth at once. It was so much cleaner in Pyu.

People bathed or washed their clothes there almost daily, the water warm and pleasant for use; they swept their wooden floors habitually, abandoning shoes and washing feet at doorways, even children treating dirt like an enemy.

Ruka's people stunk like old sweat and filth. They scratched at fleas and lice and tromped through kitchens and bedrooms with muddy boots, with even rich Northern farmers like Altan and his family grime-caked rubes by Pyu standards.

"Will your men be joining us?" Noyon asked, though they never did—eating and sleeping instead on the ship no matter the weather.

"They are too busy," Ruka said, "I'll bring them something later, if you agree."

The Matron nodded, and their ritual was finished. Entering the house at all made the islanders turn up their noses as they avoided touching benches or walls. And the smell of Noyon's cooking made them gag.

She ladled steaming pork and oat stew into a deep bowl, and Altan and his children joined them, the girls sitting far from Ruka out of custom rather than disgust. The boys' spirits were high from sharing work with their father and they tussled and joked. Ruka tried not to hate them.

"Seef bless us," muttered Altan over his bowl, always quiet with his faith as if embarrassed, perhaps because Ruka was a 'Rune-Shaman', or perhaps because the Order called him a heretic. "How's your leg?" he asked to break the following silence, then cleared his throat.

"Better, thank you."

Ruka had been exaggerating his limp for many days now to buy time. It still hurt and slowed him down, but he was more than able to travel.

They ate mostly in strained silence. After the meat though Altan opened honey wine and filled even the children's cups, the specialness and warmth loosing tongues and postures. Soon the family talked about the new house, the weather, the blankets, and the youngest twins who slopped their food, and all laughed together. All except Noyon.

Noyon did not approve of Ruka. If it were only her who'd found him then surely the local chief would already have come. But Altan had given his word. His Matron seemed to love her Chosen and respect his honor, though she was by no means bound to do so. He'd given his protection as host to

Ruka, and for Noyon this appeared at least enough to delay.

Still, they whispered at night.

"The priestesses lied. We don't know the real story, and he seems honest," his host had said the first night while Ruka sat against their house, awake in the darkness.

"The truth won't matter if the Order finds him. And what if our neighbor talks?"

"He won't."

"You can't be sure. And what about his little dark-skinned...allies? His Noss-mark? And he's a *giant*, Altan! What will we do if he turns violent? You saw what he did to the wolves."

"He swore to Nanot, my love, and I..."

"If he's done *half* the things they say he's done, do you think that matters?"

"I looked in his eyes, Noyon. He doesn't mean to hurt us. I would know."

The couple had at last worn out and slept, but whispered much the same for days. Ruka decided to summon silver from his Grove, and had handed a chunk worth two horses to Noyon after a meal.

"It...it's," her eyes had gone wide as dinner plates. "It's too much, Bukayag."

"For your kindness. And for the animals."

She'd eventually nodded, wrapped it in cloth and hidden it away without further protest. After that, she no longer voiced complaints in the night.

Later he'd brought more silver to buy supplies for Kwal, taking every scrap of lumber and rope Altan had on his beach while the man goggled at the amount. He brought more dried wood, too, along with iron nails, plugs and rods, various clamps and hammers and other tools—all of which he'd pretended to have in the ship's hold.

Soon he would need workers, and warriors—the kind of men he could take across a deadly sea to plunder and glory. And somehow he must keep hidden from the Order and the chiefs, who would surely gather and chase him down like a rabid beast to the ends of the Ascom, at least if they knew he was alive.

In the world of the living he focused half his mind on the now, smiling at the family that risked their lives when they took him in. He drained his wine-cup in a single swallow, watching the boys as they tried to do the same and choked, and Altan laughed and re-filled all.

These were good, honest folk, that was clear—rich enough perhaps to earn the dislike of Bukayag, but in the world at large they still ranked amongst the poor. Families like Noyon's were why Ruka had returned—people trapped without knowing in an icy cage.

He would free them, and open the shell of the world before them, so that the brave might choose their path.

But how do I spread the word of my return? How do I gather chiefless and teach them all the truth and rally men to my cause?

He saw no obvious answer, and blinked to stop Bukayag from staring at Ana's curves before focusing on his Grove. He would have to win back the loyalty of his outcasts, if they lived. Perhaps he would start with that.

"Let's stretch that leg a bit," said Altan just before dark. He seemed a little drunk, and made a face at his youngest twins before helping Ruka stand.

It wasn't their first evening walk, and they settled into a comfortable pace along the beach.

They listened to the waves, the chirping birds and grasshoppers, watched pelicans dive at fish along the coast, at ease in silence before one or the other picked a topic.

"The first man I killed was a fisherman," said the farmer, picking at his teeth with straw.

Ruka said nothing, waiting for the rest. He had already learned his host was a chiefless warrior from the midland hills—not much different in his youth to an outlaw.

"I was starving, course." Altan shrugged. "I'd watched him damn near sever a dockboy's head for fiddling with his rope. Anyway, I tried to take his fish. Ended up knocking his skull instead. He slipped into the water, and that was that."

Ruka sighed and stared at the mangled jaw of a walking corpse in his Grove.

"Mine was a stable-boy. I was twelve, the boy perhaps fourteen." Here he paused, not sure what else to say, except for the truth. "I'd needed a horse."

As usual the other man said nothing and didn't seem to judge. He just kept moving along mindful of Ruka's limp, and this time they went further than they had before—past the Trung ship now pulled up and hidden by trees and brush in low tide, past the jut of marshy land on the Western tip of Altan's farm, and down the edge of his huge, recently planted crops, which for now looked like dirt-fields lined with man-made trenches and flecks of shrub.

"It was before your time." Altan broke the pleasant silence. "But I fought for years in the Grain War, too. You hear of that?"

Ruka nodded, though he wasn't sure. Unlike the Pyu, Ascomi kept no written books of their history—or if they did, only the priestesses had them. Egil had told him of many things in their travels, of course—of rebel uprisings and Southern blasphemy, greedy chieftains bribing priestesses for land or favor. He'd never called anything a 'Grain War', though he'd spoken of Northern chiefs warring over farmland.

"That was what we called it, anyway." Altan shrugged. "The grain-chiefs were tired of giving away their harvests, so one day they got together and... stopped." His eyes drifted in the way of men in reverie. "It was how I met Noyon." He smiled. "Gods you should have seen her back then," he winked and cupped at pretend breasts.

"The Order gathered up a thousand killers like me and loosed us on the chiefs," he shook his head. "Just butchery, mostly. We hacked our way through soft Northern boys, killed farmers, ranchers, townsfolk, whatever, long as we got their crops moving, no one much cared." He half laughed, half snorted, but to Ruka it was a forced thing—a pretend callousness lined with regret. His eyes went far away.

"I killed Noyon's man here in this yard—handsome fellow, older. She stood an arm's length away, beautiful as you please. She had tears in her eyes and a knife but she just stared at me. Imler's cock I'll never forget that stare." He paused, as if still in wonder. "Then she points and says the words and chooses me next, right there—her dead man's blood on my sword, pack of killers and dogs behind me. I was frozen. I was hers." He shook his head and had water in his eyes.

"I never deserved peace or family, not after the things I done, the laws I broke. But the gods gave them anyway." He stopped and put a hand on Ruka's arm. "Are you...truly a shaman? Can you really speak with the gods?"

Ruka kept any reaction from his expression, but a puzzle piece fit into place. *Answers,* he thought. *Answers and guilt are the riddle of your kindness.*

He met the farmer's eyes and nodded, seeing his mother's useless piety and trying not to hate the double-edged strength and weakness of faith.

"They move my hand even now, Altan," he said, then took his walking stick and drew three perfect runes in the dirt without looking, as if his fingers were moved by some greater power.

The man's eyes widened as he watched, his tone eager but afraid.

"What...which...what do they say, shaman, please?"

Ruka paused for effect. He took a breath and looked down as if he'd drawn the runes without knowing what they were. *He wants forgiveness,* he knew, *comfort, absolution—but do I give it? And how to make that useful?*

"They say to trust the gods." He looked away, as if unwilling to be clear.

The big man gripped Ruka with both rough hands, pupils shifting back and forth.

"Please, please I beg you, shaman. Whatever it is, I want to hear."

Ruka breathed as if steadying himself. *Can't you see my deception,* he thought*? Can't you see me? Can't you see what I am?*

"That's the sign of Noss, Altan. He has marked you, as he has marked me." He put a hand as if idly to his blotchy chin. It was the best he had without warning, and hoped it would bind the man with time.

Altan swallowed and closed his eyes, as if his worst fears had been confirmed. "Marked for what, shaman?"

Ruka stared, and sneered. "One does not ask the mountain god his reasons."

The grip relaxed. "Of course, yes, of course. I'm sorry. Thank you for telling me." He backed away, looking unsure. "We should go back, it's getting dark." The farmer turned away, squinting in the moonlight.

Ruka followed. The journey back felt longer, and more lonely. He understood he could no longer be the man's 'friend', and there would be no more walks.

Altan moved in a daze, no doubt sifting fuzzy memory like a prospector, seeking signs to make his beliefs true. Their pace increased as the man forgot Ruka's limp, but it was not difficult to keep up.

Ruka had a strange feeling as they walked, the hint of moisture as if the weather changed—dark clouds formed in the distance while he waited in a windless sea. He tried to understand and perhaps seek his memory and observation just as Altan in his own way. Then in the darkness, he noticed the smoke.

"Does Noyon make a fire tonight?" he asked, intuition now tightening his chest, knowing he'd smelled it first and perhaps Bukayag had known. He saw a dim silhouette of light, and felt treachery like water in the wind.

The farmer looked up, still distracted. "I don't know." He looked at Ruka's expression and all at once came back to reality. They picked up speed together, taking a shorter path over the field, trampling green wheat barely sprouted. "She could have," Altan said, now breaking into a run. "There was enough firewood."

Ruka ignored his pain and discarded his stick to keep up. They climbed the last hill in full stride, reaching the top together panting to look out over the homestead and barn with a clear view. They saw the fire. But it wasn't where it should have been.

The house crackled and burned. Already it was half collapsed to the ground. Ruka saw men moving in the yard, others near the animals. He counted perhaps thirty breaking apart sheds and fences with swords and torches. He seized the older man's shoulders.

"There's too many, Altan, there's nothing you can do."

He searched the darkness of the coast for signs of men near his ship, seeing nothing through the distance and wind-shelter of trees.

"My axe...it's in the house," the old warrior whispered as if in afterthought, searching his own land as if lost.

Ruka thought of Ana being 'raped' or hacked apart, then remembered he was in the land of ash. The girls would be safe.

The men would belong to the local chief, or the Order, and in either case they would take the women gently as prisoners for their master's judgment.

He looked and saw Altan on the edge of breaking—a man who had all his life expected a cost for his deeds, a reckoning for his past. Now it had come.

I can't save his family, Ruka thought, *but I can save him. I can bind him to me now, and give him a new life later.*

From his Grove Ruka lifted a war-axe—one of many blue-steel creations etched and waiting in his armory for worthy men.

"Altan, son of Brandt," he spoke in his most prophetic voice, modeled after Egil and honed with use. The farmer blinked and met his eyes, and Ruka summoned the weapon from air and fire as the rain of sparks lit them both. "I told you Noss has marked you. You have been called, Midlander."

Altan gaped with an open mouth, yanked back from his horror by the brightness and sound of creation. He swallowed and lifted a trembling hand to the steel, as if unbelieving it could exist.

"I am Noss' prophet," Ruka said as he held the weapon firm, until both their hands closed around it. He met the man's stare, knowing his monstrous bright eyes would glow in the still-falling flames. "Tonight, you become one of His."

41

Altan seized the god-forged axe.

I deserve this, he thought, *I deserve destruction and misery, but not Noyon, and not her children.*

He grit his teeth and blocked the many questions of why and how that no longer mattered. There was only fear and failure left, and he would not permit either. With a nod to the prophet or maybe demon of the old world, he jogged down the grassy hill, hoping to approach his destroyed house from the side with the least warriors.

The only question left to the man or thing at his side that mattered was simple: *will you help me?*

More fire flared in the darkness, filling the giant's hands with a blue-steel blade of legend, as long and vicious-looking as any sword Altan had ever seen. The answer seemed clear enough.

Light from the burning home he'd built with his own hands lit the bandits, or whatever they were. Three stood guard on his side but mostly watched the flames. They were well-armed with swords and spears. They looked hale and thick, their faces shaved in the Northern fashion. By their postures they seemed unconcerned, as if they knew there might be more victims, but little danger.

I'll show you fear, Altan thought, *you fucking bastards.*

He charged without waiting for Bukayag's reaction, thinking with scorn of how Noyon's first Chosen hadn't even fought back.

"Here!" shouted the first at the last moment. He raised his spear, and Altan clove it in two, the heavy weapon striking through to hew the bandit's head like a piece of firewood.

The sharpness of the blade surprised him. The arc of the swing felt so natural, so familiar—the sound and feel of bone blasting away the years of cutting trees to bring Altan back to younger days of desperation and violence.

He tried to kick the body off, his balance thrown, knowing another man's charge would come.

But the others had stepped back, pale-faced terror clear as Bukayag growled and entered the fray, sword and eyes shining in the firelight.

The first seemed too distracted to fight back, falling away red as the giant's sword opened his gut. The second turned and ran, yelling bloody murder before a spear shaft lit by embers pierced his back.

"Noss sends his regards," the shaman growled. Then he pulled his bloody spear from the dying man's chest, muttering "Waste not, want not," with a crooked-toothed smile, as if in private joke to himself.

Altan had to put the madness of it all from his mind. "I don't see my family," he whispered between pants, then crept along the rounded house, hoping none of the others had heard their fellows screaming over the blaze.

Many of the bandits must have spread out searching the yard and land, leaving perhaps five more near the house. They stood just far enough away from the fire to be hard to see clearly, clumped together and talking.

Altan gestured at Bukayag, hoping he understood, then moved out from the fire into darkness, sweeping around to get closer. He caught the scent of cooking meat on the wind, and prayed to Bray it was his pigs.

He lost track of the shaman but didn't wait, creeping at the end on hands and knees to get close enough to hear, no longer bothered by swelling joints or the dull ache always in his back.

"The priestesses promised me!" Altan heard a Northern man's voice, so wrong to be familiar now.

"And I'm sure they'll hand her over when they please. But I'm to take the girls, and kill the rest. Those are my orders."

The shape of Tabin's scrawny limbs became clear in the meager light. He was tugging at his wispy beard, twisting back and forth in a restless pace as he'd done when Altan first proposed their joint merchant venture.

"What sense to walk her all day and night just to turn around and march her back?"

The black bearded man speaking glared. He was lean and sinewy, tall but broad in the shoulders, and draped in iron ring.

"I don't make orders, I follow them. Now fuck off."

"Four ounces of silver," Tabin said. "I take her now and we tell the priestesses whatever you like." He produced a chunk of ore from his pocket wrapped in cloth, and Altan realized, chest fluttering, it was the same silver Bukayag gave Noyon.

The man inspected, then unwrapped it. He raised a brow, then glanced to his men. In a single knock of Altan's fast-beating heart, he drew a sword, and pierced Tabin's chest.

"Bribing an Order guard," the killer hissed as he twisted the blade, "is punishable by death." He waited for Tabin's legs to give out before he pulled away.

"Take the girl," he said to the others, pointing into the darkness and wiping the stain off his sword with Noyon's cloth.

Altan watched it all in perfect silence, and remembered to breathe. He watched the dying man he thought his ally, and pushed down the niggling fear that Noyon was somehow involved. *She loves me, and she loves her children. Tabin must have found the silver in the house.*

He moved closer now, slow and sweating, thinking of what he could still lose. More shapes appeared in the night, and what he'd thought was five men was really more like fifteen. Even with the shaman, he thought, he couldn't possibly kill them all.

So he kept watching, startling as he saw his daughters huddled on the ground, arms wrapped around each other as if it offered some protection. The sight of them there, terrified and trapped, broke his heart.

They were so close. He could shout to them now, run to them, but it would accomplish nothing. From where they sat they must have heard everything their captors said—heard the man who all but ordered their destruction.

"Get up. Just you."

The killer pointed with his sword, and several men moved to pull the girls apart.

They tried to resist—tried to hold on to each other's hands, then dresses, some of the cloth ripping. Altan realized Noyon was amongst them.

"No, please, please, no," she cried, as if not afraid for herself, but for what would happen next.

Altan tried to rise and charge to an honorable death, but his legs wouldn't move. The begging voices that should form laughter, the soft white hands that clutched him as children but now gripped each other in panic—they were poison in his veins.

They spread a numbness down his spine that locked his limbs as he shook, the heat of rage snuffed out in an icy bath of fear and disbelief. He thought back to the passive coward he'd killed those years ago to claim this life, and felt the justice, the understanding. The horror.

"Enough," said black-beard, "she's the matron, she's responsible. You know your orders. Do it." His men didn't move.

"Goddess'll send us to the mountain, brother. Let's just leave 'er. Who's to know?"

The killer spit. "Her *priestesses* ordered it, why would she punish you? I won't tell you again. Kill her."

Still they didn't move, and Altan felt like his heart would burst from his chest. *They can't do it, they'll just take her back. Oh thank you mother of laws, thank you and please forgive me for doubting you and being a fool.*

Blood sprayed and a few drops landed warm on Altan's face. For a moment he couldn't understand from where. He heard the gurgled chokes and saw black-beard's arm rise and fall.

His daughters didn't cry out, they didn't move as Noyon collapsed, the men all still and stunned, except the killer, who cleaned his blade.

Ana screamed, and kept at it, one shrill pierce after another, the only sound in the world. She knelt down to her mother and the men were too frozen to stop her. She curled her small hands around the cut throat as if she could put the blood back in.

Altan clenched his fist around the haft of Bukayag's axe as his gut heaved. He tried to rise and still had no strength, nor could he even think of what he'd do if he had.

"Keep looking, there should be two men." The bastard frowned at his dirty cloth and wiped his sword on the grass, like a cat cleaning its claws before moving off into the night.

I'll kill him, Altan thought, though he still couldn't rise. *It doesn't matter what happens now. I'll kill just that man and die with my Noyon.*

He stood up from wobbly knees, blood flowing back from his chest to his limbs. *I'm sorry, my love*, he almost said out loud, *I should be stronger and live and try to save your daughters, but I'm a coward. I can't live with this, I can't.*

He stepped forward to his death and only idly wondered where Bukayag was.

An arm wrapped around his neck, a huge hand over his mouth. He felt himself fighting, pitifully, trying to say he had to help his family, to take revenge. He managed to look up and see the stars mixed with the smoke of his burning life, smell the salt of the sea mixed with the flesh of his pigs, and no doubt his sons. As the lights and sounds of the world faded, he used his last thoughts to hate himself, and welcome death.

"Get him on board," Ruka said as Arun dragged the farmer by his leg through wet sand.

The tide was coming in, but the ship was still completely out of water—hidden in a spot that took Altan, all his sons, both islanders and a horse to slide it to in the first place.

"We'll pull together," Bukayag offered.

Ruka snorted and watched the shoreline for bandits. There was still nothing, but surely it was a matter of time. The neighbor must have told the Order everything—his name, about the ship, the dark-skinned foreigners.

"The priestesses might not trust their dogs with such things," Bukayag said, his tone holding its normal venom, the perceived insult to his gender or upbringing that he took personally, as with all things possible.

Of course, that didn't make him wrong. These men may not know who or why they were ordered to kill—told only to slaughter everyone they found responsible. *But not the girls*, he reminded himself. The girls it seemed they would only take back to their masters.

The thought of Noyon dead, of her daughters taken as prisoners, made Ruka angry even in his Grove— enough to stop him from grabbing ropes from dead men he hoped could somehow help him do another impossible thing.

"They make no difference to our plans, brother. Forget them."

Ruka knew Bukayag was right, but still, the words annoyed him. His gaze left the beach to rest on his unconscious host.

The Midlander's weakness and failure at his family's death was surprising. Ruka could have perhaps stopped or delayed what happened—could have skewered half-blind chiefless in the dark till they panicked. At first, that was his plan.

But it had not been his test. Ruka was not interested in saving those who would not fight to save themselves. The woman's murder would harden Altan's heart; it would shake his faith in the god of law and re-shape it to older, darker idols. Now he would re-gain his purpose, or fade to nothing.

Ruka hoped for the former. He had use for the old warrior's knowledge of Northern conflict and the Midland hills, not to mention his experience as a grain farmer. He hoped he would renew himself and earn a place amongst the living, because if nothing else, Ruka liked the man's company.

As he stood debating how to move his ship, Kwal tied clever Pyu knots in rope around the farmer's round middle. He clambered up ladder-like netting past the rail, then heaved hand over hand as Arun pushed up from below.

Ruka ignored them now. He walked to the stern looking for holes, hooks, or anything at all to tie onto, unsure exactly what he intended.

Through the trees on the closest bank he heard voices and men hacking at branches as they searched. He looked to Arun, but the Ching master moved without instruction, Ruka's knife in hand and stance low as he crept into the brush.

"What's the plan, sir?" Kwal whispered panting from the deck.

You wouldn't believe me if I told you, Ruka thought.

"Raise the sails, Captain. We go East down the coast."

Kwal blinked because they were land-locked with no clear solution, two men's length at least between their ship and a drop of water. Still, he nodded, and Ruka thought: *Now there is a proper servant.*

Then he pulled thick rope from his Grove and tied it where he could with Pyu knots. He wrapped the other ends around his waist and arms, knowing the tender flesh of his still-healing hands couldn't bear the weight without tearing. *And what of my leg and ribs?* he wondered. But he had no choice. The answer made no difference.

Shouting came from the trees as Arun found targets. Other men were coming down the bank now into view. Some pointed and called out, then raced with torches across the beach.

"Now, brother, I will carry it."

Bukayag stretched his neck and flexed his shoulders, excited as always it seemed at the chance of his own destruction.

To me! Ruka called to the dead in his Grove, standing by the green-water lake surrounded by pine. The many men he'd killed gathered at his side in silence and took their places.

We must send the ropes back, brother. Somehow they must linger in both worlds as we work.

Bukayag snorted like a bull, his calves and forearms flexing as he leaned his weight back.

"Do what you like. I will hold them."

Ruka smiled at his brother's boldness, then closed his eyes and called the feel of fibers to his hands, the rough pokes and strength of the lacing threads. He looked at the patch of white sand before him in his Grove where there should be mud, remembering the feel of turning something into nothing, then reached his hands down into the river.

Follow me, he willed, and the dead clambered to plunge cold, dirty hands into colder water.

We're ready, he assured, then stood up holding a drenched line, not truly knowing where the ends went or how, knowing only they entered the waters of imagination and death and mystery and would come out in a man's rough hands in the living.

"*Pull!*" Ruka screamed, and Bukayag growled like a beast as his body went rigid, muscles flexing from toes to jaw.

Ruka seized reality with his mind, with his will, and with the weight of the dead, and pulled. *One more law to shatter*, he thought, *one more sea to cross to find a world reserved for the bold.*

All the men he'd killed found their feet and joined him, sinking down into muck as they heaved, the ropes rising and tightening in their hands. They sprung taut on Bukayag's body as he leaned forward. Heat crackled in the air as dead men's strength became the livings, all hatreds forgotten with the promise of toil.

Sand crushed under Bukayag's feet, grating as the Trung ship jerked and wobbled on its keel, then turned slightly to match the angle of the pull. With a snarl like one of Altan's dead wolves, and with Kwal watching in open-mouthed awe, Bukayag stepped one foot behind the other. The ship dragged behind him towards the waves.

42

Altan woke to a swaying, dark blue sky. He remembered only fire and a swelling sadness that stopped him from even raising his head, or trying to understand where he was.

"Good. I thought perhaps you wouldn't wake."

Altan knew at once he was alive and almost wept—no man could ever fail to recognize Bukayag's voice. With a groan he rose to a sit and stared at an orange morning horizon, then briefly at the strange, flat hull beneath him. Bukayag and one of his bizarre retainers rested against the rail as the other stood at a huge rudder at the stern.

"Some things need decisions," said the shaman.

Altan met the huge demon or half-god or maybe prophet's glowing eyes, and found them burying into his skin. "My sons…," he said, feeling as if it must be said out loud, must be acknowledged. "My matron. They're all dead."

His gut heaved at the words, as if saying them made it true. Again he saw his lover spraying blood and choking in the dirt.

"But not her daughters, Midlander. And you yet live."

Altan shook and would have screamed if the rage could escape the numbness. "For now," he said, and looked away. *As if it matters.*

He lay back down on the creaking wood, listening to gentle waves slosh against the hull, thinking *I always wanted to be a sailor.*

"Have you forgotten, Midlander?" Bukayag stepped over him and blocked the view. He seemed to fill all the world as he reached down and seized Altan's bloody shirt, lifting him to his feet with one arm and monstrous strength. In his other hand he carried a rune-covered axe. He held it reversed, as if in offering. "You are *chosen*, Altan. Do you think the waves care for your pain? The sky? Do you think it absolves you?"

Altan shivered as he met the man's merciless gaze. He looked at the blood-stained axe and wanted to spit and throw it in the sea and curse the gods. He felt tears on his cheeks, but took it with trembling hands. The shaman stepped back and met his eyes.

"The first decision is this, Altan. You can be a rich farmer who has lost all and now lies broken, wallowing in his useless, stupid misery. Or, you can be a chiefless dog, who never did deserve his luck, yet somehow still has two daughters who can yet be held to his breast—if his will and courage holds. One of those men belongs to Noss, Midlander, and each day the burning god will give him vengeance to sustain him. Now decide."

Altan swallowed and saw no mockery or deception in the shaman's eyes. There was only truth. It did not belong on the prophet of Noss, perhaps, yet did. Altan shook his head and gripped the axe tighter, willing himself to believe.

"What is to be done?" he said flatly.

Bukayag held his eyes and the axe for a moment longer before he released with a nod. "Next we decide where to sail, and who to trust. I require land and perhaps even a chief to protect my ship and efforts to recruit and gather supplies. The Order may still be looking."

Altan blinked and tried to shake the frozen hurt that clogged his mind and senses. He thought of his many brothers from a former life, the grain-war veterans who would no doubt still live in the North and perhaps serve chiefs. *Some might even be chiefs themselves.*

"I have some old allies, and some neighbors I've known for…"

"Allies like the man who betrayed us?"

Whatever tenderness had before found the shaman's tone vanished, and Altan grit his teeth. He thought of Tabin dead in the dirt, feeling only angry he would never get the chance to kill him personally.

"No." He took a deep breath. "Maybe. It's been many years. I'll have to see."

Bukayag seemed to accept this and turned to his retainers, speaking in a quick gibberish of sounds that Altan couldn't decipher. The man at the stern seemed to understand and heaved at the rudder, and the huge ship slowly turned as the wide sail angled.

"We will head to a town." Bukayag eased back to the deck with a groan, his breaths seemingly painful. "And Altan," the golden orbs turned to slits. "Now that you've decided— when Noss calls, he does not mean 'maybe'. We'd best not fail."

In the big, strangely sailed ship, the journey to the closest town took only that morning. They'd first made some distance from the shore, so as not to be spotted by fishermen or merchants, then cut towards land when they spotted smoke.

Altan saw the watchtower first, then the old abandoned wall that people said once covered half the coast.

"This is Kormet," he said, mostly to himself.

"We'll land there." Bukayag pointed to a small beach and patch of foliage West of the town, then muttered gibberish to his men. Altan had wished to ask about this strange code of theirs many times but always refrained.

"Are those words from a Southern tribe?"

Altan had heard accents before. He knew steppemen to speak so strangely their words could hardly be deciphered. But nothing he had ever heard sounded like the flowing, constant noises Bukayag and his men produced.

The shaman glanced at him and carried the hint of a smile, then turned back to watch the land. "One day I will explain this and many other things, I give you my word. But not today."

Altan found this answer strange, but said nothing. Everything about the shaman was strange. *More* than strange, and Altan's curiosity easily crumbled beneath the dull apathy of a life destroyed.

He watched the dark waters of the shore, wondering if it would hurt to drown as Bukayag and his men took down the sails and threw a huge iron anchor. Ruka tied the ship to the trees, then handed Altan a white strip of cloth.

"If you expect betrayal, wave this as you return." He put a burnt and four-fingered hand on Altan's shoulder. "The gods are watching you now. Remember that. Everything you do matters."

Dirty sand crunched as Altan stepped over the rail. The last time he was in Kormet, he'd come as little more than a bloody-fisted raider. He and his brothers killed and robbed the chief and the richest men, and the sons who didn't flee. Matrons and mothers had watched and tried to shame them with their eyes, others with their words. A few had claimed the killers as mates. At the time, Altan had only laughed.

Now his face burned at the memory. On the sparsely forested outskirts of the town he stopped and looked at his blood and dirt stained pants and sweat-marked shirt. He hadn't washed any part of himself in days.

His eyes drifted slowly to the rune-covered axe, almost forgotten in his hands. The blade was single-sided and curved, utterly smooth and polished, as if the elaborate runes simply *emerged* from the blue-grey iron instead of having been inscribed. Even the handle was iron, he realized, attached smoothly to the blade as if a single piece, only sheathed in hardened leather grips. It was a weapon out of myth, to be held by the great heroes of an ancient age.

And Bukayag pulled it from fire and air. And now it's mine.

It would be stared at, he realized, if men saw. And perhaps that's what the shaman intended. Perhaps Altan was to claim some special mission from the gods. *Or should I say little, and let them wonder?*

He smoothed his sleeves and tightened the ties of his belt, running a hand over his now untrimmed beard and disheveled hair. For a moment he tried to comb his fingers to unravel knots and scrape out dirt, then growled and walked forward.

He would know and be known by some of the men of this place, or not, and his appearance made no difference.

The pale morning light had given way to a cloudless, afternoon glare. Like most Ascomi towns, Kormet had been built largely in a ring. The houses were solid and well-kept, a reflection of Northern prosperity. A few young men laughed as they worked expanding a large house on the outer edge, some carrying carved and smoothed lumber, others laying out hammers and nails.

Altan looked away, sealing off the memories of his sons as if cauterizing a wound. No one seemed to notice him, though he didn't try to hide, walking plainly along the town's southern crossroad.

Kormet had grown since his first arrival. What had once been perhaps a few hundred seemed now closer to a thousand, merchant-houses marked with wooden signs, mothers inspecting wares with their children in tow.

He had no scabbard or belt-loop that fit his axe, so he rest it over his shoulder as he walked towards the circle-center. He passed boys tousling in the streets, chasing dogs in happy games, and meant to smile at them, but caught himself and focused on his path.

He saw the huge, curved horn attached to the strange square roof of Kormet's hall, remembering it and glad he and his brothers hadn't burned it down. *Or perhaps we did,* he realized, *and they re-built it.* In truth he couldn't remember. Either was possible.

A young man stood guard at the entrance, chewing orange root and spitting at rocks on the road. Smoke rose from the hearth-hole above him, thatch covering pushed aside no doubt till the season turned. Altan expected the chief ate inside.

He breathed and felt strange, as if he'd lived this moment before. The young retainer's face blurred with images of other young men guarding other halls, staring wide-eyed in terror as Altan and his Southern killers tore down their lives with the Order's backing, their only crime serving the wrong masters.

"Hall's closed." The guard's eyes found Bukayag's axe. "Come back… come…later…"

Altan felt himself standing taller at the attention, perhaps trying to be worthy of the weapon in the young man's eyes.

The Gods are watching. Everything you do matters now.

"My name is Altan. Go tell your chief about the axe. He will see me."

The warrior blinked and nodded, pausing slightly but pushing through the double door. He returned and jerked his head to follow, glancing around the street as if to see if anyone watched.

Altan had no memory of the inside of Kormet's hall, and perhaps he'd never gone in. A handful of young men sat at a round table eating maybe mutton with their hands. Their much older chief leaned against his high-chair at the far end.

Even sitting he looked short, and perhaps fat. A dark, patchy beard covered his round cheeks and a red neck. Altan tried to remember him but failed, until he smiled. His voice was loud, and almost shrill.

"You old cock. How long has it been?" The chief's chair legs screeched across the floor-boards as he rose, and his gut shook the table. He held out his arms for an embrace, and Altan took one arm and held it as if the axe made anything more impossible.

"Too long," he said, with a friendliness he did not feel.

"My sons," the chief flicked a hand towards the others in introduction. "Now here's a man," he said, with a prouder tone, reaching up to put his arm on Altan's shoulder, "who knew your Da in his prime." He winked and laughed. "Tell them, brother, tell them what fierce, fucking savages we were. Not like these coddled virgins."

"Fierce as you please."

The chief—Halvar, though all the raiders had called him Mouth—howled and pulled harder at Altan's shoulder. "Fierce as you please, aye." He waved again at his sons. "Now get the fuck out. Out! Not you, fool boy, you stay."

More chairs scuffed the dirty wood, and after sullen looks and grumbling, eventually the hall's door slammed. Only Altan, Mouth, and his apparently favorite son remained.

"So," the old rogue and murderer sat and poured himself more beer, "what do you want?"

Ruka brought more sail from his Grove, then focused on the silver. The dead had already found considerable stores of the metal beneath his cave, and separated the ore from rock with water, picks and scrapers. Ruka needed it shaped at least roughly into a form his countrymen would recognize and accept.

He helped the dead use his furnaces and forges and build the molds, and now they worked on their own filling small chests with different sized pieces. Others twisted strands of flax to make rope, others hammered new swords and axes for gifts. Over the years, Stable-boy-from-Alverel had become a master. He now apprenticed some of the Pyu dead on Ruka's techniques, teaching them in utter silence.

"I don't trust him." Arun watched from below the rail then ducked back down. Ruka blinked and lay his head back against the ship's rail.

"You are untrustworthy, pirate. Of course you don't trust him."

Arun snorted at that. "We don't need him. You can make our coin and supplies with...well, whatever you do. Let's just pay mercenaries. We can *buy* ships, why bother building them?"

Because my people are cut-off and ignorant and we don't have 'mercenaries' or a single ship worthy of that damn turbulent sea, Ruka wanted to say.

"Our ships are too small, pirate. We must build them bigger."

Ruka watched the beach and small patch of woods for ambush, knowing Kwal would scout for ships down the coast. His only plan was to bribe whatever chief Altan brought him. What came after would depend on the man's ambition, or his cowardice. While he waited he rubbed dirt on the silver and chests in his Grove.

"They look too new," he explained, when Stableboy-from-Alverel frowned with his eyes.

"They're coming, sir." Kwal dropped from his perch atop the mast.

Ruka blinked and returned his focus to the world of the living. "Hide below. Both of you. The ship will be strange enough for them for one day."

Kwal nodded and of course went instantly, Arun slower and with narrowed eyes.

Altan and a group of men followed the dirt path South from Kormet, their pace leisurely as they spoke and laughed. The man beside Altan stood a head shorter. He was plump and ruddy and loud, and if he was chief it meant he'd got there through cunning and charm, or perhaps ruthlessness, and not strength. Ruka sighed. He'd have preferred a big, dumb ox.

When the group came close enough to see the Pyu boat in full profile, the men stopped and silenced.

Ruka watched carefully but saw no white flag, only five armed townsfolk who looked too clean and anxious to be real warriors. Some looked little taller than their chief and were perhaps his sons.

Finally they stepped forward, and Ruka rose. He lifted a boarding plank and dropped it down from the rail to sand, then stepped carefully to the beach as the wood bent and creaked from his weight.

He watched with satisfaction as the group took him in and faltered, hands moving to still-tied scabbards and eyes shifting to their fellows.

"Halvar, meet Bukayag, son of Beyla."

The chief nodded, if only slightly. Ruka returned it.

"Is it true?" The little man called with a voice larger than he was. He cocked a brow and smiled as if he enjoyed some private joke. Ruka indulged him.

"Is what true, Chief Halvar?"

"Did you kill a lawspeaker in Alverel? Right on the bloody Noss-cursed stone?"

Ruka took this as a positive sign. He summoned the memory of Lawspeaker Bodil's judgment when he was a boy, then her terror and the soft flesh of her neck before he crushed it.

"With my own hands." He held them up, splaying his nine fingers.

Halvar looked to Altan, then to his sons, and laughed. The sound lingered and the man spasmed twice with a dry cough before he met Ruka's eyes.

"Couldn't have been hard, killing an old woman," he said with a harsher tone. Then he turned and gestured to Altan. "I came because this one said I could benefit. So tell me how before I need a shit."

Ruka stared and waited until he felt the group's discomfort. He didn't like the man's words, his petty cleverness or his tone. "I will make you rich, Halvar. Far richer than you can dream."

Halvar snorted. "A chief keeps no wealth. The matrons and the Order I protect provide."

Ruka smiled faintly at this, wondering if even a single chief in the Ascom believed or followed the official custom. He looked long and hard for some twitch or sign of greed in the man's eyes, though, and found none.

Pride is his coin, then, Ruka guessed. Or perhaps it was cruelty and simple power like Trung, but he hoped not.

"As you wish," he said, and turned. "The choice is yours. Perhaps neighboring chiefs will feel differently. Perhaps they will find uses for silver, and god-forged iron for their retainers." Ruka waved at Altan to follow as he stepped away.

"They call you heretic, 'shaman'," called Halvar. "The Order would come and cut down anyone who helped you, if they knew you were here."

Ruka stopped and spoke over his shoulder. "They may try. But then the Order says I'm dead." He turned and pointed to his new farmer ally. "They killed Altan's Matron, chief, just for seeing me. Imagine what they would do to a man."

Halvar took this in and smiled with a huge cluster of teeth, though it didn't touch his eyes. "Tell me, shaman, before I let you sail from my coast. What would you ask my rivals to do in exchange for your silver, and your…'god-forged iron'?"

You will not 'let' me do anything, little creature, Ruka thought. But he ignored this and relaxed. No doubt there would be many hurdles to come, but the man had agreed.

"I would ask them to protect my work, and keep it secret—help my men with supplies, and ship-building, and sending messages. For this simple task, such a chief would be paid his sons' weight in silver. And later, considerably more."

Halvar's eyes sparkled, then he spat. "Not so simple. And some sons are heavier than others." He snorted up another wad of phlegm, as if in preparation. "Help your men, you say. And what about you? What will the great Bukayag be doing while my rival dotes on his men and ships?"

Ruka grew bored of the negotiation now that it was finished. He turned and watched the waves, mind moving beyond the ships, and even the raid to come—to the impossible future of freedom, and conquest, and knowledge—to an armada of ash and sand, and a great plain of killers mounted on mighty steeds. The thought made him smile, as did the answer.

"Recruiting," he said, then waved at Kwal to prepare to beach.

* * *

Ruka raced through rocky hills on foot, and thought of his youth. *How far I've come,* he thought, *and yet how far I have to go.*

He pictured his first perilous journey to find Beyla's kin, only to be turned away by an old Vishan crone, dangerous indifference in her eyes. The capital, Orhus, was only a few days East now. Ruka instead turned back North to the coast, his direction set on the word of a sailor he'd met in the same fishing village he'd left for Pyu.

He intended to find his old retainers, if they lived, and would start with the bravest, and the most loyal.

"A warhorse," he'd repeated, again and again to men who shied away from his size and drawn hood. "Huge and black with a grey stripe down its face, and grey hooves."

The fishing village he'd found and stolen a ship from was little different than two years before. He'd handed out wine to the oldest men, hoping someone would remember such a beast as Sula.

"Aye, a huge black monster, I remember," said the kennelmaster, in the end. "Group o' young men found him, and he came quiet-like despite his size."

"Were they locals? Did they sell him? Try and ride him? Did they have a chief?"

Ruka had shivered to think of the mighty animal munching oats and shackled, put to stud in its prime. The kennel-master shrugged and swept his dirty floor, and Ruka handed him a piece of silver, which disappeared in the man's pouch in an instant.

"Chief Densro," he said, "in Vinskild, not far from here. If they brought him as they should, though, or just sold him, I can't rightly say."

Ruka nodded, then all but ran from the village.

He'd left Kwal, Altan and Arun with Chief Halvar to begin construction of his ships, working out the plans with Kwal and all the supplies needed first. Without Ruka to translate they would of course have problems, but the captain had more than he needed to begin, and was clever enough to make the farmer understand. Ruka couldn't be sure of Halvar's loyalty, and Arun had paced in rage and fear at being abandoned. But the risk was necessary.

"I will return with warriors. You must protect Kwal and the ships while I'm gone. I need you here."

The pirate had ground his teeth and eventually hunkered down inside his cabin, lighting tobacco. "Make sure there's plenty to drink," he'd yelled. "I'll wait, savage, but I won't do it bloody sober."

Ruka smiled at the memory, then crested the last rocky mound before a dip and almost valley-sized crater that held the outskirts of Vinskild. With the right crop and effort it would be good and fertile ground, he suspected. But instead the men of ash chose it as a village in ancient times, no doubt for protection no longer required.

Ruka watched and waited at the outskirts. When he'd seen enough to expect little danger, he climbed down the now-dry, weed-filled edge of the gully, scattering two rabbits hidden in the brush. He skirted the central road that lead to the Spiral, entering the town on the richest side, which was closest to the sea.

He squinted against the drooping sun, hoping to find some sign of a stables. Many of the houses were closed within fences and blocked from sight, but he could see sheds and barns attached to many.

Silent and still as he focused, he almost missed movement close-by. But he froze and waited, and spotted an animal climbing over the ridge of the gully.

Ruka blinked, disbelieving.

He watched a horse and rider crest the near-by hill and run across open ground—a dark horse streaked with grey, saddled, groomed and washed, shining in the early dusk.

Picking his way through the growth, Ruka watched them ride on open grass and feared they'd turn towards a road and leave the town. But he could see no supplies, and no weapons. *He rides only for the pleasure,* Ruka decided, *not to go anywhere.*

He stood and watched Sula's grace and power as he sprinted full speed, mane and tail flying in the wind. The impulse to follow and kill or at least remove the rider faded.

Sula had been treated well in Ruka's absence. He looked healthy and content, and for a moment Ruka thought perhaps he should leave him where he was.

Bukayag snarled.

"He's ours. The rider means nothing."

Ruka sighed, and in his heart knew he agreed. He followed, and as the light slowly faded, Sula and his rider turned at a trot towards home.

He may have forgotten me, he realized, frightened at the possibility.

"He's a warrior," Bukayag said without a hint of doubt. "We are his master. He will remember."

Ruka wasn't so sure. He had an urge to turn South and never learn the truth, but pushed this down and smothered it as Bukayag walked them forward.

To calm himself, Ruka strolled through Beyla's garden, which now sprawled in rows over more land than the house, filled with the green leafy spread of Ascomi potatoes and squash. Further out he'd planted three kinds of bamboo, which clustered and sprouted higher than a grown man. Beneath them taro and yam fought for false light, and Ruka found Girl-From-Trung's-Pit kneeling in the dirt pulling weeds.

He'd been so busy since he left Pyu, he felt he'd neglected her. But she looked up and smiled, shifting the scarf she now wore to hide her neck bruises. He roamed the beauty of her smooth, cool skin with his eyes, and wished he could explain how pleased he was to see her happy.

In the world of the living, Bukayag had stalked Sula's rider to a large, newer-looking house, an open view of the sea at its lone window. He climbed the pitiful fence and hid in the shadow of a small oak, and Ruka watched the man dismount.

He seemed young, perhaps only sixteen or seventeen, and had called no servants to help with the horse. He whispered to Sula and poured water to a copper jug, then moved to untie his saddle.

"The animal. It isn't yours."

Bukayag stepped into the tall, dim entrance. Sula's ears flattened, the rider startling and reaching a hand to his belt, perhaps for a sword that wasn't there.

"What is this? Who are you?"

Ruka stepped forward and lowered his hood, ignoring the boy. "Sula," he said firmly.

The stallion's nostrils flared. Its head turned back and forth as it pawed at the straw-covered earth, and the rider settled one hand on his flank, perhaps to calm him, or hold him back.

"Sula." Bukayag growled. "Come. Now."

The animal's tail twitched as if it swatted flies, one leg raised and stomped as its eyes flared. Its rider now gripped hair firmly in a fist, his shoulders flexed as he held it.

"Get out! Get out before I cut your throat," he yelled in panic.

Ruka raised his hand and smiled as warmth flooded his gut. He felt the strength of the pull now, he saw the excitement, the memory of endless fields of grass and charging terrified men in combat. "Sula," he said more quietly. "Come."

With a snort the animal shook his head and lurched his massive weight to the side, throwing the young rider to crash against the wall. He stepped forward and sniffed Ruka's hand.

Ruka seized the hard, leather pommel and lifted himself on Sula's back. He felt the strength, and the eagerness—the urge to run again across the world, no fear of the dark, or of strangeness, or of anything.

Ruka took a large piece of silver from his pouch and tossed it to the earth. "For the saddle," he called, then rode into the night.

43

For five days Ruka rode South to Alverel, hoping it was for the last time. Along the way he stopped at two towns, asking if they had seen the skald known as Egil.

Townsfolk in both shook their heads and said not for two years, and so Ruka moved closer to the last place he knew the man had been.

If Egil had survived the valley's chaos, Ruka assumed he would return to his old ways. He would ply his trade from town to town, hall to hall, filling his stomach and drinking himself to oblivion.

Or perhaps the journeying had become too hard after Ruka's torture. Perhaps he'd been forced to settle with a single chief, or a rich matron, playing in a single hall. If so, then he'd have gone to Orhus, or be close to Alverel, perhaps playing for the travelers there.

Or he was recognized as one of mine, and the Order took him, and instead he died screaming.

Ruka winced at the thought. Without Egil, finding his former retainers would be harder. Recruiting more men would be harder. *Amazing, the power of a storyteller,* he thought. *A little music, some showmanship, and oh how my cousins swell.*

Ruka admitted, as well, he also just missed the man. Perhaps not the constant greed or cowardice, nor the frequent whining. But Egil knew him. He had been there from the beginning. His face and voice and presence felt natural in a way other men's did not, and Ruka felt the urge to tell the skald all he had seen in the North—about Trung and Farahi, about the great mainland beyond with a hundred more races of men, religions and kings, and even an emperor.

The world had grown so very large since he last saw his first retainer. Perhaps in that growth the torture and past would shrink, and in the future Egil could be more than just a retainer. Perhaps he could forget the past and be like Farahi, to be a friend.

Bukayag rolled their eyes and Ruka urged Sula forward. He raised his plain, brown hood as he crossed Bray's river into the valley, expecting he wouldn't be paid much attention. His timing was good—most priestesses would be in the capital for summer elections.

On the outskirts he dismounted and asked the first unarmed men he found if they knew of any skalds in the valley. He expected the Ascom had only so many, and that most would know of the others. The men mumbled and couldn't agree and Ruka soon found himself re-tracing old steps, wandering straight into one of two great sources of the Order's power.

He wanted Sula close if he had to run, but he walked beside him rather than ride to be less visible. Many other men had horses here and moved through the crowds and merchant rings alone or in packs, and this brought him some comfort.

Alverel still stunk of packed humanity, animal dung and rotting barley. A hundred make-shift houses littered the garbage-strewn land, small herds of animals kept along the edges, smoke rising from every direction. Young warriors lounged or strolled in groups, or threw bones or fought dogs. A crowd huddled around the lawstones, an old woman perched atop doling out her 'justice'. Ruka snorted. His violence had made no difference.

It came as no surprise, but still he walked away in anger from the stones towards a drinking hall. He scanned the crowd for watchers, or danger, always moving as if he felt no concern. As he came close to the building, he blinked and stared at a young, confident man in fine, clean mail riding a warhorse, and he froze.

The rider laughed and spoke with another man on foot near-by, unstrapping the sword at his side as if in display. The blade was black steel tinged with blue, and it was covered in runes.

"Where did you get that sword?" Ruka had crossed the distance without thinking. The young man hardly looked at him, as if this sort of thing happened often.

"I was just telling this other jealous man. I killed a bear with my fists, and found this in its gullet."

Ruka felt his eyes narrow. Haki the Brave had found a magical sword in a monster's gut—it was an ancient tale in the Book of Galdra. He was being mocked.

For now he kept Bukayag's hands clean and turned away, then wandered into the crowd and waited. He followed the young man through the valley, watching as the young, peacock strut himself about the busy grounds as if some conquering hero, seeming without purpose except to be seen. As light fell the young man bought a flask of wine and turned towards the richer homes.

Ruka followed him to a barn behind the house, then seized him as he dismounted. He thrust him inside and against the thin wooden wall, one huge hand on the smaller man's neck.

"Where," he hissed, "did you get that sword?"

The warhorse's eyes blazed and it pawed at the ground. Its rider panicked, reaching uselessly for a blade as Ruka's other hand circled his wrist and squeezed.

"If I must ask again, cousin, I will shatter your arm." Ruka let Bukayag smile, and watched the man's pupils flare.

"I...took it...from a man in the South. I dueled him and killed him. The sword is mine."

Ruka doubted very much the boy had ever fought anyone, let alone dueled to the death. "And where did *he* get it?"

"I don't..."

Ruka crushed until he felt the bone crackle.

"A cripple! Not himself, but, he said he stole it, from a rich man, and he said the man bought it from a cripple! Please! That's all I know."

Ruka watched until he was sure, then stared at the agitated horse until it quieted. He released the smaller man, now on his knees, and lifted both sword and scabbard from the horse's flank.

"You are a fool, but I will spare you. To carry such a weapon marks you for every ambitious warrior seeking a name. One day, a real one would have found you, and killed you."

The rich matron's son clutched his bruised but unbroken wrist. His head snapped up as if he meant to give some retort, but changed his mind.

Ruka's mind already moved to the future and where he'd begin his search. Egil had apparently given up his trade, and become the 'cripple selling artifacts'. It would be just as easy to track this down. Ruka hoped Kwal was making progress, and that Arun and Altan would protect him long enough, and that their supplies would last while Ruka journeyed and rallied men.

In his Grove he crossed the clearing to the great, green lake he'd discovered. The banks were hard soil save for the patches of island sand he'd made by sending pieces of reality there. The dead toiled silently at the drydock—their third attempt at a larger, sturdier hull in the Pyu style. Ruka nodded to Sailor-from-the-coast as he worked on improving the sails, and finding ways to add more width.

If Kwal failed, if the Order discovered them, or if Chief Halvar betrayed and Ruka returned to nothing, he could only hope to build ships with the dead.

But let us hope not, he thought, flexing a scarred hand and imagining the strain. He still understood little of the price he paid for bringing something from nothing. *If there is a price*, he allowed, but without conviction. Ruka knew nothing of value came without cost.

A boot scuffed against wood, and Bukayag turned. He snarled, almost with glee, as if he'd been waiting, and seized the young man's arm. He held a small, clean knife he must have had concealed in a sleeve.

"My brother spared you," Bukayag hissed. "But I knew better. Oh yes, boy. *I* knew."

Ruka's would-be-killer blinked, face pale but still determined. He threw a wild strike with his other arm. Bukayag hammered the fist with his forehead.

The young man gasped and stumbled away, and Bukayag followed. He wrapped his thick arms around him as if in embrace, opened his mouth wide, and clamped down on the almost beardless cheek to chew.

Ruka sighed in his Grove. He blocked out the screams and laughter as his brother broke limbs and spit chunks of the man's flesh, thinking *cruel, and unnecessary, but such is life*. Ruka'd given him his chance.

"Tell your kin you tried to kill Bukayag," his brother hissed, leaving the half-dead valley-son whimpering and shattered on the ground. "I take your horse in place of your life."

The animal had moved to the corner of the barn in fear, but it hadn't panicked. It cowered as Ruka approached, close now to running or fighting, but unsure. It was no Sula, of course, but it would do, and Egil would need a mount.

Ruka seized the reins and tugged the animal until it moved, walking out into the night and to his own, true companion.

"Come," he said, leaping to Sula's back, feeling the new horse calm at once in a greater presence. He drank water from a skin and swished it, then spit the valley-son's blood to the grass.

* * *

Ruka hunted rune-swords for two weeks with no avail. In town after town he announced himself a shaman in a darkened hall, then hid in his cloak as he spoke to skittish valley-chiefs. None of them were useful, and it was an old builder, in the end, that led him to Egil.

"Don't know nothin' 'bout any runeswords," he'd said as he took the silver. "But, aye, I know a cripple an' 'is young matron. Built 'em a fine 'ouse by the East river last spring." He glanced about to see if anyone was watching. "Paid full in silver ore, he did, not a bit in trade or anythin' else."

Ruka said nothing and left the shop. A day's ride later in heavy rain, he stood before a grand house of red cedar and cut-stone. He marked the thick thatching and good construction, and the size of the house, noting at least three rooms.

He left both horses soggy and miserable in the downpour, and stood at the entrance. He felt suddenly strange, almost hesitant, as he had perhaps when he first considered leaving Sula to his peaceful fate. Whatever it was, Bukayag soon felt contempt for it and knocked.

A boy poked his head from a window in the darkness, staring with narrowed, wary eyes. Ruka stood still and let him inspect, liking the sharp, curious look of the boy. He was too old to be Egil's.

After thirty drops of Ruka's water-clock, the door slid open on a well-greased hinge, and the former skald stood in a soft, rich robe and held a knife. He took one look at Ruka, his eyes rolled back to their whites, and he collapsed to the fine fur rug at his feet.

Ruka sighed. He stepped into the house with hands raised in peace, for he saw a young woman he recognized holding a sword. She held it up as if to challenge him, her eyes moving unwisely to the skald as she wavered on what to do. Ruka walked straight past her towards the fire, and she went to her lover on the floor.

"Is he awake?" Ruka asked, glancing about the house, noting smooth, well-crafted chairs and tables, and an expensive pile of furs. The young woman said nothing, and Ruka took a moment to match her face with his memories. He found a young priestess from Alverel who had once opposed him with Kunla, and tried to send Aiden against him.

Egil finally groaned and placed a hand to his face before rising groggily to his elbows.

"What happened?" he muttered. Ruka spoke before the priestess.

"You fainted."

He almost laughed as Egil clenched in fear. Perhaps, in truth, he'd missed the man's cowardice a little, too.

Egil turned and bumbled a greeting to 'Bukayag', perhaps for the sake of the woman—no doubt he feared Ruka would kill her if she heard his real name.

But he wouldn't, and meant her and the boy no harm. He inspected his old retainer, finding Egil healthier, stronger, and perhaps happier. This pleased him, but it passed.

It was clear the skald loved this woman and child, and though Ruka would not harm them, as long as they could be threatened, Egil would obey. Still, it was best to be sure.

"Now tell me," he said with a menace he did not feel, "why I shouldn't just strangle your priestess."

The young woman rose with sword held before her, and by her footing seemed to have been at least briefly trained. Better to be no swordsman at all than a poor one, he thought, but simply stared at Egil's fear-widened eyes. *I'm sorry old friend,* he thought, seeing the love as plain as day, *but now you truly belong to me.*

His point had been made, so he soon softened and promised he had not come for violence. The brave ex-priestess asked what he wanted, and he told them a lie they might believe.

"More of these."

He reached a hand beneath his cloak and took a freshly minted coin from his Grove, this one made of gold—a metal the Ascom did not have. When they stared in marvel he told them pieces of his journey North through the uncrossable sea, and the beautiful islands of the Pyu.

They didn't believe him, as expected, but for now it made no difference.

"Tell me of the last two years," Ruka said later and sat forward, truly curious. "What happened after Alverel?"

Egil's eyes lost focus as he remembered. He stared into the hearth.

"We ran away. Or at least I did. Aiden and Tahar and some of the others tried to follow you. They…they fought like demons, Ruka. Two valley chiefs rallied men against them at the river, but by then most of Aiden's warriors had chosen to die at his side, and with your warriors—fifty maybe against hundreds—they charged and routed them. After that," he shrugged, "mostly, it was slaughter. When they couldn't find you they scattered. They knew they were outcasts, or at least would be. They hide on the edges of the steppes, or with Southern chiefs, or in small groups near townships or who knows where. The Order hunts them."

Ruka said nothing, and Egil cleared his throat.

"Pretending…assuming I helped you, in whatever small way I even could, what would you have me do?"

Ruka watched the priestess' hatred and rage and felt Bukayag's urge to rise with it.

"You will spread word of my return. With my wealth you will help me gather lumber, weapons, men and supplies, and find any of my retainers who still live. You will convince men to join my cause."

The fire popped and sizzled, and Ruka knew his brother was ready to kill the woman if she charged him. He would still have the boy as leverage.

"And what is it you'll do with these things?" Egil asked. "Kunla is dead. Hulbron would not be hard to burn, if you wish. Why not simply tell the world about this Northern land?"

Because they won't believe me, just like you, Ruka thought. He almost snorted in remembrance at the small dreams of his youth—the petty vengeance of a boy to burn a town or kill a single priestess.

"I will fulfill my promise," he said, thinking of his ancestors, of the future, and his mother's words. "I will destroy this land of ash, and make my followers kings in paradise."

He watched the skald's eyes—the resigned sadness. No doubt he thought Ruka mad and suicidal and no different than before. But nevermind. Ruka was alone, just as he had always been, and it must be him that bore the truth for others until they grew strong enough to withstand it. For now, only obedience was required.

"You're out of your bloody mind." The priestess' legs moved again to a warrior's stance, and Egil begged Ruka desperately with his eyes not to kill her.

I don't want to, Ruka wished he could say. *She is a victim of the past, and this place—just like me, and you, and all of us.* But he showed his grief and frustration only in his Grove.

"No. Soon enough you will see. Collect your things, I have two horses but perhaps we should buy or steal another. In the morning…"

"I'm not going anywhere!" The girl's eyes were wild as she waved the sword. Egil turned and almost fell from his chair.

"Juchi, please…"

"No!" She pointed the blade. "This is madness. Get out. Get out of my house, or I'll open your guts. And if you come…"

Ruka stood, tired of the charade, and raised his open palm in the air. In his Grove he walked to his armory, which now stretched for a hundred paces filled with tempered steel swords and axes, maces and spears, javelins and shields.

"Tell me, priestess," he smiled, knowing he should not enjoy the fear he knew to follow. "Do you believe what your own eyes see?"

He grasped a three foot sword of blued steel, and Bukayag closed his fist. The fire of creation filled the air with sparks, dim light lighting even the small, armed boy hidden in the corner, and Juchi's bright, green eyes.

As the glow faded, the priestess stared, bewildered. Ruka lurched and swung, snapping the hardened, too-brittle sword in her hand clean in half.

The boy leapt forward as if to strike, and Ruka liked him even more. Juchi held him, and made the mark of Bray.

"Tell me, daughter of the Book." Ruka closed his eyes for effect, then sent the sword back to his Grove. The sparks flickered as the steel blurred and faded like the dead from other men's memory, until Bukayag opened his empty hand. "What am I," he said without tone, perhaps a little curious himself, "what am I if not a god, or a demon, or a prophet? And who are you to challenge me?"

Egil stared, too, transfixed at the hand that had just before held steel. Ruka watched their shoulders slump as the fight drained from even Juchi's eyes. She took the knife from the boy's small hand, and sat quietly beside Egil.

44

Ruka half closed his eyes and kept the fire stoked while Egil and his family slept. In the morning they gathered supplies and clothes and tied them to the horses in silence.

"Aiden should be first," Ruka said at last. "Do you know where he is?"

Egil nodded. "Still in Husavik, incredibly enough. His crimes were all unofficial." Egil glanced uncomfortably at the two mounts.

"You and Juchi can take the mare," Ruka said. "The boy can ride with me."

The ex-priestess reddened, and the boy paled as he looked to her. "His name is Ivar. And is this how you treat all your followers? Frightening their children?"

Ruka smiled, stepping towards them until they both cringed. He turned and seized the boy, lifting him to Sula's back before leaping up behind.

"I mean you no harm," he said quietly. "You must be brave. The future belongs to the bold."

He clicked his tongue and rode East without waiting for a response, and Juchi and Egil mounted and followed, leaving behind most everything they owned. Outcasts or even townsfolk would no doubt squat or steal, but this no longer mattered. Ruka had no intention of beggaring his followers, and would make Egil a rich man one day.

Ivar trembled at first, but soon calmed as the gentle hills passed in silence, and the Noss-monster holding him didn't eat him. The morning was warm and clear, and when they reached a flat field of grass Ruka leaned down and whispered. "Stick out your arms, I'll hold you up."

The boy blinked in fear but obeyed. Ruka urged Sula into a run.

The great stallion snorted in challenge, pawing at the grass before he began. The wind whipped the boy's long hair back with Sula's mane, and even Ruka ducked as he held the boy with one hand and Sula with the other. Ivar yelped but kept his arms wide, and despite the wind he opened his eyes to see the world speed past. Ruka grinned at his wonder.

"Run, Sula! *Ha!*"

The mighty warhorse snorted again, moving full out into a sprint with pleasure across the flat ground until even Ruka clung with his thighs and at last pulled on the reins in caution. Sula returned to a trot, head raised and tail whipping, looking rather pleased with himself.

Ivar glanced up with arms still extended, his heart pounding so hard Ruka could feel it. The boy grinned, and ran his hands through Sula's hair in wonder.

Juchi called as they caught up later. "What is wrong with you? That was *needlessly* dangerous."

Ruka snorted. "So is life, Priestess. Ivar wasn't afraid, were you boy?"

Ivar shook his head, whitened knuckles clinging to the horse, forehead moist with sweat. His lips spread wide in a smile.

"You see? Like Haki the Brave," Ruka summoned the image of the boy's readiness to fight for his family in the dark again with pride. "One day he will ride down his enemies, like Egil Bloodfist, victorious on the field of Wends."

"There was a hero named Egil?" Ivar looked up again, and Ruka shook his head in dramatic disappointment.

"And to think you live with a skald. Yes, Bloodfist was a great legend. He broke his sword in the maw of a mighty beast, then killed it with his bare hands."

Ivar frowned at this. "Seems foolish. He should have carried a seax."

Ruka laughed in genuine pleasure. "Yes, he should have. Always keep yours close, and keep it sharp."

They rode towards Husavik again mostly in silence, Ivar looking comfortable, if distracted, perhaps lost in ancient stories and imagination. The daylight soon exhausted, and they made camp by a patch of bushes large enough to block the wind, eating carrots and what little salted pork Juchi had ready in the house.

"We've left our animals," she said once Ivar fell asleep. "We've left most of our things. God knows what the neighbors or just some wanderer will do while we're gone." She fluffed at the clothes she'd gathered as a bed, separately from Egil's.

Ruka shrugged. "If wealth is your concern, priestess, fear not. Your mate is my trusted retainer. I will shower him with gold and silver in the days to come. You will want for nothing."

"He's not your…I'm *not* a priestess. And my name is Juchi. Try it."

Ruka smiled, and looked at the skald, who chewed silently and stared into the fire.

"I can see why you like her, Egil. She will make a fine mother, and matron."

With that he lay against a bush he'd draped with his furs, and rested, thinking of Beyla. Bukayag watched the family, and Ruka was pleased he did not need to sleep, for he would not have liked to tie their arms and legs.

The next day took them over the flatlands and through another patch of hills, then finally to a road, and Husavik.

Ruka matched the layout of the town against the first time he saw it. A few new houses had been raised, but otherwise it looked much the same. He waited beyond the outer trench with Juchi and the boy, and Egil went inside to make inquiries. He returned pale and sweating.

"There's a new chief here. Or at a least a man who calls himself such and sits in the hall unchallenged. He's not from here. Neither are his warriors."

Ruka nodded, understanding at once the Order had declared Aiden an outlaw in truth, and installed a man from Orhus with their support.

"And this new chief has a matron? And a priestess?"

Egil nodded.

"And what do the men of Husavik say?"

The skald shrugged. "Little with their words. By their faces I'd say they're angry and prefer Aiden as chief. I didn't, well, I'm sorry Ruka I didn't know. He never said, he…"

"And where would Aiden the Outlaw go?"

Egil sighed at this and shrugged, putting a hand to his thick, black hair. "If he had any sense, far away. Perhaps further South, in or at least near a forest, or…"

"No." Ruka grit his teeth and thought of his own time as an outcast. He knew Aiden—he would not truly hide as Ruka the child had done. Nor would these Northerners fight him if they could avoid it and pretend they did not know where he was. "Aiden will be close, and the men of Hulbron will know where. Go back and ask them."

Egil blinked but nodded as his face gained a touch of pink. Perhaps he knew he had failed to comprehend the mind of the brave.

"No need," he said. "If he is truly close, I know the place."

Ruka nodded, and let Egil lead the horses East.

Less than a day's ride from Hulbron took them to a large, often frozen lake filled with algae. Old, trickling rivers sprouted from it South and West, not strong or deep enough to be much use for men, snaking along the land like old, purple veins.

Ruka walked to the bank and stood in plain view when he saw men fishing in a narrow boat near the edge of the water. They turned to face him, and he shook his head as he recognized the chief.

After a time they rowed towards him, and soon Ruka saw Aiden's hard jaw and his stiffened posture. His eyes were restless, and unsure.

"Aiden, son of Tora. I am pleased to see you alive." Ruka recognized most of the burly men in Aiden's boat, save for one older man at the prow, who was no doubt the true fisherman. The others stilled or shifted uncomfortably, and waited on their chief.

"*You* are pleased, shaman? Or are the gods?" He stepped off into shallow water with ease, paddle plunged down as a walking stick, as if he'd been born in this boat and on these shores. His men followed and together they dragged it onto dry land.

Ruka let the good humor he felt remain on his face. "It is time to finish what we started, Aiden. That's why I'm here."

The former chieftain turned, failing or perhaps not trying to mask his glare. "What did we start, *shaman*? Little and less has changed, and none of it good."

Bukayag bristled at the way Aiden said 'shaman', but Ruka kept his calm. "More than you think. Trust the gods, mighty chief, and I will show you."

"Oh I trust the gods, shaman, that has never changed."

Ruka felt his brother's jaw clench, and his eyes narrow. He knew he must be calm, and patient. But he used his brother's disdain.

"I came here by route of Husavik. So tell me, why does another man sit in your hall?"

Aiden scoffed, and tossed his paddle to the earth. "You'll give me back my seat, is that it?"

Ruka let Bukayag's sneer show plain.

"I give you nothing. A man takes what's his, or else doesn't deserve it. I offer opportunity. Follow me, and challenge this 'chief', or sit on this lake and cower."

Aiden blinked in anger and met Ruka's eyes. Like a wolf he sought weakness, or deception—any chance to strike and destroy this thing that challenged him.

"And then what?" he said low and with menace. "Will you start a new doomed rebellion? The Order will send more men. Their Northern lapdogs have a thousand warriors camped in the belt, fortified on a mountainside."

Ruka snorted and stroked Sula's nose, thinking of how much the world had changed, and how grand it could become. "No, not rebellion. One of your retainers will stay and govern Husavik's lands once we've taken them. You and I will go North."

"North? To Orhus? Are you mad?"

"Maybe. But no, not Orhus. We go North as North goes, and beyond. That is where I've been, Aiden—two years in a sun-filled paradise promised by the gods. We go now to make our claim."

The great man stared and stared, no doubt searching for madness just as Egil and Juchi's had. Ruka almost laughed.

Calm yourself, brother, he has not seen as we have, and his world was shattered in Alverel. Give him time to rage and remember his faith. He will rise to greatness yet.

"You needn't believe me," Ruka said more quietly. "Gather your men first. Do it now, today, and I will fight beside you. After this you may decide if Bukayag, son of Beyla, is a herald of the gods, or of woe. The choice is yours."

At this he clucked and climbed to Sula's back, trotting to where Egil and Juchi waited.

Aiden stood for a long moment on the bank of the lake. He shook his head and lifted the discarded paddle, then he and his men stowed their supplies and followed with baskets full of fish.

Ruka said nothing and let Aiden think as they marched to his camp. With some surprise he saw near twenty houses built in two rings on a hill surrounded by sharpened stakes. Men guarded two gated pathways holding bows, whistling as they saw the fishermen return. They opened the gate and stared, open mouthed. Ruka recognized many faces from Alverel.

"*They could betray*", whispered Bukayag, "*we could be swarmed and killed in this place.*"

Ruka agreed, but thought the chances slim. Even if Aiden had lost faith in 'Bukayag' entirely, he was still a man of honor. If he meant to kill him, he would do it himself and in clear view. Ruka had no desire for such a duel, and it would hurt his cause greatly, but nor did he fear it.

Inside the fence, women and children worked and played within the central rings, their voices light and happy as they stitched and sewed and washed. All chatter ceased when Aiden and Ruka entered.

Ruka dismounted, not wanting to sit above Aiden in what passed for his hall. He hid his surprise as he recognized several former retainers, all of whom gaped as they recognized him, then put absent hands to the hilts of rune-swords. Tahar was amongst them—a former chief made outcast, and one of Ruka's first and best retainers.

"May I speak?" Ruka asked the chief once the men had gathered, knowing he must win the man's people before he could be accepted.

Aiden watched him with obvious concern, but finally nodded. To decline would have shown he feared Ruka's words, and diminished him. Ruka walked to the top of the hill.

"I am Bukayag, son of Beyla," he called. "And I know what it is to be rebel and outlaw. I know you have suffered. I know your children have suffered, and your faith has been tested. But I know too you have had each other, and you have had a chief of your choosing. A chief freely chosen without shame. A great warrior, an honest man, bold and respected by the gods."

He waited here to see if the men disagreed with their eyes. But he saw pride, instead.

"I ask for nothing except what brought you together. I ask only for the thing that has always been yours—the thing that makes you greater than all lesser men and women of ash, no matter their houses or riches. *I ask for your courage.*" He points at Aiden. "I ask for what is honorable, and right—loyalty to this man."

He waited and met Aiden's eyes.

"Across this lake, on the other side of fertile land now growing tall with wheat and barley, a man sits in your hall. This man is a Northerner. He has never lived in these lands; he has never starved or prospered on its harvest, nor fought for its safety. His position is unearned. Would you have it otherwise?"

"I would," Aiden almost growled.

"Then there is no more to say. A time will come later for talk of past and future. But today, *now*, is the time for deed, as it has always been. Where you go, I will follow. I say no more."

He stepped from the top of the hill and walked to Sula, who glanced about the dirt and gravel for grass and huffed when he spotted nothing.

All eyes turned to Aiden now, who paused as if to consider the words. Ruka expected he was not a man of fine speeches, but even so found he could not look away as Aiden stepped to the hill. The tall warrior drew a sword from his hip and examined the edge, his voice quiet as always.

"Edda has heard your words, and mine. A thing promised need not be repeated. So. I go to Husavik. Who will match word with deed?"

Tahar stepped forward at once, eyes blazing, hand hovering over his bow. "I will match them."

Many of Ruka's former retainers stepped forwards now unsheathing rune-swords that looked well cared for and polished. "And I," they called, faces turned now as an old spark threatened to renew.

The hill below Aiden circled with drawn swords, and many of Aiden's other followers looked on with some blend of fear, and excitement.

"Tonigh' I slee' in my own huse," called an older Southerner, scarred and one-eyed and ragged. He wrapped perhaps seven fingers around an axe-haft, and spit on the road. Several sets of twins who looked like him stood and growled. More warriors stood beside them—men who had come from all over the land of ash to serve a renowned chief, then found themselves caught in heresy and dishonor and yet did not stray.

"We go in daylight," Aiden said, his voice sure and deadly. "We go outnumbered to an open field." His pleasure showed clearly now in his tone, as if he had only been waiting for this moment—the fearless madness of a man who believed his place in death assured. "There will be no retreat."

45

Egil watched the killers, outcasts and chiefsmen wait in their ramshackle line.

As promised, Aiden and his men had armed themselves and marched straight to Husavik with bloody thoughts, and Ruka had followed. They walked straight to the edge of the town into an open field, Ruka blew his horn, and there they waited.

Now the sun had peaked in its rise, and hundreds of Northerners came behind their new chief with spears and axes, leather and mail to oppose them.

"Easy now, girl, easy."

Egil's horse had been skittish from the start, but with all the men and noise about was verging on anxious panic. He stroked her neck and spoke soothing words, then wondered for a moment who Ruka killed to steal her.

Ivar squirmed in his arms and pointed at Aiden's rune-sword, or maybe at some other man beside, or maybe just couldn't keep his hands down.

"Da, look at that! Do you think they'll win? What happens now?"

Egil sighed. He'd argued with Juchi about his presence before they left. Ruka wanted the boy to come and 'see how men behaved', and ignored Juchi's protests. Once invited, Ivar was ready to bolt out from Aiden's camp and run all the way here himself.

"If Aiden or Ruka falls," Juchi told them both as she collected dried fruits/meats, "you turn that horse and run back here as fast as you can."

He'd been about to promise he would and say whatever was required to put her at ease, but stopped himself. That was the old Egil. And the new Egil told the truth, or at least to Juchi. "Aiden doesn't matter now. But if Ruka falls, I promise we'll run."

Of course he wouldn't fall, not yet, and not here, because that was not how a man like Ruka died. Egil knew that in his bones.

Juchi paced and hadn't really been listening in any case. "In fact you should run when the fighting starts no matter what. He has his men now. He doesn't need you anymore. We can run and hide and he won't care enough to find us."

Egil had closed his eyes and shook his head. "He does, my love. He'll find us and kill you and chop me to pieces unless I serve, just to make a point. And there's nothing we can do about it."

She didn't acknowledge this and kept pacing, as if to find some escape, some clever ruse or stratagem. Egil didn't blame her. She couldn't know, not truly. She'd kicked the table and thrown up her hands and turned to him with a sudden fury.

"*You're a god damn coward.* You've given up. Fine. Well I haven't, and I won't."

Her tone and words had hurt, but still he sympathized. He knew what it was like to believe, to have hope in safety and freedom and how hard it was to see it fall.

"I would die for you," he said softly, "and Ivar. I would do it gladly, Juchi. But it wouldn't help. Ruka will kill you both so the next man who thinks to disobey knows the price. I know it's hard to understand, but please believe me. The only way I can protect you is to serve. Please understand that. Please."

"He's not a god, Egil. He's just a…"

"What? Just a man? No, my love, he never was, not even as a boy. He can see in the dark, I've told you that. I've heard him kill without even enough moonlight to see my hands. In two years I never saw him sleep, not as you or I or beasts sleep."

"Yes you've said, but…"

"Every word of it was true, and more." He took her shoulders and met her eyes. "These are not the fanciful stories of a skald. He knows things he shouldn't, my love, he sees things. Did you not see him draw a sword from nothing? He's not some pious shaman. He mocks the gods with every word, he hates them. He's half man and half demon and all his fine tales are lies. But we can no more stop him than we can stop a storm. We can only weather it and survive. Please, Juchi, *please*. I want you to survive. Let me help you."

Still she'd shaken off his hands and kicked a water-flask across Aiden's guest-room. But when Egil stood still and silent, she'd come back to his arms, and wept.

"I'm sorry, you're not a coward," she whispered. "We'll all survive together."

He'd smiled for her and kissed her, hoping only he was worthy of her trust. But he did not believe for a moment he'd survive. Not this time. This time he would stand beside his master when the 'inferno' came, trapped in his death throes to the unmaking of the world. But Juchi and Ivar would live.

Now, as the sun drooped from its high zenith into a pink and orange sky, he looked out at the new chief of Husavik across the field. A hundred warriors at least gathered with him on the town's edge. They'd assembled in two lines, each as wide or wider than Aiden's, and Egil's heart raced hard and fast.

"Can we win?" Ivar turned, his face now holding some of the fear Egil felt.

"Of course we can," he said. "Numbers aren't everything."

But they're a hell of a lot. And what do I bloody know anyway. I'm a Noss-cursed skald.

He looked down the line of Aiden's warriors, though, and felt at least some hope. Most of these men were those who'd broken hundreds in Alverel. They were blooded warriors who'd killed before; they wore armor and most carried rune-swords. *And, we have Ruka*, he thought, unsure how this made him feel.

Egil turned and spotted his master instantly—the only other man on a horse.

Ruka had 'transformed' again into Bukayag the runeshaman. He'd smeared most of his head and face with ash, then drew runes in the black mask with his finger. He carried a scabbarded longsword he'd no doubt just pulled from nothing, or maybe the mountain god's hell. But—Egil realized as he watched him—he still wore no armor at all. He'd covered his thick torso and limbs only in tight-fitting cloth, without even the leather padding worn by the wildest of Aiden's warriors.

God-cursed madman, he thought, watching him. *Damned bloody arrogant fool. If he's even wounded these men will be shaken...and if he falls...well.*

But wasn't that good? Wasn't that what Egil wanted? For a long, uncomfortable moment as he watched the man, he had absolutely no idea.

Sula broke his thoughts, snorting as he stepped forward from the line. Ruka looked briefly to Aiden for approval, then shouted, his huge voice reaching far enough to scatter a few birds nesting in Husavik's houses.

"Erden of the North."

Men on both sides stopped their chatter or fidgeting and stared at the owner of such a voice. A tall youth wearing the black of a Galdric warrior stepped forward. The lines were close enough for Egil to see sweat shining on the young man's brow. He held his shield firmly, and his eyes looked hard.

"Leave this place," called the would-be chief. "You are outmatched."

Ruka smiled, and pointed a finger at Aiden.

"You have claimed this man's position, yet here he stands. Only a chieftain's blood unmakes him. You and you alone will pay your debt of honor today, or the gods will strike your men from this field."

Many of Husavik's warriors—new and old—exchanged a look at Ruka's threat. The young chief answered in a mocking tone.

"I have seen statues of your gods in Orhus, shaman. Even Vol's cock has crumbled."

Surprised laughter and perhaps pleasure at this boldness swept the Northern line. Egil could see Aiden's face redden with rage, but Ruka only waited. He let the laughter mostly die before he turned and smiled fiercely at the men, something like excitement in his eyes.

"So be it." He raised his arms. With eyes closed, Ruka looked up to the bright sky, and the air around his body shimmered. Sparks flew from his hand as it had in Egil's house. Blue-black steel emerged and seemed to 'grow' from his grasp, reaching higher and higher until Egil realized it was a huge spear, at least the length of two men.

The sparks widened and lowered until they met Ruka's body, which flared even thicker as smooth plates of iron formed over the cloth—first on

Ruka's arm, then down his shoulder, chest and back, linked together by tight-weaved mail.

Still the fire descended. With a roar like a furnace blasted with air, Sula glowed with light. The space around the animal wavered with heat and the warhorse snorted and shook its head as its body wrapped in grey steel mesh. Two iron horns grew from a skull-shaped 'helm' on its head, others from its side just below Ruka's feet. The warhorse stomped and lifted its forelegs and snorted air.

It crashed back to the earth and pawed, not a trace of panic despite the insanity of what had happened—only anger at the surprise. Ruka's other arm seethed with fire until a round-shield of thin metal blocked his left side. He leaned forward, and Sula jerked forward into a trot.

Aiden and his men stared, slack-jawed. No doubt so did the new warriors of Husavik, but Egil couldn't look that far away from his master.

Ruka roared atop his now-armored warhorse, raising his spear in challenge as he charged. Sula's hooves pounded the earth alone across the field towards a hundred men.

Egil stared, feeling somehow outside himself. He had sung many songs for chiefs and would-be heroes performing deeds of valor, and he had embellished them all. But this time, he thought—watching one man charge a tribe—exaggeration would not be required.

* * *

"Woah, boy, calm. Calm."

Ruka soothed Sula as best he could as they advanced. The warhorse balked at the fire and new weight, and Ruka nearly slipped and dropped to the earth when the animal bucked. *That would have rather ruined the effect, I think.* He almost laughed.

His feet dangled almost uselessly now, his armored thighs hindered in their squeeze. He would have to deal with that later. And the plates were too narrow, and uncomfortable, because apparently Pyu had made him fat. Had he not thought to strap himself to the saddle with leather cords, he'd have surely fallen.

But bravely done, Sula, I never doubted you.

In truth he'd doubted greatly, and feared the horse would panic and freeze or throw him when the sparks flew and the feeling and weight of the armor surrounded his flesh. Ruka had built the barding as thin and light as possible, wanting it as much for intimidation as protection. But between this and his own heavy armor, Sula's burden had doubled.

Wind howled by Ruka's bear-head-shaped helm. He tried desperately to match the rhythm and stop from bouncing in the saddle, and for good or ill it seemed the speed of the animal's charge was only mildly affected.

The enemy line grew before him. The baffled and perhaps terrified men directly ahead clutched spear-shafts or axe-handles and looked to their chief. At least two mastered themselves and held out the points of their spears forward.

Break, Ruka prayed as he closed. *Panic and spread out, curse you, or even brave Sula may not charge, and my plan will fall to ruin.*

Warhorses were brave, not stupid. When Sula saw a line of spears in his face he would turn, or stop, and whatever madness in his master's heart be damned. The men needed to split.

Ruka lined up his own spear at the nearest man and hoped the length of his weapon would save him. After that, Sula's wild rage and courage would hopefully be enough to carry them both forward through the line.

Time became measured in the moments of near weightlessness as Sula's hooves left the ground. Water-drops fell in his Grove, and all the world became two men with spears, and the weight in his hand.

Some of the men shouted and fell away or threw rocks or axes, which missed or bounced off Ruka's shield. In the final moments, he managed to see the frozen panic of the man who stood in his path. And then Sula turned.

Ruka's thrust missed its mark utterly. The few spearmen in the enemy line stayed together and did not move.

Sula turned, but he did not stop. With a snort he swerved and crashed his mighty, now-armored chest into the closest man who hadn't raised a spear.

The stricken warrior grunted and hurled aside to his fellows. Sula's legs trampled past him and leapt through the second line just as easily, crushing a man's shield into his face before stomping over him.

A few useless sword and shield swings bounced against the barding, and then Sula was through, turning without command and slowing to a rigid trot, head raised high behind Husavik's line.

Ruka checked himself for injury and found none. His hands shook, and Bukayag woke with a mocking smile.

"Spear, or sword," he said as if to himself, curious about the weather. He looked at the small cluster of ruin Sula had wrought and laughed.

You can have them, brother, all but the chief.

Bukayag growled with pleasure and lifted a spear. *"Die,"* he rasped, and hurled at the closest man.

Even from horseback, the strength was monstrous. Bukayag's javelin tore through a layer of good chain and pierced a warriors chest, still flickering with flames. Bukayag drew another and skewered his next victim straight through his shield.

The men were shouting now in rage. Others found their courage and charged from the line both ahead and behind him.

Bukayag drew a sword and rode Sula around them hacking at heads and arms, then sped away and charged again at the line's edge with a spear. When yet other men broke formation to trap him, he fled and threw more javelins, laughing and howling with every kill or failed attack from his enemy.

When at least fifteen men had abandoned the line to help surround him, firing their weak bows or throwing useless axes or spears—Ruka reminded his brother to blow their horn.

The Northerners startled in confusion, unsure whether to run back to join their shield-wall, or keep chasing the mounted shaman. But they had little time to decide. Aiden and his men began their charge.

* * *

Egil watched Ruka's mad assault with the same awe as everyone else. He watched him break through the line and fight his way free, killing many of those who gave chase. *He is truly a demon*, he thought. *And I will never be free of him.*

The new guardians of Husavik hesitated, or looked to their uncertain chief, watching the men who tried to face Ruka die, or at least fail.

Their good order fell apart as both ends of the line huddled and clumped together, not sure which way to face. Then Ruka blew his horn, Aiden drew his rune-sword, his eager pack of killers drew theirs, and forty men charged together.

Egil felt his horse surge in instinct but held the reins, then ignored the disappointed huff from Ivar. He risked moving forward slowly for a better look, knowing Ruka would expect him to see Aiden's duel clearly.

The Northern chief had regained at least some sense and the men around him formed their shield wall. His undisciplined line had crumbled though and now formed three separate groups. Aiden's line crashed screaming against them all.

The ground was entirely flat, the charge fast and brutal. Men against the two 'side' clusters cried out and buckled against it, many falling on the outside, and the rest trying desperately just to hold their foes in place. Aiden and his fiercest retainers had slowed, and now hacked furiously against the enemy chief's cluster.

Through all of it, Ruka's mad laughter pierced the din. Men skewered with javelins littered the field, some still alive and groaning, half crushed from Sula's charges, knocked senseless and trampled beneath his hooves. When he was free, Ruka charged at the would-be chief's failing shield wall. Men seemed to all but close their eyes as they swung at him, or simply turned and ran.

Aiden smashed shields apart in a rage to get at his foe, sometimes reaching with a bare hand to simply pull men out of formation while his followers deflected sword and axe blows. Chief Erden, who had till now stayed between the lines, was finally hurled forward by his men.

All fell away naturally to the flanks until he and Aiden stood on both ends of a circle. Even in the North, men of ash respected a duel.

Ruka must have seen too and blew his horn again, and the fighting trickled and ceased as Aiden's men backed away.

Aiden himself said nothing. He seized an offered shield from a retainer and clanged his runesword against it. Seeing his men's fear and failure, Chief Erden yelled and rushed bravely, slashing wildly then bashing forward with the boss of his shield.

Aiden blocked the first and met the second with his own guard, throwing his weight behind it and knocking the smaller man away. Without waiting he followed and slashed apart chunks of wood with his blade, every blow staggering Erden around the clearing.

Aiden followed him chopping with frightening precision, and even to Egil it soon seemed clear he avoided the kill. Blow after terrifying blow threw his enemy off balance, thrashing him around the circle like a child.

"*Chieftain of Husavik?*" Aiden finally cried, then cut down hard and knocked the young man's sword from his hand. The big man's chest heaved as he he spit, looking about at the men around him. He was unwounded, almost untouched.

"Chieftain of Husavik," he said, slowly and calmly again, lips curled. He dropped his shield and seized Erden by the throat. He shoved his sword straight through the man's armor, through his breastbone, then waited until the last gasps ended, and the death twitches ceased.

Most of Erden's retainers dropped their weapons to the dirt at once. Ruka dismounted and scattered some as he walked to Aiden's side.

"Do you claim his position, Aiden, son of Tora?"

The big man sneered. "It was always mine."

"Then the gods say this township belongs to the South." Ruka looked at Aiden, who nearly matched his height. "These men fought bravely. Will you spare them, and accept their fealty?"

Aiden glanced at his foes, and with menacing calm stepped on the throat of a dying man beside his foot. Egil flinched at the crunch.

"Who amongst you will re-claim your honor," Ruka called. "Who will serve this mighty chief?"

Egil expected 'serve, or die,' was understood. The sweat covered and red-faced warriors nodded and swore their grateful, eternal loyalty as a group.

"Then it is done." Ruka's sword and shield vanished into shimmering air and many watching gasped. He untied his cloak and spread it on the ground, then looked up to the heavens as he had before on horseback, and raised his arms. "Mighty Vol, Even-handed. I, Bukayag, son of Beyla, ask you justly reward your faithful champion, and the brave warriors who fight at his side."

The men looked on, glancing up at the sky as if for some miracle, and Egil felt the urge to mock them.

Had he never met Ruka he would have rolled his eyes, but now the impossible seemed possible. Just as Ivar and every man on the bloody field outside Husavik, he watched the white-clouds for a floating demi-god, or a flying horse, or some other ridiculous, immortal thing. And just as before, the impossible came.

Sparks and flame erupted from the air, this time above Ruka's head. The sun glittered off something flat, polished and grey. Along with the rest of the crowd—who had moments before been ready to kill the other—Egil watched and blinked in silence as perfect, clean, pieces of silver rained from the sky, bouncing and clinking as they filled the cloak in a pile.

"Vol blesses your courage," Ruka smiled. "Aiden, Chieftain of Husavik, your years of faith will be rewarded. Distribute this first token to your men as you see fit."

Aiden dropped instantly to a knee, his old warriors following at once. "Forgive my weakness, shaman. I ask for nothing."

Ruka placed a hand on Aiden's shoulder, then stilled and waited until the men looked to him.

"The children of Tegrin have tested men long enough. The time of faith and suffering without hope has ended, cousins. Now with courage comes reward." He closed his eyes, and the flames of Vol or maybe Noss burned an outline around Aiden's body, as it had before for Ruka and his steed.

Smooth, polished metal rings draped across the huge man's chest and limbs. He jerked in surprise, just as Sula had, then rose, eyes blinking in the false light. He stared as even his wrists sheathed in god-forged armor. Egil noticed the clasps and ties of the separate pieces—all made exactly to Aiden's form. It ended with a blue-tinged breastplate inscribed with black runes.

Ruka studied it as if reading the symbols for the first time, and looked pleased. "Rise, Champion, bearer of Vol's favor and gift. Behold, men of ash, Aiden, son of Tora, Chieftain of Husavik, Shield-Breaker."

The big warrior blinked wide, watery eyes, staggering as if he may fall again to his knees. Even before he spoke, Egil could see the utter belief, the pure fanatical devotion growing in his face. "Please…shaman, tell me Vol's will, I beg you. By…holy oath, before these men and Edda and all the gods, I will see it done."

Ruka nodded in approval, and Egil watched his pleasure and his bearing and his damned charismatic mask. And despite everything, despite all logic and all the things he'd seen, somehow, *somehow* he knew this was all a trick. It was all a trick.

Ruka closed his eyes and looked to the heavens, as if hearing divine command.

"North, Aiden. The Gods beckon. They call you North."

46

After the battle, Ruka and Aiden entered Husavik with their retainers behind them. They stayed clustered and ready for violence in case the Order had more warriors or some other deception. But they found no men, nor even boys. The streets were empty.

Matrons and their daughters stood guard at every doorway of every house. They held seaxes or axes and barred the entrance to their homes.

Egil gawked because he had heard of such a thing, but never seen it. All the remaining mates, fathers, brothers and sons of Husavik would be hiding inside, hoping Aiden and his men didn't push their way through and slaughter them.

"Peace," an old woman shouted. One by one the matrons tossed axes and seaxes onto the road as the warband passed, taking up the call. "Peace. Peace."

Aiden strode past them all towards his hall and said nothing. Egil was surprised when some of the women smiled, even waved, as if happy and unafraid and taking part in the old ritual only out of solidarity with their neighbors.

He realized for many of them, their absent mates and sons were returning victorious, having followed their old chief into the country to hide. But not all.

Many women stood frozen and pale. When a new Southern chief won his title in a duel or battle, he and his followers often killed the rival men and boys. The able-bodied might escape, or the women might send their children away on horseback if they had the wealth. But the old, the poor, and the unlucky would often perish.

Egil watched the angry, jealous eyes of some of the men and knew there would be blood. Some who had left with Aiden, he expected, had been replaced. Many of these replacements now lay dead in a field, but not all, and the Southerners perhaps began to understand their replacements were their new 'allies', and marched beside them a sword-stroke away.

Aiden reached his hall unchallenged. A mother of no more than fifteen stood before the wide, double-doors. She carried no seax, but rather clutched two infants. Her brow shone with sweat and she swayed slightly as the men approached, her eyes scanning the now god-steel clad Aiden.

"I am Ida, First Mother of Husavik," she said, almost panting with fear.

Aiden glanced at her little boys—the children of his dead enemy—then met her eyes. His expression of contempt looked much the same as it had for the 'chief' before he slaughtered him.

"I do not know you," he said in his quiet way. "Agnes, daughter of Gerta, has survived sixty winters in Husavik, and birthed fifteen sets of twins." He blinked, looking round at the watching matrons, then back to the girl. "Yet you tell me the women here have chosen *you* as First Mother?"

The girl's lip trembled but she raised her chin. "The priestesses, it was they who decided…"

"*Priestesses* are not the heart of Husavik," Aiden snarled. "*Mothers* are." He walked to the center of the town circle. "I serve the gods, and this town. Tell me who speaks for you, Matrons. Tell me your will. I will slaughter any man who denies it, that is my vow."

The young woman trembled but said nothing. An old, but still healthy looking great-matron stepped from her doorway. She waited until the other women had clucked their tongues, knocked on their houses, or nodded in approval.

"I have that honor, Chieftain. I am First Mother here."

"Agnes," Aiden nodded in respect. "A chief must have a matron. Mine is old, and long ago left for the North." He shrugged. "I'll need another."

The First Mother smiled.

"My womb is long dry, so I give up that honor. But Husavik needs strong children." She looked at the terrified girl standing before Aiden's hall, and pointed. "Ida's mate is dead. She is headstrong and arrogant, but young and fertile, and we will guide her. Will you accept her?"

To ask this was custom, and polite, but Aiden had no choice and neither did Ida. He nodded, and the First Mother's face tightened.

"She has two sons. Do you accept them?"

Aiden glanced around at his warriors and the matrons frozen in doorways, and renewed his look of disgust. "A chief punishes men, not boys. I accept them."

The women seemed to take a collective breath, some moving finally from doorways, as if the ordeal had ended. But Aiden held up a hand, and the gathering stilled.

"Now tell me, First Mother." His quiet voice hardened. "How many women in this village have taken more than one of my retainers as their mates?"

The old woman's eye twitched as she glanced at Ida, then spit orange root from a toothless mouth. She looked carefully at the warband's faces.

"Seven, Chief."

"Have them step forward."

The old woman took a deep breath and nodded. The other women looked to her with helpless panic, but she ignored them, and called out seven names.

All those who stepped forward were young, childless, or pregnant. They had no doubt been freshly made Matrons when their mates picked up and left them to follow an outlaw chief, with no idea if they would return.

Aiden's Southern retainers knocked their swords against shields or stomped their feet or rumbled a sound deep in their throats. They stepped apart and formed a circle around the town center, until only fourteen men remained inside.

Egil had never seen this either. He watched the fear on the Northern men's faces and couldn't help but feel pity, for they had no doubt followed a new chief from their homes with little choice, then to their great shock and pleasure received new, young mates with land and households. And for a few years, at least, they must have felt blessed. Then Ruka and Aiden killed their chief and tossed the coin of fate again. Now they would surely die.

Aiden's retainers ground their teeth or jerked with rage, the pleasure at the duels apparent in their eyes. All were true warriors. All had come from around the Ascom just to serve a famous chief, and their scarred bodies were thick with muscle. They held their shields with practiced comfort, and each wore an earring that showed they had killed before in a duel.

Their Northern counter-parts seemed ordinary men. These were citizens of Orhus, or at least more civilized towns where few ever dueled to the death over honor. Their frightened eyes roamed the town in horror, looking perhaps for some escape or answer.

Their women, though, could do nothing. Rejecting either man would dishonor them. For the insult, the Southerners would kill regardless. If the women instead rejected the Northerners, the men would have to fight or else be considered worthless and dishonoring their new chief. For that, they would be killed.

"One at a time. You fight to the death." Aiden stepped to the center. "Burned or buried, brothers?"

"Buried," called the Southerners together in a single voice.

The Northerners glanced at each other and around the town as if locked in some terrible nightmare. Some mumbled "Burned," quietly and huddled together.

The first of Aiden's warriors stepped forward with a growl, his opponent shakily. A woman watching wept and placed a hand over her mouth, and turned towards her house as if to go inside.

"You will watch." Ruka's voice shook the gathering. He had been silent during the exchange, but Egil looked and saw a rage swelling in his eyes. Even Aiden flinched at the call, and a few children cried at the sound. Egil saw what he thought was genuine anger in his master's face and shivered, though he was unsure why it had come. "You played your part," Ruka hissed through his teeth. "You will suffer at least this."

Both duelists glanced at the young woman, emotions splaying clear across their faces. Finally they looked to each other. Aiden stepped aside and nodded, and they both charged.

It ended almost before it began. Blood and guts spilled to the gravel before a single shield broke, and Aiden stepped into the circle and plunged his sword into the dying Northerner's chest.

Two of his followers dragged the corpse away as a cry of despair left the girl's lips. Her mother or perhaps sister held her from falling, and Egil noticed the slight bulge of her belly.

"Next." The chief kicked dirt over the blood.

Two more men stepped into the ring of bodies and fought on the stained gravel. This time they broke two shields, but another Northerner died. Dirt and rock covered the spot. The chief called, and two more men fought beneath a growing twilight.

Every new duel brought the death of another Northerner, quickly or slowly, bravely or in terror. Soon the few survivors cringed at every sword-stroke, pallors worsening as they waited their turns.

Then six men lay heaped in a pile as torches lit and the men fought by moonlight, and the last Northerner stepped onto a circle stained with his countrymen's gore. His enemy howled and charged and soon broke apart his shield.

He took another and wiped his sweat, and even Egil felt anxious for the man. He kept his guard high and sword poised and soon lost another shield.

The Southerners howled for blood and to see the thing finished, a dishonor wiped clean. Egil saw their hunger for it—the primal, communal stain wanted expunged with their brother's deeds. But the last Northerner fought well. He kept his focus, blocking and moving his feet until his third and final shield broke.

Without it, he was surely a dead man. Still he danced around the circle, parrying and narrowly avoiding his death until the crowd of men jeered, and his opponent charged to finish him. He reeled away as if caught and stumbling for escape, then with a strength and speed he had not once displayed in the duel, he swept past the larger man's guard, and cleaved through half his thick neck.

All stood silent as the favorite writhed in dying agony on the ground. Aiden stepped forward without pause, and pierced the man's heart.

"It is done," he said, then looked round at the angry faces of his original retainers—warriors who had fought beside the fallen man for years.

"He fought like a coward," said one of the other Southerners as he stepped forward and spit. "He offends me. He fights again."

Aiden stood silent as he considered, but Ruka jerked forward. Whatever rage had consumed him seemed only to have grown during the violence. His movements were forceful, his neck muscles taut.

"The duels are done. Your man is dead. Accept it."

The Southerner looked surprised but held his ground, eyes glassy with grief. He pointed his sword at the small, exhausted Northerner. "This man has offended me. He killed my brother with trickery. I will have satisfaction."

Ruka growled and drew his sword, golden eyes bright and bulging in the fading light. Egil saw the killer only ever held at bay—the thing inside his master that swallowed life with joy.

"*And your words offend* me." Ruka's chest heaved, and every man near-by seemed to take a step away. "Can offense be forgiven, cousin, or can it not? *Choose.*"

The warrior gaped and looked to his chief, who stood very still until he shrugged. Seeing no protection, the Southerner blinked until his grief-filled eyes lost some wetness. As they did, next to Ruka's menace, the man seemed to shrivel.

"It can," he said, "the day is red enough."

Ruka shook the rage from his eyes and plunged his sword back to its scabbard. The little Northerner dropped to a knee.

"I pledge my sword to you in thanks, shaman. Please accept me."

Egil twitched at the scoffs from Aiden's men. No Southerner would 'ask' for acceptance—they would simply offer. Ruka glanced at the chief, who only smiled as if amused.

"What is your name?"

"Eshen, shaman."

Ruka watched the man as if curious. "Surely you see I am Noss touched, Eshen, and not a chief. I hear the will of the gods and so men heed my words. But there is no great honor in serving me."

"I am no great man, Bukayag, son of Beyla."

Ruka grinned at this, and some of his anger perhaps began to fade. "A free man serves who he wills," he said. Then with frightening speed, he reached and knocked the kneeling man's blade from his hand. He seized his forearm and used it to lift him to his feet. The air shimmered with heat and fire as a blue-tinged, long, wavy dagger almost slithered into Eshen's hand. The dark handle held two silver runes.

"Spider's Fang," said Ruka, again as if reading it for the first time. He watched the huge eyes of his new retainer with obvious pleasure. "Noss, too, chooses His champions, often the clever, or the cunning. May it serve you well against your enemies."

Eshen nodded in reverence, and Ruka released him. He walked away from the pile of corpses, calling back over his shoulder.

"You have the night, Aiden, and tomorrow. Bring your other women and children here, and whatever supplies you have in your other camp. In two days, rain or sleet, the faithful go North."

* * *

After the duels, the warriors of Husavik went to their rest. Most matrons welcomed their former lovers with open arms—men embracing their children and mates before doors closed and happy families re-united.

Egil could only imagine the 'welcome' for the duelists.

Two years before they had left Husavik to follow Aiden into outlawry, and for whatever reason their matrons had not followed. Now these men returned to the same women, mostly teenagers, some impregnated by other men. Before even a greeting their former men slaughtered the new—the women's mates for two years—then walked through their doors for 're-union'. Now they would leave them again.

Egil put Ivar to his rest in Aiden's hall, then stood by the outer trench and relieved himself. For just a brief moment before the mad future of death ahead, he had wanted to be alone.

"Such a waste."

Egil jerked and just barely missed pissing on his fine, leather shoes. He finished and turned to see Ruka by a cart heaped with the dead. His master's expression matched his tone, and Egil thought he understood his anger.

"Don't worry, lord, we'll find you more warriors."

Ruka looked into the night and appeared not to be listening. He shook his head as he poked and prodded at the bodies, as if to take a better look at the injuries.

"They were so close," he said, voice sounding more sad than angry. "If only the women had waited. A few months with a cold bed and seven more men might have seen paradise."

Egil looked around the circle and saw no one listening. He could see no reason for Ruka to deceive, but nor were regret or concern things he expected to hear from his master while they were alone.

"They would have had no choice, lord," he said, though this seemed obvious.

Ruka looked up from the pile of dead men in confusion, though, and Egil reminded himself that for all the man's brilliance, he had never truly lived in a town with others. He didn't know many of their intimate customs.

"The women's mates were outcasts, lord, and they were young. The old mothers would have chosen for them as soon as possible. It's…tradition."

Ruka's golden eyes flicked in acknowledgment. "Honor." He spat the word. "Tradition." He breathed out and walked the town's central road, gravel crunching beneath his feet. "You're all slaves, Egil. But I will free you. I will drag you from this place kicking and screaming if I must."

His master looked to the clouds and closed his eyes, breathing deeply as if tasting fine pork. He clasped his hands behind his back, and smiled faintly.

"You will enjoy paradise, skald. But you will miss Ascomi air, I think. Enjoy it while you can."

Egil nodded as if this comment made some sense to him. But, as was often true with Ruka, he did not understand, and had no idea what to say.

By evening Aiden left for his old camp with a small pack of warriors, and in his absence asked the First Mother to host a feast in his hall for the others. Egil sat at Ruka's side throughout.

Many of the men now watched 'the last runeshaman' with an awkward, open reverence. He did not jest or make smalltalk as any chief would. His eyes looked far-away, his forehead wrinkled in concentration, as if even as he spooned mutton broth to his lips he listened to the gods.

Largely the townsfolk of Husavik seemed pleased with the day of blood. Many of their men had returned, their famous chief back in his hall. A strained silence gulfed some duelists from their mates, and Northerner from Southerner, but some, it appeared, had begun to make peace.

As the wine flowed the men around Egil spoke of their wild battle and Sula's charge. They lamented the state of the world, and described their time as outlaws. They spoke of the silver Aiden had yet to gift, and soon the crops they could perhaps hire men to work this season, and the fine prospects in their future.

Egil did his best not to show his amazement, or scoff at all their 'plans'.

Had they not heard their new 'prophet' call for the end of the world? Did they not know what 'paradise' meant? Did they not truly understand?

He supposed the end of all things could scarcely be imagined by normal men. Whether or not that meant they believed or not, he had no idea. Perhaps they thought it only in some distant future, too far to be planned for or seriously considered. He supposed he too had believed things in his youth he did not follow. All his life he'd believed Edda heard men's words, and still he had lied, and broken oaths. Had he believed he'd escape judgment, he wondered? Or did he just not care?

Throughout the feast he watched the door, waiting for Juchi and for some reason afraid she'd walk in and see him at Ruka's side.

Whether or not she actually accepted their situation as hopeless and without choice he did not know. No matter what she said he feared she would look at him and see a traitor—an ungrateful coward who spurned her love the moment his 'master' returned.

Would she hate him soon, he wondered? Would he know the moment when it came, or would she learn to fool him?

The thought felt heavy and painful, and he blinked and hid the water in his eyes. He expected one day she would simply take Ivar and run, knowing Ruka only wanted Egil. It was precisely what she should do, and if Egil were a better man it's what he would have suggested. But he did not want them to leave.

Gravel crunched outside beneath boots, and men and women's voices echoed from behind the wooden walls. Egil felt both relieved and terrified.

Aiden threw open the doors, and followers old and new greeted each other politely. Some embraced, and the hall filled with motion and speech as the men gave women seats and sat together in groups on the floor. Children and dogs ate and played, oblivious to the excitement and fear of their elders and masters.

Juchi entered with the others smiling bravely. She walked passed Egil and squeezed his hand before sitting with the women.

Warmth enveloped Egil's body at once at this simple gesture, though he nearly wept at the cruelty of fate. He decided if a man was to be stripped of everything in the world he loved, then it should at least happen quickly, and not in tiny pieces over time. An execution should be swift.

Many of the mothers came to offer Aiden their congratulations—no doubt especially those with young sons. He smiled at them and offered his support, promising to protect their land and kin. The men, too, crowded around him. They drank and boasted and mocked each other's roles in the battle, or the ease of their duels. The Southern warriors laughed and boasted the loudest. Some of Ruka's surviving retainers, now sworn to Aiden, watched and listened and said little. The Northerners mostly drank.

"Who will harvest my matron's crops?" said one man after enough wine, a little too loudly.

"Aye," agreed a few others.

Aiden held up a hand for calm. "Every man will be given silver for his matron's house. They will handle hiring farmhands and whatever else is required."

"And who will protect that land? And our sons and matron's property?"

"Aye. And what if the Order comes? They've still an army near the Beltway. Only a matter of time before they learn what happened here. Might be all of us couldn't stop them."

"And if we're to go," another man raised a skin, perhaps only half in jest, "give us a few more nights to sire sons first, aye?"

The men laughed, but Egil could sense their discomfort. Most were afraid to truly voice their thoughts and what they wanted, and felt safe only in jest. Aiden glanced at Ruka, who said nothing, still staring far away.

By now the women had heard this talk and stopped to listen as well. In the silence, the First Mother's voice rang across the room.

"Husavik's sons have been gone too long already. Will the gods not give them another few nights, perhaps even a week or a full moon with their families? Have they not earned at least that reward?"

All eyes in the hall soon dragged carefully to Ruka. Egil instead watched Juchi. He saw her grin, saw her hope grow again now that perhaps the men could sway and temper the Noss-touched demon's madness. But Egil knew better. He looked away.

Ruka swayed in his chair and blinked, as if pulled from some reverie. He looked around the faces of Aiden's hall, hearthlight flickering in his golden eyes.

"A day? A week? Why not another season?" The giant's face rippled with scorn. "Why not watch another generation of your kin die of starvation? Why not huddle in your beds in terror, afraid you won't last the winter, afraid of drought and disease and Northerners and the Steppes?"

At this he stood and hurled his chair back across the room, which stilled and silenced. He looked for dissent, for argument, daring someone to speak. None did.

"The gods will not save you, cousins. They care nothing for cowards. But I tire of watching it. I go North. I go to see that your children have more.

I go to end the fear and suffering that has plagued us all our lives." Here his tone changed, anger and judgment flickering in his voice like the hearthlight in his eyes. "But if you prefer, then wait. Stay in your homes and sleep in soft beds next to soft flesh while the future withers. Stay still, stay silent, and watch death as it comes. But you will never see paradise."

With this, Ruka looked away again as if drained. His eyes returned to a far-off stare at a darkened window, and wood cracked and splintered on the fire. Two dogs snarled as they wrestled over a bone.

Aiden broke the silence as he rose with a groan from his chair, a stiffness it seemed in his back. He clenched his jaw before he spoke.

"I go North with the shaman's guidance." He pointed at the men. "Tahar, what will you do?"

The ex-chief rose up. "If Bukayag says tonight we storm the mountain, brother, I will be first."

"And you, Eshen of the North, what will you do?"

"I go with Bukayag, Chief, to Noss if I must."

"And I," called another of Ruka's few surviving retainers.

"And me," said another.

"And what of you, Egil, great skald, what will you do?"

Egil flinched as Aiden turned to him. His chair creaked as he pushed back, standing awkwardly to his full height. He avoided Juchi's eyes with every shred of will he had.

"I go North, mighty chief, to sing songs of the brave, so their kin will remember their names forever."

Many others rose at this and clasped hands and arms, until even the Northerners stood with perhaps some small chagrin, and the men laughed and drank again and made no more jokes about the other's prowess.

Egil sat back down, forgotten, until the next time men needed glory.

I'm sorry, my love, he thought, seeing Ruka's small twitch of pleasure, no matter how he might try to hide it. *Forgive me,* he begged, though he still didn't dare to look at her. *You may think I could have stopped him now. But you are wrong. And the day I fail him, the day I turn against him, that is the day you die.*

47

Birmun, son of Canit, Chief of the Iron River, drew his sword.

"Dag, hold him down."

Dagmar, Birmun's most loyal retainer, grunted as he threw his considerable weight against the murderer in his grasp. Birmun rose his voice, and tried to sound official.

"For the crime of murder without honor, and for the High Priestess of the South, I claim this man's life." He raised the blade and waited, expecting the man to buck like a mule.

A small crowd of curious townsfolk and warriors had gathered and looked on, though most walked by, going about their day. The accused spit and threw his head back in a failed attempt to break Dag's nose, thrashing and twisting like an unbroken horse.

"Go *fuck* yourself," he hissed. Birmun sighed.

Another of his retainers smashed down with a club, and the crack of the man's forearm made many in the crowd wince.

"Noss cursed...cowards," he roared. "My brothers will *kill* you!"

The club fell again and shattered his hand with a sickening crunch. This time he screamed. His arms buckled and he fell, his neck sliding between the wooden slot in the board beneath him, and Dag threw the latch above.

The murderer howled in rage, jerking against the wooden pillory. It was made of fine carved yew, though, and he had no chance of escape.

In a smooth, gruesomely coordinated motion—well-practiced in the last year—Dag rammed the man forward from behind so his neck would stick out slightly from the binder, and Birmun cleaved off his head.

A few boys from the crowd cheered. Most of the 'temporary' citizens of the newly made town of Varhus shrugged and returned to their business. The entertainment was over.

"Well, that's that." Dag stood up red-faced from his efforts. Birmun nodded, then reached down to grab the corpse by the shoulders. "Ah let the damned nightmen take him," Dag complained. "Bugger kicked like a wild ass. Tired me out already."

By 'nightmen' he meant the lowest social order of men—so named because they were only permitted to work in darkness. They spent their lives cleaning the waste and the dead and killing rats or other nuisances, and very often had no matrons, children, honor, or hope.

Dag flushed a shade more like purple after his words, perhaps remembering his chief had been forced to live as a nightman for years. Without another word he reached down and took the corpse's legs.

Birmun masked his smile. He could have let another of his men take the corpse, but in all difficult or unpleasant things he wanted his warriors and the townsfolk seeing him do what he asked of others.

Besides, he thought, *I will always be 'The Nightman Chief'. I have a reputation to uphold.*

He placed the gaping-mouthed head on the corpse's stomach, then together with his retainer heaved it all into a near-by cart. Having dealt with such things all his life—and much worse—the distaste and revulsion clearly present on his follower's face always amused him. This time he let it pass without jest.

"God cursed messengers," Dag muttered. "When do we get more horses?" He pushed the cart, with some difficulty, through the half-dirt and half-gravel muck of Varhus's side roads. Birmun pulled from the front.

"Soon," he said, and grinned. Dag returned it, and both men laughed.

"This fucking place."

"Aye. But it'll end."

"You've been saying so for a year, Chief. No, a year and *a half.*"

Birmun had stopped counting but supposed that was true. Following the priestesses, he had come down nearly two years before to 'put down rebellion', and kill Bukayag, son of Beyla with nearly a thousand men from Orhus. Only forty or so were his own sworn retainers, the rest 'gifted' temporarily by the many chiefs in the North for just this purpose. In all that time, though, he had found little trace of rebellion, and none at all of 'the last runeshaman'.

Many of the men he'd been 'gifted' were also no such thing. They were too old or too young, drunks and rule-breakers, insolent or incompetent. The great chiefs of Orhus had taken the opportunity, it seemed, to dispose of their worst men. *And more worthless mouths to feed.*

Birmun grunted as he tripped on a rock, then shot Dag a look to ward off the grin. Their path to the outer trench was entirely downhill. Varhus, which was just as much fort as it was town, had been built on the side of a small mountain on the Eastern reach of Alverel. The idea at first was to protect their camp from attack, so they'd constructed a stockade that circled a sheer cliff and network of caves, then hunkered down and waited for their scouts.

But days and weeks and then months went by without battle or a need for the army, and the camp followers grew. The valley and surrounding towns came to feed, entertain and otherwise supply the warriors, and many never left. Life for Birmun soon became an endless cycle of miserable logistics, begging the priestesses for more coin and more supplies, and just trying to keep order.

At the bottom of their little mountain, Birmun and his men dumped their grisly cargo and sighed as they looked up the slope.

"I need a drink," Dag said. Birmun almost instantly agreed.

He had a hundred things to do, of course, but the men looked at him like little boys, and by any god you please—he needed a drink, too.

"Great Chief!"

Hooves stomped across the flat stone base of Birmun's mountain, and he turned with a sigh. An Arbman, or messenger-scout of the Order, raced towards the spear-like fence with his arm raised and a scroll in hand.

Birmun waved him in without a shred of pleasure.

He'd dealt with this rider before and recognized him, so he walked to the bored-looking warriors at the fence of wooden spikes and told them to open it. They groaned and lifted the wood and iron contraption to clear a space, and horse and rider squeezed through the almost inadequate effort.

"I bring message, chief, for big priestess." The short, little steppesman—most Arbman were small and light—dismounted and glanced up the steep incline with a grimace. "But…you may deliver."

Birmun cocked an eyebrow and grabbed the scroll. "Medek, if you send me up that damn mountain, it better be important, or I'll sit you on that bloody fence."

The horse-tribesman nodded and hunched to put his hands on his knees while he caught his breath. When he stood he glanced around and leaned forward, lowering his voice to a whisper.

"Husavik is taken, chief, by outlaw. A Great Mother sends me herself."

Birmun blinked and met the messenger's eyes. "Taken?" He lowered his voice. "By outlaws? What sort of outlaws can take a town?"

Medek grinned, as if knowing he shouldn't say but couldn't resist—a common trait, no doubt, in men who carried secrets.

"Bukayag, son of Beyla, says Mother. He leads and throws fiery spears from hell, she says, on warhorse made of iron."

* * *

Birmun left his men to drink, and ascended the mountain alone.

Almost instantly he saw a few men dumping waste in an area they weren't allowed. He ignored this and moved on, and soon saw warriors tormenting builders and no doubt stealing from them. He saw a sodomite being forced to work despite his protest, and half a dozen men waiting their turn. Such was daily life on Varhus.

He soon regretted not bringing his men, too, because he attracted a few stares and in truth he had many enemies. Every day he had to punish someone, it seemed, and though he was chief and had many loyal men, he had a great deal more who *weren't* loyal. He quickened his pace.

Halfway up the side of the walkable face of the mountain, Birmun reached the so-called 'Priestess Cave'—or as often snickered by the men —'Galdra's hole'.

The smell of damp salt hit him at the entrance and he cleared his throat to keep from chuckling at the name. The 'caves' were in fact ancient lava-beds, drilled when the mountains spewed flame and melted the stone into almost perfect, rounded tubes. Some of the walls still looked wounded from the experience, translucent crystals in whites, greens and reds showing like the rock's innards laid bare, stalagmites and stalactites framing beside like broken ribs.

Birmun nodded at the two men guarding the narrow opening before stepping past. He used only his own retainers to watch the caves, and placed all the most critical supplies within. In the deeper tunnels they'd built almost permanent homes for crates and crates of salt, tools, and vellum. And of course, Dala.

Once past the first small 'guard room', the cave opened into deeper cavern. Birmun saw a group of women in torchlight sitting on boxes in intense conversation. He entered the light and stood at a respectful distance, waiting to be noticed.

Dala saw him first, and smiled. The sight stirred him still. She had been just a girl when he met her, full of fire and life and passion. But she had a hardness, a metal spirit forged in some unknown fire beyond Birmun's understanding. For a time he'd hoped it might temper and soften, but no longer. It made no difference. He was entirely hers.

She soon rose and dismissed the women politely, but Birmun could tell the meeting had been strained. He nodded in respect and they returned it as they passed. Both were merchants who sold goods North and South down the Spiral, both from rich families who had traded for a hundred years.

"That looked interesting," he said when he and Dala were alone.

"They're threatening to leave." She sighed. "They're running out of stock and will need to buy more from Orhus or wherever else, but they're afraid our camp will disappear one day soon and leave them with far too much supply. They want a *guarantee*, somehow, as if anything in this life can be certain. Bloody merchants."

She looked over his shoulder and shouted to the guards. "Don't let anyone else in, I need to take Birmun down to storage for a moment."

One waved a hand, and she led Birmun deeper into the caves.

"Good, I should see the state of the supplies, and we're still waiting on horses, Dala. And if…"

She turned and seized a handful of his crotch, her eyes glassy.

"I want you. Now."

He blinked and saw the hunger, and felt his loins tighten even before she started massaging. With her other hand she worked at his belt, and with a growl he pulled up her long priestess' dress with both hands until he could get one under and between her legs. His heart pounded when he found she wore no smallclothes, that she was smiling at his discovery, and more than ready.

He pushed her down to a crate, spread her legs and took her right there, trying only to hide his bites and clawing where they'd be covered by her clothes. He grabbed every part of her, letting some of the wild craving he was forced to hide emerge. When they were finished, she sunk against him and wrapped her arms and legs around his body, and half groaned, half sighed.

"Just what I needed." She kissed him almost chastely on the cheek, slipping her breasts back inside their cloth and straightening her dress. Birmun watched and tried to soak up every moment in his mind to sustain him in the nights to come.

"Not that I'm complaining," she chewed her lip as she straightened herself, then leaned up and kissed him one last time. "But I assume you climbed up here for a reason?"

He nodded and slumped on a barrel, already missing the oblivion of lust. He took the scroll from his belt and held it. Now that they were so close he noticed the dark, purple smears under Dala's eyes. Her lips were dry, her hair verging on unkempt, her shoulders tense. It made him want to protect her, but he didn't know how. He tried to do what he could, to take what weight he could, but he knew it was never enough. He only hoped she could take this news and carry it, too.

"A message from the First Mother of Husavik." He handed it to her, having only the word of the messenger on its contents, since like most men he could not read.

Dala snatched it, brow furrowed with concern and perhaps curiosity as she unfurled the vellum and scanned the symbols.

"Don't worry," he said. "I'll gather the men and we'll go sort it out. Honestly something for them to do will be helpful…"

"No." Dala put the Vellum to her chest and closed her eyes. She squirmed almost like a little girl, and shouted "Thank you, Goddess!", her voice echoing around the caves.

Birmun gaped for a moment in surprise. "It won't be him, Dala. 'Bukayag's' are always popping up, and we know Aiden and his men are camped nearby. No doubt they've just caught the new chief by surprise."

"It doesn't matter. Don't you see?" She sat beside him. "This isn't some lone fool trying to make a name. It's fresh rebellion. Fresh evidence of the need for this army in the first place. I can send scouts further now, ask for more supplies."

She jerked forward and threw her arms around Birmun's neck, and in the warmth of it he was just pleased he'd decided to bring her the message himself. He stood still, not wanting to break the contact, but she pulled away and stood to pace.

"Husavik still needs to be dealt with," he said. "I'll take two hundred men. We can be there in two days."

"No. Not yet." Dala bit the inside of her cheek and looked away. "Just a few scouts for now. Just you and a few trusted men." She smiled, walking to the small table that kept most of her things. She took a quill and flattened a fresh piece of vellum , holding the corners with stones. "I want you to take a message to this 'Bukayag'."

Again Birmun felt utterly lost. *A message?* "You want Birmun, the great and celebrated slayer of Bukayag, to deliver a message…to *Bukayag*?"

Dala snorted as she wrote. "No one believes he's really dead. Anyway, as you say, it probably won't be him. You don't need to give your real name. I trust no one else to do it because it *might* be him. So it must be you."

Birmun watched her excitement and decided she *wanted* it to be Bukayag, though he had no idea why. It certainly wasn't because she wanted an end to all this—if anything she wanted more men, more supplies, and he had no idea what she did with it all besides feed her little army. He watched her hand scrawl across the vellum more carefully than her other letters.

"He won't be able to read it," he said. She paused for a moment, then shook her head.

"If it's him, he's a runeshaman, so of course he can. If it isn't, then it doesn't matter."

She rolled it carefully and placed it in a leather satchel, then stood and put it in his hands. "Do this for me, Birmun. Take Dag with you, and be careful. If it's really him, and I think it is—the goddess sends me a message. I must answer."

He controlled his expression, uncomfortable as ever with her prophetic beliefs, but unwilling to outright deny them.

She smiled in her knowing way, and moved closer, whispering "Hurry back to me," in his ear, her warm breath on his neck. Then she sealed the scroll with wax, and his lips with a kiss.

In his heart he knew she loved the Goddess more than him. But whatever her reasons, whatever her visions of the future and her goals for the Order, he would die before he failed her.

He turned back to the mountain and the dusk, and hoped his men weren't overly drunk.

* * *

"Stop whining. You'll be paid." Birmun refrained from twisting in his saddle to meet the Arbman's eyes. They'd been riding for several hours and he was already sore and tired. He focused all his attention ahead of him because he felt at any moment he might fall to his death. In fact, he'd nearly tumbled twice already.

"Pah." Medek spit orange root and looked back to Varhus, now on the horizon. He glanced at Birmun and Dagmar's horses and scowled. "You are too big, and carry too much. Old, stupid mules will need as much rest as riding."

"We'll be fine." Birmun rode on with a careless expression, but actually —after a pause, and a subtle glance at his blankets and supplies, weapons and armor—he'd likely brought too much. He supposed he could shed some weight now if he had to, though the thought of dumping perfectly good supplies galled him. *Could have said something before we bloody left*, he thought.

For now he turned and winked at Dag, who rolled his eyes.

It was only Birmun's second time on a horse. As a little boy his father once set him and his brothers together in a line on his mother's mount, and Birmun vaguely remembered crying as the big man laughed and let him and his twin down. Tears and discomfort, that was his memory. The experience had changed very little.

Every step the animal made slumped or flopped him back to fight the movement and the pull towards the earth. No matter what he did or how he fought, eventually, he lost. His already sore crotch banged against the muscled back, his thighs rubbed and stretched in their awkward pose, his lower back increasingly stiff. And the animal was only moving at a trot.

By contrast, the Arbman seemed to float on a cloud of horseflesh. He hardly touched the reins, looking at the sky in boredom as much as the horizon, sometimes almost reclining, as if entirely capable of sleeping as he rode.

They moved through the edge of the mountainous ground into milder hills with more grass and life. They let the horses feed and rest for a time while Medek cursed and made a fuss, then at last reached flatter ground, and the Spiral.

"Finally." The Arbman rolled his shoulders and sprang to life as his mount's hooves crunched the graveled stone. "There is waystation ahead. A hard ride and we make it, then swap horses and ride hard again, and we see Husavik by night time. Yes?"

Birmun swallowed down his horror, then nodded. Medek clicked his tongue and his mount snorted and moved to a run. Birmun and Dag's horses pulled forward instinctively.

The wind blew his face and hair and for a moment Birmun forgot his discomfort. But Medek was a steppe tribesman, all but born on a horse. No doubt he'd spent most of his life taking messages like this one around the world, and he would ride Birmun and Dag until they crumbled and broke apart and no doubt could ride long after.

Birmun did his best. As promised, they rode hard all afternoon and swapped at the Order's waystation, taking a short rest to eat dried rations and stretch their legs before re-mounting on new animals. Then they were off again, though every muscle in Birmun's body screamed to stop.

He had faced such moments before. As a nightman he had swung a shovel until his hands bled; he had stood hip-deep in filth from sundown to sunrise, getting human waste on his face, in his hair, even once in his mouth, all the while surrounded and choked by it until he thought the scent would burn in his nostrils. But after the long night of riding the Spiral for the second time, he'd have still chosen the waste.

"How much further?"

By the time he asked, he existed only in some mixture of numbness and nightmare, eyes blinking and staring at nothing as if reality were only a painful dream. He could force the man to stop at any time, he knew, but didn't. *Gods curse my stupid pride.*

"Nearly there, Chief. Very close now."

To Birmun the man's voice sounded as if it came through water. He closed his eyes promising himself for just a moment, and when he next opened them he saw smoke and a ring of houses. Dag whistled and pointed ahead, and the Arbman guided his horse through a wheat field, small raider-bow strung and slipped over his neck. Apparently he'd been off ahead scouting.

"We miss them. Tracks go North. Twenty, thirty, men, maybe more."

Birmun could see—even after two hard rides and in moonlight—the tribesman meant to carry on.

"We make camp," he said, admitting temporary defeat in his heart. "We'll follow in the morning."

Medek spit a glob of orange spittle that caught the moonlight. "Is bandit town, Chief. No good for camping." He ran a finger across his throat like a knife.

Dag grunted and pointed at a small valley dark with shrubs and bushes. "Chief's not asking, *scout*. There should do."

For a moment Medek stared, and though he was too exhausted to worry much, Birmun wondered if the man would just leave them here and go back North.

Instead the little tribesman shrugged and turned his horse with his knees. He shook his head when Dag stooped to gather kindling for a fire, sliding another finger across his neck. Then he finally dismounted as if it was no great hardship, lay a pack beneath his head, and starting snoring moments later.

"Guess we're taking first watch." Dag had to drag Birmun from his horse.

"I'm alright." He groaned, and pain flared from the bone and muscle in his hips, but he fought the pain. He limped as he untied his animal's bags and saddle, then slumped to the earth.

Soon he was dreaming of Dala tucked in his arms, a memory rather than a fantasy. Since the day he'd become the man responsible for killing Bukayag, they had been together again, very carefully. Two years now nearly of bliss and lovemaking in the dark, perfect were it not for all the drudgery and toil of the world between them.

Well. Not quite perfect. They had no children.

He'd voiced his quiet fear that perhaps they could never have children, despite this being a mixed blessing for now since Dala was a High Priestess. She'd only laughed without concern.

"We've lain together hundreds of times, Dala. You should be pregnant by now. Something is wrong."

She'd smiled and stroked his hair.

"Not now, my love. There is no time, so the goddess prevents it. When this is over, perhaps, and my work is done. Maybe then we'll find time for children."

As ever she'd said it with such confidence he'd at once felt calm. She'd seemed so sure. That night he'd lain down relieved, finding peace and sleep in her arms. But with the light and morning and solitude, his fear returned.

"Wake, wake. Sun is soon."

Birmun drew a seax before he remembered where he was. He glanced at the almost amused, ugly flat face of the Arbman, then nearly tripped from the pain in his lower body as he rose. He looked at his horse grazing and just the sight made him ache from stem to root.

Dag yawned and blinked red eyes, and all three men saddled their horses and broke camp in silence—the Arbman in half the time—then mounted and rode in single file.

The raw, tender flesh of Birmun's thighs flared with pain as they rubbed again on the hard leather. He tried and failed to shift, to find some position that would spare him, eventually settling into the misery as he'd done the day before.

"If I never ride again," he complained after the sun crept up, "it will be too soon."

The Arbman laughed and coughed as he maybe choked on his root. "Imagine how feel horse. You are like bear."

Following 'Bukayag' and his outlaws proved simple tracking, but difficult riding. Were it not for watching Medek do it first, Birmun wouldn't even have dared take his mount down such steep slopes and rises as they found in the valley.

In turns they'd coax the animals up or down the sides of gullies and natural trenches, often dismounted. Streams often criss-crossed the bottoms, their beds filled with slippery, moss-covered rocks. After a dozen such careful crossings the Arbman cursed.

"We never catch," he said, gesturing ahead. "Follow. This way."

With an uneasy glance at each other, Birmun and Dag followed their guide further East—out of the dried up riverland near Husavik to higher ground.

Birmun was a creature of the city and had lived in Orhus most of his life. He knew little of the world, or this part of it, and if he were abandoned here it would be all he could do to find the Spiral and home.

After several steep climbs the ground turned to hard clay and rock with hardly even any grass. Grey, lifeless, and curved, Birmun felt as if they walked on the edge of some giant skull. But beyond it a huge patch of trees climbed mountains to the East, and a red and orange sky filled the horizon.

"Ha." Medek urged his horse forward and ducked the wind as he raced across the hard, flat ground. "Come along, farmers, daylight burns us."

Birmun and Dag sighed, but did their best to follow.

All morning and afternoon they raced across the strip of hard earth between forest and valley. Bleary eyed agony dogged each clap of his animal's hooves, and several times he panicked as he nearly fell from his horse. But still, Birmun had to admit, the place was beautiful.

Cool wind refreshed him even as it stung his eyes. He found himself staring at the endless Eastern horizon of mountain peaks, so jagged and numerous they seemed like a huge trap laid for some divine and monstrous bear. He realized after some time it was the Eastern mountain range, and knew beyond it lay the sea and the edge of the world.

I am a fortunate man, he thought, smiling. In his short life and limited travel, still he had seen three of the world's edges. He had known love and revenge, brotherhood and family, and even if he died now he would die a chief.

Still, the thought of death frightened him. He had done things—terrible things. He had butchered unarmed men and boys in Orhus, he and his nightmen with Dala's knives. *And I killed a girl, and women, and their infants. Nevermind that I tried not to look and make myself forget. I killed them while they screamed.*

For his crimes, no matter what Dala told him, he knew he would not see paradise. He would go to the mountain and burn in Noss's flame, and perhaps one day be re-born.

"We rest and cross here, Chief." At last the Arbman slowed. He pointed down a ridge that would help ease their descent into the valley. "We find their trail again, yes? Should be close now."

Birmun nodded. "If so, you've done well, Medek. You'll be rewarded."

The man smiled and showed his orange teeth. They rested their horses and drank goat milk from skins, and Birmun chewed salted venison which he offered to the Arbman when he saw him staring. The man licked it and frowned, but ate it anyway.

"Waste of salt," he muttered, then rubbed his hands together and vaulted to his horse without using his arms, and urged it towards the drop.

Birmun and Dag followed, leading their mounts on foot. Dag once lost his footing and nearly pulled his horse down to trample him, but they stepped and stumbled their way back to softer, greener earth without disaster.

Their pace at the bottom, at least, was leisurely. Birmun and his retainer kept quiet and looked at the terrain as Medek concentrated, but for the most part they didn't know what to look for, and just followed him in silence as the time dragged.

"God cursed shit-eaters." When the sun began its drop, and still no sign of the outlaws, Medek began muttering. He led them West across nearly the whole valley before he turned back and said they must have passed their quarry.

"They move slow," he explained, before taking them back South, nose now gaining a hue similar to the root he chewed.

Birmun simply followed. Volus turned his eye, and the light from its glow lit the skies in shades of red and purple before the inevitable dark. Medek finally dropped off his horse, avoiding Birmun's gaze as he climbed the highest tree they could find.

"I see," he called, almost at once, stepping carefully down from branch to branch. "They stop and make god-cursed fence." He made stabbing gestures with his hands. "Horse-spears, like farmers. Yes?"

Birmun nodded, understanding but confused. "Why should they make a proper camp here? There's nothing but woods and dried up valley."

The little man shrugged, and Birmun supposed it made no difference. In single file they picked their way through the curving landscape, avoiding hilltops so as not to be seen, though since they were messengers and would soon announce themselves, he didn't truly think this mattered.

Near the final hill before the outlaw camp he said as much and climbed to the peak, wanting a good look before he committed.

They'd built a stockade as the Arbman said, and even a trench. Men moved freely outside gathering wood and water from the valley. *They'll have scouts and hunters and scavengers*, he realized, feeling an urge to run and hide as quickly as possible.

But he held his ground. He took a closer look at the men in sight, and saw they were warriors. Most had shields slung across their backs, even as they took their rest. They carried spears or swords or axes, and sometimes all three. Many had chain-linked armor or at least a leather cuirass, and the ones who didn't looked so big and armed they must have been unprotected by choice.

"We go, in *there*?" The Arbman shook his head, his forehead sweaty. "No. We no come out."

Dag cleared his throat. "I'm inclined to agree. These are hard, disciplined men, Chief, not bandits. They might just kill us for seeing that."

Both looked to Birmun, whose hand went thoughtlessly to the scroll at his side, wishing for the hundredth time he could read what it said. But whatever his feelings, he trusted Dala and would do her will. He had never failed her. He wasn't going to start now.

"We go in," he said, and smiled, enjoying the horseman's fear. "I thought you raiders had stiffer spines."

With that he reached up and un-pinned the small, silver bar through his ear that marked him as a chief, and urged his horse forward. He expected by now they'd been spotted anyway and had no choice. He turned his eyes back to the camp for one last look, and his pleasure at the tribesman's discomfort vanished.

There, waiting at the gate of wooden spikes—already directing a few warriors to move it aside—was the biggest man Birmun had ever seen. He stood in plain sight, staring at Birmun's hill. Even from a distance it was clear he wore polished iron all over his body, and had an almost bald head that looked somehow black—as if he'd smeared it with dirt, or ash.

Bukayag, he thought, hardly believing it, and suddenly afraid.

In truth he had always thought the man little more than myth—a man like any other who had rebelled and fled or died, leaving a story to live on only in skald tales. But this man watching as if Birmun was expected—this man was no myth.

Birmun raised his hands to show he meant no harm, and rode forward, perhaps to his death, and the mountain's flames.

48

Ruka watched the Galdric scouts come forward, and admired their courage. Tahar and his falconers had spotted them the day before, but Ruka told him only to watch, mostly out of curiosity, wanting to see what his enemies would do.

He knew a small army of Northerners camped on a mountain near Alverel. Egil told him they'd come down after their bloody rebellion on the lawstone, and some minor chief and a priestess scoured the beltway and some of the South and still remained after two years. *Looking for me*, he thought, amused.

He studied the men and their horses as they came towards him. One was clearly a tribesman from the steppes, his wild pony largely unburdened by gear or supplies, a small hunting bow lain strung across his lap. Men like him could ride across the whole of the Ascom surviving on nothing more than a flask of milk mixed with blood pricked from their mounts.

The others looked like Northern chiefsmen. One was young— tall, a wiry but muscled warrior only slightly older than Ruka—the other a veteran perhaps near forty. They had shields and scabbarded swords. The younger seemed ready to fall off his horse.

"I feel their fear, brother," whispered Bukayag. "Perhaps they're assassins."

Ruka resisted the shrug and tempered his brother's itch for violence. Bukayag had wanted to kill the scouts from the beginning, arguing they would simply run back to their masters when they'd seen enough, and perhaps soon hundreds of men would be hunting them in earnest.

Ruka didn't think so. Clearly someone from Husavik sent word of Aiden's attack, and if the valley army meant to respond then they'd have sent a larger force. Perhaps someone was only curious. Perhaps someone, maybe a priestess or a great chief, wanted to use this little uprising, or believed they shared an interest with Aiden, or with 'the last runeshaman'. Whatever they wanted, it would give Ruka leverage. He would manipulate them and buy time to gain more men and supplies, or just ignore them.

With the Eastern forest so close—a huge, maze of trees nearly devoid of civilization, mostly contemplated in fear by the superstitious men of ash— he had little fear of attack. With some 'divine' promise of safety, he and Aiden's men could move deep into the trees and ambush any brave enough to follow. Ruka had been here before as an outcast. He knew every cliff, valley, waterfall and cave.

So, he'd convinced Aiden, and they'd waited. With their time the men cut down trees and made rope and carts. And though the chief had seemed bewildered, since the gods demanded haste just the day before, Ruka only smiled.

"We're on the path now, Aiden. But we can not know what obstacles may come." He knew the yew trees here were good for lumber. They'd need all the supplies on the coast, and to begin preparing now would seem prophetic later.

The dead did the same in his Grove, but it seemed best to be productive in both worlds, and the wood there was different.

Aiden's retainers lifted two heavy gate-posts from their holes and moved them aside for the visitors, opening a path in the spikes.

"We are messengers," said the young warrior, his hands raised in a gesture of peace. He lowered one slowly and withdrew a scroll tied to his belt.

Ruka watched them very closely. He noticed the concern in the older man's eyes. *But not for himself,* he decided, *for the other man. Perhaps they are kin. Is it his father? Why then does the son speak?*

Egil had hobbled to Ruka's side when the men approached, as ordered, and many others watched from the hill they'd chosen as a camp. Eshen lurked by a near-by post, his new, long dagger tucked inside the cloak that shielded half his face. Aiden sharpened a sword by his tent, appearing uninterested.

"I am Bukayag, son of Beyla. Whose message do you carry?"

The young warrior tried and failed to subtly inspect Ruka's face, armor, and camp.

"Dala, daughter of Cara, High Priestess of the South."

At hearing this name, for a moment Ruka stood over the mangled corpse of priestess Kunla, waiting for death. He watched the chaos of Alverel and all the faces and terror until he found a young, pretty apprentice with a scarred cheek and determined eyes. She had, in a way, saved his life two years before.

She had ordered the Galdric warriors who pursued him to hold, and in their confusion and delay Ruka had overcome his moment of weakness and doubt, and fled North. *'We serve the same God, you and I,"* she'd told him. *"One day you will see."*

Ruka blinked and cleared the past from his eyes, then nodded. Egil limped forward to take the message.

"My mistress said she used simple symbols. Do you have a matron who can read?"

Ruka glanced at the young messenger and held back his laugh. Before touching the message he inspected the scroll. The vellum had been furled tightly around a wooden spool and tied with a leather strap, then sealed with wax. Ruka wondered for a moment if poison could be somehow rubbed or infused in the skin. He considered the herbs Beyla taught him, which he expected were all those available in the Ascom, deciding some could perhaps burn his hands, but little more.

He took the message and unraveled the leather, finding mostly common words written in a somewhat sloppy hand.

"Bukayag—if it is truly you—these messengers are my servants. If you are still the man I met in Alverel, the man who fought for a world of justice and mercy and wisdom, where love is never a crime, then I would meet you. Perhaps together we can make that world. Tell me when, and where, and I will come."

They were the exact words he had uttered to Kunla two years before. Then he and Bukayag had killed her and ripped her corpse to pieces, and Dala would have seen that, too.

Ruka took his time with the scroll, as if he found reading the symbols difficult. When he finally looked up he met the young messenger's eyes, deciding he held himself with dignity, and command.

A red sun hung on the horizon. The light colored the messenger's face, and Ruka smiled when he saw the hole lit on his left earlobe where a chief's ring should be.

"So. You are Birmun."

All three men stiffened with surprise and fear.

"No." Ruka shook his head. "She did not betray you. You betrayed yourself. Tell me, why shouldn't I kill you, Birmun, son of Canit, who has been sent to destroy me?"

Aiden perked up now, his warriors shifting forward. Some half-drew blades or lifted knives and axes. The messengers' horses sensed the danger and whinnied or pulled away as if to run, and the men had to soothe them.

"Well," said Birmun, no sign of his fear in his voice, "that depends on what's in the message."

Ruka liked this answer greatly, as he liked the man's calm. He indulged it. "Your mistress says she would like to meet me."

"And will you?"

"Perhaps."

Chief Birmun shrugged, holding the reigns of his horse idly.

"Then you have nothing to fear from me, shaman. Unless you mean her harm." He met Ruka's eyes. "Then I will kill you."

At this ludicrous threat Aiden's warriors surged. The few men who'd long ago moved to block the rider's flight drew spears. Eshen's knife slid free of his sleeve.

The messengers tensed, the sweat-covered steppesman drawing his little bow and readying an arrow.

Ruka waited and watched all the men, taking in every reaction, saving every expression to examine later. He laughed.

"Your boldness does you credit, chief. But you are correct in one thing—I have nothing to fear from you." Some of the men grinned, and Ruka turned to them. "These are messengers and my guests. They are not to be harmed." He extended a hand and felt the threat of violence disappear. "Come, cousins, your ride has been long and difficult. Sit and eat with us. In the morning, and with my blessing, you will return to your priestess."

* * *

Later, Birmun wandered near the outlaw's bonfire. He watched the hard, frightening warriors eye him, his horse and supplies, as if considering what they'd take first when he was dead.

After his somewhat tense 'welcome', the shaman's men returned to their business of cutting down trees and crafting what might have been rope. Birmun wasn't sure why, but he thought better of asking any questions.

Instead he stood with Dagmar and kept quiet, watching the hunters and cooks prepare a small feast. He watched Bukayag move about the camp alone, distracting men everywhere he went. Then he sat by the fire, and with great surprise, learned the outlaws had a skald.

Bukayag motioned and grunted, and the dark-haired and handsome man who'd taken his message climbed to a high stool near the camp's center. He smiled as some of the men cheered him on, then his fingers danced across a lyre, and his deep, strong voice sang of Haki the Brave, and the ancient world.

Birmun had heard many skalds as a boy in his father's hall, then later at celebrations in the halls of other Orhus chiefs. But as he watched this outlaw singer in an ancient woods—as he watched pink sunset light the trees of the quiet valley, he could not remember a better performance.

The men stomped their feet and cheered when the song was lively, then silenced and sat still when the skald's voice and words became forlorn. When it was over they calmed and settled and ate and drank, mostly in groups or pairs and in silence, as if the mood of all had settled.

"Damned good," said Dag with a mouth full of hard bread.

Birmun nodded and remembered where he was. He'd been just as enthralled as the men, staring and forgetting for the moment what peril he was in. When at last he looked away he blinked in amazement to see a young woman.

She stood near the tents and watched the skald, too. The warm sunlight lit her light brown hair so it looked golden red. She wore leather breeches and a long cloth shirt like a man, and Birmun saw wetness on her cheeks. She noticed his attention, and retreated inside the near-by tent.

"Eat. The catch is fresh."

Bukayag emerged from the woods like a hunting dog and Birmun almost reached for a weapon. His heart fluttered and for a moment he despised himself for the fear. He glanced and noticed Dag and even the Arbman looked similarly startled.

The shaman seemed oblivious. He settled on a log near the fire and gestured at one of the spits holding rabbit. Birmun nodded politely. He leaned forward to cut a piece with his knife, and for a time they sat and listened to the fire.

"Chief, would you bloody look at that." Dag pat a greasy hand on his knee and pointed at the camp's edge.

A group of men stood near a huge, wide elm. One was by himself near the trunk, another directly before him inspecting a flat, wooden bench. The man at the tree had a cloth tied over his eyes, and his counterpart lifted a stone from the bench, drawing laughs and cheers from the onlookers as he seemed to prepare himself to throw.

"Gods. I'd heard of this but never seen it. You mind?"

Birmun shook his head, and Dag winked and went to watch. Bukayag looked up from greasy hands and a rabbit's thigh at his lips.

"You should be careful here, chief. Even games are full of danger in the South."

Birmun glanced at the shaman's strange eyes, but he wasn't worried. Dag wasn't a young man, nor prideful or easily offended. He wouldn't cause any trouble. Still, the shaman's words stuck in his mind, and he found himself watching while he ate.

"*Bedrag*, they call it." Bukayag said later, his voice holding almost an edge of contempt. "It just means 'deceiver' in some old Southern tongue. The rules are simple. One man chooses a rock, a small knife, or an axe, the other covers his eyes. The thrower hurls with whatever strength he wishes, at whatever part of the man's body he wishes. The onlookers count and the weapon is thrown on three. The blinded man knows it will come, but not which weapon, or where. He chooses to stand, or move."

Birmun nodded, but didn't see the point. "Do they wager?"

Bukayag snorted. "Some. They do it to show their courage, to win honor, to pass the time. The men who play usually like each other." He leaned again to the fire for more rabbit. "They throw only the rock or the knife. If they choose the knife then they aim for an arm or leg, and if the man stands he takes a small wound and hides his pain. The others douse the cut in arog and toast him for a fool. Later they will sing his praises."

"Danger without purpose." Birmun shook his head. "It seems foolish."

The shaman chewed a leg and Birmun tried not to watch as his sharp, angled teeth bit into the rabbit's bone. Bukayag looked into the flame as he spoke.

"In the steppes, tribesmen make a game of chasing goats or horses into pens. There are few rules. Even boys as young as ten winters play, and all carry clubs and knives, and use them. Sometimes they die."

Birmun didn't know what to make of this, or the tone. He shook his head and shifted on the moss-covered rock he'd chosen as a seat, more uncomfortable by the moment. Bukayag almost whispered now.

"Below the beltway, cousin, mothers name infants only if they survive two winters. Some of these men here have lost as many as *ten* children to sickness and cold. Most have lost pieces of their bodies, to frost or corruption. Some have left their mates and stopped trying, choosing a simple life of serving a warrior. So tell me, chief, with such an existence, should men not grow a contempt for life? Is that foolish, or is it wisdom? How else could a man stay sane?"

Birmun watched the shaman speak and felt enthralled, just as he'd been with the skald. He stared at this strange man in the firelight, his words spoken as if the suffering were his—as if the fate he described were some burden weighing heavy on his shoulders.

At first, Birmun had wondered why Dala should want to meet and perhaps ally with this strange son of Noss. But he felt they shared something, some sense of burden, responsibility. And whatever else was true, and to his shame, he felt a sort relief—he had no desire to fight this man.

As the evening passed he stole many glances at the now silent Bukayag. His ugly features flickered in the firelight, strong jaw always chewing. He sat mostly rigid, his long limbs planted like the legs of a chair, bright eyes either staring far away, or furtive, as if watching for danger.

Purposeful, Birmun thought as he watched him. *Restless, like a hawk.*

The men still playing *bedrag* roared. Birmun turned to see one of the warriors had dodged aside, only to observe with chagrin he'd fled from a softly lobbed stone.

An older man shook his shoulders and took his place next, then tied the cloth around his eyes himself. He gestured and boasted he'd never once fled from rock or iron, and 'let whichever weak-armed coward test me as he pleases!'

A huge thrower moved opposite to many cheers and then laughs when he took the stone. When it died down and the men counted, on three he reached back his whole body and arm into a mighty hurl, and whipped the little bullet hard. It caught the old man square in the crotch.

The veteran groaned and hunched, putting his hands on his knees, and some of the onlookers cringed or covered their mouths. He took off his blindfold and looked at the thrower before he shook his head.

"I think...", he took a steadying breath, "I think I've had my last son, brothers. And good riddance."

The men howled. Even Dagmar looked to join in as the Northerners wiped their eyes and helped the old warrior sit.

"You must be very loyal to bring your priestess' message to me yourself," Bukayag said. Birmun snapped his eyes back to the shaman, and found him expressionless.

"I do my duty, as my father did."

"Ah. So your father was a chief. Do you have a matron? Children?"

"No." Birmun tossed the now meatless bone in his hands to the fire. He didn't like the shaman's tone, feeling manipulated or mocked or playing a game he didn't understand. Bukayag seemed to sense his discomfort. He said nothing for a time, then leaned forward with an almost arrogant grin.

"Dala is a very beautiful, young woman, isn't she?"

Birmun felt his face grow slightly hot and was glad the man wouldn't be able to see it in the poor light.

"We've met before, Dala and I," said the shaman.

"So she told me."

Bukayag smiled, though Birmun felt no warmth in it. "She must trust you greatly. Did she also tell you I ripped her old mistress apart with my bare hands, and that she watched and did nothing?"

Birmun fought the urge to meet the man's gaze, and also the urge to rise from his seat and run. The shaman had leaned forward, his whole face changed, his shoulders and limbs slouched as if ready to strike. Birmun kept his composure and shrugged as if it made no difference.

"She said you killed her. How is not important." With this he turned back to the fire as if the conversation were over, and for a time neither of them spoke. Bukayag broke the silence, his tone returned to something almost friendly.

"The men and their game." He pointed as another Southerner stood brazen against the tree. "There is a difference between courage, and contempt for life. But sometimes, either will do."

With that Bukayag stood, and walked toward the tents, and Birmun sat alone. He considered the strange shaman and his words. He thought on his years as a nightman, the nights of blood in Orhus as he served Dala's will, and all the strange twists of fate that led him to this place. His eyelids drooped enough he considered laying down to sleep.

"Ye callin' me a coward?"

The tone and direction of the argument jerked Birmun awake. He glanced back with interest but little concern, at first. Then he spotted Dagmar.

"No, brother, and I don't say it now."

"Ye wagered I'd move, so ye think I'm a coward. Don't hide wit' lies."

"No, I...I meant no offence. The other men..."

"Are true brothers and warriors who ha' stood before a tree. But not ye. Now I'll have satisfaction."

Birmun felt himself sweating and stood, fear coursing through his body as he looked around the clearing for Bukayag. He found the shaman standing in the dark near a tent, already watching.

"He will stand," Birmun called as he came closer, knowing there must be violence to end this. "He'll stand next at the tree. And you throw. That should be enough."

The tall, wiry Southerner turned to see who interfered. His body was slim but fashioned as if from oak, exposed limbs sheathed in hard-earned muscle. He sneered and seemed ready to reject this, but another of his brethren spoke.

"Edda hears. T'is is a fair offer, Brack. Let 'em stand. I'd like ta see."

A few others near Dagmar grunted in approval. They held flasks of arog, and moments before had been laughing and enjoying the game. It seemed they'd gotten to like the man enough to help him, or at least didn't like the disruption. The Southerner growled and gestured angrily at the tree.

"Stand 'en. We see who's a coward."

Dag glanced at Birmun, who shrugged, and the older man walked rather unhurriedly to take his place.

A dangerous tension still hung in the air, though the men returned to their jokes and drinking and many others came to watch the excitement. One of the less drunk warriors walked to the tree with a strip of dark cloth and winked to the onlookers as he tied it around Dagmar's head.

Birmun's palms sweat, but he expected this would keep his man alive. The Southerner would no doubt throw the knife or even the axe, but Dag would do the sensible thing and move. The thrower would call him a coward, the men would all have their laugh, and that would be that.

"Vol is watchin'," called one of the bystanders. A few others told Dag to go left, or right, or 'don't duck, little brother, Brack loves when a man ducks'.

Birmun was glad for the jokes, and hoped they eased some tension. The noise dimmed as Brack lifted the throwing axe. He held it up to show the crowd, and most of the men grimaced or glanced at each other but said nothing. Birmun took a breath and hoped the man didn't intentionally miss, trying to hit Dag as he moved.

The older warrior who'd apparently taken charge of the counting waited for quiet, then put his hands to his mouth like a horn. "Wune", he shouted, his accent thick and heavy. The gathering silenced entirely, and the old warrior shouted 'due', and at last 'threy'.

Birmun held his breath, and Brack spun his body expertly, throwing with all his might.

The axe spiraled through the air on target. Birmun would have shouted but he had time only to twitch and squeeze his fists as the weapon sailed end over end. Dagmar didn't move.

The weapon struck—handle first, directly into his gut.

The weight and force of the throw alone dropped him to a crouch. His hands sunk to his knees as he coughed and retched. The crowd half gasped, then half roared their approval. Men laughed and took it up, and it went on for several long moments until the anger on Brack's face became obvious to all, and Dagmar removed the cloth and stood. The thrower's voice was tight.

"You think so little of my skill, you don't even move? Do you insult me again?"

Birmun twitched and couldn't believe the old man hadn't moved, and that he'd been such a damned fool. By the frowns and grimaces from the other men, he could see they felt this insult wasn't fair. But still they said nothing.

Dag put his hands on his knees again to hold himself upright, then gestured at the other old man who'd been counting.

"Oh I'da moved," he panted, and groaned. "But you Southerners can't bloody talk. Didn't know that was counting."

Birmun blinked, and the Southern warriors took turns meeting each other's eyes. The first man's howl of laughter became a roar that engulfed half the camp. Even Brack eventually allowed a smirk and a nod, and as he turned away the threat of violence vanished like smoke into the night.

Birmun damn near carried Dag back to their fire in disbelief, and eased him to the earth.

Later, still resting together by the fire, his father's old retainer clutched his stomach, his face pale. "I know, I know," he whispered. "Trust me I know, but I was a dead man if I moved, Chief. These men are mad."

Birmun snorted, thinking *damn the shaman to hell but he warned me,* just glad the older man hadn't died in a duel. They ate some more rabbit and drank mostly water and a little arog, joking to ease the pain.

But the night wore on. Dag's groans grew louder and soon he waved away the drink. His eyes turned slick with wetness and with Birmun's help he tried to empty his bowels twice but passed only blood. On his third attempt he slipped and fell to the dirt, and stared at the night moaning his children's names. Birmun held his head and shouted for help.

Only the shaman came. He looked at Dag's gut and face and brought herbs he poured down the man's throat, but these too came back up. He spoke softly, like a loving mother in the man's ear, and soon looked to Birmun and shook his head.

Before the sun rose above the trees of their clearing, Dagmar settled and died in Birmun's lap. The shaman's herbs had stopped him from calling out in agony, and he smiled briefly at Birmun before he closed his eyes and did not open them. They sat together as the sun rose.

"I am sorry for his death," said the shaman, who then stood as if some decision had been made. "But still the light comes, and we must get started, and turn our minds to the living."

Birmun felt numb, and beneath this only a vengeful misery that hated every man in Bukayag's camp. "Started with what? Burying my retainer?"

Bukayag released a breath and turned towards his tent. "No, Birmun. These men will see to him. They will have taken no pleasure in his death, and treat his body honorably. You must start your journey home to your priestess. I am coming with you."

49

Birmun woke with the sun and forgot where he was. His hips pulsed with a dull ache and he sat up and at least remembered the days included torturous riding. Then he saw Bukayag looming over other men near the still burning fire.

The bandits or whatever the hell they were brought Birmun water and fresh-cooked rabbit, as well as some roots he couldn't identify. They'd apparently cared for his horse, removing some of the items the Arbman had criticized, and adding at least one waterskin. He felt embarrassed because he didn't know who to thank for it. He looked for Dag to ask, then remembered, and no longer felt like thanking anyone.

"Good morning." The shaman approached and nodded in respect. He wore a plain cloth shirt and trousers, with leather riding leggings and a dark cloak. "Did you get a little sleep?"

Birmun knew he should return the gesture but felt too bitter to force himself. "I'm ready, if that's what you mean."

Bukayag ignored or didn't notice his lack of respect. "I assume you'll want your…steppe-man, to come along with us?"

"My scout. Yes. Will you bring any warriors?"

The shaman's strange eyes seemed to sparkle at this, as if the question amused him. "No, Chief, the gods protect me. Now stand. The pain will get no better until you move."

For a moment Birmun couldn't believe he'd say such a thing now, then realized the shaman meant his *physical* pain. He groaned and lifted himself, feeling weak and rather small as he stood next to Bukayag.

The warriors in the camp did not hide their stares, though Birmun soon realized they looked at the shaman and not him. A man near as tall as Bukayag eventually approached them as they readied the horses. He wore a bronze circlet, and a chief's earring and Birmun assumed this must be the famous Aiden of Husavik.

"Should we not accompany you, shaman? Let me send at least a few men. Or send Egil in your stead. Surely the skald can speak for you by now. Who will tell us the will of the gods?"

Bukayag put a hand to the man's broad shoulders. "I will take Egil. I may need his silver-tongue. Make as much lumber and rope as you can, then enough wagons to haul it all North. Have no fear, I will return in four days."

The way he announced his return sounded more like prophecy than estimate, and the big chief nodded as if completely satisfied. A smaller warrior with a Northern accent came next.

"I am sworn to you, lord. Let me follow, at least."

"Serve me here, Eshen. Help these men do what is required." He grinned and nodded to the many onlookers, and mounted a riding horse.

"Come, Chief. As you can see, I have a great deal to do." He clicked his tongue and spurred the animal forward without waiting, and Birmun reluctantly mounted and followed.

He wanted to see Dag's corpse before he left, but he knew he'd be refused. He glanced around at the hard Southerners around him, their scars and cunning eyes, their impressive weapons and armor, trenches and stockade. To his shame, as he left this place alive he felt first a great wave of relief, reflected in the same look in the Arbman's eyes. He grit his teeth and put his knees to his horse's flank, and followed Bukayag out from the gate.

* * *

They rode in silence, and it soon wasn't clear to Birmun whether Bukayag or Medek was leading.

In either case both men seemed entirely comfortable on horseback, and to know precisely where they were going. Even the crippled skald rode well and looked at ease. Between the pain, the long night, and his own shortcomings, Birmun felt a growing agitation.

"It would be better if Dala knew you were seeing her," he said at last, though he regretted it almost instantly. The shaman looked disturbed from a pleasant reverie and turned his head, staring for long moments before he spoke.

"Better for who, Chief?" As usual his tone held an almost slight mocking note of arrogance, which only heightened Birmun's annoyance.

"Better for both of you. Varhus is surrounded by men who mean to kill you. No doubt she'll want to meet somewhere further away, or at least..."

"We will enter at night. Who better to lead me than the Chief of the nightmen?"

Birmun's words died on his lips, and he saw the glint of a grin on the shaman's lips. The constant feeling of being slightly ridiculed was like an itch he couldn't scratch.

"Perhaps I'll lead you to your death instead," he answered.

The words leapt out, and left him very much aware of the bigger man's strength and confidence. He forced himself to hold his gaze, hoping to at least appear as an equal.

Both the skald and the Arbman's brows raised. The shaman looked at their reaction, then back at Birmun. He tilted his head slightly, and laughed loud enough to disturb the birds.

"I like this man, Egil. But if you're going to threaten someone, cousin, it would be better if you were prepared to kill them." The shaman pointed at Birmun's saddlebags, and he looked down to realize his weapons had been stripped. The shaman smiled. "If riding annoys you so, why not walk for awhile and rest the animal? I shall walk with you." With this Bukayag lifted his leg and dismounted.

The Arbman narrowed his eyes, and spoke for the first time since they entered the stockade. "Too slow already. Much time wasted. I never agree to…"

"Perhaps we should *all* walk, save for Egil." The shaman's face and voice gained an edge of menace, and he stared until Medek seemed ready to bolt or draw his bow. When he didn't obey, the giant stopped walking. "Get off your horse," he growled, voice cracking like a whip. The Arbman sighed loudly and dismounted, and with agony Birmun did the same. Bukayag's face regained its amusement.

"Did you know a man can out-run a horse over enough distance? In fact, I have found no animal he *can't* outlast. This is quite something when you consider it."

Medek rolled his eyes in answer, and Bukayag revealed his sharp, crooked teeth. "I have run down deer on foot. And the book of Galdra describes ancient armies who could only march at their horse's pace. They both overheat, you see. I believe men's sweat prevents this. Isn't that interesting?"

Birmun felt trapped in some bizarre dream, and half nodded and half shrugged as he walked in silence. He didn't understand this strange man in the slightest, and felt constantly uneasy around him. Every so often he also remembered he bad been tasked by the matriarch herself to kill him—that he had the temporary loyalty and trust of a thousand men—at least some of whom were away from their families—for the *singular task* of killing him.

Yet Dala wished only to speak. She believed whatever threat he posed was not nearly as dire as the corruption in the Order itself. She seemed even to believe he might be her *ally,* though Birmun didn't see how.

And if he truly was, or could be, would she try to wield him as she had once wielded Birmun and his nightmen? Would she try to turn him and his killers against the chiefs and the Order? Why should he listen to her?

Whatever this Bukayag was, he was no simple man to be manipulated or toyed with. He was a leader of fierce warriors. He could read runes and everything about him was uncomfortably sharp. He was already an outlaw and free, with his own plans and resources, whatever they were.

Birmun flushed momentarily because he too had little interest in helping Dala at first. In truth, she had seduced him. He denied this for a time, telling himself that it was accidental. But he had since learned her mind and seen her manipulate the men and women of the mountain, just as she manipulated the Order. And slowly, he had admitted the truth. He glanced at Bukayag.

Would Dala try and seduce such a man as this? Or at least lead him to believe she might? How could he ever believe it was true? He was so ugly to be almost inhuman.

But then…Dala was very convincing. And if anyone could accept such a man—an outcast or heretic, Noss-touched and discarded, it was Dala. It was one of the reasons he loved her. But if she took Bukayag as a mate she would force Birmun to allow it, or to kill him. He would certainly choose the latter.

He turned subtly and roamed the shaman's long, powerful limbs with the corner of his eye, thinking: *or more likely, I'd get myself killed.*

Even so, he would not stand aside. He would fight for Dala and his own honor, even if he would lose.

Bukayag blinked and looked straight at Birmun with his obscene, knowing smile, as if he'd sensed the inspection—or as if he could somehow read Birmun's thoughts and meant to savor the knowledge of his own superiority. Then he looked away, and the moment passed.

"Perhaps a song, Egil, to pass the time," said the shaman in a pleasant tone. "Our skald is a very fine singer."

The well-groomed and dressed cripple blinked awake atop his mount. He removed a lyre from his saddlebag as if without pleasure, but changed instantly as he began to play.

Birmun listened and drifted from his own thoughts and worries for at least a moment. He resented the shaman's commands, his advice and his knowledge, his infuriating smile. But soon Birmun's legs began to feel better as the party walked. The music seemed to calm his agitation and reminded him to breathe the fine, valley air while he could. And slowly, perhaps sadly, he had to admit—whatever else was true about this shaman, whatever hell or god had spawned him, he was often right.

* * *

It took them two full days of long travel to reach Varhus. At first Bukayag had made Birmun uncomfortable, but by the end of the journey, he frightened him.

First and foremost it seemed the man hardly tired, and did not sleep. After the long, grueling days of travel, even the Arbman would slump to his rest, and Bukayag would begin clearing the camp and building a fire without a word of complaint or concern about the efforts of the others.

As night fell he collected firewood. Once, as Birmun woke in the dark for a piss, he found the shaman *whittling.*

Only a sliver of moonlight had showed the world in pale grey, and Birmun saw Bukayag's golden eyes reflecting in the gloom like an animal's.

"Would you like one?" he'd lifted his hand in the darkness.

Birmun had mumbled a thanks and took it, then later by the fire stared at the incredible detail and craftsmanship—the perfect, thin wings of some bird with huge eyes. It also had two intricate runes carved on its back, though Birmun could not read them.

"Thank you for the gift," he said again awkwardly in the morning. "It's beautiful. What is it? And what does this say?" He pointed.

Bukayag smiled and Birmun thought perhaps beyond the sharp teeth and ugliness there was genuine pleasure, if still a trace of mockery.

"It is an owl," he said. "I suppose you don't have them in the North, or in the city. It is a fine, wise hunter. The runes say 'night chief'."

Birmun cleared his throat but didn't know what else to say. He raised the carving in thanks, unbalanced again by the man's strange ways.

And it wasn't only him who noticed.

On the second day, as Bukayag stepped away to examine a plant or Bray knew what in a field, Medek moved close to Birmun and whispered. "This man is demon. He watches in night with evil eyes. I see him. I leave. Now."

Birmun looked to see if they were being watched because he thought that a very bad idea. "You promised to take us both ways," he whispered back, hoping the near-by skald couldn't hear them.

"Demon knows way, don't need me."

"I don't care, I want you leading us."

"No. I leave. Before the night. I not sleep with it watching me."

"You've been paid, and you'll bloody well…"

"Is there a problem?"

Both men silenced at the deep sound of Bukayag's voice. Birmun nodded in respect.

"No, shaman. A minor disagreement."

The Arbman glared but held his tongue, and the moment passed. Throughout the day though the tension felt strangely physical and ever-present, as if the shaman had some evil aura that wore at the tribesman and drove him mad. Medek soon took to quiet muttering, his posture stiff and alert. When night fell at last he looked almost frantic, terrified, his eyes scanning the horizon, his hands moving restlessly about his horse.

"We should camp here," declared Bukayag when the mountain was in sight. He dropped from his horse without pause or another word, and the Arbman squinted. Birmun saw sweat glistening on his neck.

With a last furtive look, the scout clicked his tongue and dug in his knees, and sprinted his mount away from the clearing.

Birmun called out in surprise, but didn't move, flinching as a light sparked near his head. It was as if a fire had been lit in the air, and he looked to find the shaman stepping forward, his body leaned back, his arm wreathed in flames.

A spear seemed to form from nothingness. It was as if it *grew* like a plant from the shaman's hand, emerging from fire and darkness. Bukayag released it with a grunt, and it sailed fast and hard across the considerable distance, piercing the Arbman's back.

Medek grunted and flailed and twisted off his mount, collapsing to the dirt. For a few moments he moaned and shifted on the ground as his horse sped on, and Birmun stood mute and stared. When he finally regained his senses, the shaman was watching him.

"He was going to betray us both, Chief."

Birmun said nothing though he felt the urge to disagree. He considered trying to fight, or flee, but rejected both as foolish.

"You knew it, surely," the shaman added. "He is not a man of honor. He would have fled straight to the priestesses and told them Bukayag the Bastard was alive and well, and that his appointed slayer and their High Priestess were both in league with him." Here he shrugged. "I don't blame him. It is true. And the Matriarch would have rewarded him well."

Birmun watched Medek's dying struggle in the grass, and couldn't resist another thought. "He despised you and called you demon, shaman. I suppose that had no influence?"

Bukayag's eyes narrowed. "I have heard such talk all my life, and far worse. As a nightman, surely, so have you. To escape it is simple, if intolerable. Simply say nothing. Do nothing. Be nothing."

Birmun met the man's eyes and felt a strange sort of shame in the words. He had known, of course, the Arbman couldn't be trusted, and now suspected Bukayag was right again. He considered his next question, and his heart raced.

"The fire, and the spear. How…how did you do that?"

Bukayag's face fell as if the question disappointed him. He drew his sword. "Rest, Chief. Tomorrow will be a long ride. You wouldn't want to be exhausted before your mistress."

With that he walked to the dying Arbman, who raised one arm helplessly, trying and failing to speak. The shaman batted it away, and pierced his heart without hesitation.

Birmun laid out a fur blanket with wide eyes and a busy mind, again feeling numb. Egil sat on a rock near-by and strummed his lyre, humming a low, deep sound. Birmun listened for a time, thinking nothing in the world could make him sleep after the last two days. Then he knew only darkness.

50

Birmun jumped when the skald woke him. He blinked and found a strange thing in the handsome bard's eyes—maybe sympathy, or pity.

"Peace, brother," he said softly. "Night is here, and my lord is waiting."

Birmun groaned and stood with some difficulty, rolling his neck and shoulders. The dull ache of travel still rippled up and down his body. He saw a small mound of dirt near the camp and realized Bukayag had buried the Arbman while he slept, leaving a stake etched with runes and a small circle of rocks.

"In the steppes," the shaman said, as if knowing Birmun watched, "men are burned, not buried. But we can not risk a fire. I made him one of Vol's rings because he was competent, that was clear."

Birmun had no idea what to say to this, so instead mounted in silence, and the other men did the same. They crossed the final distance to Varhus in silence, too, and it occurred to Birmun as they approached that he had never much worried about scouts, or even watchmen.

With a thousand warriors fortified on a mountain, the idea that someone might actually *attack* had hardly entered his mind. Having seen Bukayag and his men, even with their numbers so small, perhaps he should have.

His nerves wore thinner the closer they approached, and he realized he didn't know exactly how they'd enter. A stockade had been built surrounding the entire base of the camp with a single gate. He turned to Bukayag to point this out, but the shaman spoke first.

"I thought we'd sneak over your little fence. Is the stockade manned?"

Birmun opened his mouth, then closed it and shook his head. A few men always stood at the gate, and others guarded supplies and weapons and other things of value. But in truth he had not prepared for men attempting to sneak inside, either.

They left their horses tied to a tree a short distance from the base, then crept to the stockade.

"After you," Bukayag whispered, crouching. Birmun lifted himself to the top and looked around. He saw the littered garbage of camp life, empty carts and the mess remaining from a day of business and travel. Some few puddles of water reflected the dim light. But he saw no guards.

He put his hands on the rather dull sharpened logs and lifted himself over. Bukayag helped Egil, then almost stepped over without much effort. The fact that a cripple had simply strolled inside without difficulty made the embarrassment even worse.

They ascended somewhat carefully, but still didn't see anyone roaming. The few guards theoretically on duty must have been sleeping or in any case not at their posts. Birmun grit his teeth and realized Ruka could have easily snuck into the camp, walked all the way to Dala by himself, and in all likelihood killed her. *And perhaps*, he realized with fear, *that is still his plan.*

But if so he would not have brought the skald. Bukayag had to assist the man as they climbed the steep hill, and Birmun watched the care with which he did it, remembering how he had whispered in Dag's ear and stroked his brow at the end. It seemed so bizarre and contradictory, and like everything else about the shaman, made no sense.

They soon reached the top without challenge. Two guards stood at the entrance to the caves. Bukayag and Egil waited behind a cart, the shaman watching Birmun seemingly without concern.

"I'll get rid of them," Birmun whispered, "but give me a few moments inside to warn Dala you're coming. She's likely sleeping."

The shaman nodded, and Birmun took a breath and stepped out from the shadows into torchlight.

"Chief."

Both men nodded in respect when they saw him, and the younger man yawned.

"Go to your furs," Birmun gestured and smiled. "Both of you. I can't bloody sleep. May as well watch the hole."

The men went gratefully and without signs of suspicion. *And why would they?* Birmun waited until they'd gone down the central path and out of sight before he went inside.

Dala sat at a wooden table pouring over messages and ledgers by candlelight. She blinked in surprise as she saw Birmun, but her face transformed almost instantly to pleasure. Her tired, green eyes sparkled and her mouth curled to show her teeth. Birmun wondered if he could ever live in a world where her reaction was not so.

"There's little time," he said coming forward. "Bukayag has come. He waits outside with a skald to speak with you. There's much to tell you."

Dala nodded and waited without interrupting, and Birmun shook his head as he considered where to begin.

"Hello, Farm Girl."

Birmun twisted to see the shaman standing at the entrance. He didn't understand this greeting or how the shaman could know of Dala's origins. But she rose without concern, and nodded in respect, though Birmun could sense her anxiety.

"Thank you for coming, shaman. But surely, this is dangerous."

"Life is dangerous. It seems I must keep reminding you priestesses of this. You helped me, Dala, daughter of Cara. I don't know why, but it makes no difference. I remember my debts. What do you want?"

Birmun shook his head because he could hardly imagine any man speaking to a High Priestess in this way. Dala did not seem offended.

"I want you to work with me, shaman. I told you once we served the same God, and I will show you. Help me terrify the Order. I will keep you informed of all their movement and activities, and you will attack them where and when I say."

The shaman's face gained that hint of arrogance and maybe contempt that Birmun hated. "And why should you want that, Dala? You're a High priestess now. You're in the Goddess' favor."

Dala mimicked his expression. "The Goddess does not approve of what the Order has become. It is corrupt, and needs new leadership and change. But first there must be crisis."

"New leadership." Bukayag raised a misshapen brow. "*Your* leadership?"

"Yes. And others like me."

Bukayag smiled at this. "I'm not sure there *are* others like you, Dala. Tell me, if I made you matriarch, what would you do differently? How would you improve this *corrupt* land of ash?"

Birmun knew her answers because they had discussed it many times.

"I would ensure the priestesses do their duty," she said, some trace of her anger bubbling forth. "I would see that the men of ash were seen to, respected, and taught Galdra's true teachings, and…"

"Would you grow more food?" Bukayag almost spat. Dala blinked and seemed prepared to answer, but the shaman went on. "Would you give those who wished it land, Dala? *Decent* land? Where would you get it from? Would you spread fresh water further and stop it from freezing half the year? Would you bring more fish to these shores?"

"I…" she frowned, and flicked her eyes briefly at Birmun and Egil, "these things are…"

"Impossible? They are not." The shaman sighed. "Your Order is not the problem, Dala. They have their corruptions, as you say, but they have tried to rule this place at least with some semblance of law. In truth, they are meaningless. Vestigial, like that lump of flesh you cut from your cheek. Your aims are too low."

Birmun looked from the strange man to his lover's eyes, speechless. *Her aims are too low?! The woman means to overthrow the very structure of the world!*

Dala looked angry, too, but handled it better. "What exactly are you saying?"

Bukayag smiled, or at least showed his teeth. "I'm saying we should stop fighting over scraps. I'm saying you should turn your mind to the *potential* of this world, rather than its limits. First, I'm saying we colonize paradise."

Dala scoffed, but not rudely. "Paradise is not a place, shaman. It is a metaphor, a reward from God. It isn't for the living."

"Oh but it is, priestess, and I have seen it. I have walked on its golden shores and drunk from a warm river that has never even dreamed of frost. There is a whole world beyond your understanding, Dala, but if you have the courage, I will show you."

Bukayag held out his hand, and just as the spear pulled from fire and darkness, sparks erupted about his grip. An almost blackened iron grew downward until the tip touched the stone floor of the cave.

"I am a prophet, Dala, like your Galdra before me, and I bring word of a new dawn for the men of ash. I have sailed North beyond the sea with Egil." He gestured to the skald. "Together, we found the white-sand beaches of paradise. I have held its wonders in my hands. And I can take others."

The skald nodded his head in solemn respect. "What he says is true, priestess, before Edda and Nanot. I have seen it with my own eyes. The world is far larger than we ever knew, and nearly all of it is better than here."

Bukayag waited, perhaps for questions or argument, but Dala said nothing. "My men and I are traveling North," he said. "There we will build ships no man of this land has ever even imagined. We will sail for paradise in three months, and return with wealth, foreign women to be my follower's matrons, seeds for a dozen new crops, and many other things. When I have brought enough men to my banner, I will burn away the Order and the power of the great chiefs if they oppose me, and unite this land beneath a king. Then I will take the brave far away from this frozen hell, and their children will never know winter."

As he spoke his hands clenched around the hilt of the blade, as if his vision were some palpable thing he need only reach out and grasp. His eyes burned as if he might be ill, so purposeful that even next to Dala he seemed a zealot. *He is without doubt a prophet, or a madman*, Birmun thought, and truly had no idea which.

Dala sat and put a hand to her chin, as if this were a conversation and not insane ramblings of a lunatic. "Destroying the Order is a mistake."

The shaman blinked from his speech and shook his head, his arrogance returned. "The Order is irrelevant. I already told you."

"Yes and you're wrong. It has legitimacy, which you lack entirely except in the South. You can't overcome a thousand years of belief with anything, Bukayag, not proof, not your magic, not god herself. You're a son of Noss. I don't profess to understand exactly what you propose but it's clear your plan will require time, and help. You will need warriors, miners, builders, fishermen and who knows what else. These men have families, and matrons. They need reassurance. Your message will terrify them, and disrupt their lives. Therefore it will *not* be believed."

Bukayag's jaw clenched as he shook his head. "One can ignore reality, priestess, but not its consequences. Unlike your Order I don't require belief."

Dala laughed, now with her own look of arrogance. "Oh yes you do, shaman. You require belief that a different world is possible, and desirable, and that you can bring it without the sword. Even I don't believe that. The Northern chiefs will rally all their strength and fight you, that is the truth. Unless, perhaps, the Order accepts your tale. *They* can give you your legitimacy. They can calm the great chiefs and promise security and divine approval, and make everything easier. Wouldn't you prefer to avoid a war?"

Bukayag damn near snarled at Dala's words and to Birmun didn't look exactly like he *would* like to avoid it. But he took a breath and sat at Dala's table, eyes shifting as if he examined the potential with his gaze.

"And you wish to be matriarch," he said flatly.

"I do."

Bukayag blinked as if he'd snapped shut a book, and glanced at Birmun before he smiled.

"I see why you serve her, chief. My mother would have liked you, Farm Girl. And since my men think me mad already I shall trust you." He took another breath and glanced at his skald. "We depart from Kormet under the protection of Chief Halvar in three months. If all goes well, we will return at the end of next season. Meet me then and see for yourself what the future holds. Then you and I will discuss how we make you matriarch..." he smiled, "or should it be queen?"

Dala nodded carefully and with respect, and Birmun wondered exactly who the man meant to be king. "I look forward to discussing it," she said. "Galdra protect you."

"Come, Egil," the shaman stood. "I fear she's right, conversation with her has been most dangerous. Let us escape to the relative peace of the mountain and its warriors."

Birmun moved to follow but the shaman raised a hand. "We can find our own way, chief." He hesitated, as if in afterthought, or perhaps of two minds. "Take this as a gift, and for your retainer's life. I hope we will meet again."

Birmun glanced at Dala, then took the heavy blade. Without another word the shaman turned and vanished into the night.

Dala sagged onto the table, but she smiled when she looked at him, and her eyes still held a fire. "We're going to need to convince some of your men to turn traitor, and come up with a story. Then we'll need to be ready for Bukayag when he returns." She sighed. "We have a great deal to do, Birmun. And we'll still have to re-take Husavik or else appear suspicious."

Birmun nodded absently, busy now as he inspected the huge, two-handed blade in his hands. He touched it in awe and couldn't quite believe what he was seeing, gaze moving from the blade up to the strange looking hilt.

At the very bottom was a thin piece of metal rather than a rounded pommel, almost like another blade except too flat to be a weapon. All at once he realized what it was and held his breath—recognition flooding in a mix of emotions too deep to be conveyed—it wasn't a knife, it was a shovel, a small decorative version of one like Birmun had used all his life, just the same as the nightmen used.

Birmun shook his head to hold back the sob as he saw runes inscribed on the flat surface—not raised, but branded, as if with blue, curving scars.

Dala was looking at him now with concern, and he realized perhaps there were tears of wonder in his eyes, and not just at the weapon. The runes on his sword were the only symbols Birmun could read, taught with but a moment's effort by a strange son of Noss on the road.

"It says night chief," he said, knowing she could perhaps never truly understand—that not in all his years had one person ever taught him a symbol, not even his mother, or sisters, not even her. That as a nightman and just a man he was not deemed worthy. He whispered it again, this time only for himself, clutching the handle in his grip. "It says night chief."

51

"Did it go as you expected, lord?"

Ruka shrugged at his retainer, thinking *not at all, but it may serve.*

"I don't think my words mattered," Egil said. "She seemed surprisingly willing to accept your story."

Ruka agreed, and wondered what the strange priestess actually believed, and if all she truly wanted was to rule. "Perhaps. She's clever, Egil, and I don't entirely trust her, but we shall see."

The skald raised his brow. "You've told her a great deal about your plans for someone you don't trust."

He flinched slightly at this because it was most certainly true. "I owed her the chance to betray," he said, knowing this wasn't the whole of it. "If she does, then I will kill her. Now let us return to the horses. Watch your step."

Ruka took Egil's arm as they descended, thinking on Dala's words and finding more truth than he wished to admit. With his powers and knowledge he could certainly win, in the end, but at what cost?

He wasn't sure her plan was feasible. The Order voted on their leadership and would never choose a young woman from the South as matriarch. Even if Ruka threatened them, even if they knew by choosing Dala they stopped the marauding Bukayag, would they do it?

The children of Tegrin were poor at judging risk, just as Egil had once been with a boy he didn't understand. They would require a demonstration of their peril, no doubt, but Ruka found he did not wish to give it. Perhaps this time there would be another way. It was a problem for later.

First, he had the coast, the sea and finally Trung. *I mustn't get ahead of himself.*

"My lord."

Ruka blinked, so lost in his thoughts and his Grove he'd stopped paying attention to the one place that mattered. He followed Egil's eyes and saw torches out where their horses would be. It seemed the men of Varhus had spotted them.

His impulse was to act quickly, but he crouched and looked about the stockade, and soon realized there were more men than he hoped. Others moved about the field like ants searching for food. He glanced at the horizon and knew the sun would soon emerge and light the world and strip away his protection.

"Run, my lord," Egil turned to face him. "I'll stay and distract them. They won't know me or care about me. I'll follow to the coast when I can."

Ruka met the man's eyes and looked for the deceit. He banished the thought in any case because he still had Juchi and the boy, and while he did the skald would never betray.

There was only a quarter moon, and the light was dim. Ruka thought how far to Aiden and the men and how long it might take on foot. The distance was tremendous. But for Ruka the Outcast, it was possible.

"I will see you in Kormet, Egil."

Ruka wanted to tell him that Juchi and the boy were not truly in danger, and never would be from him. But it was useful for Egil to believe otherwise, and one more thing to bear for his purpose.

He hurried down the mountain, over a narrow edge of the stockade where men had yet to gather or watch closely. He ran out into the field in dim moonlight, striking a winding path that would take him near the horses in case he might still steal one and flee. Soon he heard a shout from the stockade. A torch flew through the air to land near his feet.

"There! I've got him! Trap him in!"

Ruka snarled, and ran.

He kept low and fled towards the closest gap in the net of warriors, picturing the terrain in his mind. He saw rocky ground with low grass, few bushes and fewer trees. He knew he had nowhere to hide.

Men were shouting now and running through the gloom in every direction. Most carried swords or spears or axes and looked like warriors. Only some had torches, and these spread themselves amongst the others, but even without them there was enough light for the sons of Imler to see a little.

Ruka counted fifteen now near his horse, these actively searching and guarding the animals, another twenty or more patrolling. All of his supplies—most importantly, his water—was on his horse. If he had brought Sula he could call and his mighty friend would ride to his aid. But he hadn't.

"There! Near the stockade!"

An arrow whistled through the breeze and struck the dirt near Ruka's feet. He couldn't see who'd shot it, but it made no difference. He threw away his sword and scabbard, moved to his toes, and sprinted at full speed. A man with a torch was closer now and shouting, and the other men came swarming like moths.

Ruka reached the first gap and escaped the net of bodies, though he heard their boots not far behind him. He pictured the mountain fort and knew he had seen no stables within. It was possible the only horses were the three the men had now captured, and if so they may not think or even know how to ride them. If they did and came at him with only three then he'd kill these and take his animal. He heard no dogs, either, though perhaps they had some in the fort and would bring them soon.

A young voice called almost excitedly from behind, the thrill of the hunt clear in his tone.

"There's nowhere to go, chiefless scum. You can't out-run us all!"

You should be more cautious, Ruka thought with judgment, *a hunter should always be wary of his prey.*

He lifted a shield from his Grove and handed it to his brother, who drew it from the air as sparks and fire forged thin iron from nothing and lit the darkness. The strange sight slowed his pursuers, and another loosed the arrow in his hand.

Ruka deflected it before looping the leather strap he'd made over his neck, then hanging the shield on his back like a turtle shell. He paused briefly on a rise to see his pursuers, who were all clumped together now, at least twenty men with other stragglers catching up.

He looked out in the direction of his camp and calculated again how long it would take to reach it, sorting through the memory of the distance and consulting his always improving map. He guessed what speed would be required, and for how long, and smiled at the difficulty of the task.

Men, he thought, shaking his head at the young warrior's confidence. Like wolves they overvalued their strength in numbers. They felt a courage and confidence in a pack that made them feel unstoppable. But only the strongest mattered, only those willing and able to strike and die for the pack, only the brave.

I'm not going to out-run all of you, Sons of Imler. Ruka smiled. *I'm going to out-run* each *of you.*

He called down to them. "If you can catch me, cousins, you deserve to."

Another arrow flew and Ruka turned and bolted, angling his path left then right to make himself a harder target. Like most Northerners his pursuers wouldn't be expert shots, and the dim light and Ruka's shield should be protection enough.

He increased his pace to add a little distance. He hadn't had to run down any animals in years, and back then he was thinner and lean as sinew. His upper body was bigger and heavier now, but he was also healthier, and compared to most any man in the Ascom, he was very well fed.

The feeling of the sprint and the cool air on his face mixed with the memories of his time as an outlaw, and in his mind he was alone again in the wilderness, one speck of warmth in a frozen steppe, hunted and alert and in danger, but utterly free.

A strange feeling of loss swept the corners of his mind. That he should miss such a thing amused him, and he supposed it a loss of innocence—a time when his purpose and been simple, even if it was terrible. To save the world would be a far heavier weight than to destroy it. But for Beyla, and her ancestors, he would bear it.

He kept his pace harsh. It would hurt him in the long run but he could handle it better than the others. When he'd made enough distance he sent the shield back to his Grove, knowing the men would have to keep their weapons, and it would slow them down further.

Already they had made a mistake in allowing him some distance. They should have hunted him like wolves—half surrounding him and forcing him back and forth in sprints while most held back and kept their strength. But his pursuers were city-folk, at best farmers or the sons of farmers. They were not hunters.

Ruka ran through the last shreds of night, until a morning sun rose with the mist over the hills. He looked back over the flatlands to see some of the men had already turned back, perhaps for dogs or more men or horses.

The rest had spread out now with the better runners up front, others trailing behind. Ruka ran them again to spread them further, then dropped to the grass, and waited just beyond a hill.

As the first man came panting, he rose up with a Grove-sword and pierced the boy's heaving chest, watching his wide eyes as he pulled him down.

"You ran well," he whispered as he held him, "quickly now, what is your name?"

The boy grunted in panic and spit blood and hissed nonsense, struggling without words before he stilled for the last time.

Ruka sighed. He took the young man's water-skin and a measured drink before thanking him for his sacrifice. He stood and moved Bukayag back to a methodic run, then oversaw the dead as they built the Northerner a grave.

"Runner-From-Varhus", he inscribed on the marker with a frown. Like so many things, for now it would have to do.

* * *

Ruka ran without pause for a night and two days. His legs trembled and his feet had numbed, his bones and joints creaking like the wooden pillars of his childhood home. His eyes grew tired, and Bukayag offered to finish the run while Ruka slept in his Grove, but he declined. Some tests were best done alone.

Many times he had re-calculated the distance and doubted himself, but always when exhaustion seemed overwhelming he knew his body would do more—that in truth it would run until shattered, and that doubt only existed in his mind. He pictured the outline of the forest on the horizon so many times he almost didn't believe when it became real.

He looked back before he entered, but knew he'd lost his pursuers long ago. They had never sent riders or dogs, and after the first day disappeared as specks on the barren plain.

Now the moon waned, and what little light it had left tangled in the canopy of the trees. To Ruka, this felt like safety.

He knew his men were close now. He sat and closed his eyes to rest before entering the camp, for it would not do to let them see him trembling and exhausted. It felt as if only moments passed, but Bukayag's eyes flared as twigs broke and leaves rustled near-by.

A few scouts with torches emerged from a clearing on a patrol, and Ruka sighed, then rose from behind his tree.

"Peace, cousins." He held up his hands. "I have returned."

The men saw him in the darkness and froze, staring at his eyes in the firelight. "Shaman...", the young scout swallowed, and collected himself. "Thank the Gods."

Ruka nodded politely in respect, and together they walked to the main camp. Ruka did his best to hide his pain and exhaustion, and didn't bother mentioning the pursuers. Aiden greeted him at the evening bonfire.

"The fourth day, as promised. But where is Egil, and the horses?"

Ruka felt a touch of his brother's anger at the greeting. *For the love of the gods*, he thought, *I have likely just run further and faster than any man in the history of the Ascom. I have walked the sands of paradise, created steel harder than anything in the world, pulled something from nothing, and with this one small setback I did not expect, these are the first words from your mouth.*

He blinked, and took a long, collecting breath. "Egil will meet us on the coast. The horses are gone." Ruka heard the shortness in his own tone and regretted it, but Aiden only nodded.

"We have made good progress. It will be slow moving North with the carts and lumber and only Sula to help us move it."

"Sula does not drag lumber," Ruka snapped. Or perhaps Bukayag did.

Some of the men standing near-by glanced at each other now. Ruka reminded himself that Southerners killed each other over even slight offence, and a man like Aiden was not disrespected lightly. He took another deep breath, knowing his own hatred of weakness was maybe a weakness of its own.

"Ignore me, chief. The day has been long. If it suits you, we can discuss our route and logistics in the morning, and of course Sula is yours to do with as you please."

Aiden nodded at once, and the tension drained. "In the morning then. Goodnight, Bukayag."

Ruka attempted a polite smile and turned to his tent. He realized, too, he was tired of being called Bukayag. He was tired of the deceptions and pretending what he did was some divine workings of the Gods instead of just the broken dreams of a dead, desperate mother, and a people who fled from paradise. *It's just the exhaustion*, he told himself. *A night of rest and our purpose will renew with the dawn.*

He could do nothing in any case but hope this was true, and staggered to his furs, collapsing in the darkness. Even in his Grove the false light of an unknown sky dimmed as he leaned against Beyla's house.

When Bukayag was asleep—only moments before Ruka—he found he wished that for one night he might forget like other creatures, that he could put away pain and love, suffering and truth, and all the dead faces and names and words of ancient men. He wished he could live again as a child relying only on his mother, and that he wasn't so alone. But within moments, he slept like his brother, and the thought was gone.

* * *

Ruka dreamt of a woman whose face he could not see. He crept towards her prone body, silent and excited, with no understanding of where he was. Despite the cool air she slept in only a thin, cloth shift, and Ruka's hands moved over her legs, then her hips and stomach and to her breasts as she slept.

As he massaged them, she startled, but at first didn't move as his hands roamed her body. He tried to pull up the cloth between her thighs and she thrashed and kicked and he was forced to hold her down. He felt a fury at being interfered with, at being rejected, and one of his hands wrapped around her tiny throat and began to squeeze. He heard whimpering across from him.

He looked and found Ivar in the corner holding a seax. The boy clutched it firmly but remained paralyzed with fear, and when Ruka looked again he saw the woman beneath him was Juchi. Her wide eyes were frozen and full of tears, and Ruka stepped away in horror. He fled for the tent-flap, and as he emerged he woke in his own furs. He sat up and put a hand to his cheek.

Tell me it was a dream, brother. Tell me we didn't terrify Egil's mate and his little boy in the night.

Bukayag sneered. "What difference to me. Still you deny us. You deny us both a simple pleasure, and why? Why, brother?"

Tell me it was a dream, brother!

"What you do in your dreams is no business of mine. I slept. I needed rest. I need it still."

Ruka listened to this answer again and again but couldn't tell if the words rang false. He winced, thinking he would see the ex-priestess and boy soon regardless, and would know well enough. Even Ando the island god couldn't force Bukayag to speak the truth, Ruka wouldn't bother to try.

He rose with a groan and stepped out into a late-morning sun. Men were already moving about the camp preparing food and packing lumber and supplies into crudely built carts. Ruka found Aiden by a pile of wood directing the men.

"Good morning, shaman. I've begun preparations. I assume we leave today."

Ruka nodded but found for the moment he didn't care. He scanned the cooking fires and dead trees for a sign of Juchi and saw none. "Where is the ex-priestess and the boy?"

Aiden shrugged. "Bathing, I think, at the stream. Do you want them?"

Ruka nearly flinched at the wording. "No." He forced his mind to the present and what mattered, picturing a route through the forest on his map, then the path through the small stretch of hills North to the outskirts of Kormet. "When the men are ready, chief, so is our path." For a moment he considered his next words, and chose caution. "If you wish to use Sula to help move supplies, of course you are welcome."

Aiden smiled. "Bored men are dangerous, shaman. Especially mine. It will be good for them to end their days exhausted."

Ruka grinned at this, glad for the courtesy, and also in agreement. Aiden walked through the camp speaking with a few of his men, and the preparations to leave began in earnest.

"I've prepared your horse, lord." Eshen brought Sula with saddle strapped and supplied, and Ruka nodded his thanks. Ordinarily he'd walk, but already he could feel the weakness in his legs and thought an afternoon mounted would be pleasant.

By the time the men were ready, pushing and pulling the crudely made carts in some semblance of a line, Ruka spotted Juchi.

He walked straight towards her, ignoring everything, eyes locked on her face. When she finally noticed him she startled a little, but said nothing.

"Egil will be re-joining us on the coast," he said. "You needn't fear for him."

Juchi's hair was still wet from the stream. She wore leather breeches and quilted gambeson much like the warriors. When she'd seen Ruka she nodded with the bare minimum of respect, but this didn't surprise him. He saw no terror in her eyes. Nor hatred.

"Thank you. But I wouldn't. Fear for him, I mean." She turned towards her tent in dismissal, but this was not unusual, and as a woman not cause for offense.

It was just a dream, Ruka breathed a sigh of relief. Had it been real she would have acted strangely, and couldn't have hidden such a thing. He mounted Sula again feeling a weight lifted from his shoulders. Then he looked on the hard, well-armed gathering of his warriors and smiled. *How far I've come,* he thought, remembering Ruka the Outcast and his tiny ambitions.

Now, because of him, these would be the first men of ash to stand on paradise in maybe thousands of years. They were close now, very close. They need only avoid roads and move unseen for three days, and if they were spotted perhaps they must kill whoever saw them.

They would need more lumber, more rope, tar, pitch, nails, and many other things. Some Ruka would bring from his Grove, and already the dead were piling nails made from hard iron in moulds Ruka designed. His silver would pay for the rest, though if he spent it too fast perhaps the value would fall and the Northern chiefs and perhaps the Order would become suspicious. But he did not need long—less than a season. Only two, maybe three months to build his first ships and make his raid.

He thought of the possible betrayals. First and foremost Halvar, who might have already done so, and Ruka might arrive to find the Order's dogs waiting. Now perhaps Dala, or Birmun, or even Egil. But he had many loyal men. They would not sell their lives cheaply, and if Ruka must, he knew, he would sacrifice it all, and survive.

Perhaps later he'd sneak into the matriarch's home and strangle her in the night. Perhaps for a few years he'd sew chaos and terror until the world of ash convulsed in fear, and in the madness begin again. He did not wish this, but his purpose transcended failure. As usual, his mother had told him the truth: a man failed in only two ways. He quit, or he died. Ruka did not intend to quit.

"Ready, shaman?"

Ruka blinked away from thoughts of the future, and looked to Aiden. He wore Ruka's gifts at all times now—the hard, blackened iron plate perfectly fit to his chest, his torso wrapped in chain. He wore them well, as he seemed to perform all the tasks worthy of respect well.

One day you will be a king, great chief, Ruka thought. *Perhaps you will rule this land of ash for all those left behind, or an entire island. But you must keep your faith, your wits, and your courage.*

He nodded, liking the man as ever for his competence, and his potential. Then he led Sula and his small army of outlaws and traitors out of the valley, and towards the future.

52

Egil glanced again at Chief Birmun and his handful of warriors, their backs loaded with supplies. *You're likely all dead*, he thought, not for the first time. *Your mistress sends you to your doom.*

He shifted on the small, unfamiliar saddle of his old, borrowed horse, and tried to look pleased. But to be honest he'd grown to like the nightman chief, and didn't want to see Ruka kill him.

After Ruka had fled out into the night, some of the men had found Egil and challenged him. His limp and lack of weapon saved him from instant death, but they'd seized him and forced him to explain he was a skald invited by High Priestess Dala herself. Still, they hadn't looked impressed, and quite literally dragged him back up the bloody mountain.

"Mistress, we found this man lurking outside the stockade. He says he knows you, that he's your 'guest'."

She'd waited much longer than Egil found comfortable, fixing him with an almost Ruka-like stare that seemed to indicate 'I can grant you life, or death, with a single word. Best remember that.'

"He speaks the truth," she said at last. "But thank you, chiefsmen, for your careful watch, and your diligence. You have my thanks."

They half-bowed in what seemed actual respect, then dropped Egil like sackcloth before leaving the cave-mouth without a word. He found a barrel of maybe salt and collapsed with a groan.

"I'm sure your cave is very nice, priestess, but perhaps your home would be better placed at the *foot* of the mountain."

High Priestess Dala rewarded him with the barest of smiles. And perhaps it was her curves and beauty, or the slight redness in her cheeks, or the small crinkle in her otherwise smooth dress, but Egil's mind began to wander to rather unwholesome things. A man's voice disturbed the darkness, and Egil understood his intuition.

"Back so soon, singer? You must have missed me."

Egil nodded at Birmun and kept all trace of carnal suspicion from his face. "Not for all the wine and widows in Orhus would I have climbed your god-cursed mountain again by choice, chief."

"Oh I'd say it's more like a hill, really."

Egil grinned but Dala's face seemed entirely unamused.

"Explain your presence here."

Egil took a breath, and did. He explained the loss of the horses and the dozen or more men who'd chased Ruka into the night. Then—when the couple glanced at one another—his complete confidence they wouldn't catch him.

"You seem very sure," said the priestess. "I didn't take you for a man of faith." Her tone maybe held an edge of contempt, but Egil didn't mind.

"I've little enough." He shrugged, trying to find some words to explain the one thing beyond his love of Juchi and Ivar that he knew for certain. "I am a storyteller, Mistress. I know a man like Bukayag doesn't die in a field in the middle of the night, and not with only young, unblooded warriors to see it."

Dala's steady gaze watched him as he spoke, so intense it overshadowed her youth. Once, perhaps, it would have shriveled him. But he no longer feared priestesses. "Is your master a good man, skald?"

Egil smiled then nearly laughed out loud. When he collected himself to speak plainly he found his own answer sobering, because he believed every word.

"No, priestess. But he is maybe a great man. I think none of us can understand him. Perhaps only later in stories will he be judged. I shall not try." *At least, not with you*, he thought, feeling a night of screams in the stumps of his toes. For this he could judge Ruka, but only him, and certainly not when and how anyone else asked.

The young woman watched him closely. She asked more questions but he shrugged or lied or answered in riddles until she grew tired of him.

"Birmun and some of his retainers will take you to your master, and stay with him," she said with some finality. The chief glanced at her with wide eyes before mastering himself. "And you will tell Bukayag he is to take them with him to paradise. They will serve him as warriors until they return."

Egil nodded slowly, knowing what he said made no difference, but really thinking 'you mean *if* they return, priestess'. Because if Ruka didn't wish it, they would most certainly not.

But, as usual, his opinion was not sought. They sent him again down the god-cursed mountain on foot, while Birmun woke men and gathered supplies, and even produced an ancient horse for Egil.

He mounted with a resigned groan, and Birmun led him with a pack of ten older and somewhat disgruntled-looking men. They traveled along the spiral for two days in mostly silent and confused company. Each night they found their places by the fire, and when Birmun found Egil eyeing his wineskin for a second night he raised it with a questioning brow. Despite promising Juchi he'd permanently abstain, Egil took it.

"By all the gods that's good." He closed his eyes and let the fire scorch his throat and belly.

Birmun smiled and produced another from his bag. "Never met a skald who'd quenched his thirst," he said, and Egil nodded as he wiped his lips. They drank for a time in pleasant silence, then the nightman chief pointed at Egil's lyre.

"How does a man learn such a thing?"

Egil blinked, surprised, then snorted as he thought of his lonely childhood. "I was a rich matron's son, born late and last, and my twin died when I was young. I had little enough to do."

Birmun nodded and took another long draught. "A good life, no doubt," he said without tone. Egil smiled politely, thinking *yes, once perhaps, it was.*

When they'd finished their skins Birmun took yet another from his saddlebag. "Where we're going I thought we'd need it," he said with a grin. Egil nearly groaned as he noticed the stars had blurred already, but took it regardless. He hadn't had a drop in over a year, and the numbness it brought felt like an old companion forgotten on the road.

"Have you truly been to paradise, skald?"

Egil nearly spit his drink at the suddenness and the man's casual tone. He meant to lie, of course, but changed his mind. "I have not," he sniffed, and took another drink.

Birmun stared for a moment. When it appeared Egil was not joking and did not intend to say anything else, the chief took another drink, sagged into his furs, and laughed.

Egil found the sound warm, and infectious. As he considered why he'd chosen the truth, he knew it was because of the cave, and the feeling in Dala's presence. He understood this man too was a slave to greater forces, just as Egil was—that his deeds and words were the last scribblings of a simple rower on a mighty ship, trapped in seething waves, never to be written in any tales. *There should be truth,* he thought, *and good humor, between the doomed.*

When they'd both settled and drunk several more generous swallows of the excellent honey-wine, Birmun spoke again.

"Do you think it exists? Or is your shaman some kind of demon, or half-god, sent to destroy us?"

Egil looked at the man's earnest eyes, and took the time to consider this properly. "With Ruka," he shrugged, "neither would surprise me." He looked up from the fire, surprised to see confusion on the other man's face.

"Ruka?"

Egil froze, and forced himself to blink and shrug as if it meant nothing. "Bukayag, I meant. Ruka...was his brother. He's dead now."

Birmun watched him but nodded, and looked away as if it didn't matter. "I had brothers, once. Did you know him? This Ruka?"

"I...no. No, I, met Bukayag after."

Damn drunken fool. But then what does it matter? It makes no difference anymore.

They spoke little enough after that and slept, and in the morning Egil woke with the familiar squint and raw mouth of his youth. Birmun's men cooked a breakfast of sheep sausage and oats, and without hurry again took to the Spiral.

As he rode Egil considered the possibility that Ruka had, in fact, never made it to his men. Despite his earlier display of certainty, the truth was he couldn't be sure—and it had been many days on foot back to the forest. Ruka would have been utterly without supplies, and chased by twenty warriors. Had it been a normal man, any *other* man....

But no, to underestimate Ruka was to be destroyed. How many times had he seen it? Ruka had lived for years as an outcast with nothing and survived. He would have survived the men of Varhus. He would survive his new Northern ally and betrayal, until he had gathered a great and terrible army and brought the world to the brink of madness. Only when all the willing and able were dead could a man like Ruka die.

But Juchi, and Ivar, on the other hand...they most certainly could be taken or killed if Halvar had betrayed. And this seemed exceptionally possible. The thought plagued him day and night. And by the time their small party saw the outlines of Kormet's buildings, Egil's gut seemed to slosh with ice. His hands and armpits sweat and he couldn't sit still on his horse.

"Are you well, skald? We could rest awhile before we enter."

Egil blinked and smiled politely. "No. I'm fine, Chief, thank you."

Birmun nodded but quirked a brow as he stepped closer and spoke more softly. "If challenged, I can say we've come for supplies. But if these men are Bukayag's allies then perhaps they'll kill us out of fear of what we'll see. So, what should I say?"

Egil clenched his jaw as he considered. He noticed his hands had gripped the reins, and did his best to relax them. *Have faith*, he thought, with a mad, mental cackle. "Tell them the truth, brother. We're Bukayag's men, come to serve. If they don't like that, you'll have to kill them."

Birmun's eyes widened slightly and Egil wondered for a moment if it had been his words he'd uttered, or Ruka speaking through him. He supposed it didn't matter.

They kept moving, and Kormet's scouts soon came to intercept them. These were typical Northern lads with brown hair and pale skin, carrying good, clean spears and swords. As a few blocked the road, others came from behind trees and bushes and tall grass, until they numbered at least twenty. Egil didn't recognize any of them.

"Peace, brothers," Birmun raised both hands. "My name is..."

"Which chief do you serve?"

The menace in the man's voice was clear, his tone and interruption disrespectful. The warriors inspected each other's weapons and armor, and Egil realized they'd have heard of Chief Birmun, 'Killer of Bukayag the Bastard', and if he said that's who he was they had a very serious issue.

Egil was the only one mounted, so most of the men looked to him. He cleared his throat.

"I am Egil, the skald. I serve no chief."

The speaker's brow raised. "Your name is known to us. You are welcome here. But these chiefless dogs, they must leave."

Egil felt Birmun and his men bristle, and if they'd been Southerners blood would certainly spill.

In truth the lack of welcome surprised him, and he realized perhaps the town's chief would prefer it if Bukayag's ranks didn't swell further. Egil took a breath, and channeled Ruka's arrogance in his voice.

"What is your name, warrior?"

The man twitched an eye and spit orange root, but said "Brun, son of Elena."

Egil nodded in respect, then crossed his arms over his saddle. "Well, Brun, these men have come to serve Bukayag. You can either bring them to him and let him decide, or I shall be forced to tell him you thought you knew better, and turned them away. Which one would you prefer?"

He tried not to enjoy the ripple of fear that washed across the men at his words. Invoking Ruka's wrath on anyone seemed unfair. The men squirmed visibly until their leader let out his breath.

"Very well, but give over your weapons."

Birmun half-drew his huge, now obvious rune-sword. "Try and take them."

The scout looked at it with huge eyes, and Egil held his breath until the man gestured to follow, and turned away.

Birmun winked, and Egil faked a cough to hide his sputtering, tension-filled laugh. Then he followed towards Ruka and whatever wild future awaited him, for a moment feeling a strange, mad sort of excitement—the way he used to feel as he walked out into the open plain, nothing ahead but horizon. But the moment soon passed.

53

Kormet looked typical enough. Egil had no doubt been through it once or twice before but now couldn't recall. The townsfolk glanced at him and the small pack of warriors at his side, but otherwise went about their business. The scouts led them on and past the hall, and Egil was about to question where they were going before he saw the coast.

Huge, skeletal hulls stretched out along the beach surrounded by men. All around them lay tools and lumber scattered in chaos, boys watching or helping their elders. Egil stood frozen as he stared at the size of the ships under construction. By the silence of the men at his side they seemed equally stunned.

"The great skald returns." Ruka's voice carried up the rise without effort as he rose from a near-by workbench. Aiden walked beside him with several armed retainers—as if they spent their days simply following the shaman, and awaiting violence.

"Lord." Egil dismounted and nodded in respect. Ruka returned it, then came forward and put a hand to his shoulder. He smiled warmly, and Egil felt the strange pull of pleasure, confusion and fear. He saw the surprise and perhaps resentment of other men at the gesture.

"You flee the very mouth of danger, Egil, and yet bring us new allies? Does your cunning never end?"

"We have come to serve you, and sail with you," answered Birmun before Egil could speak.

Ruka looked up at the interruption as if annoyed, and his eyes drifted over Birmun and his warriors while his face contorted. "I don't know you, save now that you speak when you should listen," he said harshly. The expression dissolved as he looked back to Egil. "I'm pleased to see you, skald. Your loyalty at Varhus will not be forgotten."

Egil nodded and felt a flush rise to his cheeks. He wasn't sure why Ruka should honor him here and now, but long ago he had stopped trying to understand the man, and tried to push down the pleasure he felt.

Ruka released a deep breath and inspected Birmun's men again. "What can you do?" he said at last, his tone still unfriendly.

Birmun glared for a moment, then half-lifted his rune-sword from its scabbard. Aiden saw it and twitched, and his men shifted a step closer.

"We are warriors," he answered, tone brash and appropriately arrogant.

Ruka stepped forward and smiled his predatory smile. "You carry a great weapon. But are you worthy? Will you kill? Will you die?" The smile disappeared. "If you wish to see paradise, cousin, swear that sword in service to the old gods, and their prophet. Do it now. Otherwise, I do not accept you."

Egil blinked and watched Birmun's face redden, his hand still on his sword. No doubt he had expected this conversation to take place in private

—to relay Dala's order and be quietly accepted and carry on some kind of deception.

Now he was being made to swear publicly. And though a Northerner like him likely didn't believe Edda heard a man's every word and judged him, he was a warrior—a chief, even if in secret for the moment—and few things lost a man more honor than broken oaths.

Aiden's hands twitched as if he hoped the man before him refused and became an enemy, and Egil shook his head in wonder at Ruka's never-ending cleverness.

"I...swear it." Birmun gestured, and the men behind him muttered their oaths. Ruka's menace dissolved at once.

"Good. Aiden is your new chief." He pointed at the big warrior, who stood near-by tapping a knife against his chest. "You will do as he says, and learn to sail. My ship needs a crew." He looked around at the men watching. "Enough idleness. Volus waits for no man."

The workers dispersed in perhaps some mild disappointment, and Ruka gestured for Egil to join him as he walked towards the sea.

"Juchi and Ivar await you with Kormet's matrons."

"Thank you, lord."

Ruka nodded and stopped to meet Egil's eyes. "What happened with Dala on the mountain? Will she betray?"

Egil felt his master's strange eyes pierce him, knowing to lie was pointless and in any case unnecessary. The truth was he did not know. Perhaps Birmun had been sent to kill Ruka, or at least to try. Perhaps the High Priestess even now marched her thousand warriors North and meant to obliterate Ruka and his followers all at once, and in view, then march straight to Orhus in glorious victory.

Egil supposed in his heart he had considered this. Perhaps he even hoped for it. By trusting Dala, Ruka had exposed himself in a way Egil had not expected. But even if she betrayed, Egil did not believe Ruka would be defeated. Even if he fled alone into the sea, somehow the man would survive, and his wrath would be terrible. Egil had doubted him once. He would not make that mistake again.

He scratched his beard in thought. "I believe she cares for this Birmun. I don't think she'd send him to die." He shrugged. "Unless absolutely necessary."

Ruka nodded as if he agreed. He looked to the water and his face took on the far-away expression Egil had grown accustomed to. "We are safe here for now. Return to your family. Soon you will meet men from distant islands and learn their words, and see all the splendor of a wealthy land. Together we will build a new future for our people."

The Vishan son and outcast and maybe demon smiled with a warmth that seemed genuine, and Egil returned it, feeling like a fool.

It wasn't that he didn't trust, exactly—though he didn't—nor that he didn't believe such things were possible. It was that he did not feel as if he truly smiled at a man, but a hungry bear, or perhaps at the tide as it swept him away.

* * *

"We saw no sign of a larger force, lord—only the skald and these few others came from the mountain."

Ruka nodded, unsurprised but still pleased. He looked to Tahar—one of his most loyal, competent retainers, and put a hand to his shoulder. "You've done well, chief, as ever. One day you will be a great lord, and no man will be more deserving."

Tahar swelled, and Ruka thought on his mother raising up the chief of Hulbron and his warriors with simple words. *Thank you, Beyla*, he thought, *for teaching me their ways.*

"Take your men and return to the hills, Tahar. We must know if an enemy comes in force."

"I will not fail you, lord."

Ruka nodded in dismissal, and walked to his ships. Kwal had nearly all the supplies he needed now. Ruka had brought much from his Grove, and through Chief Halvar purchased a great deal more from merchant ships from every town and port in the North, as well as the material brought with Aiden's wagons. Lumber cost little here, and so he largely purchased this, as well as the food to feed his men.

Alone on the beach in darkness, he brought crates and crates of iron nails, barrels of tar, and more specialized lumber in neatly laid piles. In the morning the men found it and gaped in awe, and Ruka smiled and said Vol was pleased, and so the construction continued.

Weeks passed without interruption. Ruka introduced Egil and Juchi to Kwal and Arun and hid his smile at their stares and disbelief. The islanders largely avoided the men of ash and stayed near the boats, but at night Ruka forced them to sit with him and his retainers by the fire, and often translated at least a little smalltalk.

Soon Ruka sent his men further and further out to sea to fish and at least delay the inevitable complaints of Halvar, and the growingly exorbitant price of meat and grain. He brought more and more silver and other supplies to trade.

"It's getting easier, brother," Bukayag had smiled as they'd finished another night of creation. Ruka found he had to agree. Each thing he brought seemed to *strengthen* his grasp and memory of turning nothing to something.

The dead dug deeper and deeper into the mines of his Grove, they cut down more trees and did more work without him even realizing. He told himself this was only natural, and efficient, that he should be pleased the dead went to their work to tame their land, just as the living. Still he felt an anxious fear.

Each day he watched the skeletal frames of his new ships, his 'Kingmakers' as he called them, gain flesh and structure. He helped Egil and Juchi learn Pyu words, and it seemed far easier for the priestesses who could already read and write.

Tahar and his men roamed the countryside every day looking for the enemy. Aiden and his warriors helped with the ships and kept the peace between the different warriors from North and South, usually by frightening them witless. Birmun and his men kept to themselves, but did what was asked and did their best to learn the ships and the toil to come.

Soon Kwal was overseeing construction of the decks, flat and raised in the fashion of Pyu warships, so that many men might stand and fight together on top with balance. The huge masts now jut from the beach like spears, and soon they would hang with cloth sails spread wide and taut in the wind like the skin of a drum.

Ruka turned his mind to the voyage to come. The islanders of Pyu knew much of the sea, and the stars, and had ways to navigate far beyond the men of ash. Still, they largely used landmarks, and sometimes a device made from wood that could be used to measure the shadow of the sun at a fixed point to know their position North and South. It was far from accurate, however, and Ruka needed each ship able to determine their direction in case of a storm—to have some idea of there whereabouts and proceed without instruction.

He knew it must be possible.

A week before Kwal said his ships would be ready, Ruka stood on the beach and watched the stars. He knew for certain the world was a sphere. He knew whatever the celestial bodies in the heavens truly were, they moved about this sphere in a predictable way. He believed they could be measured.

Ruka stood perfectly still and watched from a rise on the coast, away from the lights and smoke of Kormet. He did not turn away or sleep, and blinked rarely. Many times men came to him and sometimes he spoke, if necessary, including once with Chief Halvar who complained—as usual—then said Ruka must take his son and some men when he finally sailed. Ruka took a moment to intimidate him, but agreed.

After six days of watching the heavens—perhaps with prompting from the now greatly disturbed Aiden and a few others at a distance behind—Egil finally approached him.

"Are you…alright, lord? Do you speak with the gods?"

Ruka breathed, and let himself feel the stiff exhaustion of his body. He felt his eyes bulged with bruise, and no doubt red with dryness. But he didn't care. After the fourth day he had suspected, but by the sixth he was sure.

He broke his gaze at last and turned to Egil, glad for the pain in his eyes for at least it would mask the wetness of joy, and discovery. With all his effort, and the great gift and curse of his memory, he had mapped the stars above Kormet.

Now he took the memory of each moment and strung them together, reliving it at as the light shone and spun across the darkness in a great dance of divinity. It was like learning mathematics in Pyu—a thing that had always existed and yet Ruka had not understood, seen but not observed.

"They're so beautiful, Egil," he said as he watched the memories—a great ring circling a single, fixed point. "It's Tegrin," he said, and nearly sobbed. "Tegrin is the center. He is the key." Ruka blinked and turned to the skald, wishing someone could understand. "They *knew*, don't you see? Our ancestors. They...they followed Tegrin South. He is *fixed,* Egil. He is the guide."

Egil's eyes watched him, uncomprehending, perhaps afraid some further madness had seized the already mad prophet.

"They left him in our memories, in our stories—a star-king held in trust for thousands of years. And now...now the men of ash will follow him home."

"As you say, lord," said the singer, his tone cautious. Ruka laughed in the cool breeze of the autumn night.

No matter, he thought. One day he would understand. One day every man and woman of ash would know the history of their ancestors, and honor them—these brave survivors, these people of the sea, who crossed the waves to save their future.

Ruka walked on stiff legs to his men and put a hand to Aiden's shoulder. "The gods have spoken, great chief. We are ready."

The big man grinned, and nodded. The ships were complete, and supplied—five kingmakers loaded with enough food and water to make the crossing twice, and two-hundred warriors of ash.

Ruka went to his rest, then with the dawn stood on his flagship, now manned by Arun and Kwal, Tahar and Birmun and their men. Eshen took Sula to stow safely on board. Ruka watched the men as they prepared for their first voyage to paradise, feeling part of a grand story now as he looked to the clear sky. They deserved some encouragement.

"Are you ready to conquer paradise?" he shouted once on board. The men cried out and stomped their pleasure, then pushed out behind him into the Northern sea.

54

Farahi woke from another nightmare, or perhaps a vision, and like many it ended in drowning. As usual he was maybe fifteen years older and still a king. His remaining sons and grandsons knelt beside him with their hands bound, their faces bloody.

The Emperor of Naran stood before them all, dark hair touched with white, making his victory speech at Sulu Bay to a defeated people.

At last the emperor waved his hand, and smiled, and his sailors dropped Farahi into the sea. This time they'd bound him in rope and weighted him down with a stone, and since he could never end such dreams by choice, he sunk to the bottom, and drowned.

He had died in other worse ways. Sometimes it was a strange, foreign illness, or in battle, captured and tortured, burned on his ship. He never felt the pain of these deaths, but he did feel the fear, the helplessness and despair. Sometimes white-skinned giants on warships were the cause, invading the isles in their thousands. But usually, it was the emperor.

Farahi saw the fate of his sons, or grandsons, or great-grandsons, too. Even if somehow he managed to prolong his rule and protect the isles from outside threat, his descendants always failed. Such was the way of his visions, though he had learned over the years the future was never certain.

With a sigh he slid his legs from his simple bed and dressed for the day. He had never liked the layered silks of his station. The heat bothered him, and as a young man he wore little more than a short covering even in the dry season. *But I must look the part*, he sighed, *especially today.*

He had summoned a special meeting of the small-court—ten or so of the most powerful Sri Konese Orang-Kaya, or land-owners. He had also summoned the kin of his remaining wives, whom he had never once asked for anything. Today he would tell them Sri Kon was going to war.

Kikay despised the notion, of course. The announcement, that is, not the war.

"If it's war you want, brother, than send every ship and soldier at Trung in the night. Destroy him. Utterly. Him and all his warriors. And *then* call a meeting, and 'negotiate' with the other two of these so-called 'three-kings'."

Farahi had considered this, of course, and nearly obliged. It was the most logical action for a short-term victory, and no doubt with enough effort would succeed. But Farahi's visions taught him patience.

For many nights he closed his eyes and thought on his lessons with Ando, looking out at the tangled future, at the different threads all coiled and bound together. He imagined Trung destroyed, then imagined past it. He destroyed the Molbog, too, then made peace with Kapule, and held the isles for many years in an iron fist. But when he did, in each and every vision, in every thread no matter what else he did after, Pyu was destroyed.

So he waited. He would be patient and not act like his father or his brothers, and watch for opportunity.

He knew every great mistake might put the isles further and further down a path of destruction, every action placing him on a path with less choice. The true enemy was the future and the enemies of the isles, and to defeat both the Pyu had to stand united, and strong. *And even then...*

Farahi needed allies, not enemies. He had to somehow control his disjointed and unruly people, and bind the coastal powers to his safety, because only a union of kings and city-states could resist Naran.

To do this would require marriages and pacts, treaties and laws, trade and exchanges and a hundred other things. It would take a new generation of islanders who thought of themselves as one people, who trusted and worked with their neighbors and did not see themselves as above them. It would take Farahi all his life, he expected, and all his family's wealth. He could not afford a prolonged, damaging war in Pyu creating new hatreds, because even to win would be to lose.

He stepped from his room and took a moment to remember which wing he'd slept in, nodding to his bodyguards. The sun's rays had barely slipped over the palace walls, but the orange glow lit the stone and murals. As a younger man, Farahi would have admired the view, the scents of the morning, the moisture in the air. But Hali was dead, and she had taken beauty with her.

He dropped his gaze and tried to pull at the future, walking quite oblivious towards his study. He'd hardly crossed the first courtyard when a messenger hailed him.

"My lord!" The young man descended from the battlements, then raced to the steps with sweat gleaming on his forehead. He looked very fit, yet arrived panting. "My lord. A ship. From the South. It's Master Eka, lord. He said to wake you, he said you're expecting him."

Farahi breathed and let his mind roam. This was a rare thread. There was only one chance in fifty Arun returned alive with Ruka so soon.

He closed his eyes and tried to remember the series of threads sprouting from this possibility—trying to remember the many times he'd seen it clearer in his dreams. He felt his breathing quicken with his pulse because in the short-term the threads were few, and he knew the answer.

If Ruka returned so soon, it meant he maybe came in friendship. It meant maybe peace and alliance and a great and dangerous mind could be turned to saving Farahi's people—then to changing the world. *But not always. No, not even by half.*

Still, the possibility existed, the chances improved. Though Hali was dead and Farahi no longer hoped, he knew he must try. In his lifetime, such a chance would not come again.

He banished every trace of interest, curiosity, or expectation, and turned his face to stone to protect the future. He walked without hurry, as if nothing in the world had changed.

"Bring him to my study, if he wishes. Tell him I shall meet him there."

* * *

When Arun arrived on the shores of Sri Kon, he dropped to his knees, and kissed the sand.

"Oh, great mother Haumia. I, your wayward son, will eat all your bounty, and make sweet love to all your daughters, and never leave you again." He looked up and saw Kwal tying their catamaran to the docks, face sour and dull as ever.

"Stop your babble and hurry to the king. I'll wait because I expect he'll send us back."

Arun spit a few grains of sand, and sighed. He desperately wanted a proper meal, a proper drink, and—if he was very lucky—a wild, desperate night with Kikay. But he knew Kwal was right.

He rose up and crept along the sandbar, briefly attempting first to wash what little silk he had left. It still stunk like sea and sweat, and his heavier barbarian cloth pants smelled even worse than they looked. They itched, too, and before he stepped out into plain view along the Southern road to Sri Kon, he scratched with abandon.

"God-cursed filthy, ignorant savages! Spirit-buggering, lice infested animals!" He staggered as he gave up and tore them off, kicking them into a bush. Then without shame or concern, he marched in his small-clothes towards the palace.

The idea of facing Farahi again made him sweat, though for a time he lied to himself and pretended it was just the heat. The man's far-away eyes unnerved him—as if he were looking straight through you, beyond you, like you were just some pawn in a larger game you didn't understand. Of course Ruka's eyes were even worse.

The barbarian leader did not look beyond, but straight *inside*, as if examining every flaw in your spirit, as if with a glance he'd seen your darkest deeds and greatest triumphs, your secret whisperings in the night. Whatever he saw, his thick lips always curled just so, his wild, demonic eyes gleaming like a prophet or a madman.

At least with Farahi maybe you could know his mind. He could tell you why and what and like equals you might speak and understand. With Ruka, Arun felt inadequate—as if it might take so long for Ruka to tell him all he saw, that when he was finished Arun would have forgotten the beginning.

He put away the thought and thanked the spirits again he stood on dry land.

The same Alaku killers and guards were waiting outside the palace and pretending otherwise. They eyed Arun's half-nakedness and some smirked. He glared at them and marched without pause because the king expected him, and anyway to hell with all spies and servants.

They made him wait at the gate regardless and sent a messenger ahead. The Alaku elite pointed at his nakedness and cracked jokes, and for a moment he considered breaking a nose or three before he just smiled and gripped his manhood and said 'your mother', which made the guards laugh.

He tried to find calm but failed, as usual. Action had been the only thing that ever made him calm, and he knew rewards and riches were close now—perhaps closer than they'd ever been. Doom felt just as likely. He felt trapped between great forces, a small ship in a storm of roiling skies and brutal waves—the Savage and the Sorcerer-King.

The messenger returned, and guards soon took him inside, quickly wiping off their mocking smirks as they stood at attention. He passed through the outer courtyard and palace and outer fortress in a blur, trying to ready himself to face the shrewd king with his wits about him and some semblance of a plan in place.

Then he was at the study, and the messenger draped a cloak over him and gestured inside. Arun half-bowed as he entered to find the king at his desk scribbling, calm as a Bato breeze.

I wonder how you'll feel once you know several boat-loads of barbarian murderers are anchored not far from your shore, waiting to unleash mayhem.

"So." Farahi finally looked up as he placed down his quill. Arun cleared his throat.

"Your plan is very successful, lord. Ruka and two hundred warriors have returned. They've dropped anchor South of Halin, and I believe intend to attack at your command."

Farahi nodded but said nothing. He seemed different than Arun remembered him—paler, perhaps, as if he rarely saw the sun, his eyes duller and less interested. Arun felt uncomfortable in the silence but wasn't sure what else to say. The king returned to his scribbling before he spoke.

"Tell me, what has Ruka promised you to betray me? My sister, I assume, and riches. Or perhaps an island throne?"

Arun blinked and said nothing as he listened to the scratches of the quill and his tongue went dry. Farahi eventually stood and moved to a painting of his ancestors.

"Nevermind," he said absently. "I'm going to tell you something, Arun, something I have only ever told one person in this world." He turned, and smiled faintly. "You may not believe it, but I think you will. I think you have seen Ruka's gifts now and know such things are possible. Well, I too have a gift, like the ancient king, or the hero Rupi out of some sebu play. I can see the future."

He smiled and nodded when Arun said nothing.

"Sometimes I see it very far away, more than a lifetime, other times only days, or even moments. It isn't perfect. It comes mostly in images, though sometimes I hear and feel and know things I should not know. I see only possibilities, not truths—choices twisted together so that each can be separated like the fibers of cloth, then followed to their inevitable ends."

Arun still stared at the man in silence. He didn't know where this was headed, and of the many men he had met he would describe Farahi as mostly practical—not partial to fancy or delusion. He assumed this was all some kind of ploy, leading to a threat or bargain. The Alaku king turned, his eyes sharpened and fierce as if now the gaze itself might impale.

"Would you like me to tell you your future, pirate?"

Arun stepped away without thinking. He shifted awkwardly in the cloak covering his body, telling himself it was just intimidation. Now would come the offer and the threat if he did not obey. That's all this was.

"I have thought long and hard on your future and seen many threads," said the king. "All of them now end the same. I think that is the reason I tell you this. In a way, I trust you more than any other man." Here he smiled, but not unkindly. "Not in a single thread have you ever once betrayed me, Arun. I cannot know why." He shrugged. "Perhaps because you love my sister. Perhaps because you know she loves me more than she'll love you, and to betray me is to lose that love. I don't know. Perhaps you simply realize, no man will ever give you as much of the things you want as I."

The strangeness of it all kept Arun paralyzed, and he found himself unwilling to interrupt, though a small piece of him rejected this and wanted only to take the knife strapped to his thigh and plunge it straight through Farahi's heart.

"Oh, you could kill me," said the king, as if he'd read Arun's mind. "Some other monarch might reward you when the chaos is over. Or you could tie yourself to Ruka, but you have seen his people now, and you know Kikay despises him." The king met Arun's eyes, and again he spoke intensely, but not unkindly. "Unlike Ruka, I know the truth—you don't want to be a king, because to be a king is to be a slave, and the opposite of free. In your heart you know this. Therefore I will give you what you truly want. I will make you powerful and more dangerous than you've ever been, so that even whispering your name will make men of the isles tremble in fear. I will let you visit Bato as a man of respect and power, whenever you wish. And one day you will shed the mask of the scorpion and become an honorable man, and perhaps a happy one, whose great talents are put to dark use. That is the future I see for you, pirate, if you take my hand."

With this the king returned to his seat, and Arun stood stunned. He had felt himself rise and fall throughout the speech, wishing to disagree, to protest, to explain his own vision of the future. But he knew every word the king said was true.

"I have no guards in this room," Farahi added as he took up his quill. "You could kill me now and take my sister. I could be wrong. A king must take risks. You respect Ruka, I understand, and perhaps you fear him. I do too. More than any man I've ever known. It is my intention to make an alliance with his people, and to bind them to me. I want your help Arun. I want you to help him see a great future, and to be our friend, and to stay alive. So. Now you must choose."

Arun felt his hand move absently to his face. He felt a tingle in the air, like the moisture before a great wave. He had no urge to strike this man down. In truth he feared it would be somehow impossible, or the greatest mistake of his life.

Ruka was perhaps more man than monster, and had offered a path in good faith. Arun trusted him but feared him more. With Farahi, at least, it might be the opposite.

"What are you asking me," he said quietly.

"To be my right-hand in the shadows," said the king, "to be given all authority my sister once possessed. You will work through her when it suits us, but in truth do my will. I believe she loves you, in her way, or will grow to do so. It will soften the blow as she realizes the truth. What I am offering, *Master Eka*, is to make you the second most powerful man in Pyu. Not Arun the failed monk, or 'Noose' the pirate—but a new man. I offer this quietly, slowly, but with all my support and coin. And in the dark corners of these islands, you will rise."

Arun shivered and drew his cloak tighter at the king's words. It was as if they'd been plucked from the depths of his mind and spirit and laid bare before him. He knew instantly he would accept, and that the king knew, and perhaps had always known. The thought terrified him, but brought him comfort, too. It was as if he were finally trapped, saved from himself, the dangerous game at last over. He sat heavily in the chair laid out before the desk, and lifted the cup of water set out to his dry mouth.

"I accept," he said, and drank, and the king seemed ready to re-fill it, giving no indication of pleasure, or anything else.

"Go back to Ruka," Farahi said. "Tell him to attack on the third day. When he's finished in Halin, give him this letter." He curled the scroll and slid it across the desk. "And Eka—your first task in my employ is what I asked you when we met. It has *always* been thus. You will bring me back Trung's head."

55

Two days of waiting in the sea did not sit well with Ruka's men. Already the journey had been strange and difficult, overcome with steady toil and a feeling of glory and adventure. Heroes in stories, however, never sat in sweltering heat and waited.

After Kwal and Arun returned from Sri Kon with Farahi's plan, Ruka set as many followers as he could to fishing or maintaining the ships, and brought the captains to his boat to explain.

Following Tegrin, all at least had made the journey. Their Kingmakers had weathered a few minor storms, and only a few men were lost to the islander's sea. Now the captains stood with Ruka in the dim light of his flagship's near-empty hold, and listened intently.

"There are things you must learn, cousins." He met each of their eyes. "This new world has great wealth, but also dangers. I have already made an ally here—a foreign king, who will help us with our raid. He will distract our enemy's warriors, then we will land, force our way to his war-fort, and kill him before we plunder."

The men looked mostly confused. Aiden spoke first.

"What need of this ally? I don't fear a battle with their warriors. Are the gods not with us, shaman?"

The captains turned their earnest eyes to Ruka together, and he almost snorted at their ignorance. He knew he must be patient. They could not know.

"The gods reward the brave, chief, not the careless. You will see things in this place, things you can hardly understand. First, know this—these island kings sit behind walls of stone so tall and thick, nothing in the Ascom could defeat them. They sits upon thrones made of jewels and silver, inside impregnable forts, surrounded by water filled with flesh-eating fish. We face an army with more warriors than half the chiefs in Orhus combined."

At this the captains blinked and shifted their weight uncomfortably, none wishing to deny it as a lie, though no doubt they hardly believed. Ruka smiled.

"The gods are with us, as ever. But we must be quick, and ruthless. We must stay together and kill in haste. Do not allow your men to be distracted by the strangeness, the wealth, or the women. Half the men will follow me, the other half will guard the ships with Aiden. Plundering will come at the end. Most of the women we take will come from the fortress. Now is the time for questions."

"The women," said Tahar, half eager, half concerned, "how will we get them on the boats?"

Ruka looked into the big, deadly man's eyes, forcing himself not to laugh at the question, or at the curiosity and excitement of the other men.

"The women here..." he paused, and shrugged, unsure how to truly explain. "Island women are…more docile. Your appearance alone will terrify them. You have been taught a few words and phrases, so use them. But you may have to force them, cousins. You and your men will have to take many physically onto the ships."

At this thought the men visibly cringed. Some looked at their hands, as if trying to imagine doing such a thing.

Many of Ruka's followers had never even touched a woman, save for their kin. In the Ascom, violence against a woman meant death and suffering for eternity in the mountain. It would be easier after the killing, Ruka hoped, when their blood was up.

With no other questions he dismissed the captains back to their own ships and told them to keep their warriors in line. He took Arun aside when the men were gone.

"You've broken in before, pirate. How would you get inside?"

Arun scoffed, as if not realizing Ruka was serious. "With bribery, and then climbing hooks, alone, and at night."

Ruka stared because obviously that wasn't useful. The pirate sighed.

"Trying to get in that castle in the day while the walls are guarded is madness. The gates are thick and heavy, the walls are impossibly high. We have no time to siege them out and likely couldn't anyway. And this is not a king like Farahi. You could slaughter every man, woman and child in Halin before Trung's gates, and he would be unmoved to interfere."

Ruka sneered, knowing Trung would be more than 'unmoved'. He would stand and watch.

"You're right, pirate, he would enjoy their suffering. Even now he can't bear to be far from his precious slaves and their misery. That is why we will not attempt the castle walls, but come up inside the fortress through its master's weakness. We will go through the pits."

Arun nodded slowly as if perhaps he expected this.

In his Grove Ruka flattened a map of the fortress' underground. He had long ago labeled the servant quarters, the torture chambers, the pens, and the doors—but he had not seen everything. Trung would have portcullis and other tricks to seal every passage, if needed. But Ruka would find a way.

He turned from the map and walked to his training field where some of the dead smiths and weavers lay hooks and rope. They bound them together, and set down hammers and thick prying rods to bend metal grates, or perhaps destroy stone walls. Others placed weapons and armor in a line so that it would be easier for Ruka to choose what he needed when the moment came.

He walked along it, calloused hand drifting over the perfect, beautifully made tempered steel. A hundred javelins filled ten racks; swords ranged from short-stabbing blades to huge, two-handed greatswords and hung next to their leather scabbards.

The armor at the end, though, was Ruka's true masterpiece. With thin plating over corrugated mail, he had found the perfect balance between hardness, strength, and absorption. Nothing these islanders made could pierce it, or even harm him much without luck.

Not with every arrow and sword in Pyu could they kill him quickly, at least not in the heat of battle, save for bludgeoning him a thousand times. He had engraved the runes himself and with great care, covering every inch of the armored plates with a short version of the story of the Veeshan.

The thought already pleased him. He would carry the riddle of the islander's guilt on his chest—the answer to their butchery, the reason for their deaths plain and bare to their eyes if only they could read it.

In the world of the living, Ruka walked to the railing of his ship, eyes pointed towards the speck of paradise in the distance. He was close now, very close. He felt as if justice were some physical thing just beyond his grasp, and if he were patient than sooner or later he would take it in his fist.

Trung is yours, brother, when the time comes. Cleave through these warriors with me and give our followers a legend. And then I give you my word, the king is yours.

He froze the image of Trung's face watching him in the pit. The fat, over-stuffed limbs, the contented smugness, the hard, cruel eyes. Ruka didn't know what his brother would do to the man, or how long it would take, but imagining it made him smile.

Before the first day of waiting ended, it began to rain. At first the men of ash were pleased and set out their barrels to be re-filled with fresh water as they laughed in the downpour.

It helped cool the air and disrupt the endless, unbearable heat that chased the men below deck in turns, burning their skin, and sapping their energy. But if men of ash were not accustomed to such heat, nor were they used to an endless, flood-making wet.

Ruka hoped it would end but knew in the rainy season it likely wouldn't. What mattered was if it disrupted Farahi's plans. Would the king expect Ruka to know what rain meant to his navy, if anything, and delay? He couldn't be sure. Nor did he wish to wait. Instead he hoped that after so many victories at Chahen, the wily king would correctly guess Ruka's actions.

After two days of the ships swelling and rocking in the drizzle, with sodden, miserable men hunched together below decks, Ruka ordered the assault as planned. The various crews went to their work, weighing anchor and setting their sails, others moving to rowing seats in case of temperamental winds. They started forward, and Ruka tried to hide his anxiety as he watched from the deck.

When he could stand it no more he went below deck to ready Sula, finding the stoic creature restless and angry in his stall.

"You will soon run free, my friend." Ruka extended a hand and tried to calm him enough to place the saddle, but feared if he stepped inside he might be kicked or thrashed against the hull. At last he stepped back and stilled, growling until Sula felt the challenge and watched him. "You are a warrior," he said low, angry for a moment with the usually unshakeable beast. "You will live, or die, but not as some trapped and helpless coward, not mewling in fear."

He raised his tone, and watched the black pool of the creature's eyes until he could see his reflection. Sula snorted, calming, and Ruka laughed. "Forgive me," he said, understanding the truth. The beast showed only the anxiety of its master. He stepped forward and stroked his friend's nose.

"Forgive my weakness, mighty Sula. We will succeed, or die together. Let lesser creatures worry which."

He unbound and saddled him, and ordered Eshen to bring him up as they approached the shore. He saw the man's fear of the animal, and smiled.

"Live only in this moment, cousin, and know the brave live forever. This is easy to forget when a man has something to lose. Even for me."

Eshen smiled and nodded, and when Ruka returned to the deck he felt renewed. He walked to the front of the ship, noting Birmun's quiet calm with a nod, smiling when he saw Egil and even the now obviously-pregnant Juchi taking a place at the oars.

He smiled at his crew not to please them, nor to comfort, but because he imagined the possibility of success, and even the chance of it seemed not so long ago a dream within a dream.

The coast of Halin soon spread large in his vision. Part of him already imagined it in flames, but another part saw huge, wide docks filled with trade ships—a great island fortress connecting Pyu and the Ascom, islanders and men of ash. They worked together in this dream, built families, learned each other's ways and found new, better methods to explore and tame their worlds.

"Bring my horse," he called over his shoulder, and Eshen went below.

He turned to Halvar's son—Folvar—who had been quiet much of the journey, but whose eyes Ruka liked. He thought, with the right guidance, the boy could be made a useful man.

"Folvar," he called, and the young man broke his wide-eyed gaze away from the beach to return Ruka's stare. "Race behind me, chiefling, if your will holds. Show your men the way with courage and they will follow you to hell."

Folvar blinked then looked back to the shore, but Ruka thought his jaw set with determination rather than contempt or fear, and he nodded in respect.

Ruka recalled the first time he had seen white-sand and gentle slopes— the first sight of palm trees with leaves so green and wide a man could lie atop them, a thousand houses and buildings with two or even three floors, protected by beautifully tiled roofs and walls made of brick, marble and stone. He knew what his men saw, the beauty of it all, and didn't blame them for their wide-eyed stares.

Catamarans drifted about the coast. Soon, Pyu fishermen stood on their little hulls, hands blocking the sun as they stared in utter confusion as men of ash came from an endless sea. They abandoned rods and nets, frozen at the sight of Ruka's small fleet of Kingmakers. Few fled, equally enthralled by the cloth sails wide and taut, rows of oars splashing through open sea in a navy charge.

Ruka almost laughed at the pure, wild chaos to come—the changing of the world beneath him. He knew Halin had no guard-towers on the South side, but he could still see many men on shore.

Some would run to the castle or at least begin to warn the soldiers, and as he stared he realized that some of the ships at the docks were actually scouts and small warships. They weren't manned, however, nor ready to sail.

No doubt the navy used this side of the island to train—removed as it was from the sight and presence of the other islanders. A cluster of these men had stopped to watch the ships, too, and now many were shouting and running towards open-sided buildings that looked more like stables. Ruka grit his teeth as he understood—they were attacking barracks.

Eshen came to his side with Sula, and Ruka mounted on the widest curve of the deck. In his Grove, Boy-From-Alverel finished clasping him in his armor, but he waited to give it to Bukayag.

He breathed, feeling his men's eyes on him, feeling their overwhelmed senses and fear. He felt their courage, too. He waited until the ship skimmed the bottom of the beach, finally striking island sand in earnest.

"Ride!" He lifted his sword. Without hesitation, Sula leapt from wood to sand, snorting as he sprinted up the gentle slope.

Bukayag woke and laughed his laugh, sensing blood and glory and vengeance. Ruka gave him his armor, wrapping his body in flames as he charged towards the first doomed men to stand.

Regardless of the outcome, he had already won. With this landing, his people had left their frozen world since their first flight in Tegrin's shadow— the first anyone had seen them in force since history could recall. The men of ash had come to paradise. Ruka intended to make it memorable.

56

Arun sat in confusion on the barbarian's ship. He saw the mad, wild excitement of the men, but felt none of it himself. In fact he had debated not returning at all to Ruka's ship, or being part of this, joining neither Farahi nor Ruka and instead fleeing to the continent and starting a new life away from everything.

But as he'd walked down towards the coast, his feet had taken him back to Kwal, and Kwal had taken him back to the ship. And here he was.

Now he watched the awe, confusion and terror in the people of Halin, which until this moment he would never have considered *his* people. But compared to the men of ash, they certainly were.

Islanders all liked to think of themselves as different, but were so thoroughly mixed it was almost impossible to know a man's roots. They spoke in some small different dialects and even language, but all spoke the 'Common' words of Sri Kon. They had the same gods, or close enough, the same traditions and calendar and ways. In this moment, next to the men of ash, to claim any true difference felt ridiculous.

The barbarian ships moved closer, propelled by a fine wind and long oars rowed by huge men. They struck the gentle slope of the sand without pause and started gathering to make their assault.

Ruka—mounted on his monstrous animal he called a 'horse'—and with a last, crazed look to the men behind him, leapt off the ship onto the beach.

The savages all screamed and followed him, most carrying shields and swords, many others a motley of axes and spears, picks and hooks. Arun moved quietly behind, unable to see much of anything for all the huge backs of the larger men around him.

There appeared to be two gatherings of Halin marines on the beach, but Arun realized they were recruits. They were boys, really, clustering now into unorganized packs behind red faced and terrified sergeants.

Ruka raced past them with a wild shout, his body wreathing in flames as he threw spears from the air in a now-familiar miracle, like some demon straight from hell. The islanders fled before him in raw, instant terror, and his warriors cried out and raced to follow.

Fishermen, merchants and warehousemen began to scatter, with some few fools too frightened or confused to run simply hacked apart.

Another group of young men near the beach began to muster, coming out of barracks and mess halls with knives and spears, some few with bows. These rallied other near-by men, growing bolder as more men of ash left and split their forces near the boats.

Arun looked at the young men readying for a fight—half naked and soft, armed with old, dull weapons made of more wood than iron. He knew none would have ever killed, never seen war, or death. Then he looked at the men of ash.

These were warriors forged as hard as their iron; they were killers who knew only suffering and violence, and even as they looked out over this strange, new world with awe, he saw their readiness for death and murder. They watched the islanders but did nothing to build their own nerve. They stood together almost at ease, calling to each other in their harsh, foreign words, all eyes on the giant 'Aden', who stood before them sweating and covered in iron, but smiling in genuine pleasure.

They are wolves in a sheep-pen, Arun thought, feeling some strange mixture of embarrassment and pride in the boys who stood ready to oppose them. He knew what was about to happen here, and did not wish to see it. He raced after Ruka and his attackers.

The fortress attackers had kept in good order though they struggled to walk in the sand. They marched over a few corpses left by their prophet, slaughtering some few too slow or too foolish to escape them. They went largely unopposed, straight to the plaza—the flat, clear section of volcanic rock surrounded by merchant stalls just before the entrance to the pit.

Arun realized it was festival season, and by the looks of the active stalls that perhaps it was a slave-fighting day. If yes, there would be hundreds of men and women inside for the show.

Ruka waited for his men at the entrance, massive and terrifying on his animal, spear held high like the tip of some dark spire. Most of the merchants had already fled, though one hung skewered and sagging from the cave wall.

The savage leader called to his men in the barbarian tongue, and Arun didn't need to know the words to hear their meaning. His tone was harsh, brutal, and merciless. The warriors of ash matched it with war cries, and raced inside.

Arun went with them and soon saw the gamblers. They were shouting, the noise and excitement of an ongoing fight so loud it had drowned out the death outside. Ruka led his warriors around the pit without a hint of pause, and the slaughter began.

For a moment Arun wondered if the crew of the Bahala were here, but supposed it didn't matter. They were pirates and murderers and did they not deserve this fate more than most? They had lived their whole lives ruining others because they were stronger, and because they could. Surely this was the spirits' reckoning.

Arun himself didn't take part in the killing. He stayed close to Ruka to 'protect' him as promised, but this quickly became a joke. Ruka wore armor that seemed nearly without weakness, and in any case faced an enemy that didn't fight back.

When the gamblers realized what was happening, confusion and fear spread like a plague. Men ran for the doors, or tried to get around the attackers to the cave mouth. But other Ascomi were waiting, and killed every man without hesitation. The women they ignored entirely.

"Pirate." Arun blinked and realized Ruka was staring at him. His armor was already soaked in blood, golden eyes bright in the gloom of the cave. "There is a way to the fortress through these passages. Do you know it?"

Arun nodded. It was secret and maybe shut, but in his many bribes before rescuing Ruka from the prison, he'd been told a way.

"Good. Take these men and find it," he gestured, then spoke to several warriors briefly in his foreign words. "Find Trung, if you can. My path is through the pits. Hopefully one of us succeeds."

Ruka's hand sprayed fire as a metal hook and maybe rope dangled in his open grip. With a mad grin, he turned, attached it to the railing, and leapt down into the arena.

* * *

Ruka stood in the sands and smiled at the wretched gladiators cowering in the corners. His men began climbing down the walls more slowly to join him, and while he waited he inspected the bronze arena door.

While imprisoned he had inspected every door and lock he could find, and noted the shape of the guard's keys. He'd quickly realized they were all the same, but the arena doors could only be opened from the inside. It would require brute force.

From his Grove he summoned the long, thick pry bar of tempered steel he had made for this purpose, and jammed it through the grate. The thinner, lesser metal creaked and bent and by the time his warriors had gathered behind him, Ruka reached his arm through the hole, unlocked the crossbeam latch, and pushed open the door.

The guards who should have been inside were gone. Whether these had simply fled, or run up to help contend with the madness they'd heard in the arena, Ruka did not know. Nor did he care. Sweating now in his armor from the exertion and heat, he walked out into the dark, dirty slave pens, remembering the smell.

He looked back to his warriors and held up a hand, pulling three keys he'd forged in his Grove.

"Open the cells, but don't harm them, and leave them inside."

Eshen took the keys and nodded, and Ruka walked on. He followed in his own footsteps—the same path once cleared by Arun when he freed him, walking through slave pens he had once shuffled through bare foot.

He felt the hard leather sole of his boots tap against the stone, and breathed the fishy scent of what he now knew were whale-oil lamps. He thought of Trung in his hands, and ran the metal of his blade along the stone corridors, every step bringing him closer and closer to his prize.

Servants poked their heads from behind open doors ahead. Most screamed when they saw Ruka and his warriors, then turned and fled up the winding passages. Ruka didn't chase them because he had no need to follow. He knew the way.

He followed the map in his mind until he emerged into the huge, tapestry-filled dining room where he had seen his first painting, and his first sculpture. This time it was guarded.

Ten warriors stood ready for whatever might come from the tunnels below. They held their thin, pitiful shields forward, their small, curved swords of brittle iron or bronze in their other hands. They looked ready and calm enough, though they wore only a leather cuirass. Their arms and legs were unprotected, their heads uncovered, their feet in open sandals.

"We are demons sent from hell for your master," Ruka said in the Sri Kon dialect. He drew a wide, round shield from his Grove, the sparks flaring from an invisible forge. "Run," he pointed his sword, "or die."

The guards' eyes widened and some looked to their fellows. Only the gods knew what they thought of their enemy, but to their great credit, and courage, they stood. The prince behind them ran.

"Forward," Ruka growled in Ascomi, then advanced first in the narrow corridor. He raised his shield and charged without caution, throwing his body and all his weight at the first barrier in his path.

Three guards tried to hold him. Two of their shields thrashed against his then fell away as Ruka burst into the room. The men behind recovered and attacked, and Ruka spun and slashed as he carried his momentum. He felt a sword ring against his side, his thigh, then another against his shoulder. Through the mail and padding he hardly felt it.

His men followed behind screaming, slashing wildly to catch him, shield-charging and smashing the men away so they could move inside. The guards fell back and protected themselves as soon as one of them fell, withdrawing further and further until they'd all but moved to the great tapestries. The men of ash kept coming.

Ruka simply waited, curious now, watching the eyes of Halin's guard as ten then twenty giants crowded the room. As every new warrior entered the guardsmen fell back, and back, until they'd withdrawn to the rich fabric and the barred windows behind them. Ruka could see their terror, the slow understanding of how outmatched they were.

Men called from another corridor, and more islanders charged with the prince who'd fled. Folvar growled and turned to them, the men he'd brought close behind. For a moment it seemed the sides were almost matched in number, both formations eying the other as if to decide who held the upper hand. But this was an illusion.

Ruka's warriors had been culled by hardship, surviving when so many before them had fallen. They were killers and fanatics, desperate men with nothing to lose. In this moment of violence they howled only for their gods to watch them kill, or die, believing only the brave would be rewarded. They charged without fear.

Wooden shields shattered and bamboo spears shivered and cut as iron showed its strength. The bravest islanders died first, hacked to pieces with nowhere to flee, trapped between flesh and stone. The men behind them fled.

Ruka saw the Trung royal amongst these and gave chase, leaving Folvar to finish the survivors. *Run, run little prince*, he thought, *show me where your father hides*.

He threw off his helm so he could hear the footsteps better, racing down gray corridors then up several flights of stairs. Even in his armor he could have likely caught the man, but kept his pace matching as he only tried to follow.

Eshen caught up behind him with two others, though many might have been separated and lost. It made little difference now. The fortress would be cleared, and soon enough there would be time to collect slaves and plunder, and return to their ships. Farahi had obviously succeeded in drawing out Halin's soldiers. Ruka would assume he had the day.

As he gave chase, he realized the windows and floor-sizes were shrinking, and that he'd nearly reached the top of the fort. He picked up his pace and caught sight of the prince, who had stopped before wide, open double doors of iron to glance behind.

"Inside, my prince!" shouted a voice from the inside. The island royal turned to flee, and next to him, as if from nothing, hands seized his arms.

Arun stepped out from the only shadow darkened by the hallway's tapestry and pulled him down to the corner screaming. Ruka ran and lunged for the iron doors, but the men inside shouted, and slammed them shut.

"He has ten guards with him," said Arun, as he slowly squeezed the air from the prince's throat and held him fast.

Ruka scanned the walls of the room and soon understood they were built of thick, solid stone. The doors would be all but impossible to break, designed as a last stand to buy time. Trung and the rest of his family would be inside.

Bukayag shouted and seized a hammer from Ruka's Grove, ramming it uselessly against the door, hitting again and again as he panted with rage.

We will find a way, brother. Be calm. I'm thinking.

Bukayag dropped the hammer and leaned against the wall like a petulant child. "Trung won't bargain for his son," he growled.

I'm aware of that.

Ruka wondered if the island king would build some secret passage as an escape, and even now fled down beneath the bowels of his fortress. Certainly, that is what Farahi would have done, but this king was arrogant and proud. He wouldn't plan on running.

Instead he would sit behind his iron door and hope his men would return and save him before Ruka got inside. He thought of the man's cruelties, his torture, his unworthiness as a leader and king, and the idea of leaving him alive nearly incensed Bukayag again. But Ruka repeated the thought again and again, knowing such a king would be despised by many servants. Particularly honorable ones.

He looked out the window and saw several on the tower, knowing his words would be heard inside. He raised his voice.

"One of you will be the captain of Trung's guard. You will remember me. We stood together in a pit, you and I. You honored your word, and I mine." He waited with no answer, but to try cost him nothing. "You are well trapped now, my friend, as I once was. Soon enough this door will be undone. Your choice is this: open it, and I will spare you and all your men. Or wait, and die with Trung."

Arun looked at him as if he were wasting his time, and perhaps he was. He wondered next if he could try to take the door or a part of the stone back to his Grove, despite not having created them. This felt like a risk, but he was about to try when he heard voices from the tower. They raised in volume, growing more and more agitated.

The voices followed by ringing metal and screams, and with a creaking shudder, metal snapped on stone, and the huge door unsealed. It pushed open slowly, and behind it stood 'Kaptin'—the one man in this hell who had treated Ruka with respect. His face was pale and dripping. He looked on Ruka's armor and the men behind him with stark, naked terror, and backed away.

Ruka stepped alone into the room. The captain's men held Trung at spear point, as well as three princes, four daughters, and at least ten other relations.

"These warriors are not to be harmed," he called in Ascomi to his men. "Eshen, you will go with them from the palace. Ensure they are not killed by our other warriors. They are under my protection. Understood?"

"Yes, lord."

Ruka nodded, and turned to Trung's guard. "These men will take you to safety. Keep your weapons, if you wish. Now go."

The captain swallowed, and his men lined up behind and gave panicked, trembling bows as they sped from the room.

Ruka swept his eyes over the plush furniture, the children's toys, the jugs of wine and plates of fruits and sweet-meats, as if the family were having a picnic. A big cooking pot sat in the center of the room, and Ruka smiled as he looked at it. At last he met Trung's eyes.

"Hello, Chief of the Pits," he said. "Remember me?"

* * *

Bukayag shivered at Trung's fear. Ruka thought of Kunla and how killing her had been so unsatisfying—how it had removed his meaning and left him with nothing. This time, though, his purpose was far larger. It would take all his life, no doubt, and in any case far outlast Trung and Halin. But he could still enjoy the little things.

"I am much more use to you alive," said Trung, huddling against the further corner. Sweat beaded on his red neck, fine silks sticking to the folded flesh on his torso. "I have many riches buried. I...I can help you, whatever you're after. And I know secrets, many secrets, things worth a fortune. You're clever, I can see that. Be clever now."

Ruka stepped closer and pictured Kunla as she said much the same. She had been very brave in death, Ruka had to give her that. He did not think Trung would go as admirably.

"There is but one thing I want to know from you, *great king*. If you can answer, I will let you live. As you can see," he gestured towards the path of the still-living guards, "I am a man of my word."

Trung swallowed, and his eyes darted but looked dubious. No doubt he was the kind of man who might taunt his victims in such a manner, knowing no matter what they did or said they would still be butchered. Ruka, though, meant every word.

Bukayag almost shook with impatience and the thought of losing his kill, but Ruka was the master. He closed his eyes and lifted a newly-crafted iron rod in his Grove, pulling it to the world as he raised his arm and formed it in Bukayag's hand. He had spent many hours on the detail of the head—sculpting the curves and angles, particularly the face. He had made Girl-from-Trung's-Pit sit for him as he scraped the edges just so. It was very fine work.

"What is the name of this slave girl, king, the one you sent to die in my hands like a dog? Tell me that, and I will set you free."

Ruka walked to the girl's grave with a marking stone holding her hand. He had prepared a sign, in case the man knew, but was confident he did not. He looked into the king's terrified eyes and saw the desperation, the naked duplicity as it formed so clearly, lie swelling from the man's lips like a bruise.

"Iliana," he said, "it was Iliana." He met Ruka's glare forcefully, as if to bludgeon him into belief.

Ruka looked at Girl-From-Trung's-Pit, and she shook her head sadly. He touched the scarf hiding her neck, wishing she could speak, or at least write, but it seemed the dead could do neither.

He did not lie to himself and claim no responsibility for her death. One day for this and all he had done, he would be judged, just as Trung. When he had served his purpose he would pay without complaint. In the meantime he would honor them, give meaning to their sacrifice, and carry on their deeds. If he could, he would give them justice.

Ruka stepped forward and took Trung's arm, then swung the perfect, beautiful visage of the man's dead slave, and broke it at the elbow. The king of Halin screamed and would have collapsed, but Ruka held him. He swung again and broke the other arm.

"Know this as you die," he hissed over the sound, "if you had been a better king, you would not be suffering this. It was within your power, Trung. The fault is yours."

Ruka looked back to his men, doing all he could to control Bukayag, feeling the raw urge to tear this man and his whole world apart.

"Kill the men. Take the women. They won't want to see this." He turned to Arun and spoke in the island tongue. "Find the king's harem, pirate. All the women there will be taken as matrons."

His chest heaved and his hands opened and closed in anticipation. The pressure on his mind began to lift at last, a great urge on the edge of fulfilled.

Alright, brother. He's yours. He's all yours.

Ruka took Pit-Girl's hand and led her to his garden, letting the dead dig the graves for the guards he had killed.

"Would you like to see my homeland's Road Roses? I have a new row by my mother's statue."

She smiled, and nodded, and together they walked the clean, flat path towards Beyla's garden, where Ruka would put yellow and blue flowers in her hair, and perhaps they'd lie on the cool, moist grass and sleep for a time.

Ruka could vaguely hear the screams, and taste the blood, but had never enjoyed such things. He focused on the girl's pretty smile.

57

The men of ash slaughtered Trung's male kin as if cutting firewood.

Arun walked away from the wailing and smells in a daze to explain to the weeping, retching women that they would not be harmed, but they would be coming with the killers.

"Show us to the harem." He grabbed the arm of what he thought was one of Trung's daughters, and she cringed. "Don't make them angrier, you damned fool. Do it quickly."

She glanced at the others, and they huddled together and moved to the open iron doors. The men of ash—finished with their grisly work and covered in blood—then transformed.

The giants stepped aside and lowered their heads as if in respect to the women, gesturing at the corridor. None of them made a move to touch, though the royals wept at their every gesture. In fact the men hardly *looked* at the royal ladies, and when they did it was only in stolen glances, as if the tears they caused confused and shamed them.

Arun didn't bother trying to make sense of it. He lingered briefly at the door as the party left, his eyes transfixed on Ruka, and his prize.

During the butchery, the leader of the ash-men had never wavered in his attention on the king. He had cornered the man and begun to beat him with an iron rod, shattering bone and crushing tissue until the king collapsed, his face a pale canvass of suffering.

Arun had thought this simple cruelty, then blinked in memory, seeing Ruka beaten in Trung's prison with bamboo in the exact manner. At last the savage dropped the weapon and muttered words in his own tongue, as if to himself. Then his lips curled as he growled. He dropped to his knees, seized the older man's head, and tore a chunk of flesh from his cheek with his teeth.

Trung's horror and the eating became the only sounds left in the room, and Arun knew no amount of rum would ever purge it from his mind.

"Stop," he said, finding his nerve. "Farahi needs his head."

Ruka's face turned back slick with gore, his eyes wild as they'd been in Bato's temple. Again it was as if he didn't recognize Arun at all. He growled and bared his now red, crooked teeth, then lurched forward as if he meant to cross the room and rip Arun apart with his bare hands.

Instead he stopped and blinked until his face and eyes cleared. He shuddered with a long, deep breath, and lifted a near-by discarded sword as he stood. Trung—still alive—wept and begged pitifully until Ruka seized his hair, swung the blade, and struck the king's head in a single blow.

"Go with the men," he said, tossing it to Arun's feet as if it no longer mattered. "I will leave Trung's successor a little message. Help the warriors get the women aboard. They will find it awkward. I shall see you at the boats."

Arun wandered in a daze to the harem. The hundred and fifty-odd women and girls at first stared at him and the noblewomen in confusion, as if perhaps this were all some elaborate ruse. Arun broke his trance and screamed at them and brought five men of ash to help gather their clothes, and the women wept and obeyed.

Soon they were paraded through the fortress, stepping over dead guards and servants, collecting some of the terrified serving-girls on the way. The men of ash killed every man except the few Ruka spared.

They hacked Trung's guards and male servants apart without mercy, seeming annoyed at their feeble attempts to fight back. They pointed at corpses and joked amongst themselves as they passed. Again Arun felt himself in a daze, barely understanding anymore how he'd come to this place, or how he would escape it.

Many of the women retched as they were led out through the gambling hall and the pits. A hundred corpses or more lay strewn about like garbage after a storm, many shoved into corners or against walls to clear a walking path. The warriors left outside welcomed the palace-raiders by banging their shields and stomping or raising deep and feral voices to chant their savage songs. They left the fortress of King Trung as conquering heroes, and Arun supposed they were.

These men had sailed an unknown sea, stormed the beach of a powerful king, and with only a handful of losses, they had killed him. Now they marched on foreign sand with a line of young, beautiful women behind them.

Arun was forced to scream and holler and throw women forcibly onto the boats when they realized their fate. The men of ash formed a wall of flesh and iron to block their flight, but otherwise tried not to touch them, or interfere. Arun and eventually Kwal helped load the women and settled them below, then returned to the beach exhausted and trembling.

They glanced at each other but said nothing. Arun lit a cigar with shaking hands and removed a flask of rum, passing both to the stoic captain. For the first time, Kwal took both. They shared something nameless on the beach, perhaps a feeling of dread that what they did now could not be undone, and one day they'd wish it was otherwise.

Together they watched as smoke and then fire begin to rise from the palace, and the city around it. They watched the men of ash return in their twos and threes from elsewhere on the island, soaked in blood and carrying plunder. As the sun froze and began its dip in the sky, at last Ruka approached.

More men trailed behind him carrying chests marked with Trung's seal, and Arun understood they had robbed the treasury. The big warrior 'Aiden' silenced the men around him at Ruka's approach and dropped to his knee. The others followed, and soon every man of ash sunk an armored leg to the sand.

Ruka raised his hands and spoke foreign words in his elemental voice, then came forward and took Aiden and raised him up with wet eyes as he gestured at the men. Soon all were on their feet, chanting and screaming in what could only be called religious fervor.

Arun stared at their strangeness—so many of them brothers, even twins who looked almost the same. Their pale, ruddy skin made them resemble corpses, their wild beards and hair and dirt-covered bodies making them appear as savage as their deeds. He saw the terrible threat of them, the foreign strangeness, the joy in killing men just like Arun. All he could think was *what have I done.*

"You've done well," Ruka said to him and Kwal later as they boarded his flagship. He pointed at a smaller catamaran scout-ship on the shore, his men dragging it towards the water. "Take this back to your king," he said, putting a hand to Kwal's shoulder. "I have met few men as competent as you, my friend, on land or sea. Go with my people's thanks. I hope to see you again."

Kwal bowed stiffly, then moved towards his next task without a word, as was his way.

"Pirate." Ruka smiled as he met Arun's eyes. "It seems our bargain is finished." He took Farahi's letter from his pocket, which Arun had decided to give him in advance. "I have read your king's words, and so it seems I cannot give you what I promised. If you wish you may come with me now, at my side until I have paid you in some other fashion. But, I think you won't. So go back to Farahi and your princess, and live in their favor. Like you I am Farahi's ally. But I remain in your debt."

Arun nodded and did his best not to race at full speed towards the catamaran and escape. In a grotesque, inexplicable way, he still trusted Ruka. Perhaps he even liked him.

It seemed impossible to reconcile the honorable man before him and his now-perfect words to the savage who had come before. He saw the sorcerer who could make miracles, and the disfigured beast who fed on men's flesh. He couldn't separate it, any of it. Ruka was all of them.

"I will tell him," he said as he hoisted the cloth sack holding Trung's partly-eaten head. Then he forced himself to his full height, and to step forward and extend his hand as a man respecting another man. Because in truth, he did. Ruka seized it, and grinned.

"Keep the dagger, pirate, and be careful. Kikay is treacherous, and Farahi plays a game of Chahen with his servants as pieces."

With that he turned and gestured at his men to make ready. But as Arun left the deck and walked to the catamaran, Ruka called to him from his flagship.

"And tell your king—I have written on his letter what supplies the land of ash will require, and what we will pay. Tell him I will expect his first shipment in the spring."

* * *

Ruka and his men sailed with fair winds and clear skies for two days. Going South was far easier, because even if they were far separated in a storm and blown off course, following Tegrin would still bring them to the wide land of the Ascom.

The men maintained their almost boyish excitement for a time, then faded to a quiet pride and perhaps a disbelieving numbness. The wounded were praised, stories of violence spread up and down the ship and repeated over with fresh exaggeration, until even the tellers laughed at their own wild tales.

All agreed Folvar had fought bravely and led his men with courage. The legend of Aiden spread as some relayed his prowess on the beach. Only Birmun seemed uninterested in the many tales of glory, but his silence did not concern the others.

The captured women required tending. Men argued and came up with a dozen systems to decide who would be given the privilege of taking their meals, helping them to the buckets, or walking them on deck. Ruka had taught them 'loa', 'please', and 'thank you'. And though everything the men of ash did seemed to terrify the islanders, the mumbled words and gentleness kept them calm enough.

Their small fleet faced a storm on the third day, but with the men bailing and the sturdy design of Ruka's kingmakers, they soon came through and kept their course.

Ruka was no longer permitted to do things for himself. The men scrambled to care for Sula, to bring him water or bread and dried pork on a barrel lid, bowing and scraping like cursed island slaves whenever he approached. He tried to tell himself it was necessary, or at least inevitable, but found the change appalling.

On the fourth day he sat in his cabin alone. He had all of Farahi's words still locked in his mind forever, and summoned the feel of the letter again to his fingers, and the smell of the ink. He read it again in his mind.

"My friend," it started, which made Ruka smile. "If you're reading this, I hope it means Trung is dead, or will be shortly. To me his death is a solemn pact between us—a trust sealed with blood. Like you I have often felt alone in this world. I did not expect to be joined in vision by a gifted man from a land of ice and snow.

"I, too, have gifts, which perhaps a man like you can hear and believe. My gift is to see the future of this world. I see the possible, and the likely, great and small—the future of nations, and the choices of my opponent in a game of Chahen. I see it best in my dreams, my friend, and in my dreams I have seen two very different worlds.

"In the first, your land of ash and the people of Pyu go to war. What follows is always death, destruction and starvation—hatred and fighting until one side or the other is destroyed. That is the most likely future. If it isn't in our lifetime perhaps it will be in our children's, or theirs. That is the easy future. To bring it you and I need only do nothing, and one day my nightmares will become reality.

"But there is a second world—as unlikely as a disfigured boy surviving the Ascom, crossing an uncrossable sea with the greatest mind of a generation, and befriending a lonely king. It is a world where islander and ash-man come together in brotherhood, very carefully, and with open eyes—where Pyu grain-ships bring life to frozen shores, and giant warriors sail in Pyu warships. Over hundreds of years they marry and mix until they face this world as one. In this world, after many hardships, our people might form the greatest sea-power ever seen, and turn their eyes to distant shores.

"This is the future I wish for my descendants. It is a future perhaps possible to forge with your help, with your mind, and your great gifts. It will be hard, Ruka, and take all our lives. It will be bloody in both your lands and mine, because the great power of Naran must be resisted and to do so will bleed us both. One day it will come with all its might, with all its warriors and allies, and both our people will require many changes to resist. You and I will have to trust each other and speak many times of our plans and schemes and be ready to kill and lie and sacrifice. But for my part, I vow to see it done. The choice is yours."

'Your friend,' it ended as it began, and Ruka wiped his eyes as the wetness threatened the page. He laughed as he remembered every loss in Chahen despite immense mental calculations and different strategies, feeling always a step behind.

What he believed, exactly, he wasn't sure—but he believed enough. He believed the island king saw the future better than any; that he was a good man who would help Ruka's people, and that his true enemy were conquerors like Naran, nature itself, and man's ignorance.

Ruka wanted only an excuse to join Farahi, and now their purposes aligned. The Enlightened and all those who had doomed the Vishan were long dead and gone. Their descendants were no more responsible for their fate than Ruka's were theirs. The brave were the brave, and if a foreign empire would set their feet on paradise than let them come and take it. Ruka did not blame them. But by every god or spirit, the men of ash would make their claim.

Remember us, said the Vishan. And Ruka would, but the good must be remembered with the bad.

His ancestors had survived. For this they would always deserve praise, but they had lacked the strength to hold their islands. They'd been destroyed by a greater force because after all fine words and the spectacle of civilization, what truly mattered was strength. And the men of ash were strong.

Ruka had read many books on war and empire in Farahi's study. To face Naran and anyone else who threatened them his people would need their own fleet. Not just warships, but transports—the strength to invade an enemy and destroy his land and cities. They would need to learn how to fight armies and navies and build walls and navigate the seas, to siege castles and negotiate with kings. But they would learn. Ruka would ensure it.

He looked up to the darkening skies, knowing another storm formed on the horizon. His kingmakers would survive this as their creators had survived. They would reach land and Farahi would keep his word, and between them they would prepare their people for the hardness of the future.

Then would come the true storm—a storm building for two thousand years, made of the sons and daughters of once bitter enemies, an alliance between the lost children of paradise—a storm of ash and sand.

Part III - Kings of Ash

58

"Land, shaman. Kormet is ahead of us, I see the horn."

Ruka glanced at Eshen swaying in the crow's nest in the afternoon sun, then gripped the rail as he watched for the coast. He closed his eyes and breathed as the fear of ruin subsided.

More luck, he knew—another crossing of the uncrossable with fairer weather than any man deserved.

"Signal the captains. I'll speak with them before we land."

Birmun nodded and motioned to one of his men, who waved the agreed flag that meant gather. It would take time and use what little daylight remained, but Ruka preferred to land in near darkness anyway.

The ships paddled and eased their way into some semblance of a line, and the captains used shore-boats or gangplank to cross to Ruka's flagship. They followed below, and soon Ruka hunched beneath his Kingmaker's hull—not far from his many, huddled prisoners—in a circle with his captains and retainers.

He looked at each of them and did not rush the moment. Aiden had taken to carrying a scabbarded rune-sword at all times in one hand, as if ready at any moment to kill for the gods. Despite the burden of the weight, Altan carried his axe strapped to his back, his eyes still unfocused, as if he barely clung to life. Eshen watched the stairs, the prisoners, and even the other men, ever-vigilant. Tahar's beard had gone grey since Ruka met him, but the same impatience and fierce cunning lay in his eyes. Folvar had begun to transform after Halin, new purpose straightening his spine and squaring his shoulders. Birmun was competent and looked calm, but was the only 'retainer' Ruka did not yet trust.

He looked to Egil last. Their history still brought him shame, and one day he knew he would pay for it. But like the many lives ruined by Ruka's purpose, this justice would have to wait.

"It is possible our landing will not be welcome," Ruka explained, "and that we are already betrayed." Some of the men nodded, but said nothing. "Folvar has told me his father never believed we'd return, and if we did he fully intends to inform the Order the moment it benefits him."

The young man nodded, and Tahar sneered. "Then let us land in the darkness and finish him, shaman."

Aiden's eye twitched in displeasure, and Ruka understood why.

"Halvar gave his word, and so did we. He may betray but he has not yet. For now we owe him what we promised. We will land and greet him as an ally. But we will be cautious, and ready." Here he took a breath, then met Birmun's eyes. "High Priestess Dala may also betray. The Order might be waiting, and if they are then we will be forced to sail elsewhere. We will have to start again and find new allies and it will all take time, and be difficult."

Birmun gave no reaction, though whether this was because he agreed, or knew speaking otherwise was meaningless, Ruka did not know. In any case the others took note. Some had not trusted the man from the start—Tahar in particular. Aiden's quiet voice broke the silence.

"Shaman. You have taken us past the edge of the world, and shown us paradise in this life. I will see you to the mountain, if that is the path, and kill any who stand before you. That is my vow." His eyes strayed for the briefest moment to Birmun as if in threat, and Ruka smiled gratefully. The others nodded or grunted their approval.

That he he had earned such loyalty from a great man moved him, but Ruka wished he did not need to deceive. He met the eyes of his followers one by one again, knowing his own golden pupils would look strange and monstrous in the dimness of his kingmaker's hollow, but that these few, perhaps, no longer cared.

"Make ready, cousins. This is only the first step on a long and difficult march. One day I will tell you everything, all that I know, as well as I understand it. Until then you must try to keep an open mind, and to trust what you've seen."

"And the gods?" Aiden smiled.

Ruka forced himself to return it. "And the gods. Now let us go and greet our 'ally'."

The men grunted or nodded their respect, then made their way up the stairs to return to their ships in order of their reputations. Only Egil lingered.

Ruka raised a brow, and his oldest ally or maybe prisoner blinked as if unsure, his body half turned towards the stairs perhaps prepared to run. At last his eyes flicked to Ruka's face.

"We have walked a long road, you and I, haven't we?"

Ruka hesitated, unsure where this was going. Even now he could see Egil as he once had been—the handsome skald roaming at his will, drinking and rutting his way across the land of ash. He saw the man's dread as he ran for his life from wolves, and the greed as he offered a strange child of the Vishan a story, and an ill-fated plan.

"Yes," Ruka said at last, still hearing in perfect detail the sound of Egil's screams.

He will ask to leave, he realized. *He will say he has done as much and more as any man, and that now he wishes as a free man to take his family away from this. And I must allow it.*

Despite all the years and memories, Egil's expression seemed almost new, and strange—emotional, but unafraid. He smiled at last and broke his gaze, then turned with his slight limp to ascend the stairs. He stopped and spoke over his shoulder.

"I did not know your mother, Ruka, but…I think she would be proud of you."

With that he climbed and left Ruka alone with the captive women in the gloom. For a long moment, he stood very still. In his Grove he sat in his mother's garden, staring at her likeness etched in stone. He sat feeling numb, thinking on his life, on all the dead and the weight of history and the hope and terror of the future.

Would you be proud, Beyla?

He did not know. He did not know either how to change the world without a great sea of blood and misery. Would Beyla approve of that, too?

Yet without intervention, the children of ash would go on starving and freezing until perhaps their own ignorance destroyed the land that sustained them. So what was right? And who should decide?

Ruka stared at her image until the tears came.

Soon Girl-from-Trung's-Pit came and stood beside him. She had wrapped her scarf tightly to protect his eyes from the bruises he'd left, and she smiled as she took his hand. He turned and sunk into her arms, picturing Beyla's smile as he wept like a child.

In the world of the living, Bukayag walked to the deck in silence, and watched the coast loom closer in the darkness.

* * *

"Good evening, ally." Ruka spoke in a neutral tone, staring from the almost moonless night outside the chieftain's hall.

Chief Halvar stumbled from the front of the double doors. 'Bloody shite!' he called, looking about himself as if for a weapon. His equally surprised sons, and a few of his warriors, huddled up around him. They stared at Ruka and his retainers flickering in the torchlight.

"We have returned," Ruka said, because it seemed the man could not believe his eyes. "Our raid is successful."

Halvar's face at last seemed under his control, and one of his hands found the handle of his sword. "So you have," he said. "I congratulate you. But things have changed, shaman. My matron and her sisters ask too many questions. They want to know how I have acquired so many swords and shields and why more men are asking to serve me. A priestess and her dogs have come and gone, too. I didn't like the way she looked at me, or spoke to the townsfolk."

Ruka listened to the pop and gentle waving of the torch-flame as it blew in the wind, both groups of men utterly silent. "I told you there would be risks," he said quietly. "I have come with your share, as promised. Now I require supplies, shelter and labor. I require what you owe."

"*Owed*, shaman." Halvar glanced at his men as if Ruka were speaking nonsense. "I protected your little venture and my part is done. I'll have what I'm due and keep silent. Then you and your men will leave on your ships. You'll have to re-supply elsewhere. And that's the end of it."

The squat chief straightened and took a half-step away, though Ruka made no movement. For a moment he said nothing, only holding the smaller man's eyes.

"The gods punish oathbreakers, Halvar. Edda heard your words as she heard mine. Falsehood must be answered with deed."

More voices came from the hall, and Halvar glanced behind as more of his warriors approached the gathering out of curiosity. He sneered, clearly bolstered by their presence.

"You Southerners and your gods. Don't threaten me, I have *twice* your warriors, and the Order's protection. If it weren't for Altan I'd never have given you more than a moment's thought. Go back to your ships, outcast, and get me my treasures, or else I'll fuck your Edda in her filthy arse."

A few of the chief's half-drunken men laughed, but most put wary hands to the hilts of daggers or swords.

Ruka raised an arm to hold Aiden back. Despite the chief's claims, he knew he could burn Kormet to the ground. He would suffer losses and gain little, though, riling up the Northerners and the Order and making everything harder. So many didn't deserve to die for one foolish coward.

"I make no threat," Ruka said. "I only warn you, as I warn all men of ash. Now is the time to look to your deeds, son of Imler. Only the brave live forever. That is the truth."

With that Ruka nodded in respect and stepped away, and the two groups of warriors began to separate before Halvar called out to his son.

"Boy, come here. I will hear of what you've seen in this 'raid', and accept your renewed oath of loyalty now before these men and your brothers." He held out his hand, and his other sons grinned and waited for what was all but public humiliation. The other warriors stopped but Ruka could see in their eyes many thought their chief foolish to test the moment again.

Folvar grit his teeth and held his ground. It was clear he had intended to return to the ships with Ruka. His father's face grew impatient, and he opened his mouth to speak. His eyes went wide, and one of his hands jerked as he stumbled forward.

A hooded man stepped from Halvar's line as quick and quiet as Arun. Ruka slowed the moment in his Grove, blinking through the memory until he saw the dagger flash in the torchlight. In three heart-beats, the attacker crossed the dirt between the warriors and vanished into Aiden's line, and Ruka knew it had been Eshen in a stolen cloak.

All watched as Halvar moaned, then collapsed to his knees. Blood spurted from his neck just above his shoulder, and his sons and some of his warriors reached for him and held him up as he thrashed and failed to speak.

"The gods have spoken," Ruka hissed. "Dishonorable death, for a dishonorable man."

Halvar's warriors drew swords and axes but held their ground, their chief dropped and dying in the dirt.

"I am the eldest." One of his sons stepped forward with sword raised. "I claim his title." He pointed it at Ruka. "You will give me my father's murderer, and every coin you owed, unless you're an oathbreaker, too."

Ruka nodded as his mind raced. "I will honor my word. Kormet will receive what it is owed." He smiled as he saw the answer. "To *whichever* man is its steward."

The boy snorted. "Not *whichever* man, shaman. Me. Malvar, son of Halvar. I claim the title, who would challenge me?"

Again Aiden moved forward with death in his eyes, and again Ruka held him back. Instead he looked to Folvar.

Already the young man's forehead glistened with sweat. He met Ruka's eyes, and nodded, then took a deep breath. His lids drooped as he mastered his fear.

"I challenge." The young man stepped forward. "You're no better than that fool in the dirt, brother. *I* have seen paradise. *I* have crossed into the realm of the gods and returned. I will take the men of Kormet to their glory, if they have the courage."

Silence grew as the twins stepped before the warriors and took each other's measure. Ruka wondered again at the strangeness of fate or chance or whatever power moved the world, not sure what he would do if Folvar lost. It would be better, he decided, to ensure he did not.

"Well spoken." Ruka stepped beside his favored champion, placing a hand on his shoulder, then turned to the crowd of men.

"Look now, men of ash, to the power of the gods you've forsaken. Look to a man gifted for his deeds, and for his boldness. See your brother rise." Ruka lifted a round-shield of tempered steel in his Grove, its face etched with runes. In the land of the living he seized Folvar's forearm, head bowed as the fires of creation flared. The young man's arm trembled at the sight, and as the weight of the wood, steel and leather wrapped itself around his flesh. His hand gripped the handle.

"This is Efras, Hunter of Men." Ruka drew his own sword and glanced at the other would-be chief as he smiled. "But it will kill boys just as well."

Aiden growled low from his gut, and his men stomped their feet and clashed swords against the hall or their shields until the racket broke the other men from their trance. The threat of group violence vanished in the spectacle of a duel, and the warriors stepped closer together to form two half-circles.

Folvar took Ruka's sword with wide, glistening eyes. He stared at the edge until his jaw hardened, then he clanged the iron against his shield. The sound echoed in the cool, night air like a ringing bell as he stepped into the circle. Aiden's men roared.

His brother entered with far less fanfare. He drew his sword and yelled at his brothers until one of them passed him a wooden shield. His face had gone pale, and he stared at Folvar's rune-covered shield in disbelief, and perhaps terror.

They stood apart too long. The crowd of warriors began jeering and calling for blood until the frightened Malvar tried to boost his courage with a war-cry. Then he charged.

Folvar jerked forward and their barriers clashed, the metal boss of the wooden shield ringing against steel. Both brothers pushed and shoved and tried to knock the other off balance, but both held. They separated and took turns slashing at the other's guard and trying to find some path around. It became clear they were evenly matched—that they had fought many times, practiced under the same warriors, and knew the other's tricks.

After several blows, Malvar's shield began to splinter. Chips flew from the edges, and the boss angled as the frame around it warped. The bearer saw it clearly. He licked his lips and attacked wildly, exposing himself as he swayed from side to side to find an opening, swiping his shield across to knock away his brother's guard.

The thin wood protecting him held incredibly well, and he staggered Folvar to the edge of the crowd with desperate strength, crying out now with every blow as if he'd won.

All at once, Folvar planted a foot, lurched forward with saved strength, and rammed Efras through his brother's chest.

In the frozen moment of victory and defeat, both men dropped their shields and almost embraced, staring into each other's eyes. Malvar coughed blood, and Folvar eased him to the ground and held him, using his free hand to touch his brother's face and stroke his hair and speak soothing words.

The blood-lust and shouting of the men died to nothing. Folvar rose stained with his brother's blood, and in the fighting the half-circles had come together, all threat of violence gone. Both sides of warriors stomped or knocked their shields or called their praise.

Folvar closed his eyes, then opened them and looked to the night sky. For an endless, fleeting moment, all around him basked in the bittersweet glory, and at the wonder and tragedy of life.

"What is this? What have you done?"

The warriors almost collectively sighed, turning towards the hall as the moment broke. A group of women stood outside the main doors, a grey-haired matron in the shift of a First Mother standing before them. Folvar stepped towards her.

"I have returned, mother, from beyond the edge of the world. I have stepped on the shores of paradise and killed men in battle. I have gained allies and wield a weapon of the gods." He pointed Efras at the body of his father. "And I have claimed the title of this unworthy man. Unlike him, I will see the matrons of Kormet see the rewards they are owed."

The First Mother swept her gaze over Ruka and his men, then over the corpses and the eyes of her town's warriors, before returning them to her son.

"And your brother? Was he unworthy, too?"

Folvar grit his teeth. "No, mother. Your son sought his title like a man. He fought bravely, and honored himself. He will be re-born."

Many of the men grunted their approval at these words. His mother sighed but said nothing, then looked to Ruka.

"I have heard of you, shaman. The Order calls you criminal, and heretic. Is that what you are? Have you corrupted my kin? Are you here to destroy all our sons, fathers and brothers?"

Ruka stepped into the circle. In his Grove the dead were already digging a grave-marker for Malvar, who he agreed had fought bravely.

"Can you read, First Mother?"

The woman's eyes narrowed as if she meant to spit a retort, but thought better of it. "I can read runes enough, son of Noss."

Ruka nodded. "Hold up your shield, Folvar."

The boy stooped and lifted it, and clearly it had not even been scratched in the duel. The matron's eyes squinted as she looked, and Ruka feared she couldn't truly see.

"It reads courage," he said, as much to the crowd as the matron. "Vol etches it with his marks, for only bravery will truly protect your men, and shield them against whatever comes. Your son has it, First Mother, as has every great man since Turgen Sar brought us forth." He pointed. "Look on your son. Look on the heroes who stand at his side. It is these who will take your daughters to paradise, if their will holds true." He raised his voice to be heard even in the hall. "Look on their deeds, mothers of Kormet. Look on the spirit shining like star-gods from their eyes, and tell me—have I corrupted them, or have the priestesses? Have I not set them free?"

The men rose up with pride at his words, and made it true. The matron looked, and looked, emotions and thoughts rising and falling in ways Ruka could never know. When she turned to her son, her face did not hide her approval.

"Your silver tongue may be our doom, shaman. But if my sons will follow you, then the daughters of Kormet will stand with them. You will need a matron, Folvar. We will go and choose." She looked one last time at her dead child. "Return him to ash, chief. He was young and strong." Her eyes passed over her mate of many years, and only a wave of scorn rippled across her face.

She turned and the matrons followed her towards the hall, no doubt for a long night of bargaining and discussion and harsh words—a battle of persuasion and will to calm worried minds, and find a path to harmony. Ruka smiled. *A matron's duel.*

He saw the men who had before looked frightened and wary now seem content, and thought again on Dala's words. She had been right, he knew that. He would need the approval of the women of ash as much as the chiefs. He would maybe even need the priestesses, for he could not truly intimidate the matrons with violence, and he did not wish to kill all their sons and fathers.

The thought did not give him peace, for he had lost power he thought he possessed, and Dala's had grown. He did not know if she lied, or if she would betray, and could not know until the moment arrived. But even if and when it did, what exactly could he do?

59

Two days after Folvar's rise to chieftain, Ruka stood gathered with all his men and allies on the beach beside his Kingmakers. He stood with his captains and stared at a crudely drawn map, sketching the outline of the Ascom, and the coasts of Pyu.

If he wished of course he could have drawn a perfect map of the known world by Naranian reckoning, but these men were not ready for such things. He would strive to give them the essence of the truth for now, and leave the detail for later.

"The land of ash must change," he said, squinting in the mid-morning light. "Some of you have seen the future. You have seen the warm shores of paradise and its wealth. But to take it, and hold it, will be difficult. It will mean managing a new world full of many peoples and warriors, kings and ships. And there is more to this world even than you have seen. This new land is made of many islands, cousins, but there is another, even vaster land beyond them. To face these things the men of ash must be united."

Here he paused to gauge their reaction, which seemed mostly bewilderment. Egil cleared his throat, knowing his role after so many years now without instruction.

"How would we do this, shaman?"

Ruka looked away, as if the gods spoke to him even now. "First, we seize the fertile ring." He swiped his quill and drew a line across the map, separating the farmlands and the peninsula from the rest. The men all stared, somewhat awkwardly, until Altan spoke.

"Isn't that what Imler did, shaman?"

Ruka almost grinned, thinking *yes, because it is the only way.*

"Imler didn't have ships," he said instead. "We'll use ours to seize the coasts quickly, take over the farms, and stop all trade through the Northern sea. The Order and the chiefs have nothing in the water to stop us." He waited again though he didn't much like the expressions he saw. *What did you think,* he wanted to shout, *did you expect we'd defeat the Northern chiefs with words?*

"So, who will do this?" he called. "Who will step in the footsteps of a fallen king?"

He knew the answer, of course, but was not disappointed. Aiden nearly surged forward like Sula in battle, eyes blazing with the promise of glory.

"I will, shaman. I will clear the chiefsmen guarding the peninsula, and clear the sea. The fertile ring is my gift to you."

Ruka nodded. "Well spoken." He looked to his other retainers. "Altan. You know better than any of us the foolish waste of the breadlands. So tell me, if you had no quotas, and no masters, what would you do with every field on the peninsula?"

The Midlander was clearly surprised to be called on, and looked about before he shrugged. Then he squinted and seemed to actually consider it. "Disease must be controlled, shaman. It is rampant from so many seasons of mostly wheat." He shook his head, as if it were all foolish talk. "Much of the crops should be burned and given a year of fallow. At the very least, we should know who is planting what, and where, and separate it with other crops, flax, peas, and so on. Some farmers know this and try it now, but it's difficult with different chiefs controlling the land, all of who are rivals and do not speak of such things."

Ruka smiled. "Go with Aiden, Midlander. You are the Master of these lands now. You will work with the farmers, and between you decide what is best."

Altan blinked and glanced around again, as if it were madness to simply declare such a thing. Ruka had just announced he was in control of the richest land in the Ascom.

"Won't Orhus and all the chiefs come for us?" Birmun said, standing largely on his own. "Aren't we breaking most every law there's a punishment for?"

Tahar sneered openly, which was not useful but neither easily dealt with. Ruka spoke without rebuke.

"First the laws, then the lawmakers" He looked to Egil. "The great skald will go to Orhus. Many of the chiefs there already bear my gifts. I don't expect this to give them much pause, but Egil will present my terms—enough grain to replace the best harvest their lands have ever had, delivered by ship come spring, along with silver and other gifts. All I will ask is that they do nothing—drag their heels and wait until spring. Some at least will listen and reduce the forces against us. We will need only two seasons."

"That won't stop them," Birmun said, undaunted. "Orhus has thousands of warriors. Once you've taken the ring, they'll come in force, and we'll be slaughtered."

Tahar looked on the verge of drawing his sword now, and other men muttered too until Altan spoke over the din.

"Nevermind that, we can't deliver on such a promise, shaman. If I do what you've asked with the land, it will take a whole year to deal with disease and produce a harvest, and only then with a bit of luck. In the meantime, the Ascom will starve. So what do we do about food?"

This was a very reasonable question, of course, but then Altan did not know about Farahi.

"Let me worry on that, Midlander. We'll have enough. More than enough. In fact," he looked to Kormet's new chief, "we will need to begin construction of new warehouses and bins—enough to hold an entire harvest at least from the peninsula. I will help your builders with the foundations, but then I have a task elsewhere."

The young man nodded without complaint, though many others looked concerned. Ruka had not addressed the threat of attack at all, but he did not yet intend to.

"What will you be doing, shaman?" Aiden asked, his tone polite, as if only curious. Ruka smiled as most of the men watched him with wide, eager eyes, as if he would tell them the next act in a great story, their trust in him almost complete. He glanced at the sea.

"I'm going to need three ships, mighty chief. And Folvar—I will require all Kormet's fishermen and their boats. You can tell them they may earn a place in paradise without ever lifting a sword. It's time the men of ash overcame another kind of fear. Sigun has given his blessing. We're going to hunt the great beasts of the sea."

* * *

Ruka watched the spray of the narwhales rise as high as a Kingmaker's mast, then raised a hand to signal the ten fisher ships. In his Grove he stood next to a line of harpoons, though he hoped to need only one.

"Let's get their attention." He smiled, and the old captain with him nodded, crinkled skin wet as their ship splashed through the waves. The spear-throwers in every boat rose to their task, and the other crew splashed their oars and readied the ropes.

His three Kingmakers waited beyond, further out to sea, with little to do but wait and if necessary try and chase the whales back towards land.

Ruka held until the fearsome creatures came as close as he dared. The crew moved opposite to balance as he leaned over the side, arm back and body taut with strain as he gathered every ounce of momentum and arc in the cramped space. He held back his weapon, and released with a grunt.

The javelin slipped into the foam then vanished in a swirl of white and red. Their boat rose and lurched as the creature spasmed and thrashed. A huge, grey tail rose, then slapped down hard to spray water over their ship. Ruka could only hold on and trust to the ropes wrapped around his waist and legs.

Almost in unison, as if the pack of whales had heard some horn of war, the bulls turned and circled around the females and their young. Ruka's men roared and smacked the sea with their oars and threw their spears down the line, moving forward now in a mad hope the beasts would flee.

The ropes attached to Ruka's target snapped taut as it tried to dive. The men seized the pommel and tried to keep the wood and steel from coming apart. They dropped their oars, no longer needing to row. From here out, they would be dragged.

Ruka looked at his terrified but still controlled men and laughed. "Scream, cousins! Scream like you burn in the mountain! *We're* the hunters, not them! Now s*cream!*"

The men saw his excitement and took up the shout, the line of fishing boats releasing their sails as the rowers pumped like madmen in pursuit, some few with lines attached to their own targets.

Ruka had both feet planted firmly in the thrower's nook, gloved-hands on his rope, arms straining as the waves pummeled the ship and soaked him again and again. It felt as if he or the ship or the spear might come apart at any moment, as if everything he had ever built could fall to ruin in the blink of the sea god's eye. He had never felt so alive.

The whales fled straight before them, panicked and surprised to be hunted by some creature they couldn't see or understand from above. Many of the stronger and faster beasts turned and slipped past the long line of ships and escaped. Most did not.

Ruka thought back to an open plain of grass with nothing except sky and field and the hunt. He had once chased a full-grown buck on foot with nothing but a knife, overcoming a great runner in its prime, facing strength with strength and wits as a lone hunter.

But like dogs and wolves, men were pack animals. They were not meant to hunt alone. There on the waves, with the calls and tools of the sons of Imler and the men of ash, for a pure moment Ruka felt the strength of his tribe beside him.

With his body focused and steady as it bent to his task, he looked at the brave, competent men doing a thing their ancestors had never imagined. He felt the kinship, wanting them to succeed and to be part of it. He looked at the other men battling with the whales and the waves, their bits of wood and rope and nails propelling them madly through forces so huge and elemental they should bring only terror. He looked on their courage with pride.

The shore loomed ever closer. The men's voices cracked and broke from the screaming, their red faces twisted with agony as they strained beyond mortal endurance, or sanity, until only their grit and purpose gave them the will to hold on.

With a soft, almost gentle slide and crush of dirt and sand, the first whale struck the beach in panicked flight, and beached.

Men from the shore raced into the water throwing spears and ropes. More whales swam at full speed into the coast, their weight carrying them the length of ten men into water too shallow to escape. First there were five, and then ten.

Ruka and his hunters came up behind them but did not help in the killing. Instead they dropped to the dark sand, or lay back in their boats with heads resting against bloody hands, or the trembling backs of their fellows.

Ruka stepped out and held up his captain's arm, and the men on shore laughed and started the cheer that swept the town of Kormet, most of whom had come to the docks to watch a thing never seen in the land of ash. Children and matrons cried out their praise, knowing the feast before them would keep all from hunger for weeks, and with enough salt, maybe months.

In his mind, Ruka saw the ever greater potential of a land and people behind for so long. They were behind the rest of the world in so many ways, especially in knowledge. But their suffering, he knew, had made them strong.

The threat of a greater world perhaps would unite them as nothing could. Farahi would send grain, and Ruka would teach them. All was possible now. They had crossed an uncrossable sea, they had hunted Sigun's beasts. It would take time but they would rise from the snow and ash like Tegrin, or Noss from his mountain of fire. *You were right, mother, as usual*, he thought. *The stories of the book were true, in their way. They were true after all.*

* * *

In the two days it took to butcher the whales and figure out what to do with the meat, bone and oil, Orhus attacked.

Several scouts came first. They moved openly through the hills led by an Arbman on horseback, almost brazen in their loose formation and movement in the day. Tahar and his men spotted them long before they arrived.

Ruka had to at least applaud their ambition. By their numbers it seemed a single chief had come for glory with a hundred men, thinking to seize the opportunity before his rivals acted. They had near as many men as Ruka, of course, with Aiden away. And if they'd attacked in broad daylight in good order Ruka might very well have considered running to prevent his losses. Instead they moved to the village outskirts, and waited.

Their main force hid on a rise before the sloping ground of Kormet, and Ruka quickly realized they meant to raid at night.

He told Folvar and his men to get ready—to gather every bow and every spear or axe made for throwing, and to have their matrons prepared to extinguish every flame in every house. The young man quirked a brow.

"There is little moon, shaman. We will be as blind as they in the dark." The new chief spoke without reservation and showed no fear, and Ruka's pleasure in his rise increased.

"A seer can see where other men are blind," he answered. "I will reveal your enemy with fire. When you see them, you will attack."

Folvar frowned, but nodded, and did as he was told. As the light faded Ruka waited until Kormet's warriors crept to hide behind houses and fences, or along the hills and high grass, waiting for his signal.

He waited until the sun descended entirely beneath the horizon, knowing the enemy would give the men of Kormet time to drink, relax, and sleep. Then in the heart of darkness, they would come quietly over the rise like a pack of wolves, throwing torches at houses, slaughtering any man who fled the flames.

When they had killed or chased away every last man, they would march to the hall and wait for the matrons, and offer them their 'protection'. They would expect to be chosen by the women and replace their mates, or else they'd slaughter their boys, too.

But Ruka would not let them reach the town at all.

In the darkness, he moved out quietly to the sloping ground with wineskins filled with whale oil. He emptied one after another on the rocky ground in a circle, and for his own amusement and perhaps for the gods, if they existed, he drew a rune in oil that meant 'surprise'.

He walked out into the deep darkness of the night, around the edge of the enemy's hill until he came close enough to see them fortifying their courage with drink, readying their weapons and torches and looking out for ambush.

A man patrolled the edge of their camp. He stared straight into the dark and squinted, then smirked and nudged his fellow. "A coyote, eh? Maybe a wolf? Brave to come so close to men."

The other looked, too, and Ruka stared. He could see them clearly. The tiny glint of moonlight peeking through the clouds cascaded over the earth for his eyes, lighting it in a cold, gray light. Ruka knew he belonged to that shallow gloom—beyond the day creatures of Galdra, a pale black reflection. It had maybe always been thus. Like Noss' wolves in the night he would cull the weak of mankind, and make the whole stronger.

He raised his hand. A shower of fire spewed from the air as Bukayag drew his first javelin from the realm of the dead. The men blinked and stepped away in panic, and Ruka hurled his weapon through the first man's chest. He drew a long, cutting sword and rushed, hacking at the other's back before slashing indiscriminately at confused and idle warriors sitting with skins.

"Ambush!"

The warning sounded and the men rushed up all at once. Some loosed arrows in panic at rocks or bushes, others threw axes or knives. Ruka stepped away and faded again into the darkness.

He rushed over the rise and down towards Kormet, hearing the men's angry shouts, knowing they might decide instead to withdraw. He hoped they would. Many lives might be spared, and perhaps many more men of ash might see paradise. But if they came as planned, if they raced ahead to burn homes and threaten little boys, he would slaughter them without mercy.

Their chief growled and shouted and stepped over the hill, and his men followed. Ruka watched, and waited.

So be it.

At the edge of the oil-sodden earth he held his horn to his lips. The men advanced towards the distant lights of Kormet in a cluster, the men on the outskirts already formed in a shield-wall. Ruka was impressed by their discipline. They came down the slope together, and he waited in silence before them. He drew another spear from his Grove, and the sparks flew and floated to the earth, lighting the oil. He blew his horn.

Fire spread through the fuel and raced over the ground. At the sound of the horn, every campfire in Kormet began to extinguish, until the only light in the world burned beneath the men's feet.

Ruka heard the arrows before he saw them. Folvar and his men came from their hiding places in the grass and hills and began loosing missiles.

Some of the raiders panicked and fled from the flames, others kicked dirt and came together behind their shield-wall. The chief was calling for his men to come to him and backing away. Ruka waited in the night. He cut down any man who strayed too far from the fire, cleaving any who thought to find safety in the shadows.

Arrows struck man after man and Ruka circled throwing javelins. The fire lit him as Bukayag growled and laughed, and a few men charged together. He took two swords and met them in the flickering light. He spun between them breaking shields and roaring, his body sheathed in steel rings and padding that mocked their blades.

"To the hills!" cried the raider's chief.

Bukayag kicked the man before him down, took another javelin, and threw it through the chief's throat.

All those around him cried in alarm and fell back or scattered. They held their shields above them as arrows fell dark and terrible and unseen. Most broke and ran, the wide fear of prey now in their eyes, lost to the mindless fear of flight.

Ruka let his brother chase and kill several who stumbled on the uneven ground. He watched the others running terrified and left them because they weren't truly his enemies. He turned back, and put the worst of the wounded from their misery.

Two thirds of the raiders lay dead or bleeding on the rocks. The men of Kormet had gathered now, staring at Ruka and the field of corpses. They looked at his eyes, the blood covering his armor, and the men lying flat and skewered by javelins pulled from nothing. But Folvar had seen it all before. He unstrung his bow, and met Ruka's gaze with courage.

"Should we bury them, shaman?"

Ruka glanced at the carnage but put it from his mind. It was done, and more would follow. For now they must act.

"Burn them," he walked back towards the village. "You men will need your strength. Tomorrow, we start on the trench."

"What trench, shaman?" called the chief after a pause.

For now Ruka said nothing. In his Grove he carried more rock with the dead, waiting for them to plaster a layer of mortar so he could start on the next level. Unlike the living, the workers in his Grove never tired, which in this case was all. They had little time, and a great deal of work to do.

60

"We need a priestess, shaman. Too many of the women are sick. You must come."

Ruka sighed and leaned on his shovel, looking up from the trench. It was a relatively cool day, and much more pleasant working here than Sri Kon in the baking sun. He supposed Hemi wouldn't have thought so, and memories of the man made him smile.

"They are likely just tired, cold and miserable," he said, preparing to rise. "And the priestesses know far less of herbs and medicines than I, Folvar. But if you wish, I will come." With a groan he stepped over the edge and looked back. They had made reasonable progress. From the beach to the site of their battle, ground was being dug and flattened in a straight and measured line. The men had stared in disbelief when Ruka told them the task.

"We must build a trench," he'd said at the light of dawn. "It will need to be the length of two stakes, and as deep as a half. It must run from this coast to the other edge of the peninsula."

Folvar had squinted and looked up from Ruka's crude map drawn in the dirt.

"What do you mean."

"I mean what I said, chief. I need a trench that crosses the fertile ring."

Still he balked. "The whole...the *entire* peninsula?" When Ruka said nothing more he shook his head and snorted. "That's...I'm sorry but that's impossible, shaman. That's too far. I have only two hundred men, it would take us...I don't know, months, maybe."

"We have one week. It will require your matrons and children, and the women we took from paradise. I have sent for more men."

"What good is a trench, shaman? We can fight at the edge, of course, but...not across the whole peninsula at any rate. They'll still get around."

This was rather reasonable and true, but Ruka was not willing to say more. They had argued for a time, but in the end, as usual, Ruka's miracles allowed him to overcome good sense.

Soon enough the people of Kormet had come with their children, their spades, picks and shovels, gathering all along the line Ruka had marked with stakes, and begun to dig.

Now Ruka looked up at the growing cloud and hoped it wouldn't rain. He stepped from the dip in the earth and rose up towering over Folvar, then followed him towards the town. They passed the newly started bases of the rounded grain bins, which would have to wait now for the trench. But they would not be needed until spring in any case. Ruka only hoped they *were* truly needed—that Farahi would come and do as he hoped. For if not, than the Ascom would starve, and all Ruka's work would fall to ruin, death and war.

Worrying, however, made no difference. Ruka could forget nothing but he put this concern to a corner of his mind and left it like a stone moved from a well-trodden path. "Why are we going to the hall?" he asked when he realized. He had assumed the sick women would be recovering in the houses of the matron's who had taken them in.

"There's too many now," said Folvar. "Only the hall was big enough."

This hurried Ruka's steps.

Kormet was largely abandoned now save for new mothers and their infants, and some few of the old and sick, so the way was clear. Ruka saw the empty streets and sped to a run. He raced along narrow gravel and dirt roads to the huge horns sprouting from Kormet's hall. The smell hit him as he pulled open the doors.

The foreign women of Halin lay in blankets or huddled around the main hearthfire. Their wan, sagging faces turned up towards the sudden light with bleary eyes. Ruka saw waste buckets near them, others by his feet, yet more near the floor-hole used to dump waste outside.

"It is as if they drank foul water, shaman," explained Folvar, panting. "But they drink what we drink, and none of us are sick."

Ruka nodded and stepped inside. He thought this a wise observation. The water in Pyu had been clean beyond belief. Perhaps the women's constitutions couldn't handle the sediment or some other impurity from the rivers and wells of the Ascom. *But Arun and Kwal had seemed fine.*

"What is your name?" He leaned down to one of the women strong enough to help the others, then dropped to a knee to be of equal height. Like most of those taken she was young and beautiful with dark hair and eyes. She cowered as Ruka approached, but when he spoke in her native tongue she blinked and looked to the others.

"Lia...Liana, lord."

"Good. I am called Bukayag, a priest to my people, not a lord. You need not fear me for I will not hurt you or allow you to be hurt. Tell me of your illness, please."

She looked worn, uncomfortable, and perhaps skeptical. He did not blame her. Since the raid and capture she had known only weeks at sea—only misery and fear since meeting the men of ash. Ruka had always known some would not survive the process, whether because of illness like this, or a destruction of spirit. One day he would pay for it.

With a deep and determined breath the girl lowered her eyes and spoke of the vomiting, the loose bowels, the rashes and myriad of other symptoms. Ruka nodded throughout and asked her what they had been eating and drinking and how their hosts had been treating them. Nothing seemed unusual.

"Thank you, Liana," he said when she had answered, then he went to stand but paused. He met the girl's eyes, and saw a courage within. "We have wronged you. But soon enough you will be given houses. You will be allowed to choose husbands and live as respected wives and mothers here, protected and more or less equal to other women. Life is unjust, but you can survive and even prosper, if you have the will."

The girl watched him, emotion he could not understand rippling over her foreign face. She wiped a tear as it spilled from moist eyes, but he decided her shoulders were strong, her back straight. She would overcome; she would survive.

Ruka moved to another girl and asked her similar questions. Then he told Folvar to fetch jars and cups, water and any herbs the matrons had. He told the women they must keep drinking, and to boil their water over the fire first, then showed them what he meant. He mixed a potion his mother had taught him, then added a few things he had learned in Pyu, hopefully to help with the vomiting. When he had made enough for all the almost two hundred women, he stretched and glanced at the open hall doors, and saw a womanly figure leaning against the wood.

The sun hovered behind her and lit her silhouette. Ruka blinked his light-sensitive eyes, for a moment paralyzed as he swore he saw his mother before him, blondish hair sparkling in the afternoon sun. The woman smiled.

"Smith, shaman, sailor, warrior, herbalist, scout. Is there anything you *can't* do, Bukayag?"

Ruka blinked until his mother vanished, replaced by a young girl in a shack full of dead orphans. This image too blurred with the memory of a High Priestess of Galdra dressed in matron's clothes. Dala had come.

"Priestess." Ruka stepped forward with a menace he hadn't intended. He listened for footsteps, or for the clanging of iron or wood or the scrape of leather scabbard as the Order's servants leapt inside to kill him. But he heard nothing.

"I am alone," she said, as if reading his thoughts. "I've come, as promised. And I'm pleased to see you alive, truth be told."

Ruka stepped forward until he stood an arm's length from his 'ally'. He looked out from the hall and saw no sign of men, though of course they could be hiding behind houses and fences. Ruka felt his brother's urge to draw cold steel from nothing and hack her down. Dala met his stare and did not flinch, or shrink away.

"Truth be told," he echoed, collecting himself. "An odd expression for a priestess."

She snorted and stepped past him. "So. These are women from paradise?" Her eyes went over the islanders' skin and hair, and she frowned. "I thought they'd be taller. You and your men have been treating them with the proper respect, I trust? Do they speak our language?"

Ruka frowned, reminding himself his people were ignorant of the world, and could have no concept of the many tongues and their difference.

"They do not. But I can speak to them."

Dala's eyes narrowed, which gave Ruka the urge to smile. He waited, wondering if her pride would stop her from asking how, or if it was just that she believed he'd lie anyway. She eventually shrugged.

"I'm pleased you're caring for them. But we will need more."

Ruka blinked, surprised and uneasy at the woman's words and manner as usual.

"More *what*, priestess?"

"More matrons. You are hopelessly outnumbered. I assume you realize that."

He did, of course, though her saying it so plainly annoyed him. He had his plans, but for the moment they were weak and vulnerable. If Orhus came soon, and in force, he could not stop them.

"I have no method of winning matrons," he said, and shrugged. "I am not popular with women."

Ruka had considered what he might do or say to convince the matrons of Orhus. But with the exception of threatening their mates, fathers and sons with death, he couldn't think of much. He glanced back at Dala and found a look of unconcealed humor.

"No," she said, laughing openly, "no I imagine not."

Ruka almost snarled at her open contempt. That she should mock him so plainly risked his brother rising like some demon out of hell and choking the life from her throat. He stepped out to fresh air that didn't smell of human waste to control himself.

"Bukayag!"

He turned to find Dala had chased him. Her hand moved to his arm.

"I've offended you." He nearly recoiled at her touch, but stilled when he saw regret and perhaps sympathy in her eyes. "I hadn't meant..." she sighed, "I thought you spoke in humor. If the women of ash don't see your value, than they are fools. It is they who I blame. You will take their children to paradise, shaman, I truly believe that. I admire you."

Ruka watched her eyes for deception. His brother's accusing stare searched her for the lie, expecting, perhaps even hoping for any sign of false praise or mockery. He found none, and did not know what to say.

"The problem remains," said the priestess, as if unaware or unconcerned with his inspection. She sighed, and a few strands of golden hair blew in the wind, sparkling in the fading sun. "Without powerful matrons and their land and families, we will only ever attract the fringes to our cause."

"You have a suggestion," Ruka said dryly.

Dala smiled, and he could no longer pretend not to see the beauty in it. "The Matriarch has a cousin, Valda—the most powerful matron in the world. She despises the order and always has. If we can convince her, then, perhaps, others will follow."

Ruka turned back towards the ditch to hide his sneer. That a powerful matron should despise the matriarch perhaps should not have surprised him, but it did. For all their words of sisterhood, peace and unity, Ruka supposed power was not so easily shared. Trying to convince Valda in particular appealed less than digging in dirt.

"Do you agree?" Dala called. "If so, we should leave at once. On horseback we could be in Orhus before morning."

Ruka kept walking and wanted to say no. He wanted the power to ignore these women and their politics and words and scheming favor. But he knew he couldn't. *You must learn to hold men's minds with your piety, and sway them with your devotion*, Beyla had told him.

She had meant devotion to the old gods, the gods of men—gods of darkness and terror, blood and iron and deed. She said nothing of Galdra's God. Beyla had never taught him how to sway women's minds, perhaps because she'd assumed he had no chance. No doubt she was right. She usually was.

"If you wish it, priestess, we will go. But I do not expect to succeed. As much as Valda might despise the Order, their world maintains her power and wealth. We offer risk and disruption to an old woman." He ground his teeth. "It will be no more welcome than the disfigured son of a fallen granddaughter."

He stopped and turned to see Dala's confusion, and sighed. "We have met before, briefly. Long enough for an old, rich woman to destroy a boy's hope of safety or comfort. I was only a child then, with no one in this world." Ruka re-called the image of the old woman's face. The idea that he'd need to ask her for help again was enough to make him wish the world burned instead. He saw Dala's stubborn curiosity and knew she wouldn't leave it alone.

"Valda is my kin, priestess, my great grandmother. She rejected me at birth, again when my mother died. Now she will do it for a third time."

Dala still said nothing, though it was clear she listened intently. Ruka was impressed she could wait in silence, letting him rise and fall on his own without words. So few seemed able.

Perhaps because of this he found himself wishing to tell her more—tell her how it felt, what he did after, and the many details of his life from then until now. But Bukayag was impatient and perhaps wise not to trust. Instead he turned to their trench.

61

Valda, daughter of Valdaya, rolled her rheumy eyes at her great granddaughter's tears. It seemed sometimes she had endured a lifetime of women's tears. *No, two lifetimes*, she thought. And Galdra's tits if she'd endure any more.

"Sasha." The girl's head snapped up at Valda's tone. "Wipe your face and sit straight. You will collect yourself in my presence."

Sasha snuffled and tried to do as commanded, breathing sharply to control her sobs. "Yes, Greatmother," she said, when her voice was useful.

Valda shifted on her pillow. "So. You've lost another child. Always a tragedy. It will be hard for Chief Oda with the boy so close to his name-day, and hard for the boy's brother to be alone. But that is why we have twins. I have outlived ten children, Sasha, and fourteen grandchildren. I have buried hundreds of kin. Do you know what I've learned?"

"Please tell me grandmother." The girl was wracked by a renewed choking sob, and Valda grasped her hand.

"I *endure*. That is matronhood. It is our duty to look to our other children, to our kin, to *survive* death and tragedy so as to keep our families going. Now comes the only test that matters. Can you bare it? That is what your mothers and grandmothers whisper, their faces stained black with tears and the ash of their children's bones. Can you bare this life, descendant? Can you earn your place with us?"

The girl sat transfixed at the words and the tone, but returned to her weeping. Valda hunched forward and seized her chin hard in a skeletal hand.

"Well?"

"Yes, greatmother, I will bare it," the girl sobbed. Valda watched her eyes until she believed it might be true.

"Good. You are Valdaya, and Vishan, and we more than any other carry this responsibility. In public you must be without tears. You must go lie with your mate and smile and tell him of all the other children you will make together to ease his mind that these things happen and are expected. You will stand straight in your home and hall and in the streets of Orhus until other women look on you and think 'By God, how can she be so strong?' When you notice this you will smile as if it is nothing. Not for you. Not for a grand-daughter of Valda. And then privately, *very* privately, in the company of your sisters, you may weep. Do you understand?"

"Yes, greatmother."

"Good girl."

Valda blessed her descendant with the mark of Bray, Goddess of life and beauty, and Edda, goddess of words, for the Valdaya had long held to the old ways even as they embraced the new. "Now collect yourself. Go to your mother, and your children." She took a milk-sweet from her tray. "And give this to Mina. Tell her she's my favorite."

Sasha spasmed with a broken laugh. "I will tell her, but she already knows."

Valda smiled. "That's why she's my favorite."

Her great-grand-daughter rose with grace and shook off her obvious sorrow in less time than Valda feared. She bowed with respect and courage as she walked tall to the door, squaring her fine shoulders as she stepped out of the bedroom.

Valda hoped it had been enough. She wished the girl's mother had as much sense and spine and the wisdom to teach such lessons herself. But nevermind, that was the function of kin. Some would always be stronger than others and in different moments. After Valda died Sasha would perhaps be a great matron and first mother herself, and she would do admirably enough.

Valda waved a hand at her great-great grand-daughter and attendant. She wasn't as sharp as the girl taken by the god-cursed Order, but she would do, and Valda could bear the loss as she could bear anything. She lay back and closed her eyes before the next girl came with her tears and her 'problems'.

The closer to death she got the less patience she had. But a nap always helped.

* * *

Valda woke to a chill and licked the drool from her chin. She hugged her shawl to her shoulders and glanced at the open window wondering who would be so foolish in these cool evenings. It reminded her still of the Time of Troubles—of death and murder in the night and every man and woman of Orhus afraid of the dark. Even her powerful kin had been affected. She had lost grandsons in duels, distant relations butchered in the streets. And one Vishan family had been almost entirely slaughtered, even the women and babes killed in their home.

Valda maintained guards ever since, even at night. The events had troubled her far more than the Order. The priestesses seemed to pass it off as just chief's taking their quarrels too far, or maybe some outcasts seeking revenge. Valda knew different.

Some of the greatest chiefs in Orhus whispered of war. They knew the Order was weak and unable to solve the growing problems of the North. Valda saw the power of the priestesses slipping as their rules seemed more elaborate and arcane and useless every year.

The crops of the ring were worsening, that was a fact; the fishermen's catches shrunk every season, the South grumbled of rebellion and even the old horse tribes hid their numbers, no doubt simply waiting for a single man or strong tribe to unite them.

It was Valda's sons and men like them who dealt with it all—it was they who fed and housed the Ascom, protected it from the cold and the savages, from flood and wind and snow. *Men* ran Valda's world, that was the truth, they just couldn't agree how to *rule* it. Thus the Order had a purpose.

But for those trumped up figureheads to forget this purpose and believe themselves responsible for the world was to believe their own stupid lies. They played their role, just as the chiefs and the matrons did. Somehow they had begun to believe themselves the architect. The damn fools. While the people had food in their bellies they might be thankful, but the day they didn't, they would know exactly who to blame.

Valda shivered and reached for the bell that summoned her attendant, then realized it wasn't there. She stared, confused, for despite her age her memory had always been very sharp and clear, and she knew she'd left it on the table.

"I thought it best if we spoke alone."

Valda froze.

A huge, dark figure stepped from the shadow of a corner and spoke in a deep, sonorous voice. He wore a black, hooded cloak over his towering frame, and stooped until his face was level with Valda's. His bright eyes shone in the gloom, sharp and active and faded gold like the sun behind a mist. They were the eyes of a little boy born to a once promising child.

"You're Beyla's son," Valda said after a long pause, fighting to keep her voice controlled. "So you are this 'Bukayag'. I thought perhaps you might be."

Valda watched the surprise wrinkle across the man's Noss-groped face, and felt at least some measure of control. She settled into her chair. "Come to kill me, have you?" She snorted. "I'll go soon enough without your help."

Her great-grandson's hands moved to his knees as he stooped to his haunches. He smiled, and his strange, golden eyes sparkled in the dim hearthlight. He said nothing, and Valda's opinion of him rose.

"Your mother taught you patience, then. Very good."

"If I were you," he said, his smile vanishing. "I wouldn't speak of my mother again."

Valda opened her mouth to snap at that but saw the raw, wounded look on the boy. She closed her mouth, and nodded. Perhaps he had earned her silence on the topic.

"What do you want?" she said instead. "An apology? We're all prisoners of the same rules. I played my part. You played yours. Words are meaningless."

She felt slightly resigned as she said this, expecting him to do whatever he came to do. The thought of torture brought a stab of fear, but she would scream with her old lungs and men would come running, and he'd be forced to kill her quickly. If that was her fate, then so be it.

Beyla's son leaned forward and smiled with sharp teeth. "There we agree. But for all our sake, let us hope we are wrong."

She met his eyes and felt as if she stared into the hungry gaze of a well-trained wolf—as if all he wished were to butcher her with his bare hands, but held himself at bay. A knock at the door startled her, and her attendant whispered through the oak.

"Greatmother, there is a woman here to see you. She is dressed like a matron, but says she is a priestess from the South. Shall I let her in?"

Ruka nodded, and stepped back into the darkness.

"Yes, but leave us."

"Yes, Greatmother."

Valda felt the real pull of interest and surprise now. Success and tragedy had a way of becoming routine when you were as old as she. But, still, her curved spine felt a tingle.

Boots clattered on the floorboards, and a curvy woman in the plain brown of a poor matron entered Valda's room. She bowed low with respect, then pulled back her hood to reveal a pretty, youthful face, wind-burnt and touched by the sun. She closed the door behind her and sat in the chair set out for guests.

"My name is Dala, High Priestess of the Southern Prefect. I come with an offer, and for your help. You've met my ally."

Valda recognized the girl. It was the apprentice who had carried a bag of heads to the spring festival and slopped them beneath the matriarch's feet. Valda would have liked her just for that, but she had also come boldly proclaiming rebellion and terror and called for men to stop Bukayag and his outlaws. In an afternoon, she had rallied more men than the Order in a generation.

Valda looked from the priestess to the outlaw she had promised to stop, wondering exactly how and when they had arranged their plotting and collusion. She supposed it didn't matter.

"Well done, girl." Valda laughed, which brought on a small coughing fit. "Oh very well done," she said more quietly when it was over. "But I don't care about your Order or who rules it. You've made a mistake coming here."

The girl smiled politely, her hands resting at ease on her lap.

"I don't think so," she said. "The Order is only a stepping stone." She gestured towards 'Bukayag'. "Your grandson has sailed North, across the endless sea, and found land. It is a new world of wealth beyond imagining. We intend to create a new future for our people. But the task will be hard. We will require help. *Practical* help."

Valda watched the girl's eyes for trickery or madness and couldn't be sure. She had of course heard reports already of the strange ships off the North coast of the peninsula. Her sons had already asked their builders if such a thing could be done, and long before this she had smiths studying the incredible, rune-covered weapons being fought and dueled over all across the Ascom. None of it meant a new world, of course, but it seemed Beyla's son was clever, very clever. Could he have tricked this High Priestess? Could the ships and the weapons be entirely his own?

"Let's assume I believe you," Valda said at last. "Why come to me? You have a ship and some followers. Go, then. Sail away to your new lands."

Dala looked to Ruka, so Valda did too. He stared into the small hearthfire and sighed.

"We are but one small corner of a vast and complex world, Valda. These new lands have people and kings, great cities that could hold ten of our capitals inside them. They have armies and armadas of ships that make us look like the scattered savages we are. We will not be welcome. To claim our place in these lands will take strength we do not possess." Here he paused, and smiled as he turned to Valda. "But it could also unite us. I can give your chiefs more glory and enemies then even the most ambitious could ask for. Together, we might give them a vision grander than any ancient book or ancestor ever dreamed. With your blessing, perhaps they will seize it."

Valda felt a trickle of drool on her chin and wiped it. She stared into the strange eyes of her kin, unsure of what made him and the few other children like him. Her ancestors said it was the god of chaos. She did not think so, and this brought her fear, and shame. Most such children were put to the sword since she was a girl, and no doubt long before. Even still, they were often abandoned.

"You have proof? Of any of this?"

Ruka rose, his head cocked. He held out an open, empty palm, and looked into her eyes with the hint of a smile, as if he could see her thoughts. "You are studying my weapons, yes?"

Valda made no reaction, and Ruka's smile widened.

"See now how it is done." His voice grew louder, more dramatic. "See yet another world you stand apart from in ignorance."

Light flared from his hand. Even in the fog of her rheumy eyes she saw the sparks and the forming cylinder of a blade appearing from nothing in the air. Ruka's thick fingers clamped around its hilt.

"You were right, Valda, daughter of Valdaya—you have played your part, and I mine. But the story must change. A new age has begun."

Valda stared at the weapon and forced her mind to settle in reality. In truth, she had already believed him. She had felt the shifting of the world for years, and now the blunt and honest nature of this man, nevermind his words or stories. He was the sort who could tell truth with lies.

"Will you shepherd your people to this new world?" he said, as if he had practiced this speech a thousand times. "Or will you be ground to dust before the endless wheel of time?"

Valda felt a smile form and did not stop it—a pleasure formed of pride for her fallen grand-daughter, who had saved this creature at birth, and raised it into this man.

Few warriors of ash could resist his message, Valda believed that. And so the time had come for a king. Strange, she thought, that it would not be a great chief who had conquered his enemies, or a mighty warrior who won a hundred duels. It would be a son of Noss, a rune-shaman of old who could bind the South with the North. But no matter—it would still be a Vishan, and Valda's kin.

She pushed down the fear of change and risk and lifted a cup of water to soothe her old, dry throat. "I am Valdaya," she answered, then grimaced in her seat as if annoyed. "I will always help my people. But I have one condition." She considered this and changed her mind. "Make it two."

Ruka's narrowed eyes glanced at Dala.

"When there is new land to occupy," Valda said, "you will ensure my kin are given choices as befits their support. And before I shrivel up entirely and expire, you will show me this paradise."

At this a slow grin formed on Ruka's face, but still he said nothing.

"And since I'm an old woman you'll permit me a third condition I'd forgotten," she said, and he nodded slowly. "We will speak of your mother and you will tolerate it. Because here is a truth and I'm far too old to lie. Beyla was my favorite grand-daughter. I have not been pleased to treat her memory as outcast."

The giant twitched, and his eyes flared. For a moment Valda worried she had stepped into a buried pool of madness too deep to be expunged. But if he could not agree to this, then perhaps the madness would be too strong for the greatness to thrive, and so in any case it would be best to refuse and destroy him. She watched the struggle in the young man's face, and at last, the mastery of his own demons. She released a breath.

"As you wish," he said, as if the struggle had not been obvious. "But Beyla was never an *outcast,* Valda, for no one banished her. It was me you did not accept. For that she chose to leave you. Not once did she mourn this choice, nor did she wallow in misery, or speak of regret." His eyes looked far away and moist with pride, as if he could see his mother now. "A lioness cares nothing for the shriek of jackals, old woman. Now hear this, and hear it well—if she had raised me to hate, I would kill you and all your kin, and no man or god could stop me. Until the end of days, Valda, remember: your line lives by Beyla's grace."

With this he turned and vanished through the gloom of the window, his movement sure and controlled in the dark. Valda watched him go, then sat in silence.

She sat long after the priestess rose politely and left her with words of thanks and promise, and Valda mumbled something polite in return. She let the fire dwindle and did nothing, angry then sad then numb, and finally at peace.

Ah, life, she thought, *what a wonder.*

She had heard the truth in Ruka's words because she was too old to bother avoiding it. Sending Beyla away had been a mistake, she'd felt it then, yes she'd known, but not how deep the mistake had been.

Valda thanked whatever gods of ash existed, and that in their wisdom they made their children different, so that when some were wrong others might redeem them. Beyla had been the promised child, and her son had seen it clearly. He had been made by love, then saved by it, and now it had saved Valda, too. She smiled, because in all her years she had never had a favorite grand-son.

She lay against her chair and wished for the thousandth time she could live forever, which was perhaps the last childish thing she had never given up. She sighed as she settled. Instead, she would die soon, far too soon, her part in the great story finished and left to others. But she would do what she could for her kin now, today. Or at least tomorrow. She closed her eyes and slept, because the morning would be very busy, and a nap always helped.

62

Dala walked beside Valda with a growing tension in her gut.

In many ways, this moment was the culmination of years of her blood, sweat, and planning. But she did not know exactly what the old matron intended to do, or say. This concerned her.

After their 'meeting', Valda had rallied seven of her grandsons to escort them across Orhus. Two were great chiefs of the capital, another lesser—the others warriors of various renown. The ancient matron had first argued with these men behind closed doors, perhaps explaining her position while Dala and Bukayag waited anxiously in the morning fog. Loud voices and grumbling drifted unintelligible through the wood. But whatever their protests, they had come.

Now Bukayag walked amongst them with a plain hood drawn, and shoulders hunched.

They walked together across Orhus at the slow pace of the ancient woman, who refused to ride or be carried. "Never do for someone what they can do for themselves," she snapped, then focused on the road with a glare as if at some old foe, placing foot after tiny foot as she crunched gravel and dirt.

Many citizens of the richer chiefdoms noticed them. They stared at Valda—Vishan crone and great matron of the North—and at two mighty chiefs and a pack of rich, older men with swords. But like most of the warriors at her side, despite his attempts to remain hidden, Dala couldn't help but steal glances at Bukayag.

Here stood a son of Noss in the depths of power. He was an outcast who had murdered priestesses—who had been declared heretic, and was hunted by nearly every civilized warrior in the world. *No, in the Ascom*, she corrected herself, *not the world.* And yet here he stood in plain sight, in the capital, strolling to the source of law itself, surrounded by thousands of enemies. And he did not look afraid.

What a man, she thought, watching him, with a warmth rising in her gut. His face was monstrous, true, but not his body. Even hunched, Bukayag 'the last rune-shaman' stood above the warriors around him. Dala had seen him shirtless and covered in runes at Alverel, and she had seen lean, sculpted, hardened flesh. Since then he had grown and filled out. Now the cords of his neck sprouted like the bones of some winged bird preparing to rise. He walked like a predator, purposeful and dangerous—the owl preparing to shred nightingales with its claws. Ruka was a lone wolf in the shape of a man, and the truth was, Dala wanted him.

And if Dala wanted him, then perhaps God herself intended it. What better way to bind him? To guide him? No doubt he'd never felt a woman's touch.

For now she ignored these thoughts. They crossed the iron river to the old city, and she felt an anxious flutter because she would likely have to enter the Order-hall alone. The High Priestesses and Prefects would be huddled together inside Galdra's Hall already, counting votes and scheming. For weeks they would jostle for position, bargain and bribe, until the old matriarch called it to an end, and the final tally was counted and the new yearly rankings decided. This year, as determined every five, they would even decide on a new matriarch.

Of course a new matriarch was never chosen. The reigning priestess closest to God was always re-elected unless her health or mind had crumbled, because the position gave such power and advantage that to unseat her was nearly impossible. Dala would not bother to try. She would instead convince her which way the wind was blowing, keep her position as High Priestess, and ask for the Order to do what was sensible. They were a practical institution, despite their corruptions. They would see reason.

"There are many Galdric guards, grand-mother." Valda's son, Marnuk, frowned as the Order hall came into view. Valda had finally allowed him to at least support her as she walked, and she turned her head this way and that with squinted eyes trying to see. With a sigh she sat on a near-by bench.

"If they will not let me pass, will you kill them?"

The big man chewed at the thick hair on his lip, then looked at his kin. "No. Not unless we are attacked, grandmother. To start a fight with Galdric guard...it isn't honorable. It would damage our reputations. It would hurt our family name."

Valda blew air and shook her head. Dala's breath caught as Bukayag pulled back his hood.

"I will kill them, Valda, if you ask me."

The old woman looked at him and smiled, and Dala wondered at the exact nature of that smile.

"There are at least ten men," spoke Marnuk, as if addressing Bukayag brought him pain. "We...can't help you."

The shaman met the chief's eyes, then looked him up and down as if judging his worth. "It was not I who asked for your presence, son of Imler. Do whatever your courage allows."

Dala felt the tension flare—the men's pride curling at the stink of insult. Bukayag seemed oblivious, or at least didn't care.

He extended his arms high like a madman, or a seer, as if beckoning the sky for some purpose. Dala would have gawked with the others if she had not already seen, and did not know what was coming. Still, she stared.

The air sizzled like fat burning on a skillet. All at once his body seemed to swell and grow, and as Dala blinked at the light she saw his skin had turned grey. She blinked again and saw where there had been nothing now sat smooth, iron plates connected by mail. A dozen runes of power decorated the metal. Dala stood wide-eyed with the others.

Bukayag turned and strode towards the hall, and Valda followed, elbowing her grandson back to reality.

The Order guard came to life as they saw Bukayag. They moved from their rest and formed a line before the hall, hands resting on scabbards, dark tunics and cloaks moving to show good mail and leather beneath. A man wearing a bronze circlet of renown and the silver earring of a Captain stood before the door—the point of a V formation like a flock of birds. His sharp eyes moved over the group, beginning and ending on Bukayag.

"You come armed to a holy place. Leave it quickly, or die."

Dala was surprised at the instantly aggressive tone and words. For a moment she saw Bukayag smile, but she stepped before him and threw back her hood to reveal the Galdric shawl about her shoulders. "I am High Priestess Dala of the South. I've come for the elections, and to address this holy gathering." She gestured at the old matron. "This is Valda, daughter of…"

"I know who she is." Again the man's tone shocked her and she knew something was amiss. "Only a priestess enters the hall." He looked directly into Dala's eyes, which was almost always considered rude for a man not her kin. "You are welcome, High Priestess. But know that you are accused of several crimes. You will stand trial on the rock inside."

Dala nodded slowly, at last understanding. She had known this was possible. It was not uncommon to be accused of crimes before elections for political reasons, though the disrespect of the Captain suggested her accusers had already established her 'guilt'. It would make little difference to her argument, though perhaps increase the price if she failed. She intended to respond but the Captain spoke again.

"This abomination must be Bukayag. It would seem the accusations against you are true, priestess." The man's hand moved to his scabbard, and the shaman's grin widened, but it was not friendly.

"We have met before, Captain. Or, at least, I have seen you."

The wiry soldier glared but said nothing. Bukayag went on.

"You don't remember. I don't blame you. You were busy killing an unarmed woman named Noyon, matron of the fertile ring. You killed all her young sons, as well, and took her daughters." The shaman's pretense of humor disappeared, and it was clear to Dala the man recognized what he was saying. "The night was dark, and quiet," said Bukayag. "But the Gods were watching. Now here we stand outside the hall of Nanot. A fitting place, I think, for a man to be judged."

Valda cleared her throat. "There's no need for unpleasantness. Stand aside, captain, and we will…"

"Oh we are *long* past unpleasantness, Greatmother." Bukayag's bright eyes bore into the man as he sneered. "These sons of law won't give you the justice you deserve, Captain. But Noss will see it done."

Whatever 'tension' had existed between Bukayag and the chiefs was like a thin broth compared to this. The air felt thick, and oppressive, and Dala's skin tingled with the threat of violence. The captain stood very still.

"I think I'll feed those cursed eyes to my dogs," he said, "come forward, heretic."

Bukayag did not move. They stood across the road from one another, the Galdric warrior with many men at his back, the shaman on his own. Bukayag watched them all, and laughed

"I like you, captain, such a shame. You have been blessed with strength, skill, and courage. But you have abused those gifts. I think it is Vol who will judge you."

The captain's eyes rolled, and he glanced at his fellows as Bukayag raised his arms in the air.

Again, the air shimmered. This time Dala felt the heat on her face as the wind whipped through the street. Bukayag flared with light as if beside a roaring fire. Metal grew before him like a huge mushroom from the earth, curving and screeching as it seemed to bend into shape. When it was finished, it looked like a giant bow lay flat and placed on an anvil, or some kind of stand—a strange weapon the size of a man pulled from nothing but air. Everyone stared.

In its center, an arrow the size of a man's leg faced the hall. Ruka had his hand on a metal stick protruding from the side of the weapon. His head quirked as he inspected it, then he pulled.

A sound thrummed like a hammer striking a bell. The echo hung, and the arrow released and flew. The captain drew his sword in a blink, then the arrow struck his chest.

It knocked him back, ripped him from his feet as if rammed by a bull. He hurled backwards and smashed the door, blood splashing from his body like water thrown from a cliff. The entrance to the hall cracked and splintered as it flew from its hinges to rattle on the stones inside.

An attendant priestess turned from the corridor with a panicked stare.

"Vol has spoken," the shaman growled, then turned to his great-grandmother. "The way is open, Valda." He quirked a brow and looked back to the Galdric warriors. "Unless another man would like to be judged?"

The guards glanced at each other, then to the twitching corpse of their captain. They stepped away.

Valda snapped her fingers and Dala blinked. "Come along girl. I won't live forever."

They walked arm and arm inside, stepping over the door and the mangled corpse of the captain, whose torso had almost ripped from its body. Dala looked at the impossible wound and the huge arrow leaning against the gaping hole and realized there were runes etched onto the shaft. They were stained slightly with gore, but she could still make them out. In a simple, but elegant hand, they read: "Altan's Justice."

* * *

It was the first time Dala had ever entered the Hall of Nanot. She had been made High Priestess in absence at the nomination of the matriarch, and accepted her new power quickly and without strangeness. But now, walking inside the huge, cavernous den of legal authority, she felt rather small—again like the scarred up farm girl in an unwelcoming city.

She looked at the faces of the most powerful women in the world, Priestesses and Prefects, positions arranged in descending benches like circular steps, all surrounding the seat of the matriarch. Every face was turned towards Dala and her entourage. All of them were staring.

Dala still felt shaken from the death of the captain, and the strange, divine weapon used to kill him. Long ago she had accepted the power of God in the mortal world, and that Bukayag too served Her will. But to see it employed so...*directly*...

She breathed, controlling her movement as she tried to focus on the now and calm her nerves. *Bukayag is God's greatest warrior*, she thought, *why shouldn't she grant him feats of divine might?*

This thought, at least, calmed her. Now she had to face these women and overcome their complaints and objections, all the while with Valda and Bukayag waiting, and watching. But she had survived worse.

She looked to the angry eyes of the matriarch, the old woman so much like Valda, perched on the twin of the holy rock at Alverel. She sat next to a bench covered in stones and counting bowls and a box Dala knew to be stuffed with peat for burning if a new matriarch was chosen. No doubt it was several years old.

The strangeness of the moment seemed close to broken. The matriarch looked ready to rise and speak, and Dala knew the time was now, or never. She had to seize control of the room, and quickly. Valda turned to her.

"If it is alright with you, priestess, I would like to address the gathering first. You are welcome, of course, to interrupt. But I think what I have to say will please you."

Dala's mind raced. Every instinct told her not to cede control. But then, this woman was her ally. She had agreed, and with great peril to her own position and wealth, and had brought her sons here and obviously challenged the Order.

So what would she say? Only God knew for sure. There was so much at risk, so many unpredictable things. Dala couldn't decide. *Send me a sign, Goddess, I need you now. I'm so close. Is this to be? Will she betray?*

At last Dala nodded, tight-lipped, because time was short and she could think of no better solution. Valda dipped her head in thanks, and stepped to the edge of the lowered, angled benches. She gestured for Bukayag, who now stepped behind her and clearly into view. The women gasped, or cursed, or stood.

"We are here for the elections, cousin," Valda shouted as she leaned on her cane. The matriarch rose, veins stretching across her red face.

"I hope for your family's sake you are that man's prisoner, Valda. You are not welcome here." Her tone rose with every word. "You have no authority. You have no right."

Valda extended a hand as if to acknowledge this and calm her kin. "I am no man's prisoner. But I tire of having no vote in this room, cousin. So now I'm going to speak, and you're going to listen, or else I'm going to let my mad, heretical dog here slip his leash. As I understand it, he doesn't much like priestesses."

Bukayag smiled to reveal his teeth, playing his role all too well. Dala wondered for a moment what the real man was like beneath it all, what drove him, and how he'd been made. He stalked behind his great-grandmother as if he could barely contain his violence, and Dala wondered if that were true.

The matriarch's jaw clenched in rage but she said nothing. No doubt she wanted to know very much where her guards were, and how exactly Bukayag had gotten inside. Valda sat on a near-by bench, forcing the priestesses to give her room. She groaned at the exertion and removed a wad of orange root from the pocket of her dress.

"An old habit," she said, as if in apology, stuffing it in the corner of her cheek. She spoke casually, like a conversation between kin. "I must tell you, sisters. I've not been very happy with you. Not with the farming quotas," she spit orange saliva to a clean, white step, "Not with your unwillingness to go South, with meddling in matron pairings, with politics and chief-making." She spat again, this time alarmingly close to a woman's feet.

The matriarch looked like she might interrupt, but delayed at a look of pure malice from Bukayag. Valda kept on as if she hadn't noticed.

"Yes, yes, I know, most of it is to prevent a king, or was. Such a waste. So terrified you all are of a man with power! God knows why. I have known many men who would have made fine kings, and I've had children with three of them. But sisters, and you must listen to me, men...they are not like us. They *want* a king. It is quite natural for them. Always men are asking who is strongest, who is best. That is what drives them, sisters. You have no children or mates and so you don't see this. How could you? They are not interested in your bland unity. They don't want your forced peace and harmony. And sooner or later, with or without you, they will have their king."

She took a moment to glance about the gathering, as if to let that sink in.

'*With or without you*, sisters," she said, as if she didn't believe it had. "And why shouldn't they? We are not their enemies. Are we not their mothers, sisters, daughters, and matrons? Is the moon goddess not the partner of Volus? Does he not fear *her* wrath and jealousy even as he turns his eye to Zisa's beauty? Why would he fear her if she is not his equal?"

"Spare us ancient stories. Imler taught us what a king will do," growled the matriarch. "The chiefs will *destroy* themselves, and all of us with them. It *must* be prevented."

"What will they destroy?" Valda rolled her eyes. "All around you my men build and maintain this world. They build your houses, they grow and hunt your food, they fight the cold, the waves, the weather, nature itself. Why do they do this?"

"Because they are born to do it," said the matriarch, "but like dogs they must be trained, or become dangerous."

The old matron sighed, and spit juice, lowering her voice. "I pity you, Ellevi, truly. They do it for their families. They do it for their matrons and children and gods. For me. And yes, for *you*. And yet here you stand, protected by a ring of such men, one of whom just died for your cause, and you stand in judgment. How can my sons be my enemies? Have you all gone truly mad?"

"You think *that* man is our ally?" The matriarch pointed at Bukayag. "You think he is yours, cousin?"

The old woman craned her neck to look at him, and a smile spread across her toothless jaw. "He has discovered a new world, cousin, and for reasons beyond my understanding, he has returned to take us there, despite our treatment of him. So yes, he is our ally. Perhaps he is the greatest ally we will ever have."

Dala looked at the shaman and saw the crinkled brow of surprise and perhaps emotion, the mask of the crazed dog slipping.

"There is no world except this land of ash," said the matriarch, eyes hard in contempt. "You have been tricked by a monster, a son of chaos. Only God knows why he does what he does."

Valda released a wheezing breath. "Ah yes, your precious book. It has less use than you think, and this son of chaos has already proved it wrong. Accept it. I am rarely tricked, cousin, because I cling to few illusions. I speak plainly and not in endless riddles like you and your ilk. So let me be plain now." She spit, then groaned to her feet and pointed her cane.

"Your order has taken its last daughter of Valdaya. I and all my family—all my men and land and matrons—are going to join this heretic." She smiled, perhaps at the shock in the room. "And then we are going to set your world aflame."

Most of the priestesses rose at this, shouting vulgarities or exchanging words Dala couldn't possibly hear. Valda struck the stone with her cane, and the room quieted as the sound echoed. She spoke again, the menace clear, old voice rising above the growing din at every word.

"We will kill your brothers, and your fathers, until Orhus runs red with their blood. And when all your men are dead, we will burn your holy places, and we will destroy you."

By the end of her threat the gathering had silenced again, such madness beyond all imagining to be uttered by a matron as eminent as Valda. She shrugged.

"Or, you can vote Dala, daughter of Cara, as your new matriarch. You can do it right now."

Dala blinked, and almost flinched as every eye turned to her. She looked back at Bukayag, who grinned.

"Do this," said Valda, "and I will trust Dala to begin a new era of Galdric leadership—a leadership that accepts the chiefs and matrons will decide how they will be ruled, *assisting* us as possible. If elected, girl, can I believe that?"

Dala nodded because she didn't trust her voice, trying to keep her chin high enough to seem confident, but not too high to seem proud. The old woman winked.

"Good. Now, while I'm here, I will also be taking my grand-daughter. Talia, come girl." She held out her arm, and a young woman with a fierce look stood instantly from the back of the hall. She cast off her shawl as if it were nothing, and stepped with a wide smile towards her grandmother.

"And the daughters of Noyon," Bukayag added, his deep voice rolling about the rafters. "They were taken against their will, and belong with their father."

The old woman glanced at him with a raised brow, but nodded, and two more girls rose from the servant ranks at the edge of the circle, shyly coming forward towards Valda. "Come girls, let's leave the priestesses to their business." She glanced one last time about the circle. "I await your decision. We'll be just outside."

With that she turned and limped towards the broken entrance with her granddaughter's shoulder as a crutch. Bukayag raised a brow at Dala as if to ask 'should I stay?'. She shook her head, despite secretly wishing he would. He nodded in respect, and followed his kin.

Dala stood alone at the edge of the circle, some small murmuring sounds and whispers moving about the priestesses. The matriarch had turned a shade of purple.

"This is blasphemy," she hissed. "The Order will not be strong-armed by matrons and their lapdogs. Every one of you will burn for this. Do you think us powerless?"

"Yes," Dala said, not worrying about the many whispers. "But power is not the role of the Order. It is guidance—true guidance to God through Her prophet. A role you have forgotten."

Dala glanced around the room. She saw some familiar faces, but no allies. Then she saw Priestess Amira—the woman who had been in charge of Dala's conclave when she'd become a priestess. She had helped her then, and as she saw her eyes, believing more than ever Amira and maybe others were true servants of the goddess. The woman smiled, and stood.

"I believe we should do what she says. For the Order, and the Ascom, we must bend."

Some of the women around her made at least weak noises of

agreement, though others scoffed or looked away. Dala had intended to convince them—to make them see the great future more suited to the aims of all. But sometimes, perhaps, Bukayag was right. Sometimes words didn't do much of anything, and the women already understood their peril.

They knew Valda could rally enough support to plunge the Ascom into civil war, and probably win. Their whole existence depended on preventing such a thing, for why else did the chiefs and matrons provide for them?

"Perhaps we should begin the vote," Dala called over the voices, then descended slowly towards the old woman on the lawstone. She abandoned all pretense of humility, head high as she met the woman's eyes as an equal. She thought back to the spring festival, knowing even then the old priestess failed to understand the change happening all around her.

"No need for tablets," Dala called, "a show of hands will do." She stepped onto the stone, crowding the matriarch who seemed ready to push her away, but looked in Dala's eyes, and at the seax on her belt, and changed her mind.

Dala stared at the faces that had intimidated her as she entered—the women she thought together understood the message and teachings of God, and helped guide Her flock. She saw their fear—the very mortal fears of loss of power and position, and not the fear that perhaps they might have failed in their duty. She lost all anxiety and concern for winning their loyalty, then. They would serve, or she would go to God's true servants and her allies, and start the cleanse.

"Time to vote," she said, with as much brutal threat as she felt. The matriarch looked about the room as if hopeful, as if failing to understand her time and everything she believed were at an end. "Who chooses Dala, daughter of Cara? Raise your hands."

Dala felt she was at her ceremony again, standing before her peers waiting to be judged. Then, as now, she had brought men with cold iron. And then, as now, she would not hesitate to use them.

One by one, the women looked to each other and raised their hands. Dala knew as they did that it was truly over—that Dala the Noss-touched, the waste of beauty, the scarred up Southron prude, would be the holiest woman in the Ascom. It was her time, and she would do God's will. *And woe to those who stand in my way.*

She spared a glance at the pale-faced, now former matriarch, whose jaw hung slack to reveal only a few, yellowed teeth. Dala stared until the old woman stepped away from her lawstone. She glanced to the matriarch's attendants.

No, she corrected herself, *my attendants.*

"You wouldn't want our allies to get the wrong message," she said. When the girls didn't move, she raised her voice. "Burn the damn peat."

The attendants blinked and looked frantically about the room. Seeing no objection, support, nor any sign of other orders, they hurried for the dusty box.

63

After Orhus, Ruka returned to Kormet, and prepared for war.

Despite Valda or the Order's words, he knew many chiefs would not agree without a fight. Many would not yield unless to a warrior. And so they would come, and he must be ready.

He left Orhus alone and quickly, returning to the trenches to find far more men than he expected, and far more progress.

"It's the nightmen," said Folvar outside the hall in report. "Birmun brought them. They dig like animals, working even in darkness."

Ruka smiled at this. Birmun must have moved quickly to gather them. With Dala's obvious support, he no longer worried about the nightman chief's loyalty. But still, he felt uneasy, and it did not take long to figure out why.

He wanted the priestess, that was the truth. But he banished the thought instantly as foolish nonsense. Dala was his ally, and perhaps even friendly with him, but no woman with any kind of choice could want him as a mate. His humor worsened at the thought, and dropped more as the chief went on with his report.

"Some of the foreign women have died, shaman. Most recovered, though, or have at least improved."

Ruka nodded and followed him behind the hall to the few shallow, unmarked graves. Some of the other women wept near-by.

"I thought you might wish to see the bodies," Folvar explained. "But… we will burn them now, unless you say otherwise, or, would they want some other ritual?"

Ruka shook his head. The Pyu buried their dead but made little of it except for their kings. He uncovered the women's corpses so he could mark which had perished, and asked the other women for their names. In his Grove the dead dug graves and made signposts with Pyu symbols, then he let the men burn their bodies.

Perhaps they would not appear in his Grove, for he had not killed them, and did not wish them dead, but still they had died because of him. One day he would grieve, and accept the price for all the lives snuffed for the great cause of the future, and suffer whatever came. But not today.

He checked Sula and found him well-fed and bored, then greeted Aiden who had returned from the peninsula. The mighty chieftain of Husavik grinned and took Ruka's arm with a respectful nod.

"The farms are secured, shaman. They had few guards, and fewer ships. Now they have none. I left Altan with some guards to work the land."

Ruka nodded. The raider-turned-farmer would do what was right. He would have time to re-unite with his children later, and until then, Ruka would keep them safe in Kormet. He met with Tahar and his men next, who had been busy chasing Northern scouts and Arbmen near the border of the fertile ring.

"Nothing yet in force, lord." The ex-chief came stained with sweat, dirt and blood, his eyes rimmed with bruises. "But we have seen many tracks. And a man looks first where he means to go."

Ruka agreed. "Rest. Eat. Then return to the hills," he said. "You've done well, Tahar, though I expected nothing less."

The capable warrior withdrew with pleasure in his eyes—though perhaps less than Ruka hoped. It took recognition *and* reward to bind men like Tahar, but Ruka could provide both soon enough. A foreign bride would be a fine start.

Eshen soon followed in silence and became Ruka's shadow. He had never had a bodyguard, but found with so much on his mind it did put him at ease. He reminded himself that ambush and betrayal was most possible, and that if he died now the dream of paradise and a future for the Ascom would crumble to dust in the wind.

"How did they receive my gifts, and message?" he asked Egil later as night fell, when he returned from his errand to the chiefs.

"Well enough." Egil grimaced, and drank water from Folvar's table in large gulps. "The number of rune-blades now in Orhus has hurt the worth of each, but still they are very valuable, and the risk of owning them at least has reduced."

Ruka nodded, and waited, caring more about which chiefs would wait, as requested, and which would try and seize glory.

"I don't know is the short answer," Egil glanced to ensure they were alone, then shrugged. "If I must guess, I would say Valda's kin will obey her and give you time. So will most of their allies. But this is a chance for many others who hate the Valdaya to undermine them. Chief Balder and Hoden in particular. They will come, I think, with like-minded men. They may even band together in the attempt."

"No, they will try alone." Ruka looked away as he imagined the best ground between him and Orhus to fight. "How many men do they have?"

"A thousand between them. More, maybe. I don't know."

Ruka felt his jaw clench. With Aiden, Folvar, Dala, and even the nightmen, he had only half that.

"You've done well, Egil, now as ever. Go to your family tonight. I have but one last task for you, then you are free from all of this."

His first retainer's eyes widened, his hands frozen on unbroken bread.

"Go back to Orhus. Tell every influential man and woman, chief or priestess, to gather at Alverel. Tell them in ten days I will speak on the mountainside like the heroes of old. Tell them to bring their warriors, if they wish. But they must hear. I will speak of the future. I will speak, and then together they will decide if I lead them to it, or if I die instead on the cliffs. Whatever they say, I will obey."

Egil watched him, utterly frozen. Then he shrugged and tried to pass it off as nothing. "In ten days we may all be dead. What will you do until then?" The skald's tone was careful, his eyes piercing and full of conflict.

Ruka wished he could explain. He wished he could express his hopes and fears and sorrows as a man might to a friend. But without Beyla, he was alone, save perhaps for Farahi. Only Farahi at long last might understand and be as kin of the mind.

The thought warmed and comforted him, because perhaps he had learned a sort of faith, faith in a man—Farahi would come. He would help the men of ash join the larger world, and for this they would be his ally as he asked, because unlike the Empire to the North he did not seek slaves. But the Ascom must be ready.

"I will do what is required," Ruka said after a long pause. "Good night, Egil." He stood and left the hall, nodding to Folvar's warriors guarding the door. He walked out into the cool night air and breathed, seeing in his mind the great works required in the future, the courage, the commitment, as well as the possible disasters.

His people would have to learn to speak new languages, to sail, to make war, to co-exist with islanders who did not think or worship or behave as they. They would face the sea and its great waves, then kings and armies. And, he now realized, there would be sickness on both sides.

Disease might sweep the old and the young and the weak like a harvester's scythe, no matter how peaceful their intentions, or how they tried to prevent it. The thought sickened him. It weighed his spirit as an anchor of iron, dragging him beneath the waves.

Or we can do nothing, he thought. *We can stay on our frozen patch of meager land and let the rest of the world change and struggle as it will.*

This too seemed intolerable. And in either future, in either choice, there would be suffering and death, and one day the sickness would spread regardless. But how could men stop disease without becoming afflicted and letting the weak die? Surely there was a way, even if Ruka did not know it.

No matter what, it was not only him who must choose. Despite his purpose and Beyla's words, he was beginning to believe it was not only his will that mattered. He would stop the pointless battle, and protect the most ambitious men for a time from slaughtering the other. But he knew he must stop the deception and lies. For what use to save a people with trickery, when one day the true test of their will would come?

* * *

In three days, the trench was ready. The thousand men, women and children that formed Ruka's allies had dug and flattened the ground from sea to sea. They were exhausted and filthy, with many hands torn and raw.

Tahar returned from the hills to say several hundred chiefsmen were marching from Orhus in two groups. They would arrive before nightfall.

By his tone it was clear he thought they should run. It was also clear that he and all the warriors thought Ruka's trench useless, and maybe madness. Folvar asked with heavy lidded eyes if he should ready his men for battle.

"No, chief. There will be no battle. Have your people stand before the trench in a line, spaced from coast to coast."

The man blinked in tired confusion, but had committed to it all already, and went to obey. The gap at the entrance to the peninsula was narrow. Each side of the sea could be seen by a man standing in the middle, so that is where Ruka stood.

In his Grove, the dead placed the last stones atop the wall. They had used largely limestone from the quarry, moving the huge, base-rocks atop logs rolled in unison in the Pyu style. They had lashed them with ropes and winches and pulleys and lifted them one atop the other, then filled in the rest of the height with smaller stones and mortar.

Now the wall of the dead stood twenty 'ri'—a unit of measurement from Naran—and the exact width of the 'fertile gate'.

Ruka put his hand against the cold, hard stone, and closed his eyes. The dead stood in a line, just like the men and women of ash. Boy-from-Alverel grinned with his eyes, broken jaw flopping in excitement. He had led the work on the gate, making it from as much iron as wood, even drawing the runes now displayed proudly in defiance.

Ruka was ready, but waited. If he failed here then all his plans would fall to ruin, and he must flee and perhaps start again. But if he succeeded, it would be best if all could see.

As Volus climbed to his highest peak, the first warriors of Orhus crested the rise to the lowlands. Hundreds of men in a haphazard line carried swords and spears and shields, wearing the finest armor bought by rich and powerful chiefs.

Many of Ruka's retainers looked on them in fear, but they did not run. Some turned to see Ruka, perhaps for courage, and he grinned at any who'd meet his gaze.

"Have faith, cousins," he shouted to any close enough to hear. Still he waited until more of his 'enemy' had gathered and readied themselves to charge. He wanted them close enough to think their victory assured, to be looking out at the thin line of half women and children with disbelief. He held out his hands.

In his Grove, the more obedient dead placed their palms against the stone. Some had broken fingers or shattered arms, and so placed their foreheads or backs instead. Many still hated Ruka for what he'd done. He saw it often as they passed him, moving to their endless toil with deep scowls and bitter eyes. But they did not hate life or the living. Even in death their old purpose and habits sustained them, or perhaps their love, or just their memories of honey and sunshine.

"It will stand for a thousand years," he called. "It will last longer than every creature on this field, a great monument to the dead. And today it will save these people."

Most of the walking corpses seemed appeased by this, and Ruka only hoped it was true. He still did not know the limits of his Grove. Could he do anything he could conceive? Was the only limitation his knowledge, and his means? And why could Ruka alone do such things?

He did not know, nor did he assume any answers. For now he could only imagine, and test.

First, he imagined a wall. He imagined every detail, from the huge, solid base that would sit on the flattened ground of the trench—to the crenelations and the ramparts above. *Protect us*, he prayed to the dead, *protect your kin. One day we will share your fate, but let it not be today.*

Other corpses moved to the wall as if they understood. They forced broken bodies past nerve and sinew with only the will that moved them, and Ruka watched with pride.

The living owed them so much already. They owed the Vishan fleeing across the sea, then those suffering to survive and have children, taming the land and building tools one by one over thousands of years. They could owe them a little more.

Take it back, brother, use it. Stone does the dead no good.

Ruka put both sets of hands to the wall, and both worlds around him trembled.

It started with Bukayag. Heat came without fire, then a slow rise from the soil, a hill growing from a rumble that should have meant a fissure—an earthquake in reverse.

Ruka felt the will of the dead mingling with his own, their purpose crossed and strengthening his until it spread through the trench. It felt directed, but unstoppable, like releasing the Kubi. Heat and purpose flowed like a river across the land of ash, and the air shimmered and shook as if it were water rippling across a pond.

All along the wall, Ruka heard screaming. He did not know why, but it made no difference. It could not be stopped.

As the stone released he could only stand in witness, helpless and meaningless next to the reality of such creation. Where there had once been nothing now rose a great wall of the dead, thick as a man, tall as four, spewing from the air and the earth like a landslide going up. The noise consumed all, growling and roaring as elemental forces clashed and ground together.

It lasted only ten drips of the water-timer, and yet forever. All at once the rumbling of the sky ceased, and the dead in Ruka's Grove stepped away from the crushed line of ruined grass now open before them.

In the land of the living, Ruka stood at the open, iron gate of a massive stone wall, as if it had grown from his hands. He looked to the sides, and saw that it stretched along the trench from sea to sea, blocking off the entire fertile ring.

He looked to the men and women along it and saw many had fallen, though he did not know why or to what end. Some had their hands placed over ears or chests. Some bled from their noses. Others had perhaps stepped too close, and Ruka saw several bodies thrown back and shattered.

They will be honored, he thought, stepping forward to hide his own shaken spirit. His gut trembled with fear and confusion, but he had to be strong in this moment. They would look to him for answers, and whatever the cost, the wall had worked. A few dead townsfolk had saved thousands.

Ruka stepped out so the men could all see him clearly. The approaching chiefs had stopped, the men staring in awe at the huge barrier. Ruka walked inside the open portal—the only way to enter now save for the high rocky cliffs at the edges of the peninsula, or the frigid and dangerous waters guarded by Aiden and his ships.

He pulled the clever Pyu winch with a screech of greased steel, and the rune-covered gate slammed shut.

64

The dead dug more graves. Ruka had lost track of them now, but he preferred not to look if he could avoid it.

"How…what *was* that, shaman? How is this possible?" Folvar gestured at the wall, his face pale, his hand trembling.

Ruka's retainers had crowded around him. Fifteen people were badly wounded—some deafened, others shattered. Nine more had been killed, including two women and a child. All, it seemed, had been badly shaken.

"I felt…I felt…something. A coldness. It was as if I was being suffocated," Folvar whispered. "It felt…like the hand of Noss, choking me, shaman."

Ruka nodded but shrugged it away, as if this were expected. In truth he was greatly disturbed. He did not know the rules of his Grove, nor indeed even of the world he could see with his eyes, or any other world beyond it. He did not know if the coldness had been the dead grasping at the living, or some force required to create the wall—if it had been necessary, or if it was over. He did not know the price of such power.

But there was no path but forward, and all greatness came with sacrifice. He ignored the fear and told Folvar and the others to keep preparing the granaries, to keep building ships, and to guard the coasts.

"I must go to the valley now, chief. But you may keep every warrior."

The young chief's concern showed plain. "The valley? Why, shaman? We've already won. We are safe at least for a season. We can hold this wall against ten times our number. Even if the chiefs agreed and banded together now, it would take months to build enough ladders to get over with enough force to dislodge us. The peninsula is ours."

"Yes," Ruka nodded, then turned to the stables. "We are safe. But the gods require more than safety. They demand strength, and courage." With that he walked along the edge of the town towards the stables, and perhaps his death. The few townsfolk at their labors watched him, staring like rabbits as a predator passed. He did not blame them.

If a man could make such miracles, blocking a whole army with his will, was he even a man anymore?

Ruka did not feel any different in his body. In his mind and Grove, if anything, he felt less in control, more like a son of chaos than ever, trapped in a whirlwind or a great wave and only playing his part as Valda claimed. And yet, what else could he do? He had one last role to play.

"We'll go together, old friend." Ruka put a sloped brow to Sula's cheek and used the Pyu word. The animal snorted but did not pull away—tolerance the closest he came to affection. Ruka smiled regardless. He considered it respect.

"Ah, mighty Sula. What a man you'd have made." He patted the muscled flank, then placed his saddle and tied the cinches. If anything, the warhorse had grown since his arrival—hale and healthy and thick as he ate lush grass and waited. In his time in Kormet, Sula had also sired several colts, and for the greatness of the future Ruka hoped he sired many more.

And what of me, it made him wonder. Would Ruka die childless? Would Beyla's line end with him?

Perhaps that was to be his punishment. If so, he would not complain. Perhaps in another thousand years a man like Ruka would come, or with the changes made already then in another generation the sons and daughters of ash would turn North on their own. Perhaps Ruka had already planted the seed of change, and even if Farahi betrayed and Ruka was destroyed, then a bright future may yet still come.

It put his mind at ease, and he mounted, riding from the stables South towards the mountain and the valley of law. The ride would be short along the Spiral, and it would give him time to rest and work in his Grove while his brother followed the well-kept gravel and stone.

Ahead and blocking the road he spotted a cluster of warriors at the edge of Kormet. For a moment he considered riding to the chief's hall, but recognized Aiden and his men armed and dressed for battle.

"We go with you, shaman," said the great chief of Husavik as Ruka approached.

Beside him stood Tahar, Birmun, Folvar and many of their warriors. Ruka nodded to them, and smiled.

Near every warrior carried a rune-blade, spear or axe. Most were Ruka's oldest retainers—men who had lived difficult lives, then been led into the valley and abandoned. They had survived as outlaws, re-taken Husavik, sailed to paradise, then captured the richest land in the Ascom. Had their deeds been recorded in the book of Galdra, already they would be heroes.

"You are all free men," Ruka said with a shrug, trying to control his voice. "You may go where you please."

The big chief grinned. Hoofbeats clopped through the square behind him as Dala, Egil, Juchi, and a host of Kormet's matrons rode to the warriors in traveling clothes.

"We come, too, shaman," said the newly minted matriarch, her smile radiant as an island dawn. "I would not miss the great Bukayag as he speaks before Alverel."

Ruka nodded in respect to her and the other women, then turned towards the valley. He did not wish the crowd to see the wetness in his eyes.

In a slow, comfortable pace, he rode towards the stones that had destroyed his life. For thousands of years Alverel had been the holiest patch of earth in the Ascom—the great mountain looming to the clouds, a frozen monument to the gods. It was where all great heroes had spoken, their words captured and re-told mostly by illiterate men and women for an age.

Ruka knew every word of every story. As a child he had played in the woods pretending to be Egil the Brave as he rallied five towns against the nomads; or Haki the Fearless as he promised to stop a mighty beast, then succeeded.

But Imler the Betrayer too had spoken at the valley. He had promised greatness and peace, delivered somehow with blood and iron. Ruka knew that perhaps the heroes did not exist at all—that they were simply stories told to create a vision of the world the men and women of ash could understand, emulate, or avoid.

Yet Tegrin could still guide a ship, shining like a lighthouse in the heavens. Runes etched by ancient hands could still be read by a long lost son. So whether real, or fiction, the stories in the book were rooted in truth. Imler's was a dark tale of a man who killed because he could—who took because he wanted, whose love of power was lodged deep in the breast of most honest creatures.

In this way Ruka knew Imler to be as real as a brother who hated all the world. And whatever that meant, whatever the truth or the meaning of things—Imler had spoken at the valley, too.

* * *

Ruka said little to his men on the road to Alverel. They had seen him perform 'miracles' many times now, of course, but the wall was clearly different. When he approached they hushed and lowered their heads, scrambling to give him room or to see if he was thirsty, staring as if awaiting some grand pronouncement. Ruka had never felt more alone.

In a way he envied their faith in him—their comfort in believing some grand design, some powerful prophet that gave them meaning and purpose. Ruka had only his hope that the past did not guarantee the future—that with enough effort and sacrifice, a man might change his world with his own two hands for the better.

In quiet moments he missed Hemi and his builders and drinking rum together at the end of a long, simple day of sweat and labor. He missed Arun and Kwal and all foreign men of competence who knew much of the world. And he missed Farahi—his patience, his cold, careful eyes. He even missed losing at Chahen.

"Something has pleased you, shaman? Do the gods speak?"

Ruka blinked and looked to Aiden's earnest expression at his side. He felt the genuine smile slip away.

"No, chief. I was imagining the new lawspeaker's face as I approach her stone."

Aiden grinned, and glanced at the men who had witnessed Ruka strangle the old lawspeaker. Soon all were laughing and wiping at their eyes, and for a moment, at least, Ruka felt like a man again instead of a prophet, even if it was at the expense of an old, dead woman.

But it didn't last. On the second day, as they neared the valley, Ruka rode alone at the front with his entourage behind. Only Dala dared push through to ride by his side, and for a moment he loved her for it.

"This should be interesting," she said, grinning. Together they looked out at the huge gouts of smoke rising from the crowded valley. The crowds had already grown and swelled beyond usual in the make-shift markets and the gathering place that had all but become a city. "Shall I speak to the Lawspeaker for you?" Dala's brow quirked in amusement, but it was clear she meant it.

Ruka felt the impulse to decline and take offense at her humor, but he knew this now as weakness grown from a life of scorn. He nodded respectfully.

"That would be useful. Thank you, priestess."

The sun lit the road and valley save for the great shadow of the mountain, and Ruka urged Sula forward. He followed the edge of Bray's river to the Western edge of the valley, the low hum of humanity cascading from stone cliffs, growing louder and louder until the party reached the first bridge. Fishermen and herders stopped to watch them.

Ruka had come in the full panoply of his guise. He had shaved his head and covered it in ash, tracing runes with his finger before wearing a thin helm of mostly iron bars. From his Grove he had brought a thin layer of mail covered in flat discs drawn with the name of every major god. Even Sula he had covered as if for war in steel—his proud neck shielded by spikes raised from dark, leather barding. *If I am to be feared*, he thought, *let it be for good reason.*

Many in the valley's outskirts fled before him as they saw.

He did not change his pace, and ignored the warriors mustering on the edges of the crowd, desperately donning armor in small packs. He marched his entourage deep into the valley before the chief protecting it this year had rallied enough men to try and oppose him.

These formed a shieldwall directly before the lawstone, and soon a hundred men stood haphazardly, others still running from every direction to join their ranks. Ruka had ordered his retainer's weapons sheathed unless they were attacked.

Of course the crowd did not know that, yet many came closer than reason would dictate, clinging still to their belief in law, and the illusion of its safety. Ruka had the urge for violence just to teach them sense.

Dala clucked her tongue, and rode forward. "Bukayag, son of Beyla, has come for words at the peak. Stand aside."

A short, but thick man at the front of the shieldwall gawked at Dala's shawl, then at Ruka, and at the pack of warriors covered in runic arms and armor. Ruka saw his chief's earring, but by the look of his soft arms he had earned his position with more words than deeds.

"Yes…mistress. Of course. Except…have you…," the poor fool's face contorted in perplexed anxiety, "have you come here *willingly?*"

Ruka almost smiled as Dala's eyes flared.

"I do not move anywhere *unwillingly*, chief. I am chosen as Nanot's Highest Servant by the holy Order of Galdra. I am *Matriarch*."

The little man's face paled. "Yes...yes, Mistre...Holy Mother. Yes of course." He wiped sweat from his face with the sleeve of his sword arm, then gestured to his confused men to collapse their shieldwall.

Ruka nodded to his ally, enjoying the display perhaps more than he should have. He rode on, feeling the eyes everywhere upon him, the mix of fear and loathing, interest and excitement.

At the foot of the mountain path, he told Dala to have the Lawspeaker and the valley-chief distribute the rarely used voting stones—flat rocks taken from the river, one side painted white. Each man and woman in the valley would be given one to hold up when the moment came. Paint meant yes, rock meant no.

Ruka waited for a time, but soon his feet were on the legendary path—a winding mixture of cut-stone steps and sloped mountain, gentle enough to climb without tools. Ascending it was not easy, which he expected was intentional. As he rose higher, with every rock avoided or flat surface used, he wondered if a great hero had done the same.

When he at last reached the peak, he looked down at the gathering of Alverel, which seemed closer than he expected after the hike. His ancestors had chosen this place because the mountain and the valley slopes would carry a voice further, naturally mimicking the echoing halls of the islander courts.

Ruka waited without stepping forth and watched the crowd. The richest matrons and even many priestesses had clustered near the front. Richly dressed warriors stood behind them, no doubt many of them chiefs or their trusted retainers. Perhaps five thousand people and maybe more packed the space around them.

To see such a crowd of the powerful from Orhus, and formed so quickly, gave Ruka at least some hope. No doubt they had all whispered of the wall, the new matriarch, the weapons, the ships and the capture of the fertile ring. They would know their world was changing around them, and that soon there must be words or blood to re-align it. Ruka felt a sense of pride, too, for Egil the Skald, who had gathered so many with so little time. It seemed words were not so meaningless after all.

At last Ruka stepped out to the edge to speak, and the crowd began to hush. He had practiced this many times, and intended to convince the wealthiest, most powerful citizens of ash to turn all their efforts to a single purpose—to prepare one day to abandon their homes, and push out to a sea they'd been told was endless, working for a day many years in the future on his word alone. Unlike the past, it could not be a rebel cry to desperate men. He could not play on the weakness of the trodden.

This time he intended awe, and wonder—the power and promise of the gods to take their children to paradise. But as he looked out at the crowd, he considered the lies he would utter and carry, and the many years he'd carry them, and he could not speak.

He realized if he lied to them now, if he tricked them into salvation, he would be no different than the Order. His new world would be built on a foundation of sand, and one day, it would crumble. In his heart Ruka believed no people requiring a lie to save them deserved to live at all.

He took off his helm, dropping it off the cliff, and spoke from his gut as Egil had taught him.

"You know who I am." He waited. "I came to impress you with trinkets, and deeds. Yet what have I accomplished? The land still freezes, still starves. No matter how many words I give, next year it will go on freezing, and starving." He paused and surveyed the crowd, and found them rapt. "So I offer one truth, and one choice, and the truth is this: North, beyond the sea, is land. This land is already filled with people, cities and kings, living under warm suns with good, black earth wider than the steppes. Some few men and women amongst you now have seen it, but they too offer only words. I have brought strange people and trinkets from this new world, but these things could be tricks. I do not ask you to believe. I offer only a choice.

"You can ignore me. This choice is easy. You can go on freezing and starving, telling your children stories of Bukayag the Bastard and his madness. Choose this and risk only the loss of the one chance in your lives to give those children something better. Do this, and I will do what my mother failed to do—I will hurl myself from this cliff, and die." He looked away from the crowd, the height of the cliff suddenly dizzying. His fear of it angered him, and hardened his tone. "Today my life is in your power, cousins, and mark it well, for it is the last time you will have it." He waited here for the muttering and whispers, but still the crowd watched, almost too surprised to speak.

"Or," he shrugged, "you can follow me into this new world. This choice will be hard. You will have to wait many years for the road is long, and in the meantime treat old enemies as allies. You will have to toil and sacrifice and one day face the unknown with courage. Some of you will die in the attempt. You will have to listen to a son of Noss, though what the future holds not even I can say. But whatever it is, choose to face it, and it belongs to you. I say no more."

With that he gestured to Dala, who after a pause did the same towards the Lawspeaker at her stone. Ruka stepped to the precipice.

The crowd came alive, murmuring and shouting for they had expected a speech that went on far longer. It was clear many were not ready to vote, no doubt wanting details of how, and when, and who would make decisions and what about the land and the harvest and a thousand other things.

Ruka let them whisper and argue. Some even yelled and pushed at his followers at the bottom of the rise, as if they meant to come up and lecture this upstart shaman properly. Ruka finally shouted over it all, voice harsher now, the power of it booming across the valley.

"*More words will not help you.* You can not bargain with winter, you can not negotiate with death. There is no comfort, no safety, nothing to be found in soothing voices. We are the children of the dead. When faced with sickness, with bitter cold, with deadly creatures bent on their destruction, our ancestors could have chosen to hide in their caves, but they did not. They went forth upon this earth and faced their doom. They made their choice. Now so must we. Choose."

Ruka looked below again to the rock that would be his death. Still he heard the arguments from the crowd, the muttering, even fighting, and he thought perhaps they would fail. He felt Bukayag's rage swelling inside him at the thought, struggling against such a foolish errand, wanting only to go down the way they'd come and begin a campaign of terror against such unworthy things.

"It is their failing," his brother hissed, "not ours. This is *weakness*, brother. We do not ask. We do not beg. We *demand*."

Ruka closed his eyes and breathed, thinking *no, not this time, this is not our decision.* Men were pack animals, and Ruka alone could not redeem the dead.

In his Grove, the corpses stood around him staring. They had come in his distraction, surrounding him, their eyes filled with regret, or hatred, love or sorrow. Boy-from-Alverel could not smile with his broken jaw, but Ruka could still see it in his eyes.

Redeem us, Ruka almost fell to his knees and cried out to the men and women of ash. *Make worthy all I have done, and all I must do. Redeem us, redeem me, I beg you. Please.*

He feared instead he would die here and now, and fail, for he had meant every word. If hell existed then that is where Ruka would go, but he would not complain. He had earned it with his deeds, and if the afterlife were fair, he would accept it. But he did not want Beyla's people to die.

As if some great serpent shedding its skin, the crowd before him swayed and steadied, almost in unison, shifting across the valley as men and women whispered and turned their faces.

Ruka blinked, trying to understand. He looked and saw the lawspeaker had raised her hand—this one just another old priestess, another creature of the Order that had doomed a little boy to misery and death. He expected nothing different from before, and almost laughed because he thought perhaps this time it truly was justice.

The old crone exposed her bony grip, and Ruka blinked as he realized it held the painted stone. He turned his gaze to see Dala had raised her first, as had all his retainers at the foot of the mountain.

The color of fresh snow swept from the lawstones through the matrons and the chiefs, back through the crowd, into the valley from East to West, until the yellowed grass beneath them had all but disappeared.

Ruka collapsed upon his knees on the precipice, and did not try to hide his tears. His body wracked with sobs two decades in the making, and he saw wetness even in the eyes of his followers as they watched him, perhaps surprised by the emotion the same as he.

The children of ash held their stones in the air far longer than was needed, trapped or perhaps enthralled by the moment as a son of Noss wept upon the peak of heroes. Ruka could not speak, though he wished to praise them—to tell them of the Vishan and how they honored them now with their courage.

Holding their white stones visible to the star-gods, his mother's people had spoken—the children of Tegrin had at last come of age, and with their first words, they had chosen life. They would live. And they deserved to.

You were right Beyla, Ruka thought, on his knees now in his Grove too before her image, his hands trembling as they touched her feet. *I am not a demon, I am not a mistake.*

Beyla had spared him, she had redeemed him, and now her people would live, so she had redeemed them, too. This she had done without blood, and without words. She had used only the love for her child, strong and demanding, without bitterness or hate. With only this, Beyla had saved them all.

65
Three months previous, in the palace of Sri Kon

"Brother? Fara-che? *Farahi*? Roa take me, leave your daydreaming for one bloody moment and answer me!"

Farahi blinked, and forced himself away from visions of the future. He sat in one of the royal wing's dining rooms in a simple chair across from his sister. The servants had been sent away. His food remained untouched on his plate.

"Brother my spies tell me you've ordered every royal family in the isles to attend your court." Kikay looked more perturbed than usual. "That you did this days ago. And yet, you and I have sat together and eaten our meals, just like this, and you have not breathed a word."

Farahi blinked again and frowned. He had been close to the end of a useful thread. "I don't discuss every little detail with you, sister."

She stared at him as she cut her pork with far more effort than required. They'd been having this same conversation in various forms since Hali died, but this was the most important thing he had denied her.

"What are you planning, and why aren't you telling me? I only mean to help you, to protect you."

"I don't need your help in this, sister, nor your protection."

"As you didn't need it when they almost gut you in father's chair?" She sliced her pork in half. "When you almost died retching in my arms? Have you forgotten that, brother?"

"No," he said, half-closing his eyes again to search for the end of the vision. He heard her knife clatter.

"No?" She jerked dramatically. "No. Just 'no'." She sneered. "Father was right, you can be so cold, so closed to the world. I feel like I'm speaking to a stone."

He sighed, thinking *here we go*.

"Do you know what Father called you privately, brother? Farahi the Fish. Mother said he could never make you laugh. He'd make faces and strange voices and you'd just stare at him with those eyes, as if judging him. And then you grew older and you never changed, always watching, always judging. 'No joy in life' he said. 'No love in him.' Maybe I just felt sorry for you, maybe that's why I paid so much attention. But now I know it's true. After everything I've done, still you can shut me out like I'm nothing."

Farahi let his sister spend her rage. To use their father as a weapon meant she was out of other options and desperate, which gave him no pleasure. In truth he had wanted to tell her all along. He missed her advice, and support. But he couldn't trust what she might do.

Kikay would never accept the future he was choosing. She hated Ruka, and so he could never tell her his true goal. This knowledge made him feel more lonely than he had ever been, for despite her flaws, Kikay was the only person in the world Farahi trusted besides Hali—the only kin he had besides his children. As a boy she had been the color in his gray, cautious world, the spark of life he watched in awe and sometimes shared in.

It was why he had stopped her from getting on the boat with father those years ago, and saved her life. Early on he had seen the possibility of a future without her, and warned her of every danger out of habit.

Since that day she had believed somehow he knew what would happen to the rest of their family. She did not speak it, but he knew she suspected his involvement—that perhaps he had given word to his father's enemies. She had believed the very worst of him, the same rumor spread by common men—that all along, even as a boy, he had wanted to be king, and was a kinslayer.

Had he truly known he would have tried to stop it. As a child his visions had been confusing and this was long before Ando's help to focus them. He had seen only a future without the sister he loved, and thought perhaps it was the sea that claimed her and her alone. He had not feared for his entire family.

Farahi finished his pork and wiped his face with a napkin, then pulled back his chair. Long ago, with their feet dangling in the Lancona, Ando had told him: *'To be a king is to be alone'*.

"You will know what I've done as I present it in court, sister. One day I will tell you why. Perhaps in the meantime you'll consider trust is not a river and does not flow one way. Perhaps you'll try to remember I am king, and give me at least the benefit of the doubt."

He rose as she clattered her fork across the room. He knew her rages could be deadly but decided this time she would eventually calm. And if not, at least he had Eka.

He stepped out into the morning sun knowing so many important threads depended on the result of this single day. Sometimes, he thought, it would be easier not to know. Easier to live like other men, going through life without the constant fear of misstep, afraid that if only he had thought longer and more carefully the future might have been saved.

All his life he had been watching, preparing, and waiting. But not today.

He closed his fists and cleared his mind as Ando taught him. For many years he had acted the part and made few errors and stayed alive. Now came the end of that caution. Now came choice and deed and a great risk in his private game of Chahen. Now he would choose a future for his people.

* * *

"Tell me again." Farahi stood outside the entrance to his court next to his newly appointed 'speaker'—a sebu actor he'd picked from a good family.

His father never would have used such a man. He had been a loud, gregarious speaker who loved playing host and ringmaster, and took every opportunity. But Farahi had thought he looked like a fool—self-aggrandizing and narcissistic. And most importantly, not threatening.

Farahi had always thought a king's voice should be uncomfortable. It should be like violence—rare, shocking, and ultimately, decisive. Let the lesser men of state prattle and charm.

The guests had all arrived now—many just representatives and not the royal families themselves. Save for the Molbog, his allies had come, their lesser families as well. The turn-out was not as impressive as he hoped, but far better than he feared.

"I am not to announce you," the speaker repeated. He looked nervous, but confident. "I will stand at the dais while the royal family seats, then I will invite the priests to perform their ritual. I will not smile, and I will say nothing to the guests."

Farahi nodded, and gestured inside, and the speaker collected his bearings and entered the courtroom to take his place.

Kikay and Farahi's wives and children would enter through the usual door and take their places next. Farahi would enter alone through the furthest gate.

For the first time in public he had not worn the royal wrapping-silks of his station, but rather a simpler, thinner silk dyed almost black. He wore a silver circlet rather than the Alaku crown, and removed all rings or jewels, as well as the amulet around his neck. He did not wish to appear in any way to compete with the others, because he did not intend to. After today, he would be beyond these things.

He put his forehead against the cool stone wall and breathed. Much of what had to be done had already been done. The game had begun, the future hurtling forwards faster than any man could plan. Farahi had designed it.

This was the moment all his friends, enemies, everyone in the isles, and soon the coastal nations and beyond would see his opening gambit. Despite his visions and many predictions, he could not truly know how they would react.

Finally he stood tall and walked with his hands behind him. He had chosen hard leather shoes with a metal layer under the heel, so his steps would clack through the arch and all along the path to the dais. At his slow, clicking steps the court began to notice and quiet. By the time he had crossed the halfway point, he walked in silence.

He climbed the steps with great care, then looked out at the court as if he'd only just noticed they existed. He sat in his new throne—a simple, metal chair with a thin cushion. He sat erect with his arms and legs spread at ease, and nodded to the speaker, who gestured to the priests.

The Alhunan priests from Sri Kon's temple lit their incense sticks and waved their chimes, and the Batonian monks began their throat-chant. Both rituals would be familiar to the guests—though something they only experienced at temple. The priests placed their bronze statue of the first Alhuna—the first benevolent spirit, who had helped protect men from the gods, and a sort of stand-in for the Enlightened.

At last the sweating priests turned to the attendees just as they did at temple. The speaker asked if the families rejected violence—they did. If they rejected lies—they did. If they embraced the central path that connected all things, and believed that only the race of men could protect the world from destruction. They did.

"Then with courage, and humility," said the speaker, "let us seek the wisdom of the Enlightened."

"*Alhun*," spoke the court rotely, though with an awkward pause and not in unison. From the rear of the pack of monks stood an old master holding a purple cloak—the Cloak of the Traveler—though, of course not the original. This was a ceremonial artifact said to be worn by the Enlightened when he first arrived in the isles, and was only ever put on display. Farahi stood and bowed his head, and with proper solemnity accepted the cloak around his shoulders.

The monks and priests took their places, and Farahi returned to his seat to observe a silent, staring crowd.

By their expressions, it seemed they had no idea what to make of this. No king had ever worn the cloak. It had always represented a link to the divine, and to the spirit world—to the destructive power of the gods themselves. Pyu rulers did not associate themselves with the priests save to pay their respects, and ask for protection, because no man dared tempt the gods by claiming influence beyond the realm of men. Many would think doing so was the very height of hubris, and that doing so was to invite disaster.

"The king thanks you for your attendance," said the speaker, his voice well-controlled, his bearing strong. "He has asked you here for two momentous reasons. The first, to receive a copy of new laws which will affect all islands. And the second, to hold an important vote." Here he bowed, and withdrew with a hand extended.

Farahi waited, and did not rise. He watched the royals in attendance bristle at the word 'laws'.

"You will all understand," he said at last, keeping his voice low enough the audience would strain to hear, "that pirate raids have become as common as raindrops, both on land and sea."

Already many in the crowd shifted. 'Pirate raids' was now all but short-hand for 'nobles making quiet war on their neighbors' while the great kings quarreled and didn't stop it.

"Trade in the isles suffers," Farahi continued. "More importantly, trade with our coastal neighbors suffers. This can not be allowed to continue. I have therefore drafted several laws of the sea to return our waters to order."

He gestured to the Speaker, and thirty servants entered with stacks of scrolls to be distributed to every attendee. Farahi waited as they received them, knowing they would think it all meaningless and no one would obey them anyway. He imagined himself a stone jutting from the waves, and wondered which wave would crash first.

"With all due respect." Tama of the Keala—King Molbog's cousin and a powerful Orang Kaya from the Eastern islands—stood. When he spoke he looked more to the gathering than at Farahi. "We are not your vassals. Halin's ships protect us. And while we appreciate your concern for trade and peace, we are not subject to your laws."

This was, of course, true. Nearly every island had its own system of laws and governance and allies. None of the islands owed the Alakus official loyalty and never had. For a hundred years all recognized their ascendance and obeyed them informally, but not always. Farahi did not so much as blink.

"It is a shame King Molbog was unable to attend. How his island is ruled or indeed yours is none of my concern."

Tama's mouth quirked in a sly smile, and again he spoke more to the court than to Farahi. "Oh I'm sure he *deeply* regrets his absence, great king. But may I ask, if you do not mean to apply your laws to his island, why he *should* regret it?"

Many in the crowd snickered. Farahi waited until long after it ended.

"The laws before you are *sea* laws, Tama, and will now apply to every sea that bears my name. Halin is surrounded by those seas, as are the Eastern islands. But have no fear, you need not read that entire document, these laws are quite simple." Farahi finally raised his voice. "Piracy is now punishable by death. To give safe harbor to pirates is now punishable by death. To purchase supplies or goods knowingly from pirates is now punishable by death." The crowd was already murmuring and rising but Farahi kept speaking. "Every merchant, every city, and every king who uses an Alaku sea will now pay a sea-tax to help keep these laws enforced."

Even Farahi's allies looked tinged with red as the Orang-Kaya and petty lords and ladies looked to one another in astonishment, or perhaps offence. Tama's face twisted.

"Perhaps we should unburden the Alaku family from such responsibility." No one quite dared to cheer this on, but it received a few grunts. "I expect my cousin will be happy to protect our seas without any 'tax' on his neighbors. But thank you for the offer, great king."

Farahi smiled now, and he could see it unnerved his enemy. He gestured at the speaker, who waved at the far entrance to the court.

Eka entered alone and in the robes of a priest, which Farahi had to admit suited him best. Before him, balanced on a large, silver tray, he carried the severed, slightly eaten, decomposing head of King Trung.

He walked so smoothly and calmly, Farahi reminded himself the man was a master of the Ching. With the long fabric dangling to the floor, he almost drifted more than walked, hovering down the aisle until he ascended the dais and placed the tray on one of several small, round tables.

The crowd stared, and Farahi spoke into the silence with a tone of barely held contempt.

"It saddens me to inform you, that King Trung is unable to protect anything, because King Trung is dead."

Tama stared along with everyone else, all eyes roaming the gruesome scene and no doubt trying to determine if it was real. Farahi stopped smiling.

"Crown-Prince Trung is also dead. And Prince Turi. And Prince Rata." He paused, and raised his brow. "Alas, a man could sail for many days in any direction, and he would not find a single person bearing the name Trung. It seems even the women are gone."

Tama blinked, looking again and again at Trung's head, his face sweating as the crowd watched him, as if hoping he would see that it wasn't truly his ally and some kind of trick.

"You've attacked a peaceful city?" he whispered, then raised his voice. "You've slaughtered women and children? In the last few days?"

Farahi bristled. "I did not say *I* killed them. But then if I did there would be no laws forbidding it, would there? In any case you will have all seen Sri Kon's navy has not left her port, and has fought no battles."

Farahi had made sure of that. Everyone in attendance had been invited to arrive at his royal port, which currently housed his entire navy—complete, and freshly maintained, without even a speck of damage.

The strangeness and the brutality of the head was still doing its work, and the court officials were dabbing at sweat and looking at exits, no doubt growing concerned how all of this would end. Trung had been the second most powerful man in the isles. His family lineage was as old as Pyu.

"We all know Trung was a man of unwholesome tastes," Farahi said with a shrug. "He loved violence, and ignored the Way. The temple of Halin is crumbling and corrupt. If people accept such behavior from their king, surely they invite calamity. We must be wiser, my friends. We must be pious, and civil. We must obey the laws."

Tama remained on his feet. "If you didn't kill him," he said without a shred of belief, "how *exactly* do you have his head? Did it fall from the sky, my lord?"

Farahi sighed as if repentant. "I'm embarrassed to admit. But you all know King Trung and I have been having our differences. In a low moment of frustration, I freely admit I whispered into the darkness, and once asked the spirits for Trung's head. I did not mean this literally, you understand, and on reflection regretted it at once. But words are important, oh yes, and intentions. One day, while eating my breakfast and playing with my children, here it arrives. I feel responsible. I have already begun to atone as the priests command."

Throughout this speech Tana looked increasingly disgusted. He looked at the attendants around him, spewing air and perhaps spittle. "You asked the *spirits*? Spirits brought you the head of a king? You expect us to listen…"

"Yes." Farahi's voice snapped short and harsh and brought silence. "And spirits left Halin in flames, Tana, which I expect you will be hearing reports of very soon. Speak to the survivors. Speak to the guards. They will tell you what they saw. Some have already brought me word from Halin's navy. The admirals too seek atonement for their previous ways, their *lawlessness*. They wish peace with Sri Kon on behalf of whichever new family is chosen to rule them. Of course I accepted. It seems Halin's treasury was also emptied, so I have offered to maintain Halin's fleet, and pay her sailors. I will continue do so until order is established."

At this, even Molbog's cousin was struck dumb. To lie about such a thing would make Farahi a fool, and whatever the men in this room thought of him, they did not think him a fool. They would think it must therefore be true.

That Farahi could afford it would be terrifying enough. That it had been agreed to and already done—that the Alakus could now command the second greatest navy in the isles to at the very least remain idle, and perhaps even fight for them, made Sri Kon untouchable.

And now the killing stroke.

Farahi looked one of his few remaining public enemies in the eye. "I have also informed our great partner, Kapule of Nong Ming Tong, that no more pirates would interfere with his grain ships on my seas. To give him comfort, I have promised to guarantee all his shipments from my treasury. He will therefore no longer be trading rice with the other islands. But have no fear, you may purchase through Sri Kon, and I will ensure my merchants are fair. I will take a modest fee, of course, but as piracy ends, you will see prices will still go down."

At this pronouncement, the court no longer murmured or complained, for this was not politics as usual. If what Farahi said was true, the major source of conflict and opportunity in the seas was gone. Coastal piracy was a great source of island income, but he had promised death to anyone who tried. He had forced every island to rely on him for food, which they required every year, and he had killed his greatest enemy, all in the space of an afternoon.

Farahi decided it was time to make his exit. *A king's words should be violent, not torturous.* He rose, and at this signal the speaker smiled at the crowd and cleared his throat.

"The king thanks you all for coming, friends and allies. He has prepared a feast in your honor. He looks forward to seeing you and all the other members of the royal families next gathering of the court, which will be taking place more frequently in the next several years."

Farahi had already stepped from the dais. He smiled at the thought of the final course of the feast—a very specific type of fish heads, found only near Halin.

"You said there would be a vote," Tana called, a bit less fire in his voice, perhaps, if no less hatred. "I must return to my family immediately, so what is it."

Farahi stopped and turned with a tap of his metal soles, and smiled politely.

"I give you a great responsibility, my lord. Please lead the discussion with my blessing. You must decide whether we meet now for court at Matohi, or some other time of the month going forward. Whatever you choose will be acceptable, but please consider everyone's convenience."

With this he signaled the speaker to bring the first course and walked from the hall, already thinking on the future and relying on the silent Eka to watch for danger. The ex-monk had already begun to hire his own network from pirates—pirates that would soon need other work. He had a devious mind, and no compunction with getting his own hands dirty. Farahi could not have been more pleased.

Next he would deal with the Molbog, perhaps surrounding their ports and sinking a few ships to make his point. Then a few of his own more disloyal lords needed to be tamed, because he was positive at least Lord Sanhera was actively against him, and had been the third 'king' in the so-called 'Three-kings'.

He had little fear, however, at least in the short term. The 'war' of the isles was over before it began. Word would spread of Trung's death like wildfire, and though no one would know what had happened or how, they would assume Farahi did it. They would hate him more than ever but he had learned he could not overcome this with reason or good governance, so he would rule with harsh laws, and fear.

Soon he would accept a ward from King Kapule to seal their bargain, which was expected in such an important agreement. He would take a young, and meaningless daughter to signal his trust, perhaps a girl Kale's age. He would ask Kikay to be responsible for her because she had never had children and perhaps it would help temper her.

Farahi found he could not even look at Kale without thinking of Hali. A single glance sometimes reignited the dwindling love still fighting for life in his chest. Unfortunately, he could not afford it. He had given the boy siblings, now he would give him a play-mate and an aunt, and later the best tutors in the world. It was not a replacement for a father's love, he knew, and unfair, but such was life.

He knew he must be quick and focused now, and turn his attention South. Ruka had asked for supplies come spring, and the timing would be difficult. He would have to push Kapule for large shipments early, then operate with as much secrecy as possible, perhaps letting Kwal lead the ships with skeleton crews and swear all to secrecy. Eka would ensure they didn't talk too much.

Farahi followed the threads of his venture South as best he could as he walked through his halls, the silent Eka drifting beside him. There were many possibilities of disaster, including storms, betrayal, even the failure of Ruka before Farahi's ships ever arrived.

Far beyond this and overlaying all were the oppressive strands of the Naranian empire, covering all as if unstoppable, heavy as iron chains, no further than fifteen years away. There was so much to do. Only a powerful people united and ready could resist the empire.

Still, Farahi would try. And at least now he was not alone.

He wondered where Ruka was and what he was doing. The image of the man's threads sprouted before him, terrifying and radiant, the sea shining with a rising dawn.

No, Farahi was not alone. Incredibly, defying all the many threads of treachery and doom, now he had Ruka. And in the time he had, in the decade and a half or more before disaster, Farahi would wrest control of his rebellious islands, then stand between two threads and try to balance one against the other. Though Hali was dead and the greatest hope of a pure future gone— if he managed it, perhaps, his people would survive.

66

Ruka stood on the beach of Kormet as Altan fell into his daughter's arms. The farmer had returned from the peninsula, his face slick with tears the moment he'd seen them from his boat. Ruka left them to their reunion, but later his retainer had come to him and Egil in Folvar's hall

"Things are progressing as planned," Altan spoke in private, "though the farmers fear what will happen come harvest." He shook his head and shrugged. "We should use more of the bloody North for farmland, shaman. Most of Orhus is on good, rich soil, and so are some of the other towns and villages. The lines were drawn by city folk who knew nothing."

Ruka nodded and had thought the same. "Then we will move them. And I've been thinking we will split Bray's river. Two, maybe even three forks should be sustainable. That should help with irrigation and several other things."

He grinned as both the skald and farmer's mouths gaped. "All is possible now." Ruka looked to the hearthfire, eyes and mind far away as he worked in his Grove. "What we must do will take many years. Maybe even a whole new generation of ash that can sail, read and write, and fight like soldiers. We're going to build pipes beneath the earth," he almost whispered, "vast works reaching every house, so we can move water further South without it freezing, and dispose of waste in one of the riverforks. We're going to hunt whales further out to sea. We'll build better, warmer houses with clean beds, and show our people ways to keep their teeth, and clean their water, and prepare their food."

The bewildered men said nothing, until the Midlander frowned. "What are 'pipes'?"

Ruka blinked, and laughed. "Nevermind. One day at a time. We will re-build this place, cousins, even as we prepare to go to new lands. You will see."

And he meant it. Alverel had changed everything. Progress could happen now as fast as men could build, supply, and communicate their efforts, and already families were coming from all over the Ascom for work. It was a good problem to have, but the logistics were a nightmare.

Ruka's shipbuilders needed more lumber, and different kinds of lumber. He sent men to the smaller but closer Western forest to cut as many as required, knowing he would have to pay the local chiefs. Kormet's builders needed nails for ships, bins, and more houses for all the new matrons. They needed more tools, more food, more water, more cloth for sails. More *everything*.

Each night Ruka stood on the coast and summoned from his Grove, but even so it was not enough. He sent requests to Dala for supplies from Orhus and across the Ascom, the quantities boggling the minds of his Arbmen messengers, which Dala had given him full authority to direct.

Some would ask again or for clarification, and Ruka would patiently repeat himself. He paid in silver, hide, or furs, lumber and stone, iron and tin, all of it from his Grove. He managed, but barely.

A season passed in steady toil.

Ruka gained thousands of men, many who came with their chiefs, others on their own or with families and all their supplies loaded into wagons. He began the process of moving near-by towns and villages, despite the anger and confusion it caused.

Dala had sent him a priestess to help him with the matrons—a woman named Amira she said could be trusted. So far this seemed the case. Whatever insane request he put to her, the priestess nodded and said she would convince the First Mothers and inform the Order.

The new matriarch herself was busy in Orhus. For every mad change Ruka planned, she would have to soothe rich matrons and priestesses and convince them to part with supplies or alter their trade routes and habits to support the 'dream of paradise'. She and Ruka exchanged messages almost daily, and he had begun to hear her voice even in her written words. When he told her the people of ash would need more sons and daughters to confront the larger world, her answer had been astounding.

"I am ordering every Galdric daughter below the rank of High Priestess to take a mate, shaman, and creating new fertility festivals. If you can feed us, I will stress the duty of every matron to bear children. Please inform your men."

He'd laughed out loud when he read it, thinking her as crazy as he and a worthy ally indeed. He'd expected something akin to rebellion from this, but soon enough, women of the Order came to the swelling town of Kormet to pick mates and houses and become something like matrons—just as the women from Pyu had already started.

Dala had also offered many outcasts and rebels pardons, including, of course, Aiden of Husavik, and all of Ruka's followers. She had permitted the 'nightmen' of Orhus to work in the day, and to carry weapons like any other man to prove their point. She had even 'encouraged' older priestesses to take them as mates.

Of course, there were problems. As Southerners, Midlanders and Northerners mixed, tensions rose, duels and brawls happening regularly. Chiefs who had lost half or more of their followers began to wonder exactly what they were chief of, and if the old territories even mattered. Southern towns were abandoned. Thievery was rampant and forced Ruka to protect supplies and waste men who might be more useful. Builders in the North did not understand their work, and Folvar reported injury after injury in all the moving and re-building, often with inexperienced men.

Ruka's whalers and all the Northern fishermen were pressed harder and harder to provide for so many new mouths, and even so there was never enough food. Animals were being slaughtered faster than could be sustained, and Ruka tried not to consider what would happen if Farahi did not come in the spring.

None of Ruka's followers left him, save for Altan, who returned to his farm with his daughters, and Birmun who returned to Orhus. Despite Ruka's dismissal, Egil stayed, moving into a home in Kormet with Ivar, and Juchi, who soon gave birth to their twins.

Aiden sent many of his men home to Husavik, but stayed by Ruka's side, rune-sword held as ever, hand ready for violence. Tahar took a Pyu mate, a house, and a well-earned rest. Eshen brought his matron from Husavik, but otherwise stayed as Ruka's vigilant shadow.

Ruka himself remained ever-busy. On Sula's back he traveled up and down the length of the Ascom, seeking to improve the salt and iron mines, the lumber camps, and the many forges and workings of the textiles made in Orhus. He chose ground for changes to the river and farmlands, areas to plant new trees, and hoped one day to ride to the steppes to make allies of the horse-tribes, and perhaps even the far-South.

The Ascom weathered a fall and then a winter with no harvest from the fertile ring. They slaughtered animals, stretched the crops from the Midlands to the brink, and relied on fishing more than ever. They survived.

Ruka counted every day. By Pyu reckoning he marked the moon by Matohis, trying to put the fear from his mind that all would end in ruin if not for one foreign king. His huge, empty bins stood ready in Kormet, soon to be either a sign of the great future of plenty ahead, or a sad, useless landmark—testament to a broken hope, and the beginning of another war over grain.

Ruka returned to Kormet the day before spring.

More than ever he was treated as some kind of prophet, or demi-god, avoided with panicked respect by most except his retainers. His wall had become a religious artifact, attracting pilgrims from Orhus all the way to the South, travelers coming to leave trinkets or scratch runes on the stone, or beg the gods for favors. Ruka only regretted the land it had made useless.

Every day he helped his builders or shipmakers, but in the mornings he stood on the beach and watched the horizon, eyes tricking him with every glint of light or dot of ocean spray until he resigned to his work.

The stores of food ran lower daily. If Farahi failed, or betrayed, no words of comfort or promise would hold back the madness of starvation that followed. Not even Dala could stop the matrons and great chiefs from doing what they had to feed their children and themselves. War would be inevitable, and it would soak the children of ash in blood.

Spring progressed. Warmth returned to the soil, flocks of birds coming from the North to whine at fishermen and mate on the beach. Ruka now sailed with the whalers trying to help and find new sources. They moved out further and further, took more risks and lost more men. Soon he forced himself to consider what to do without Farahi—thinking perhaps they could hunt the horse herds of the steppes, though he knew it would mean war and death for the tribes who lived there. Instead he chose a kind of faith, and waited.

He worked every moment of every day—with whalers in the light, and alone building houses in the dark. Once a week a collapsed to his furs in Folvar's hall to rest his body. But even so, he worked in his Grove. Or at least he tried.

In the final days of spring, Ruka was jerked awake by panicked footsteps, and a young man's shouts. He had only vague memories of a nightmare, starving to death on a deserted island.

"Shaman!" Folvar burst into the hall panting. He looked terrified. "Shaman. From the sea. There are *warships*. Come quickly."

Ruka wiped the sleep from his eyes and bolted after his ally, feeling only a lingering sense of dread. He ran beside Folvar to the beach, fearing some deep and awful treachery—some unforeseen Chahen move that would disrupt his careful strategy and end their game. But he could not understand why.

What could Farahi gain by making war on the Ascom? Was it simply to destroy a nascent threat? Or could it be some other island king who had learned of the secret? In a kind of panic, he realized: *perhaps it is Kikay.*

He splashed into the shallow water of the beach, squinting as he looked out to sea. His eyes were not as good as Folvar's in the light, but soon he saw the blue and silver flags of the Alakus, huge sails curved in the wind. They were clustered together, and as they came Ruka saw more, and more.

He almost choked as he saw them more clearly, and realized the truth. He put a hand to Folvar's shoulder. "Those are not warships," he said, knowing the man had seen the size and assumed. Ruka felt the smile coming and did not fight it. "In the new world, cousin, those are transports."

He waited and watched the cluster as a single ship broke and sailed to the coast, releasing an even smaller vessel to come ashore.

Ruka watched the young, beardless, square-jawed man at the helm, his face impassive and perhaps impatient.

"Loa, sir." Captain Kwal stepped onto the dark sand of the Ascom for the second time. Several rowers behind him watched the shore and the foreigners with ill-concealed amazement. Kwal held a scroll in his hand, which he waved as he spoke.

"This contains the full contents aboard my fifty ships. Beyond considerable rice and salted pork, there is wheat-seed, fennel, mustard...," he shrugged in disinterest, "I know nothing of farming, sir, but Farahi's man said there is a mixture of crops that might survive in colder weather and provided details. I have also brought the king's Chief Builder, and some of his men. My lord says they are to serve you until next spring when we return with more supplies. I am told you can perhaps provide us with some silver, and iron. But he says this year whatever you can give will be adequate, though I will also need fresh water. Next year we will expect more in trade, and for assistance in war if he calls, but he says, and I quote 'I don't expect to'."

Ruka met the mostly blank expression of the man who had just brought an entire people life, and salvation. He took the scroll and inspected it for a moment, then laughed and stepped forward, lifting the surprised islander in his arms. Kwal eventually grinned, and returned the squeeze.

"You stink like rum," Ruka said, face buried in the man's shoulder, unable to stop the full-toothed smile.

Kwal sniffed. "I'm a marine, sir. We all stink like rum."

Ruka laughed and set him down, lost for words as he looked at the fleet of transports. He tried and failed to imagine the cost, the effort, the absolute impossibility of what Farahi had done.

"I assume I may tell my lord you accept his trade and friendship?" Kwal lifted a brow, as if there were some chance of rejection.

Ruka bowed as low as his pride would allow. "You may tell your lord he has made an eternal ally. Assure him we will make the Alakus ever more famous for silver. And may his enemies tremble in fear."

Kwal smiled politely and turned towards his boat. "We'll begin unloading, sir. But I have few crew. Yours will need to do most of the work."

Ruka nodded absently, flooded now with a relief so great he could hardly stand. His hands trembled and with the sensation he felt his brother fading, as if preparing for a long sleep like the plants and beasts, perhaps knowing he would not be needed. Ruka thought it wise, for he had another brother now, a brother of the mind across the sea. Farahi had come.

The men of ash would at last have time, and support. They would rebuild their frozen lands, and Ruka would find ways to stop the sickness and disease that spread between them and their new allies. He would forget the past and the old hatreds that could form with a room of runes and the legacy of the Vishan. One day he would give the full history to his people, but it could wait. Farahi had come.

Ascomi and islander would work together in peace, and prepare for the future Farahi had seen. If he was right, it would not be easy. They would mix their fates and fortunes as perhaps they had been mixed since the day the Enlightened came. But the past need not decide the future. One day Ruka's and Farahi's people would face the larger world together, and preserve the legacy of their ancestors.

He looked to the birds circling over the islanders' ships—the same birds that had once led an outcast North, and smiled. *Welcome home, clever cousins*, he thought, *welcome home.*

67

A cold, dark place. 15 years later. The present.

Kale woke to a crackling fire, and a deep, sonorous hum. Above him he saw carved beams holding a painted, wooden roof. The planks serving as walls had been decorated with many drawings of animals, most strange and unfamiliar, but all made with incredible detail and skill. Many shelves held wooden figurines, also of real or imaginary beasts, so intricate and perfect they looked alive.

"The sleeper wakes."

Kale blinked and jerked to his elbows. He lay in a bed twice his size, covered in what looked like thick, dark fur. His head pulsed in agony and he could see cloth bandage covered parts of his exposed torso. The giant with bright eyes sat next to a fire stirring an iron pot.

"I have covered your wounds in ointment, and bandaged them. I have also given you a tincture to help with the pain." He pointed at the pot. "This is mostly rabbit, and potatoes. But I have many Pyu spices now and attempted to make something that will taste familiar to an Alaku prince. That is, if you are hungry."

Kale blinked. His own family name formed in his mind as the giant spoke it.

"You know who I am?"

At his words, the giant jerked and spilled some of his soup. He stared until his eyes grew watery.

"You can speak. I...I had thought you had, but wasn't sure. I didn't think you were dead, but...you can speak. Yes I know who you are."

Kale found the man or creature's reaction strange, but lodged in the far stranger reality of his surroundings he paid little attention. "Where am I? And who are you?"

The giant stirred his pot, and sighed. "Those are complicated questions. My name is Ruka." He squinted and gazed around the house. "Once I believed this place a child's fantasy, a harmless day-dream to house a troubled mind. But it is more. Like the other world you know it is governed by rules I don't truly understand. How you have come here, even how I created it, I am not certain."

He dished a ladle full of soup into a wooden bowl and set it on a nearby table. "Eat," he said, but made no attempt to move it closer.

Kale had to rise to get it. He groaned and pulled off his furs, setting his feet firmly on the floor. He decided he must still be dreaming, or unconscious, or hallucinating, though he didn't remember ever doing so this vividly. It was a very strange dream. His vision blurred but he stood steadily enough and held out his arms to keep his balance.

'Ruka' watched him and nodded as if pleased, but still made no move to interfere.

Kale thought eating imaginary food no more unusual than anything else in this dream, so he sat at the sturdy table and spooned dream-soup to his lips.

He realized he was famished. He leaned forward to gorge as if he were back in the navy, burning the roof of his mouth but beyond caring. His host watched and said nothing, and Kale's world became only chewing and filling his stomach until the bowl emptied and he took a breath and leaned back in his chair.

"Almost like coconut soup," he said as he realized, and the strange dream-creature smiled. Kale found himself staring at his host's ugliness—made worse by the beauty of the small, but comfortable home.

"So bizarre," he said.

"What is, prince?"

"That I'd imagine such a frightening man as you, and all the details here. I've no memory of anything. Yet I expect I'll soon wake in my bed in the palace."

'Ruka' blinked and his eyes sparkled in the firelight. His grin faded, and despite knowing he was really just talking to himself, Kale felt a bit embarrassed at his choice of words.

"Perhaps you would like to use those legs, and have a tour."

Kale shrugged, then nodded politely. They rose together and Kale wobbled a moment before steadying. The giant watched him but made no move to support. Instead he walked to the door and opened it, his eyes narrowing slightly at a squeak from one of the hinges.

"Come, island prince. See what else your sleeping mind has made."

Kale nodded in thanks as he passed through the held-open door, stepping out into lush, green grass. The air struck him—cool, and dry, like a palace cellar, and a fog sat heavy over a world of colorful and varied plants. Rows of vegetables separated and labeled with wooden stakes ran all around the multi-leveled house. Beyond them built in rings were huge, foreign trees, mixed with palms and maybe figs and mangoes in a pattern so thick they blocked sight. The canopy stretched up into the fog and Kale couldn't see the sky, save for perhaps a few bright spots of stars.

He looked at his host, who had closed his eyes. As he did, a chanting music drifted from the heavens. Kale listened and realized it was Pyu and perhaps Batonian monks, their voices mixed with a deep, throaty hum, and the quiet strumming of some instrument with strings. The sound was slow, and sad, but peaceful. It rose and fell as Kale watched the giant sway to the sound as if in rapture. He opened his eyes again.

"This way, young Alaku." The giant moved onwards, breathing the air as if he too had just come to this place anew, and Kale followed in fascination.

They walked through an elaborate garden of bushes and flowers and fountains. The flowers all seemed in full bloom, reds and blues and violets built as if in paths to guide the way over flat, smooth stones laid perfectly together.

"It's beautiful," Kale whispered, because it was, and the giant smiled.

"It is for my mother. The house as well, the garden, and other things." He pointed to a clearing, and Kale's eyes widened. In the center stood the most life-like, perfect sculpture he had ever seen. A woman carved from stone emerged from the garden's core, one hand raised to the heavens, the other over a small, maybe pregnant bump on her belly. Even the lines in her face were visible, her long hair grooved with tiny strands—every piece of the stone rounded or etched or carved until it seemed all but alive.

"You must have loved her very much," Kale managed, overwhelmed at the sight. "I never knew my mother. She died when I was young."

His host glanced at him, then looked away as if embarrassed. He turned and led down one of the many paths away from the clearing, and they walked in silence for a time. Kale felt a little as he had on Bato—a peaceful sort of escape from life, too perfect to let simple worries intrude.

The giant turned to him abruptly and frowned. "I do not deceive in this place. I knew your mother, Kale. I tried to save her, and failed. The poison had gone too deep. I am sorry."

The trance of the music and the garden broke. Kale met his host's strange eyes. "My mother died of illness. And what do you mean you tried to save her?"

The giant looked confused first, then annoyed. "I assure you she died of poison. Your father's second wife mixed it in her tea. Hali died in the evening, beneath a half but bright moon, and it broke your father's heart."

Kale stared, unsure what to make of it. He saw no purpose in arguing with a dream, however, so he followed on towards the path of flowers, which had now turned yellow and green like water-lilies on land, giving him the distinct feeling of entering water.

At the end he found a dark, still river, then snorted in surprise when he recognized an almost perfect replica of the Kubi near Sri Kon's palace. It had the same bridge, even the weir—or 'drowning steps', a dam-like structure he had once shown to Amit of Naran as he walked him to the palace. He shook his head as he inspected it.

"Why should this be here. It bored me in life, one would think dreams could be more exciting."

Ruka stepped beside him. "It was practice," he said quietly, then walked across the bridge to another wide, trim field of grass.

Kale followed because he didn't know what else to do. Once crossed, all around him, emerging from the fog he saw wooden racks of weapons, and armor. There were swords, spears, and axes—some as long as a man—and pieces of heavy, iron plating as he had once seen in Naran, all shaped in a hundred different ways. They lay arranged in perfect rows, or adorning stands and draped across the wooden constructs of men.

Kale twisted his head because he thought he saw something move in the fog, but it disappeared.

"We're close," said the giant, who had followed his gaze. Something in his tone changed and gave Kale pause.

"To what?" he asked.

"You will see."

Kale felt an anxiousness now—a desire to turn and run, and not to see whatever this strange man or creature had to show him. He knew this was a dream, but he knew dreams could still be dangerous—no man was truly safe from himself. He followed anyway.

They walked along the river, on a path of the same round, flat stones laid so precisely in the garden. The bank of the murky water had been built up with wide, stone structures like the sides of a pipe; as Kale looked down, he saw several holes in the sides, with more pipes or perhaps caverns disappearing beyond. Ruka saw his interest.

"Nothing is more important than clean, running water." The giant frowned as he looked at it. "But it would be better to be covered. In the world of sun, heat evaporates the water, and much is lost."

Kale nodded, utterly confused. Again as he looked at the detail of this place, and the strangeness of it and of his host, he felt a sense of wrongness—as if it had all come from a mind not his own. He tried to remember what he'd been doing before he slept and couldn't. But he began to realize that he had not been at the palace, and hadn't been in some time. He remembered being banished, traveling to Nanzu, the Naranian capital, and learning of Ru and meeting Asna and Osco and Li-yen...

And, oh God, what had become of Li-Yen? He saw her smile, her soft, gentle hands, and heard her voice. Had the emperor learned of their relationship? What would he have done, if he had?

More movement caught his eyes in the fog. At first he thought them formless shadows, but soon he saw arms, shoulders and the backs of heads. They were men.

The fog seemed to lift slightly as they pushed on, and he saw some with shovels digging into the earth; others pushed carts or wheelbarrows, moving dirt or carrying stones. All the stones were white, smooth slabs, and soon Kale saw rows of these planted in the earth in careful lines like Ruka's garden. They were marked with symbols.

"It is a graveyard," Ruka explained.

As he did the fog seemed to recede further, until Kale stood before a whole field of graves and wooden stakes, as wide as a palace courtyard.

More men and women stood amongst them. Some turned to look, as did the others who moved about their toil in the earth. They began to stop, or come forward in twos and threes.

Kale looked at them, and no matter how he blinked or shook his head, he began to see broken faces. Some of their limbs were angled strangely. Others he now realized had open wounds, or broken bodies and all had pale, frozen faces. He saw some had pupils rolled back, and blood staining their eyes.

"They are the dead," said the giant, his expression cold. "This is a land for the dead."

Kale felt sweat on his brow. He stepped from Ruka looking for another path, some kind of escape, some direction away from these abominations.

"In truth, I would be pleased with a companion who could speak," Ruka said, following him back into the fog. "But you mustn't linger here, Kale. Out of love for your father; for the mother I could not save, I must help you. You must leave this place, prince. You must return to the world of the living."

The voice followed him further into the fog, but he ran on, though he knew not where.

"Wake up," he whispered, feeling a tightening in his chest that clouded thought and sense and brought a tremble to his lips. *Wake up, wake up, wake up and end this nightmare, wake up!*

He ran with nowhere to go. He ran away from the river, into more darkness that led to torches and a huge, wide cavern of stone. Everywhere he found more walking corpses. Some were holding picks and hammers and crawling like ants about the rock. Other rolled huge chunks along felled trees with rope. These turned to watch him, and he fled this too.

He ran until in the distance he saw a sight as horrifying to him as the dead—an almost perfect replica of the palace of Sri Kon. It loomed large in his view with more corpses moving about its walls, painting and building, pruning and gardening. It was like some grotesque parody of his childhood, servants bound to their endless tasks forever in hell.

Ruka's golden eyes found him again in the gloom. Kale fled until the fog again overtook him, and soon all he could see beyond the grass and the stars were two golden slits gleaming in the meager light. He screamed.

He was lost and felt helpless, raising his hands as if to stop some fatal blow that never came. He squeezed his eyes shut and burned his thoughts.

This is a dream, he told himself again, a nightmare, yes, but only a nightmare. And anyway he was nothing as everything was nothing, and why should death make him afraid?

He began to remember a purpose, though, a purpose more important than his life. *Control your thoughts, you are nothing, we are all nothing, and there is only suffering and love.*

He slowly began to remember Nong Ming Tong—flying into the sky at the coast, plunging into a dark pool that took everything he had and was and snuffed it out without a moment's pause. He had left a great task unfinished. Threads of power had firmed like iron bars in his hands, mocking all attempt to pull them. But he felt no pleasure in remembering— because of his failure, many would die.

"It doesn't matter," he told himself, sinking to the grass. "It's all meaningless."

The giant growled, as if in contempt. "Ask a starving man if food is meaningless."

Kale blinked as the giant approached. He considered the words, thinking yes hunger was suffering and therefore existed, and better by far not to experience it. But this still felt empty, and hollow, inadequate to justify the world as it was.

The giant sneered as if he'd read his thoughts. "Your life is not just yours," he hissed. "You owe the dead more than most, prince of paradise. You speak the words they've given you, you live in the peace carved from mystery and chaos with their blood and toil. You have accepted their gifts, and so you bear the burden of their deeds. Lay down and die if you wish, but your debt remains for your descendants."

Kale looked at the terrible gaze of the giant, knowing in some way what he said was true. "I may fail," he whispered. "I've taken on too much. Those who need me and those I've made promises to will pay for it."

'Ruka's' face contorted again. "Success is not your obligation, boy. Success is often luck and to think otherwise is arrogance. Your burden is only to try. Face your path with courage, and let come what may."

Kale shook his head. "You don't understand the difficulty."

Ruka's brow raised, and he laughed. "All think the same, and all are right. One day you will die and there is no escape. For now the task of life remains. Go around it, little Alaku. Go beside it, over it, look again from every angle until the strain snaps your spirit, until you've reforged a hundred times. Most of you is deadwood, boy, burn it. Rise again and see what remains beneath the ash. Try until the blood drips from your veins and your mind is broken in madness. Then will you die in honor. Perhaps your children will do better."

Kale shivered at the words, so harsh, so oppressive. He stared at the giant, feeling naked before an unbending will. He felt judged, but not all wrongly.

"Stand up as if you had some dignity," the giant growled. He leaned until his eyes bore into Kale's "You were born with a great name, princeling. All your life you have rested at the feet of giants. Now stand. Earn it. *Live.*"

"If this is not a dream," Kale whispered, "how do you know me? Who are you? *What* are you?"

"Just a man, Prince Alaku." Ruka smiled, but it was not comforting. "Look to your deeds, son of Farahi, son of Hali. Courage calls, and only the brave live forever. Now *stand.*"

Kale felt as if pulled to his feet, but he had risen on his own. The act itself gave him strength, and though it had only been moments he felt almost shame for staying seated so long.

"I don't know how to leave," he shrugged, "I don't know where to go."

At last Ruka seized Kale's arm, leading him back onto the grass and into the fog. He looked to the heavens. "You know very well. You came from that sky. Return to it."

Kale shook his head. "There are shadows, some dark terrors in the void that rend flesh. I saw no light but here."

"You have not been listening," the giant growled. "A man fails in only two ways. He gives up, or he dies. Are you dead?"

"No." Kale looked up and shivered as he thought of the heat and the near-invisible creatures that had clawed at his back. *At least I don't think so*, he thought. "I am nothing," he whispered, "but it matters why." The giant snorted.

"Piss on your humility. You are alive, and all around you are dead. Deserve that life, or lose it, for many here should like to take your place. Go quickly. I will help you rise again if you fall, that is my vow."

With that Ruka stepped away, and waited, bright eyes like a Pyu lighthouse shining in the dark.

Kale felt no deception in the words. He felt shame again for judging the man's appearance when all he had done was help. At last he looked to the small dots of light visible above, and breathed.

He imagined a dark, empty beach and his fire, then burned all thought except what he must do. He didn't know how long it took, but at last he opened his eyes, and reached out for his body, trying to sense it. All at once, he knew where to go.

He turned to his strange host with hope, and smiled, then wondered again why he was here.

"Are you dead too, Ruka?"

The giant blinked, and his jaw clenched as he seemed to consider. "Perhaps a part of me. I am the shadow of a man, or he is mine. It no longer matters."

Kale nodded though he did not understand. "Thank you, Ruka, for helping me." He didn't know what else to say, nor what was happening or why he was here. He looked into the almost bestial eyes of his savior and saw no malice, hatred, or resentment. They were too hard perhaps to ever be beautiful, or even kind. But they were strong, and Kale thought maybe even held a tinge of pride.

The giant bowed slightly in the Pyu fashion. "Goodbye, Prince Alaku. We will meet again, I hope. But not too soon."

Kale returned the bow then outstretched his hands, finding that even here in this foreign place, beneath the void, there was power. *I am nothing, he thought, and weigh nothing, and the sky and the fog and the creatures in my path are nothing. There is only what I must do.*

Kale rose with the ashes of his thoughts, rising above the fog and the strange land of beauty and death, and flew towards the light.

68

"He's awake. Get the healer!"

Kale opened his eyes and saw the white, alabaster tiles of King Kapule's guest room. He smelled incense and tasted blood, and his joints and muscles ached as he sat up.

"Calmly, islander. You've been unconscious two days."

The blurry shape of Osco kneeled by Kale's bed. Apparently he'd helped him sit up.

Shapes that might have been Asna and several Mesanites in full armor stood at the room's door and windows as if waiting for danger. They seemed to search an old man in robes as he entered, inspecting even his hair before allowing him inside.

The old man tolerated this all in silence. Once inside he smelled Kale's breath, then looked in his mouth, his eyes and in his ears, poking or prodding in several spots before getting his attention.

"What is your name?" he asked, in a rather horrendous version of the island tongue.

Kale rolled his eyes, feeling progressively better with each passing moment. He kicked his legs off the bed and gently slapped away Osco's hands. Despite his thirst, a slight headache, and general soreness, he felt fine. More than fine. He scooped a jug of water off the table beside his bed and drank half of it.

"Right." He gasped. "I'm going back to the sea." He wiped his face and stood, swaying slightly before the world steadied.

"There are riots," Osco explained, his eyebrows deeply opposed. "Your...previous attempt, terrified any who witnessed it, and still there is no rain. Kapule will wish to speak and..."

"Asna." Kale stepped past his friend and towards the door. "I'll need a cloak to cover myself. We're going down to the sea." He looked back to the Mesanite. "Anyone who wishes to assist me is most welcome. But by all means, stay here if you prefer."

The general's son stared, and now that Kale was looking directly at him he realized half his friend's face was reddened as if burned. The observation softened his gaze a little—no doubt it was his efforts that had caused it. He glanced and saw the Mesanites too had been singed, or maybe half-frozen.

Asna on the other hand looked fine. He searched the cabinets until he found something suitable, than draped it around Kale's shoulders with a wink.

"You near make other friend shit self on beach, prince. It great and historical event. Asna remember for always."

Osco turned his glare to the Condotian, then barked an order in his tongue at the Mesanites. They stomped and massed at the door.

"Very well, *King* Alaku." The general's son sighed and came forward with sword half-drawn. "But if it's all the same to you, I'll be standing well away this time, and behind a shield. Maybe a few shields."

Kale nodded, thinking that most reasonable. He held back his grin.

Getting out of the castle proved rather difficult. Kapule's usually open and welcoming palace had apparently become a fortress of guards and locked gates. It seemed easier going out than in, at least, and the first few blockades let the group of mostly Mesanites pass easily enough. At the main exit to the courtyard, however, a captain and his host of warriors held their spears.

"No one comes in or out without the king's permission," said the young man, his face hard.

Kale drew back his hood and stepped forward, and the man's eyes widened in recognition.

"I'm going to the sea, captain, to try again to bring the rains. I may fail. I may die. But every moment of delay is further suffering for your people."

The captain stepped back, putting a hand to his sword. His men glanced at each other and some readied bows or lowered their weapons with pale faces and widening eyes.

"I...I have my orders, Prince Alaku."

"I understand." Kale smiled politely and closed his eyes as he held out his hands. As he did, one of the guards panicked and released an arrow, and Kale let the air seize it and hold it motionless. The men gasped as Kale gestured—entirely for show—and the gate unlatched, the heavy wooden doors opening with a creak.

"I am here to help your king, and his people. I will speak with him, but first I must give him what I promised." Kale walked forward without another word. As he reached the guards they stepped aside to let him and his warriors pass.

In the courtyard, the huge grain-bins had been closed. The outer gates were shut, and what had before been an open bazaar was now silent and lifeless. All that disturbed the stillness of a grey, hot morning was the clamoring of those wishing to be allowed inside. Kale took a deep breath.

"Your men will have to wait here, I think."

He knew if he tried to go through those gates with his soldiers he'd make a riot. Many would be injured and maybe killed.

"Islander," Osco's brow shone with sweat. "You will need protection. Last time you dropped where you stood and Asna carried you to the palace. My men and I cracked a hundred skulls to get you out. You can't possibly..."

Kale's crossed his legs as his body rose from the ground. His spirit pulled him forward with the smallest of threads, and he reached back and put another to his friends, smiling as they shouted in alarm and rose behind him.

Asna blinked in panic but soon steadied and drifted gracefully, while Osco swore and waved his arms and half-spun as he fought for control against the uncontrollable. *We are all nothing*, Kale thought, *compared to the heavens and the earth. You cannot fight it, my friend.*

He soared over the wall but didn't bother rising out of sight. He took the moment to feel the cool wind wash over him, to look out again over Ketsra and enjoy the color and sounds and all the life that would exist with or without him. He saw the few citizens looking up and pointing as he flew towards the sea, and he wished those with their eyes raised could join him—that they could fly and see the threads of power and help him, and that mankind could venture into this new world together.

But they couldn't, he knew, at least not yet. Some few must first cross into strange waters alone, forging a path for those behind. For now, that task lay with him.

His sandals touched on the yellowish sand of the Tong coast. The tide surged towards the beach, and he walked out until the water washed over his feet and shins and rose to his knees. He breathed in the salty air and thought of his childhood, of his brothers and Lani, Aunt Kikay and his nursemaids, and yes, even his father.

"I have lived a good life," he said with tears of joy in his eyes for what he already had. He had loved and been loved. He had flown through the sky and swum for his brothers and shared in the victory of expendable sons. He maybe even *had* a son, if the boy yet lived. But he burned this thought at once.

There were so many questions, so many truths yet to discover, so many deeds undone. But before he could do more, seek more, by God or Gods or spirits, he would bring these people their rain.

A man fails in only two ways, he heard the strange, forceful giant. *He quits, or he dies.*

Kale shivered as he thought of the land of the dead. Another riddle, another mystery he couldn't explain, like Ando the boy who was not a boy, Master Lo and his shadow, and Master Tamo who had taught him to dance the Ching in a room of symbols and light.

What a strange, and wonderful world it is, how full of mystery and beauty, and not only suffering.

Kale looked out past the gentle waves to the deep, roiling power of the sea. *What makes the waves*, he had asked his oldest brother Tane as a child. *A great beast churning in the deep*, he'd said.

Kale laughed, though he wished he knew the answer because the answer mattered, but not today. Today all that mattered is what Kale did. And today he would bring the rain to Nong Ming Tong, or he would die.

He was ready, and perhaps understood Osco better now than he ever had. It wasn't a desire for death—only a declaration of intent, an acceptance of meaning. *I am mortal, fragile, and flawed*, Kale thought, *but that will not stop me from doing what I must.*

His spirit rose far above him and reached out for the dense, cords of power stretching out far beyond the mountains to the West. He wrapped one arm inside them, thinking of what he'd tried before and how it had failed.

Go around, go over, go through, said the giant. 'Ruka's' golden eyes stared at him from the roiling sky as they once had from the fog. Kale thought of Osco fighting the threads of power in the air, flailing and helpless because he sought only control. He must not try to control it, to fight it, that was impossible.

He knew instantly he'd been an arrogant fool. One did not try to control the world—but rode atop it, like the pontoons of his people's ships, cutting and skimming above the waves, using the force of the sea and the wind, the master of nothing except himself.

Kale reached his other arm into the sea. As he touched the cords of power beneath he could almost feel the desire to be one, the pull of the wetness of the rain and the sea as two pieces of a massive puzzle, sloshing against their walls to one day mix and drain to the same gutter.

He cried out as he pulled. This time, he tried only to bend the threads of the world, not break them. He saw the water seething with foam as he did, waves swirling unnaturally against it, as if fighting yet some greater force. He almost laughed because for the first time he truly understood the story of Rangi and Roa.

Perhaps his ancestors, trapped between the sky and the sea, could only pass this understanding on through their stories because everything else fell away. In that story, the hero Rupi had not been some mighty warrior, nor a sorcerer who mastered miracles, nor a fearsome king who mastered man—he had been a trickster. Rupi had cut the sun and spilled its warmth, stolen fire as he had stolen the heart of the sea, fleeing beneath the waves. He used great power, he did not contain it.

Kale tried to do the same. He stood inside a maelstrom of power, between great forces that would punish a misstep, or a single moment of arrogance. He let them wash over his body and spirit, teasing them closer, always closer, until the moment of clash arrived, the two beasts rising to a mutual challenge. Then he ran.

The force collapsed as if trying to crush him until the sky touched the sea, and cracked like thunder. For a moment Kale blew away in the single flash of lightning, the waves and the clouds lit in perfect daylight, silent and still and beautiful.

Both his spirit and body blasted away from the power. He lay on the beach, looking up at the swirling colors of the endless sky, threads layered like a rainbow as infinite as the stars.

"Are you alright?"

Osco was checking him for wounds as thunder rumbled from the West.

The clouds swelled and darkened until even Kale's spirit lost sight of the threads beyond. He raised his hands as the first raindrops fell, and laughed like Rupi when he'd outrun death.

He knew he was just a man. Yes, he knew that, and men were nothing. But he thought again of Ruka the maybe-dream giant, scowling in the dark. *Piss on your humility*, he'd said, *you're still alive*.

Kale watched the sky moving faster than seemed possible, clouds pulling towards the sea bringing water and life and salvation for a million thirsty mouths. It was not *his* power that saved them, because it came from the earth.

But still, he, Ratama Kale Alaku, with the help of the sea, had called the monsoon. Maybe for this one act he would become a legend, a myth come to life out of some ancient book. The fourth prince, they would say, the expendable son—like Rupi cutting the sun-beast, or tricking Roa before him—Kale the Sorcerer-Prince had called the sky, and the sky-god answered.

69
Not far across the North Alaku Sea. The present.

"Look at the water, shaman!"

Ruka grunted at Eshen's voice without looking. He stood on the Northern beach of Sri Kon in the sweltering afternoon sun, leading a group of young Ascomi warriors in their drills.

"Spearmen," he growled, "double line."

The teenage boys—all from what the men of ash now called the 'Galdric generation', or the sons of priestesses after Dala required them to mate—panted but leapt to obey. Sweat poured down the red flesh of their uncovered faces and necks, and they shuffled apart from their massed formation and spread out as ordered. Ruka turned and walked to the water.

He blinked, confused by what he saw as he approached. He raised a hand over his brow to block the sun and stared at the sea, thinking perhaps it was some kind of trick of the eye. But it lasted too long. And the sound—the sound of the sea itself was wrong.

The warmth of the day vanished as a coldness spread through Ruka's gut.

In the distance, the sky roiled with thick, dark cloud, and perhaps warned of a storm. This was not so unusual of the season in the isles, but Ruka soon understood what had caught Eshen's attention. It was the tide. The tide had stopped entirely.

Beyond and further out to sea, the North Alaku itself seemed stilled like a pond in calm wind. Flat, unbroken water stretched from the white sand as far as Ruka could see. He knew this was impossible. Yet, he could see it with his own eyes.

"What does it mean, lord?"

Ruka was about to shake his head, then jumped as the sky crashed with a thunderous roar. As if leashed by some godly chain, the dark clouds in the distance mashed together far in the North, then flashed with thick lightning, followed by a hundred pale echoes of the first boom.

Eshen held up his hand and made the mark of Bray, and for the first time in his life, Ruka was tempted to join him. Instead he shook his head, caught for a moment in awe.

Ripples began in the water, and soon the tide surged and foamed and white spray followed waves as the water renewed its attack against the sand. Within several more heartbeats, all seemed returned to normal.

Ruka stared for a long time at the images and sounds because he did not understand. The image of a man soaring through the sky like a meteor, crashing headlong into the land of the dead refused to leave his mind. But he put it away. For now he would assume nothing, and if any man could give him answers, it was Farahi.

"Drills are over. Go back to your posts." Ruka turned to find the young warriors had managed both to obey his order to form lines, and also face themselves to the coast to watch the spectacle. Despite his concern, it made him smile.

But as usual he had no time for pleasant things. He jogged towards the palace, Eshen close behind him with an open stack of letters and notes. He had learned to read and write with the Galdric generation, and known Ruka long enough now not to further question the sky, or the sea, and instead focus on the things requiring attention.

"Aiden has returned from the Molbog, shaman," he said without panting from their run. "He said the list of nobles for execution were all found save for one, who he believes fled to the continent."

Ruka nodded, not really caring about individual island lords. "How many losses?"

"Fifty three dead, a hundred or more wounded."

"So many?" Ruka snapped his attention to his retainer at this, and spoke more loudly than he intended. "What the hell happened?"

"Mostly dead at sea, lord. The Molbog had several warships. They fought bravely."

Ruka's hands twitched and his pace increased. *Damn these islands*, he thought, damn Farahi's complex world and all his nobles and all their petty problems. Already there was so much stupid waste. So many executions for island lords or Orang Kaya because Farahi said it must be so, because 'they would turn traitor when the empire came', and because he was usually right. Even in paradise, the wealthy squabbled over whose plate should be the fullest.

We were supposed to come in peace, he almost growled. But Farahi said the island lords would not accept it—that even now the Alakus had too many enemies, and in every vision of the future he saw assassinations, piracy and even outright alliance with Naran no matter what he did. Better to have the Ascom 'attack', he'd assured—better to kill Farahi's enemies in pretend 'raids', and when all the 'problem lords' were dead, make a lasting peace thereafter.

So as always, Ruka had done what was required. Farahi had sent nearly his whole navy away on 'training exercises', and Ruka had landed to 'capture' Sri Kon's open gates in darkness. For months now he and his men had purged the island lords, and the death and waste continued to mount. *Fifty three more*, he thought. Fifty three more brave men of ash who had come so far would never enjoy the fruits of their labor.

Ruka tried to put this from his mind. He passed out of the navy district and into the edges of Sri Kon proper. The streets bustled with trade as usual. Ascomi and Pyu civilians did their best to communicate and had since the occupation began. It did not always go smoothly, but things had improved.

Warriors stood at their posts—or at least hid in shade close to their posts—and after so many months of largely peaceful control, the islanders had returned to daily life. After the initial fear and hiding, the Pyu women in particular had begun to realize the white-skinned giants meant them no harm, and indeed, even feared them. Though they had a tendency to stare.

Ruka had ordered his men to avoid violence since the beginning. Most obeyed, though incidents happened. Food supplies were still adequate because Farahi had stockpiled, though with the drought lasting so long this could change.

All of this was only distraction, though—the true problem was disease.

Since the first cases with Trung's concubines, Ruka had done all he could to understand how it spread and how to treat it. He had learned there was more than one illness. For ten years and more he had experimented, tested, made potions and herbal remedies, isolated and listed symptoms and every possible combination he could try. Still, the diseases spread. The worst began with a skin rash and fever, then vomiting and diarrhea which could be treated but not stopped. The very young or very old often died before it ended.

The men of ash too began reporting strange illnesses, though far less severe. Different kinds of spots and rashes formed on their skin. Eyes turned bloodshot, fevers came and went, as well as any number of minor ailments. He had brought only strong and healthy men so far to the isles, however, and few of them died.

It was the children of Pyu who fared worst. Ruka had spent nearly all his time since landing trying to treat them and keep them alive. Farahi tried to tell him it was inevitable and not his fault, that with time all would strengthen and resist the illness. But it seemed so unjust. It was as if no people so different could come together without death, regardless of their intentions—that whether they meant war or peace, trade or plunder, their very nature rejected their aims.

Each day Ruka forced himself to walk amongst their graves. Farahi had set up 'military districts' far in advance to serve as quarantines, and this at least controlled the spread. The men of ash served the sick islanders as nursemaids and cooks, and at least some of those who survived perhaps would come to see their 'invaders' differently.

Ruka entered the busy city streets with Eshen and several bodyguards, and the islanders stared. Many fled before him, as usual, the street thinning as citizens pushed to the edges and clustered near buildings.

He meant them no harm, of course, and never had, but he did not blame them. He wore the island silks but had covered himself in dyed, dark runes just to intimidate. Better they be frightened, he thought, then build the courage to rebel and force him to put them down. He carried a sword and shield at all times, and he knew his bald, disfigured face frightened even his own people. The islanders knew he was one of the invasion's leaders.

Ruka crossed the Kubi and nodded to the few workers setting up the beginnings of a sewer. Ironically, the Ascom's new capital and Northern towns were now far more advanced in their irrigation then Sri Kon. Over a decade they had constructed copper pipes beneath the earth stretching all the way to Turgen Sar, and every home in between had access.

In the few months he'd been in the isles, he had already begun a project to improve the flow of fresh water, as well as more barriers against flooding in the rainy season. His old friend Chief Builder Hemi even helped, though he had retired and could hardly move from his ill health after a lifetime of bad habits.

Ruka grinned as he approached the young Ascomi guards outside the palace gates. They'd huddled and lay prone in the shade of the wall, and when they noticed him they turned an even deeper red as they found their posts and stood tall with spears at the ready.

"Be calm," Ruka said quietly as he passed, "I will not tell your chief."

Their 'chief' was Tahar—who Ruka had placed in charge of the island's security, and the relatively soft, young boys of the North and the new generation soon learned the iron of an old Southern outcast.

"Thank you, shaman," said the elder of the twins. Ruka knew his name, just as he knew the name of every man who had come across in the 'First Wave'. He pat the boy's shoulder and moved through to the courtyards, dismissing his guards at the gate.

A skeleton crew of servants still maintained the palace. Since the initial attack, these were mostly women because Ruka's warriors were less likely to cause an issue. His overzealous raiders had also killed many of the men in the attack.

As he cleared the first courtyard, Ruka followed his mental map of Farahi's fortress. He knew every hallway now, every false room and secret door in perfect detail. Farahi kept most of his unpleasant rooms together in the same wing, and so Ruka was forced to pass through the torture chamber on his way to the prison, flexing his four-fingered hand in memory. He pushed down the exactly recalled feeling of pain, then the taste of the torturer's flesh, summoning the pleasure of saving Arun, instead.

"Loa pirate." Ruka grinned as he reached the cells.

Arun, or Eka as he now preferred, had begun his evening stretches in his 'cell'. He held his body inches from the stone floor, contorting himself strangely. Despite being at least forty now, the exertion seemed hardly to bother him, and in truth his body looked little different than it had in his late twenties.

"Loa savage," he said, without a trace of physical strain.

"I'm in a hurry." Ruka tapped the bars, and the ex-monk frowned as he stood.

"Your guards are..."

"Yes, yes I left them at the gate, open the bloody door."

Most of Ruka's people were not privy to the alliance and deception, thinking they had truly invaded to prove their point. This was far easier for a culture of warriors to understand.

"You used to be much more lively," Ruka said.

Farahi's spymaster smiled politely and flipped his secret lever, and the trap door clicked at the same time as the gate. "So you've said," he answered, as if neither annoyed nor pleased. Ruka entered the cell, then lifted the bed to descend the secret stairs.

A thin red covering of carpet began at the bottom of the steps. Dim light lit the bare stone walls of a narrow corridor, and Ruka emerged into the only opening.

"You're early," muttered the king of Sri Kon. He sat at his favorite desk in his favorite chair with a simple cushion, surrounded by books and parchments, inks and quills. He pinched his nose and blinked in the comfortable gloom of his candles and fireplace.

Ruka frowned. "I knew I would regret giving you a water-clock. I need your talents."

Farahi shrugged and returned to his scribbling. "Well I'm not ready. I have three messages for families in the Eastern islands yet to finish, and another short list of names for proscription."

"Another bloody list?" Ruka grunted and took the only guest seat. "Nevermind. Forget your letters, this is more important." He sighed in pleasure at the cooler air in the 'dungeon' and wiped sweat from his brow with the fine, silk fabric of his shirt.

The island king's brow furrowed at Ruka's tone. "Has the sickness spread again? Is my grand-son all right?"

"No, and yes." Ruka waved a hand in annoyance. "I've come from the coast." He met his old friend's eyes and held them. "I saw a miracle today, or at least some act of nature I can not explain. I watched dark clouds swell like pooling water over Nong Ming Tong. I heard thunder without lightning. And I watched the sea itself become still. I can't explain, but it felt... controlled. As if by something, or someone. I thought perhaps you would know more."

Farahi's eyes narrowed as he leaned back and drifted far away. The man could hide his feelings better than most anyone Ruka had ever known, but at Ruka's words, the stone-face had cracked with something more than surprise.

He said nothing, however, and from experience Ruka knew his friend would always win a war of patience. He rose and paced while he waited, then considered working in his Grove, but the dead had long moved past needing his help.

"I know you've seen it. What does it mean?" he said when he could wait no more.

Farahi blinked but otherwise remained frozen, no doubt still searching his visions. Ruka flexed his hands and took a breath, looking at the few paintings of his ally's ancestors. The work was done well enough, but the canvass left something to be desired, and the likeness seemed too angled.

The king finally released a breath. "Yes. I've seen it before. I thought it was a dream."

"Aren't all your visions 'dreams'?"

Ruka had learned much of Farahi's visions over the years. He knew, for whatever reason, his friend could see the future, at least *his* future, or that of his descendants. Usually he saw it best while sleeping, but could do so awake if he let his mind stray.

Much, however, could hide from his sight. As he explained it, he saw 'possibilities', and it took a great deal of time and effort to narrow these down and decide which was most likely. He could never truly be sure, and Ruka thought he relied on them too much.

"I will need time to see beyond it," said the king, rather carefully. He fiddled with his papers.

Ruka scattered pieces from the half finished Chahen board on his desk.

"You're all out of time," he hissed. "I lose men every day to your proscriptions. I need more people and to send transports back with food. And we need to start working with Kapule now, and bringing in your sons, and all the other coastal nations to restore Sri Kon under our new leadership. The time for caution and thinking and plotting is over, Farahi. It is time to *act*. Now tell me what you've bloody seen, because I must prepare for it."

Farahi's mouth opened and snapped shut. He was a guarded, careful man, and sometimes required pushing.

"There's more," Ruka said, picking up some of the pieces, "I've seen your son."

The king blinked and his face contorted slightly in anger. "I thought we'd agreed to keep Tane in the dark until *after*. He's still imprisoned at least?"

"Your youngest son, Farahi. Kale has somehow come to me in my Grove, or perhaps he was lost. I don't know how, or why."

Farahi blinked again, sitting back as if he'd been struck. Ruka did not blame him. His ally knew much of his own 'gifts' to create, but little of his Grove—save that it was filled with the dead.

"He is alive," Ruka said after a pause. In his heart he had known the moment Kale fell from the sky and could speak that something in the world was different. Then he'd seen the storm. Now Farahi's reluctance. He watched his ally very carefully. "I think your son has gifts, Farahi, like his father. And I think he's coming home."

The king flicked his gaze to Ruka's eyes. He abandoned the Chahen piece in his hand, leaning back to look at the only portrait in the room of his family.

"Life is so strange," he whispered, lifting a mostly untouched bottle of rum from a drawer in his desk, as well as two small glasses. "A man can be so careful, Ruka, he can plan for a hundred likely things, neglecting one, and it is that neglect which destroys him."

Ruka watched every detail of his friend's face to lock in his mind and examine. He took a deep breath at his words, and a large swallow of rum. The island king was not a dramatic man, nor prone to sloppy words. Farahi sipped and kept looking at his portrait, a small grin perhaps on his lips.

"Tell me what it means," Ruka said, losing his patience. "How do I prepare?"

Farahi snorted, and shook his head. "I don't know. Not for certain. I have dreamed of my death in a storm and never seen the cause." He moved to the images of his sons, and smiled sadly. "I can see my descendants future, Ruka, but never while I'm alive."

"Tell me what it means, Farahi."

The man clenched his jaw and his eyes watered as he drank. "In all my dreams, I have never once seen Kale from *his* eyes. I had always thought… I thought he might die young, or at least before me. In truth perhaps because of this I tried not to love him, or perhaps it was just because of Hali. In any case I thought I would lose him, and that there was nothing I could do."

"Spit it out, damn you. What do you see?"

The king met Ruka's eyes. Etched on the stoic rock of his face lay some mixture of pride and sadness, exasperation and fear.

"I see a fleet of my ships. They carry an army to re-take this island. I don't know when they'll come, or who leads them. But all around them is rebellion and chaos and death, and behind them a great storm that blots out the sun and the stars. This storm sweeps your ships from the sea, and your men from the beaches. I don't see a thread to stop it."

"It is Kale," Ruka said, "Kale is the storm?"

Farahi met Ruka's eyes but said nothing, as if he couldn't himself yet believe. Ruka watched the boy again in his Grove—his plummet through the mists, crashing headlong into soil with the power of a meteor.

He found me there, he thought, *wherever I am. And he could speak. What does that mean?*

"I'll have to stop him, Farahi. We've come too far for this."

"You can't stop the storm in my vision, Ruka, it's…," Farahi's eyes faded again as if in awe, "it's like a God. Like the power of a great wave directed by a man. Not even you can stop it."

Ruka stood and clenched a fist. "Unlikely. You have always relied too much on your visions. I'll test this 'storm', and if the boy is truly so powerful, you must convince him. He is your son, Farahi. Speak to him."

The king took a deep breath. "We parted very badly. He may not listen to anything I say."

"You're his father. He will rage, but he will listen. Perhaps we can use this army. You can re-emerge now, sooner than planned. I can call a peace and we can establish an alliance as intended."

Farahi blinked, and nodded stiffly "Maybe. I can try. But there's so much Kale doesn't know and won't understand." He paused, and shifted in his seat. "You could surrender to him. Let him enter the palace a conquering hero, then you and I will have the time to speak and convince him."

Ruka almost snarled at the thought. His people had come for land and new lives in a larger world. They had sacrificed and toiled, suffered and died. They had not come to kneel.

"Every week I kill island lords because you say they will not bend," Ruka tried to control his contempt. "Your people are not the only ones with pride, Farahi. The men of ash are not here to surrender to an untried, angry boy who barked at them. The chiefs would be dishonored. They will never agree and I am not a king to command them. It is impossible. If Kale brings warriors, so be it, they will be tested. Every one of my men would rather die than kneel without a fight. Peace requires respect for your enemy's strength, and he will learn it."

Farahi met his eyes, then gave a tight smile. "Let us hope I am wrong. And if not, that Kale has learned patience, and is wiser than his father."

Ruka released some frustration with a breath, then nodded and turned to the stairs. He would save his ships and instead prepare a force on the beach. If Kale had some kind of sorcerous power, surely he wouldn't use it unless he saw sufficient threat. He must therefore be threatened.

As Ruka emerged from the cells and walked towards his men, he felt his steps quicker and lighter than they'd been in months. His body moved with a strength he hadn't known in many years—with a purpose, perhaps, other than that of saving others. By the time he'd cleared the gate and signaled a meeting with the chiefs, he had to admit: all his life he had wanted to humble a god. Perhaps now he would get the chance.

70

The rain over Ketsra turned to a deluge as the monsoon moved. Kale had felt the windows of his spirit-house all but close as he spent every scrap of will to coax the sea.

"Where should we go?" Osco called over the howl of the wind.

"To my people," Kale yelled, doubting his friend even heard. It didn't matter. He struggled just to keep his eyes open, and felt more than saw his friends lift him up by his shoulders and carry him towards all that remained of Sri Kon's navy.

He fought sleep despite the exhaustion, reveling in the thick droplets of water falling into his face. Soon he saw vessels ranging from ten-man scouts to large, hundred-man warships moored and lashed in various states of readiness. Shirtless sailors swarmed over them tying down sails or stowing provisions.

One marine in particular caught his attention. He was standing on the sand pointing and screaming as he directed others. It was a young man, Kale realized, half-naked in nothing but an island loincloth, stomping footprints in the wet beach with muddy feet as he moved.

Kale recognized him, and couldn't help but smile: it was Haku—one of the captains who had served with Kale in training school, and saved his team from utter failure when they'd been betrayed and dumped in the sea.

"Take me...to him." Kale pointed. As they got closer, Haku turned and stared, his momentum of screaming interrupted as he blinked in surprise.

"Captain...Prince Alaku...," something near the ships caught his eye, and he seemed torn between protocol and rage. "Take him aboard." He pointed at a near-by flagship, and gave the briefest of bows before spinning back on his men with obscenities.

Even half-conscious Kale grinned and would have hugged the young man if he could. If Haku lived, then maybe so did the others. Maybe Thetma and Fautave and Lauaki. He realized he should very much like to see them again.

Asna and Osco dragged him past several staring marines without a word, then up the boarding ramp and out of the rain and into a cabin without knocking. The officer rose from his bunk as if to scream bloody murder, then inspected the intruders more closely and silenced.

Kale mumbled a half apology as the man helped Osco set him down. He'd meant to ask the sailor's name, but soon heard only the creaking of wood, the howl of the wind, then all was blissful darkness.

Admiral Mahen visited him in the night. After giving his apologies and inquiring after Kale's health so many times he'd have impressed the most tedious Naranian diplomat, he came to the point.

"We're almost out of supplies, my lord. Since your...efforts on the beach, the Tong have stopped bringing grain. We fish, of course, though the locals despise us for it and there's more than a few incidents. But…we have to move. Spreading out down the coast is wise, I suggest all the way to Samna. We will have more desertion, but there's too many men in one place to feed, and…"

Kale raised a hand and sat up. He was feeling stronger already, though he could still sleep for a week.

"Tomorrow I'll speak to the men, Admiral. We've waited long enough. It's time to go home."

Mahen clenched his jaw and looked as if he wasn't sure whether to speak. "I'm sorry, my prince, but we can't. We will lose. Even if we beat their fleet or surprise them and land, and even if we beat whatever fighting men they have, we don't have the supplies. They'll hole up inside the palace, and we have no way to breach the walls. We would be forced to plunder our own people for food and water—which, the enemy has likely already done. Sooner or later we'll be forced to withdraw."

Kale forced himself not to interrupt the man, knowing this was all likely very reasonable. He knew the admiral didn't believe he'd brought the monsoon—that the rains were due and had simply come now on their own accord.

"I can get us in the gates, or through the walls," he said. "I can also cause great damage to the enemy's fleet, or their army. Once we've landed, the people of Sri Kon will rally to our cause. I'll help there, too." He smiled. "And you've not seen my Mesanites in battle, Admiral. They're worth five times their number. Likely more."

He glanced at the older man's expression and saw his opinion hadn't changed. Another miracle might do the trick, he thought. But the truth was the officer owed him his loyalty no matter what he deemed their chances, and Kale was already tired of trying to convince him.

"That's the last I'll say of it. I am your king." He stared until Mahen met his eyes. "We are at war, Admiral. You have two options. Do your duty." He had intended to say 'or be stripped of command,' but the severity of their situation, and perhaps his anger, changed his mind. "Or die."

With his spirit he whispered to Asna and opened the door, and the Condotian entered with a hand resting on one of his many knives. The admiral glanced back, then returned his gaze to Kale, as if assessing the seriousness of that claim. Kale truly hoped he didn't test it.

"As you say, my king. I will do my duty." Mahen displayed not a shred of pleasure, but Kale believed him a man of honor. He would do as he pledged. With that he turned and stooped to leave the cabin, and after a nod from Kale, Asna stepped aside.

"Don't let anyone else in. I need to rest."

The mercenary grinned and closed the door, and Kale lay back and blinked away the tears, feeling every moment, even in his thoughts, he became more and more like Farahi. *Another sorcerer king*, he thought, *rising to power at the death of all my kin.*

The part of him still a boy and not a prince or king cried out in frustration. He didn't want it, any of it. Yet tomorrow he would ask thousands of men to risk their lives to make it so. And one way or another, he would lead them to bloody slaughter.

* * *

In the morning, Kale changed into a navy uniform. He woke feeling stronger and clearer than he had since Nanzu, remembering the strange dream-giant's words of purpose.

Your life is not yours alone. You owe the dead, prince of paradise. You have accepted their gifts, and so you bare the burden of their deeds.

It made him realize there was more at stake than just suffering, and the lives of his people. He must honor all they had built already, and so too must all the islanders. It made him feel less responsible for the violence to come, as if in a way it were inevitable, and required. Like the admiral—it was his duty.

He stepped out from the flagship's cabin into an almost flooded beach. The sky was still so dark it was difficult to tell if it was morning. The rain still poured, though it had lessened slightly.

Sailors were hard at work dealing with the weather and swelling tide. They covered everything in tarps, lashed supplies, wrapping ropes over masts and sails until nothing moved but the hulls in the water. Kale kicked Asna's foot, who was sleeping outside the door beneath a canopy. He jerked awake and pulled a knife in each hand, then grinned and stood with a stretch by Kale's side.

"Look good, islander. Healthy, neh?"

Kale smiled and stepped out into the rain, using but a tiny thread to protect himself from getting soaked. He breathed and flew out with his spirit, feeling restless already, eager to test the power he felt hanging all around him.

He walked amongst the men, soon finding Osco and all his Mesanites camped and waiting under the closest trees. They looked soaked, and rather miserable.

"Don't see this in the hills, I imagine?" he shouted. His friend's eyebrows twitched like a soggy cat's whiskers.

"Can we sail in this?" Osco pointed, and Kale grinned because the Pyu could sail in damn near anything. He waved to follow, and the general rallied his men.

Together they crossed the beach attracting stares from waking or waiting men. For a moment he considered telling Mahen and some others to get the navy moving and maybe gathered first so he could make a speech. But he realized—he didn't need them gathered. He could speak to every man whenever he wished.

Kale walked in full view, straight and with purpose—like a navy man and maybe like the prince he was. Osco and Asna kept at his side, near five-hundred Mesanites in full, soggy kit around him. The sailors outside his ship were now awake and moving, but stood still and silent as they watched him approach.

"Where is your Captain?" he called. The sailors looked at each other.

"Dead, lord. Don't have one. Not official-like."

Kale held back a smile because he knew all about unofficial captains. Haku stepped out from below deck, and the men cleared him a space.

"Still doing what needs doing, eh marine?" Kale spoke in a neutral tone. Some of the sailors looked confused and rather impressed, and all eyes turned to Haku.

"I try, lord."

Kale grinned. Up from the stairwell, several heads bobbed and cluttered each other with grunts as they pushed to the top. Soon beside Haku came Fautave and Thetma, faces cracking into shit-eating grins.

"Well aren't you a bloody sight for sore eyes," said Thetma, whose sun-dark farmer skin had gotten even darker since training.

"He always was the pretty one," added 'Big' Fautave, who'd gotten bigger.

At this the other sailors almost cringed, and even Fautave looked concerned he may have overstepped. Kale laughed, and the tension diffused.

"Your mouth was always bigger than your brain, you penniless son of a whore." His friend grinned and looked at his fellows as if he'd been picked out for some special honor. Kale turned back to Haku. "Would you and your miserable men do the honor of carrying me and my allies to Sri Kon, *Captain*?"

Haku bowed in formal navy fashion. "With great pleasure, lord."

Kale winced as he glanced back at the Mesanites. "We'll need another ship or two, you pick them, with my authority. And…while my allies are brave, and fearsome warriors, they…" He failed to find the right words to finish this, and frowned. "They have never been on a ship."

Haku and many of the sailors slowly cracked grins, and looked over the silent ranks of heavy infantry, who of course had no idea what they were saying.

"We'll tuck them below, sir," said Haku, "right as royalty till we reach the shore."

Kale laughed as he imagined the hillmen sloshing around below, sick as cadets. "Very good, Captain." He noticed Osco's impatient eyebrows, and realized it was even possible the Mesanite spoke his language and had never revealed it. Kale nodded, and the general's son shouted an order. In near unison the hillmen stomped and broke into lines to enter the ships with spears held low, shields tucked before them.

The islanders all stared in some mixture of awe, fear, and mockery, until Haku started shouting all into panicked action. They began clearing space in the hull in a cleaning frenzy, next moving to the sails while others ran off to commandeer several more ships. Kale thought he'd help them there.

With his spirit, he whispered in the ears of every man on the beach.

"I am Ratama Kale Alaku, called by some the Sorcerer-Prince. Today I am your king. By sacred right I take command of this navy in the name of my forebears. By the claim of blood I declare war on whatever cowards have attacked my island. Get off your damn asses, sailors, and make ready. We leave for our city today, right now. We're taking back our home."

He watched many men go from terror to surprise to resolve in the few short words, and some even cheered, then sheepishly checked if others heard voices. Kale thought it would serve.

Action soon swept the beach. Sailors and marines started loading, rigging and tying down. They checked the hulls and the sails, the oars and the pontoons, swarming over the boats with the skill and precision that marked the Pyu as the greatest sailors in the world. Kale mostly stood on his deck to watch, visible and—he hoped—looking kingly.

From his relatively calm vantage, he soon saw a pack of Kapule's men descending from the palace. He counted maybe fifty in total, armed and ready and walking in a protective circle. Kale resisted the urge to inspect them with his spirit, instead predicting it was a messenger. He took the time instead to decide what he'd say.

As he waited, further down the beach and coming behind the cluster of initial men, he saw hundreds of spear-tips glistening in the rain.

Growing more concerned, he floated his spirit towards the approaching soldiers, and found at least several hundred—maybe upwards of a thousand, all wearing thick cloth gambeson, armed not only with spears, but shields, and long knives.

"Osco," he whispered, "get your men off the boats and in formation. We may have to fight our way free."

The general blinked but did not hesitate, calling at his men as he bolted upright and raced for the ramps leading to the sand, the sound of boots soon behind him. The smaller party of Tong thread their way through the staring Pyu sailors and marines, and walked straight to Kale's ship. Kapule himself stepped out from his bodyguards.

"I've come to wish you luck," he announced, somewhat strained grin cracking the round edges of his pudgy face. He wore the silks of his station, wrapped from toe to neck despite the wet heat. His men looked as nervous as he did.

"Thank you," Kale said in a neutral tone. "Surely that message could have been delivered without a beach full of soldiers." He gestured towards the growing outline of the block of spears.

The Tong king glanced in their direction, and his grin spread into a smile. "I saw you *fly* away from my palace, young Alaku."

Kale shrugged. He bit back his first impulse to say 'yes, and not all the soldiers in the world could protect you from me'. The king almost crept forward until he reached the railing of Kale's ship, waving a hand at his bodyguard, whose eyes whipped back and forth like an anxious mother.

"I thought to myself: if he can do that, then what else is possible? I think you did bring the rains. I believe it's true. And so for that I thank you. These soldiers are yours to command young Alaku because your father is my ally, and if he's truly dead than I hope his son is still my ally. I am on your side, Kale, and I hope you're on mine. I feel no shame in declaring this hope is now based on both respect, and fear! Soon, I think, we will meet again. Go to your people and give them my goodwill. And if you see your father tell him what a slippery snake he is, and…" here he paused, and looked more like a father than a king. "If you see my daughter, tell her that her mother worries greatly."

Kale searched the man's words and eyes and found no malice or great deception. He saw the Tong soldiers stopping a safe distance from his men so as not to alarm them, their weapons held at rest, their backs loaded with supplies. He had no words to thank this man.

"You need never fear me, my lord," he said, controlling his voice. "You have proved your friendship twice over. My people will not forget."

Kapule smiled, and patted Kale's hand on the rail. "Nor will my accountants, young Alaku, I assure you."

With that he turned and gestured at his entourage, and Kale held back his laugh as the squat king waddled towards the hill where his servants already constructed a sort of viewing tent of plush fabric and cushions, protected by silk drapes.

Kale turned back to his men, brow raised as he gestured to get back to work. All at once Haku roared back to life, ushering Mesanites to their hold, and marines to their ships.

By mid-morning, the remnants of the Pyu navy floated gently on the Northern edge of the Alaku sea. Smaller scout ships pushed out in a wave, dizzying in their pattern and chaos as they rushed South through the waves to test and spot for the enemy.

In a huge, unbroken line, the greatest warships full of marines blew their horns and pushed out into the sea, oarsmen sweating and pulling hard.

In battle these would use their sails if wind allowed, but did not need them. If the enemy came they would loose flaming arrows covered in pitch, throw hooks and javelins, ramming and boarding to charge their marines across if necessary. Just as skillfully, they would fall back, letting the scouts and smaller ships distract and sew chaos in a controlled, but frantic attack of fire and missiles so confusing and precise most enemies hardly knew what was happening.

No doubt when the enemy first scattered the fleet they'd caught it utterly by surprise. Wherever they came from, and however they even existed, the king's navy wasn't ready. This time they were.

The islanders of Pyu had sailed since time immemorial; they were born to loving and hating the sea as the Tong loved and hated their farmland. In a thousand years they had never lost a battle on the waves. Kale intended to show this *ambusher*, this honorless thief in the night, exactly why that was.

"So this is sailing."

Kale blinked as Osco lurched to the rail beside him. His face was pale, and he clenched his jaw as he swallowed burps.

On a different day, in some other context, Kale would have found pure joy in the stoic warrior's discomfort. Today he needed him at his best, and wished there was another way. Still, he felt a small grin.

"It'll get worse if there's a fight, and your men will be useless. Fortunately, we won't need you. Once we've landed you'll recover soon enough."

Osco's eyebrows didn't like being called 'useless', but he said nothing, then squinted.

"Why 'if'? Are your powers not…useful here? Shouldn't you be out looking with your spirit-eyes already?"

Kale looked back to the waves and the ships and nodded. He breathed and felt the sway of the water, knowing beneath him were currents so long and powerful they would terrify anyone who could understand. He felt the monsoon, he felt heat trapped in the water, air whipping over it blown from the North.

"The scouts will do their work," he said. Already an anger built the closer he came to home. He found he couldn't truly burn the thoughts of his family imprisoned or slaughtered now, his people attacked by some foreign foe. Not knowing anything about his enemy made it worse—it made them some nameless evil, their attack of an innocent people who had never even heard of them so unambiguously wrong. He tried to feel some understanding or compassion for them but failed. He saw no reason to show restraint.

"My father's fleet is the greatest in the world," he said. "And my 'powers' are stronger here than they've ever been. I hope they send their ships, Osco. I truly do. I hope they send every last one of them, filled with their warriors. Because if they do I'm going to rip them timber from timber, and leave their men for the sea god."

He looked at the young warrior who nodded weakly, caught in another bout of nausea. He thought of his friend's view of the world, and no doubt the view of all warriors, including the conquerors of Sri Kon—the notion that the strong ruled the weak, and this was simply the way of the world.

Fine, he thought, feeling drenched in elemental forces, endless and terrifying, invisible and only for him. *If power rules, let's see what these usurpers think of me.*

71

All day the winds rose. The sea swayed, but still Sri Kon's navy moved in formation behind their scouts, unhindered by the growing storm.

Osco, on the other hand, kept up his vomiting, then went back down to suffer with his men. Asna stood beside Kale and beamed, showing not a hint of sickness.

"I like this sailing," he said in Naranian. "When Islander is king, he should make Asna...Chief Captain Pirate."

Kale grinned but otherwise ignored him. He watched the horizon, his nerves growing a little unsteady.

His scouts had not seen a single sign of the enemy, and he was tempted to start looking himself. The coast of Sri Kon was close now, other little islands already forming on the horizon. But his confidence in his scouts hadn't changed. If they hadn't found anything, no doubt he wouldn't either. Perhaps the enemy was afraid of the storm.

"No, no," Asna continued in self reproach. "Captain is small thing. Admiral. Pirate Admiral Asna Fetlan. Terror of sea, Destroyer of Ships, Capturer of Virgins! Your enemies will tremble, islander."

Kale sighed and pushed away from the rail. "Alakus kill pirates, Asna, though not as well as the sea. We'd best find you something else."

The mercenary frowned but nodded sagely, then leaned off the rail again like a child trying to catch the spray.

Kale was beginning to suspect there would be no sea battle at all. Perhaps his enemy's ships were all hidden on the other side of the island, to be brought forward only when sure. Perhaps they'd all gone back to wherever they came from. Most likely they hid from the winds. In any case it seemed they didn't fear their enemy making a landing, and that thought was sobering.

"It's time we readied the soldiers, I think." Kale said mostly to himself. Asna was nodding and saying 'You can rely on Asna,' as he headed down towards the hatch. But Kale didn't need his help, or anyone's. He reached out with his spirit and spoke to every ship at once.

Prepare to beach. Form up in your groups as determined by Admiral Mahen. My men will form the vanguard.

He hoped no one panicked at the sound of his voice suddenly appearing in their mind again. And by 'my men' Kale meant both the Mesanites and now Kapule's spearmen. In truth, both were far more experienced soldiers.

Pyu were very good sailors, and it was prestigious to be in the navy, but only the worst, poorest, or most desperate souls joined the army. With limited need, even these were poorly trained and equipped. Most carried short-spears, bows and knives. They had no armor worth mentioning, rarely had shields, and fought in what might charitably be called 'loose' formation.

Osco would say 'disorganized mob'.

Kale's scouts had approached Sri Kon now, then turned down the coasts to watch for enemies further out. The main warships waited for a report, but seeing no flag of warning, dropped anchor and released their transports.

Kale loaded in beside Asna and Osco and some of his men on the first deployment. He sat still and calm as the waves buffeted their ship, until the sail was out and the pontoons deployed, and they started moving in a calmer rhythm.

"How are you feeling?" Kale asked. Osco only groaned in response.

The coast filled with hundreds of transports, a thousand men rushing the beach with oars at once. All involved were at their most vulnerable now, for if they were attacked they'd be abandoned by the warships, who themselves were at risk unless they pushed out to sea for more room to maneuver. Kale was still not afraid because the scouts would have warned them. He kept his eyes locked on the empty coast.

This surprised him again. If the enemy had seen them and intended to fight, they should already be forming on the beach. The longer they waited the better chance for an invader to gather and face them on open ground and with coordination. Yet Kale still saw nothing. At last he lost his patience and burned his thoughts, sending his spirit up and over the water to inspect the coast.

He realized as he did that it was the first time he'd inspected his home from above as a spirit. He wished he did it only for pleasure, and that he could laze about the sky as he spotted old childhood landmarks. But for now he put this from his mind.

As he looked he realized there was nothing damaged at all. He saw no burnt shells of warehousing laying like skeletons, no destroyed docks or houses or merchant stalls that had been overturned or destroyed. The only strangeness to his eyes was the absence of life, for he could see no people. Houses looked clean but closed up, most windows shuttered. Kale hovered down to look inside one that was open, and heard a mother chastising her children.

"Get away from there! There'll be fighting! Didn't you hear your uncles? Go back to your rooms!"

Kale blinked, for a moment confused, then pulled back and flew towards the coast. He used his real eyes and saw his and many other boats had already reached the shore. Men were leaping out and pushing the transports back into the water, others forming up into lines. Some of the Mesanites kissed the sand.

He felt an anxious panic but could see nowhere for the enemy to hide save inside the coastal buildings themselves, but even so, not very many. There was simply no enemy close that he could see. Infantry could of course be hiding further out on the island, or in the city, but by the time they arrived Kale's forces would be gathered. It made no sense.

More and more boats kept arriving and the infantry soon numbered in their thousands. They started forming up into three groups as ordered, Kale's men standing out front on the slight rise of the hill towards Sri Kon, most of the others on the flanks of the flat beach.

Kale was nearly ready to order the advance and start heading into the city when he heard something—or rather, *felt* it. Sand moved against his feet like insects leaping off the ground, jittering and shaking as if alive. After a moment, he believed he knew what it was. The islands suffered not only great waves and mighty storms, but also earthquakes.

Kale had felt many in his life. He outstretched his hands for calm when he saw Osco's eyebrows panic. He called a warning as he braced his feet when the tremble started, thinking in truth it felt rather weak compared to most. He put his spirit's hands down into the earth to feel the great forces moving below him, but he couldn't sense it. The threads seemed solid and still, undisturbed and sleeping. Then he heard the shouts.

Men on the East flank were screaming and calling out in terror. Kale hovered up with his spirit to see dust rising from the beach. He stared and squinted because though he could see it he didn't understand. Leading the dust, moving so swiftly across the flat white sand it didn't seem possible, looked like half-men, half-beast creatures with four legs.

The beasts' charge shook the earth, and Kale's mind reeled, blank, because they approached so quickly.

His friends were down there on the East flank because he'd put them there. He wanted them in the back, hidden away so the real soldiers could do the fighting. Instead, they were directly in the path.

The distance between the strange enemy and Kale's unformed islanders vanished with every moment, and he had no idea what to do. He called out with his spirit, telling his helpless Mesanites to cross the ground, to prepare, somehow, to do something, *anything*, before he flew closer to try and help the men himself. He gathered threads of power as he moved, but he knew he would be too slow.

* * *

Ruka felt the warm sea breeze rushing over his brow as he charged. He and his men had waited for the enemy just past the curve of the first trees until the landing fully gathered. He had hidden all his infantry, and kept his cavalry waiting until the islanders felt safe. He knew they would not look so far for an enemy force—they did not know any soldiers on land could close such a distance so quickly. Ruka and the chiefs had waited, and waited, then rode like the wind.

Amongst his first great fleet he had brought two-hundred and fifty warhorses from the land of Ash. These were one of his secret weapons—a might never seen in this New World, which had nothing truly like them. For years he had trained them to charge behind the bravest in a staggered line, to shatter infantry like a spear, or ride along them taking heads. They were designed to face Naranian spearmen, of course, but these would serve. They had never been tested.

He led them himself on Sula's back. Despite the animal's twenty-odd years, there was still none braver, nor greater. Sula had a great many colts now, and many rode at his back carrying the great chiefs of ash and their sons—men who wanted glory as desperately as others wanted life.

Their courage was bolstered by their own legend already spun, as yet unearned. Egil had taken to crafting stories of 'The Prophet's cavalry', though Ruka had rolled his eyes. He learned to tolerate it, however, because of the name. Egil had called them the 'Sons of Sula'.

"We break their will, cousins." Ruka roared over the wind. "Hit them, then ride past and away. We are here to terrify, not kill. Follow mighty Sula. For the Ascom. For the dead."

"For the dead," growled Magnus, a great chief of Orhus, bloodlust steeling his eyes. The men whooped and clanged long-spears against shields or iron armor or barding. All had waited a decade and perhaps all their lives for this moment—for an enemy to kill that wasn't their countrymen, a target for their skill and fury that would win them great fame and glory and place them with the heroes of old.

They were heavy and sweating in the heat, weighed down by armor, spears, swords, and javelins. But they would charge over the dryest sand, and the fight would be short. The enemy would have no concept of what was coming. If Kale had magic, he would surely use it here. If so, Ruka would see with his own eyes, and then his men would withdraw.

Two hundred coursers in steel and leather trampled the beach, crushing drywood and crabshells and the corpses of dead fish as they shook the earth. They rounded the last bend and saw the edge of the enemy. Ruka's men took up their shouts, growing wild with the excitement. Ruka felt it, too.

There was maybe a god on that beach.

"Ride Sula," Ruka hissed, drawing a flaming lance from the realm of the dead, holding it high before lowering it to charge. He had drenched it in pitch so it would burn long after being summoned. Both he and Sula were covered in rune-stained steel, made with fangs and spikes as if to resemble a demon out of hell. He wanted every man before him to see his doom, and flee.

But he did not hate his enemy. He did not believe they deserved the death they'd be given, yet nor were they innocent. They were soldiers who had come here to destroy Ruka and take away his people's dreams—to impose their will and arms against his, no matter their reasons. If a man lifted a spear, he should not be surprised to die by one.

Ruka snarled as the final moments arrived. The islanders panicked long before contact, but didn't know where to run. Men on the edges pushed against the others. Many ran straight back towards their boats or simply fled into the sea. Ruka saw wide eyes and frantic movement as they looked back towards their leaders. Some few held their short spears towards the enemy.

The charge at last struck. A thousand bodies stood in opposition, and Sula did not disappoint.

Without slowing, the great patriarch of the Sons trampled the first man with his iron chest. Ruka skewered the spearman beside him, ripping a half-naked soldier from his feet by the shoulder as if with a battering ram. All around him islanders screamed and fell to the sand even before being attacked. The Sons behind him threw javelins and cried out as they rammed spears into their enemy. Ruka kept them moving forward.

He saw the three groups of Pyu soldiers and marines and intended to ride along them, keeping to the coast. To his left, raised on a hill, he saw real spearmen and soldiers in tight formation with shields and armor. Already they were advancing to intercept, and he would have to move quickly or the rear of his formation would be caught.

"Ride! Forward!" Ruka threw down his spear and drew a long, heavy-ended sword made for this purpose. He kicked Sula's flank, hacking as if with a sickle at any man brave enough to stand in his path. Arrows zipped about him now, some striking Sula's barding or his armor uselessly. Others threw their spears or knives or even rocks rather than come any closer. Their weapons were crude and equally useless.

Ruka did not turn from giving death. The men of ash could not have peace without respect, and they could not have respect without fear. First they would bloody this would-be hero, and show their strength. Only then would they talk.

Their charge shattered the first group and snaked past them towards the second. Ruka glanced back to see his men in good order. These were leaders of men and they knew how to follow. He snarled and spun his sword as he pushed into the saddle, his feet dug deep into the stirrups, his blood up and his next targets clear. They were all but unopposed, and he saw nothing to challenge his charge.

He blinked as the air all around him blurred. He felt the moment frozen, as if only a memory, a scene from his youth plucked from his mind to be examined. Thunder cracked as if beside his head, and the world seemed to turn upside down.

Grains of sand raised from the beach without being touched, hanging suspended in the air. All at once Ruka's vision clouded as more of it swirled to life. He cried out and covered his eyes as Sula slowed and reared. A storm of sand engulfed them, blinding and pelting his armor hard enough the sound was deafening.

Hairs stood all over his body. Force seemed to surge all around him followed by thunder. Even in his Grove the sky darkened with lightning crackling high above. Bukayag woke all at once. He screamed as if in rage, or maybe agony, though Ruka did not know why. He knew only he must not stop.

"Show them your courage," Ruka tried to yell over the storm, "ride Sula, forward!"

Whether the animal could hear him he did not know, but he dug in his heels and flicked the reins, and Sula ran. In only moments his vision cleared. With stinging eyes he and Sula burst again into open ground, turning away from the second group of islanders to bolt straight for a gap.

With a shudder, he looked back towards his men and saw only a cloud of swirling sand. Above it lay thick, dark clouds far too low to the ground. They loosed lightning into the dust storm over and over, thunder blaring like a hammer striking iron. Ruka saw several shattered men, burnt and fallen bodies of horse and rider outside the unnatural force. He turned his eyes away and towards the cluster of spearmen moving down the hill, and he saw the source.

Farahi's son floated in the air like the sand. He was the same young, thin man Ruka saw in his Grove, though he wore Alaku colors now. His hands were outstretched, his face calm but pointed towards the sky. As he hovered there above his men, face almost serene, his enemy trapped in his power, Kale certainly *looked* like a God. Ruka resisted the urge to summon a spear.

Instead he turned and fled. He did not know how many of his men managed to escape behind him or perhaps another route, but there was nothing he could do for them now—not against such power. Incredibly, Farahi was right.

Ruka's ride back to the palace was very long, and very strange. All his life he had been surrounded by lesser things—creatures ultimately weaker and frailer than he. He had felt some guilt in opposing them, some feeling of cruelty as a wolf might feel eating the fawn instead of the doe. But here, finally, was a different sort of life. This was no fellow wolf or any beast Ruka knew. It was not a man, not truly, but a flood, or a flashfire. No sane thing stood against it.

Now that the chiefs had seen it, they would understand. Farahi would have to convince his son to join their cause, or they would surrender. The men of ash would not begrudge peace with a god. *And what a world we might make with such power,* he thought.

Perhaps even the great feats Ruka had imagined could be surpassed. Perhaps together they could re-shape the land and the sea for the betterment of mankind, learn all the secrets of their hidden worlds, and who knew where it might end?

He closed his eyes as he rode, giving thanks to the warriors and animals who gave their lives in that terrible storm. In a way, he thought, no man should have such power. But that was not up to him. Even the strange might of Ruka's grove frightened him, and for many years had made him wonder if he could wield it and still be just a man at all.

But next to this boy, his powers were insignificant. Ruka re-visited the memories of the miracle on the beach, in awe as it seemed somehow Kale could alter the very fabric of the world. It frightened him in a way he had not considered since meeting Ando of Bato—another mystery one day to solve.

For what man could wield such power with wisdom? What might he do in a fit of rage? At the death of a lover, or a child? *What would a man like Bukayag do?*

Such thoughts plagued him even as he arrived safely at the palace, telling his men to hide within while he spoke to his prisoners. He and Farahi perhaps would go out together to meet the boy, and maybe even bring his brothers and son. With time, and patience, they would convince him.

Ruka had long suspected he'd meet other men with gifts like his, or like Farahi. But he could not have imagined. The world had changed in a heartbeat—a world he thought he knew and was working to improve. But perhaps like the great mountain Turgen Sar, in a rage spewing lava and ash, or a huge wave striking the beach, this boy could take it all in his hands and destroy it. Though he tried to hope, Ruka felt his brother clench their jaw.

72

Most of the strange warriors and their beasts scattered and fled Kale's storm, though maybe only half escaped alive.

Kale stood on the beach with his men as they stared in horrified fascination, or looked to their own people's corpses. Osco moved about the fallen with a furrowed brow, checking for survivors amongst the enemy.

"Do you speak Naranian?" he tried, then again in a dozen other languages, before eventually trying Pyu common.

"I bloody knew it," Kale muttered without any feeling. Osco ignored him, and so did the enemy.

The huge warrior was almost white-skinned as the messages had claimed. He had thick black hair on his head and face, now stained with blood and sand. He lay beside his even more massive animal, a curved blade clutched in one hand. He looked up at Osco with a mouth full of blood to spit, then lay flat with a groan.

The Mesanite frowned. He lifted one of the attacker's spears, tested the point, then clanged it against his blade. He shook his head. "Their weaponry is...incredible," he held one up in awe. "I've never seen anything like this. Their armor, these animals, and that *charge*." He glanced at Kale with eyebrows more excited than they'd ever been.

"I'm going to see how many of my men just died," Kale snapped. "And if my childhood friends are amongst them. By all means, keep enjoying yourself."

He turned and walked towards the site of the first slaughter, and Osco followed, looking suitably chastised. Together they spoke to Admiral Mahen, who said it looked like at least a hundred were dead, or near enough, with four times as many wounded.

"I thought it would be worse," the admiral said, clear remnants of fear still haunting his eyes.

Kale had the bodies lined up on the sand and walked amongst them, horrified at the grisly wounds. Most had been trampled and crushed rather than struck by a weapon. He stopped when he found Fautave.

The big boy's eyes were closed in death. A spear had been rammed straight through his torso from the side, and looked to have pierced his heart. Over the pull of his own grief, Kale thought at least he hadn't suffered long.

"He stood," Thetma said, already kneeling beside. His eyes were red and his chest smeared with blood. "He should have run like the rest of us. He always was a stupid bastard, Captain." He wiped at his nose with a fist, and Kale put a hand to his friend's shoulder and tried to smile.

"Brave, too."

Thetma nodded reluctantly. They took a moment to touch his body, but Kale already felt Osco's impatience behind him and knew they were still in danger. He had little time for this.

"Let's get off this damn beach," he said, rising and turning towards the outer edge of the city. Despite the power he'd used against the invaders, his strength had hardly dimmed. All around him threads of creation surged with strength, as if begging to be pulled, or changed. "They can't charge with those god-cursed…animals, if we're in the streets, I expect."

Osco nodded slowly. "It will disrupt our formations, islander, but I agree."

Kale used his spirit to whisper the plan to his soldiers, hoping the first encounter hadn't already broken their morale. He thought maybe a speech might help but frankly he wanted only to move forward and start ripping giants apart with air. Let the men do what they will.

He walked ahead and heard some following—at least Osco and Asna, but soon the Mesanites and perhaps the Tong spearmen on their heels. Kale roamed with his spirit as they moved.

Sri Kon still looked largely as it should, with almost no signs of looting. It seemed the invaders had closed off the military districts, though, placing small groups of men all around the closed gates. After spotting no army anywhere else in sight, Kale flew inside one out of curiosity.

The first thing he found near the border confused his eyes. All along the wall were stakes, or wooden signs, placed in row after row. Some few women moved or knelt about them, placing little white stones at the base. It was these that made him realize, and with horror—he'd found a graveyard.

In Sri Kon, children were always buried with white stones, turned towards the sky so Rangi might see them and feel ashamed. At least half of the hundreds of stakes and headstones before him were covered in them.

Most of the women amongst the graves wept openly. Kale wanted to speak to them, but feared his spirit would terrify. He took a breath and whispered to one old woman who looked more stoic.

"Do not be afraid, grandmother. I am a good spirit of the sky. Tell me, what has happened here?"

The old woman startled and looked first to the clouds. She shook her head, and put gnarled, bony hands to her face. "There is evil here, spirit, such evil. Monsters make us drink potions and tinctures. They poisoned my grand-daughter. They're not even men. They rape young girls and eat their flesh. They sacrifice children to their dark gods. And they say nothing, never. They never speak. Help us, spirit, help us, I beg you." The woman bowed low to the sand and moaned in grief, tears running freely from her eyes. Kale could think of no words of comfort as his mind reeled. He felt bile in his throat. It was worse even than he'd feared.

He flew on and found more of his people huddled inside cloistered buildings. Many lay in poses of agony, as if starving or poisoned as the woman claimed. They were sprawled on beds or lain out on the floors, and outside every house and entrance stood white-skinned giants with weapons, as if holding them prisoner.

"There, islander, we should take the main road to the palace. If they come with their giant donkeys we can fall away to the side-roads." Osco pointed, and Kale blinked and returned to his senses.

He felt a rage building inside him now, far worse than he'd expected— far worse even than he'd felt for an unknown foe with selfish intent. These pirates had attacked a peaceful people without provocation, without explanation. Now they were holding them as prisoners, subjecting them to maybe rape and torture, and if nothing else trapped in fear. *And they are killing our children.*

"I've seen enough." Kale trembled now with an impatience, his hands clenching as he felt the urge for violence in a way he had never believed himself capable. "There's endless power here. I'm not wasting more effort on pawns or sending men to die." He pointed at the palace. "Their leaders will be in there. Tell the men to hold their ground and guard the ships. I'm going to end this. I'm going to rip it all apart until I find whichever bastards are responsible. Are you coming with me?"

Asna stepped forward and half-drew his sword to make sure it was free, a grin spreading across his face. "More fly? I will be prettiest bird in paradise." He fluffed his plumage for emphasis.

Osco made a long, drawn out sound, and turned to his men as he shouted orders. "I recommend against it," he said simply, then spread his legs as if in a battle stance to fight the air.

"Noted." Kale closed his eyes. With a tiny thread he lifted them all into the power-filled air. As the men watched in awe, he flew them over Sri Kon proper wondering if the citizens were watching. He hoped the enemy saw a prince soaring over their heads and learned to fear—a little taste of their helplessness.

With his spirit he raced ahead, hungry for blood, and called out to the palace, to anyone and everyone, knowing it would translate to any man no matter what language he spoke.

"I am prince and sorcerer of this city, pirates, and now I return. Get back on your god-cursed boats. Run like the cowards you are, or I swear on the graves of my people, every one of you is going to die."

* * *

Kale couldn't be sure where the enemy would stay, but he could guess. Farahi's only opulence lay in the main throne room, on the second level of the palace. To reach it required penetrating the outer courtyard, then climbing a winding flight of stairs and breaching another gate, all the while surrounded by murder holes and archers hiding above. Kale flew over all of it.

As he did he saw hundreds of men waiting in the grass below. Even from a distance he could see they wore armor and carried weapons like those found on the beach, and he fought the very strong urge to start raining death. He would kill them happily, but he'd rather they fled. First he would rip their leaders apart, scattering the bodies down like chum, and perhaps they'd get the message.

Two giants stood guard before the iron doors. They were already wide-eyed and sweating, staring at Kale as he floated ahead of them. One opened his mouth as if to speak, but Kale was not interested in talk. He seized both with two threads of power, and flung them screaming from the rampart to the courtyard below. With another, he ripped off the door.

Asna landed gracefully behind him, while Osco shouted and spun, dropping to his knees on the stone with a curse.

Kale knew without looking there would be men waiting inside to ambush. He considered sending his spirit inside to find the men he needed, but he was all out of patience. He wouldn't wait one more moment while his people suffered at the hands of these beasts. His chest heaved with ragged breaths, something like a righteous purpose settling inside him, making everything easier. With a tangle of threads he could never have touched a year ago or in a place with less power, he seized the entire roof of his father's palace.

The thought of the enemy beneath made him picture vermin cowering inside, protected from his sight only by stolen stone and pitiful darkness. But they couldn't hide what they'd done. Not anymore.

Voices cried out in terror as Kale lifted the throne room ceiling. Wood and stone cracked as he tore the marble from its pillars and frame, letting it crash to the side as rubble rained and one of the walls sagged outwards

Kale felt no weakness from the effort, no limitation, as if the justice of his cause became bitter fuel, and he almost chanted, *it matters why*.

He flew forwards, seeing two more pirate guards emerge from the ruins holding swords. He took their bones, and shattered them.

He floated over the iron door feeling energy crackle all around him, gathering more threads of power from the sky as he dragged clouds over the exposed palace, ready to smash back anything and anyone that came too close.

Several warriors stood in the waiting room, and Kale raised his hands to seize them before the door burst open and another man emerged.

"Don't harm them, Prince Ratama. I am here. It's me you want."

Kale blinked as he heard Pyu common. He looked at his enemy, and like the others he was a white-skinned giant, but his head was entirely hairless. His face was darkened as if by dirt or soot. He held his hands raised as if in submission, four fingers on his left. And his eyes, his eyes were yellowed gold.

"You...", Kale felt the rage inside him falter. "You're...the giant. You're Ruka, from my dream."

'Ruka' nodded. He spoke in a foreign tongue to his men, but Kale understood with his spirit.

"Put your weapons down and leave slowly. Do not approach me, and do not approach him. Everything will be fine."

The men showed concern as if for their leader, but obeyed, and Ruka backed into the throne room. Kale descended slightly and followed, Asna and Osco close behind him.

"I did not expect you so quickly, and am unprepared. We must speak," said the giant. "There is much to explain."

Kale's faltered rage returned and grew. His dream was irrelevant next to reality.

"Speak? *Now* you wish to speak? As you wanted to speak on the beach? As you wanted to speak before you attacked this city? Now when you're at my mercy, *now* you want to speak?"

Tendrils of power wrapped around the abandoned weapons as if on their own, and Kale bent and twisted the metal apart.

"Your father is alive. He is coming now," the giant looked at the weapons and winced. "He brings Lani and your son, all your brothers, Kikay. None of them have been harmed, I assure you."

"Oh very noble," Kale hissed, unable to process this and anyway not impressed. "You kept your hostages intact. And what of the common people, *Ruka*? What of the field of graves of children I passed? What of my dead men trampled on the beach? What of the hunger and starvation from the trade you've ruined on every coast of the world? Have you harmed *them*?"

"You're angry." The giant continued to withdraw. His tone seemed almost unrepentant, unafraid, the same iron will from Kale's dream. Less than a day before the man's advice had been useful, and this alone nearly made Kale rip him apart. "But you do not understand," the giant continued. "The situation is complex, prince, you must be patient and listen."

"Be patient? You…*lecture* me? You think to tell me *anything*?" Kale saw threads drifting beneath his father's useless throne, and ripped it to shreds. He lifted guest chairs and broken pillars and flung them just past the giant's head. "I should kill you." He grit his teeth. "I should rip you and all your savages apart and leave you as bloody stains in my ancestor's sea. That would be the justice those children deserve."

Ruka watched him and at this seemed to show at least a morsel of regret. "Disease knows no justice, Kale. But if you wish vengeance, then take it now. I am a killer, yes that's true. Every corpse you saw in your 'dream' was dead because of me." The man's golden eyes moved back and forth as if he were seeing them now. "Many wailed or begged, yet I did not or could not spare them. I have tortured. I have deceived and broken laws which should never be broken. So yes I am a monster, prince, punish me. But my people are blameless. They have come only for a better life. If you destroy them you are the same as me."

Kale looked on the giant's ugliness and now felt repulsed. "We are nothing alike. Your *people* will be allowed to get back on their boats and go back where they came from. That is the mercy I offer them."

The child-killer's jaw clenched. "What you offer is not mercy. There are fates worse than death, Prince of Paradise. You would not know."

Kale said nothing because words would not change what had been done, and he would not change his mind. The giant's face twisted. Though he was within a single effort from death, still he had the arrogance to speak with anger.

"You have no *right*. You think now you've seen *suffering*?" He laughed a desperate sound. "You who rip apart the great walls built by your forefathers? Who disdains all they have given you? Your safety, your wealth, your words? *Do it*, then. Use that strength and kill me. But don't you stand in judgment. Not you, prince of nothing. Make your claim with might. Look into the eyes of those you doom to misery and say 'I choose life for mine, and death for yours.' For that is your right, but spare me your indignation."

Kale twitched, disbelief at the man's tone. He felt only a white-hot killing rage being prodded by an insect, and that words meant nothing to dead children. Only the man's help in a strange dream world gave him pause. The giant saw it, and sneered.

"Still a child. Do it, *sorcerer*. Do it because if you do not I will kill you and end this farce."

Ruka drew the sword from his back and came forward, and Kale seized threads all around him. Still he felt a strange reluctance, but thought of Osco with a blade to his throat telling him to act, or die.

Despite the confusing, irrelevant words, Kale already knew enough. No 'complexity' could justify what had been done. He grabbed the threads hanging all around him to make it brutal, but quick, seized the man's almost blurry shape as it loomed before him, and pulled.

73

Ruka stood in his Grove with his arms out, and waited for death. He knew his tone with Kale had been wrong, even foolish. But since Bukayag had woken on the beach he felt an old part of him renewed—a part that had always wanted to die, perhaps, and in this moment felt relief.

It was finally over. Since Beyla's death he had always wished to pay a price. Since the day he had dragged a knife through his mother's throat, he had done many things to raise the cost. All his life he'd been willing to pay, and felt no bitterness.

Kale was angry now, but killing Ruka would sober him. Beneath it all he was no doubt a good man, and with time Farahi would convince and educate him. The alliance would stand. Kale would use his magic to help protect them all and maybe stop Naran, and who knew what else was possible. Ruka had done enough.

The dead crowded around him as he waited, and he could see pleasure in some of their eyes. No doubt they would laugh, if they could. If they could speak they would spit and froth as they wished him eternity in hell for what he'd done. But not all.

Boy-From-Alverel stood before Ruka with tears in his eyes, and Ruka reached out to wipe a drop from his cheek.

"Perhaps there is another place for the dead," he smiled. "If you have no family, we can live together there and build with wood and iron, stone and clay. You have become a master craftsman, my friend. The greatest smith in all the world." He felt his own tears and blinked them away. "I am sorry for your death. But…I am so glad you were with me, all these years, right to the end."

He took the boy in his arms, then looked to Girl-From-Trung's pit, who waited behind. She smiled and touched his face as he looked to the others. "I am sorry," he called, voice cracking. "I…tried. I tried to make it worth something, to make our deaths matter. I do not ask for forgiveness, for I know there is none. Goodbye."

Already he could feel Kale's power surging into his body, but he did not close his eyes. Ruka opened every sense in awe of the power, wishing only that he could understand it—this, and so many things—before he died.

The world remained so full of potential, and he wished he could have spent his life unraveling its secrets instead of washing it in blood and bringing a people across the sea. *Perhaps I will be re-born*, he thought hopefully. *Perhaps, after my suffering, Noss will spew me from his mountain to try again. I would like to be a bird, I think.*

"Goodbye, brother," he whispered. Bukayag still lay mostly dormant, yet twisted in rage—a beast trapped behind bars and poked with spears it couldn't reach. Ruka had overcome him long ago. He faced his death with arms open and head high. Paradise or hell, he was not afraid.

The magic closed around him, searching, crushing, unraveling. The boy's eyelids narrowed, his face slackened as if in intense concentration. The world changed from storm clouds and tapestries of Alaku silver to red, and Ruka's face sprayed with his own blood.

But he felt no pain. For a moment the land of the living and the dead seemed equally still, as if both waiting to observe the damage after great disaster. Ruka opened his eyes.

In his Grove he blinked and tasted wet copper. He looked down and saw the mangled, half-exploded corpse of Boy-From-Alverel, who lay on the grass in peaceful repose, more dead than he had ever been.

Ruka looked on the Sorcerer-Prince in the land of the living and saw confusion. The handsome young man's eyes twitched, and his hands balled to fists. The air in Ruka's Grove shimmered with heat, and two more dead men ripped apart.

Bukayag woke. As if his cage had been smashed by whatever the prince had done, he burst from his shackles screaming like Noss, ready to fight and kill anything and everything.

In both worlds the sky roiled and descended as a mighty storm approached. Ruka did not know how or why he was still alive. But it made no difference. He walked to his armory and lifted a metal club. He thought of the moment after he had killed Priestess Kunla, thinking to let a boy strike him down and end it there. But then, too, the fool hadn't been up to the task. Ruka would not stand idle and die to incompetence.

"Protect yourselves," he spoke to the dead, "make ready and get to the fortress, the river, and the estate. Whatever comes." He felt his pulse race—the same as it had when he'd sailed North to an unknown sea. He had always thought to face a god with his own two hands, and die as some legend of old.

"Stop me," snarled Bukayag, his voice hoarse from disuse, "and you deserve to."

* * *

Kale tried again to rip the giant apart. As he pulled at the threads and forces attaching him to the world, the man's body shimmered. A darkness seemed buried beneath his skin, flickering with black patches that soaked up Kale's threads of power. Now the darkness emerged, a shape the same size as the giant, pulling forward with difficulty, as if trapped in chains.

Claws extended from the huge warrior's gnarled hands. His golden eyes mixed with red blotches, his thick lips and angled teeth sprouting into a maw of fangs. The shadow sprang forward, consuming the threads of power around it—a shadow seen only with Kale's spirit, a shadow like the one that spoke to Master Lo outside the Batonian temple. As it came free, it howled.

Kale had no time to think. He seized more threads and didn't try to be precise, or cautious, or humane. He simply gathered as much power as he could reach quickly, trying to shatter the giant and everything around him.

The shadow hissed and growled, but just as before, the energy entered it, and simply vanished. Ruka charged forward. A weapon grew from the shadow's fingers until it rested in the man's hand.

Kale watched the armored frame of the foreigner loom ever closer. A part of his mind told him he could fly, that he could destroy the palace beneath their feet, or do something else entirely—but for that single deadly moment, his body froze in fear, an animal staring as a predator struck.

He blinked as metal clanged against metal and a wheezed breath followed. Kale twitched and fell back, and the giant staggered a pace as Osco's shield slammed against his chest. The Mesanite's shorter blade knocked the killing blow swinging away, and the high-pitched ring lingered in the air.

Stopped you, said the Mesanite's eyebrows. He rolled his shoulders, and moved between them.

Rain pattered on stone from the open ceiling, and Asna drew his blade and cracked his neck. Ruka breathed as he stood to his full height. He breathed the wet air as if he had not smelled it in a decade. Then, incredibly, he grinned.

Kale's spirit watched as threads of power sucked into the man's shadow and vanished entirely. Ruka's body wreathed in flames, then sheathed in iron. It grew up his arm until it formed a shield, and watching the process, Kale could only imagine it as the shadow *eating* the world.

In two huge steps Ruka crossed the distance, his sword slashing with such strength and speed the air hissed with the blade. Osco sidestepped and deflected it, returning with his own hit against the giant's shield. They sprang apart, taking a similar stance, almost mirrored for a moment— though the Mesanite was two thirds the size of his opponent.

"Kill him, islander. And do it quickly." Osco didn't take his eyes from the giant.

Kale breathed and stepped away until his back was to the wall. He tried to eject as much fear and frustration as he could, summoning his beach, darkness, and a calming fire by the sea. "I'll need a moment."

Asna snorted as he circled Ruka's flank. "This next moment is very long moment," he said, and even Osco's eyebrows smiled a little.

Kale looked at his friends and saw something like pleasure in their eyes —as if this were some glorious moment to be glad for. Not for the first time, spirits help him, he thanked fate he'd befriended warriors.

He burned his thoughts and focused on his breathing. His spirit rose up into the roiling sky he'd summoned, and reached for every thread of power. He gathered it around him like armor, swimming in it, abandoning himself to it. He already had his reason, and he no longer needed tricks or even a spirit-house. He gave himself to the power and danced amongst the threads, ready to direct, or to command.

He could tell he'd hurt the shadow before, though it seemed it could absorb power similar to Kale. No doubt it weakened like he did, too.

So be it, he thought. *You've come to the wrong place.*

All around him energy seethed and twisted—brought by the rains, dwelling in the seas and beneath the earth. Even if Kale had to pull it all apart, he'd fill this dark 'spirit' to bursting.

Let's just see how much you can take.

* * *

Ruka's brother ignored the flanker, shield-charging the man between him and his goal. The steel of his heavy round-shield clashed with wood and bronze and cracked it as he pushed. It seemed near impossible for the smaller man to resist, and yet he did. The prince's little bodyguard jerked and pushed with his whole weight, angled and straight like an oak beam.

Bukayag snarled, abandoning his charge and striking, but the warrior ducked and swiped at his feet and pushed him away in reflex. As he stepped back his enemy shield-charged in return and sent him staggering to keep his balance.

The other warrior—'Dog-Nose'—leapt and tried to pierce his side. Ruka took one look at the light blade of shoddy iron and ignored him entirely. It struck mail, then again before the warrior leapt away. Bukayag almost laughed.

The heavens above them both flared and roared with light and sound. In his Grove, the gentle fog had condensed, the space above them consumed with thick, dark cloud so heavy even Ruka's eyes couldn't pierce it. Wind howled through the world like baying wolves. Lightning struck the earth, igniting fires in the grass and gardens and the raised wooden infrastructure of the mine. The dead ran to the river, gathering brackish water in pails to fight the flames, even as they ripped apart or jerked and spasmed, their bones seeming to try and escape their bodies.

"We have to stop him," Ruka shouted over the noise, "and quickly." He ran to his armory and stood before a hundred tools of war, letting his brother understand. *Anything you need*, he thought, looking at Beyla's house as the foundations shook. *He must be stopped.*

Bukayag growled, maybe this time in pleasure. He had waited a long time for such a moment. He seized a javelin first, stepped back from the warrior in his path, and threw.

The hardened spike sailed on target, but the bodyguard spun and slashed his sword in a perfect strike, deflecting the spear enough it pierced the stone wall by Kale's arm.

Bukayag snarled and seized a war-pick—two feet of steel spike made to punch through shields, or armor, or almost anything. He spun first to thrash his shield against Dog-nose, who still hacked increasingly painful blows against his back. The man danced away, throwing a red, silk cloth in the air as if to cover his retreat. Bukayag blinked in confusion, and barely turned aside as two knives flew through the fabric and narrowly missed his face.

He flinched as lightning struck the earth near his feet, a thunder crack knocking him to a knee and throwing over several tables lined with weapons. It hurt his opponents more—both flew away and cried out as they sprawled.

Bukayag rose first, throwing another javelin. This time it somehow bent in the air and missed as if blown by the wind. He snarled and charged, but the air itself seemed to hold him back like deep water. The bodyguard leapt before him again, and Bukayag sunk his pick straight through the pitiful shield.

The warrior grunted and pulled away as Bukayag thrashed and tore the protection from his arm, seeing blood stain the grip. He threw the pick aside and pushed on, ignoring the man's sword as it bounced off the chain guarding his neck.

He dropped his own shield and seized the bodyguard's throat, lifting him and carrying him forward into the harsh, unnatural winds as he squeezed.

"Spear," squawked the warrior in Naranian, both his hands now on Ruka's, trying desperately just to stop his life from being crushed. But Bukayag was too strong. He raised him high, then reached for another javelin as he turned his gaze to Kale.

Ruka heard a voice calling over the storm, and kept his brother still. It was Farahi.

"My son! Stop! Stop this, Kale!"

Ruka's hesitation enraged Bukayag, who fought only to throw and crush and kill.

"Stay back, Farahi!" Ruka called, knowing all around him—even the air could destroy other men. Behind Farahi stood Lani, Tane, and Kikay, wide eyes taking in the half-destroyed palace and the magic spewing from the boy they had known since childhood.

Kale didn't seem to notice any of it. He looked utterly enthralled, eyes rolled back, arms before him, feet hovering over the stone. Still, Farahi pushed into the storm.

"My son! I beg you! For our people, for your family. Please!"

Ruka watched it as if in memory, or in a dream. Even in the center of it all, he felt helpless and terrified, grip forgotten on the warrior in his hand. He screamed, perhaps, before it happened.

Kale's power rippled through him, through his Grove, impossible and god-like, only the tiniest surge missing its target. Farahi lifted from his feet, plunged sideways instead of downwards, thrown against the hard stone wall like a mason's scrap.

Bukayag seized his moment. He threw two, then three, then four spears while Ruka stood numb, until the last one pierced Kale's field of power and cut a trench through the prince's arm.

Pain lanced Ruka's side, and Bukayag released the bodyguard. He twisted to find his own spear jammed into his chain, and swung but missed as Dog-Nose danced away.

Bukayag howled and turned back to Kale, but his enemies flew back, then rose into the sky like birds. He threw spear after spear screaming in rage, but each was plucked as if by the hand of god, and tossed easily aside. Kale and his warriors soared up from the shattered palace, and out of sight, gone in moments.

Ruka absently touched the spear and sent it back to his Grove. The wound was shallow, and had surprised more than harmed him. He walked in a daze to Farahi, knowing without looking what he would find.

Kikay already knelt at her brother's side. It was clear his head had struck the stone, the side caved and red. He seemed to speak to his sister before his eyes rolled back, then the great king of Sri Kon lay still and shattered, far beyond the help of any healer.

"What did he say?" Ruka took his friend's hand and felt the tears. "It might be important, Kikay. What did he say?"

The great matron of the isles looked on Ruka with such disgust, such hatred, it overshadowed her grief.

"He asked for you," she said, wiping a hand over her face. "He asked for you, and then he died."

With that she stood and left them both to return to what remained of her family, and Ruka leaned down to his brother of the mind. The king who had saved the Ascom, who had found a savage people and extended his hand, had been killed by his own son. Ruka kissed Farahi's cheek, testing for the breath that was no longer there. It was over. It was all over.

"For love of your brother," he said, maybe in Bukayag's voice, "I will spare you, Kikay, and all your kin. You need not fear me."

She stared at him with such loathing he knew he should kill her. But it didn't matter. Very little mattered now.

"Shaman, are you alright? We came...we came as quickly..."

Aiden's voice called from the entrance, and Ruka saw he had brought many warriors. Egil and most of his retainers were amongst them, their eyes roaming the corpses, the all but obliterated throne room.

"The prince has fled." Ruka explained as he rose.

His men exchanged careful glances, their brows raised as they again surveyed the ruin, and the naked display of god-like power.

"Should we...chase him, shaman?" Aiden's sword was already drawn, his hard eyes already staring at Farahi's family. "Our men are still hidden all over the city, or on the ships. They could be brought forward quickly."

Ruka thought on all the careful planning gone to ruin, mind yet incapable of moving far beyond Farahi.

He looked at Lani staring at the dead king in terror, clutching her son as she had when they'd first met. She had been promised to him for many years by Farahi, who had long known his eldest son preferred men. Kale had given her the child, he knew, which shouldn't have mattered and hadn't before. Now it felt like poison in an already fatal wound.

This boy had everything. He had Farahi for a father, a life of comfort, brothers. He was handsome, had a beautiful girl who loved him, and beyond all of this a world-shaping power. How unfair life was. *And God curse him,* Ruka thought. The stupid, ignorant boy. He had destroyed Farahi and shattered his own people's chances to resist Naran.

Ruka had no strategy without Farahi. The Alaku king was required to unite the islanders under a single banner. He had old alliances with the Tong and other coastal nations. He had friends and history and a reputation forged over decades. Ruka was just an unknown conquering pirate.

He knew instantly he should sue for peace. He should somehow befriend Kale, convince him, unite perhaps in grief. But the thought enraged him. Now, after everything, after a *lifetime* of work, he had to ask a boy-god for permission. And of course Kale could simply say no. He could start ripping men of ash apart with air, and in his ignorance start breaking quarantines. Who could say how many more would die?

Ruka took a long, settling breath, and looked to Aiden. The mighty chief had never failed him—not once in all these years. "Bring the ships," he said. "The infantry. What is left of the cavalry. All of it. We're going to wipe these soldiers off our island."

The big man nodded, and from behind him Tahar muttered 'about bloody time'. Ruka glanced at Tane, whose eyes had never left his father's corpse. He watched the now recovered Kikay, and the still terrified Lani. Their futures had changed, too. "Take them to the cells," he flicked his eyes to Eshen, who nodded.

"Pirate," he said towards Arun in Pyu common. "I consider you my ally. What will you do?"

The ex-monk smiled politely and with infuriating calm, as if nothing in the world were amiss. "I will go wherever the princess goes, savage. But I thank you."

Ruka nodded and gestured for them to be taken away before turning back to Aiden. "The sorcerer is our only target. We must distract him, and kill him. His men are meaningless."

"As you say. He fled from you once, shaman. The gods will protect you again."

For once Ruka wished this were so, and that the gods existed. He looked at the destruction in his Grove, and wondered what would happen if it were truly destroyed. He found he feared this more than death.

"I can take it, brother," Bukayag breathed, hand opening and closing in excitement. Aiden's brow lifted, and Ruka coughed before turning towards the stable.

He pictured the Northern beach in his mind and the best way to attack it. Kale would not fight him in the city because it would endanger the people. He would stay on the beach because he was either going to flee, or would want his enemies clearly in his sight. In either case it made him vulnerable. The Sons would ride again, no doubt to their doom, with all the speed they could muster. Mighty Sula would lead one last glorious charge.

74

Kale's feet touched the white sand of Sri Kon's Northern beach, then he sagged to the earth. He groaned as Osco tore open his uniform.

"Surgeon! Damn fool islanders. God curse sorcerers, magic and all foreigners. Why warn you if you just let it hit you?"

Kale couldn't help but laugh. "I didn't *let* it. And I was a little busy flying, and trying to kill something apparently almost unkillable, oh and keeping your neck from getting crushed. You're quite welcome."

Osco frowned as he doused the wound in alcohol, then did the same to himself. His hand and forearm were oozing blood. "We are both very lucky," he said, eyebrows drooped in focus. "That man's throw would have ripped out your heart, and his pick almost took my hand. What in god's name is he."

Kale had no idea, and was about to say something clever, but without warning Osco started stitching his arm.

"What...wait, fucking hell."

He lay against a rock and tried to meditate, soon giving up to look around his make-shift camp. Mesanites and all his men were fanned out and waiting.

Thetma eventually found him, leaned over to inspect the wound and made a face. "So it went well, then."

Osco snorted, and Kale looked from one to the other and shook his head. "Do you know I once called a monsoon? That was yesterday. It was about the most amazing thing I've ever heard of. I honestly impressed myself."

"They have a sorcerer," Osco explained before yanking another stitch through.

"Yes," Kale hissed, "but I didn't see him ripping the world apart. His powers are more...damnit...defensive, and I was hurting him. I could tell."

"Your own injuries require less spiritual insight." Osco said flatly.

Kale couldn't argue there. He'd fled because he'd been so focused he didn't think he could keep his friends alive. Despite all the power he'd soaked in from the world, the giant and his shadow took it. He'd found himself taking more risk than he should have, grasping further and faster than seemed safe to draw, though he'd again perhaps increased his limits with the test. And he couldn't explain it, but he knew the shadow was... thinning, somehow.

His magic was killing it.

Osco had stopped stitching and met Kale's eyes. "We should withdraw, islander. We don't know what we're dealing with. Teach us your miracles, bring more men. Or just starve them out with your ships."

"No." Kale didn't bother adding 'them' included Kale's people, who would starve right alongside the enemy. "I was hurting him. Even if I can't kill him, you and your men can. I'll stop his warriors, who are *clearly* not resistant."

Something in the Mesanite's eyes caught Kale's attention—some kind of deception. "You're tired…," he said, "your men are frightened. I advise…"

"I'm fine." Kale was more restless than tired. In truth he wanted another chance at that shadow. His body felt exhausted, that much was true, but his spirit was almost energized by all the power in this place.

"Their weapons and armor, Kale. It's a metal I've never seen. We could hardly hurt him, and if his men have something similar…"

"It didn't stop me." Kale was getting angry now, reminded of his conversation with Mahen. "I'll tear his God-cursed men apart. You and yours just stop him. One man, Osco, can you fight one man?"

Osco's eyebrows didn't much like that. Kale twitched as the Mesanite yanked a stitch and cut the thread. "I have sworn to help you, islander, and all my men will fight and die for that oath. But that does not mean I must be a silent fool. I advise you withdraw."

"Noted." Kale stood. "We stay. I'll not allow these men more time to butcher my people. We prepare ourselves, and attack."

Osco nodded and turned to his men, calling in his own tongue. They raised a cheer and stomped their feet in the sand, and Kale was pleased at the quick acceptance. He knew he could not motivate his own men so easily, and wouldn't try. He looked to Thetma, who waited at his side.

"Tanay, ka?" he said—'do men not drown' in the old dialect, as he had said in their fight on the beach those years ago.

"Ka, my lord." The farmer's son grinned. "Now let's go kill the bastards."

* * *

Osco stood in the wet sand and rolled his aching shoulders. "Are you ready to die, brothers?" he'd called, and every man had shouted 'yes!'.

Their instant loyalty moved him, but he did not wish to throw away their lives. Already he re-lived the battle in Pyu's throne room—watching the huge iron spike near sever his arm as it punched through his shield, the ancient sword of House Magda bouncing off the man's armor, bent and blunted without effect. Only in his nightmares would he recall the strength in that giant's hands.

Now he and his men were in formation again in the center of Kale's army. Though they had planned originally to attack, it became clear the invaders were coming faster. Their infantry poured from the houses of the city and began forming on the outskirts into tight, semi-disciplined lines.

"There, General." Osco's second in command pointed at the ridge, and he nodded in acknowledgment.

Osco cleared his bruised throat. He glanced at the islanders guarding his flanks and knew they were almost useless against this enemy. He'd had no choice but to form his men into a square formation, preparing for the inevitable.

All the giants Osco had seen were huge, well-armed, and real warriors. As he watched them he saw they were not equipped with uniformity, and by their slow mustering did not appear to be proper soldiers, or at least poorly trained. But that would not matter. Osco knew as he saw them that unless Kale's miracles carried the day, he and all his allies would die on this beach.

"Stay close, islander." Osco looked to his friend until he returned it. "That sorcerer is coming for you, and your infantry will not be adequate. Make sure there are always Mesanites in his path."

Kale nodded absently. His eyes were already glazed and no doubt he roamed the battlefield with his magic. He blinked and seemed present again. "It'll be like before, Osco. The power I'll use will be…destructive. You'll have to keep your distance."

Osco nodded and released a breath. He had wondered at first if Kale knew what he'd done. The prince had been so focused in the throne room he hadn't seemed to notice his family's arrival. His magic had nearly ripped the palace apart, and even Osco and Asna had felt their peril.

It was clear now he did not know his father was dead. Telling him did not seem wise, now, or maybe ever. Osco felt a moment of fear at the thought of his ally for the first time, but this was not helpful either. He turned his mind to the now, to the ground they'd chosen and shedding all their supplies. He hoped his assumptions were correct.

The tide was still coming in and the sea directly behind them. The sand was wet and would churn to mud in the battle. But Mesanites were trained to fight in mud and sand. If their formation held they could fight all day and night in it without rest or water. Osco's enemy on the other hand were large, heavy, and on the attack. They would like the sand far less.

"Be ready for the beast-riders, and save your…strength, if you can," Osco said, still thinking *fly away, you damn fool, fly away to your ships and safety and forget this place and these monsters, it is your miracles that truly matter!*

He knew in his bones the giant sorcerer was coming for Kale, and Kale alone. The bloodlust and maybe rage he'd seen in those golden eyes would haunt his dreams. All his life Osco knew the minds and habits of warriors, but he had never seen such raw, murderous intent.

If the giants had any sense, they would send everything they had, all their strength at once to overwhelm Kale's magic and distract him for the kill. That is what Osco would do.

Kale smiled as if unconcerned, and his confidence gave Osco at least some comfort. God only knew what the island prince could do when pushed to the limit. Every moment, every encounter seemed only to grow his power and understanding. Perhaps they need only protect him, and keep the deformed giant away. If they could buy Kale time, there was a chance.

The enemy had mustered thousands of men now, spread across the outer city and the gentle slopes leading to Sri Kon. But here they waited, and Osco was about to question why when he heard the horns.

"It's the scouts," Kale said as he looked to the sea. "One means enemy sighted." Another horn blew. "Two means many." The men silenced on the beach as they listened, and Kale's jaw clenched even before the third horn sounded. "Three means they're coming. It seems the enemy doesn't intend for us to withdraw."

Osco hid his concern, because it seemed his enemy was not some mindless barbarian. He put a hand absently to his neck and cleared his aching throat, then scowled and spit to the sand.

"We've apparently upset them," he said, then glanced to his friend. Kale had a strange look in his eyes. It wasn't anger, for Osco had seen that look before—it was something more familiar, something ugly—the dull glaze of a soldier in combat, blank to the horrors while he did what was required.

"Just hold them back," Kale turned to the sea, and spoke now as if only curious. "We'll see who decides to run."

Osco nodded, feeling a shiver at the tone. Any soldier understood the will to kill, of course, and even fostered it. But in Kale's acceptance of his own power came something frightening, something inhuman. For a moment Osco imagined what it would be like to be his enemy— to be charging across the beach in the sight of a god, killed by power you could not see.

The thought disturbed him, but he needed all his will and courage for the battle, so he put it from his mind.

* * *

Ruka watched from Sula's back as the men of ash advanced on their enemy. His warships moved forward in a single block, though in the end he had only sent half. They were outmatched and undercrewed, told to withdraw after a short fight. Ruka required only distraction.

The infantry advanced in three blocks—Aiden led the center for not even Ruka could convince him otherwise; Tahar took the right flank, Folvar the left. Their warriors were a mix from across the land of ash—Northerner and Southerner, Midlander and outcast. Chiefsmen stood beside rebels and once chiefless raiders, now all volunteers who had come to risk their lives and do the hard work of first colonists. Some had come for glory, others escape, some loyalty or hope. But whatever their reasons, what they shared was courage. They would do what needed to be done.

Some few islanders already loosed arrows, and the men of ash raised their shields. The Pyu marines shouted warcries and pounded the sand with their spears. Their real warriors stood in perfect formation in their center. Ruka realized as he saw them that they were 'Mesanites'—a tribe or city of warriors from West of Naran he had read of in his time in Pyu.

As the ashmen approached, these loosed their javelins. Most struck steel shield, deflecting or falling away. Ruka smiled, unsurprised. His men were clad from neck to shins in good chain, with thin but near unbreakable shields made wide and tall. They would not fall easily.

The sky above the battlefield again cracked with thunder, and Ruka clenched his jaw. Clouds from every direction blew towards it as if from a circular gale, yet not even a breeze touched Ruka's face. The dim sun darkened further, light flashing as the clouds came together. Lightning flared, then blasted the Ascomi's left flank.

Many screamed. Some flew from their feet, others collapsed where they stood as if struck instantly unconscious. The sea behind the enemy stilled. Sand swirled into life before them, slashing at the men in coiling strands like swinging rope. Ruka watched his brave warriors walk forward and meet their enemy regardless. They stayed together and did not charge, and soon the lines came together in cries and clashes of iron and bronze, flesh and wood.

Ruka turned to the skald at his side. Egil was older now, as they both were, and a father of four sets of twins. All had survived to join a generation of ash with one fifth the deaths of children than any before it.

"We have traveled a long road, you and I," Ruka said. Egil met his eyes. His black beard was touched now with grey, the lines and wrinkles on his face somehow enhancing his fine looks, and showing his wisdom. His face twisted with a mix of emotion Ruka expected could never be untangled.

"Wait awhile longer, lord. This sorcerer will tire."

Ruka smiled, wishing he could say so much more—how grateful and sorry he was, and how much he would miss his timid, talented, wonderful friend. Instead he turned to what was left of his cavalry.

A hundred-odd 'Sons of Sula' remained from over two-hundred. Some were his kin, or at least Beyla's—the great-great-great grandsons of Valdaya, who had stepped foot on paradise in the four hundred and twenty ninth year of Galdra, in a special trip just for her, two weeks before her death at the age of eighty-three.

Many of the men were already wounded, some so badly they'd been strapped to their horses. But their eyes still held fire.

"We go to this sorcerer, cousins," Ruka shouted so all would hear. "We go for our kin, and their future." He met his retainer's eyes, and perhaps saw a wetness there. Whether it was joy, or grief, he did not know.

"You asked me once how the story of Ruka, son of Beyla should end, skald. Do you remember?"

Egil nodded very slowly. His expression slackened, as if he had heard some great and horrible truth. Ruka looked to the battle, the swirling storms of magic, knowing behind it all stood a man who thought himself a god. He lowered the iron bars of his visor, and smiled.

"One last task, Egil, and your work is done. Tell our people how the son of Beyla dies."

* * *

Ruka raced across the white sand of Sri Kon, warm breeze drying the sweat on his brow. He had tossed his helmet to the beach perhaps to serve some bold and clever crab. He would need to see his target clearly.

The Sons scattered now in many directions. Most would charge Kale alone, getting through the line any way they could. Twenty remained and rode at Ruka's back in formation towards the islander's East flank, and would help clear him a path.

Ruka hoped the prince was too distracted to stop them all. He slowed Sula to a cantor and glanced at the sea, seeing many Ascomi warships already in flames. Others still closed with the larger ships trying to board. Pontooned scouts swarmed them like flies, and the skies above them looked unnaturally darkened and hostile. *Thank you for your sacrifice,* Ruka thought, expecting they were doomed. *I will redeem your courage, or die trying.*

On the coast, his infantry were faring far better. Despite the magic ripping many apart, already they were breaking the islanders on both flanks as they cut a path towards the sea. Half-naked marines and poorly equipped Tong spearmen still fought desperately for their lives, but were uncoordinated and weaker, both individually and as a group. The Ascomi shieldwalls bashed and hacked them to pieces whenever engaged, and the sand churned red with island blood.

Ruka waited and waited until he saw some of his riders breaking through the line, hurling spears at the rear of the Mesanite block. Those that did fell instantly, and Ruka knew where the sorcerer was. His breath quickened because the moment had arrived, or it never would—all of Ruka's life sharpened to a single jagged point.

"Ride, men of ash! Give me my enemy! Show the gods the strength of their sons!" He raised his spear, and the warriors around him cried out, surging forward behind Eshen, who refused to leave Ruka's side.

Ruka urged Sula into an impatient run, rising over the small crest he'd hidden behind, straight for the crumbling flank of the enemy.

Many brave islanders stood before their approach, and all of them died. With spears and iron beasts the Sons trampled over the outer edges, breaking through to race along the coast behind them. They sprinted hard through the shallow water, flinging wet sand from heavy hooves as they maintained their charge. The perfect square of the Mesanites loomed, spears sticking out from every angle like a well-built palisade.

Ruka saw the prince behind them now. He was floating again, his arms outstretched, air shimmering around him in seething waves. Ruka readied a spear.

Again as he came closer the moment froze as sound seemed muffled—sand shook and leapt to the air, this time ahead of them, swirling like a living thing as it transformed into a cyclone of grit.

Every horse reared up in panic. They screamed and turned away from the roar of air and sand before them, scattering and skirting the edges into the sea, or into the rear ranks of men.

Every horse panicked, that is, except one. Ruka snarled and raised his shield, feeling Bukayag's excitement to feel the sand tear at his flesh. Sula ran straight into the storm.

75

Osco could no longer hear the battle over the sound of Kale's magic. His summoning of a monsoon had been impossible and terrifying enough. Somehow, this was different.

Kale's head lolled in exhaustion, or maybe rapture. He floated a man's height from the ground, pulsing with a blurry miasma of maybe steam. Behind him, the sea had stilled. The sky cracked again and again, the battle shrouded in unnatural darkness from clouds that leapt and surged like living things. Osco's breath frosted in the air as if he stood on a mountaintop, and the rear ranks of his square shivered from the cold. But he had little time to worry.

The giants had now engaged three sides of his square as the islanders crumbled. For now the Mesanites held, though the huge enemy bashed against them almost heedless of counter-attack—partly due to their armor, partly because they were stark, raving mad.

The enemy fought like demons. Covered in mud and blood—sometimes while being torn apart by invisible magic—they pushed on, as if all that existed was the next foe. Despite their obvious tiredness they fought with fury, hacking at Osco's men and breaking apart shields. The fight, Osco realized, would go to total exhaustion. Or at least it would have.

Kale's magic raked the beach in horrifying waves. The enemy sometimes flew back, thrown by the hand of an angry god. Others collapsed, blood and bone bursting from the cracks in their armor, or burning alive as lightning struck them from above. Sometimes the sand itself opened and swallowed them, vanishing into the earth without time to scream. Still their brethren continued the assault.

"Hold," Osco yelled, not knowing if any could even hear him properly. "Your city's honor stands behind you! This ground is your oath! Not one step back!" He turned, not yet joining the rotating formation, eyes scanning the beach for riders.

"Be ready," he called directly in the ear of his Second, who nodded, and managed by gesture to break off a small pack from the rear to move closer to Kale's painful aura.

Beast-riders were breaking through the islanders, and Osco's men took turns bringing them down with javelins as they charged. The giant mules were fast, but predictable, and like anything else did not run far with four feet of bronze and iron spike plunged through their necks and legs. The Mesanites killed the fallen riders on the ground.

Again Osco turned to the beach, this time as the ground beneath him trembled. He could not know if it was Kale's magic or a charge like before, but he scanned with every speck of battle awareness hammered into him since childhood.

"West flank," he shouted as he saw them, "second unit!"

The unit leaders screamed and shoved at the giants until twenty more men could break loose from formation to stand between Kale and the riders. Osco counted the enemy as quickly as he could.

It was a packed cluster like before, hurtling at impossible speed straight through the chaos, islanders bouncing away from them like nothing. He looked to his already hard-pressed infantry and knew he could spare no more without risking collapse. It wasn't enough.

"Islander," he screamed, pressing into the freezing air towards Kale. "There's too many! West flank!"

Kale's lips didn't move.

"I see them."

Air rushed off the sea, and sand swirled into life to protect the flank, covering the ground all the way from water to the edges of Osco's square like a wall of cyclones.

From his angle, Osco could still see the riders, and breathed a sigh of relief as he saw the beasts panic and flee from Kale's magic, turning aside to stumble into packs of islanders. He left ten men to watch for stragglers, then turned back to support the square.

* * *

Bukayag and Sula snarled as the sand whipped against their flesh. Ruka closed his eyes as grit buffeted his face and hands and felt like ice driving against him in heavy sleet.

The sound and feel of it overwhelmed his senses. Sula stumbled blind, and Ruka knew at any moment he could be struck down by something he couldn't see.

But like most fear, in moments it was gone, and the storm with it. Ruka burst through to see Kale floating before him in plain view, bodyguards arrayed in a line. Sula charged without instruction.

The surprised men scrambled to intercept, wrapping somewhat around the edge towards the water, no doubt fearing he would try to skirt their flank. But Ruka did not intend to go around.

Bukayag threw their first spear, the weapon flying straight and true until the air itself seized it and tossed it aside. Ruka charged on, picking up speed despite the heavy sand clinging to Sula's hooves. With every moment he drew closer, hands twitching, body held high in the saddle, ready to jump. The enemy infantry threw their spears.

Ruka raised his shield and a solid hit clanged and bounced against it. Most struck Sula. The barding stopped nearly all of it, but one entered the animal's cheek, ripping through the other side to stick and jut like a crossbeam. Others gouged his lower legs and carried off chunks of flesh and bone. Two more struck the leather saddle and lodged deep into his side. Still, Sula charged.

In a wild rage, the stallion rammed into the spears turned against him, his barding shivering the points, chest hammering men and weapons aside with all his massive weight. His breathing was ragged, his body pierced, but still he broke through the line. Mighty Sula thrashed his head in victory, spraying blood even as he stumbled to the sand. Ruka leapt screaming and ready from his back.

He banished his armor to his Grove because it weighed him down. He kept his feet and ran on, feeling a pitiful cold in the air no worse than a single moment of Hulbron winter. He felt a weight, oppressive and thick, as if every step now were trudged through the river of tears, swift and unfreezing though it burned like fire. He was only steps from his prey.

All of Kale's power turned against him.

His grove shook as trees all around it burst into flames. Dead men collapsed before his mother's house as the walls cracked from the fury of a sudden wind. Weapons and armor flew from his armory, caught up in a cyclone to spin and collide with the dead and the walls. Beyla's statue cracked and broke, and Ruka screamed as it vanished into the swirling mists in a vortex of air.

In the land of the living, the Mesanites were trying to intervene, but couldn't. They fell and cried out as they approached, helpless in the aura of the sorcerer's power. All around him the air seethed with heat, or iced in frost, or crackled with lightning—as if the world tried all it knew to bring Ruka down.

Bukayag roared, and trudged them forward. Through the weight, through the agony, step by step, impossible but true, he pushed into the flames like Noss leaping into the mountain. The dead seized Ruka's arms in his Grove, mustering behind him, propping him against the terrible wind, dragging him like a ship to the sea.

"Why...won't...you...die!"

Kale's voice boomed across the beach, deafening and elemental, ringing from the heavens in the land of the living and the dead, mocking the noise of mortal war. The prince raised his arms and began to move higher, as if he meant simply to fly far above and rain his murder from the safety of the clouds.

Bukayag snarled, and leapt.

Ruka's brother wrapped a four-fingered hand around the ankle of Farahi's killer, and dragged him down. The sword in their other hand burned so hot it seared his flesh, and Ruka released it, closing his fingers into a fist. Kale struggled and kicked, but with a single pull, Ruka brought the island prince within his reach, and struck with a closed fist.

Kale's handsome cheek shattered. His eyes rolled as he fought unconsciousness, and the destruction in Ruka's Grove ended as quickly as it began. He ran from his mother's broken house to the fields of his armory, and lifted a knife. His brother seized it.

Together they turned Kale in their arms to stand wobbling, using his body to shield them from the Mesanites stumbling to their feet. The moment felt so calm. The sounds of battle were almost peaceful as Kale's power drained from the world.

Ruka held the young prince forward. He felt his brother's eyes roam the boy and felt his resentment. The prince of paradise had been born alone, but never accused of eating his brother in the womb. He had not been called a monster, nor been forced to become one in truth in a frozen wasteland. His ancestors had not left him a room with all the weight of history sagging on his shoulders. Perhaps he was so small and light because he did not bear the weight of the dead.

It isn't fair, Bukayag tried to scream.

Ruka thought on the words echoed by Kale's magic—the harsh nature of such a powerful force with its will turned against him after everything. After *everything*.

"Why won't I die?" he hissed. "*Why wont I die?* he shouted, loudly enough for the Mesanites to hear. "I am not a man, Prince of Paradise. I am a thousand years of children buried nameless in rotten earth. I am the rage of their helpless mothers, weeping beneath an empty sky. I am the bitter fruit of frozen tears."

Bukayag took the knife from the prince's throat, and withdrew his arm. It was not difficult, in the end, for Ruka need only stand aside, and in silence. He need only do nothing.

"See what they reap," his brother whispered. It was Bukayag who drove the blade.

* * *

Osco watched the blood-slick iron emerge from his friend's chest and knew it had pierced his heart. The giant threw Kale forward, all the way to land at his protector's feet.

The sandstorm collapsed, just as all around his Mesanites islanders broke or fled in panic to the sea. For a moment Osco considered making his last act revenge on this sorcerer—surrounding him with his ten exposed men and bringing him down, searching that damned armor for every chink. But it made no difference. Kale was dead. And even if all his men were next, Osco would not throw away their lives.

"Formation," he ordered. The soldiers around him lifted the fallen prince and withdrew to reinforce the square, placing Kale inside.

Osco could see that most of his allies had already broken, with only a few small packs of the Tong still fighting. Those that could swim dove into the bloody waters of the North Alaku Sea, perhaps just to float there in safety, or perhaps to swim all the way to their ships.

Safely tucked behind a wall of his men, Osco knelt beside his friend. He met the still-dazed, frantic eyes, and took his hand.

A small, desperate part of him thought he might see another miracle— that Kale would rise from the sand, mending his flesh as power surged all around him. But as his friend's gaze focused, tinged with regret and terror,

Osco knew it wasn't so.

"Go in peace," he whispered, "your brothers will join you soon."

Thus went the words of all Mesanite commanders to the fallen, but just for Kale, Osco smiled and shed a tear.

The prince's eyes relaxed, as if he prepared some final mental effort, and Osco stiffened. In truth he believed it still possible. Perhaps he truly was going to create some final miracle, overcoming death itself. Kale gasped and stared at the sky as he squeezed Osco's hand. He met his gaze, and seemed now only sorry, and not afraid. He blinked and lay back on the sand, and his grip relaxed. His chest stilled, and Osco closed his lids.

"What now, other friend?" Asna paced back and forth, thus far safe in the Mesanite formation. Since the battle started he'd been like a caged animal, watching with frantic looks, entirely useless. Osco stood and flexed his wounded shoulder, strapping on his shield.

"We die. Or you can swim away like the damned Condotian dog you are."

The mercenary frowned and glanced at the roiling sea. "Asna the Great is not murdered by water. No." He drew his sword.

Osco nodded because it made as much sense as anything. He dropped his visor and put an arm to the closest back, taking his place in the formation. It hurt to hold his shield, but nevermind. It seemed he would not be the one to save his people. But it had always been a madman's hope.

He would not see Liga again, or the children they would have made. These were small, and minor regrets for a man whose whole life had been war.

"Brothers, it's my honor to die with you," he shouted over the din. "You have earned your names. Woe to our enemies!"

"Woe to the enemies of Mesan!" cried his brave warriors together in strong voices, and without hesitation. Osco of the Magda nearly wept in thanks, for though he had failed, and perhaps his family had failed, his culture had not. He would go to his death with pride.

76

Ruka stood on the gory beach and watched the sea. It seemed the Pyu had proved their reputation. All the ships he'd sent were on fire, fleeing, or destroyed—the islanders' smaller scouts and transports already coming to collect as many soldiers as they could. Tong and islanders fled into the deeper waters, most swimming, some drowning—all abandoning the unbroken block of Mesanites.

Ruka watched them fight for a time. His exhausted men pushed and hurled themselves against the smaller warriors, who managed at every turn to push back and defend their position. The hillmen and their clever formation switched and rotated so that the fighting rank would be as fresh as possible, while Ruka's men cluttered each other and fought their own trying to get at the enemy. By a quick count, perhaps half of the Mesanites were dead. Their equipment was failing them, shields breaking, spears and swords denting and bending against Ascomi steel.

Ruka tried and failed to care. He felt as he once had outside Alverel with Priestess Kunla dead at his hands. It was as if he had succeeded and yet failed. He had brought his people to paradise, killed a man with the power of a god, yet he had lost all.

Farahi was dead. The alliance was dead. If the island king was right—which he usually was—the empire of Naran would invade the Tong in less than a year. The emperor would destroy Pyu's trade routes, ravage and subdue her allies, and when there was no one left to oppose him, at last he would come for Sri Kon.

Without Farahi's ships and the Tong's grain, the Ascom would starve. In the past ten years their population had further outstripped their ability to feed themselves. If they could not secure land and begin shipping new colonists into paradise as promised, perhaps the chiefs would lose faith, and the Order betray. Many more than expected had already died. Now things would get worse.

As he watched the waves, Ruka felt a great urge to simply walk into the sea.

"I tried, Beyla," he whispered. "I have tried."

It seemed the world was as dark and cruel as she'd once told him. Even in triumph hope was snatched and crushed beneath the waves of fortune and tragedy. Ruka did not know how to resist. How could he face the suffering of life when all his plans and dreams turned to ash in his hands? How could he go on when what waited was death? Always death?

In his Grove, he stumbled through the devastation Kale had wrought. Beyla's statue was gone, her garden destroyed, her house half pulled from its foundations, mostly scattered around the Grove. The mines looked collapsed. The bridges had crumbled, the sewer cracked, the armory scattered like iron leaves. Many of the dead were proper corpses, and Boy-

From-Alverel, his oldest friend, was truly gone.

Girl-from-Trung's-Pit found him, and he ran to her and took her in his arms as he wept.

"You're alive," he whispered. When her brow raised he shook his head and laughed. "I'm sorry, I mean you're still with me. I'm…I'm so pleased. Are you alright?"

She smiled, but her scarf was gone and seeing the bruises on her neck reminded him he still had not paid for all his deeds—that even given the real chance to die at Kale's hands, instead he had chosen survival.

He had to admit his willingness to die was only words. Every time he was tested he had allowed Bukayag to save him. That was the truth. He despised himself for this, and for his self pity and hopelessness in this moment.

"A man fails in two ways", he heard his mother's voice. They had been hungry, and cold, huddled in a dirty shack alone and forgotten, and Ruka had wept in misery. "He quits," she said, squeezing his little but full-fingered hand, "or he dies. Are you dead, my son?"

"No, Momma."

He smiled at the memory, picturing Beyla's face. She had lost everything, all at once, and still had strength enough for him. *The statue is nothing*, he knew, clinging to the image in his mind. The book of Galdra he had once burned had been nothing, just as all a man's possessions were nothing, and only things. Things could be re-built.

Ruka looked to the dead who remained, already idle as if waiting for instruction. They did not look tired, or dejected. Even in death they looked ready, their broken bodies set to renew the world for as long as their will held true. Ruka shook his head in wonder.

"Yes, I see," he called to them, feeling chastised. In the end his failure and misery made no difference, nor even his mortality. He had been given a single task, perhaps by star-gods, perhaps by life itself—'stoop and build your broken world with callused hands, again and again, no matter the price'.

This he would do because maybe some other fortunate thing could know a love like Beyla's, if only for a time. That was all. That was the why. That was everything.

Ruka sent the dead to their work, and turned back to the fighting, lifting the horn from his neck. As he blew the withdraw, his men fell back from the enemy in bits and pieces, most seeming grateful as they did. The Mesanites did not follow, instead using every spare moment to throw corpses, broken shields and weapons from their line, re-forming to fill any gaps. Ruka shook his head, and called to his own men.

"Here are foes worthy of Vol's attention. Shall we spare them, if we can?"

Aiden, still alive and soaked in blood, clanged his sword against his breastplate, and the men followed until the sound filled the air in a ring around their former enemy. Ruka looked on them with pride, and called in the island tongue.

"They honor you, men of Mesan."

For a moment he feared they did not understand, or would not speak. But a strong voice answered.

"Come closer and we'll honor you back."

Ruka recognized the man from the hall, and smiled. He told his men what was said, and they laughed and cheered their enemy's boldness. It was clear the Mesanites were utterly confused by the display.

"I am Bukayag, son of Beyla. What is your name, warrior?"

The man stared and did not answer at once, but glanced at his men and spoke. "Osco Magda, but that is irrelevant. We will not surrender."

Ruka nodded. "I do not ask. Men who fight so well and bravely are not my enemies. The beach is yours, with my congratulations. I will withdraw and allow your allies to collect you, but I have a request. Will you carry a message?"

He could see his words confused the commander, but he rallied quickly. "If your message is that you've defeated Mesanites in battle, I'd prefer to die, but thank you."

Ruka smiled, liking the man more with every word. "No, and I don't believe we did, Osco Magda. What I wish is for you to tell King Kapule the Alakus are finished. Tell him that I, as the new king of Sri Kon, will uphold all of Farahi's laws. I will keep these seas clean of pirates, and…"

"Will you be using those ships, king of Sri Kon?" The Mesanite commander pointed at the small fleet in flames on the water.

Ruka glared as his smile faded. "I have more ships. And the island fleets will be mine soon enough."

The young commander's rather emotive brow raised, and Ruka was suddenly glad his men didn't know what was being said.

"Tell Kapule I will also honor his bargain with Farahi. I will marry his daughter, Lani, and maintain the alliance. Tell him for this we will even come to his aid in battle, if he requires it. Will you carry my message?"

The Mesanite's hands seemed to grip his spear as he considered, but again he looked at his men, and softened. "We will carry it."

Ruka could see the man's distaste. No doubt he had lost a friend today, and who knew what else. Ruka felt no pleasure in that but nor could he offer any solace. "You served your ally well," he said, "and you fought like lions. We hold no ill will against your people."

With that he turned away, gesturing to Aiden that the fight was over. The exhausted men of ash sheathed their blades and started moving to their dead, and Ruka walked to Sula and knelt.

The stallion had somehow managed to skewer a Mesanite with the spear sticking from his jaw, then collapsed on another as he died. Ruka laughed as he wiped away the tears, running a hand over his old friend's bloody nose. His retainers came to his side one by one.

"Forgive me, lord, I have failed you again." Eshen almost wept, and Ruka put a hand to his knee.

"No, cousin. Every man on this beach fought like the heroes of old. You have never failed me."

The others said nothing, silent as they looked to the death and glory, lost in the feeling of their own survival. Egil broke it softly.

"It seems your story hasn't finished after all, my lord."

Ruka thought he could hear pleasure in the skald's voice, and almost groaned with relief. "So it seems. We have destroyed one enemy, but gained many more. The islands will have to be secured. We will need more men, more horses, more ships. Aiden—you must return to the Ascom and maintain peace. You'll need the matriarch and the Order to help keep the chiefs in line. I must remain here."

"As you say, shaman. But there are other great chiefs. Why should they listen to me?"

Ruka smiled. "Because you are no longer a chief, Aiden. You are now First Chief and lord of the Ascom. You will bear a message for Dala and the matrons and they will crown you in Orhus. Tell them it is the will of Nanot. It was always so."

Aiden seemed to swell at the words as men had once swelled at Beyla's. "And you, shaman? What will you do?"

Ruka considered his answer and what it meant, feeling as trapped as Bukayag.

"I will pacify these islands and become their king by right of conquest. You and I will rule both lands together." His retainers all grinned knowingly, as if they'd only waited for this to be so. "We must hurry, cousins. Our enemy from the mainland will begin his war soon. If we do not fight him, all our efforts will fall to ruin."

The men nodded as if without concern, though destruction surrounded them on every front. They didn't know about Farahi's visions, of course, but they'd been told long ago of this enemy, and long accepted Ruka knew things he shouldn't.

"Go. See to the dead," he told them. As they dispersed, he did the same.

* * *

Ruka had many new graves to dig. Several burnt trees had fallen amongst the graveyard, and by himself he chopped them and dragged the pieces away. As usual he did not know the names of those he'd killed. He labeled all 'Pyu soldier', or 'Tong soldier', then gave them numbers and a place together under a name for the battle.

As he worked he considered what must be done in the land of the living. A piece of him knew Farahi's son Tane could be placed as the new king. By all accounts the young man was well-liked by local lords. He was an Alaku with an heir, already married to Kapule's daughter, and in nearly every way was perfect. Except Ruka did not trust him.

With time, perhaps, he could be convinced, and for honor and the love of Farahi Ruka committed to try. He would protect the islanders now as he did own people, though in truth he did not wish to be king. Rulership was ugly lies from pretty faces; it was coddling those too timid to face the hardship of the world. Ruka had not been made for such things.

If he had the power he would wave his hand and remove the threat to his people, help them colonize new lands or at least travel them, all without war. After that, he would let other men rule.

Ruka wanted to build, and explore—to race ahead of other men and mark the way. With the rest of his life he wanted to complete the map of the world and find its limits, work to understand its secrets, and answer as many questions as he could.

Instead he dug men graves.

When he came to the last, a piece of him hesitated. For a moment he questioned why he even returned the dead to his Grove. It was supposed to be honor. It had begun as a way to recognize a fallen foe, or at least a fellow living thing that died; it was remembrance, and gratitude—a final thanks for eternal sacrifice. But what was it now?

He stooped to the earth one last time, and dug. When he'd finished he took a plain stake no different than the others and placed it at the end. The signpost was wider than the others, because this time Ruka knew his victim's name.

Ratama Kale Alaku, he carved in runes and then in the island tongue, *Prince and Sorcerer of Sri Kon, son of Hali, son of Farahi.*

He stood with a heavy heart and did not brush the dirt from his hands. Then very slowly, and with a reluctance he had not felt for any other grave, he turned and looked at his field.

Kale stood before him in simple robes. He looked like a Batonian monk rather than an Alaku prince. His left cheek was still shattered, but otherwise he had died very cleanly.

"Loa," Ruka said sadly, expecting the prince to join the ranks of those who hated him. He had been young and powerful, with a long and beautiful life yet to be lived, and Ruka had stolen all with his knife. One day he would pay the cost.

The island prince put his hands in his sleeves as he looked about the Grove. He turned away, as if only curious, and unlike most of the others did not seem interested in the toil, or indeed in Ruka himself. As with Arun, the boy's apathy was unnerving.

"I'm sorry," Ruka called to him, thinking now he could explain all he'd not had a chance to say in life, and that this might make some kind of peace between them.

A small breeze touched Ruka's face, which felt pleasant but bizarre because he had not meant to call it, and he controlled almost everything about his Grove. He blinked and saw the islander had managed to smile, despite his jaw.

"No," whispered the wind, a voice emerging as if from contact with the trees. *"You aren't. But I think you will be."*

Ruka blinked and dropped his shovel. Even the dead men working near-by stood and turned to look at the source of the words. The prince walked away, Ruka's eyes boring into him. His damaged face was serene, almost peaceful as he strolled the grounds, but he soon vanished in the deep mists of the Grove, lost from Ruka's sight.

End of Book Two.

Epilogue

Epilogue

Emperor Yiren Luwei invited his newest spymaster to report from a suicide pan. The man's predecessor had been asked to join his ancestors in the same manner, and so it was with some surprise the new man entered without a shred of obvious fear.

"Welcome, Master Zao-Yu. You come most highly recommended by the Grand Chamberlain. Your presence is an honor."

Zao-Yu bobbed his head respectfully, and Yiren next inquired after his health and his day because these things were polite, and the correct behavior even from an emperor was politeness.

Zao-Yu responded briefly and with equal politeness. He bowed perfectly and knelt in his Seat of Honor before prostrating equally perfectly. He was very plain looking, which was true of most of the greatest spies, and despite his somewhat baggy formal attire it was clear his body was lithe and strong. Yiren found himself unable to decide even how old the man was.

"This worthless servant is embarrassed by such praise and attention, divine lord," Zao-Yu said after the correct length of time. "Please accept my humble report."

Yiren nodded, and an attendant visible from Zao-Yu's prostrate angle also nodded.

"This servant's network informs him of two important matters, divine lord: first, Prince Ratama Alaku is killed in battle, and second, the conquerors of Sri Kon have presented terms of peace and alliance to King Kapule."

Yiren nodded politely to hide his surprise. His own network had learned of the sorcerer's death, but not of the terms offered to his enemy. To have learned this and revealed it so quickly meant Zao-Yu was incredibly impressive, ambitious, or foolish.

He must have a spy in Kapule's inner circle, he thought, *or connected with them.*

Yiren wondered exactly *who,* though, because his network had found the court most impenetrable. The Tong king was as careful with his advisers as he was with his rice.

"Can you trust this information?" Yiren asked.

"Oh yes, lord, with my life."

Yiren frowned because of course his life was the risk. But then perhaps Zao-Yu was simply indicating he was most aware of that fact, yet offering the information anyway. Impressive, then, *and* ambitious. Yiren would have to be careful.

Not for the first time, he contemplated the death of Ratama Alaku and squirmed on his throne. He knew little of these 'conquerors' save that they were large, pale, and couldn't speak any civilized tongue. He found it difficult to believe they existed at all, let alone that they had done a thing Naran itself could not do. Yet he could see no other explanation. *Where* such an enemy had come from seemed equally impossible, and yet also without other explanation—they had come from beyond the map.

"And will King Kapule *accept* this peace and friendship, Master Zao-Yu?"

"I do not know, lord."

Yiren grunted, satisfied because he had not asked the man to elaborate or speculate. The answer in any case was 'yes, if at all possible', because Kapule had little other choice. The monsoon had come and soon his silos would overflow with grain, and he would need to honor his commitments and sell down the coasts, which he could not do without ships because Yiren would ensure 'bandits' attacked any and every caravan as usual.

For years he had done the same with ships, too, but in the last decade Farahi Alaku had seized control of his waters with an iron fist. Now not a single pirate or island lord could be paid enough to accomplish much. But perhaps things had changed.

"Thank you, Zao-Yu, that will be all. Please return to your duties."

The spymaster closed the gap between his head and the floor and held it before rising from his suicide pan. He backed out smoothly and correctly with lowered eyes, and Yiren decided he was pleased for now with the appointment. More than ever he would need men of competence to face this new world already forming. He would have to tolerate a little risk.

"It's time for a walk," he announced as he rose.

Body-servants, bodyguards and councilors bowed and scrambled, lifting the silk train of his robe, holding his slippers steady as he poked his feet inside.

"General Cao," he spoke over his shoulder, and one of his five chief military men came forward. "Please assemble a war council. I would like several different invasion strategies for Nong Ming Tong to read this evening. Please assume minor to moderate rebellion in the provinces, as well as conflict with these new invaders."

"Yes, lord."

Yiren next waved to High Priest Sanfeng, his representative from the Order of Two Waters, who bowed his ancient back in response.

Yiren did not like the man's title or the ancient religions and customs it had sprouted from, but he had not yet found the time to deal with it. The priests of Two-Waters had existed for a thousand years or more, and their secrets were largely their own. Yiren stepped carefully and with a polite smile along his carpet, following the man to the rarely used descending staircase.

Another priest from the same order stood ready inside. He bowed and lit a torch, but Yiren allowed two of his bodyguards to go first, with another two behind him. These and his hundred other bodyguards were the only men Yiren truly trusted—soldiers trained since childhood for their task, paid well and assisted with their marriages, their entire extended families living on royal land.

The hiss of flame and the shuffling of feet accompanied them all the way down the several flights of stairs into the gloom, and they emerged into a wide cavernous hall that stunk like mildew and old sweat. Already Yiren felt his mood dampen so far from Ru's sight.

He couldn't see much, but knew the dark hall was decorated with the ancient spirits and gods, massive stone pillars carved with monstrous faces and long snake-like beasts that could fly and breathe flames.

The small party walked in silence until they reached several rectangular tables arranged like a soldier's mess hall. Chairs all around them were filled with robed apprentices eating plain rice from small bowls more fit for children. They stood and bowed low as Yiren and Sanfeng approached, and the old priest beamed and gestured towards them.

"Fifty-two apprentices have now demonstrated aptitude to the holy flames, lord," he said, clearing his ancient throat. "Two are already ranked high enough to be considered ready as Flameweavers in war. Twelve more are very close."

Yiren chose not to react. When he had first become emperor, the Order of Two Waters had approached him secretly and told him of the 'holy iron' beneath the palace—the ability to transform it into fire, and the carefully guarded process of training Flameweavers. Yiren had eventually asked them to begin training more, but he had certainly never said why—whether it was war, his own amusement, or anything else.

He would not tolerate such presumptuousness from any of his other servants. But then, that was the problem. The priests of Two-Waters did not see themselves as his servants.

"Thank you, High Priest Sanfeng, very impressive. But I would please like that number doubled in three months. Please also inform the temple in Nanzu to begin a new testing program. They should declare Ru will choose five anointed, and have the academy gather volunteers from any province, class, race or occupation. They should test only for aptitude with the metal, the training as priests can come later."

The old man stared for a moment before glancing very subtly at his colleagues and apprentices. Water dripped from the cracks in the ancient ceiling and Yiren felt damper and more oppressed with every sickening breath.

"Surely, my lord," the old priest hardly hid his scoff, "surely so many are not needed against the Tong. And to resort to such extreme measures, and so quickly?"

Yiren blinked for a moment without comprehension because no one had uttered a single protest to his commands since his uncle Amit had died.

He turned very slowly to regard the old priest, considering the stooped back, bald pate and liver spots. No doubt he was old enough to have seen the fall of the previous emperor—to see Yiren's father, a trumped up merchant and farmer, crowned the new son of heaven. The thought galled him.

He smiled politely and ignored the issue for now. "Perhaps first just a demonstration. I would like your two finest students to compete against each other, please."

Sanfeng raised a brow, looking almost impatient, as if he were educating a child. "Competing is very dangerous, lord, and it's wasteful to harm an anointed. We can certainly demonstrate in the testing area, though, and have them…"

"*Am I not the son of heaven?*" Yiren snapped in calculated rage.

The priests, apprentices and even his bodyguards tensed like startled rabbits, and Yiren wondered how many sphincters he had clenched. Sanfeng looked perhaps slightly chastised, but not afraid.

"Yes, of course lord, but…"

"*Do I not then speak with the will of god?*"

The old man paused far longer than he should have, finally almost jerking forward with the proper bow as he muttered, "Yes, lord."

Yiren paused to let that settle. "Thank you. Now I require your two finest students to compete. The loser will join their ancestors. Please step forward." He gestured to the apprentices.

The priests exchanged looks and did nothing, and for a moment Yiren wondered if they planned some kind of refusal or rebellion. At last a young man and woman stepped forward from the tables with fierce looks of pride. Yiren inspected them both, thinking one was an old blooded Naranian from the capital, the other little more than a peasant from the Northern provinces. He smiled with pleasure.

"Very good. I've changed my mind. A demonstration will be adequate."

Priest Sanfeng almost sagged with relief, pitifully attempting a renewed look of humility. Yiren spoke in his most polite, and therefore dangerous tone, as a signal of deadly intent to his bodyguards.

"Honored Priest Sanfeng—please stand in the testing area. I welcome your two apprentices to demonstrate their immense power by assisting you in joining your ancestors."

Yiren watched very carefully as the priests and their apprentices froze. He thought if they intended to disobey him than now would be the moment. If the Fireweavers were loyal, they would be most dangerous, but his bodyguards would move quick and strike them first. He knew their power took a little time.

"I am a high priest of Two Waters," the old man croaked. Unbelievably, he met Yiren's eyes. "No emperor has ever dared to order such a…."

Two of Yiren's bodyguards charged forward and clubbed the old man across the neck. As the apprentices gasped, the soldiers lifted him up and carried him to a stone pillar, wrapping a leather strap around him to keep him standing. He groaned and wavered feebly. Yiren turned to the two chosen students.

"Please assist Priest Sanfeng in joining his ancestors. Do you have what you require?"

By 'what you require' Yiren meant the holy iron beneath the palace that produced Ru's miracles.

"Yes lord," said the young woman, producing the holy metal from the palm of her delicate hand. Yiren watched her eyes for threat, or betrayal, and debated having her killed before she could work her power.

He knew only the very skilled held the metal to their actual flesh, rather than in a pouch or container of some kind. He looked to his bodyguard, who he trusted also to see danger. None gave indication. He felt sweat sticking his robes to his flesh, but gestured for her to proceed. The young man moved beside her, his brow red and jaw clenched.

Yiren breathed sharply, aroused by his own fear. He watched in fascination as the young couple clasped their holy icons, raised their other palms, and scrunched their faces in concentration. After a few moments that stretched like the ring of a palace bell, each sent a thin stream of fire snaking through the air, two rippling rivers of flame.

Two waters, he thought with amusement, thinking of the stream that ran through the base of the cavern, and the water-like appearance of the miracle. *How clever.*

The heat of it sent him back a step, yet he couldn't look away. He stared in fascination as the fire reached Sanfeng, roaring to life as it enveloped him. Despite his half-conscious daze, the old man screamed.

In moments, the blackened, charred flesh of what used to be a man collapsed from the burnt strap, and Yiren closed his eyes in the terrified silence.

"What are your names, apprentices," he whispered. The couple blinked and turned away from their handiwork, hands still clasped hard on the holy iron as they answered.

"Thank you," Yiren said genuinely. "You will both be promoted to High Priest and serve me directly. Please inform the other priests of your new roles, and know you have my full support. We will speak again soon."

"Thank you, lord," they mumbled together, and Yiren turned back towards the stairs.

He had taken a risk, but risk would be required in this new future. Next he would change his mind a dozen times about the number of students, the appointments, the timelines, and many other things. Most people were simple and stupid and assumed a thing once said or planned was true—to confuse them was always best.

The Order of Two-Waters required a cleansing, and soon. Yiren would see it done. He thought again on the priest's question of using Fireweavers against the Tong, and almost snorted as he began ascending the stairs.

Stupid man, Yiren thought. Amazing how someone could spend all their lives with books and learning yet be so naive and ignorant. Yiren could have destroyed the Tong years ago. He could send a vast army trained by his uncle for decades; he could strangle their trade, terrify or turn their allies, and bring Kapule to his knees. Yes it would be better if Amit were alive to lead it all instead of his mostly noble-born and simple generals, but nevermind. The task was straight-forward enough.

Yiren did not need Fireweavers for the Tong. He needed them because Ratama Alaku had been a miracle worker, and now he was dead. Somehow, despite his great power, these strangers from across the sea had killed him.

Unlike the stupid priests, the moment Yiren had been taught about Ru's metal he had wondered if it existed elsewhere. When he had learned of the island prince's miracles, it had only cemented in his mind that divinity could be brought from heaven onto earth and duplicated by man.

This knowledge, though, did not frighten him. Yiren had always thought it unlikely Ru was the only god. Even Naranians had other gods before him, so only a fool thought their divine lord alone in the cosmos. What mattered was that Ru was the greatest—that his prophets, servants, and teachings would soon hold dominion over all lands touched by his light, overcoming all others. Ru's servants would be ready.

After they conquered the Tong, Naran's borders would stretch from sea to sea to sea—the ancient analects all but realized, the sun god's dominion over every land touched by his rays. Yiren had believed it would take many more years, but his chance had come.

He would move the world almost to perfection, until earth reflected heaven, and in so doing enshrine the name Yiren Luwei in history forever. As he left the cold, damp squalor of the priests' pits, his mood brightened, and he sucked a proper breath of air. *Heaven on earth*, he thought with pride, *with its greatest son as its herald.* He could not imagine anything more important.

Acknowledgments

As it turns out, second books have a lot more people to thank. Perhaps this is because my first involved mostly just me alone in a basement with the occasional phonecall from my mother wondering if that little book project is done yet.

Well. Not so number two! Many good friends and new acquaintances have helpfully cracked the whip. Some even gave the impression my family might see more utility with this work than burning the pages in a zombie apocalypse.

Writing a book is great, and satisfying, but if no one reads it you've built an artistic bridge to nowhere. That is just a painful truth, and thus would have been the fate of Kings of Paradise and now Kings of Ash without a great horde of book barbarians - also known as generous, brilliant bloggers and podcasters, megaphone-waving readers, fellow writers, and general fiction and fantasy lovers of many stripes. It's not nearly enough, but for those who help strangers turn dreams into reality, and particularly those who have helped me, I intend to at least thank you here.

Let's start with the colleagues. Yes I have some of those now. Thank you ML Spencer, Rebekah and Jesser Teller, Charles Phipps, Rob Hayes, Michael Baker, and all the other wonderful Grimdarklings for welcoming me into your dark, murky midsts, giving good advice, and for shooting the writing shit. Thanks to Josh Erikson, Dave Woolliscroft, and William Ray also for their advice and chats.

Thank you to the bloggers and reviewers, first generally for your time and insight, and for the heroic work of separating wheat from chaff. Thank you more specifically to Lukasz Przywoski and HiuGregg for leading the KoP Reddit discussions, to Anton Baboglo for your early support, James Tivendale for your many chats (and free books!)—to Samir Karajic, and Jordan (Lostinliterature), and Petrik Leo for helping to spread the word. Thanks to Lynn Kempner for the ARC interest, and Mihir Wanchoo for making me read the Mahabharata (or, you know, *some* of it).

Special thanks to Brittany 'the matron saint of indie' Hay, for taking the chance on my book so early on, and pulling it up from the depths. No one ever forgets the hand when they needed it most, and yours was mine. Thank you, truly.

Thanks to Adam Weller for tireless support, brilliant insight, professional level beta reading, dad-quality jokes, and just for being a stand up fella. Thanks to Jon Adams for all the same, plus proofing, minus the last bit. Also thanks to Michael Nedelcov, Tyler Yaehne, Steve MacDonald and Scott Mckague for their time, support and internet skillz.

Finally a thanks to the many readers who've supported me, making everything else possible. Thanks in particular to those who've taken the time and energy to send me notes of encouragement, leave reviews, or otherwise get in touch. The older I get, the more I realize whenever one gets the urge to say something positive to another human being, one should do it. Many wise readers seem to have realized this long ago, but you'll forgive me—I've always been a late bloomer.

I hope you've enjoyed this latest installment, and that this note finds you well. I also hope to give you many more.

-Richard

P.S. - To those I've neglected and inevitably missed - I apologize. Please take a future opportunity to shame or guilt me to your own benefit.

Where to Find More...

The final book in the series, Kings of Heaven, is available now on Amazon.

You can sign up to the author's mailing list for the latest updates (and get a free novella), at:

www.richardnell.com

Or get in touch...

Email: rich.nell2@gmail.com

Twitter: @rnell2

Goodreads: search for my name

On Reddit: you can usually find me on r/fantasy (as richnell2)

Printed in Great Britain
by Amazon